Intervention

Julian May is the author of the bestselling *Saga of the Pliocene Exiles: The Many-Coloured Land, The Golden Torc, The Nonborn King* and *The Adversary*, as well as a guide to the saga, *A Pliocene Companion*, and these are all available in Pan. She now lives in Washington with her husband.

Julian May

Intervention

A root tale to the
GALACTIC MILIEU
and a *vinculum* between it and
THE SAGA OF PLIOCENE EXILE

Pan Books in association with Collins

First published in Great Britain 1987 by William Collins
This edition published 1988 by Pan Books Ltd,
Cavaye Place, London SW10 9PG
in association with William Collins
9 8 7 6 5 4 3 2 1
© Julian May 1987
ISBN 0 330 30309 0
Phototypeset by Input Typesetting Ltd, London
Printed and bound in Great Britain by
Richard Clay Ltd, Bungay, Suffolk

CONTENTS

To Robie Macauley

Evolutionary creativity always renders invalid the 'law of large numbers' and acts in an elitist way.

Erich Jantsch
The Self-Organizing Universe

At the still point of the turning world. Neither flesh nor
    fleshless;
Neither from nor towards; at the still point, there the
    dance is,
But neither arrest nor movement. And do not call it fixity,
Where past and future are gathered. Neither movement
    from nor towards,
Neither ascent nor decline. Except for the point, the still
    point,
There would be no dance, and there is only the dance.

T. S. Eliot
'Burnt Norton'

PROLOGUE

Hanover, New Hampshire, Earth
17 February 2113

The proverbial February thaw did not materialize for the 203rd annual Dartmouth Winter Carnival, and the temperature was around −10° Celsius when Uncle Rogi Remillard emerged from the sanctuary of the Peter Christian Tavern into a blustery, festive night. Cheered by a late supper of turkey-apple soup and a Vermont cheddar omelette, not to mention a liberal intake of spirits, he was damned if he would let the Family Ghost keep him from the fireworks display. The thing couldn't possibly do anything blatant in the midst of such a mob.

The northeast wind blew leftover snow about thronged Main Street and down the tavern's stairwell. Rogi had to push past revellers who tried to crowd down the steps as he climbed up. When the full blast caught him, he gave his long red-wool muffler an extra twist to wrap it partially about his head. Thick grizzled hair stuck out of the scarf folds like a scraggly fright wig. Uncle Rogi was tall, skinny, and slightly stooped. His youthful face was disfigured by great bags under the eyes and a slightly mashed nose, which dripped when forced to inhale the arctic air of unmodified New Hampshire winters. More fastidious Remillards had long since given up pleading with Rogi to fix himself up. The family image? Ça ne chie pas!

He stood in the partial shelter of the tavern building and looked warily around. The melting grids for both the streets and sidewalks of downtown Hanover had been turned off to preserve a properly old-fashioned atmosphere for the celebration. A six-horse team pulling a snow-roller had tamped down the worst ruts; and now sleighs, farm wagons full of hay and carousing students, and chuffing antique autos equipped with antique tire chains drove towards the College Green in anticipation of the pyrotechnics display. No modern vehicles were in sight. One could imagine it was the 1990s again . . . except that among the human pedestrians in their reproduction winter gear from L. L. Bean and Eddie Bauer were slower-moving groups of exotic tourists from the nonhuman worlds of the Galactic Milieu. All but the hardy little Poltroyans were snugly sealed inside environmental suits with visors closed against the harsh Earth weather. The Poltroyans romped and chortled in the stinging cold, and wore fish-fur mukluks and oversized Dartmouth souvenir sweatshirts over their traditional robes.

Rogi searched the night, using his watering eyes rather than his farscan ultrasense. The damn Ghost was too clever a screener to be spotted with the mind's eye – or at least *his* mind's eye. Perhaps the thing had given up and gone away. God, he hoped so! After leaving him in peace for thirty years it had given him a nasty shock, accosting him there in the bookshop just as he was getting ready to close up. He had fled out into the street and it had followed, importuning him, all the way to the Peter Christian Tavern.

'Are you still here, mon fantôme?' Rogi muttered into his scarf. 'Or did it get too cold for you, waiting outside? Silly thing. Who'd notice a ghost in a crowded bar with mulled cider and hot buttered rum flowing like Ammonoosuc Falls? Who'd notice a dozen ghosts?'

Something insubstantial stirred in the tiny plaza fronting the Nugget Cinema just south of the tavern. Whirling powder snow seemed for a moment to slide over and around a certain volume of empty air.

Bon sang! It had waited for him, all right. Rogi farspoke it:

Hello again. Beats me, Ghost, why you don't simply put on a psychocreative body and sit down to supper with me like a civilized being. Other Lylmik do it.

The Ghost said: There are too many alumni operants in the Peter Christian tonight. Even a Grand Master or two. In their cups, the older ones might be unpredictably insightful.

'And that would never do, eh? Some really big operator might see through you in the worst way!' Rogi's whisper was scathing and his mental façade, fortified with Dutch courage, no longer betrayed a hint of unease. 'Well, I'm going over to watch the fireworks. How about you?'

The mysterious presence drifted closer, exuding

restrained coercion. Oh, yes — it could force its will on him any time it liked; the fact that it didn't had ominous implications. It needed wholehearted cooperation in some scheme again, the sneaky bastard, and very likely over some considerable span of time. Fat chance!

The Ghost's mind-voice was insistent: We must talk.

'Talk between skyrockets,' Rogi told it rudely. 'Nobody invited you here tonight. I've been waiting for this all winter. Why should I give up my fun?'

He turned his back and set off into the crowd. Nothing restrained him physically or mentally, but he was aware of the thing following. Bells in the Baker Library tower struck ten. A brass band was playing 'Eleazar Wheelock' over in front of the brilliantly lit Hanover Inn. The leafless branches of the ancient elms, maples and locust trees around the snowy quadrangle were trimmed in twinkling starlights. Streetlamps had been dimmed so the pseudoflames of the energy torches set up around the campus were the major source of illumination. They cast a mellow glow over the cheerful waiting throng and the ranks of huge snow sculptures in front of the college residence halls. In this centennial year of the Great Intervention, whimsical takeoffs on Milieu themes predominated. There was a flying saucer with its Simbiari crew marching down the gangplank, each exotic carrying a bucket of frozen green Jell-O. A hideous effigy of a Krondaku held out a tentacle to take a candy cane from a smiling human snow-child. Gi engaged in their favourite pursuit were posed in a Kama Sutra ensemble. Sigma Kappa had produced Snow White and the Seven Poltroyans. Out in the middle of the College Green was the festival's monumental theme sculpture: a bizarre armoured humanoid like a fairy-tale knight, astride a rampant charger that was almost — but not quite — a horse. This statue was almost eight metres high.

The Ghost observed: A fair likeness of Kuhal, but the chaliko's a bit off the mark.

'The Outing Club tried to get him to be grand marshal of the cross-country ski parade,' Rogi said, 'but Cloud put her foot down. Spoil-sport. And you can't fool me, Ghost. I know why you showed up tonight instead of some other

3

time. You wanted to see the Winter Carnival yourself.' He groped inside his disreputable old blanket-coat and found a leather-bound flask of Wild Turkey.

There was a *choong* from a cleared area over beyond Wentworth Street. The first rocket went up and burst in an umbrella of pink, silver and blue tinsel extending from horizon to horizon. The crowd yelled and applauded. Rogi moved into the lee of a giant elm trunk to escape the wind. He held out the flask. 'Une larme de booze?'

Nobody noticed when the container left his gloved hand, tilted in the air, and then returned to its owner.

Good stuff, said the Family Ghost.

'As if a damned alien Lylmik would know,' Rogi retorted. 'Gotcha!' He took three hefty swallows.

Still seeking solace in the bottle instead of the Unity, I see.

'What's it to you?' Rogi drank again.

I love you. I wish you joy and peace.

'So you always said . . . just before you gave me a new load of shit to shovel.' He took another snort, capped the flask, and put it away. The expression on his face as he watched scarlet fire-flowers bloom above black branches was both cunning and reckless. 'Level with me. What are you, really? A living person or just a manifestation of my own superego?'

The Ghost sighed and said: *We're not going to start that all over again, are we?*

'You're the one who started it – by coming back to bug me.'

Don't be afraid of me, Rogi. I know there were difficult times in the past —

'Damn right! Least you can do is satisfy my curiosity, settle my mind before you start in all over again with the botheration. Put on an astral body like your damn Lylmik compères. Show yourself!'

No.

Rogi gave a derisive sniff. He took a bandanna handkerchief from his pocket and mopped his nose. 'It figures. You're not a real Lylmik anymore than you're a real ghost.' Wind-chill tears blurred the purple and orange comets that

4

chased each other overhead like she-elves with their hair on fire.

The Ghost said: I am a Lylmik. I am the entity charged with the guidance of the Family Remillard through your agency, just as I've always claimed to be. And now I come to you with one last task —

'Shit – I knew it!' Rogi howled in mortal anguish. Three stunning detonations from aerial bombs announced a flock of golden pinwheels. They zoomed heavenward in a tight formation, fissioned into hundreds of small replicas of themselves, then rained down towards the skeletal treetops, whirling and whistling like demented birds. There were vocal and telepathic cheers from the crowd. The brass band in front of the inn played louder. Metapsychic operants among the students were mind-shouting the final verse of the old college song with drunken exuberance:

Eleazar and the Big Chief harangued and gesticulated.
And they founded Dartmouth College, and the Big Chief
   matriculated.
Eleazar was the fa-cul-tee, and the whole curriculum
Was five hundred gallons of New England rum!

'All my life,' Rogi moaned, 'haunted by a damn exotic busybody masquerading as the Family Ghost. Why me? Just a quiet man, not very clever, hardly any metabilities worth mentioning. No world-shaker, just a harmless bookseller. Most insignificant member of the high and mighty Remillard Dynasty. Why me? Persecuted! Pushed around without any common consideration. Forced into one dangerous situation after another just to carry out your damn Lylmik schemes and forward the manifest destiny of humanity . . . unless it all hatched in my own unconscious.'

Like starry dandelion puffs, colossal pompoms of Dartmouth green and white exploded high over the Old Row. The wind strengthened, stirring more and more snow into the air.

Patiently, the Ghost said: You and your family were the key that opened the Galactic Milieu to the human race. The work required an exotic mentor because of the psychosocial immaturity of Earth's people and the pivotal role of you

5

Remillards. And while I admit that you were called upon to endure mental and physical hardship —

'You should be ashamed, using me that way. Playing goddam God.' Rogi gave a maudlin snuffle. He had the flask out again and emptied it with a single pull. 'Nobody ever knew I was the one – your catspaw. Always another pot you wanted stirred, another piece of manipulation, meddling with this Remillard or that one. Uncle Rogi, galactic agent provocateur! And you used every dirty trick in the book to keep me in line, tu bâton merdeux.'

The Ghost said: Your family would have been aware if we had tried to coerce them, and they never would have accepted direct counsel from nonhumans – especially in the pre-Intervention years. We had to work through you. You were the perfect solution. And you survived.

A cascade of white fire poured from the sky behind the library, silhouetting its lovely Georgian Revival tower. Psychokinetic adepts among the spectators took hold of the falling sparks and formed them into Greek letters and other emblems of college fellowship. The crystal dust of the blown snow began to mix with heavier flakes running ahead of the predicted storm.

Rogi's eyes glittered with fresh moisture. 'Yes, I survived it all. A hundred and sixty-eight winters and still going strong. But good old Denis had to die before he ever reached Unity, and Paul and his poor Teresa . . . and Jack! My Ti-Jean, the one you exotics call a saint – for what good it does him. You could have prevented all their deaths, and the billions of deaths in the Rebellion! You could have had me warn Marc, shown me some way to stop him. You could have used me properly, you cold-hearted monster, and nipped the conspiracy in the bud before it ever came to war!'

The Ghost said: It had to happen as it happened. And in your own heart, Rogatien Remillard, you know that the tragedies brought about a greater good.

'Not for Marc! Not for poor Marc the damned one. Why did he have to end that way? My little boy! I think he loved me more than his own father – nearly as much as he loved Ti-Jean. He almost grew up in my bookstore. My

God, he teethed on a mint copy of Otto Willi Gail's *By Rocket to the Moon*!'

The Ghost said: So he did . . . I remember watching him.

'And yet you stood by and let him become the greatest mass murderer in human history – that brilliant misguided man who could have done so much good, if only you'd guided *him* instead of using an impotent old fart like me as your puppet.'

The fireworks were reaching a crescendo. Great jets of vermilion fire rose from the four points of the compass behind the trees and nearly converged overhead. In the dark at the zenith, in the midst of the glare, there appeared a dazzling white star. It vibrated and split in two and the paired lights began to orbit a common centre drawing intricate figures like laser projections. The stars split again and again; each set drew more detailed designs about the central focus until the sky was covered with a blazing mandala, a magical pattern of spinning wheels within ornate wheels, white tracery in ever-changing motion.

Then it froze. It was fire-lace for a moment, then broke into fine shards of silver that still held the wondrous pattern. The night was webbed in a giant constellation of impossible intricacy. Down on the campus the crowd released a pent-up breath. The tiny diamond-points faded to darkness. The show was over.

Uncle Rogi shivered and pulled his muffler tighter. People were hurrying away in all directions now, fleeing the cold. The band finished playing 'The Winter Song' and withdrew into the shelter of the Hanover Inn, there to drink the health of Eleazar Wheelock and many another Dartmouth worthy. Sleigh bells jingled, the wind roared in the white pines, and fresh falling snow curtained off the tall sculpture of the Tanu knight on the Dartmouth College Green.

'Whatever you want,' Rogi told the Ghost, 'I won't do it.'

He darted off across rutted Wheelock Street, dodging a Model A Ford, a wasp-coloured Ski-Doo, and a replica post-coach of 1820 vintage carrying a party of riotous Poltroyans.

7

The unseen presence dogged Rogi's heels. It said: This is the centennial year of the Intervention, 2113, and a year significant in other ways as well.

'Et alors?' sneered Rogi loftily. He headed back on Main Street alongside the hotel.

The Ghost was cajoling: You must undertake this last assignment, and then I promise you that these visitations will end . . . if at the end you wish it so.

'The devil you say!' The bookseller came to a sudden stop on the brightly lit sidewalk. There were roisterers all around, shouting to one another and filling the aether with farspoken nonsense. The celebrating students and visitors ignored Rogi and he in turn shut out all perception of them as he strained his mental vision to get a clear view of his tormentor. As always, he failed. Frustration brought new tears to his eyes. He addressed the Ghost on its intimate mode:

Thirty goddam years! Yes, thirty years now you've let me alone, only to come back and say you want to start all over again. I suppose it's to do with Hagen and Cloud. Well, I won't help you manipulate those poor young folks – not even if you bring a whole planeful of Lylmiks to lay siege to my bookshop. You exotics don't know how stubborn an Earthling can be till you try to cross an old Canuck! To hell with you and your last assignment – et va te faire foutre!

The Ghost laughed. And the laugh was so different from its characteristic dispassionate expressions of amusement, so warm, so nearly human, that Rogi felt his fear and antagonism waver. He was overcome by a peculiar sense of déjà vu.

Then he was startled to discover that they had already reached South Street and were just across from The Eloquent Page, his bookshop. In this part of town, away from the college buildings and drinking establishments, the sidewalks were nearly deserted. The historic Gates House, with his shop on the first-floor corner and the white clapboard of the upper storeys blending into the thickening storm, had only a single lighted window in the north dormer: the sitting room of his third-floor apartment. He hustled up the steps into the entry on Main Street, pulled off a glove, and thumbed the warm, glowing key-pad of the lock. The outer door swung open. He looked over his shoulder into the swirling snow. The laughter of the Ghost still rang in his mind.

'Are you still there, damn you?'

From inside the hallway, the Ghost said: Yes. You will not refuse me, Rogi.

The bookseller cursed under his breath, stepped inside, and slammed the door. Stamping his feet, he shook himself like an old hound and untwined the red muffler. 'Go ahead – coerce me! But sooner or later I'll break away, and then I'll sic the Magistratum on your self-righteous, scheming ass! I'm a Milieu citizen and I've got my rights. Not even the Lylmik can violate the Statutes of Freedom and get away with it.'

The Ghost said: You're half drunk and wholly ridiculous. You've worked yourself into a frenzy without even knowing what my request is.

Rogi rushed up the stairs, past the doors of darkened offices on the second floor, until he came to his own aerie. He fumbled in his pocket for the famous key ring with its gleaming red fob.

'You've set your sights on Hagen and Cloud – or on their kids!' he said wildly. He flung the door open and nearly tripped over Marcel, his great shaggy Maine Coon cat.

The Ghost said: My request does concern them, but only indirectly.

Outside, the snow hissed against the double-glazed windows. The old wooden building responded to the storm's pressure with dozens of secret little noises. Rogi slouched into his sitting room. He dropped his coat and scarf over a battered trestle bench, sat down in the cretonne-covered armchair in front of the standing stove, and began to take off his boots. Marcel circled the bench purposefully, bushy tail waving. He broadcast remarks at his master in the feline telepathic mode.

'In the right coat pocket, probably frozen stiff,' Rogi told the cat. Marcel rose on his great hind legs, rummaged with a forepaw that would have done credit to a Canada lynx, and hooked a doggie-bag of French fries left over from Rogi's supper. Uttering a faint miaow, incongruous for such a large animal, he transferred the booty to his jaws and streaked out of the room.

The Ghost said: Can it be the same Marcel, food-thief extraordinaire?

'The ninth of his line,' Rogi replied. *What do you want?*

Once again the strangely evocative laughter invaded Rogi's mind, along with reassurance:

You have nothing to be afraid of this time. Believe me. What we want you to do is something you yourself have contemplated doing from time to time over the past twenty years. But since you're such a hopeless old flemmard, you've put it off. I've come to make sure you do your duty. You will write your memoirs.

The bookseller gaped. 'My . . . my memoirs?'

Exactly. The full history of your remarkable family. The chronicle of the Remillards as you have known them.

Rogi began to giggle helplessly.

The Ghost went on: You'll hold nothing back, gloss over no faults, tell the entire truth, show your own hidden role in the drama clearly. Now is the appropriate time for you to do this. You may no longer procrastinate. The entire Milieu will be indebted to you for your intimate view of the rise of galactic humanity – to say nothing of Hagen and Cloud and their children. There are important reasons why you must undertake the task immediately.

Rogi was shaking his head slowly, staring at dancing pseudoflames behind the glass door of the stove. Marcel strolled back into the room, licking his chops, and rubbed against his master's stockinged ankles.

'My memoirs. You mean, that's *all*?'

It will be quite enough. They should be detailed.

Again the old man shook his head. He was silent for several minutes, stroking the cat. He did not bother to attempt a thought-screen. If the Ghost was real, it could penetrate his barrier with ease, if it was not real, what difference did it make? 'You're no fool, Ghost. You know why I never got around to doing the job before.'

The Ghost's mental tone was compassionate: I know.

'Then let Lucille do it. Or Philip, or Marie. Or write the damned thing yourself. You were there spying on us from the beginning.'

You are the only suitable author. And this is the suitable time for the story to be told.

Rogi let out a groan and dropped his head into his hands. 'God – to rake up all that ancient history! You'd think the painful parts would have faded by now, wouldn't you? But those are the most vivid. It's the better times that I seem to have the most trouble recalling. And the overall picture – I still can't make complete sense of it. I never was much good at psychosynthesis. Maybe that's why I get so little consolation from the Unity. Just a natural operant, an old-style bootstrap head, not one of your preceptor-trained adepts with perfect memorecall.'

Who knows you better than I? That's why I'm here myself to make this request. To give help when it's needed —

'No!' Rogi cried out. The big grey cay leapt back and crouched with flattened ears. Rogi stared pointedly at the spot where the Ghost seemed to be. 'You mean that? You intend to stay around here prompting me and filling in the gaps?'

I'll try to be unobtrusive. With my help, you'll find your own view of the family history clarifying. At the end, you should understand.

'I'll do it,' Rogi said abruptly, 'if you show yourself to me. Face to face.'

Your request is impossible.

'Of course it is . . . because you don't exist! You're nothing but a fuckin' figment, a high-order hallucination. Denis thought so, and he was right about the other loonies in the family, about Don and Victor and Maddy. You tell me to write my memoirs because some part of my mind wants to justify the things I did. Ease my conscience.'

Would that be so terrible?

Rogi gave a bitter laugh. The cat Marcel crept back on enormous furry feet and bumped his forehead affectionately against his master's leg. One of Rogi's hands automatically dropped to scratch the animal's neck beneath its ruff. 'If you're a delusion, Ghost, then it means that the triumph of Unified Humanity was nothing but the result of an old fool's schizophrenia. A cosmic joke.'

I am what I say I am — a Lylmik.

'Then show yourself! You owe it to me, damn you.'

Rogi . . . nobody see the Lylmik as they really are, unless that person is also a Lylmik. We are fully perceptible only to minds functioning on the third level of consciousness — the next great step in mental evolution, which you younger races of the Milieu have yet to attain. I tell you this — which is known to no other human — to prove my commitment to you. My love. I could show you any one of a number of simulacrum bodies, but the demonstration would be meaningless. You must believe me when I say that if you saw me truly, with either the mind's eye or that of the body, your sanity would be forfeit.

'Horse-puckey. You don't show yourself, I don't write the memoirs.' A tight little smile of satisfaction thinned Rogi's lips. He patted his lap and Marcel leapt up, purring. The old man watched the dancing artificial flames. He whispered, 'I've had my suspicions about you for years, Ghost. You just *knew* too much. No probability analysis, no proleptic metafunction can account for what you knew.'

The Seth Thomas tambour clock that had belonged to Rogi's mother struck twelve with familiar soft chimes. Outside, the storm winds assaulted the north wall of the building with mounting vigour, making the aged timbers groan and the clapboards snap. Marcel snuggled against Rogi's stomach, closed his wildcat eyes, and slept.

'I'm bound and determined to know the truth about you, Ghost. Read my mind! I'm wide open. You can see I mean what I say. I'll work with you and write the memoirs only if you come out in the open at last — whatever the consequences.'

Rogi, you're incorrigible.

'Take it or leave it.' The old man relaxed in the armchair, fingering a silken cat's ear and toasting his feet at the stove.

Let me propose a sublethal compromise. I'll let you see me the way I *was*.

'You got a deal!'

Rogi realized that the thing was invading his mind, flooding him with the artificial calm of redactive impulses, taking advantage of the liquor's depressant effect, triggering endorphins and God knew what-all to bolster him in anticipation.

And then Rogi saw. He said, 'Ha.' Then he laughed a little and added, 'Goddam.'

Are you satisfied?

Rogi held out a trembling hand. 'Are you going to tell me the way you worked it?'

Not until you complete your own story.

'But — '

We have a deal. And now, good night. We'll begin the family history tomorrow, after lunch.

Part I
The Surveillance

From the Memoirs of
Rogatien Remillard

I went down to walk along the icebound Connecticut River very early today before beginning this chronicle. My wits were more than usually muddled from overindulgence, and I had received an emotional shock as well – call it a waking dream! – that now seemed quite impossible out here in the fresh air and the revitalizing aetheric resonances of the rising sun. As I went west along Maple Street the pavements were still patchy wet and steaming; the melting network had been turned back on precisely at 0200 hours. In the business district and throughout most of the college precincts the −25° chill would be gentled by area heaters, but in this residential part of Hanover it was still fast winter. The night's brief storm had given us an additional ten or fifteen cents of snow, piling small drifts in the lee of fences and shrubs. Out here only a few wealthy eccentrics had force-field bubbles over their houses to screen out the elements. It was early enough so that the gravo-magnetic ground-cars and flying eggs were still locked away in their garages.

Down in the sheltered strip of woodland alongside frozen Mink Brook the scene was even more reminiscent of the New England I knew when I was a kid in the 1940s. The snow under the tall hemlocks and birches was almost knee-deep and level as a marble floor. I'd brought decamole snowshoes in my coat pocket and it took only a moment to inflate them, slip them on, and go slogging down to the shore path that paralleled the silent Connecticut.

The great deep river was locked under a thick ice mantle, reminding me that winters are colder now than in my youth – if not always so picturesque. Thanks to the storm, the snow-cover of the Connecticut was again without blemish, swept clean of the tracks of skis and power toboggans and the footprints of foolish rabbits seeking a better climate on the other bank, over in Vermont. I 'shoed north for nearly two and a half kloms, passing under the Wheelock Street

Bridge and skirting the Ledyard Canoe Club. Finally I reached that awesome patch of forest preserve where white pines tower eighty metres high and little siskins and nuthatches whisper mysteriously in the brush thickets. The scent of conifer resin was intense. As so often happens, the odour triggered memory more strongly than any effort of will ever could.

This snow-girt wood I had not visited for three decades was the place where the boys used to come.

The Gilman Biomedical Center of the college was only a few blocks away – and the Metapsychic Institute, and the hospital. Young Marc, an undergraduate already showing the promise that would someday make him a Paramount Grand Master, used to coerce the nursing staff in the intensive care unit and take Jack away. The beloved baby brother, slowly dying of intractable cancers that would devour his body and leave only his great brain untouched, rode in an ingeniously modified backpack. Marc and Jack would spend a morning or an afternoon talking, laughing, arguing. Stolen, pitiable hours of pine and pain and the contention of those brother-minds! It was then the rivalry was born that would bring thousands of inhabited planets to the brink of ruin, and threaten not only the evolution of the Human Mind but also that of the five exotic races who had welcomed us into their peaceful Galactic Milieu . . .

Close to the shore where the snow lies drifted, it is not easy to tell where granite ends and the frozen river begins. The juncture is veiled. Molecules of water have slowed to the solidity of stone, apparently immutable. My deep-sight easily sees through the snow to tell the difference, just as it pierces the icy lid of the Connecticut to perceive black water flowing beneath. But I am not strong-minded enough to see the subtler flux of the ice molecules themselves, or the vibration of the crystals within the granite boulders, or the subatomic dance of the bits of matter and energy among the nodes of the dynamic-field lattices that weave the *reality* of ice and grey rock in the Cosmic All. My vision of the winter river in its bed remains limited, in spite of the abstract knowledge science lends me.

18

And how much more difficult it is to apprehend the greater pattern! We know we are free, even though constraints hedge us. We cannot see the *unus mundus*, the entirety that we know must exist, but are forced to live each event rushing through space and time. Our efforts seem to us as random as the Brownian movement of molecules in a single drop of ultramagnified water.

Nevertheless the water droplets come together to make a stream, and then a river that flows to the sea where the individual drops — to say nothing of the molecules! — are apparently lost in a vast and random pooling. The sea not only has a life and identity of its own, but it engenders other, higher lives, a role denied to water molecules alone. Later, after the sun draws them up, the molecules condense into new water drops or snowflakes and fall, and sustain life on the land before draining away to the sea again in the cycle that has prevailed since the biogenesis. No molecule evades its destiny, its role in the great pattern. Neither do we, although we may deny that a pattern exists, since it is so difficult to envision. But sometimes, usually at a far remove of time, we may be granted the insight that our actions, our lives, were not pointless after all. Those (and I am one) who have never experienced cosmic consciousness may find consolation in simple instinct. I know in my heart — as Einstein did, and he was justified in the long view if not in the short — that the universe is not a game of chance but a design, and beautiful.

The great white cold takes hold of the amorphous water droplet and turns it into an ice crystal of elegant form. Can I organize my memories into an orderly ensemble and give coherence to the tangled story of the Family Remillard? I have been assured that I can . . . but you, the entity reading this, may decide otherwise.

C'est bien ça.

The chronicle will begin in New Hampshire and conclude in interstellar space. Its time-span, willy-nilly, will be that of my own life; but I will tell the story from a number of different viewpoints — not all of them human. My personal role in the drama has not always been prominent, and certain Milieu historians have forgotten that I existed, except for grudging footnotes! But I was Don's fraternal twin and close to his wife and children, I was with Denis and Lucille at the Intervention, and I know what drove Victor and the Sons of Earth to their infamy. I was privy to the secrets of the 'Remillard Dynasty' and to those of the Founding Human Magnates. I watched Paul 'sell' New Hampshire as the human capital of the Milieu. I stood by Teresa throughout her tragedy. I know what kind of demons possessed Madeleine. I can tell the story of Diamond Mask, since her life was inextricably entwined with that of my family. Marc's tormented presence and his Metapsychic Rebellion will pervade these memoirs and climax them.

Above all, however, this will have to be the story of Jon Remillard, whom I called Ti-Jean and the Milieu named Jack the Bodiless. Even though he was born after the Intervention, his life is prefigured in the struggles and triumphs of the people I will write about in this book: the first human beings to have full use of their higher mind-powers. But Jack would be their culmination. He would show us the awful and wonderful course our human evolution must take. He was the first Mental Man. Terrified, we saw in him what we will eventually become.

Saint Jean le Désincarné, priez pour nous! But please – let us not have to follow your example for at least another million years.

2

Observation Vessel Chassti [Simb 16–10110]
9 August 1945

'Look there,' cried Adalasstam Sich. 'They've done it again!'

The urban survey monitoring system had zeroed in on the terrible event at the moment of the bomb's detonation, and at once Adalasstam stabbed the key that would transfer the enhanced image from his console to the large wall-screen. The other two Simbiari on duty saw the fungoid growth of the death-cloud. A blast wave spread away from it, obliterating the beautiful harbour.

'O calamity! O day of despond! O hope-wreck!' intoned Elder Laricham Ashassi. Thin green mucus poured from the scrobiculi of his fissured countenance and outstretched palms. Being the senior member of his race present, it was his duty to express the sorrow and vexation of all Simbiari at the catastrophic sight – and its implications. The telepathic overtones of his keening brought the observers of the other Milieu races on watch hurrying into the oversight chamber.

The two little humanoid Poltroyan mates, Rimi and Pilti, who had been at work in EM Modulation Records next door, were followed closely by the monstrous bulk of Doka'-eloo, the Krondak Scrutator of Psychosocial Trends and a magnate of the Concilium. The horror unfolding on the wall-screen was so riveting that none of the entities thought to prevent the entry of the ship Gi, NupNup Nunl, until it was too late. The creature's great yellow eyes rolled back into its skull as the mass death-shout from the holocaust filled the chamber. NupNup Nunl uttered a wail in a piercing progression of minor sixths, lost consciousness from shock, and proceeded to collapse. Doka'eloo caught it with his psychokinesis and lowered it gently to the deck, where it lay in a dishevelled heap of silky filoplumage, gangling limbs and pallid genitalia. Aware that their supersensitive colleague's mind had withdrawn safely into the consolation of the Unity, the others paid no more attention to it.

Elder Laricham, still dripping in ritual mourning, let dismay sharpen into indignation. 'One atomic bombing was dire enough. But to devastate *two* cities — ! And with peace feelers already sent forth by the wretched Islanders!'

'Barbaric beyond belief,' agreed Chirish Ala Malissotam; but she held her green, as did her spouse Adalasstam. 'But it was just about what one might expect of humanity, given the escalation of atrocities among all participants in this war.'

'By using this appalling weapon,' Adalasstam said, 'the

Westerners prove they are no less savage and immoral than the Island warmongers.'

'I do not agree,' Doka'eloo said ponderously. He paused, and the others knew they were in for a lecture; but the Krondaku was their superior officer as well as a magnate of the Concilium, so they steeled themselves. 'While it is true that the Islanders at this time have expressed a certain inclination to sue for peace, prompted by the first display of atomic weaponry, their gesture was by no means whole-hearted. The Island military leaders remain determined to continue hostilities – as our Krondak analysis of their high-level signals has confirmed. The Westerners are partially aware of this intelligence. Even without it, however, given the Islanders' record of perfidy in past dealings, plus the warrior-ethic forbidding honourable surrender, one might hold the West justified in thinking that the Islander High Command required a second stimulus' – he nodded at the fire-storm on the screen – 'to bring the truth of their situation home to them beyond the shadow of a doubt.'

'Bring home indeed!' exclaimed the scandalized Chirish Ala. 'Oh, I agree that this second atomic bombing will end the stupid war, Doka'eloo Eebak. But by taking this course the planet Earth has signed its metapsychic death-warrant. No world utilizing atomic weaponry prior to its cooperative advent into space has ever escaped destruction of its primary civilized population component. The coadunation of the global Mind has been set back at least six thousand years. They'll revert to hunter-gatherer!'

'We might as well pack up the mission and go home right now,' old Laricham said. The other two Simbiari murmured agreement.

'Precedent tends to support your pessimism,' said the imperturbable Krondaku. 'Nevertheless, we will await the decision of the Concilium. Debate has been lively since the atomic bombing of the first Island city. This second incident, which I farspoke to Orb promptly, should elicit a vote of confidence concerning our Earth involvement.'

'The Concilium's vote is a foregone conclusion,' Adalasstam said. 'The Earthlings are bound to blast themselves to a postatomic Paleolithic within the next fifty orbits or so, given their abysmal state of sociopolitical immaturity.'

'Perhaps not!' the male Poltroyan, Rimi, piped up. He and his mate had been watching the mushroom cloud hand in hand, with tears in their ruby eyes and their minds locked in mutual commiseration. But now they showed signs of cheering up.

Pilti, the female Poltroyan, said, 'Earthlings have been atypical in their accelerated scientific progress as well as in their aggressive tendencies. Certain segments responded to this war with a great upsurge of solidarity, setting aside petty differences for the first time in human history as they worked together to oppose a clearly immoral antagonist.'

'By Galactic standards, they're ethical primitives,' Rimi said. 'But they have *amazing* metapsychic potential. Isn't that right, Doka'eloo Eebak?'

'You speak truly,' the monstrous being assented.

Now the fallen Gi began to stir. It opened its enormous eyes while keeping its mind well screened from distressing resonances. 'I do hope we won't have to write Earth off,' NupNup Nunl fluted. 'It has such gorgeous cloud formations and oceanic shadings – and its inventory of presapient life is rich beyond measure and quite resplendent. The birds and butterflies! The oceanic microflora and the glorious sea-slugs!'

'Pity the sea-slugs aren't candidates for induction into the Milieu,' snorted Adalasstam.

NupNup Nunl climbed to its feet, assisted by kindly Rimi. The Gi settled its plumage and untangled its testicular peduncles. 'Human beings are quarrelsome and vindictive,' it conceded. 'They persecute intellectual innovators and mess up the ecology. But who can deny that their music is the most marvellous in the known universe? Gregorian chant! Bach counterpoint! Strauss waltzes! Indian ragas! Cole Porter!'

'You Gi!' Elder Laricham exclaimed. 'So hopelessly sentimental. What matter if the human race is an aesthetic wonder – when it so obstinately resists the evolution of its Mind?' Laricham turned to the two Poltroyans. 'And your optimistic assessment, Rimi and Pilti, is supported by nothing more than a naive view of the synchronicity lattices. The Arch-College of Simb has recognized Earth's unsuitability from the very start of this futile surveillance.'

'How fortunate for humanity,' Rimi remarked suavely, 'that our federation of worlds outranks *yours* in the Concilium.'

Chirish Ala could not resist saying, 'Poltroyans empathize with Earthlings merely because both races are so revoltingly fecund.'

'So speed the great day of Earth's Coadunate Number,' Pilti said, lowering her eyes in piety. And then she grinned at the female Simb. 'By the way, my dear, did I tell you I was pregnant again?'

'Is this a time for vulgar levity?' cried Adalasstam, gesturing at the wall-screen.

'No,' Pilti said. 'But not a time for despair, either.'

Rimi said, 'The Amalgam of Poltroy has confidence that the human race will pull back from the brink of Mind destruction. In friendship, let me point out to our esteemed Simbiari Uniates that we of Poltroy belong to a very old race. We have studied many more emerging worlds than you have. There has been at least one exception to the correlation between atomic weaponry and racial suicide. Us.'

The three green-skinned entities assumed a long-suffering mental linkage. Elder Laricham acknowledged the point with cool formality.

'Oh, that's so true!' burbled the Gi. It wore a sunny smile, and its pseudomammary areolae, which had been bleached and shrunken by its horrific experience, began to re-engorge and assume their normal electric pink colour. 'I'd forgotten what bloodthirsty brutes you Poltroyans were in your primitive years. No wonder you feel a psychic affinity to the Earthlings.'

'And no wonder *we* don't,' Elder Laricham growled. He crinkled his features to stem the flow of green. 'Earth is a lost cause, I tell you.' He pointed melodramatically to the screen. 'The principals in the current conflict, Islanders and Westerners, are certain to remain deadly antagonists for the next three generations at the very least. There will be fresh wars of vengeance and retaliation between these two nations so highly charged with ethnic dynamism, then global annihilation. The Galactic Milieu's overly subtle educative effort has been in vain. We will surely have to abandon Earth – at least until its next cycle of high civilization.'

'It's the Concilium's decision, not yours,' Rimi said flatly. 'Any word yet, Doka'eloo Eebak?'

The fearsome looking officer sat motionless except for a single tentacle that flicked emerald blobs towards the floor scuppers in nonjudgemental but relentless tidiness. Doka'-eloo opened his stupendous farsensing faculty to the others so that they might envision the Concilium Orb, a hollow planetoid more than four thousand light-years away in the Orion Arm of the Milky Way. In the central sanctum of the Orb, the governing body of the Coadunate Galactic Milieu had finally completed its deliberation upon the fate of Earth's Mind. The data had been analysed and a poll of magnates was taken. The result flashed to the receptor ultrasense of Doka'eloo with the speed of thought.

He said, 'The Poltroyan Amalgam voted in favour of maintaining the Milieu's involvement with Earth. The Krondak, Gi and Simbiari magnates voted to discontinue our guidance – giving a majority in favour of disengagement.'

'There!' exclaimed Adalasstam. 'What did I tell you?'

'We can't let their music die,' NupNup Nunl grieved. 'Not Sibelius! Not Schoenberg and Duke Ellington!'

But the Krondaku was not finished. 'This negative verdict of the Concilium magnates was summarily vetoed by the Lylmik Supervisory Body.'

'Sacred Truth and Beauty!' whispered Elder Laricham. 'The *Lylmik* intervened in such a trivial affair? Astounding!'

'But wonderful,' cried the two little Poltroyans, embracing.

The Gi shook its fluffy head. Its ovarian externalia trembled on the verge of cerise. 'A Lylmik veto! I can't think when such a thing ever happened before.'

'Long before your race attained coadunation,' Doka'eloo told the hermaphrodite. 'Before the Poltroyans and

Simbiari learned to use stone tools and fire. That is to say, three hundred and forty-two thousand, nine hundred and sixty-two standard years ago.'

In the awestruck mental silence that followed, the Krondaku signalled Adalasstam to change the image on the wall-screen. The picture of the devastated Island city melted into a larger view of Earth as seen from the Milieu observation vessel. The sun shone full on it and it was blue and white, suspended like a brilliant agate against the foaming silver breaker of the galactic plane.

'There is more,' Doka'eloo said. 'The Lylmik order us observers to commence a thirty-year phase of intensified overt manifestation. The people of Earth are to be familiarized with the concept of interstellar society – as a preliminary to possible Intervention.'

The three affronted Simbiari fell to choking on green phlegm. The Poltroyan couple clapped their hands and trilled.

NupNup Nunl controlled itself heroically, quieting its reproductive organs to the magenta state, and uttered a luxurious sigh. 'I'm so glad. It's really a fascinating world, and there *is* a statistically significant chance that the people will shape up. Very long odds, but by no means hopeless . . .'

It extended a six-jointed digit and activated the ambient audio system, which was patched to Vienna radio. The climaxing strains of 'Verklärte Nacht' filled the oversight chamber of the exotic space vessel.

Invisible, it continued the Milieu's surveillance of over sixty thousand years.

3

From the Memoirs of
Rogatien Remillard

I was born in 1945, in the northern New Hampshire mill town of Berlin. My twin brother Donatien and I took our first breaths on 12 August, two days after Japan opened the peace negotiations that would end World War II. Our mother, Adèle, was stricken with labour pains at early Sunday Mass, but with the stubbornness so characteristic of our clan gave no indication of it until the last notes of the recessional hymn had been sung. Then her brother-in-law Louis and his wife drove her to St Luke's, where she was delivered of us and died. Our father Joseph had perished six months earlier at the Battle of Iwo Jima.

On the day of our birth, clouds of radioactivity from the bombing of Hiroshima and Nagasaki were still carried around the world by the jet-stream winds. But they had nothing to do with our mutations. The genes for metapsychic operancy lay dormant in many other families besides ours. The immortality gene, however, was apparently unique. Neither trait would be recognized for what it was until many years had gone by.

Don and I, husky orphans, had a legacy from our mother of a GI insurance policy and an antique mantelpiece clock. We were taken in by Onc' Louie and Tante Lorraine. It meant two more mouths to feed in a family that already included six children, but Louis Remillard was a foreman at the big Berlin paper mill that also employed other males of our clan (and would employ Don and me, in good time). He was a stocky, powerful man with one leg slightly shorter than the other, and he earned good wages and owned a two-storey frame apartment on Second Street that was old but well maintained. We lived on the ground floor, and Oncle Alain and Tante Grace and their even larger brood lived upstairs. Life was cheerful, if extremely noisy. My brother and I seemed to be quite ordinary children. Like most Franco-Americans of the region, we grew up speaking French to our kinfolk, but used English quite readily in our dealings with non-Francophone neighbours and playmates, who were in the majority.

The Family Ghost, when I first met it, also spoke French.

It happened on an unforgettable day when I was five. A gang of us cousins piled into the back of an old pickup truck owned by Gerard, the eldest. We had a collection of pots and pans and pails, and were off on a raspberry-picking expedition into the National Forest west of town, a cut-over wilderness beyond the York Pond fish hatchery. The berries were sparse that year and we scattered widely, working a maze of overgrown logging tracks. Don and I had been warned to stick close to our cousin Cecile, who was fourteen and very responsible; but she was a slow and methodical picker while we two skipped from patch to patch, skimming the easily reached fruit and not bothering with berries that were harder to get.

Then we got lost. We were separated not only from Cecile and the other cousins but from each other. It was one of the first times I can remember being really apart from my twin brother, and it was very frightening. I wandered around whimpering for more than an hour. I was afraid that if I gave in to panic and bawled, I would be punished by having no whipped cream on my raspberry slump at supper.

It began to get dark. I called feebly but there was no response. Then I came into an area that was a dense tangle of brambles, all laden with luscious berries. And there, not ten metres away, stood a big black bear, chomping and slurping.

'Donnie! Donnie!' I screamed, dropping my little berry pail. I took to my heels. The bear did not follow.

I stumbled over decaying slash and undergrowth, dodged around rotted stumps, and came to a place where sapling paper birches had sprung up. Their crowded trunks were like white broom-handles. I could scarcely push my way through. Perhaps I would be safe there from the bear.

'Donnie, where are you?' I yelled, still terror-stricken.

I seemed to hear him say: Over here.

'Where?' I was weeping and nearly blind. 'I'm lost! Where are you?'

He said: Right here. I can hear you even though it's quiet. Isn't that funny?

I howled. I shrieked. It was *not* funny. 'A bear is after me!'

He said: I think I see you. But I don't see the bear. I can only see you when I close my eyes, though. That's funny, too. Can you see me, Rogi?

'No, no,' I wept. Not only did I not see him, but I began to realize that I didn't really *hear* him, either – except in some strange way that had nothing to do with my ears. Again and again I screamed my brother's name. I wandered out of the birch grove into more rocky, open land and started to run.

I heard Don say: Here's Cecile and Joe and Gerard. Let's find out if they can see you, too.

The voice in my mind was drowned out by my own sobbing. It was twilight – entre chien et loup, as we used to say. I was crying my heart out, not looking where I was going, running between two great rock outcroppings . . .

'Arrête!' commanded a loud voice. At the same time something grabbed me by the back of my overall straps, yanking me off my feet. I gave a shattering screech, flailed my arms, and twisted my neck to look over my shoulder, expecting to see black fur and tusks.

There was nothing there.

I hung in air for an instant, too stupefied to utter a sound. Then I was lowered gently to earth and the same adult voice said, 'Bon courage, ti-frère. Maintenant c'est tr'bien.'

The invisible thing was telling me not to be afraid, that everything was now all right. What a hope! I burst into hysterical whoops and wet my underpants.

The voice soothed me in familiar Canuckois, sounding rather like my younger uncle Alain. An unseen hand smoothed my tousled black curls. I screwed my eyes shut. A ghost! It was a ghost that had snatched me up! It would feed me to the bear!

'No, no,' the voice insisted. 'I won't harm you, little one. I want to help you. Look here, beyond the two large rocks. A very steep ravine. You would have fallen and hurt yourself badly. You might have been killed. And yet I know nothing of the sort happened . . . so I saved you myself. Ainsi le début du paradoxe!'

'A ghost!' I wailed. 'You're a ghost!'

I can hear the thing's mind-voice laughing even now as it said: *Exactement! Mais un fantôme familier . . .*

Thus I was introduced to the being who would help me, advise me – and bedevil me – at many critical points in my life. The Family Ghost took my hand and drew me along a shadowy, twisted game trail, making me run so fast I was left nearly breathless and forgot to cry. It reassured me but warned me not to mention our meeting to anyone, since I would not be believed. All too probably brother and cousins would laugh at me, call me a baby. It would be much better to tell them how bravely I had faced the bear.

As the first stars began to show, I emerged from the forest on to the road near the fish hatchery where the pickup truck stood. My cousins and the fish men were there and welcomed me with relieved shouts. I told them I had flung my berry bucket in a bear's face, cleverly gaining time to make my escape. None of them noticed that I stank slightly of pipi. My brother Don did look at me strangely, and I was aware of a question hovering just behind his lips. But then he scowled and was silent.

I got double whipped cream on my raspberry slump that night.

I told nobody about the Family Ghost.

To understand the mind of our family, you should know something of our heritage.

The Remillards are members of that New England ethnic group, descended from French-Canadians, who are variously called Franco-American, Canado-Américaine, or more simply Canuck. The family name is a fairly common one, now pronounced REM-ih-lard in a straightforward Yankee way. As far as I have been able to discover, no other branches of the family harboured so precocious a set of supravital genetic traits for high metafunction and self-rejuvenation. (The 'bodiless' mutagene came from poor Teresa, as I shall relate in due time.)

Our ancestors settled in Québec in the middle 1600s and worked the land as French peasants have done from time immemorial. Like their neighbours they were an industrious, rather bloody-minded folk who looked with scorn upon such novelties as crop rotation and fertilization of the soil. At the same time they were fervent Roman Catholics who regarded it as their sacred duty to have large families. The predictable result, in the harsh climate of the St Lawrence River Valley, was economic disaster. By the mid-nineteenth century the worn-out, much-subdivided land provided no more than a bare subsistence, no matter how hard the farmers worked. In addition to the struggle required to earn a living, there was also political oppression from the English-speaking government of Canada. An insurrection among the habitants in 1837 was mercilessly crushed by the Canadian army.

But one must not think of these hardy, troublesome people as miserable or downtrodden. Au contraire! They remained indomitable, lusty, and intensely individualistic, cherishing their large families and their stern parish priests. Their devotion to home and religion was more than strong – it was fierce, leading to that solidarity (a species of the coercive metafaculty) that Milieu anthropologists call ethnic dynamism. The Québec habitants not only survived persecution and a grim environment, they even managed to increase and multiply in it.

At the same time that the French-Canadian population was outstripping the resources of the North, the Industrial Revolution came to the United States. New England rivers were harnessed to provide power for the booming textile mills and there was a great demand for labourers who would work long hours for low salaries. Some of these jobs were taken by the immigrant Irish, themselves refugees from political oppression and economic woe, who were also formidably dynamic. But French-Canadians also responded to the lure of the factories and flocked southward by the tens of thousands to seek their fortunes. The migratory trend continued well into the 1900s.

'Little Canadas' sprang up in Massachusetts, New Hampshire, Vermont, Maine and Rhode Island. The newcomers clung to their French language and to much of their traditional culture, and most especially to their Catholic faith. They were thrifty and diligent and their numerous offspring followed the parents into the family occupation. They became American citizens and worked not only as mill-hands but also as carpenters, mechanics, lumberjacks and keepers of small shops. Most often, only those children who became priests or nuns received higher education. Gradually the French-Canadians began to blend into the American mainstream as other ethnic groups had done. They might have been quite rapidly assimilated – if it hadn't been for the Irish.

Ah, how we Franco-Americans hated the Irish! (You citizens of the Milieu who read this, knowing what you do of the principal human bloodlines for metapsychic operancy, will appreciate the irony.) Both the Irish and the French minorities in New England were Celts, of a passionate and contentious temperament. Both were, in the latter nineteenth and early twentieth centuries, rivals for the same types of low-status employment. Both had endured persecution in their homelands and social and religious discrimination in America because of their Catholic faith. But the Irish were much more numerous, and they had the tremendous social advantage of speaking the English language – with a rare flair, at that! The Irish parlayed their genius for politicking and self-aggrandizement into domination of the New England Catholic hierarchy, and even took over entire city governments. We Francos were more aloof, politically naive, lacking in what Yankees called 'team spirit' because with us it was the family that came first. With our stubbornly held traditions and French language, we became an embarrassment and a political liability to our more ambitious coreligionists. It was an era fraught with anti-Catholic sentiment, in which all Catholics were suspected of being 'un-American'. So the shrewd Irish-American bishops decreed that stiff-necked Canucks must be forcibly submerged in the great melting-pot. They tried to abolish those parishes and parochial schools where the French language was given first place. They said that we must become like other Americans, let ourselves be assimilated as the other ethnic groups were doing.

Assimilate – intermarry – and the genes for metapsychic operancy would be diluted all unawares! But the great pattern was not to be denied.

We Francos fought the proposed changes with the same obstinacy that had made us the despair of the British Canadians. The actions of those arrogant Irish bishops during the nineteenth century made us more determined than ever to cling to our heritage. And we did. Eventually, the bishops saved face with what were termed 'compromises'. But we kept our French churches, our schools and our language. For the most part we continued to marry our own, increasing our homozygosity – concentrating those remarkable genes that would put us in the vanguard of humanity's next great evolutionary leap.

It was not until World War II smashed the old American social structures and prejudices that the Canucks of New England were truly assimilated. Our ethnocentricity melted away almost painlessly in those postwar years of my early childhood. But it had prevailed long enough to produce Don and me . . . and the others whose existence we never suspected until long after we reached adulthood.

4

South Boston, Massachusetts, Earth
2 August 1953

He was on his way home from the ten-o'clock at Our Lady, toting Sunday papers and some groceries Pa had remembered they were out of, when he got the familiar awful feeling and said to himself: No! I'm outside, away from her. It can't be!

But it was. Sour spit came up in his throat and his knees went wobbly and the shared pain started glowing blue inside his head, the pain of somebody dying who would take him along if he wasn't careful.

But he was outside, in the sunshine. More than six blocks from home, far beyond her reach. It couldn't be her hurting and demanding. Not out here. It never happened out here . . .

It happened in a dark room, cluttered and musty, where a candle in a blue-glass cup burned in front of one Sorrowful Mother (the one with seven swords through her naked pink heart), and the other one lay on her bed with the beads tangled in her bony fingers and her mind entreating him: *Pray a miracle Kier it's a test you see he always lets those he loves best suffer pray hard you must you must if you don't there'll be no miracle he won't listen . . .*

The full force of the transmitted agony took hold of him as he turned the corner on to D Street. Traffic was fairly heavy even at this early hour, when most of Southie drowsed or marked time until the last Mass let out and the sandlot ballgames got underway and the taverns opened; but there wasn't another person in sight on the dirty sidewalks – nobody who could be hurting demanding calling –

Not a person. An animal dying.

He saw it halfway down the block, in the gutter in front of McNulty's Dry Cleaning & Alterations. A dog, hit by a car most likely. And Jeez he'd have to go right by it unless he went way around by the playground, and the groceries were so heavy, and it was so rotten hot, and the pleading was irresistible, and he *did* want to see.

It was a mutt without a collar, a white terrier mix with its coat all smeared red and brown with blood and sticky stuff from its insides. Intelligent trustful eyes looked up at him, letting pain flood out. A few yards away in the street was a dark splotch where it had been hit. It had dragged itself to the kerb, hindquarters hopelessly crushed.

Kieran O'Connor, nine years old and dressed in his shabby Sunday best, gulped hard to keep from vomiting. The dog was dying. It had to be, the way it was squashed. (Her dying was inside her, not nearly so messy.)

'Hey, fella. Hey, boy. Poor old boy.'

The dog's mind projected hurtful love, begging help. He

34

asked it: 'You want a miracle?' But it couldn't understand that, of course.

The dog said to him: *Flies*.

They were all over the wounded parts, feeding on the clotted blood and shit, and Kieran grunted in revulsion. He could so something about them, at least.

'No miracle,' he muttered. He set the bag of groceries and the paper down carefully on the sidewalk and hunkered over the dog, concentrating. As he focused, the iridescent swarm panicked and took wing, and he let them have it in mid-air. The small green-backed bodies fell on to the hot pavement, lifeless, and Kieran O'Connor smiled through his tears and repeated: 'No miracle.'

The dog was grateful. Its mind said: *Thirst*.

'Say – I got milk!' Kieran pulled the quart bottle out of the grocery bag, tore off the crimped foil cap, and lifted the paper lid, which he licked clean and stowed in his shirt pocket for later. Crouching over the ruined body in the sunshine, holding his breath and letting the pain lose itself inside his own head, he dripped cool milk into the dog's mouth.

'Get well. Stop hurting. Don't die.'

The animal made a groaning sound. It was unable to swallow and a white puddle spread under its open jaws. From the brain came a medley of apology and agony, and it clung to him. 'Don't,' he whispered, afraid. 'Please don't. I'm *trying* — '

A shadow fell over the boy and the dog. Kieran looked up, wild-eyed with terror. But it was only Mr Dugan, a middle-aged bald man in a sweat-rumpled brown suit.

'Oh,' said Dugan shortly. 'So it's you.' He scowled.

'I didn't do it, Mr Dugan. A car hit it!'

'Well, can't I see that with my own two eyes? And what are you doing messing with it? It's a goner, as any fool can see, and if you don't watch out, it'll bite.'

'It won't — '

'Don't sass me, boy! And stop wasting good milk on it. I'll phone the Humane Society when I get home and they'll come and put it out of its misery.'

Kieran began to recap the bottle of milk. Tears ran down his flushed face. 'How?' he asked.

Dugan threw up his hands impatiently. 'Give it something. Put it down, for God's sake. Now get away from it, or I'll be telling your Pa.'

No! Kieran said. *You go away! Right now!*

Dugan straightened up, turned, and walked away, leaving Kieran kneeling in the filthy gutter, shielding the dog from the sun.

'Put you out of your misery,' Kieran whispered, amazed that it could be so simple. (Why did Mom try to make it complicated?) He'd never thought of it that way before. Bugs, yes; he didn't care a hoot about them. The rats, either. But a dog or even a person . . .

'You wouldn't take me along, would you?' Kieran asked it warily. The pain-filled eyes widened. 'Stop loving me and I'll do it. Let go. Lay off.' But the dog persisted in its hold, so finally he reached out and rested his fingertips on its head, between its ears, and did it. Oddly, all of the hairs on the dog's body stiffened for an instant, then went flat. The animal coughed and lay still, and all pain ceased.

Kieran wondered if he should say a prayer. But he felt really rotten, so in the end he just covered the body with the want-ad section of the newspaper. His Pa never bothered with that part.

5

From the Memoirs of
Rogatien Remillard

I was not to experience another manifestation of the Family Ghost for nearly sixteen years. That first encounter in the twilit woods took on a dreamlike aspect. It might have been forgotten, I suppose, had not the memory been rekindled every time I smelled raspberries or the distinctive pungency of bear scats. But I did not brood on it. Truth to tell, I had more important matters to occupy me: my own developing metafunctions and those of my brother.

I have already mentioned that Don and I were fraternal twins, no more closely related than any singleton brothers. Many years later, Denis told me that if we had both hatched from a single egg, our brains might have been consonant enough to have attained harmonious mental intercourse, instead of the clouded and antagonistic relationship that ultimately prevailed between us. As it was, we were of very different temperaments. Don was always more outgoing and aggressive, while I was introspective. In adulthood we both were tormented by the psychological chasm separating us from normal humanity. I learned to live with it, but Don could not. In this we were like many other natural operants who came after us, our successes and tragedies blending into the ongoing evolutionary trend of the planetary Mind studied so dispassionately by the scientists of the Galactic Milieu.

In our early childhood, following that initial stress-provoked incident of farspeech and farsight out in the woods, we experienced other near-involuntary telepathic interchanges. Once Don scalded himself with hot soup and I, in the next room, jumped up screaming. I would have a furious argument with a cousin and Don would come running up, knowing exactly what the fight was about. We sometimes dreamed the same dreams and shared unspoken jokes. Eventually, we attained crude telepathic communication as well as a kind of shared farsight and mutual sensitivity. We experimented, 'calling' to each other over greater and greater distances, and exercised our farsight with variations on games such as hide-and-seek and hide-the-thimble. Our cousins were blasé about our talents, ascribing them to the acknowledged freakishness of twins. They learned early not to play card games with us, and casually utilized our farsensing abilities to track down lost items and anticipate impending adult interference in illicit activities. We were a little weird, but we were useful. No big thing.

On one of our first days at school I was cornered by a bully and commanded to hand over my milk money, or suffer a beating. I broadcast a mental cry for help. Don came racing into the schoolyard alcove where I had been trapped, radiating coercive fury and saying not a single word. The bully, nearly twice Don's size, fled. My brother and I stood close together until the bell rang, bonded in fraternal love. This would happen often while we were young, when each of us was the other's best friend. It became rarer as we approached adolescence and ended altogether after we reached puberty.

By the time we were nine (the age, Denis later explained to me, when the brain attains its adult size and the metafunctions tend to 'solidify', resisting further expansion unless painful education techniques stimulate them artificially), Don and I had become fairly adept in what is now called farspeech on the intimate mode. We could communicate across distances of two or three kilometres, sharing a wide range of nuance and emotional content. Our farscanning ability was weaker, requiring intense concentration in the transmission of any but the simplest images. By mutual agreement, we never told anyone explicit details of our telepathic talent, and we became increasingly wary of demonstrating metapsychic tricks to our cousins. Like all children, we wanted to be thought 'normal'. Nevertheless there was a good deal of fun to be had using the powers, and we couldn't resist playing with them surreptitiously in spite of vague notions that such mind-games might be dangerous.

In the lower grades of grammar school we drove the good sisters crazy as we traded farspoken wisecracks and then snickered enigmatically out loud. We sometimes recited in eerie unison or antiphonally. We traded answers to test questions until we were placed in separate classrooms, and even then we still managed to cooperate in uncanny disruptive pranks. We were tagged fairly early as troublemakers and were easily bored and inattentive. To our contemporaries we were the Crazy Twins, ready to do the outrageous to attract attention – just as in our baby years we had vied to attract the notice of hard-working, hard-drinking Onc' Louie and kind but distracted Tante Lorraine. (But our foster parents had three additional children of their own after our arrival, for a total of nine, and we were lost in the crowd of cousins.)

As we grew older we developed a small repertoire of other metafaculties. I was the first to learn how to raise a mental wall to keep my inmost thoughts private from Don, and I was always better at weaving mind-screens than he. It provoked his anger when I retreated into my private shell, and he would exercise his coercive power in almost frantic attempts to break me down. His mental assaults on me were at first without malice; it was rather as if he were afraid to be left 'alone'. When I finally learned to block him out completely he sulked, then revealed that he was genuinely hurt. I had to promise that I would let him back into my mind 'if he really needed me'. When I promised, he seemed to forget the whole matter.

Don amused himself by attempting to coerce others, a game I instinctively abhorred and rarely attempted. He had some small success, especially with persons who were distracted. Poor Tante Lorraine was an easy mark for gifts of kitchen goodies while she was cooking, for example; but it was next to impossible to coerce the redoubtable nuns who were our teachers. Both of us experimented in trying to read the minds of others. Don had little luck, except in the perception of generalized emotions. I was more skilled in probing and occasionally picked up skeins of subliminal thought, those 'talking to oneself' mumblings that form the superficial layer of consciousness; but I was never able to read the deeper thoughts of any person but my twin brother, a limitation I eventually learned to thank God for.

We developed a modest self-redaction that enabled us to speed the healing of our smaller wounds, bruises and blisters. Curing germ-based illness, however, even the common cold, was beyond us. We also practised psychokinesis and learned to move small objects by mind-power alone. I remember how we looted coin telephones throughout two glorious summer weeks, squandering the money on ice cream, pop and bootleg cigarettes. Then, because we were still good Catholic Franco-American boys at heart, we had qualms of conscience. In confession Father Racine gave us the dismal news that stealing from New England Bell (we didn't reveal our modus operandi) was just as much of a sin as stealing from real human beings. Any notions we might have had of becoming metapsychic master-thieves died aborning. Perhaps because of our upbringing, perhaps because of our lack of criminal imagination, we were never tempted along these lines again. Our fatal flaws lay in other directions.

The first indications of them came when we were ten years old.

It was late on a dreary winter day. School was over, and Don and I were fooling around in what we thought was an empty school gym, making a basketball perform impossible tricks. An older boy named O'Shaughnessy, newly come to the school from a tough neighbourhood in Boston, happened to come along and spot us working our psychokinetic magic. He didn't know what he was seeing – but he decided it must be something big and sauntered out to confront us.

'You two,' he said in a harsh, wheedling voice, 'have got a *secret gimmick* – and I want in on it!'

'Comment? Comment? Qu'est-ce que c'est?' we babbled, backing away. I had the basketball.

'Don't gimme that Frog talk – I know you speak English!' He grabbed Don by the jersey. 'I been watching and I seen you gimmick the ball, make it stop in midair and dribble all over your bodies and go into the hoop in crazy ways. Whatcha got – radio control?'

'No! Hey, leggo!' Don struggled in the big kid's grip and O'Shaughnessy struck him a savage, sharp-knuckled blow in the face that made my own nerves cringe. Both of us yelled.

'Shaddup!' hissed O'Shaughnessy. His right hand still clenched Don's shirt. The left, grubby and broken-nailed, seized Don's nose in some terrible street-fighter grip with two fingers thrust up the nostrils and the thumbnail dug into the bridge. Don sucked in a ragged agonized breath through his mouth, but before he could utter another sound the brute said:

'Not a squeak, cocksucker – and your brother better hold off if he knows what's good for the botha you!' The fingers jammed deeper into Don's nose. I experienced a hideous burst of sympathetic pain. 'I push just a little harder, see, I could *pop out his eyeballs*. Hey, punk! You wanna see your brother's eyeballs rollin' on the gym floor? Where I could *step* on 'em?'

Queasily, I shook my head.

'Right.' O'Shaughnessy relaxed a little. 'Now you just calm down and do a repeat of that cute trick I saw you doing when I came in. The in-and-outer long bomb.'

My mind cried out to my brother Donnie:

DonniewhatgonnaDO?

TricktrickDOit! DOitGodsake —

Thenhe'llKNOW —

O'Shaughnessy growled, 'You stalling?' He dug in. I felt pain and nausea and the peripheral area of the gym had become a dark-red fog.

'Don't hurt him! I'll do it!'

Trembling, I held the ball between my hands and faced the basket at the opposite end of the court. It was fully sixty feet away, more than eighteen metres. I made a gentle toss. The ball soared in a great arc as though it were jet-propelled and dropped into the distant basket. When it hit the floor it bounced mightily, came up through the hoop from beneath, and neatly returned to my waiting hands.

'Jeez!' said O'Shaughnessy. 'Radio control! I knew it. Thing's a gold mine!' Raw greed glared out of his eyes. 'Awright, punk, hand over the ball and the gimmick.'

'Gimmick?' I repeated stupidly.

'The thing!' he raged. 'The thing that controls the ball! Dumb little fart-face frog! Don't you know a ball-control gimmick like that's gotta be worth a fortune? Get me outa this backwoods hole and back to Beantown and my Uncle Dan and – never mind! Hand it over.'

'Let my brother go first,' I pleaded.

The big kid laughed. He crooked one leg around Don's ankle and simultaneously pushed. My brother sprawled helplessly on the floor, gagging and groaning. O'Shaughnessy advanced on me with hands outstretched. Two of his fingers were bloody.

'The ball and the gimmick,' he demanded, 'or it's your turn, punk.'

'The only gimmick's inside my head,' I said. 'But you can have the ball.'

I drove the rubber sphere at him with all my psychokinetic strength, hitting him full in his grinning face. His nose shattered with the impact and the ball burst its bladder. I heard a gargling scream from O'Shaughnessy and a throaty noise like a Malamute snarl from somebody else.

Help me get *him Donnie!*

The torn and flattened ball like some writhing marine organism clamping itself across a horror-stricken face. Savage sounds and big hands clawing and punching at me. The brother mind poured out its own PK spontaneously to meld with mine, strength magnified manyfold, cemented with mutual loathing, fear and creative solidarity. Somebody shrieking as the three of us struggled beneath the basket. Then a grotesque figure like a scarecrow, its head a red-smeared dented globe. *Go for it Donnie man HEY togethernow togethernow allezallez SLAMDUNK THE BASTARD* . . .

They found O'Shaughnessy bloody nosed and half out of his mind with terror, stuffed headfirst into the basket so that the hoop imprisoned his upper arms. The broken basketball encased his head and muffled his cries a little, but he was never in any real danger of suffocating. We had been caught, literally red-handed, trying to sneak out of the gymnasium. O'Shaughnessy blamed us, of course, and told the story pretty much as it had happened – leaving out his own extortion attempt and assault with intent to maim. He also accused us of owning a mysterious electronic device 'that the FBI'd be *real* interested in hearing about.'

His tale was too outlandish to be credited, even against us, the Crazy Twins. We maintained that we had found him in his weird predicament and attempted to help. Since we were obviously both too small to have boosted a hulking lout three metres above floor-level, it was evident that O'Shaughnessy had lied. His reputation was even more dubious than ours: he was a bad hat who had been shipped off to relatives in the New Hampshire boondocks in the vain hope of keeping him out of a Boston reformatory. Following the incident with us he was retransported with alacrity and never heard from again.

We, on the other hand, were clearly not telling all we knew.

Many questions were asked. Odd bits of circumstantial evidence were noted and pondered. In the midst of the uproar we remained tight as quahog clams. Our cousins who knew (or could deduce) a thing or two rallied round loyally. The family came first – especially against the Irish saloperie! After some weeks the incident was forgotten.

But Don and I didn't forget. We hashed over and over the glorious experience of metaconcert, the two-minds-working-as-one that had produced an action greater than the sum of its parts, giving us transcendent power over a hated enemy. We tried to figure out how we had done it. We knew that if we could reproduce the effect at will we would never have to be afraid of anyone again.

We thought about nothing else and our schoolwork was totally neglected; but we were never able to mesh our minds that way again, no matter how hard we tried. Some of the fault lay in our imperfect metapsychic development, but the greatest failure was grounded in a mutual lack of trust. Our peril at O'Shaughnessy's hands had been sufficient to cancel our jealous individuality; but once the danger was lifted, we reverted to our deeper mind-sets – Don the driven, domineering coercer and I the one who thought too much, whose imagination even at that young age whispered where the abuse of power might lead.

Each of us blamed the other for the metaconcert failure. We ended up locking each other out in a fury of disappointment, thwarted ambition, and fear – and we barely missed flunking the fifth grade.

Onc' Louie called us to him on a certain spring evening and displayed the fatal report cards. Our cousins were all outside playing in the warm dusk. We heard their laughter and shrieks as they played Red Rover in a vacant lot while we stood sulkily before our uncle and faced the time of reckoning.

'Haven't I done my best to rear you properly? Aren't

you as dear to me as any of my own children?' He brandished the cards and his beer-tinged breath washed over us. 'A few failing grades, one could understand. But this! The sisters say that you must make up these failed subjects or repeat a year. All summer long, you must go to the public school in the morning. What a disgrace! Such a thing has never happened before in this family. You shame the Remillards!'

We mumbled something about being sorry.

'Oh, my boys,' he said sorrowfully. 'What would your poor parents say? Think of them, watching from heaven, so disappointed. It's not as though you were blockheads who could do no better. You have good brains, both of you! To waste them is an insult to the good God who made you.'

We began to sniffle.

'You will do better?'

'Yes, Onc' Louie.'

'Bon.' He heaved a great sigh, turned away from us, and went to the sideboard where he kept the whiskey. 'Now go out and play for a while before bedtime.'

As we fled on to the front porch we heard the clink of glassware.

'Now he can get stinko in peace,' Don hissed bitterly. 'Rotten old drunk. Never expect him to understand. He talks about *us* being a disgrace — '

We sat together on the bottom step, putting aside our enmity. It was quite dark. The other kids were dodging around under the streetlights. We had no wish to join them.

I said, 'Plenty of people flunk. He didn't have to drag Papa and Maman into it . . . or God.'

'God!' Don made the word a curse. 'When you come right down to it, the whole darn mess is his fault.'

Horrified at the sacrilege, I could only gape at him.

He was whispering, but his mental voice seemed to shout inside my skull. 'God made us, didn't he? Okay – our parents made our bodies, but didn't *he* make our souls? Isn't that what the nuns say? And what's a soul anyhow, Rogi? A mind!'

'Yes, but — '

'God made these weird minds of ours, so it's his fault we have all this trouble. How can we help it?'

'Gee, I don't know,' I began doubtfully.

He grabbed me by the shoulders. The voices of the kids mingled with crickets and traffic noises and the sound of a television programme that Onc' Louie had turned on inside.

'Didn't you ever stop to think about it, dummy?' Don asked me. 'Why are we like this? Why aren't there any other people in the world like us? When God made us, what in hell did he think he was doing?'

'What kind of a dumb question is that? That's the dumbest thing you ever said! It's probably some kind of sin, even. You better shut your trap, Donnie!'

He started to laugh, then, a smothered squeaky sound loaded with an awful triumph, and he mind-screamed at me:

He did it it's not our fault we didn't ask for this he can't blame us nobody can hell with all of them hell! hell! hell! . . .

I closed my mind to him, slamming the barrier into place as though I were locking the door of a cellar that threatened to spew out black nightmares; and then he began to snivel and beg me to open up to him again, but I got up from the steps and went back into the house, into the kitchen where Tante Lorraine was baking something and the lights were bright, and I sat at the table and pretended to do my homework.

6

Observation Vessel Spon-Su-Brevon [Pol 41–11000]
10 November 1957

The Poltroyan commander's ruby eyes lost their twinkle and his urbane smile faded to a grimace of incredulity. 'Surely you jest, Dispensator Ma'elfoo! Personnel from my ship?'

The Krondaku's mind displayed a replay of the incident,

complete with close-ups of the miscreant Simbiari scouts taken flagrante delicto. 'As you see, Commander Vorpimin-Limopilakadafin.'

'Call me Vorpi. Do you mind telling me what you were doing in the vicinity of the satellite anyhow?'

'My spouse, Taka'edoo Rok, and I were doing an unscheduled survey in order to include details of its fascinatingly crude design in a report we have prepared. Our transport module was totally screened, as is the invariable custom of the Krondak Xenocultural Bureau when visiting pre-emergent solar systems. The scout craft with the Simbiari was also screened heavily, but this presented no particular obstacle to Grand Master farsensors such as Taka'edoo and myself. We considered replacing the stolen property. However, the scouts had meddled with the biomonitoring equipment, and there was a chance that the satellite might have transmitted some anomalous signal to the Earthside control station. And so we contented ourselves with taking the scouts in charge, together with their booty, and bringing them to you.'

'Love's Oath,' groaned Commander Vorpi. 'Our tour's nearly over, and we had an almost perfect disciplinary record – up to now.'

'My condolences.' The Krondaku politely refrained from stating the obvious: When vessels of his own methodical race were in charge of planetary Mind observations, nothing *ever* went wrong.

'I must request that you testify at the disciplinary hearing,' Vorpi said. 'And perhaps you have suggestions for redress.'

'Our time is limited, Commander Vorpi. We are due back on Dranra-Two in the Thirty-Second Sector for a conference on primitive orbital biohabitats, derelict and functional. We postponed presentation of our paper and sped here at maximum displacement factor when we learned that Sol-Three had just entered this phase of astronautic achievement. (Most of our investigations have involved the orbiters of extinct civilizations.) However, it will not be convenient to prolong our stay . . .'

'Oh, I'll call the silly buggers on the carpet right now.'

Vorpi sent out a thought on the imperative mode: GupGup Zuzl! Have Enforcer Amichass bring in those two scouts on report. And don't forget the contraband. I'll need you to log the hearing. Snapsnapsnap!

Dispensator Ma'elfoo glanced about the commander's directorium. 'A handsomely appointed chamber,' he remarked politely. 'The artifacts are from Earth?' One tentacle palpated the multicoloured animal-fibre carpet while another lifted an Orrefors crystal vase from Vorpi's monitoring desk.

'Souvenirs.' Vorpi waved a violet-tinted hand. 'The drapery textiles from the serictery secretions of certain insect larvae; the rug painstakingly knotted by hand-labourers in a desert region; the paintings by Matisse and Kandinsky, rescued from a Parisian fence; the settee by Sears Roebuck; the liquor-dispensing cabinet by Harrods. May I offer you some refreshment, by the way?'

'I would esteem some Bowmore Scotch,' the Krondaku said. 'My deep-sight perceives a bottle hidden away.'

Vorpi chuckled as he left his desk to do the honours. 'Distinctive treatment of alcohol, the Scotches. I predict a wide market for them in the Milieu – provided the Intervention does take place. Mixer?'

'Just a splash of liquid petrolatum.' The two entities toasted one another. After savouring his drink, Ma'elfoo exhaled gustily. 'Yes, it is as I remembered. Ten orbits ago I visited Sol-Three to participate in a comparative study of aircraft evolution. We went on a survey to the British Isles and I acquired a taste for this beverage, among others. Earth technology has developed apace; but one can be grateful that the distilleries cling to tradition.'

The connoisseurs enjoyed a momentary mental rapport. 'Have you ever sampled the genuine rarities?' Vorpi asked softly. 'Bunnahabhain? Bruichladdich? Lagavulin? Caol Ila?'

The fearsome Krondaku uttered a whimper of ecstasy. 'You're not joshing me, you fire-eyed pipsqueak? *Caol Ila*?'

Vorpi lifted his shoulders, let a tiny smile crease his lips.

The door of the directorium slid open. The Gi GupGup Zuzl, secretary of the mission, stalked in, followed by two very young Simbiari scouts and an enforcer of the same race. Vorpi went back to his desk and sat down. The Gi declaimed:

'Commander, the prisoners taken by Grand Masters Ma'elfoo and Taka'edoo Rok herewith submit to disciplinary inquiry. Defendant names: Scout Misstiliss Abaram and Scout Bali Ala Chamirish. Charges: On this Galactic Day La-Prime 1–344–207, the defendants, on a routine inspection of the Second Earth Orbital Vehicle, did mischievously interfere with said orbiter in contravention of divers Milieu statutes and regulations, removing its subsapient passenger with intent to smuggle said creature on board the Spon-su-Brevon.'

The male and the female scouts stood at attention with screened minds and dry, impassive faces. Bali Ala had a harder time of it than her comrade because the small animal in her arms was squirming wildly and resisting her attempts at coercion. The Simbiari enforcer scowled and added his coercive quotient, but the beast only struggled harder, gave a sharp yap, and jumped free. It made a dash for the still-open door and would have escaped if Ma'elfoo had not zapped its brainstem very gently, paralysing it in its tracks.

Enforcer Amichass, mortified and glistening with green sweat, retrieved the creature and set it like a stuffed toy beside the two crewmen on report. 'I'm sorry about that, Commander. A recalcitrant species that resists — '

'Never mind,' Vorpi sighed. 'Get on with it. What do you two have to say for yourselves? Of all the sophomoric idiocies – pinching the damn Russian dog!'

'Her name is Laika,' Misstiliss said.

Bali Ala said, 'The power-source of the vehicle's environmental system was almost exhausted. The animal was about to perish from oxygen lack. We – we shorted out the biomonitoring equipment and took Laika after making certain that Soviet ground control would have no indication of any anomaly.'

Misstiliss added, 'The orbit of the satellite is very eccentric and decaying rapidly. Sputnik II will burn up on reentry, obliterating any trace of our interference. Laika has endured nearly a week in orbit, and we thought she might provide us with valuable research data — '

'Half-masticated lumpukit!' swore the Poltroyan commander. 'You wanted to take the thing back with you as a souvenir! As a pet!'

A green droplet hung from Misstiliss's nose. He fixed his gaze on a point where the wall behind Commander Vorpi met the ceiling. 'You are correct, of course, sir. We admit our guilt fully, repent of the infraction, and stand ready to accept discipline at the Commander's pleasure.'

'So say I also,' Bali Ala murmured. 'But we really didn't do any harm.'

'Won't you youngsters ever learn?' Vorpi was out of his chair and pacing in front of the pair and the dog, waving his glass of Scotch by way of punctuation. 'We realize that these long surveillance tours of exotic worlds can be tedious – especially to youths who, like yourselves, belong to a race imperfectly attuned to Unity. But think of the importance of our work! Think of the Milieu's noble scheme for planet Earth and our hope that its unique Mind may eventually enrich the Galaxy!'

The Krondaku addressed Commander Vorpi on his intimate mode: *At least that's what the Lylmik keep telling us.*

'Young people,' Vorpi went on, 'remember your history. Think of the poor planet Yanalon, Friin-Six, that was hurled back to barbarism on the very threshold of coadunation merely because a careless botanist on a Milieu survey vessel contravened regulations and picked a single piece of fruit and spat out the pips . . .'

She was a Poltroyan, as I recall, said Ma'elfoo.

'The work we do, coaxing these primitive worlds towards metapsychic operancy and coadunation with our Milieu, is excruciatingly delicate. It can be jeopardized by a single thoughtless action, even one that seems harmless. This is why every infraction of the Guidance Statutes for Overt Intervention must be considered a most serious matter. One doesn't meddle frivolously with the destiny of a sapient race.'

And tell that to the Lylmik as well! Ma'elfoo suggested.

His peroration at an end, Vorpi resumed his seat and said, 'Now you may respond.'

'We would not deliberately contravene any scheme of the Concilium,' Bali Ala said stiffly, 'even in the case of a patently unworthy world such as Earth, which has been showered with far more Milieu assistance than it deserves. But . . . the Earthlings will never know that we saved the little dog, and it has a very appealing personality. Far more appealing than that of the average human, when it comes to that! We farspoke Laika on all three of our inspection tours of the satellite, and I admit that we both became bonded to her.'

The Gi smiled and whiffled its cryptomammaries. 'It really *is* adorable.'

Misstiliss said, 'When we saw that the planetside controllers meant to let Laika die, we were outraged – and we acted. I'm sorry we violated the Guidance Statutes, but not sorry we saved the little dog.'

Commander Vorpi tapped the side of the empty Scotch glass with the talon of his little finger. 'A grave matter. Yet, as you said, it would seem no harm was done.'

'I haven't yet logged the hearing,' GupGup Zuzl insinuated slyly. 'And we have enjoyed a perfect duty tour up until now . . .'

Vorpi fixed the Krondak scientist with a meaningful gaze. 'However, the violation was witnessed and reported by two citizens of unimpeachable status.'

Did you say Caol Ila, my dear Vorpi?

I only have two bottles.

One for me and one for Toka'edoo Rok.

'What is your disposition of this case, Commander?' the Gi secretary inquired formally.

'I don't find any infraction of Milieu statutes,' Vorpi replied, 'but these crewmen are clearly derelict in not having filed a report on their last inspection of the satellite Sputnik II. Let a reprimand be entered in their files, and they are sentenced to six days on waste-water-recycling system maintenance. The animal can keep them company. Dismissed.'

The Krondaku cancelled his coercive grip on the dog,

which came to its senses as Misstiliss scooped it up. It lapped at the Simb's glistening green face.

'Likes the way we taste,' the scout said sheepishly. He and Bali Ala saluted and hurried away, taking Laika with them.

7

From the Memoirs of
Rogatien Remillard

Belatedly, at the age of twelve, I discovered that I liked to read. It was early in 1958 and every American kid was passionately interested in the new 'race for space'. Our older cousins bought science-fiction magazines and left them lying around, and I picked them up and immediately became addicted. They were much more exciting than comic books. But it was not the tales of space travel that fascinated me so much as the stories that dealt with extra-sensory perception.

ESP! For the first time I was able to put a name to the powers that made Don and me aliens in our own country. I got all worked up over the discovery and made Don read some of the stories, too; but his reaction was cynical. What did that stuff have to do with us? It was fiction. *Somebody had made it up*.

I ventured beyond the magazines, to the Berlin Public Library. When I looked up ESP and related topics in the encyclopedias, my heart sank. One and all, the reference books acknowledged that 'certain persons' believed in the existence of mental faculties such as telepathy, clairvoyance, and psychokinesis. One and all, the books declared that there was no valid scientific evidence whatsoever for such belief.

I went through all the books in the juvenile department that dealt with the brain, then checked the adult shelves. None of the books even mentioned the mind-powers that Don and I had. The Berlin library was rather small and it had no serious volumes about parapsychology, only a few crank books listed under 'Occult Phenomena' in the card catalogue. Hesitantly, I went to the librarian and asked if she could help me find books about people who had extraordinary mind-powers. She thought very hard for a moment, then said, 'I know the very book!'

She gave me one of the old Viking Portable Novel collections and pointed out Olaf Stapledon's *Odd John* to me. Concealing my disappointment at the fiction format, I dutifully took it home, read it, and had the living hell scared out of me.

The book's hero was a mutant of singular appearance and extremely high mental power. He was Homo superior, a genius as well as an operant metapsychic, trapped in a world full of drab, commonplace normals, most of whom did their fumbling best to understand him but failed. Odd John wasn't persecuted by ordinary humans; there were even those who loved him. And yet he was tormented by loneliness and the knowledge of his uniqueness. In one chilling passage, he described his attitude towards other people:

I was living in a world of phantoms, or animated masks. No one seemed really alive. I had a queer notion that if I pricked any of you, there would be no bleeding, but only a gush of wind. And I couldn't make out *why* you were like that, what it was that I missed in you. The trouble really was that I did not clearly know what it was in *myself* that made me different from you.

John's alienation led him to set up his own self-centred moral code. He financed his ambitions by becoming a ten-year-old burglar; and when he was caught at it by the friendly neighbourhood policeman, he had no compunction about murdering the man to escape detection.

Later, when John was in his teens, he merely treated other people as pets or useful tools. He thought great thoughts, used his remarkable talents to make a lot of money, and travelled around the world in search of other mutant geniuses like himself. He found a fair number and proceeded to establish a secret colony on an island in the South Seas. (The inconvenient original inhabitants of the place were coerced into mass suicide; but the superfolk held a nice feast for them first.) Once John and his mutant friends were secure on their island, they set out to organize a combination Garden of Eden (they were all very young) and technocratic wonderland. They were able to utilize atomic energy by 'abolishing' certain nuclear forces through mental activity. They had all kinds of sophisticated equipment at their command, yet chose to live in rustic simplicity, often linked telepathically to an Asian guru of like mind who had remained at home in his lamasery in Xizang.

The colony made plans for the reproduction of Homo superior. The young mutants 'reviewed their position relative to the universe', attained a transcendental quasi-Unity called astronomical consciousness, embraced the exotic mentalities inhabiting other star-systems – and discovered that they were doomed.

A British survey vessel stumbled on to John's island in spite of the metapsychic camouflaging efforts of the colonists. Once the secret was out, the military powers of the world sent warships to investigate. Some nations saw the colony as a menace; others coveted its assets and schemed to use the young geniuses as political pawns. Attempts at negotiation between Homo sapiens and Homo superior broke down permanently when the Japanese delegate put his finger on the basic dilemma:

This lad [Odd John] and his companions have strange powers which Europe does not understand. But we understand. I have felt them. I have fought against them. I have not been tricked. I can see that these are not boys and girls; they are devils. If they are left, some day they will destroy us. The world will be for them, not for us.

The negotiating party withdrew and the world powers agreed that assassins should be landed on the island, to pick off the supranormals with guerrilla tactics.

Odd John and his companions had a weapon, a photon beam similar to an X-laser, that they might have used to fend off an invasion attempt; but they decided not to resist, since then 'there would be no peace until we had conquered the world' and that would take a long time, as well as leaving them 'distorted in spirit'. So the young mutants gathered together, focused their minds upon their atomic power station, and obliterated the entire island in a fireball . . .

'You've got to read this story, Don,' I pleaded, with my mind leaking the more sinister plot overtones that had frightened me – the hero's icy immorality that contradicted everything I had ever been taught, his awful loneliness, his totally pessimistic view of ordinary mankind faced with the challenge of superior minds.

Don refused. He said he didn't have time and that I shouldn't get worked up over a dumb, old-fashioned book. It had been written in 1935, and by an Englishman! I said it wasn't the story itself but what it said about *people like us* that was important. I bugged him about it and finally wore him down, and he waded through the novel over a period of two weeks, keeping his mind tight shut against me all that time. When he finished he said:

'We're not like that.'

'What d'you mean, we're not? Okay – so we aren't geniuses and we'll never be able to make a million bucks on the stock market before we're seventeen like John did, or invent all that stuff or found a colony on an island. But there are things we do that other people would think were dangerous. Not just the PK, but the coercion. You're a lot better at it than me, so you ought to know what I'm talking about.'

'Big deal. So I fend off guys in hockey or nudge Onc' Louie to cough up a little money when he's half lit.'

'And the girls,' I accused him.

He only snickered, dropped the book into my hands, and turned to walk away.

I said: DonnieDonnie when people findout they'll hate us just like they did OddJohn!

He said: Make sure they *don't* find out.

Don and I were late bloomers physically, puny until we graduated from grammar school – after which we shot up like ragweed plants in July. He was much better looking and more muscular, with a flashing grin and dark eyes that went through you like snapshots from a .30–06. His use of the coercive metafunction that used to be called animal magnetism was instinctive and devastating. From the time he was fourteen girls were crazy for him. Don Remillard became the Casanova of Berlin High, as irresistible as he was heartless. I was his shadow, cast by a low-watt bulb. Don was husky and I was gangling. His hair was blue-black and curled over his forehead like that of some pop singer, while mine was lacklustre and cowlicky. He had a clear olive skin, a dimpled chin, and a fine aquiline nose. I suffered acne and sinus trouble, and my nose, broken in a hockey game, healed rapidly but askew.

As our bodies changed into those of men, our minds drifted further apart. Don was increasingly impatient with my spiritual agonizing, my manifest insecurity, and my bookish tendencies. In high school my grades were excellent in the humanities, adequate in maths and science. Don's academic standing was low, but this did not affect his popularity since he excelled in football and hockey, augmenting genuine sports prowess with artful PK and coercion.

Don tried to educate me in that great Franco-American sport, girl-chasing, but our double-dating was not a success. I was by nature modest and inhibited while Don was the opposite, afire with fresh masculine fervour. The urges awakened in me by the new flood of male hormones disturbed me almost as much as my repressed metafunctions. In Catholic school, we had been lectured about the wickedness of 'impure actions'. I was tormented by guilt when I could no longer resist the temptation to relieve my sexual tensions manually and carried a burden of 'mortal sin' until I had the courage to confess my transgression to Father Racine. This good man, far in advance of most Catholic clergy of that time, lifted the burden from my conscience in a straightforward and sensible way: 'I know what the sisters have told you, that such actions bring damnation. But it cannot be, for every boy entering manhood has experiences such as this because all male bodies are made the same. And who is harmed by such actions? No one. The only person who could be harmed is you, and the only way such harm could come is if the actions become an obsession – as occasionally happens when a boy is very unhappy and shut away from other sources of pleasure. Keep that in mind, for we owe God the proper care of our bodies. But these actions that seem necessary from time to time are not sinful, and especially not mortally sinful, because they are not a serious matter. You recall your catechism definition of mortal sin: the matter must be *serious*. What you do is not serious, unless you let it hurt you. So be at peace, my child. You should be far more concerned with the sins of cheating on school exams and acting uncharitably towards your aunt and uncle than with these involuntary urgings of the flesh. Now make a good act of contrition . . .'

When I was sixteen, in 1961, I emerged a bit from my broody shell and had occasional chaste dates with a quiet pretty girl named Marie-Madeleine Fabré, whom I had met in the library. She shared my love of science fiction. We would walk along the banks of the beautiful Andro-scoggin River north of the pulp mills, ignoring the sulphurous stench and taking simple joy in the dark mirrored water, the flaming maples in autumn, and the low mountains that enclosed our New Hampshire valley. She taught me to bird-watch. I forgot my nightmares of Odd John and learned to react with forbearance when Don mocked my lack of sexual daring.

There were still five of us living at home: Don and I and our younger cousins Albert, Jeanne and Marguerite. That year we played host to a grand Remillard family reunion. Relatives came from all over New Hampshire, Vermont and Maine – including the other six children of Onc' Louie and Tante Lorraine, who had married and moved away and had children of their own. The old house on Second Street was jammed. After Midnight Mass on Christmas Eve there was the traditional réveillon with wine, maple candy and barber-poles, croque-cignols and tourtières, and meat pies made of fat pork. Tiny children rushed about shrieking and waving toys, then fell asleep on the floor amid a litter of gifts and coloured wrappings. As fast as the big old-fashioned Christmas tree lights burnt out, assiduous boy electricians replaced them. Girls passed trays of food. Adolescents and adults drank toast after toast. Even frail, white-haired Tante Lorraine got happily enivrée. Everyone agreed that nothing was so wonderful as having the whole family under one roof for the holidays.

Seventeen days later, when the Christmas decorations had long been taken down, there was a belated present from little Cousin Tom of Auburn, Maine. We came down with the mumps.

At first we considered it a joke, in spite of the discomfort. Don and I and Al and Jeanne and Margie looked like a woeful gang of chipmunks. It was an excuse to stay home from school during the worst part of the winter, when Berlin was wrapped in frigid fog from the pulp-mill stacks and the dirty snow was knee-deep. Marie-Madeleine brought my class assignments every day, slipping them through the mail slot in the front door while the younger cousins tittered. Don's covey of cheerleaders kept the phone tied up for hours. He did no homework. He was urged by the high school coach to rest and conserve his strength.

Everybody got better inside a week except me.

I was prostrate and in agony from what Dr LaPlante said was a rare complication of mumps. The virus had moved to my testicles and I had something called bilateral orchitis. The nuns had been right after all! I was being punished.

I was treated to a useless course of antibiotics and lay moaning with an ice bag on my groin while Tante Lorraine hushed the solicitous inquiries of little Jeanne and Margie. Don slept at a friend's house, making some excuse, because I couldn't help communicating my pain and irrational guilt telepathically. Marie-Madeleine lit candles to St Joseph and prayed for me to get well. Father Racine's common sense pooh-poohed my guilt and Dr LaPlante assured me that I was going to be as good as new.

In my heart, I knew better.

8

Verkhnyaya Bzyb, Abkhaziya ASSR, Earth
28 September 1963

The physician Pyotr Sergeyevich Sakhvadze and his five-year-old daughter Tamara drove south from Sochi on the Black Sea Highway into the unique part of the Soviet Union called Abkhaziya by the geographers. Local people have another name for it: Apsny, the Land of the Soul. Its mountain villages are famed for the advanced age attained by the inhabitants, some of whom are reliably estimated at being more than 120 years old. The unusual mental traits of the isolated Abkhazians are less publicized; and if questioned, the people themselves generally laugh and call the old stories outworn superstition.

Dr Pyotr Sakhvadze's wife Vera had done so until less than a week ago, on the day she died.

Still numb with grief, Pyotr drove like an automaton, no longer even bothering to question the compulsion that had taken hold of him. It was very hot in the semitropical lowlands and Tamara slept for a time on the back seat of the brand-new Volga sedan. The highway led through tobacco fields and citrus groves and stands of palm and eucalyptus, trending further inland south of Gagra, where the mountains receded from the coast in the delta of the great River Bzyb. The road map showed no Upper Bzyb village, but it had to lie somewhere in the valley. Pyotr turned off the highway on to the Lake Ritsa road and pulled in at a village store at the lower end of the gorge.

'I'll buy us some bottles of fruit soda here,' Pyotr said, 'and ask the way. We don't want to get lost in the mountains.'

'We wouldn't,' Tamara assured him gravely.

Pyotr's laugh was uneasy. 'Just the same, I'll ask.'

But the woman in the store shook her head at his inquiry. 'Upper Bzyb village? Oh, there's nothing for tourists there, and the road is nothing but a goat-track, suitable only for farm trucks. Better to go to the lovely resort at Lake Ritsa.'

When Pyotr persisted she gave vague directions, all the

while maintaining that the place was very hard to find and not worth the trip, and the people odd and unfriendly to boot. Pyotr thanked her and returned to the car wearing a grim expression. He handed his daughter her soda. 'I have been told that the road to Upper Bzyb is impossible. We simply can't risk it, Tamara.'

'Papa, don't worry. They won't let anything happen to us. They're expecting us.'

'Expecting — ! But I never wrote or telephoned — '

'Mamenka told them we'd come. And they told me.'

'That's nonsense,' he said, his voice trembling. What was he thinking of, coming here? It was madness! Perhaps he was unhinged by sorrow! Aloud, he said, 'We'll turn around at once and go home.'

He started up the car, slammed it into reverse gear, and stamped on the accelerator so abruptly that the engine died. He cursed under his breath and tried again and again to start it. Damn the thing! What was wrong with it? With *him?* Was he losing his mind?

'You've only forgotten your promise,' the little girl said.

Aghast, Pyotr turned around. 'Promise? What promise?'

Tamara stared at him without speaking. His gaze slid away from hers and after a moment he covered his face with his handkerchief. Vera! If only you had confided in me. I would have tried to understand. I'm a man of science, but not narrow-minded. It's just that one doesn't dream that members of one's own family can be —

'Papa, we must go,' Tamara said. 'It's a long way, and we'll have to drive slowly.'

'The car won't start,' he said dully.

'Yes it will. Try.'

He did, and the Volga purred into instant life. 'Yes, I see! This was also their doing? The old ones waiting for us in Verkhnyaya Bzyb?'

'No, you did it, Papa. But it's all right now.' The little girl settled back in her seat, drinking the soda, and Pyotr Sakhvadze guided the car back on to the gorge road that led deep into the front ranges of the Caucasus.

The promise.

In the motor wreck a week earlier, as Vera lay dying in her husband's arms, she had said: 'It's happened, Petya, just as little Tamara said. She told us not to go on this trip! Poor baby . . . now what will become of her? I was such a fool! Why didn't I listen to them? . . . Why didn't I listen to her? Now I'll die, and she'll be alone and frightened . . . Ah! Of course, that's the answer!'

'Hush,' the distraught Pyotr told her. 'You will not die. The ambulance is on its way — '

'I cannot see as far as Tamara,' his wife interrupted him, 'but I do know that this is the end for me. Petya, listen. You must promise me something.'

'Anything! You know I'd do anything for you.'

'A solemn promise. Come close, Petya. If you love me, you must do as I ask.'

He cradled her head. The bystanders at the accident scene drew back in respect and she spoke so low that only he could hear. 'You must take Tamara to my people – to the old ones in my ancestral town of Upper Bzyb – and allow them to rear her for at least four years, until she is nine years old. Then her mind will be turned towards peace, her soul secure. You may visit Tamara there as often as you wish, but you must not take her away during that time.'

'Send our little girl away?' The physician was astounded. 'Away from Sochi, where she has a beautiful home and every advantage? . . . And what relatives are you talking about? You told me that all of your people perished in the Great Patriotic War!'

'I lied to you, Petya, as I lied to myself.' Vera's extraordinary dark eyes were growing dim; but as always they held Pyotr captive, bewitching him. He knew his wife's last request was outrageous. Send their delicate child prodigy to live with strangers, ignorant mountain peasants? Impossible!

Vera's whisper was laboured. She held his hand tightly. 'I know what you think. But Tamara must go so that she will not be alone during the critical years of mental formation. I . . . I helped her as best I could. But I was consumed with guilt because I had turned my back on the heritage.

You know . . . that both Tamara and I are strange. Fey. You have read Vasiliev's books and laughed . . . but he writes the truth, Petya. And there are those who will pervert the powers! Our great dream of a socialist paradise has been swallowed by ambitious and greedy men. I thought . . . you and I together, when Tamara was older . . . I was a fool. The old ones were right when they counselled watchful patience . . . Take Tamara to them, to the village of Verkhnyaya Bzyb, deep in the Abkhazian mountains. They say they will care for her . . .'

'Vera! Darling Vera, you must not excite yourself — '

'Promise me! Promise you will take Tamara to them!' Her voice broke, and her breath came in harsh gasps. 'Promise!'

What could he do? 'Of course. Yes, I promise.'

She smiled with pallid lips and her eyes closed. Around them the gawkers murmured and the traffic roared, detouring around the accident on the busy Chernomorskoye Chaussée just south of Matsesta. In the distance the ambulance from Sochi was hooting, too late to be of any use. Vera's hands relaxed and her breathing stopped, but Pyotr seemed to hear her say:

The few years we have had together were good, Petya. And our daughter is a marvel. Some day she will be a hero of the people! Take care of her well when she returns from the village. Help her fulfil her great destiny.

Pyotr bent and kissed Vera's lips. He was calm as he looked up at the medical attendants with their equipment, introduced himself, and gave instructions for the body to be taken to the medical centre for the last formalities. With his wife's death, the enchantment was broken. Dr Sakhvadze put aside the morbid fancy that had taken hold of poor Vera and himself and resumed rational thinking. The promise? Mere comfort for a dying woman. Little Tamara would stay home where she belonged with her father, the distinguished head of the Sochi Institute of Mental Health. Later, after the child had received appropriate therapy to assuage grief, they would scatter Vera's ashes together over the calm sea. But for the present, it would be best if Tamara was spared . . .

When Pyotr came at last to his home that evening, the old housekeeper greeted him with eyes that were red from weeping and a frightened, apologetic manner. 'She forced me to do it, Comrade Doctor! It wasn't my fault. I couldn't help it!'

'What are you babbling about?' he barked. 'You haven't broken the news to the child, have you? Not after I instructed you to leave it to me?'

'I didn't! I swear I said nothing, but somehow . . . the little one knew! No sooner had I put the telephone down after your call, than she came into the room weeping. She said, "I know what has happened, Mamushka. My mother is dead. I told her not to go on the trip. Now *I* will have to go away." '

'Idiot!' shouted the doctor. 'She must have overheard something!'

'I swear! I swear not! Her knowledge was uncanny. Terrible! After an hour or so she became very calm and remained so for the rest of the day. But before going to bed tonight she – she forced me to do it! You must believe me!' Burying her face in her apron, the housekeeper rushed away.

Pyotr Sakhvadze went to his daughter's room, where he found her sleeping peacefully. At the foot of Tamara's bed were two large valises, packed and ready to go. Her plush bear, Misha, sat on top of them.

The Lake Ritsa Road followed the Bzyb River gorge into the low range called the Bzybskiy Khrebet, a humid wilderness thick with hanging vines and ferns and misted by waterfalls. At one place, Tamara pointed off into the forest and said, 'In there is a cave. People lived there and dreamed when the ice came.' Again, as they passed some ruins: 'Here a prince of the old ones had his fortress. He guarded the way against soul-enemies more than a thousand years ago, but the small minds overcame him and the old ones were scattered far and wide.' And when they arrived at a small lake, glowing azure even under a suddenly cloudy sky: 'The lake is that colour because its bottom is made of a precious blue stone. Long ago the old ones dug up the stone from the hills around the lake and made jewellery from it. But now all that's left is underwater, where people can't get at it.'

'How does she know this?' muttered Pyotr. 'She is only five and she has never been in this region. God help me – it's enough to make one take Vasiliev's mentalist nonsense seriously!'

Up beyond the power station the paved route continued directly to Lake Ritsa via the Gega River gorge; but the storekeeper had told Pyotr to be on the lookout for an obscure side road just beyond the big bridge, one that angled off eastward, following the main channel of the Bzyb. He slowed the car to a snail's pace and vainly scanned the dense woods. Finally he pulled off on to the exiguous verge and said to Tamara:

'You see? There's nothing here at all. No road to your fairy-tale village. I was told that the turning was here, but there's no trace of it. We'll have to go back.'

She sat holding Misha the plush bear, and she was smiling for the first time since Vera's death. 'I love it here, Papa! They're telling us, "Welcome!" They say to go on just a bit more. Please.'

He didn't want to, but he did. And the featureless wall of green parted to reveal a double-rut track all clogged and overhung with ferns and sedges and ground-ivy. There was no signpost, no milestone, no indication that the way was anything more than a disused logging road.

'That can't be it,' Pyotr exclaimed. 'If we go in there, we'll rip the bottom right out of the car!'

Tamara laughed. 'No we won't. Not if we go slow.' She clambered into the front seat. 'I want to be here with you where I can see everything – and so does Misha. Let's go!'

'Fasten your seat belt,' the doctor sighed.

Shifting into the lowest gear, Pyotr turned off. The wilderness engulfed them, and for the next two hours they bounced and crawled through a cloud-forest of dripping beeches and tall conifers, testing the suspension of the Volga sedan to the utmost. The track traversed mountain bogs on a narrow surface of rotting puncheons and spanned brawling streams on log bridges that rumbled ominously as the car inched across. Then they came to a section of the road that was hewn from living rock and snaked up the gorge at horrific gradients. Pyotr drove with sweat pouring down the back of his neck while Tamara, delighted with the spectacular view, peered out of her window at the foaming rapids of the Bzyb below. After they had gone more than thirty-five kilometres the canyon narrowed so greatly that Pyotr despaired. There could not possibly be human habitation in such a desolate place! Perhaps they had missed a turning somewhere back in the mist-blanketed woods.

'Just five minutes more,' he warned his daughter. 'If we don't find signs of life in another kilometre or so, we're giving up.'

But suddenly they began to ascend a series of switchbacks leading out of the gorge. At the top the landscape opened miraculously to a verdant plateau girt with forested uplands that soared in the east to snowy Mount Pshysh, thirty-eight hundred metres high, source of the turbulent Bzyb. The track improved, winding through alpine meadows down into a deep valley guarded by stands of black Caucasian pine. Stone walls now marked the boundaries of small cultivated fields and in the pastures were flocks of goats and sheep. The track dead-ended in a cluster of white-painted buildings sheltered by enormous old oak trees. Twenty or thirty adults stood waiting in a tight group as Pyotr drove the last half kilometre into Verkhnyaya Bzyb and braked to a stop in a cloud of dust.

In this place the sun shone and the air had an invigorating sparkle. Weak with fatigue and tension, Pyotr sat unable to move. A tall stately figure detached itself from the gathering of villagers and approached the sedan. It was a very old man with a princely bearing, dressed in the festive regalia of the Abkhazian hills: black karakul hat, black Cossack-style coat, breeches, polished boots, a white neck-scarf, and a silver-trimmed belt with a long knife carried in an ornamented silver scabbard with blue stones. His smiling face was creased with countless wrinkles. He had a white moustache and black brows above deep-set, piercing eyes. Eyes like Vera's.

'Welcome,' the elder said. 'I am Seliac Eshba, the great-great-grandfather of your late wife. She left us under sad circumstances. But her marriage to you was happy and fruitful, and I perceive that you, Pyotr Sergeyevich Sakhvadze, also share the blood and soul of the old ones – even though you are unaware of it. This gives us a double cause to rejoice in your coming.'

Pyotr, craning out the car window at the old man, managed to mumble some response to the greeting. He unsnapped his seat belt and Tamara's and opened the car door. Seliac Eshba held it with courtesy, then started around to Tamara's side; but the little girl had already opened her door and bounded out, still keeping a tight grip on Misha the bear. At that same moment more than a dozen young children carrying bouquets of late-summer flowers dashed out from behind the crowd of adults calling Tamara's name.

She ran to meet them, shouting gleefully. 'Nadya! Zurab! Ksenia! It's me! I'm finally here! Hello, Akaky – what pretty flowers. I'm so hungry I could almost eat them! But first, take me to the little house before I burst!' Giggling and chattering, the children led Tamara away.

Pyotr, white-faced, said to Seliac, 'She knows their names! Holy Mother, she knows their names.'

'Your daughter is very special,' Seliac said. 'We will care for her like a precious jewel. Be of good heart, grandson. I'll tell you everything you must know about us in due time. But first let me take you to a place where you can refresh yourself after your long drive. Then we invite you to join us for the special meal that we have prepared in your honour – and Tamara's.'

It was not until the middle of the afternoon that the last toast was raised by Great-Great-Grandfather Seliac, the tamadar.

'To the soul – which now must pass from the old ones to the young!'

'To the soul!' chorused the banqueting villagers, lifting their glasses. But then Dariya Abshili, who was Tamara's great-great-aunt and the chief organizer of the feast, exclaimed: 'Hold! The children must also drink this time.'

'Yes, yes, the children!' everybody shouted. The young ones, who had been segregated at their own table in the outdoor dining pavilion where they bounced up and down and celebrated in their own fashion during the long meal, now left their seats and filed solemnly up to stand on either side of Seliac. Grand-Uncle Valeryan Abshili, a stalwart of seventy years, poured a small portion of rich Buket Abkhaziy wine into each child's glass, coming finally to Tamara, who had the place of honour closest to Seliac. The old man bent and kissed the girl's brow, then let his electric gaze sweep over the assembly.

'Let us drink now to the soul . . . and to this little one, the daughter of our poor lost Vera, who is destined to announce our ancient secret to the world and open the door to peace.'

This time the villagers responded without words. Pyotr, befuddled with a surfeit of wine and food, was surprised to find that he had no difficulty at all hearing them:

To the soul. To Tamara. To the secret. To peace.

They drank, and there was much cheering and clapping, and a few of the oldest women wiped their eyes. Then the indefatigable Dariya began to direct the clearing of the table. Younger men drifted off to attend to certain necessary chores before the next phase of the celebration, which would include dancing and singing. Old folks ambled out of the open-air shelter to take their ease, the men replenishing their pipes and the women gossiping softly, like pigeons. When Pyotr thought to look about in search of Tamara, he discovered that she had run off into the golden sunshine together with the other youngsters. A pang of loss touched his heart as he realized that she belonged to the village now. She was part of the soul.

Seliac arose from the table and beckoned Pyotr to come for a stroll. 'There are still some questions of yours that I must answer, grandson. And a few that I would ask you.'

They followed a path among the houses that led into a grove of venerable walnut trees, their branches heavy with green-husked fruit. Pyotr said, 'I will have to begin my return journey soon. The thought of negotiating that road in darkness freezes my balls.'

'But you must stay the night! I offer you my own bed.'

'You are very kind,' Pyotr said with distant formality. 'But I must return to my duties in Sochi. There are patients at the Institute for Mental Health requiring my urgent attention. I bear heavy responsibilities and the – the loss of Vera will make my workload that much greater until adjustments can be made.'

'She was your comrade as well as your wife.' The old man nodded slowly. 'I understand. You were well suited to each other both in temperament and in the blood. Instinctively, Vera chose well even as she defied us. The ways of God are ingenious.'

The two walked in silence for a few minutes. Somewhere a horse whinnied and children let out squeals of laughter. Then the old man asked, 'Are you of Georgian heritage entirely, grandson? Your flame-coloured hair and fair complexion suggest the Cherkess.'

'I am descended from both races,' Pyotr said stiffly. His spectacular hair, now mercifully greying, had been somewhat of an embarrassment to him throughout his professional life. He had passed it on to Tamara, who gloried in it.

'The Caucasian people are all rich in soul,' Seliac observed, 'even though some of the tribes scanted its nurturing as modern ways overcame the ancient customs . . . And is it not true that one of your ancestors belonged to a group even more brilliantly ensouled than the folk of Apsny? I am speaking of the Rom. The Wanderers.'

Pyotr looked startled. 'There was an old scandal whispered about my maternal grandmother, that she had been impregnated by a gypsy lover before her marriage. But how *you* should know that — '

'Oh, grandson,' laughed the 123-year-old patriarch of Verkhnyaya Bzyb. 'Surely you have guessed by now why I know it, just as you know what kind of special human being your late wife was, and what your daughter is, and why you were commanded to bring her to us.'

Pyotr stopped dead, turning away from the old man in

a fury, willing himself to be sober again, free of the thrall of this bewitched village Vera had rebelled against so many years earlier, when she had run away to the Black Sea Coast and civilization . . .

'Vera left us,' Seliac said, 'because she did not love the man we chose to be her husband. And she took seriously the tenets of dialectical materialism presented in the school-books, with their naive, romantic view of the perfectability of human nature through a mere socialist revolution. Vera came to believe that our ancient soul-way was superstition, reactionary and elitist, contravening the basic socialist phil-osophy. And so she denied her birthright and went to Sochi just before the Great Patriotic War. She threw herself into hospital work and studies, remained a valiant maiden, and seemed wed to Party loyalty and her profession of healing. She almost managed to forget what she had been, as others have done when distracted by the turmoil of modern times. Over the years we called out to her, but there was never an answer. We mourned her as lost. But all unknown to us, quite late in life she had found you, her ideal mate, and when she was forty-two your marvellous child was born.'

'Tamara . . .'

Pyotr still refused to face the village elder. He stood on the stony bank of a brook at the edge of the walnut grove, looking over the countryside. The steep little fields and pastures were a green and golden patchwork on the slopes. Crowded against their low rock walls were hundreds of white-painted hives, piled high like miniature apartment complexes, the homes of mild-tempered Caucasian bees that flew about everywhere gathering late-season nectar for the aromatic honey that provided the village with its prin-cipal income. Thyme was still blooming, and hogweed and melilot and red clover, filling the crisp air with fragrance. Grasshoppers sang their last song of doom before the frost, which had already whitened the highest northern ridges below the spine of the Bokovoi Range. It was here in these mountains that Jason had sought the Golden Fleece; and here that Prometheus stole the divine fire; and here that defiant tribes guided by sturdy centenarians withstood wave after wave of conquering outlanders: Apsny, Land of the Soul, a place of legends, where human minds were said to accomplish wonders that conventional science deemed impossible! But not all scientists scoffed, Pyotr recalled. There were other believers besides the egregious Vasiliev. The great Nikolai Nikolayevich Semyonov, who had won the 1956 Nobel Prize for Chemistry, had spoken in favour of psychic research, and it was studied seriously in Britain and America. But even if such things as telepathy and psychokinesis did exist, did they have *pragmatic* value?

Seliac Eshba bent and picked up a green walnut fruit from the ground.

'Does this?' he inquired, his dark eyes twinkling. 'It is a thing with a tough husk; and if you break into it, it stains the fingers badly, and then there is a second inner shell that must be cracked before the meat is reached. But the walnut is sweet and nourishing, and if a man is patient and long-sighted he may even plant it in the ground and someday reap a thousandfold.' Seliac scrutinized the green ball and frowned. 'Ouff! A weevil has been at this one.' Cocking his arm, he flung the useless thing over the brook into the pasture. 'Perhaps the goats will eat it . . . but for the finest trees, one must choose the best possible seed.'

'As you have?' Pyotr's laugh was bitter. 'You draw a striking analogy. But even if it's a valid one . . . Tamara is only one little girl.'

'But a mental titan. And there are others – not many yet, but increasing in numbers – all over the world.'

Pyotr whirled about to lock eyes with the village elder. 'You can't possibly know that!'

'We do know.'

'I suppose you claim some kind of telepathy — '

'Only a little of that, and not over great distances. The real knowledge comes because of our close rapport with the earth, with her seasons and rhythms, those of the year and those of the aeon. This land round about you with its hidden fertile valleys and secret caves is the place where humanity first learned to dream. Yes! It happened here, in the Caucasus, as the great winter ebbed and flowed and primitive people honed their minds yearning for the glories of spring. The hardships they endured forced them towards the long fruition. Do you know that walnut trees will not bear fruit in the tropics? They need the winter. In the old days, they needed it twice! Once to stimulate the fruit to form, and again to rot the thick husks so that the inner nut would be set free to germinate. Our human cycle is much longer, but we, too, have passed through our first great winter and attained the power of self-reflection. Over the ages our minds have ripened slowly, giving us greater and greater mastery over the physical world, and over our lower nature.'

'Oh, very good! And now I suppose the superior nuts are ready to fall! The winter of nuclear war that threatens – is this what will bring about your mental revolution? Are we to look forward to supermen levitating over glowing ashes, singing telepathic dirges?'

'It might work out that way,' the old man admitted. 'But think: One doesn't have to wait for the walnut husks to rot naturally, not if one is determined – and not afraid of stained hands.' Work with us, grandson. Help us prepare Tamara to meet her peers, to use her great gifts worthily. There will be a price you and I must pay, but we dare not wait passively for the terrible season to do our work for us . . .

Seliac held out his brown-dyed hand to Pyotr, smiled and waited.

9

Berlin, New Hampshire, Earth
21 October 1966

The notion of killing Don insinuated itself into his mind as he was clocking out of the paper mill that Friday afternoon, and the other office workers called out to him.

The women: 'Night, Rogi! Save a pew for us at the wedding.'

The men: 'See you at the Blue Ox tonight. We'll give that big stud a sendoff he'll never forget!'

And the snide crack from Kelly the Purchasing Agent, Rogi's boss: 'Hey – don't look so down in the mouth, fella. The best man always wins, even when he loses!'

Rogi grinned lamely and muttered something then plunged into the stream of exiting employees with long strides.

After the bachelor party. He could do it then. Don would be so drunk that his mental defences would be shaky and his offensive coercion and reflexes slowed. The two of them would have to cross the bridge over the Androscoggin on the way back to the rooming house.

(Am I going crazy? My God, am I seriously considering killing my own brother?)

My PK would be strong enough. It had been the last time, when the fishing boat tipped in Umbagog Lake. Only my *will* had been too weak.

(An accident! Of course it had been an accident. And unthinkable not to haul Don up from the depths, swim with him to shore, and pump life back into him . . .)

A car went by Rogi as he walked through the parking lot, windows down and radio playing. His throat constricted. The song was 'Sunny', and that had been his private, precious name for her. But she had willingly surrendered it to Don along with all the rest.

Rogi went down to walk along the wide river. It was a fine evening. with the sun just gone behind Mount Forist and the trees touched with colour from the first light frosts: the kind of evening they had loved to share, beginning with the days they had walked back from the library. There was a certain grove of trees down by the shore, on the other side of the CN tracks, and a large flat rock. The trees muffled the noise from the traffic along Main Street and gave an illusion of privacy.

He found himself coming upon the place, and she was waiting for him.

'Hello, Rogi. I hoped you'd come. I – I wished you would.'

And my mind's ear heard you!

He only nodded, keeping his eyes on the ground.

'Please,' she begged him. 'You've avoided me for so long

and now there's no more time. You must understand I want tomorrow to be a happy day.'

'I wish you every happiness, Sunny . . . Marie-Madeleine. Always.'

Mentally, he saw her hold out supplicating hands. 'But it'll be spoiled if you're miserable at the wedding, Rogi. If you blame Don. He couldn't help what happened any more than I could. Love is without rules. Quand le coup de foudre frappe . . .'

He laughed sadly. 'You're even willing to use French when you talk about him. But with me, you pretended you didn't understand. It made me bold. I said things to you that I'd never dare to say in English. Very casually, so the tone wouldn't give me away. Sneaking les mots d'amour into ordinary conversation and thinking what a sly devil I was.'

'You were very sweet.'

'And of course you really did know how I felt. From the start.'

'Of course. And I learned to love you. I mean — to love being with you. No! Oh, Rogi, try to understand! With Don it was so different. The way I feel about him — '

He clenched his teeth, not trusting himself to speak. His eyes lifted and met hers, those innocent blue eyes lustrous with tears. His mind cried out to her:

You were mine! It went without saying. All we had to do was wait until we were old enough. That was sensible, wasn't it? And he had so many others to choose from, so many other girls he could have taken. *Did* take. Why did he need you, too, Sunny?

She said, 'Rogi, I always want you to be my dearest friend. My brother. Please.'

The temptation had been strong before but now it became overwhelming, a compulsion thundering in his brain that battered away the camouflage of abstraction he had erected to disguise it. Kill Don. Tonight.

He said, 'Don't worry about me, Sunny. It'll be all right.'

She was weeping, clutching the strap of her shoulder bag in both hands and shrinking away from him. 'Rogi, I'm so sorry. But I love him so much.'

He wanted to take her in his arms and dry her tears. He wanted to shout: You only think you love him! You don't realize that he's bewitched you – coerced you. When he's dead you'll come to your senses and realize that the one you really love is me. You'll cry bitter tears for him, but in time you'll forget that you ever loved anyone but me.

Aloud he said, 'I understand. Believe me.'

She smiled through the tears. 'Be his best man tomorrow, Rogi, and dance with me at the wedding. We'll all drink champagne and be happy. Please tell me that you will.'

He took her gently by the shoulders and kissed the top of her head. The smooth hair was as pale and shining as cornsilk. 'I'll do whatever it takes to make you happy, Sunny. Goodbye.'

Dave Valois nearly ruined the plan when he insisted on driving the two of them home after the bachelor bash at the Blue Ox. But Rogi pointed out that walking a mile in the fresh air was just what Don needed to sober up.

'Gotta burn off some of that booze. Ol' Donnie's got such a skinful, he'll be in a coma tomorrow 'less he walks it off. Father Racine won't 'preciate a zombie groom. No, sir! You just leave ol' Don to me.'

It was three in the morning, the Ox was closed tight, and the gang was dispersing in dribs and drabs, bidding farewell with honks and convivial hollering. Valois and some others protested a bit, but gave in when Rogi took his twin's arm and started slowly down Main Street with him. Don was all but unconscious. Only Rogi's coercion kept him upright and plodding along the sidewalk. Dave circled the block in his Ford and came back to yell, 'You *sure* you don't want a ride?'

'Damn sure,' said Rogi. 'See you in church.'

A few minutes later, he and Don were virtually alone, walking slowly towards the bridge. It was a chilly night with no wind. The Androscoggin was a wide pool of ink reflecting a flawless duplicate of upside-down streetlights and the omnipresent pillars of steam that rose from the pulp mills.

Under his breath, Rogi chanted: 'Pick 'em up and lay

'em down. Pick 'em up and lay 'em down. Attaboy, Donnie. Just keep slogging.'

'Argh,' said Don. His mind was a merry-go-round of fractured images and emotions – hilarity, triumph, anticipation and erotic scenarios featuring Sunny and himself. He didn't suspect a thing. Rogi had thrown off most of the effects of inebriation and was concentrating on maintaining his mental shield and keeping Don moving. The two of them made slow progress to the centre of the bridge. A few cars drove along Main Street, but none made the turn to cross the river.

Rogi came to a halt. 'Hey – looky here, man! Look where we are.'

Don uttered an interrogatory grunt.

'On the bridge, kid,' Rogi carolled. 'The good old bridge. Hey, remember what we used to do in high school? Walk the rail! Drive the other guys nuts. They didn't know we could use our PK to balance.'

Don summoned concentration with a mighty effort. He giggled, exuding good-natured contempt. 'Yeah, I 'member. You were chicken, though, till I showed you how.'

'I'm not chicken now, Don,' Rogi said softly. 'But I bet you are.'

The railing was not exceptionally high. It was of metal, wide and pipelike, interrupted every nine metres or so by a lamp stanchion. The two young men stood by one of those stanchions now and Rogi wrapped Don's arm around it so he wouldn't fall down.

'Watch this!' Grasping the lamppost in one hand, Rogi vaulted up. 'I'm gonna do it now, Don. Watch!' He extended his arms, teetered a little, then began walking steadily along the pipe. The deep Androscoggin was a star-flecked black mirror nearly twenty metres below. Don could swim, but not strongly. It wouldn't take much mental strength to keep him under in his present condition. The tricky part was getting him off the bridge without laying a hand on him.

'Wah-hoo! Boy, that's a kick!' Rogi skipped along the pipe, which was a hand's span in width. When he reached the next stanchion he hugged it and swung himself around and around, cackling madly. 'Oh, that's great! C'mon, Donnie. Now it's your turn.'

Rogi jumped to the pavement and faced his brother, tensing.

Don blinked. His teeth gleamed in a crooked grin. 'Don't wanna.'

Rogi's guts lurched sickeningly. God! Had he leaked the hostility after all? Given himself away? 'Aw. What's matter, Don? You too scared to walk the rail? Or maybe your li'l heart's throbbin' too hard, thinkin' about Sunny.'

'Ain't my heart throbbin',' Don said, lecring.

Rogi kept a grip on himself. 'Then you're chicken.'

'Nope. Just drunk 's a skunk.'

'Well, so'm I – but I walked the rail. I'm just as smashed as you and I walked the fucker. Thing is, I don't lose the power when I've got a snootful – and you do.'

'Like hell!' Don balled a fist. 'Famme ta guêle!'

'I'll shut up when you walk, pansy!'

Don gave a bellow, seized the stanchion in both hands, and hauled himself up. It was perfect. Even if someone saw them there could be no suspicion of foul play. Rogi was ten metres away and Don had taken his first step.

'So long, Don,' Rogi said. 'I'll take good care of Sunny.'

He exerted both PK and coercion with all his strength.

Don screamed and his feet flew out from under him. For a split second he hung unsupported except by his own panic. Then he fell, but he caught the railing and clung to it, kicking. His heavy boots clanged against the ironwork. Rogi concentrated on his brother's hands, lifting the fingers from the dew-slippery metal one by one.

Don was crying his name and cursing. His fingernails broke and his hands slid down the uprights and scrabbled at the toe-plates and the rough concrete footing. Black blood from his lacerated skin splattered the front of his windbreaker. There was a long cut across his right cheek. Don's PK seemed to have deserted him but he still clung to the bridge with all his considerable physical strength, no longer wasting energy in kicking. Waves of rage and imperfectly aimed coercion spewed from his brain.

'Let go, damn you!' Rogi cried. He felt his own powers beginning to weaken. His skull seemed about to burst. He would have to take a chance – get up close and stamp on Don's hands —

He was blind. Deprived of both vision and farsight.

A voice said: *No, Rogi.*

Unable to perceive his target, Rogi found that his coercion and psychokinesis were useless. He let out a shout of despair and relief and dropped like a dead man to the pavement. The voice that addressed him was calm and remote:

Once more it seems that I am fated to intervene. How interesting. One might conjecture that Don survived in some other fashion, and yet the proleptic foci show no asymmetry as a result of my obtrusion.

Rogi lifted his head and groaned. 'You! You again.'

It said: Your brother must live, Rogi. He must wed Marie-Madeleine Fabré and beget children of her according to the great pattern. One of those children will become a man of high destiny. He will not only possess mental powers more extraordinary than his father's, but he will understand them – and help the whole human race to understand them. This child unborn will have to overcome great hardship. He will need consolation and guidance that his parents will be unable to supply, and the friendship of another operant metapsychic. *You* will be that child's friend and mentor, Rogi. Now get up.

Nonono goaway let me kill him Imustonlyway must KILL —

Rogi, get up.

Better perhaps weboth die freaks damned unrealmen unrealhuman   kill   them   kill   them   BOTH intowaterdowndowndissolve —

Du calme, mon enfant.

Best. Would be best.

You know nothing. Nothing! Get up, Rogi. You will remember everything I have said and you will act upon it at the appropriate time.

'You're not *my* Ghost at all.' The realization filled him with irrational sorrow.

The thing said: All of you are my responsibility and my expiation. Your entire race.

With great difficulty, Rogi climbed to his feet. He was no longer blind and he could see Don standing under a lamp, swaying, one hand over his face. Poor old Donnie.

The Ghost said: Your brother has forgotten your attack. His injuries are healed. Take him home, put him to bed, and get him to the church on time.

Rogi began to laugh. He rocked and roared and stamped his feet and howled. He wouldn't have to do it after all, and he wouldn't be damned. Only poor Donnie, not him. The Ghost, that meddling shit, had turned 'Thou shalt not' into 'Thou canst not' and set him free! Oh, it was so funny. He couldn't stop laughing . . .

The Ghost waited patiently.

Rogi finally said to it, 'So I let Don have his way. Then later on I become a kind of godfather to his child prodigy.'

Yes.

Fury took hold of him suddenly. 'But you couldn't let *me* be the kid's father! You couldn't let me marry Sunny and beget the superbrat myself. Don's genes are Homo superior and mine are — '

The Ghost said: You are sterile.

Don was walking shakily towards him. A single car turned off Main Street on to the bridge, slowed as it passed them, then accelerated again when Don waved mockingly at it.

'I'm sterile . . .'

The Ghost said: The orchitis you suffered five years ago destroyed the semeniferous tubules. Your self-redactive faculty was inadequate to repair the damage. You function as a male but will sire no offspring.

No little Odd Johns to dandle on his knee? Rogi was quite unconcerned. The responsibility for unleashing the freaks on the world would be Don's, not his! But pride made him say, 'Heal me! You could. I know it.'

It is not possible, nor is it appropriate. When the design is complete you'll understand. For now, let it be. But take heart, because you have a long life to live and important work ahead of you.

It was drunken lunacy! A nightmare. And all at once Rogi was deathly tired. 'I don't know what the hell you're talking about. Go away. For God's sake, leave me alone!'

I'll go for now, but I'll be back . . . when I'm needed. Au 'voir, cher Rogi.

Don came stumbling up, a bleary smile on his face. 'Hey, Rogi, you look bad, man. Never could hold your liquor. Not like me. C'mon, man, let's go home.'

'Right,' Rogi said. He draped an arm over his brother's shoulder. Supporting each other, the two of them went off into the night.

10

Excerpts from:

Address given by Dr J. B. Rhine
at the Annual Convention of the
American Psychological Association

Washington, DC, Earth

4 September 1967

Some impression of the spread of psi research over the world in recent years can be had from facts connected with the McDougall Award. This annual event, like the Parapsychological Association, was initiated at Duke in 1957 and was later adopted by the Institute for Parapsychology when it took over the laboratory. The Award is granted each year by the Institute staff for the most outstanding contribution to parapsychology published during the preceding year by workers not on the staff of the Institute. During the ten years in which the awards have been made, two have been given for American contributions and two for British, with one divided between the two countries, one award each was made to Czechoslovakia, India, the Netherlands, South Africa and Sweden.

Another indication of the expansion of parapsychology may be had from the establishment of new research centres.

A number of these have had the sponsorship of psychiatry, such as the one at Maimonides Hospital in Brooklyn, one at the Department of Psychiatry at the University of Virginia, and a third at the Neuropsychiatric Institute at the University of California at Los Angeles. Others with more physically and technologically oriented connections are located at the Newark College of Engineering in New Jersey, the Department of Biophysics at the University of Pittsburgh, and the Boeing Research Laboratories in Seattle.

The centre in Leningrad is in the department of physiology; that at Strasbourg, in psychophysiology; and the laboratory at St Joseph's College in Philadelphia, in the department of biology. Psychology-centred psi research in the university is found mainly in foreign countries rather than in the US. City College in New York has what may rightly be called a centre; and at Clemson University, as well as at branches of the University of California (Los Angeles, Berkeley, Davis), psychologists are allowed to do psi research. But something more like centres have long existed in Europe at Utrecht and Freiburg. More recently work has begun that seems firmly planted in psychology departments at the Japanese Defence Academy and the Universities of Edinburgh, Lund and Andhra (India). Some recognized research, of course, is not connected with any institution whatever, as, for example, the work of Forwald in Sweden and that of Ryzl while still in Prague.

One of the noteworthy changes taking place in the present period is the development of more teamwork with workers in other branches and the use of skills, knowledge and equipment of many other research areas. Some of the psi workers today are working with physiological equipment or with computer analyses, others are depending on electronic apparatus in the measurement of psi performance or utilizing new devices in statistics. Numbers of them are using psychological tests or perhaps working in a laboratory of microphysics, or of animal behaviour. . . .

Psi research is obviously of special concern to those who are interested in the full range of the unexplored nature of man, over and above the existing subdivisions of science.

As has happened already in many of the smaller branches, parapsychology is certain to find itself grouped sooner or later with other fields in one or more of those composite sciences which are reshaping the modern structure of knowledge – groupings such as the space sciences, the earth sciences, the microbiological sciences, or such major disciplines as medicine, education and the like. When we come eventually to the stage when the *sciences of man* take a pre-eminent position, we shall find that one of the places around the conference table will have to be reserved for parapsychology.

If the findings are as important as they seem to workers in this field, we shall need no great concern over future recognition by the academic world, by the larger bodies of the sciences, and by other institutions that matter. Rather, the urgent needs today have to do with holding on to the firm beginning psi research has made. This research science needs to operate for the present mainly in the freer terrain of the independent institute or centre, or with such semi-autonomous attachments as may be found in hospitals, clinics, engineering schools, smaller colleges, and industrial research laboratories. In time its own roots will make the attachments that are right, and proper, and lasting. Such growth is slow, but it can be assisted by careful effort and understanding and by recognition of its significance.

11

From the Memoirs of
Rogatien Remillard

After the wedding of Don and Sunny I was miserable for months. I toyed with the notion of moving out of town and went so far as to peruse the 'Help Wanted' column in the Manchester and Portland newspapers. But by Christmas the entire family knew that Sunny was pregnant, and I presume that my subconscious was in thrall to the Ghost and its great expectations for the unborn – and so I stayed.

Since that night on the bridge, Don and I had erected virtually impregnable mental bulwarks against one another. Our social relationship was affable on the surface, but mind-to-mind communication was now nonexistent. I avoided Don and Sunny as much as I decently could. It wasn't difficult, since they had moved into a circle that included mostly young married couples like themselves. I saw them during holiday get-togethers and at the funeral of Tante Lorraine late in March. They seemed to be happy.

I continued at my job in the purchasing department of the mill and Don worked in shipping some distance away in another building. I feel certain that he was doing as I was during those days: trying to live as much like a 'normal' as possible. I no longer used psychokinesis, and I confined my coercive manipulations to feather-light nudges of the office manager, a dour Yankee named Galusha Pratt, who looked upon me as hard-working, ingratiating and deserving of advancement when the right spot came along.

During my leisure hours I practised cross-country skiing and went hiking in the mountains, and I continued to read whatever books I could find that dealt seriously with paranormal mental activity. My researches were still on the impoverished side, however, and would remain so until the 1970s, when the legitimate science establishment finally began to concede that 'mind' might be more than an enigma best left to philosophers and theologians.

The child was born on 17 May 1967, some seven and a half months after his parents' wedding. He was a small baby with an oversized head and the charitable consensus was that he was premature. My first sight of him was eleven days later, when I drove him to church for the baptism. He looked pink, adequately fleshed, and not at all unfinished. Sunny's sister Linda and I renounced Satan and all his works on behalf of the infant, and then father Racine trickled cold water over the hairless, swollen little skull and baptized him Denis Rogatien.

Little blue eyes with shocked, dilated pupils flew wide open. The baby sucked air and let it out in a wail.

And his mind clutched at me.

What I did was instinctive. I projected: [Comfort].

He protested: !!! [cold] + [wet] = [discomfort] *CRY!*

I said: [Discomfort]. CRY. [Reassurance].

He was dubious: ? !! *CRY!*

I amplified: Soon MOTHERyou soon youMOTHER. [Comfort].

He was figuring it out: [Heartbeatwarmsecuregraspmilk suckLOVE] = MOTHER? Cry . . .

I said: [Affirmation]. MotherGOOD. CRY. [Comfort + reassurance].

He said: LoveYOU. [Acceptance trust peace].

Then he went back to sleep, leaving me reeling.

It amazed me when the baby demonstrated telepathic ability at such an early age; but I didn't realize just what *else* was amazing until I thought the thing over lying in bed that night, and did a crude replay of the incident. There in the church, distracted by the ceremony and the relatives standing around, I had not been consciously aware of the feedback taking place between my mind and the infant's. But the replay made it clear – and explained why I still felt an uncanny closeness to that small mind asleep in its crib on the other side of town.

I jumped out of bed, turned on the lights, and rooted through my boxes of books until I found several on developmental psychology. They confirmed my suspicion. Not only was my nephew a telepath, but he was also a *precocious* telepath. His mind had displayed a synthesising ability, an intellectual grasp far above that of normal newborn infants. He was hardly out of the womb, and yet he was thinking, drawing conclusions in a logical manner.

I knew what I was going to have to do. I spent the rest of the night thrashing and cursing the Family Ghost and in the morning I called in sick at work. Then I walked to the little rented house on School Street to tell Sunny what kind of a brother-in-law she had, and what kind of a husband, and what kind of baby son.

It was a glorious day. Spring flowers bloomed in the little front yards and even dingy Berlin looked picturesque instead of shabby. She came to the door with the baby in her arms, an eighteen-year-old Madonna with long fair hair and an unsuspecting smile of welcome. We sat in the kitchen — bright yellow and white enamel, café curtains, Formica counters, and the scent of chocolate cake in the oven — and I told her how Don and I discovered we were telepaths.

I wanted to make the revelation as gentle as possible, so I did it in the form of a life history, starting with the incident of the bear in the raspberry patch. (I left out the Ghost.) I explained how my brother and I only gradually came to understand our singularity, how we experimented with mindspeech and image projection and deep-sight even before we started school. I demonstrated how easy it is to cheat on exams when farsight enables you to read a paper lying open ten feet away — behind you. I told her about psychokinesis and r vealed the secret of how young O'Shaughnessy got stuffed into the basketball hoop. I discreetly moved a kitchen chair around the floor to demonstrate the PK faculty. (She only smiled.) I explained why Don and I had early decided to keep our abilities secret. I went into detail about *Odd John* and my fearful reaction to it. Some instinct warned me not to mention the coercive metafaculty to her — and of course I said nothing about my conviction that Don had used some mesmerizing power to win her away from me. Of the terrible events that took place on the eve of the wedding I spoke not at all.

My long recital took most of the morning. She listened to it almost without speaking but I could feel the tides of conflicting emotion sweeping over her — affection for me and fear for my sanity, disbelief coupled with profound unease, fascination overlaid by a growing dismay. As I talked, she made us lunch and fed the baby. When I finally finished and sat back exhausted in my chair, she smiled in her sweet way, laid her hand over mine, and said:

'Poor dear Rogi. You've been awfully troubled these past months, haven't you! And we hardly saw you, so we didn't know. But now we'll see — Don and I — that you get help.'

Behind those dear blue eyes was a flat refusal to even consider the truth of what I had told her. Adamant denial. And worse than that was a new kind of fear. Of me.

God . . . I'd bungled it. I projected meekness, nonthreat, pure love. Sunny, don't be afraid! Not of this thing. Not of me.

Very quietly I said, 'I can't blame you for being sceptical, Sunny. Lord knows it took years for Don and me to come to terms with our special mind-powers. It's no wonder that the notion seems outrageous to you. Crazy. Frightening, even. But . . . I'm the same old Rogi, and Don is still Don. The fact that we can talk without opening our mouths or move a thing round without touching it doesn't make us monsters.'

As I said it, I knew I was lying.

She frowned, wanting to be fair. Early-afternoon sun streamed into the small kitchen. On the table were cups with dregs of cold tea, and plates with cake crumbs, and a bowl of fragant lilacs making a barrier between us. She said, 'I read once about some studies that were made at a college. Extrasensory perception experiments with flash cards.'

I seized the opening eagerly. 'Dr Rhine, at Duke University! You see? It's respectable science. I have books I can show you — '

'But no one can read another person's mind! It's impossible!' Her panic stung me like a whip and there was outrage, too, at the possibility of mental violation. 'I couldn't bear it if you knew my secret thoughts. If Don did!'

I summoned all sincerity. 'We can't, Sunny. It's not like that. You normals – I mean, people like you – are closed books to telepaths. We can feel your strongest emotions and sometimes we receive images when you think about something very intensely. But we can't read your secret thoughts at all. Even with Don, I can only receive the farspeech he *wants* to transmit.'

Partial truth. It was difficult to decipher the innermost thoughts of normals; but often enough they were vaguely readable, especially when highlighted by strong feelings. And then many persons 'sub-vocalized' — mumbled silently to themselves — when they weren't talking out loud. We could pick up this kind of stuff rather easily. The problem was to sort it, to make sense of the conceptual–emotional hash that floated like pond-scum at the vestibule of an undisciplined mind, confusing and concealing the inner thoughts. Most of the time, you instinctively shut all that mental static out to keep from being driven crazy.

I said, 'You never have to worry that I'd spy on you and Don through his mind, either. We put up mind-screens automatically now to shut one another out. It's a trick we learned years ago. I'd never pry into your life with him, Sunny. Never . . .'

She flushed, and I knew I'd seen through to at least one of her great fears. She was a conventional, modest young wife and I loved her for it.

'These so-called superpowers,' I said, 'aren't really any more unusual than being able to play the piano well, or paint beautiful pictures. They're just something we were born with, something we can't help. You've read about people who seem to predict the future. And – and waterdowsers! My God, that's an old New England thing that nobody around these parts thinks twice about, but it must seem like black magic to people who aren't used to it. I think there may be lots of other telepaths, too, and psychokinetics, but they're afraid to admit having the powers because of the way normals would react.'

(But if there were others, why hadn't we been able to contact them? And why hadn't researchers like Rhine found them – instead of the unreliable and ambiguously talented 'psychics' who participated in his experiments?)

Sunny said, 'I *want* to believe you, Rogi.'

'There was a particular reason why I came here today. It wasn't just to unburden my own mind. I'd never have intruded on you for my own sake. Not even for Don's. But now there's Denis.'

She sat there frozen with fresh disbelief. 'Denis?'

'Yesterday at the christening I felt a wonderful thing. The baby's mind communicated with me. No – don't look shocked. It was marvellous! He was startled by the water poured on him and I reached out telepathically without thinking, used the kind of mental soothing Don and I used to share when we were little kids. And Denis responded. He did more than that! There was – a kind of creative flash, something very special. At first I only transmitted formless feelings to him, trying to calm him and make him stop crying. He grabbed at the comfort but it wasn't enough, so I let my mind say, "Soon you're going to be back with your mother, and everything will be all right." Only I said it in the kind of mental shorthand that Don and I sometimes use, not projecting real words, just the concept of mother and baby together and happy. And do you know what Denis did? He made a connection in his mind between his own notion of mother and the image I projected! It's what psychologists call a mental synthesis, a putting together. But . . . a baby as young as Denis shouldn't have been able to do that yet. He's too young. In another month or two, yes. But not yet.'

She said coldly, 'My baby did nothing of the kind.'

'But he did, Sunny. I'm certain of it.'

'You're imagining things. It's ridiculous.'

'Look,' I said reasonably. 'You go get Denis and I'll try to show you. He's not even asleep in there. He's listening — '

'No!' She radiated a fierce, protective maternal aura. 'My baby's normal! There's nothing wrong with him!'

'He's more than normal, Sunny. Don't you see? He's probably some kind of ESP genuis! If you really want proof, you could probably have him tested at one of the colleges or hospitals that are doing — '

'No, no, *no*! He's just an ordinary baby!' She jumped to her feet and the fear came pouring from her like a cataract of ice. 'How can you say these things to me, Rogi? You're sick! Sick with jealousy because I married Don and had his child. Oh, go away! Leave us alone!'

Exasperated, I began to shout at her. 'You can't hide your head in the sand! You know I'm not crazy and you know that what I've told you is the truth! Your own mind gives you away!'

'No!' she screamed.

I gestured. The vase of lilacs on the table rose two feet in the air. I sent it soaring across the kitchen to the bowl of the sink and let it fall with a crash. In another room, the baby let out a terrible cry. Sunny came at me like a tigress with her hands clenched into fists and her eyes blazing.

'You freak! You bastard! Get out of my house!'

I had never in my life touched her with my coercion, but there was nothing else to do.

Sit down.

Her voice choked off and she turned into a statue, except for her widening eyes. Her face was a tragic mask, open-mouthed in silent screaming.

Sit down.

Somewhere the baby was howling like a wild thing, reacting to the emotion of his mother. Sunny's eyes implored me but I held her fast. Two tears rolled down her frozen cheeks. She let her eyelids close and volition evaporated. She sank slowly on to one of the chairs. Her head fell forward, veiled by the long blonde hair, and she wept without making a sound.

Don't be afraid. Stay right there.

She wasn't hearing my precise telepathic words, of course, only their meaning filtered through the larger coercive impulse. I went and got Denis, wrapped him in a blanket, and handed him carefully to his mother. Then I freed her mind from the compulsion and projected reassurance at the baby.

CRY. [Tranquillity.] 'It's okay, Denis. Maman's fine now.'

I extended my hand to the child, pointing my index finger, and exerted the lightest invitation. The baby's eyes were still swimming but his tiny mouth curved in a smile. A bare doll-like arm came out from under the blanket, reached unerringly, and clasped the end of my finger in a firm grip. I said:

ROGI [touch] DENIS. I/Rogi – you/Denis. Rogi [love] Denis.

There was a sudden radiant concordance. Even Sunny must have sensed it for she gave a slight gasp. The baby cooed.

'Your name is Denis,' I said.

The baby made a small sound.

'Denis,' I repeated.

The little face shone. His mind said: DENIS! His voice uttered the same funny little noise.

'He's trying to say his name,' I explained to Sunny, 'but his vocal cords and tongue really aren't hooked up properly to his brain yet. But his mind knows that he's called Denis.'

Sunny rocked the child without speaking. She was still weeping softly but the horror was gone, leaving only bewilderment and reproach. Oh, Sunny, I'm so sorry you were afraid, so sorry for my clumsiness . . .

'But I had to do it,' I told her, no longer coercing but pleading for understanding. 'I couldn't let you go on denying. It wouldn't be fair to Denis. You're going to have to be brave for his sake. He's a *responsibility*. He probably has all the special mental abilities that Don and I have – plus more. I think he has superior intelligence, too. If that giant brain of his has a chance to develop properly, he'll grow up to be a great man.'

She was now entirely calm. The infant basked in self-satisfaction and yawned. She held him tightly against her breast. 'What am I going to do, Rogi? Will – will they take him away from me?'

'Of course not! For God's sake, Sunny – when I said you could have him tested by scientists, I only meant that you could do it if you felt you had to. To prove he was – what I said. But nobody can force you to give Denis up for experiments. No way! Not in this country. If he was my son — '

She looked at me expectantly.

I was standing so close to her and the child that their combined aura enveloped me. There was relief and dependency emanating from her, and from the baby a strengthening variant of the harmonious bond I had felt earlier.

Denis [love] Rogi.

Oh, Denis, you can't! You're not mine. She's not mine. It's Don you have to imprint on. Your real father. Not me . . .

She asked quietly, 'What would you do if Denis was your son?'

I heard myself speaking dispassionately. 'The people who run those ESP labs wouldn't have the faintest idea how to give this baby what he needs. They're only normals. They've only dealt with normals. Denis needs to be taught by others like himself. Only his father and I are able to mindspeak him, so Don will have to – will have to — '

DENIS/ROGI!

Mind to mind the bond was forging whether I willed it or not. The child was catching me just as he had earlier caught his mother, as all babies form a linkage with their nearest and dearest.

Denis, no! Not me! (Bless me, Father, for I have sinned. Attempted murder. Yes, we'd both been drinking. Yes, I was out of my mind for love of her. Yes, I'm sorry sorry sorry . . . thank you. No, Don never even knew. It was all in my mind? No, I don't think so, but perhaps – perhaps – I don't know. Two months' fast and abstinence and a good act of contrition and it's over and gone and I'll never forget never . . .)

Sunny was saying, 'Don help me teach the baby? Well, I suppose we could ask him. He loves Denis, of course, but he's terribly old-fashioned. I can't get him to change diapers or even give Denis his bottle. What would Don have to do?'

My heart sank. I might have known. The Family Ghost knew all along, of course. If it *was* a ghost.

'Well, Don would have to spend time with the baby. Talk to him, mind to mind. Show him mental pictures. Help him learn control of his faculties.'

She made a dubious little moue. 'I suppose I can try.'

'This is important, Sunny! Listen. When Don and I were babies, Tante Lorraine hardly had time to give us the love and attention ordinary babies need – and God knows, she wasn't a telepath. So we grew up stunted.'

Sunny opened her mouth to protest, but I held up my hand and rushed on.

'Stunted in our use of the ESP powers, I mean. Look. Have you ever read about feral children, ones raised by animals or locked away from human contact by criminal parents? When they get out at last into the normal world they're hardly human at all because they were deprived of a certain kind of education they needed when their young minds were most impressionable. Don and I seem to be normal men – but we're cripples, too. We should have had somebody to teach us how to use our special mind-powers when we were tiny babies. All my psychology books say that the first three years of life are critical for mental development. That must hold true for special powers even more than for ordinary ones. Don and I discovered our powers accidentally and developed them in a haphazard way. We've never been comfortable with them. Don doesn't really understand them at all and I'm – I know a bit more about them than he does, but not enough.'

'You would have to explain to Don what had to be done.'

'Yes, of course. I'll work out some kind of general outline. Denis would need to interact with both of you. There'd be a lot of things you could do alone, Sunny – reading aloud to him, just talking to him. I have a book by Piaget, a famous French child psychologist, that I'll let you read. It gives the step-by-step progress of a baby's learning. Really fascinating.'

She nodded, holding the child close. The little boy's eyes were fixed on me and there seemed to be an air of puzzlement about him. I realized then that I had erected a mental barrier against his persistent reaching out. He was rooting against the obstruction like a puppy trying to dig under a wall.

No child no.

ROGI!

He forced himself on me. I tried to break eye contact with him and found that I could not. There was a strength and determination in him that was formidable, for all his immaturity, and I felt myself weakening. Babies! They have ways to insure their survival that even the normals are aware of. Mental ways. Why else do we think a helpless, noisy, smelly, demanding, inconvenient little travesty of a human being is almost irresistibly adorable?

No!

ROGImyROGI. [Love.]

My mental armour was dissolving. And then Denis smiled at me, and the trap closed.

Sunny said, 'We mustn't let any outsiders know the truth about Denis for a long time. Not until he's old enough to protect himself from people who might exploit him. We'll teach him to be cautious – and to be *good*.' She cuddled his head against her cheek. 'Strange little superbaby. How will I ever keep up with him? I wonder how Mama Einstein managed?'

'Little Albert was a disappointing child,' I told her. 'He didn't even speak until he was four.'

I went to the sink and began to gather up the broken pieces of the lilac vase. It was quite a mess.

Don came home from work that evening and found Sunny and me sitting with the baby on the front porch. While she made supper, he and I had our first telepathic interchange in more than a year. I told him what I had done, and why.

At first he laughed, and then he was enraged when I told him it was his moral duty to undertake the special education of his son. We got into a shouting match in the living room and Sunny came running to put herself between us. Then she proceeded to beat down every objection Don could think of, all the while radiating such passionate devotion to him and to Denis that I was astounded. It was plain even to a fool like me that coercion was not the force that bound Don and Sunny – nor had it ever been.

As she finished telling him of the plans she and I had worked out for the first course of instruction, Don lifted his powerful arms in a resigned shrug. 'All right! You win! I think it's a mistake to treat the kid special – but what the hell. I'll mindspeak him the way you want. But don't expect me to turn into a goddam kindergarten teacher, okay?'

Sunny flung herself against him joyously and kissed him long and hard. When he broke away from her he looked over her head and gave me a sardonic grin.

'This business of working with the kid in the evenings. The flash cards and all that crap. I'd be lousy at it. Tell you what, Rogi. You help Sunny and me teach the kid. It's just the kind of thing you'd be good at – and the whole damn thing is your idea, after all. How about it?'

'What a wonderful idea,' Sunny said warmly. 'Say you will, Rogi.'

From the bedroom came another plea: a formless mental one.

It was hopeless. The Family Ghost had won. I said, 'All right.'

'Well, that's settled,' Don said. 'What's for supper, sweetheart?'

12

Excerpts from:

Final Report of the Scientific Study of Unidentified Flying Objects

Conducted by the University of Colorado under Contract to the United States Air Force

9 January 1969

The idea that some UFOs *may* be spacecraft sent to Earth from another civilization, residing on another planet of the solar system, or on a planet associated with a more distant star than the Sun, is called the extraterrestrial hypothesis (ETH). Some few persons profess to hold a stronger level of belief in the *actuality* of UFOs being visitors from outer space, controlled by intelligent beings, rather than merely of the *possibility*, not yet fully established as an observational fact. We shall call this level of belief ETA, for extraterrestrial actuality. . .

Direct, convincing and unequivocal evidence of the truth of ETA would be the greatest single scientific discovery in the history of mankind. Going beyond its interest for science, it would undoubtedly have consequences of surpassing significance for every phase of human life. Some persons who have written speculatively on this subject profess to believe that the supposed extraterrestrial visitors come with beneficent motives, to help humanity clean up the terrible mess that it has made. Others say they believe that the visitors are hostile. Whether their coming would be favourable or unfavourable to mankind, it is almost certain that they would make great changes in the conditions of human existence . . .

The question of ETA would be settled in a few minutes if a flying saucer were to land on the lawn of a hotel where a convention of the American Physical Society was in progress, and its occupants were to emerge and present a special paper to the assembled physicists, revealing where they came from, and the technology of how their craft operated. Searching questions from the audience would follow.

In saying that thus far no convincing evidence exists for the truth of ETA, no prediction is made about the future. If evidence appears soon after this report is published, that will not alter the truth of the statement that we do not *now* have such evidence. If new evidence appears later, this report can be appropriately revised in a second printing. . .

Whether there is intelligent life elsewhere (ILE) in the Universe is a question that has received a great deal of serious speculative attention in recent years . . . Thus far we have no observational evidence whatsoever on the question, so therefore it remains open . . . The ILE question has some relation to the ETH or ETA for UFOs as discussed in the preceeding section. Clearly, if ETH is true, then ILE must also be true because some UFOs have then to come from some unearthly civilization. Conversely, if we could know conclusively that ILE does not exist, then ETH could not be true. But even if ILE exists, it does not follow that the ETH is true.

For it could be true that the ILE, though existent, might not have reached a stage of development in which the beings have the mechanical capacity or the desire to visit the Earth's surface . . . We have no right to assume that in life-communities everywhere there is a steady evolution in the directions of both greater intelligence and greater technological competence. Human beings now know enough to destroy all life on Earth, and they may lack the intelligence to work out social controls to keep themselves from doing so. If other civilizations have the same limitation, then it might be that they develop to the point where they destroy themselves utterly before they have developed the technology needed to enable them to make long space voyages.

Another possibility is that the growth of intelligence precedes the growth of technology in such a way that by the time a society would be technically capable of interstellar space travel, it would have reached a level of intelligence at which it had not the slightest interest in interstellar travel. We must not assume that we are capable of imagining now the scope and extent of future technological development of our own or any other civilization, and so we must guard against assuming that we have any capacity to imagine what a more advanced society would regard as intelligent conduct.

In addition to the great distances involved, and the difficulties which they present to interstellar space travel, there is still another problem. If we assume that civilizations annihilate themselves in such a way that their effective intelligent life span is less than, say, one hundred thousand years, then such a short time span also works against the likelihood of successful interstellar communication. The different civilizations would probably reach the culmination of their development at different epochs in cosmic history . . .

In view of the foregoing we consider that it is safe to assume that no ILE outside of our solar system has any possibility of visiting Earth in the next ten thousand years.

13

Leningrad, USSR, Earth
5 March 1969

'We have saved the best for the last, Comrade Admiral. Please be seated here at this table with the microphones . . . You other comrades may take the chairs nearer the observation window. Dr Valentina Lubezhny, our specialist in biocommunications phenomena, will bring the subject into the Faraday cage in just a moment. There is a small delay.' Danilov offered an apologetic smirk. 'The little girl was very nervous.'

Kolinsky gave a curt nod and lowered his ample buttocks to the hard wooden chair. Scared children! And you are the most frightened of all, Comrade Doctor Asslicker, and rightly so, considering the flimsy quality of entertainment offered thus far in your extremely expensive laboratory. Dull demonstrations of the human bioenergetic field. A Chukchi shaman able to stop the heart of a rat (but not the heart of any creature weighing more than four hundred grams). A neurasthenic blind youth reading printed matter with his fingertips. A modern Rasputin (sanitized) laying hands on tortured rabbits and healing their wounds. A housewife doing psychokinetic tricks with cigarettes and water glasses. A gypsy who peers into a Polaroid camera lens and produces blurry 'astral photos' of the Petropavlov-skaya Fortress, the Bronze Horseman, and other local land-marks. (That one had looked promising – until Danilov admitted that the subject could only 'envision' places where he had been. So much for psychic espionage!)

Sternly, Kolinsky said, 'We have been most interested to see how far you have progressed in the area of pure research, Comrade Danilov. Still, it was not the *existence* of psychic powers that we hoped to prove. Unlike the sceptics of the West, we are quite willing to concede that the human brain is capable of such activities. However, we had hoped that after five years of work you might have uncovered a bioenergetic effect of more immediate military significance.'

Danilov fiddled with the microphones, set out a pad of paper and marker-pens, saw that the naval aides Guslin and Ulyanov and the GRU attaché Artimovich were settled in. 'In just a few minutes we will demonstrate the talents of our most remarkable subject. I don't think you'll be disappointed, Comrade Admiral. By no means!'

Down in the test chamber on the other side of the glass a door opened. A white-coated female scientist appeared with a redheaded girl wearing a school uniform. The child had an extraordinarily pretty face. She eyed the men in the observation booth with a certain apprehension.

Danilov hurriedly addressed the admiral and the other officers. 'The girl is very sensitive to adverse mental attitudes – even more so than the other subjects you have seen today. For this experiment to succeed, we must have an atmosphere pervaded with kindness and goodwill. Please try to banish all doubts from your minds. Cultivate a positive attitude.'

Commander Guslin coughed. Ulyanov lit a cigarette. Artimovich, the intelligence man, sat bolt upright with a fixed smile on his face.

Danilov picked up a microphone with blue tape wrapped around its stand. 'I will introduce you, Comrade Admiral, and then perhaps you will speak a few words to the child and reassure her.'

Kolinsky, who had seven grandchildren, sighed. 'As you wish.'

Danilov pressed the microphone stud. 'All ready now, Tamara!'

The girl's voice came to them over a ceiling speaker. 'Yes, Comrade Doctor.'

'We have a special guest here today, Tamara. He is Admiral Ivan Kolinsky, a great hero of the Soviet Navy. He is eager to see how well you do your biocommunication exercise. The Admiral would also enjoy talking to you.' The scientist made a formal gesture. 'Admiral Kolinsky, may I present Tamara Sakhvadze.'

Kolinsky took the microphone and winked at the little girl. 'Now, you must not be nervous, devushka. We will leave the nervousness to Dr Danilov.' The child giggled. She had marvellous white teeth. 'How old are you, Tamara?'

'Eleven, Comrade Admiral.' Great dark eyes, rose-petal mouth.

'You have a Georgian name. Where is your home?'

'I live in Sochi – I mean, I used to live there before they found me and brought me here to work and go to school. Sochi is on the Black Sea.'

Ah, yes – a Celtic Caucasian girl, one of that ancient

breed famed through history for their beauty and bewitching ways! 'I know Sochi very well, Tamara. I have a vacation villa there, a very pretty place. It must be spring in Sochi now, with flowers blooming and birds singing in the palm trees. What a pity both of us are here in wintry Leningrad instead of in your pleasant hometown.'

And if I were there, I could sail my little boat – or sit at a small table in Riviyera Park, sipping a cold mix of Georgian champagne and orange juice and baking my tired bones in the sunshine. Gorgeous young things (your older sisters or cousins, Tamara!) would stroll by, tall and bare-legged and bold of eye, and I would admire and remember old pleasures. When that palled I would plot the destruction of Gorshkov, that prick on wheels, and the KGB schemer Andropov, whose hobbyhorse this whole bioenergetics farce is, and put an end to it, and get on with the Extremely Low Frequency Broadcaster, just as the Yankees have done. Psychic forces as weapons! What superstitious peasants we Russians remain, in spite of our thin veneer of science and culture. One might as well speak of enlisting the terrible Baba Yaga and her hut on fowl's legs . . .

The girl laughed out loud. 'You're so silly, Comrade Admiral!'

The woman scientist standing beside Tamara stiffened. Danilov said hastily, 'The child is overexcited. Please excuse her rudeness. Let us begin the experiment — '

Kolinsky studied the girl narrowly. 'Tamara and I have not yet finished our little talk. Tell me, devushka, what special talent do you have that interests the doctors at this Institute?'

'I read thoughts. At a distance. Sometimes.'

'Can you read mine?' the admiral asked softly.

Tamara now looked frightened. 'No!'

Danilov implored him. 'It is most important that the child be calm, comrade! If we could begin now . . .'

'Very well.' Kolinsky put the blue-marked microphone down.

Danilov signalled to his colleague. The woman took Tamara by the hand and led her to a large cubicle of copper screening that stood in the centre of the test chamber. Inside it was a plain wooden chair.

'The enclosure is called a Faraday cage,' Danilov explained. 'It is proof against most forms of electromagnetic radiation. We have found that Tamara works best when shielded in this way. The emanations from her mind do not seem to be in any way connected to the energies of the electromagnetic spectrum, however. The 'bioenergetic halo effect' that we monitored for you earlier on your tour seems to be a side effect of the life-energies rather than part of their primary manifestation.'

Kolinsky nodded, barely concealing his impatience. Within the test chamber, the girl Tamara was now completely enclosed in the copper-screen cage, sitting with her hands clasped in her lap. Dr Lubezhny had withdrawn, and within a few minutes came into the observation booth.

'All is in readiness,' she reported. 'Tamara feels confident.'

Danilov picked up a second microphone from the table. The tape marking it was bright scarlet. Activating it, he said, 'Danilov here. Are you standing by?'

Masculine accents overlaid by static responded. 'This is the diving tender Peygalitsa awaiting your instructions.'

'Please give us your approximate position,' Danilov requested.

'We are standing approximately nine kilometres due west of Kronshtadt Base in the Gulf of Finland.'

'The divers are ready?'

'Sublieutenant Nazimov and the Polish youth are suspended at the required depth of ninety metres and awaiting your bioenergetic transmission.'

'Okhuyevayushchiy!' exclaimed Commander Ulyanov.

Danilov flapped a frantic hand. 'Please! No extraneous remarks! All of you – think the most refined and peaceable thoughts.'

Commander Guslin smothered a chuckle.

'Stand by, Peygalitsa, we are prepared to transmit.' Danilov set the red-marked microphone down.

The admiral murmured, 'You are a man of surprises, Dr Danilov.'

'The experiment has worked before,' the scientist said in a strained voice, 'and it will work again – given the proper conditions.' He glared at the two aides and the GRU man.

Kolinsky wagged his right index finger at the trio. 'Not a peep from you, minetchiki.'

The scientist expelled a noisy breath. He explained rapidly. 'The girl Tamara is what we all call an inductor. A telepathic broadcaster, the most talented we have ever found. The percipient or receiver is a seventeen-year-old Polish lad named Jerzy Gawrys, another gifted sensitive. Gawrys wears cold-water diving dress. He is holding an underwater writing pad and a stylus, but he is *not* equipped with telephone apparatus, as is his companion, Sublieutenant Nazimov. The only way that the boy Gawrys may communicate is by writing on his pad. Nazimov will relay the pad's message to the reader. The tender's radio operator will relay the data to us. Our own receiver picks it up and broadcasts it through the room speaker.'

'Understood,' said Kolinsky. 'And what data are to be transmitted!'

Danilov lifted his chin proudly. 'The data of your choice.'

The aides muttered fresh exclamation of amazement.

Danilov said, 'May I suggest that you start with a few simple shapes – stars, circles, squares – then pictures, then a few words. Use the pad of paper in front of you and the ink-marker. As you finish each sheet, hold it up so that Tamara can see it . . . and send the message.'

Kolinsky compressed his lips and bent to the pad. He drew a five-pointed star, raised the paper, and smiled at Tamara.

The girl stared intently.

'Star,' said the diving tender Peygalitsa.

The admiral drew an arrow.

'Arrow,' said the faraway relay operator.

The admiral drew a clumsy cat in profile.

'Cow,' the speaker reported.

Everybody in the booth laughed. Kolinsky shrugged and drew a circle with pointed rays around it.

'Sun.'

The admiral waved jovially at Tamara. She smiled and

waved back. He wrote the seven Cyrillic letters that spelled a familiar greeting in Russian and held it up. The girl concentrated on them for some time.

The speaker cleared its throat, then said: 'We receive from Sublieutenant Nazimov the letters zeh–deh–oh–er–oh–uncertain–oh.'

Danilov picked up the red microphone. 'Stand by, Peyga-litsa.' He told Kolinsky, 'You must remain mindful that our percipient is Polish. It may be difficult for him to receive complex messages written in our script. Please keep the words as simple as possible.' He alerted the boat to receive the next message.

Kolinsky printed carefully, 'Tamara sends greetings.' The words were returned, letter by letter, over the speaker.

'May I congratulate you, Dr Danilov, Dr Lubezhny.' The admiral beamed on the scientists. 'A splendid break-through!' And so Andropov had been right after all. A billion-to-one gamble seemed to have paid off and he, Kolinsky, would have to eat his ration of shit. If Tamara's talent could be taught to others, the Soviet Navy could scrub its own Extremely Low Frequency Broadcaster Project. Let the Americans use the long-wave radio system to send messages to deep-lying missile submarines – a system that worked, but was so slow that a three-letter word might take nearly a half hour to transmit. The Soviet Union would talk to its submarines via mental telepathy, in moments! As to the KGB's use of psychic powers, the less said . . .

Danilov was babbling. 'You are very kind, Comrade Admiral! I know that little Tamara and the boy Jerzy Gawrys, who have worked so hard, will also be gratified by your praise. Perhaps you would like to tell them so yourself.'

Kolinsky said, 'First we will test one other message.' He bent to the pad, then held it up to Tamara. The lovely little face glowed at him through the copper mesh, so pleased that everything had gone well, so eager to show her skill.

She saw: FIRE MISSILES.

Tamara sat still. Her dark eyes opened wider, like those of a cornered doe.

Admiral Kolinsky tapped a finger firmly against the paper.

They waited.

Finally, Danilov addressed the red microphone: 'Attention, Peygalitsa. Do you have a message to relay?'

'No message,' said the loudspeaker.

Kolinsky regarded the little girl without expression. So that's the way of it, little Tamara! Can one blame you? You have hardly lived at all, and the true purpose of your work did not occur to you. You are shocked and revolted. You shrink from adult wickedness. But one day, will you see such wickedness as duty? As patriotism?

'No message,' said the loudspeaker.

Danilov apologized. 'Perhaps the girl is tiring. Perhaps Jerzy has temporarily suffered diminished sensitivity — '

'No message,' said the loudspeaker.

'I will go and speak to her,' Dr Lubezhny suggested.

'No,' Admiral Kolinsky said. 'Don't be concerned. I've see quite enough for today. Please be assured that I will urge full funding of your continuing efforts here at the Institute, and I will commend your work most highly to the Council for National Defense.' The admiral rose from his seat, tore the sheet of paper into small pieces, and let them sift from his hand on to the table. He beckoned to his aides and strode out of the door after having given one last wave to the motionless little girl.

Dr Danilov's eyes met those of Dr Lubezhny. The woman said, 'If only she were younger. Then it would be a game.'

'She will bend to larger considerations in time,' Danilov said. He picked up the red microphone and keyed it. 'Attention, Peygalitsa. The experiment is ended. Thank you for your cooperation.'

'Message coming through,' said the loudspeaker.

Danilov almost dropped the microphone. 'What's that?'

The amplified voice was brisk. 'We receive another set of letters. It spells . . . nyet.'

'Nyet?' exlaimed Danilov and Lubezhny in unison.

Down in the Faraday cage, Tamara Sakhvadze looked at them and slowly nodded her head.

14

From the Memoirs of
Rogatien Remillard

I came to Don and Sunny's house every Tuesday, Thursday and Sunday evening for nearly three years. We would have supper, and Sunny would stack the dishes. Then she would bring little Denis into the living room for the educational sessions that we came to call 'head-lessons'.

At first Don tried to work along with me. But he had very little empathy with the infantile mind and his attempts at telepathic rapport were so crude as to be little more than mental puppy-training: Here it is, kid – learn or else! He couldn't resist teasing the baby, looking upon our work with him as an amusement rather than serious business, treating the child like some glorified pet or a sophisticated toy. The occasional mental quantum leaps made by the boy could be very exciting and then Don was all praise and affection. But there were tedious times as well, the nuts and bolts of teaching that Don found to be a colossal bore. He would put pressure on Denis, and more often than not the session would end with the child crying, or else stubbornly withdrawn in the face of his father's mocking laughter.

As I expected, Don got tired of the teaching game after only a few weeks. Not even Sunny's pleas would move him to continue serious participation. So he watched television while Sunny and I worked with the child, and looked in with a proprietary condescension during commercial breaks. This might have been a satisfactory solution – except that babies have no tact, and little Denis couldn't help showing how much he preferred my mental tutelage to that of his father. Don's pride was hurt and he began to broadcast bad vibes that the sensitive baby reacted to, setting up a kind of mind-screen that threatened to cut him off not only from his father but also from me. I had to tell Don what was happening, dreading his reaction. He surprised me, however, and said, 'What the hell! Teaching kids is no job for a man like me.' And he began going out to the Blue Ox right after supper, leaving me alone with his wife and son.

I found out some time later that a burly tavern habitué named Ted Kowalski dared to make a suggestive crack about this unorthodox domestic arrangement. Don decked him with a single uppercut. Then he made a little speech to the awed onlookers at the Ox.

'My egghead brother Rogi is writing a book. It's about the way the little kids' minds work. Me and Sunny are letting him use our son Denis as a kind of guinea pig. Rogi runs tests on the kid using blocks and beads and pictures cut from magazines and other suchlike crap. Sunny helps. I used to help, too, but it was dull as dishwater. That's why I'm here, and why my brother and my wife and kid are at home. Now would anybody besides the late Kowalski care to comment?'

Nobody did, then or ever.

Don got so fond of the Blue Ox that he took to spending evenings there even when there were no head-lessons scheduled. Sunny was sorry about that but she never reproached him. She did cook especially fine meals for him on the nights that I visited, and kept urging him to stay with us and see what Denis had learned. When Don refused, as he almost invariably did, she kissed him lovingly goodbye. When he returned two hours later in a haze of alcohol, she kissed him lovingly hello. His drinking became heavier as the months went by and the baby made spectacular progress.

At Remillard family gatherings, Don boasted to one and all that he was proud as hell of his son, the genius. Denis, carefully coached by me, let the relatives see him as a child who was plainly above average – yet not so advanced as to appear bizarre. We let him start speaking in public when he was thirteen months old, three months after he had actually mastered speech. He learned to walk when he was a year old; in this and in other purely physical development he was very nearly normal. In his appearance he favoured the Fabré side of his family, having Sunny's fair skin and intensely blue eyes but lacking her beauty. He was never sick, even though he had a deceptively frail look about him. His temperament was shy and withdrawn (which was a vast disappointment to Don), and I believe that he was by far the most intellectually gifted of all the Remillards, not even excluding such metapsychic giants as Jack and Marc. There are some Milieu historians, I know, who mistook his gentleness for weakness and his innate caution for vacillation, and who say that without the psychic impetus furnished by his wife, Lucille Cartier, Denis's great work might have remained unaccomplished. To counter these critics I can only present this picture of the young Denis as I knew him, surmounting the emotional trials of his youth with quiet courage – and almost always facing those problems alone, since I was only able to aid him during his earliest years, and circumstances conspired to separate us during his latter childhood and adolescence.

I must not minimize the role that Sunny played. Denis learned to read before he was two, and she saved her housekeeping money in order to buy him an encyclopedia. Since the child had a never-ending thirst for novel sensations and experiences, she wheeled him all over Berlin in a stroller during the warm months and toted him on a sled in the winter. Later, she drove him about the countryside in the family car, until the rising cost of gasoline and Don's precarious financial situation put an end to her expeditions, and their growing family left her less and less time to spare.

The metapsychic training of Denis was left almost entirely to me. I worked hard, if inexpertly, in the development of his farsenses and wasn't surprised when his abilities quickly surpassed my own. He learned the art of long-sight amplification all by himself – and tried in vain to pass the skill on to me. His mental screening function very early became so formidable that neither Don nor I could penetrate it; aside from that, Denis seemed untalented in coercion. Psychokinesis didn't interest him much either, except as an adjunct to manipulation when his little fingers were inadequate for handling some tool, or for supporting books too heavy to be held comfortably. It was an eerie thing to come upon the child, not yet three years old, still sucking his thumb as he perused a levitated volume of the *World Book Encyclopedia*; or perhaps sitting in unconsidered wet diapers, studying a disassembled transistor radio while a cloud of electronic components and a hot soldering iron floated in thin air within easy reach.

But I had even more disquieting experiences in store for me.

One February night in 1970 Don returned from the tavern a bit early. He was no drunker than usual, and unaccustomedly cheerful. He said he had a surprise for me, and admonished me and Sunny to stay right where we were with Denis. He went into the kitchen and closed the door.

Denis was deeply engrossed in a new book on the calculus that I had just bought, thinking we might learn it together. Sunny was knitting. Outside the little house on School Street a frigid wind from Canada howled down the Androscoggin Valley and solidified the old snowdrifts into masses like dirty white styrofoam. I hated to think of walking home.

Don came back into the living room sans outdoor wear, carrying a cup of steaming hot cocoa. Grinning, he held it out to me. 'Just what you need, Rogi mon vieux, to warm you up on a truly rotten night.'

My brother making a cup of cocoa was an event about as unprecedented as me doing a tap dance on the bar at the Blue Ox. I probed his mind, but the usual barriers were in place. What was he up to?

Little Denis looked up from his differentiation formulas. His eyes went first to his father, then to his mother. His expression was puzzled.

Sunny gasped.

Don held out the cup to me.

'No!' Sunny cried. She sprang from her chair and slapped the cup from Don's hand. It made an ugly brown splash on the wall. I was flabbergasted.

Denis asked me gravely, 'Uncle Rogi, will *you* tell me why lysergic acid diethylamide makes cocoa taste better?'

Don started to giggle. Sunny regarded him with a terrible expression of outrage. His mind-screen, shaken by her unexpected action, wavered just enough to let me see what kind of joke he had intended to play on me. Little Denis had had no trouble penetrating Don's psychic barricade when it was still firm, and he had perceived the name of the drug emblazoned on his father's short-term memory trace as on a lighted theatre marquee.

But how had Sunny known?

Don's laugh was louder, more unsteady. 'Hey, it was only a gag! This hippie came into the Ox lookin' to deal, and we were ready to throw him out on his ass when I remembered ol' Rogi jabbering about altered states of consciousness. And I thought – hey! Whole lotta talk about the wild side of the mind, but never any action. That's you, Rog.'

I said, 'You were going to slip the LSD into me and supervise my trip.'

His grin became a grimace of pure hate. 'You been experimenting. I figured it was my turn.'

Sunny grabbed his arm. 'You're drunk and you don't know what you're saying!'

He shook Sunny off as though she were some importunate kitten and took one step towards me, big hands opening and closing. Denis whimpered, abandoned his book, and scuttled aside.

'I know exactly what I'm saying,' Don blustered. 'You and your fuckin' mind-games! You turned my own kid against me! And my wife – my wife — ' He faltered, looked at Sunny in a dazed fashion. His mind walls were down and I could see the wheels turning as he made the connection about the cup of cocoa and Sunny's frustration of his plan.

'You *knew*,' he accused her. His tone was confused, the anger momentarily sidetracked. 'But how?'

She straightened. 'Denis asked me about the LSD before he asked Rogi. Our son has been teaching me telepathy. It was to be a surprise for you and Rogi.'

I was stunned. None of my books on parapsychology had prepared me for a mind capable of exercising psychoredaction, the 'mental editing' faculty that is so taken for granted in Milieu pedagogy and psychiatry. I cried:

Sunny – is it true?

She didn't respond.

Denis said: Mommy can only mindspeak me. She can't hear you or Papa. You aren't strong enough.

Don looked down incredulously at the little toddler in corduroy overalls and a miniature lumberjack shirt. Denis was on his hands and knees. His lower lip trembled.

'I'm not strong enough?' Don roared. He stooped to seize the child, ready to shake him, to slap him —

Sunny sensed what was coming and I saw it clearly in Don's mind. We both started to intercept him. But it wasn't necessary.

'Papa won't hurt me,' Denis said. He climbed to his feet and stood in front of his father. His head was about on a level with Don's knees. 'You won't ever hurt me, will you Papa.' It wasn't a question. The boy's magnetic blue eyes were rock-steady as he looked up.

'No,' said Don. 'No.'

Sunny and I let out suppressed breath. She bent down and lifted Denis in her arms.

Don turned to me. He moved like a man in a dream, or one in an extremity of pain. His mental walls were back in place. I had no idea what message Denis had transmitted, what coercive interdict the child had used. I knew that Denis would never be harmed by his father – but the protective aegis did *not* extend to me.

Don said, 'You won't have to bother coming over in the evening any more, Rogi.'

'I suppose not,' I said.

The child reached out to comfort and reassure me. In those days I knew nothing of the intimate mode of farspeech, that which tunes directly to the personal mind-signature of the recipient; nevertheless, I was aware that Denis spoke to my mind alone when he said:

We will find a way to continue.

'Denis has had enough coddling,' Don said, 'and Sunny's

going to be too busy to play games with you two. Did she tell you she's expecting again?'

She held Denis close, her eyes brimming with tears. She hadn't. And I'd never noticed the knitting. 'Congratulations,' I said in a level voice.

Don was at the front closet getting my coat and things. He held them out to me, a defiant smile twisting up one side of his mouth, his thoughts unreadable.

He said, 'I plan to take care of the next kid's training myself.'

15

Edinburgh, Scotland, Earth
28 January 1972

He climbed, as he often did when the tensions became too great, clutching at slippery rocks and gnarled heather stems with frostbitten hands gone numb.

HALLOO!

Revelling in the height, the separation from the world of ordinary mortals, he scrabbled for precarious footholds. His mud-clotted, soggy waffle-stompers abrading the fresh blisters on his heels, adding to the welcome ensemble of pain.

HALLOO OUT THERE!

His heart was banging in his throat fit to brast. The wintry gusts blowing into the steep defile called the Guttit Haddie froze his hurdies and his ears and his chin and his nose.

HALLOO! OI! IS THERE A BODY CAN HEAR ME?

He climbed like a man pursued by demons invisible, never looking down. The spreading sea of city lights seemed to undulate dizzily below – glittering currents of traffic, dirty backwaters of tenements and shops, the up-thrust reefs of church steeples and castle ramparts and the perilous shoals of the University.

HALLOO!

Down there ran the Pleasance and on it stood the building with the laboratory. It had a grand name: the Parapsychology Unit of the Department of Psychology of the University of Edinburgh; but it was only a big dreary room up under the eaves, partitioned into cramped wee offices and carrels for the endless testing. It was presided over by the eminent Dr Graham Finlay Dunlap, whose staff – alas! – consisted only of two graduate assistants, William Erskine and Nigel Weinstein, and him: James Somerled MacGregor, a silly gowk of twenty, by virtue of his fey talents awarded a bursary at one of the finest universities in Britain – and for all that bored and wretched and wanting only to go home to Islay in the Hebrides.

HALLOO! WHAT'S NEW? DAFT JAMIE SAYS: SOD YOU!

Climb up laughing at the uselessness of it. Climb above the winterfast reeky city towards a louring sky still scarlet in the west. Climb up the steepest, most dangerous way in shifty twilight, hurting all the while. Scramble up rocks. Creep along the igneous ridge all frosty and windblasted. Climb finally to the top of that ancient crag, that sentinel of Dun Eadain beloved of tourists and sentimentalists and trysting lovers. Climb up to Arthur's Seat!

HALLOO! HURRAW! EXCELSIOR! . . .

The near-gale blowing up the Forth from the North Sea now smote him squarely. To escape he sprawled belly-flaught, face cradled in his arms, and let rattling gasps from his parched throat soften while his heart tripped over itself and slowed. He licked cracked lips and tasted salt from wind-tears and wool from his sweater. The sheepy taste and the ocean taste and the smell of wet cold stone and moorland! The thrill of climbing in the high air, the pain of it, the happiness . . . and see – the humour was coming on him again, just as it used to so easily in the early days when he was still excited with the novelty of demonstrating his uncanny powers to the psychologists. He felt it coming. He knew that he was going to be able to do it again.

The thing he thought he'd lost. What they'd been coaxing him vainly to do again down in the damned laboratory for nigh on a year.

The out-of-body thing.

I'M AWAY!

Oh, aye, it was grand! To soar up and see himself left prone below, a husk without a soul. He sped into the sunset, across West Lothian's black fells and crouching Glasgow and the Firth of Clyde, over Arran and Kintyre and tiny Gigha, beyond the sea to home. To Islay, to his private place. Like a sea bird he hovered, seeing the surf crash against the shoulder of Tòn Mhór. A few sheep skirted the bog on their way downhill. Somewhere one of the dogs was barking. The ruins of the old croft near the bay sheltered a shaggy red longhorn stot. In his own snug home the lights were on and a thread of smoke rose from the chimney. Suppertime on a winter's Friday night, and Granny portioning out the sweet while Mum dished up savoury haddock and fried potatoes. Dad and Colin and old Iain came trampling in tired and famished and red-cheeked.

He watched them, full of joy and with all pain abolished. Then he concentrated on the well-known dear aura. He said:

It's me! I'm here!

Granny looked up from the trifle she'd made that day for a special treat: Jamie my dear laddie. It's been so long. And how are you then?

Ah Gran I'm that miserable here at university I could die I think!

Such blether.

No no they're all fools and Dr Dunlap the biggest of all with his testing testing testing as if he didn't *know* my powers exist but had to prove it over and over endlessly with his damned statistics and I get so tired and impatient and I feel the hostility from the other undergrads because I'm a privileged character and allowed my special academic track here in the Psychology Department and Gran dear Gran this queer mind of mine sometimes does its tricks and sometimes not but what's the use it's not as though I could use the Sight or the Speech or the Out-of-Body Thing to earn a good living as a bookie or a blackmailer or a spy Lord knows the powers are too unreliable and me too conscience-tender for that but Gran I'm beginning to think

I don't want to be a psychologist either not even to study the powers if it means this endless dull dull testing not only of me but of *common* folk and Dunlap and his two assistants nattering on about 'extrachance performance' and the 'psi-missing effect' (which means can you believe it test results so rotten that the psi experts have decided they must be significant) and they keep trying to find a theory in physics to fit the powers and nothing works and still they write their papers and look wise and pretend it all *means* something when we know it doesn't have to and what I'd really like to do is chuck the whole thing and go off and be a stage magician or a mind reader on the telly and make a packet like Uri Geller or the Amazing Kreskin . . .

Jamie Jamie ungrateful gorlin the time's come to stop playing with the powers selfishly as I've told ye for now they must be put to use for all mankind. And if the good Professor can't solve the problem of making the powers fit into real science then maybe the job's meant for YOU Daft Jamie MacGregor!

Ah Gran. Dunlap's department doesn't have the money to do the job proper. Ah you should see what a threadbare wee place this Parapsychology Unit is. If we were in America now it might be different for there all the colleges are rich but here in Edinburgh the two doctoral candidates working under Dunlap must live on cheese sandwiches and beer I'm all right of course eating in the Pollock dining room but —

It's time for us to eat here as well so stop your whinging. You must fulfil your part of the bargain so bear with Professor Dunlap and his perjinkities and study hard and be a credit to us. Then later if you can't abide parapsychology you can shrink silly neurotics and get rich.

Ah Gran.

Ah Jamie. Go back now. Your poor body's freezing in the haar and one of your good friends has come searching for you . . .

He opened his eyes. He was back in Holyrood Park on the pinnacle of Arthur's Seat and stiff as an iced halibut. He stood upright, tottering in the east wind, tucked his bare hands into his warm crutch, and stamped his feet. The pins-and-needles effect was exhilarating.

It was too dark now to climb down the way he'd come, for the western side of the small mountain was steep and trackless down the Haddie. And besides, the lights of Edinburgh were turning yellow and fuzzy. It was the haar, as Granny had warned him, sneaking in from the Firth to swaddle the city in freezing mizzle. He'd have to go back the long way, down the easy east path to Dunsapie Loch, and then along the Queen's Drive to the Dalkeith entrance to the park where he'd come in. A dreary mile and a half, but there was no helping it.

He came down the east side of the knoll into thickening fog. The temperature was dropping and he moved as rapidly as he could along the footpath, comforting himself with the thought that antibiotics easily cured pneumonia these days —

'Jamie!'

He heard the thin shout from below. Gran had said a friend was looking for him, hadn't she! But nobody knew where he'd gone! He cantered down a precipitous stretch of track and saw an amber light bobbing about: someone with a torch coming up to meet him.

'Oi!' he shouted. 'I'm here!'

And there was a familiar stocky figure pouring out vibes of relief only slightly tainted by peevish mutterings.

'Nigel!' Jamie exclaimed delightedly. 'Did you track me with psi? The hill's strongly magnetic, you know. I would've thought that — '

'Oh, put a sock in it, you young idiot, and let's get down to the car before we both freeze.' Nigel Weinstein unwound a long striped muffler from his own neck, flung it at Jamie, and glowered. 'You and your magnetism! Dunlap was pissed to the wide when Wee Wully Erskine told him you'd aborted the afternoon magnetometer session and run off. You bloody ass! We had a devil of a time getting that test set up with the physics boys – and now, thanks to your silly-buggery, we can go back to square one.'

'I'm sorry, Nigel.' The two of them came to the road. Dunsapie Loch was lost in the murk. They turned right and hurried towards the car-park at the south end. 'Were you really worried about me?'

'You might have broken your neck,' the graduate assistant snapped. 'Where would we find another test subject with your talent? You know we're all chewing nails worrying about the new research grant.'

The underlying fear leaked through his gruff words: And who knows what kind of stupid thing a morose young Celt might get up to on a slippery crag in the dead of winter?

'I'm not *that* depressed,' Jamie told him. But thanks for caring. 'As for the tests, they'd have been no good anyway. The morning runs wore me down and I just didn't have the heart to keep on. I keep telling Erskine that it's no good endlessly repeating really tough mind manoeuvres. I lose motivation and get to swithering and then the powers wonk out. I'm not a bloody computer, you know. And Wee Wully's attitude is no help – Mr Objectivity, plug me into the circuit and work me like a damn dray-horse!'

Weinstein heaved a sigh. 'Dr Dunlap would say you're suffering from a psi decline. Me – I'd label you a prima donna.'

'So'd my Granny,' Jamie admitted, grinning.

They found Weinstein's battered Hillman at last and climbed in. There was no traffic at all on the one-way Queen's Drive that encircled Holyrood Park and the fog was getting so thick that the car's headlamps were worse than useless. Nigel muttered a curse, switched them off, and navigated with the ambers. He drove little faster than a walking pace. Outside was a world of dull-glowing golden cotton wool.

Jamie said, 'Tests like those we were doing today are a waste of time. So I try to move drinking straws with psychokinesis and the instrument measures the perturbation of the magnetic field around my head. Super! A needle wiggles, the field gets slightly bent, and it's all recorded for posterity . . . which won't give a tinker's damn.'

'The research adds to the body of parapsychological evidence.'

Jamie rolled his eyes. 'How much evidence do you need,

man? It isn't as though the magnetic measurements told you anything *useful*. You still haven't a clue about the nature of mental energy – what forces operate during PK, how telepathic messages are carried, what mechanism enables me to travel without my body. There's no scientific theory for any of it.'

'We're still assembling data. Eventually we'll fit psi phenomena and the whole notion of mind into the reality framework.'

Jamie huddled closer to the warm air beginning to come from the car heater. 'Weird powers have been around since caveman days. How come Australian bushmen and Eskimos and African witch doctors and fire-walking Hindus can use the powers and not worry about it – but scientists can't? Science flies to the moon, but it diddles and daddles and wrings its hands when the mind performs its psychic tricks, and needs to be convinced over and over again that it's not all a sham. As far as useful theory goes, we're not much wiser today in 1972 than we were in 1572 – when people blamed it all on the devil and burnt blokes like me at the stake . . . For God's sake, why can't we simply buckle down and *use* the powers without the endless havering!'

Weinstein laughed. 'Science likes things it can measure. Psi powers are too slippery for comfort. So we must try to analyse them, try to formulate theories and test them. And if psychic research had the kind of financial backing that astronautics has, we'd get results.'

'I used to think so,' Jamie said slowly, 'but I've chewed over the matter a lot lately. And I've about concluded that there may be a basic flaw in the entire concept of psi research – one that makes our kind of research futile.'

'Bosh!'

'No – listen to me, Nigel. All over the world scientists have been doing serious studies of psi effects. The Russians are keen on it because they think it might make a weapon. Give them credit for a pragmatic attitude, anyhow! The Yanks are a touch leery just because the Russkies believe in it – but they have quite a few dedicated research groups, and the American Association for the Advancement of Science *did* finally admit the Parapsychological Association to membership. Our British teams are going full throttle. There's good work being done by the Dutch and the Indians and the Finns and the Japs and the Germans. Nobody who matters laughs at us any more or calls us crackpots. The consensus in scientific circles is that psi effects are real. But . . . the net *practical* result of nearly twenty years of activity has been just about nil! You still get untrained people finding water with forked sticks, and fakirs treading hot coals, and faith healers laying on hands and curing the sick, and all the rest of the disorganized clamjamphrie of PK and telepathy and precognition and all the rest – unreliable and unexplainable – while trained researchers still have no coherent results from their experiments.'

'That's no reason to label our work futile — '

'What if the human race had the eyesight of a mole? Could we develop a science of astronomy? Of course not! The appropriate sense organs would be too weak even to notice the stars, much less organize scientific data concerning them. I think that's the way it is with psi and normal humanity right now. Most human beings have some kind of parapsychological capability, but it's so weak and undependable that it might as well not exist. The few people like me who have stronger powers are still too ill-equipped to demonstrate much that's useful. I think that science won't get off the ground analysing higher mind-powers until really efficient psychic operators are born.'

'You're saying that our data will remain essentially incomplete until . . . mental giants come along. Until the brain evolves further.'

'Exactly. When people have full control of their paranormal faculties – whether they're born with it, or develop control through training – *then* we'll be able to do valid testing. Nigel, I know I'm right! I'm one of the flawed ones myself – not totally eyeless, but still only seeing the stars as off-again, on-again blurs . . . Just look at the fog outside this car of yours. Would you know there was a great city all around Arthur's Seat if you spent your entire life in a car, cruising around and around this misty drive, only catching a rare glimpse of the lights outside? And with

Edinburgh only a half-seen mystery, would you even dream that other cities existed?'

They glided through mustard-coloured murk, searching for the exit road. And then a gust of wind blew the swirling vapours aside for a moment and they saw the junction ahead, and both of them gave exclamations of relief, and Nigel said, 'You see? Breakthroughs do happen. Take a lesson, Jamie.' He turned the regular headlamps back on and made the turn.

'You want us to keep travelling our research road, no matter how foggy, until we find a way into the hidden city – and maybe a body with radar eyes.'

'A muddled metaphor, but thine own.'

Jamie grinned at the older man. 'You poor buggers working under Dunlap are luckier than most. At least you've got me. Not quite as blind as a mole. More in the hedgehog class, maybe.'

Weinstein sighed. 'And to think I'm basing my doctoral thesis on you! I'd do better to creep back to the family tog-shop on Duke Street.'

Jamie said, 'I'll quit mucking up, Nigel. Just promise me . . . when you do get your degree, stay on at the university. Work with me on *useful* experiments, not this codswallop that Dunlap insists on. You came out to get me tonight knowing exactly where I was. We know what that has to mean. Let's train my clairvoyance and yours, too, instead of stifling it with trivia. Let's show the world that psychic powers are serious business.'

'Conceited little twit. All you want is my life, eh? All right – you're on!' Weinstein peered through the windscreen at indistinct blobs of light marking Dalkeith Road. 'Now suppose you use your clairvoyance, or your out-of-body faculty, or *some* damn thing to find us a nice pub.'

16

River Forest, Illinois, Earth
9 June 1973

Aldo 'Big Al' Camastra stepped out of his air-conditioned study into the muggy music-filled evening and closed the French doors behind him. He was smiling, for the business with the union reps and the party bagmen from Chicago had gone very well indeed. Now he was free to circulate among the guests like a proper host, just as Betty Carolyn had begged him to do. Family business came first, of course; but he wanted to keep her happy on their Twenty-Fifth Anniversary, and besides, there were some people around that he should glad-hand.

Nick and Carlo were patiently waiting on patio chairs, ever alert. Big Al nodded to them. 'Party going good?'

'Really swinging, Al,' Carlo said. 'Joe Porks even brought this broad who sang on the Johnny Carson show. Terrific! Sort of a Cher, but with boobs.'

Big Al laughed, adjusted his silk cummerbund, and shot his cuffs so the big gold links just peeked out from the sleeves of his dinner jacket. 'Did Rosemary get here?'

'Frankie drove her in from O'Hare about an hour ago,' Nick said. 'Her plane was delayed. She went to change.'

They went down the flagstone steps with Carlo leading and Nick bringing up the rear. The big garden behind the Camastra mansion was lit with skeins of Japanese lanterns in addition to the bronze lamps illuminating the rose beds. A marquee for refreshments had been set up near the west wing and there were throngs of guests moving about inside of it. Another considerable crowd had gathered around the portable dance floor where tables and chairs made an outdoor cabaret flanked by flower beds. The big band was playing 'Leaving the Straight Life Behind'. Some forty couples gyrated to the music without ever engaging in body contact.

Big Al grimaced contemptuously at the sight of them. 'They call that dancing? Everybody doing their own thing, bumping and grinding like a buncha Clark Street hookers?'

The two soldiers guarding the patio steps greeted the Chicago Boss respectfully and stepped aside so he and his bodyguard could enter the crush of the party. The bolder guests began to converge immediately – businessmen and politicians and lobbyists and fellow mobsters and their expensive women. The relatives and smaller fry hung around in the background, clutching drinks and waving.

'Happy Silver Anniversary, Al!'

'Mazel tov, Al baby!'

'Wonderful party, Mr Camastra. Quite a showplace you have here!'

'Lemme get a glassa spumante for you, Al.'

'Mr Camastra, I think we met in Springfield at the last session — '

Shaking hands, smiling and returning compliments, he wove expertly through the crowd. Nick and Carlo were always a few steps behind. He accepted the best wishes of a Chicago alderman, kissed his wife's sister, gave a polite brush-off to a hollow-eyed banking executive, told a dapper monsignor that he'd be delighted to contribute to the parish carillon fund, and congratulated a visiting New York consigliere of the Montedoro Family for having beaten a federal conspiracy rap.

Then he was at the edge of the dance floor, and all the well-wishers and importuners were swept away as if by magic. He kissed his wife Betty Carolyn, who looked terrific in clinging white Bob Mackie evening pyjamas with silver fringe, topped off with a coiffure like sculptured meringue. And there was his grown daughter Rosemary, laughing as he swept her up in a bear hug.

'Hey, Rosie, my little princess! You look great. How's the art-gallery business in the Big Apple? We were afraid you'd miss the party with your plane delayed — '

'Al, the most exciting thing!' Betty Carolyn squealed. 'Rosemary didn't say anything when she called from the airport so's we wouldn't worry, and anyhow by the time the plane landed it was all over, and her wonderful hero of a boyfriend even cooled off the US Marshals so she and him don't even have to make a statement until tomorrow when the skyjacker is arraigned.'

'What?' The word was like a soft explosion. Big Al held his smiling daughter at arm's length. 'Your plane was *skyjacked?* Jesus Christ!'

'Poppa, I'm all right. No one was hurt and the skyjacker was captured – thanks to Kieran. Kieran O'Connor, a very dear friend of mine.'

Carlo and Nick were still fending off guests, and the band was working itself into incipient apoplexy as it approached the climax of 'Jeremiah Was A Bullfrog'. Rosemary drew forward a slender dark-haired man who had been standing behind her. He was about thirty years old, clean-cut and with conservatively styled hair. He wore designer jeans and an open shirt with a gold neck-chain, the usual summer formal wear of his generation. His smile was diffident and his eyes cast down as Rosemary said:

'Kieran subdued the skyjacker single-handed, Poppa. He took away the man's gun and – and somehow knocked him unconscious with a single blow! Karate or something.'

Big Al seized the hand of Kieran O'Connor. 'My God! How can I thank you? You gotta tell me everything. My own daughter skyjacked! What's this damn country coming to? Your name's O'Connor? You a frienda Rosie's from New York? Let's find a place to sit down and — '

The band, having brought 'Jeremiah' to a rousing conclusion, now blared out a fanfare. People started tinkling their glasses with spoons.

'Ooh,' cried Betty Carolyn. 'I told the band leader that when you came in, he should quick finish up whatever they were playing and then announce our special dance. Al, you know everybody's been waiting for you to come down. And then we cut the cake — '

'Lay-deez and gentlemen!' The amplified voice of the band leader boomed through the festive summer night. 'And now, by special request, in honour of the Silver Wedding Anniversary of Mr and Mrs Aldo Camastra . . .'

The opening strains of Big Al's favourite tune, 'The Godfather Waltz', throbbed from a single violin. The guests broke into applause and cheers and Betty Carolyn tugged at her husband's left hand. The right one was still in the grip of Kieran O'Connor.

'Al, we gotta dance. Come on!'

But Big Al stood unmoving, his mouth open in an expression of incredulity and his eyes locked upon those of the young man standing before him. Kieran O'Connor's lips were moving, but the noise from the crowd and the now fully instrumented waltz music made his voice inaudible to Betty Carolyn and Rosemary.

Big Al heard every word.

I have wanted to meet you – or someone like you – for a long time, Mr Camastra. The skyjack was a charade. An introduction and a demonstration. I brought the gun aboard the aircraft myself, and I selected the poor devil who would play the skyjacker role and made certain that he played it. Wouldn't you like to know how I did that, Mr Camastra? I have a number of other useful talents at my command. If we can come to an amicable arrangement, I am willing to put them at your disposal.

'Malocchio,' whispered Big Al. Sweat had broken out on his forehead. 'The Evil Eye!' He tried to cry out to Carlo and Nick. The young Irishman's hypnotic voice reproached him.

You don't have to be afraid, Mr Camastra. My offer is entirely legitimate. I need you, and you stand to profit considerably through use of my special services.

'Al, come on!' said Betty Carolyn.

The voice in his mind was genial. The paralysis that had fettered his body eased, but still that entrancing gaze held him. Malocchio!

I'll let you dance with your lovely wife in just a moment, Mr Camastra. I just want to assure you that there is no possible way for you to harm me. We are going to be friends. Your daughter and I are already very good friends.

Big Al felt himself being pulled on to the dance floor. Betty Carolyn's body pressed against his and they began to waltz to the sad, lilting melody. Rosemary stood arm in arm with a pleasant, very ordinary-looking young man – who still exerted his mental wizardry from more than twenty feet away.

Ever since I finished law school at Harvard I've been researching the economics of the nationwide organization operated by you and your Sicilian colleagues. I found it fascinating. I know every signifi-

cant detail of the Five Families' operations back in New York, including a manoeuvre currently being orchestrated to your disadvantage by a certain Mr 'Joe Porks' Porcaro of the Falcone Family. We'll talk about it later. Enjoy your dance, Mr Camastra. It's really a great party.

17

*From the Memoirs of
Rogatien Remillard*

I continued to act as the surreptitious confidant of Denis Remillard throughout his early childhood in spite of my brother Don's antagonism. The boy's long-distance farspeaking ability improved with each passing year; and my own telepathic faculty, through our constant interaction and mental symbiosis, also advanced far beyond the level I had previously achieved with Don.

Little Denis soaked up knowledge like a human computer and my role as simple tutor soon became obsolete. Nevertheless I still had an important job to do educating Denis in human relationships. At times he seemed almost like some naive little visitor from an extraterrestrial civilization, overflowing with data about Earth, its science, its culture and its people – yet unable to fully comprehend how the human race *worked*. I could not help but recall Odd John, who was similarly bewildered. Not that Denis had any of the fictional character's inhuman alienation – far from it. But the murkier ins and outs of human psychology – especially the irrational elements playing a part in human decision making – tended to perplex and bemuse him. Brilliant though he was, he was handicapped by overly logical attitudes, social inexperience, and the inevitably self-centred mind-set of a very young child. It would have been futile to try to form Denis's conscience, for instance, by referring him to treatises on ethics or moral theology; he needed to develop a sense of values by observing the actions of others, analysing them, and judging their good or evil in

121

a context that was not only social but personal. Practically speaking, it amounted to talking things over with me.

Looking back on our relationship from my present perspective, 140 years later, I can only be grateful that at the time I did not fully appreciate the crucial importance of what I was doing. If I had, I doubt that I would have had the courage to undertake the job – Ghost or no Ghost.

With the birth of Don and Sunny's second son Victor in 1970, Denis was relieved of a good deal of paternal constriction. Don became obsessed with the new child, who was strapping and handsome and the very image of his father, and lifted his earlier prohibition of contact between Denis and me. With Sunny's cooperation I was able to spend many hours each week with the boy. Our meeting place was the old apartment on Second Street, where ageing Onc' Louie still lived with my unmarried cousins Al and Margie.

It was in 1973, when the time came for Denis to enter school, that the next crisis took place. After careful negotiation (and a bit of coercion!) I had managed to wangle a partial scholarship for Denis at Northfield Hall, a prestigious private boarding school in Vermont that specialized in gifted children; but when the time came to finalize the arrangements, Don balked. He was in a precarious financial position. His alcoholism affected his job performance and he had been passed over for promotion. Furthermore, Sunny was pregnant again, and Dr Laplante predicted twins. Don's share of the tuition at Northfield would entail considerable sacrifice on his part – and he also professed an objection to the philosophical orientation of the school, which was ultraliberal and permissive and not at all congenial to the old-fashioned Catholicism of our family. Don dragged the entire Remillard family into the row. We split into those who wanted the best for Denis (me, Sunny, Al and Margie), and those who maintained that no educational opportunity was worth 'endangering the child's faith at some godless, left-wing school for spoiled rich kids (Don, Onc' Louie and about twenty-five other cousins, uncles, aunts and in-laws).

In vain, I argued that Denis's religious instruction could

be assured by special arrangement with a church near Northfield. Don declared that the Berlin parochial school had been good enough for him, and it should be good enough for his older son – genius or no genius. When I volunteered to share the tuition expenses Don stubbornly refused. A last-ditch attempt on my part to garner a full scholarship for Denis was shattered when Don made a truculent phone call to the school's headmaster. Northfield washed its hands of us volatile Canucks.

Of course nobody had asked Denis what *he* wanted.

Frustrated and disgusted by the debacle, I decided to go on a weekend backpack in the Mahoosucs to cool off. I could usually restore my spirit by climbing in the mountains, and I have since known many other metas who felt the same way. Perhaps it is merely instinctive for the psychosensitive to ascend as high as possible above the walls and confining rock formations that tend to block the free ranging of our minds; perhaps it is more – a yearning to be where the light is brightest, where the trees merge and the extent and shape of the forest can be known, where mean and mundane concerns are blotted out in flatland haze. I suppose I am moderately devout, but I don't feel impelled to pray in the high places. (I'm more likely to cry out of the depths!) Instead, I climb upward to bask. Sky-ey energies seem to pour through me when I stand on a peak like a human lightning rod; they renew me, and in some mystical fashion revitalize the Earth I stand upon.

On that day in mid-August I climbed Goose Eye Mountain, a 1170-metre pinnacle some fifteen crow-flight kilometres from Berlin, just across the border in Maine. When I reached the top I farspoke Denis and shared the summit experience with him. For two years now he had begged to accompany me on my wilderness rambles, but Sunny felt he was still too young and frail for strenuous hiking and I reluctantly had to agree. I took Denis along with me mentally instead, and he told me it was almost as good.

After I'd let him borrow my senses, I asked: What are you doing?

Baking CAKE allbymyself (OK Mom supervises) Papa goneout so he won't laugh took Victor they lookingfor birthdaypresentPapa outboardmotor tomorrow Papabirthday I make cake Mom&me privatejoke not tell Papa cake goingtobe *magnificent*.

OmyGod forgot completely tomorrow August12. My birthday too 28yearsold just like yourPapa.

! [Dismay.] BUT YOU HAVE NO CAKE.

Laughter. Waitwait in backpack gooeycreamfilled Feuilleté! Tomorrow put littletwigs in light sing HappyBirthday toMe.

[Mindshout broken off.] Cake done! Goodbye Uncle Rogi . . .

I'll try to speak you tomorrow MountSuccess. Goodbye Denis.

And he was gone, caught up in his great confectionery adventure. Of course it would have to be kept secret from Don, who would ridicule his little son for doing 'women's work'. It was typical of my brother that he should take three-year-old Victor, his pet, with him while he shopped for his own expensive birthday present. Small chance he would have saved the money for Denis's education.

I cursed quietly. If only the tuition at Northfield Hall weren't so exorbitantly high. If only the great state of New Hampshire hadn't let the gifted-child programme go down the drain in a budget cut. If only the local Catholic school weren't so stodgy and inflexible. Sister Superior was willing to 'see what could be done' about assigning Denis some special courses of advanced study, but she was adamant about having him start in first grade just like all the other six-year-olds. It was necessary that he 'gain the requisite social skills and learn good work habits'.

Denis now probably knew more than I did. And how would *I* like to spend a year twiddling my thumbs in first grade? Doux Jésus!

I slithered down from Goose Eye and picked up the Appalachian Trail. I had intended to spend Saturday and Sunday browsing about this region of the Mahoosucs, a rather modest weekend ramble; but now renewed fury at Don's selfishness and my own inability to help Denis kindled a perverse need to push myself to the limit. I checked my watch. It wasn't quite noon. Sunset would not

124

be until around eight o'clock. My AMC map showed a more challenging itinerary, a fourteen-kilometre hike to Gentian Pond Shelter. That section of the trail was quite rugged, involving the negotiation of steep ridge and valley terrain and several scrambles over areas with great blocks of granite. I was a strong hiker, however, and my legs are long. I figured that by pushing myself I could cover the distance and arrive at Gentian well before dark – dead tired and no doubt chock-full of self-justification.

So I set off.

It was a fine day in spite of the heat. A tricky descent along the southwestern flank of Goose Eye commanded my attention. Then I flushed a few languid spruce grouse down in a hollow, and was further distracted by a harsh call that sounded like a raven, a species formerly rare in New England but now making a comeback. My bird-watcher's instinct perked up and I tramped along more cheerfully. In time I reached Mount Carlo and made my way up its rough northern shoulder. The eminence was as sombre as a chunk of Labrador tundra, but there was a good view back to Goose Eye and ahead to Mount Success. I tried to hail Denis telepathically but there was no answer. No doubt Don had returned home and the child had been obliged to take refuge in the mental sanctuary he customarily erected against his father's barbs and disparagements.

Damn Don! He couldn't hurt Denis physically, but he could certainly do enormous emotional damage. The boarding school had seemed the perfect solution, taking the boy out of Don's orbit for nearly nine months of the year and providing him with an environment where he could continue his self-education, while at the same time learning to get along with other bright youngsters and sympathetic adults. With that escape vetoed, there seemed to be only one other solution to Denis's dilemma.

I would have to reveal his metapsychic gifts.

Every instinct in me warned against it. The child would be exploited, pressured, treated as a freak if not as a menace. Once the truth came out, the psi laboratories at the various institutions would squabble over him. And I had read recently about a psi research facility at the US Army's Aberdeen Centre . . .

No. There had to be another way.

I hiked on, agonizing, entertaining one preposterous idea after another. I would steal Denis away. I would poison Don's liquor just enough to put him in bed, under my coercive thumb. I would confide Denis's secret to the nuns at school and enlist their help. (But the truth would leak out. The unsophisticated sisters could never deal with it.) I would write to Dr Rhine himself! To our bishop. To the Governor of New Hampshire. To President Nixon. To the *New York Times*!

Occupied with these thoughts, I crossed the steep notch of Carlo Col and slogged into New Hampshire again, beginning the long climb to Mount Success, that ironically named central point of the little Mahoosuc Range. Success wasn't very difficult to master. It wasn't high, only interminably broad. Up around the summit were treacherous patches of thinly crusted bog where a false step put you boot-top-deep in black muck. I finally snapped out of my distraction when I missed my footing and fell headlong into a pocket of the stuff. It was only by the skin of my teeth that I missed tumbling over a kind of rock-slab retaining wall into a lethally steep ravine.

I had managed to wrench my knee, I was half soaked, and clinging black glop slathered me from stem to gudgeon.

I crawled out swearing at my own stupidity – and at the whimsical topography of my native state, where bogs appeared at the tops of otherwise arid mountains. They were a consequent of the local weather pattern, formed when moist air driven by strong winds collided with the small peaks. In summer there might be thick mist or drizzle or even sleet at the higher elevations while the lower slopes remained warm and dry. The same terrain and weather factors made for extremely violent thunderstorms.

I recalled this as I sat on top of Mount Success changing my wet pants and socks in a rising wind while towering cumulus clouds billowed up behind the two Bald Caps in the west. Now I knew why I had met so few hikers during the last three hours – and those hiking in the opposite direction. Anybody with any brains was already holed up in a shelter; but I was caught halfway between the Carlo Col hut and Gentian Pond. It was almost five in the afternoon, my knee hurt like hell, I had no tent in my pack, and shelter was four hours away in either direction . . . for an able-bodied hiker.

I limped off in the direction of Gentian, moving as fast as the knee permitted. As the clouds humped higher and darker, I looked for a likely bivouac. I found nothing but windswept open ledges, knee-high tangles of scrub spruce and balsam (but no wood large enough to cut into a walking stick), and tumbled rocky slopes that had to be traversed with the utmost caution. Clouds hid the sun and wind whipped the miniature evergreens viciously in a prelude to the arrival of the storm front. Off in the southwest, the sky was purplish black.

As I slid downhill into a brushy washout my knee buckled. I went over sideways, but managed to land on my pack. The pain was intense. I lay there with my eyes shut listening to the tinkle of a tiny rivulet a few metres away. Then came a faint grumble of thunder, raindrops splattered my face, and I said, 'Oh, shit.'

Now what? I was going to have to get out of that ravine, for starters, since it would probably become a torrent once the storm began in earnest. Shedding my pack, I hobbled around gathering sticks to splint the knee. When the joint was immobilized I rested for a few minutes, trying to concentrate my metapsychic healing ability on the injury. But it was no good. I was too distracted and anxious to focus my mind properly. I put on my Gore-Tex jacket, the only rainwear I had, shouldered my backpack again, and began a long and awkward climb.

The rain came on fast and so did the fireworks. There was a real danger of being zapped by lightning if one remained in an exposed position during one of these big storms, and an outside chance of getting killed on the slippery granite rocks. I was still a good hour and a half away from Gentian Pond Shelter and I didn't have a hope of making it before nightfall. I'd have to hole up somewhere; but as I rummaged frantically in my memory trying to recall this section of the trail from my last-year's hike, it seemed that there was no real refuge to be had, not along the trail proper. And if I went sidetracking in the dusk I would certainly get lost.

I stood still in the driving downpour and tried to exert my farsight, seeking some cranny or marmot hole where I could gain at least minimal shelter. My ultrasense refused to function. Perhaps it was the lightning that blazed all around me; perhaps it was the pain of my sprained knee, or sheer funk. Whatever – I farsaw nothing. I remember crying out mentally to little Denis in my desperation, having some notion that his superior brain might be able to locate a hiding place where mine had failed. But Denis didn't respond. I suppose my telepathic howl was too feeble and too circumscribed by the dense granite rock that surrounded me. I was stuck.

Alors – j'y suis, j'y reste! Unless . . .

What happened next seems, in retrospect, to be almost a prefiguring – if not a parody – of the great event that would take place forty years later. Trapped on that damned mountain in a thundering deluge, I lifted my head to the sky and yelled:

'Ghost! Get me *out* of this!'

Between lightning blasts, the landscape was now nearly pitch black. I cried out to the Fantôme Familier a second time. The wind roared and my knee gave me hell. I was drenched all over again in spite of the Gore-Tex, since the rain was somehow blowing uphill. I unfastened my pack and sat on the streaming rocks, my splinted leg jutting awkwardly.

'Ghost, you son of a bitch! Where are you when I need you?'

And it said: *Here.*

I gave a violent start. Hallucination? But the wind had fallen off abruptly and the rain spigot was turned off. I was aware of a hazy glow surrounding me. The lightning's glare was almost lost in it, only visible now as slightly brighter pulses of light in an overarching luminescence.

I whispered, 'Ghost?'

À vos ordres.

'Is it really you?'

Poor Rogi! When you have legitimate need of me, you have only to call. Someone will hear and summon me. I thought you understood this.

I cursed the mysterious presence roundly in French and English, then demanded that it do something about my knee. Voilà! The injury healed instantly. Giddy with triumph, I told it, 'Now dry me off – if you can.'

Nothing easier.

Pouf! Clouds of vapour poured out of the sleeves and from under the lower edge of my rain jacket. I pulled the thing off and watched my pants and sweater steam dry in a couple of minutes. Even my socks dried.

'Hot damn!' I chortled. 'Now let's have a nice cup of tea with plenty of brandy in it.'

The Ghost's mind-voice was slightly caustic: I believe you've used up the customary three wishes. You have your Bluet stove and the makings in your pack.

Laughing like a loon, I pulled out the things and got cooking. The Ghost had charitably dried off a few rocks in the immediate vicinity so I just sat where I was, waiting for the pot to boil and munching a Granola bar. The glow from what I now know was a psychocreative bubble cast a friendly light over the dripping skunk-currant bushes.

After I had managed to calm down a little I said, 'It's a good thing you did show up. A man could die in this kind of a mess. Poor little Denis has had enough hard luck without losing his favourite uncle, too.'

The Ghost seemed surprised: Hard luck?

'The boarding-school thing I arranged for him fell through. Don and most of the family are dead-set against it. I should think you'd know.'

I have been . . . elsewhere. Do you mean to tell me that Don objects to Denis being taught by the Jesuits?

'Jesuits! Hell, no. He objects to the kid going to that school for budding geniuses in Vermont – Northfield Hall.'

The Ghost seemed to be ruminating: So! It seems that further direct intervention is called for, with the probability loci focused by this minor contretemps of yours. An interesting manifestation of synchronicity! Of course Denis never spoke of this failed arrangement, so how was one to know?

The thing's jabbering made no sense so I brewed tea and tossed in a hefty slug of Christian Brothers. Half joking, I held out the small plastic flask. 'I don't suppose you'd care for a nip?'

It said: Merci beau.

The flask floated away, tipped briefly, and returned. I hastily swilled my tea and had a fit of coughing. If the Ghost was a delusion, as I was beginning to suspect, my unconscious mind had a rare imaginative flair. I said: 'What's this about the Jebbies?'

It said: Two priests named Jared Ellsworth and Frank Dubois are opening an experimental school intended to serve gifted children from low-income families. It is called Brebeuf Academy and it is located just outside Concord, on the grounds of a small Jesuit college. You will find that the fathers will readily accept Denis, under full scholarship. You yourself will take care of the boy's incidental expenses. Don will give his consent.

A euphoric warmth, not from the brandy, began to suffuse me. 'Didn't I read something about Ellsworth in *Newsweek* a while back?'

But it ignored me and continued: After Denis has attended Brebeuf Academy for one year, you will tell Father Ellsworth the full truth about the boy's supranormal mental faculties. He will know what steps must be taken to protect Denis during his minority. You may then safely leave the boy's guidance in this priest's hands.

My brain spun. For over six years I'd devoted almost every moment of my spare time to the education and encouragement of my nephew. The rest of the time I'd merely worried myself sick over him. Was the Ghost telling me my job was done?

It said: Not done. Denis will always need your friendship. But you have fulfilled very well the first charge I placed on you, Rogi, and for a while you'll have time for yourself.

For a while?

Peace! Ne vous tracassez pas. There are years yet.

I shouted, 'How can I believe you? What *are* you?'

You may as well know. It won't hurt. I am a being from another world, from another star. I am your friend and Denis's friend – the special guardian of the entire Remillard family, for reasons that will eventually be made clear to you. Now I will see to your safety before I go. The storm will last far into the night.

All I could think of were the flying-saucer flaps going on all over the world for the past several years. And my Ghost was some kind of extraterrestrial?

I blurted out, 'What *did* happen to Betty and Barney Hill on the old Franconia Highway?'

The Ghost uttered its dry little laugh: Perhaps we can discuss it another time! I must go now. Adieu, cher Rogi . . .

Glowing mist closed in about me. I was captive for a few moments inside a pearly sphere and then there was a dazzling lightning bolt and a clap of thunder. Rain sprayed me as though I'd stepped beneath a waterfall and the terrain was completely different. I was standing about three metres away from a log cabin with lighted windows that was perched on a rock shelf above a wind-whipped little body of water. People moved around inside. A sound of singing and concertina music drifted through the night.

I was still holding my teacup, which was now half full of rainwater. My backpack lay at my feet. I dumped the cup and retrieved the pack, then strode up to the Gentian Pond Shelter and pounded on the door.

18

Observation Vessel Krak Na'am [Kron 96–101010]
24 June 1974

Ra'edroo slithered into the surveillance chamber, saluted her Krondak superior on the intimate racial mode, and bid the other three entities on duty a courteous vocal 'High thoughts, colleagues.' An unspoken query was prominent in her mind's vestibulum: Why have you summoned me,

Umk'ai? The Russian Salyut space laboratory is not scheduled to be launched for at least another five hours.

Thula'ekoo said aloud, 'That is true, Ra'edroo. But another event is about to take place below, one that happens every year . . . in New Hampshire.'

The Simb and the Gi who were working at the think tank laughed at some private joke.

Thula'ekoo reproved the pair with the slightest mental tap on their itch-receptors. He addressed Ra'edroo and a young Poltroyan who had a puzzled smile on his greyish-purple, humanoid face. 'I know that both you and Trosimo-Finabindin are keen amateur xenopsychologists. Since you two are new to the Earth tour, you'll be interested in this rather typical example of the current North American mind-set with respect to exotic encounters.'

'Perhaps not *wholly* typical,' sniffed the Simb, who was a statistician and inclined to be overpunctilious. 'Our current sampling among Status Seven Earth indigenes shows that 49.22 per cent believe that UFOs do exist, and that they originated on other inhabited planets. Some 9.91 per cent think they have personally seen one.'

A brief wave of amusement passed over the Gi, DriDri Vuvl. 'We're getting to be positively old hat. I suppose it was inevitable.'

'I should think,' Ra'edroo said, 'that those figures demonstrate that the thirty-year familiarization scheme has been a resounding success.'

'You've got a lot to learn about Earthlings, colleague,' said the Simb.

DriDri Vuvl added, 'These Americans, for instance. Their capacity for ennui in the face of the marvellous is mind-boggling. Why, they've very nearly lost interest in their space programme! Major funding was cut off in order to finance some idiotic war. And now all their leaders seem concerned about is a tacky political scandal and threats by Status Three nations to cut off the petroleum supply. *Petroleum!* I ask you.'

The Simb passed judgement. 'Excretory orifices, the lot of them. How can they be expected to coadunate their world Mind?'

Thula'ekoo was busy at the monitor and chose to ignore the crude chaffing. When the image was well centred, fully dimensioned and computer-enhanced for all eight Krondak senses (a pity young Trosi would miss out on the pla'akst, which enriched this type of observation so; but that was life), he transferred the scene to the large wall-screen.

Twenty-three humans, fourteen men and nine women, sat in a circle on the weathered rocks near the summit of Mount Adams in New Hampshire's Presidential Range. It was 5° Celsius with a cutting westerly wind, overcast skies, and visibility of about twenty kilometres. The people were dressed in nondescript outdoor gear obviously chosen for warmth. Most of them were talking quietly, with three or four engaged in solitary meditation. One woman offered plastic cups of hot cocoa from a thermos and had a few takers.

'Down from last year's gathering,' the Simb noted with wry satisfaction. 'Way down.'

The Gi rolled its saucer eyes. 'The faithful are defecting to macrobiotics, pacifism and whale watching.'

'Silence!' said Thula'ekoo. 'They are about to begin.'

Ra'edroo and the Poltroyan, Trosi, were completely absorbed in the scene. The human leader, a female of commanding aspect, had directed members of the circle to join hands. She said:

'Fellow Aetherians, the time has come. Empty your minds of all earthly thought. Prepare to divorce yourselves from your fleshy bodies and take on the astromental configuration. Banish all physical discomfort. Close your eyes. Shut out all sounds except that of my voice. Feel nothing but the Presence of the Universe. Join with me as I call to it. Let our thoughts arise with a single voice. Call out! The Universe sees us and loves us. It is alive with powerful and friendly spirits who are watching us even at this moment. If we only have faith and strength of will, these extraterrestrial beings will answer when we call. They will come and save our world from the death that threatens us. Call out! Bid the otherworld creatures come! Let them know they are welcome. Together, now, with me . . .'

Come.

'Why, she's a borderline suboperant!' Ra'edroo exclaimed. 'The others are hopelessly latent, but what meagre faculties they can project are actually in a loose mind-meld with the leader. How extremely interesting!'

Come.

Trosi was radiant. 'The dear things – what a splendid effort.' His voice broke with compassion. 'What a pity that the subsidiary humans are so inferior in mind to the leader.'

Thula'ekoo said, 'All humans possess latent metafaculties to a greater or lesser degree. In this case, only the leader has the projective farspeech capacity to penetrate the ionosphere. At this distance, none but the Krondaku and the Poltroyans can detect the metapsychic emanations of the subordinates in the meld.'

'Thanks be to Sacred Truth and Beauty,' muttered the Simb.

'I agree with Trosi,' offered Ra'edroo. 'that the effort of this little group is most affecting, a foreshadowing of the metaconcerted request that must take place before Intervention.'

COME.

'Hah!' scoffed the Simb. 'A futile mockery of such an effort, rather. One might as well compare a chorus of chirping insects to a symphonic ensemble. These poor things are one of a handful of cranks who periodically attempt to make mental contact with exotic beings – what they so quaintly call extraterrestrials. They are only unique in having a meagrely talented latent as their leader, which is about what one might expect in New Hampshire.'

COME!

'Again I detect overtones of satire in your remark, colleague,' Ra'edroo said.

'Oh, the place is crawling with latents. Even imperfect operants. It's one of the irruptive metapsychic nuclei of the planet. This world's Mind isn't evolving overall, but breaking out in spots. Quite grotesque. Makes it devilish hard for the immatures. It's a wonder any of them reach adulthood sane.'

COME!

The sentimental Gi clapped a hand over its central heart.

Its intromittent organ glowed crimson in empathetic passion. 'Oh, feel the goodwill in the female entity's cry, citizens. The yearning! One longs so to console her.'

Come come come.

'Hold your honey, colleague,' the Simb jeered, 'until you've travelled down below the planet's ionic shell as we Simbiari have, and experienced the full unsavouriness of its puny knots of consciousness – the selfishness, the irrational suspicion separating one nation from another, the perverted male sex-dynamic that keeps them endlessly at war.'

'What you say may be true, Salishiss,' little Trosi said, 'but the fact remains that these people have the greatest metapsychic potential in the galaxy, according to the Lylmik.'

'The Lylmik tell us a lot of things they never bother to prove,' grumped the Simb. 'I'm no magnate of the Concilium, only a lowly number-cruncher. But my trade gives me a certain insight into social dynamics. Left to itself, this world Mind would inevitably destroy itself.'

Come. Please come.

'So far humans have refrained from using atomic weapons in battle,' DriDri Vuvl noted, 'even though they've had them for thirty years. They keep making more and bigger weapons, but they don't use them. It seems to be a sort of threat-display mechanism.'

'Oh, yes?' Salishiss gesticulated at the view-screen. 'What do you think that group on the mountain is so worked up about? They're convinced that only a galactic civilization can rescue their world from atomic suicide. That's why they call out to us in this pathetic fashion. Of course, they have no conception of what Intervention would *really* mean, with the vast majority of Earth's population still metapsychically latent and socially infantile. Why, we'd have to occupy the planet and play nanny to it for more than a hundred orbits until its Mind matured – and the humans would oppose our proctorship almost every step of the way. The very thought of if makes me cringe.'

The Krondak officer, Thula'ekoo, said, 'The picture is by no means as bleak as you paint it, Salishiss. Large numbers of Earthlings already experience feelings of universal fellowship, the precursor to true coadunation. And the Lylmik profess to be gratified by the accelerating mental evolution.'

'And who would dare question the ineffable judgement of the oldest and wisest race in the galaxy?' the Simb inquired archly. 'Those architects of the Milieu, those masters of absent-minded subtlety? Hard luck for the rest of us that Lylmik reasoning is sometimes just as ethereal as their bodies . . .'

Come!

'The human leader is weakening,' said Ra'edroo. 'It must be very stressful on that cold mountain top for such high-metabolism creatures.'

'So few in the little group now.' DriDri Vuvl shook its ruff of filoplumage sadly. 'They may not show up at all next Midsummer Day.'

Come oh come.

Trosi the Poltroyan leaked compassion from every neuron. 'If only we could encourage them – let them know that we're out here, and we really do care.'

Great Thula'ekoo responded with implacable authority. 'Even if every human being now living on Earth called out to us, we could not answer. It would violate the scheme of the Concilium.'

'Just some tiny gesture,' Trosi begged. 'Something that wouldn't warp the probability lattices. Love's Oath – we do enough manipulation of them, what with the mental analyses and the technical experiments and the flybys. How about a simple gesture of friendliness for a change?'

'Statute Blue-4-001,' Ra'edroo said respectfully to her superior, 'gives the officer of the watch certain discretionary powers. Thou and I, Umk'ai, have the expertise to direct a most delicate farspeech beam in metaconcert.'

The circle of humans still held hands and had their faces raised to the clouded sky. Their attempt at mental synergy was crumbling. The leader urged them to one last effort.

Come!

Opaque membranes flicked over the accessory eyeballs of Thula'ekoo. His primary optics glowed an intense blue and seemed to suck in the willing psyches of his fellow

Krondaku, the eager Poltroyan, and the Gi. After a nano-second's hesitation, the Simb Salishiss blended into the fivefold brain, and it broadcast a mental chord that blended tranquillity with patience – and the merest hint of Unity:

Persevere.

For just an instant, the uplifted human faces were trans-figured. Then the spell was broken and the twenty-three startled people turned to each other with whispers. The female leader buried her head in her arms. Several others crowded around her anxiously, touching her. She finally looked up, not seeing her companions, lifted an arm to the sky, and smiled.

Then she started off down the Star Lake Trail to the Madison Huts. The others came straggling after.

19

Bretton Woods, New Hampshire, Earth
25 June 1974

'Wake up, Denis. We're here.'

The Volkswagen Beetle slowed for the left turn and swung into the hotel entrance road. The seven-year-old boy was immediately alert, straining against his seat belt to see over the dashboard of the car. Ahead of them to the east was a majestic panorama, several hundred acres of rolling lawn fronting a wooded rise that hid a tantalizing glimpse of white and red. Beyond this, a vast slope that stretched almost from horizon to horizon culminated in a mountain rampart, dark with timber in the middle reaches and a gleaming pewter along bare summit peaks that reflected the early-morning sun. This was the Presidential Range of the White Mountains. Even though it had been ground down by ice-age glaciers, it was still the highest part of northeastern North America.

The child cried: Wherehotel? Wherecograilway? Look thatmountain SNOW top in June!

That's Mount Washington. The one we're riding to top of today.

Studied allmountain names let's see: JeffersonClayWashingtonMonroeFranklinEisenhowerClinton north/south. (Not all presidents!) Why Eisenhower so dinky UncleRogi?

He got his mountain last and beggars can't be chosers. State changed name MountPleasant to Eisenhower. Once tried change name MountClinton to MountPierce honour only president born NewHampshire. Try never amounted to much. Neither did PresidentPierce. People still call mountain Clinton.

Laughter. Why thesemountains look bigger from here than from Berlin? What that funnystreak MountWashington? When we see yourHOTEL?

Rogi laughed out loud. 'Take it easy. You've got three whole days to ask questions. Batège! I'd nearly forgotten what a frantic little quiz-kid you are.'

'You haven't forgotten at all.' The child was complacent. 'I see inside your mind how much you missed me. And I missed you, too.'

The car slowed beside a guard kiosk painted a spotless white, decorated with window boxes of scarlet petunias. The old watchman stuck his head out. 'Morning, Roger. Got your nevvy here all safe and sound, I see. Plenty time yet for breakfast.'

'Morning, Norm. Yup – give him a treat before we go up the cog. Say hi to Mr Redmond, Denis.'

'Hello, Mr Redmond.' Why hecallyou ROGER UncleRogi?

'See you, Norm.' Because that myname here: Roger Remillard. Bettername man works bighotel easier people remember&pronounce than Rogatien. (And Rogi sounds naughty.)

Appreciative mirth.

The car swung around a long curve and the famous old White Mountain Resort Hotel came into view. At first it looked as though it must be a toy castle, or a chateau made from white spun sugar with the glistening roofs of the towers and wings coloured like cherry jam. The hotel had more tiny windows than you could count, and little flags

138

flying, and a candy-spill of flower gardens amidst miniature trees in front. The actual size of the place only gradually became evident as the driveway seemed to stretch on and on, with the hotel growing steadily larger until it blotted out the mountain vista entirely. The five-storey building was made of white stuccoed wood. It had a two-tiered colonnaded verandah curving from the central porte-cochère all around the entire south wing.

'It's a palace,' exclaimed the overawed boy. 'Are you really the boss?'

Rogi shook his head, laughing. 'Hardly. I'm only the assistant convention manager.' [Explanatory image.] 'But I get to live here where I work, and I like this job much better than the one I had at the paper mill. It pays better, too.'

They drove past the grand main entrance, which was crowded with autos and tour buses and guests and bellmen scurrying to load and unload people's luggage, and pulled into the employees' parking lot behind a screen of tall shrubs. Denis insisted on carrying his small suitcase himself. They entered an annex building that housed resident staff members. A man dressed in a white jacket and bow tie hurried past them, greeting Rogi and mussing Denis's mousey brown hair.

Rogi said, 'That was Ron, one of the waiter captains. Just wait until you see the dining room here. There are two of them, but we'll eat in the biggest one where Ron works this morning.' They climbed carpeted stairs.

'You like it here a lot, don't you, Uncle Rogi.' There was a tinge of dejection in the boy, imperfectly screened.

'Yes. But I can come visit you in Berlin while you're home for the summer. It isn't even an hour's drive.'

'I know. Only . . .' Uncle Rogi I miss you. Miss mindspeech. Miss friendadult questionanswers fearcalming. Teachers at Brebeuf nice kids notbad but not same YOU.

Comfort. Denis you know grownups must work sometimes goaway oldhome.

Understand. But can't speak you through mountains down Concord school can't speak you from Berlin whileyou here either.

There's your Maman & littlebrotherVictor to bespeak.

Denis stopped at the top of the stairs. He averted his eyes, clumsily trying to conceal a dark emotional coloration. 'Mom's changed since last fall. When I came home from school last week she could hardly mindspeak me at all any more. She was like that when I went home at Easter, too, but I thought it was just because of the new babies. Now she – she just doesn't *want* to share her thoughts with me the way she used to. She kisses me and says she's busy and tells me to go play.'

'Your mother has a lot to do taking care of Jeanette and Laurette. Twin babies are a terrible handful unless you have older children as ready-made baby-sitters, the way Tante Lorraine had with your Papa and me . . . Have you been able to mindspeak with your Papa?'

'Not very much. I thought he'd be pleased at the way things worked out at the academy. My good grades, and the way I was auditing classes with the college kids, and how Father Ellsworth has been getting me parapsychology books and publications from the library at Brown University, and how I'm learning archery, and how to play the piano. But he wasn't much interested. He doesn't like me, you know. Not like he does Victor.'

The hallway was deserted and quiet. Rogi knelt down to face the boy. 'Your father does love you, Denis. The thing is – Victor's only a little boy and he needs more attention right now.'

But Victor*dumber*thanme! Weakfarspeech/farsight/farhearing/PK. (Strong coercion though.) And he fights and swipes things and mindpinches new babysisters awful when thinks nobody looking. Tried mindpinch me HA! myshield reflected pinch back *him*.

'Victor is probably jealous of his new sisters. Maybe even jealous of you now that you're going to school. Four-year-olds are still pretty uncivilized. It takes time for them to learn right from wrong.'

'He already knows,' Denis said darkly. 'I can tell. He hurts the little twins anyway whenever their minds make telepathic noises that bug him. You know how little babies are.'

140

Rogi made a comical grimace. 'I remember.'

'Jeanette and Laurette can't help being pests sometimes. But Victor doesn't seem to be any good at putting up a protective mental shield, so the baby-thoughts drive him crazy. I told Mom how he was tormenting the twins and she told him to stop – but there's really not much she can do about it.'

'I see.' (Poor Sunny, retreating into fatalism and saying her beads and watching soap operas on television! Inside a year she would be enceinte once again.)

'I tried to explain to Papa why Victor shouldn't harass the babies. I told him it would discourage them from developing their own ultrafaculties – maybe even make them *normal*. He laughed.'

Rogi stood up, keeping a tight lid over his own thoughts. 'I'll talk things over with your father when I take you back. Don't worry.'

Denis smiled at him. 'I knew you'd help.'

'My room's right down here. Let's hurry. We want time for breakfast, and the shuttle bus to the cog is at ten.' (And what *can* I say to Don to show him how he's poisoning his younger son and endangering his daughters and breaking the older boy's heart? The only time he opens to me is when he's drunk. His precious Victor can do no wrong.)

They went into the small suite that was Rogi's apartment and left Denis's suitcase on the rollaway bed that had been brought in for his visit. The child inspected the premises gravely and admired the sweeping vista from the windows.

'That's a view that costs the hotel guests at least two hundred dollars a day,' Rogi told his nephew, 'but I get it for free. Of course this place of mine is pretty small, and I have to walk up a lot of stairs. But I have a nice office over in the main part of the hotel with room for my books, and when I sit up here and watch the storms play around the mountains I have a show that beats anything on television.'

They went downstairs, crossed a courtyard, and entered the hotel's north wing through a side door. Denis's eyes popped at the sight of apparently endless corridors with pillars and chandeliers, ornate Edwardian furniture, potted palms, gilt-framed mirrors, and fireplaces – large enough

for a boy to stand in – that now had bouquets of red and
yellow peonies in the grates instead of flaming logs. They
looked into a great ballroom with green velvet drapes and
standing silver candlesticks as big as hat-trees. Two men
ran polishing machines across a floor that looked shiny
enough to ice-skate on. Rogi told Denis there would be a
Midsummer Night Ball there that evening. Another salon,
lush with ferns and tropical flowers, overlooked a golf
course and the approach to Mount Washington.

When they came at last to the dining room, Denis was
struck dumb. It was fancier than any restaurant he had
ever seen in his life. Ron, the captain who seated them,
treated Denis like a grown man and called him Sir when
he gave him a menu. There were weird things for breakfast
like kippers and steak, and eight different ways of having
eggs, and twelve varieties of fresh fruit including New
Zealand gooseberries. The table was set with crystal and
shining silver and monogrammed damask napery. There
was a vase with a single mauve rose, so perfect in form and
so outré in colour that Denis had to touch it to be certain
it was real. The sugar came in hard lumps wrapped in
embossed gold paper. (Denis stole two.) Milk was served
in a faceted goblet, sitting on its own small plate with a
paper doily underneath. They ate eggs Benedict and had
mini-croissants and strawberries Wilhelmine, and were
served funny little cups of espresso, which Denis drank
politely but didn't much care for.

When they had finished, Denis sighed and said, 'I expect
you'll stay here for ever.'

Rogi laughed and touched his lips with his napkin. 'I'll
tell you a secret. What I'd really like to do is save my
money until I have enough to buy a little bookstore in a
nice quiet college town. I could stay in a place like *that* for
ever.'

The check came. Rogi signed it and he and Denis stood
to go. The boy said, 'That doesn't sound very exciting – a
bookstore.'

'I'm afraid I'm not a very exciting man, Denis. Most
people aren't, you know. Movies and television shows and

books are full of heroes, but they aren't too common in real life any more.'

The boy thought about this as they walked through the lobby. It was crowded with guests on their way to the day's activities, most of them middle-aged or elderly, but with a sprinkling of young couples and well-dressed parents with children. There were people in tennis togs and riding breeches and hiking boots, and a group of little old ladies in polyester pantsuits carrying shawls and heavy sweaters, and old men in loud sports jackets hung about with camera bags and binoculars. A pretty tour guide was calling for their attention, please.

'I used to think it would be neat to be a hero when I was just a little kid,' Denis said. 'An astronaut or a jungle explorer or a hockey star like Bobby Clarke or Gil Perreault. But I guess I'm not a very exciting person either. Father Dubois kids me about it sometimes. He says I should quit sitting around like a stuffed owl, contemplating the infinite.' The boy chuckled. 'But the infinite's *interesting*.'

They went out of the front door of the hotel to the shuttle bus. Rogi said, 'Don't take his teasing seriously. Be what you are. You've got a brain — maybe one like nobody else in the whole world. Explore that.'

The mob of old folks and the tour guide followed Rogi and Denis into the bus. The guide counted her charges, then signalled the driver. The bus drove off.

Denis said, 'There are doctors who study the brain — take it apart and poke needles and things into it to find out how it works. But I don't want to do just that. What I want to learn about isn't how the brain works but *why*. Why do those electrical impulses and chemical exchanges result in thinking? No electroencephalograph shows the thoughts in a person's mind. And how do brains control bodies? It's not my brain that commands my fingers to grab this bus seat, *it's me*. A brain is nothing but a lump of meat.'

'With a mind in it.'

'That's right,' the boy agreed. 'Mind! That's what I want to learn about. A mind isn't the same as a brain.'

'Some scientists would argue the point – but I don't think the two are identical.'

Denis said: People like you&me would give scientists fits! How mybrain speak yourbrain? No radiowaves other energy pass between us! Through whatmedium propagates coercion/PK/farspeech? How farsight/hearing/smell/taste/touch impulses transmitted? Received? What energysource powers PK? Why can't farsense through granite? Why easier farsense at night? How mymind influence another in coercion? How mymind heal mybody? . . . Iknow mymind controls mymind. This means: mymind controls chemistry&electricity in brain. The nonmatterenergything dominates the matterenergything! HOW?

Rogi said: Denisdearchild find out! Explore your mind and mine and Don's and Victor's. Explore other minds as well minds of normals find way bridge gap separating them/us. What an adventure . . . more exciting than mountaineering deepdiving oceantravelling flyingouterspace!

[Good-humoured juvenile scepticism.] But not anything like as dangerous.

Rogi squeezed the thin little shoulder. Aloud, he said, 'Of course not.'

The bus bounced over the frost-heaved macadam road that twisted through a forest of maples and hemlocks. Around Rogi and Denis, the little old ladies twittered like wrens.

The cog railway that ascends the western slope of Mount Washington is unique in North America, one of those mad Yankee notions that never should have worked but somehow did, for more than a hundred years. Denis took one look at the chunky coal-fired locomotive, oddly lopsided on level track since its boiler was designed to be horizontal when the train climbed the steep grade, and cried: 'It's the Little Engine That Could!'

The old folks simpered fondly.

There were many other tourists of all ages waiting at the base station to board the train. The engine pushed a single car, painted bright yellow. Traction came from a rack-and-pinion mechanism beneath. Between the regular narrow-gauge rails was a central track that resembled an endless ladder of thumb-thick iron rods four inches long. This rack was gripped by twin cog gears on the engine's drive mechanism, which powered the train up the mountain with an earsplitting clatter while the engine chugged and hissed and belched an air-polluting cloud of ebony smoke such as Denis had never seen before in his life.

As they crept upward through scrubby trees the entire Bretton Woods area was visible behind them. 'This is neat!' Denis yelled over the racket. 'Look down there – it's your hotel!'

Rogi said: I watch little trains go up&down mountain from my window. Sometimes when cloud clamps down on summit trains look like they're heading into sky never to return . . . Man who invented train went to state legislature in 1858 asked it to grant charter so he could build railroad. Lawmaker proposed amendment permitting inventor to build railroad to Moon after he finish one up MountWashington.

Laughter. Getting really cold. Glad brought jacket. Glad we can mindspeak can hardly hear WOW whatanoise!

You know about mountainweather? It can change in flash: bright sunshine to freezing cold even now in June. Snow any month. Wind blows hurricane fast on summit $1/3$ days year.

Yes I read book school worldclass record MountWashington wind 231 mph! Know also Indians thought mountain home GreatSpirit afraid to climb no wonder.

You hear story ChiefPassaconaway?

?

Lived NewHampshire early colonial times. Great wise leader also famed wonderworking magic allkinds wizard tricks. When Chief Passaconaway died legend says wolves pulled body on sled to top MountWashington. There fiery coach carried him away into sky.

Like *flyingsaucer?* Awww . . .

Lots of other stories. You ever hear Great Carbuncle?

?

Supposed tobe huge shining red jewel hidden mountain worth zillions. Glowing ruby light lures greedy people come search for it. They follow light get trapped terrible storms never able get hold carbuncle. Die. NathanielHawthorne used legend in story.

I'll get book BerlinLibrary this summer . . . UncleRogi you don't believe flyingsaucers do you?

Never saw one. But ElmerPeabody man drives tractor-mower at hotel says he did. Sensible man Elmer. Lots of reputable people say they see UFOs. Funny. NewHampshire seems have awfullot those things confounded UFO plague!

I read two books kindof scary. Onebook man&woman driving FranconiaNotch just west here say they abducted by saucermen. Doctor got story years later by *hypnotizing* people! Saucerman told lady came faraway star meant noharm. Anotherbook guy saw big saucer with redlights over Exeter nearcoast. Went to police. Police saw it too! Also wholebunch other people. What think?

I think . . . it may be possible.

Ahh. Littlegreenmen visit Earth but not make official contact? Why they want do such crazything! Why keep secret instead reveal selves rightout to world?

Dearchild *why do we?*

The little train crawled slowly to the region above timber-line, leaving behind gnarled and crouching dwarf trees and passing into a place where carpets of subarctic flowers, pink and white and pale yellow, bloomed in the midst of sedge meadows and a desolation of grey crags. There was still snow in shadowed hollows and the western side of the rocks was encrusted with thick hoarfrost. The summit buildings came into view. They passed a cluster of water tanks and saw a simple painted board:

LIZZIE BOURNE
PERISHED 1855

'She was twenty-three,' Rogi said. 'Nearly seventy other people have died on this mountain – more than on any other peak in North America. Some died from accidents, some from exposure. The mountain is deceptive, you see. People come up on a beautiful day like this, without a cloud in the sky, and decide to take a little hike. Suddenly clouds of icy fog come racing in and you can't see two feet in front of you. There might be snow or hail or freezing rain with a wind-chill factor way below zero. The worst weather on Earth short of the polar regions happens right here in our own state, on a mountain only sixty-two hundred feet high. I've been up here lots of times – on the cog, driving up the eastern side on the Carriage Road, even hiking up from the hotel. But I never feel quite comfortable. The top of Mount Washington is an eerie place.'

The train drew to a halt in front of a drab, barnlike wooden building that the trainman proudly indentified as the famous Summit House Hotel. He warned the passengers that they would have only forty-five minutes to explore. The return trip, like the journey up the mountain, would take more than an hour.

A strong, cold wind was blowing and Rogi told Denis to watch his step on the slippery gravel. There was very little snow on the ground, but the windward side of every structure, rock, railing and guy-cable was thick with dazzling white rime. The giant frost crystals looked like otherworldly marine growth, a crust of twisted tabs and plates and knobs and opaque lenses of ice.

The Summit House Hotel held no interest for Denis. He wanted to climb the cone-shaped rock mass that marked the absolute high point of the mountain. Then he raced off to see if the weather observatory or the TV and radio transmitter buildings were open to the public. They weren't. As he squinted up at the ice-wrapped antenna tower, the boy projected to Rogi dramatic imaginary pictures of the way this place might look in a howling blizzard with the wind blowing two hundred miles an hour. His mind was charged with exhilaration as they walked to a rocky spur and looked south, down a leg of the great Appalachian Trail, and saw a group of tiny lakes and a hikers' hut more than a thousand feet below.

'Those are the Lakes of the Clouds,' Rogi said. 'Maybe on one of your later visits we can hike up to them from the Hotel, on the Ammonoosuc Ravine Trail.'

'Wow! That'd be great.' Denis squinted, studying the

area immediately below the spur. 'What are those piles of rock with yellow paint on top?'

'Cairns marking the trails. You have to watch very carefully for them in some places to keep from getting lost. The trails on this mountain don't look like the woodland paths you're used to – at least not in the high parts. They mostly go over bare rock. That's one of the reasons why Mount Washington can be treacherous.'

They went back to the northern area of the summit to see if they could see Berlin. Sure enough, the steam plumes from the paper mills were little tan feathers rising from the Androscoggin Valley. The air was so clear that they could see Umbagog Lake and Bigelow Mountain over in Maine, and the Green Mountains of Vermont to the west, and beyond the White Mountain Resort Hotel was a pimple on the horizon that was really Mount Marcy, 150 miles away in the Adirondacks of New York.

'I see hikers,' Denis said, pointing to a line of people toiling up alongside the cog railway line. He instinctively magnified the tiny figures with his farsight and projected the picture into Rogi's mind.

' . . . eighteen, nineteen, twenty . . . twenty-three of them.'

'It's a popular place to hike. Over there is the main trail leading to Clay and Jefferson and Adams. There are overnight huts between Mount Adams and Mount Madison, too.'

Denis shaded his eyes. He was shivering in the unrelenting wind. The vision of the climbers faded from Rogi's ultrasense. And then the child uttered a gasp of disbelief, and there came a surge of fear from him that made Rogi cry out in concern.

'Denis! What's wrong?'

A trembling, bluish finger pointed at the line of people. They disappeared behind the shoulder of the mountain for a moment as the trail dipped, then came into view again. The mental picture was huge.

'Uncle Rogi, the lady in front. I *hear* her.'

'What?'

The boy burst into tears. 'I hear her mind. She's like us!

Another person like us! Her mind projection is very faint and it doesn't make much sense . . .'

He dashed the moisture from his eyes and hugged himself as he tried to stop shuddering. Swiftly, Rogi unzipped his down-filled jacket and wrapped Denis in it. He knelt beside the child on sharp stones, feeling no cold, only a gut-churning hope. 'Concentrate! Try to share the farspeech with me, Denis. Help me hear what you hear.' He put his arms around the boy and closed his eyes.

Oh my God.

She was singing a wordless melody, some classical fragment that Rogi was unable to recognize. A joyful song. Now and then a subvocalization floated above the music like gossamer spider-threads against sunlit air:

Answered . . . they answered . . . out there . . . surely . . . the others may doubt but . . . answered . . .

The clairaudient emanations and her farseen image cut off as the woman followed the trail into another hollow, but his memory would never relinquish that first picture, and whenever he thought of her after she was lost to him, this vision of windblown vitality would always come to mind: a strong-featured face, striking but not conventionally pretty, slightly sunburned across the bridge of the nose; eyes of a blue so pale that they were almost silver; an exultant smile – my God, that smile! – that was the external sign of her mind's rejoicing; strawberry-blond hair escaping from a green woollen watch cap; a body tall, slender and strong.

Denis was trying to squirm out of his paralysed arms. 'Uncle Rogi – your jacket! You'll freeze!'

He came to himself. The hikers were still out of sight and Denis was looking up at him, face tear-stained and twisted with emotion. Rogi spoke urgently. 'That woman. You're certain that the music and farspeech came from her mind?'

'Absolutely certain. She really is another one like us. No – wait! She's not as controlled as we are. Not aware. I don't think she knows what she's doing when she mindspeaks. Perhaps she's never had any other telepaths to speak to. But she *is* like us! Uncle Rogi, we're not all alone . . .'

'And that she should be the one,' Rogi whispered. 'C'est un miracle. Un vrai miracle.' Sunny's voice came to him, an echo of a long-ago apology: *Quand le coup de foudre frappe —*

The train whistle blew. Once, twice, three times.

'Oh, no!' cried the boy. 'We can't just go and leave her!'

Rogi lifted Denis in his arms. 'The hikers are coming this way, probably heading for Summit House. They should be here in half an hour. We'll wait for them.'

'But the train —'

'Another train will come.'

Rogi stumbled over the frosty rocks, drunk with happiness, for the first time realizing what Sunny had been trying to tell him about her love for Don. *When the thunderbolt strikes* . . . there is no logic, no resisting. And thus the marvel of the woman hiker's telepathic ability was lost in a greater wonder. He scarcely heard Denis say:

'If there's one mind like hers, there must be lots more! All we have to do is figure a way to find them.'

Wind sang in the antenna guy-wires and the humped little engine in front of the hotel renewed its hooting. Tourists called to each other and Denis shivered, radiating a fearful exultation that was almost as intense as Rogi's own. Rogi carried the boy up the stairs into the heavily insulated entry of the small hotel. A bearded man in climbing gear held the door open, concern on his face.

'Little fellow's not hurt, is he?'

Rogi set Denis back on his feet, unwrapped him, and said, 'All we both need is a bit of warming up.'

'Try the dining room,' the man suggested. 'Nice fire, fantastic view. You can watch the train go down the mountain while you stoke up with hot food and drink. Best thing.'

Thanking the man, Rogi led Denis into the Summit House lobby. The boy was recovering fast and he eyed the souvenir counter with interest. 'Can I buy a guidebook and some maps? And maybe we better get some Kleenex. My nose is running and so is yours.' The small, wan face looked up with a critical frown. 'You should comb your hair before she gets here, too.'

150

Rogi burst out laughing. 'Mais naturellement! It wouldn't do to look scruffy.'

'I – I just want her to like us,' Denis protested.

'If she doesn't, we'll try coercion.'

'Be serious, Uncle Rogi! What are we going to *say* to her?'

'We'll have to think about that, won't we? But first, let's clean up and then find something to eat.'

Hand in hand, they went looking for the men's room.

20

From the Memoirs of
Rogatien Remillard

Her name was Elaine Donovan Harrington.

She was thirty-one years old and separated from her husband, and she lived in a 'little country place' just outside the state capital of Concord, where she edited and published a journal for UFO buffs called *Visitant*. I found out later that she had inherited her strawberry-blond hair – and probably her metapsychic traits – from her late father Cole Donovan, a dynamic real-estate entrepreneur. From her late mother, who was of Boston Brahmin stock, she had a legacy of natural elegance and sufficient old money to support a lifestyle far above any that Remillards of that day and age could even imagine.

Scraping an acquaintance with her was the easiest thing in the world, thanks to Denis.

We waited in ambush at a table in the rustic dining room of Summit House; and when Elaine and her party of trail-weary Aetherians arrived, the boy picked her brains. In retrospect, I am appalled at his redactive expertise, for I realize now that he must have been able to monitor every thought that passed between Elaine and me. But at that time I had nothing but admiration for the child as he trotted up to Elaine all primed with pilfered data from her memory bank and claimed to be a reader of her magazine who had recognized her from her masthead photograph. She was charmed by the precocious, well-spoken lad, and engaged him in conversation on sundry flying-saucerish topics while her friends settled down to order a meal.

At an opportune moment I came up to retrieve my young relative. Denis introduced me, explaining, 'My Uncle Rogi – Roger – works at the White Mountain Resort Hotel. Do you know it, Mrs Harrington? That big old place like a palace down at the western foot of Mount Washington.'

'I'm staying there,' she said. The corners of her mouth lifted in a little smile. 'It's rather a family tradition, the White Mountain Hotel. How do you do, Mr Remillard?'

I had barricaded my unruly emotions behind the sturd-iest mind-screen I could muster; but when that silvery gaze focused on me I might as well have tried to hide behind a shield of cellophane. The rapport was instantaneous and I was unable to utter a word. God only knows what thought I projected.

She laughed and enclosed my warm hand between her two chilly ones. 'Do you mind? My fingers are still like icicles and you seem to be powered by some sort of atomic furnace.'

'I – of course I don't mind,' I mumbled idiotically. I had the sense to bring up my other hand to complete the electrifying clasp. Denis was grinning at us like a young chimpanzee and several of Elaine's companions threw quiz-zical looks in our direction.

When our hands finally fell apart, she asked casually, 'What do you do at the hotel?' I told her, and she seemed almost relieved. Being a part of management – even very junior management – gave me at least a minimal cachet. She asked: 'Are you interested in cosmic visitations, like your nephew?' I assured her that I was a fervid aficionado of all matters UFOlogical, even though I had unfortunately never come across her magazine. She nodded at that. 'We've had such trouble getting general newsstand distri-bution for *Visitant*. Perhaps I could give you a copy of the latest issue when I get back to the hotel. We'd be so glad to rustle up a new subscriber.'

'That would be wonderful! I mean – I'd like that.'

The quirky little smile deepened and her eyes had a knowing glint. 'It will have to be late . . . Shall we say tonight about ten-thirty, in the Grotto Lounge on the lower level of the hotel?'

Denis piped up, all solemn and regretful. 'I'm afraid I'll be in bed by then, Mrs Harrington.'

She gave him an amused look. 'Well, I'm sure your Uncle Roger will share the magazine with you tomorrow. And now I must go and eat. I'm dying for some real food after two days of freeze-dried trail rations. So nice to have met you both.'

She wafted off, the very embodiment of aetheriality in spite of her heavy climbing boots and insulated jacket, leaving my mind full of voiceless music and my heart hopelessly lost.

She was only a few minutes late for our rendezvous, and as she entered the crowded rathskeller-style bar, breathtaking in a clinging white floor-length gown with a single bare shoulder, I thanked God for the craftiness of my nephew, who had insisted that I wear black tie rather than the casual jacket and slacks I had thoughtlessly laid out.

'She'll want you to take her to the dance,' Denis had said. I didn't bother to ask how he knew. He had nodded his approval when I finished dressing and said, 'It's a good thing you're so tall. She likes tall men. And you look so nice in those clothes that it doesn't matter that you're not handsome.' I had told him: 'Ferme ta boîte, ti-vaurien!' and left him giggling. But he had been right . . .

Elaine and I drank cognac, and I studied the copy of *Visitant* she gave me while she expatiated on the authenticity of UFO visitations and the pigheadedness of the US Air Force, which persisted in denying the 'incontrovertible evidence' in favour of extraterrestrial encounters. Her organization, the Aetherians, was about what you would expect: a collection of quasi-mystical fanatics whose zeal outpaced critical judgement. My darling Elaine was as willing to accept the crackpottery of a Von Däniken as she was the serious studies of researchers such as Dr J. Allen Hynek and Dr Dennis Hauck. She and her friends were convinced that Earth was under intense surveillance by otherworldly intelligences, entirely benignant, who would reveal themselves to humanity if we would only 'have faith' and embrace a pacifistic 'astromental' way of life.

She leaned over the small table towards me, enveloped in the intoxicating fragrance of Bal à Versailles, and spoke with surprising coolness. 'And you, Roger . . . What do you think of all this? Am I a credulous fool, as my ex-husband and my family have always said? Am I hopelessly romantic and visionary and deluded by swamp gas and moonshine?'

My mind cried out: You are romantic and utterly captivating, and in a crazy backhanded way you're *right*!

But that would never do. Not yet. A false note, and she'd be off. I found myself studying the situation with the detached cunning of a master seducer, my normal awkwardness with women having been somehow miraculously electrocauterized by the thunderbolt. I rolled up the UFO magazine and tapped it meditatively against my balloon glass. What would be the most judicious way of snaring her? Perhaps – the truth?

'Elaine, what I'm about to confess to you I've never dared to tell another person. I was afraid to, afraid of ridicule. There have been so many jokes about spaceships and little green men . . .'

Her face shone. 'Roger! Not – an encounter? You've *had* one?'

I let my eyes fall and made a deprecating gesture.

'You have!' she whispered. 'Oh, tell me.'

I let it out with becoming hesitancy, well edited. 'It was last summer. I was in the mountains, hiking, and a violent storm came up. I had hurt my leg. It was rather a serious situation. Night was coming on and I had no shelter. Suddenly there was a strange kind of light and the rain stopped in an unnatural way. And this voice – this inhuman voice — '

'Did you see their spaceship? Did it land?'

The crowded bar all around us had faded to an unfocused blur. Our faces were nearly touching. Her misty red hair was caught back in a smooth chignon and the only jewellery she wore was a pearl and diamond ring on her right little finger. Her deeply tanned skin with its touch of sunburn made a sensuous contrast to the white silk of her simple gown. In the fashion of the times, her breasts were free. The nipples had come alive with the intensity of her emotion.

My composure threatened to disintegrate completely. I took a hasty gulp of cognac and resumed my tale.

'I didn't see any ship. I didn't even see the – the being who spoke to me. Perhaps I was blinded by the light. But he healed my leg instantly. And he told me without equivocation that he came from another star.'

And there it is. Dear Elaine, you want so much to believe in marvels. But I could show you marvels that would make flying saucers insignificant, marvels inside your own mind and mine, and within our bodies . . .

'Don't stop – go on!' she pleaded. 'What happened next?'

I lifted my shoulders. 'I seemed to fall asleep. Perhaps I lost consciousness. It was very confusing. But when I awoke I was standing just outside a trail shelter, although I swear I'd been more than two miles away from it when I had my – my encounter. That's really all there is to it. A very improbable story. I probably dreamed the whole thing.'

'Oh, no! It's quite plausible, even the part about your losing consciousness. The aliens may have taken you aboard their craft and *examined* you.'

I managed to look startled. 'I don't remember any such thing.'

'You wouldn't!' She was intense. 'Try to put yourself in the aliens' place, Roger. To them, we're a primitive people – easily frightened, scientifically unsophisticated, possibly even dangerous. They'd want to study us but their activities would have to be discreet. They wouldn't want to disrupt our culture . . . Have you ever heard of the Cargo Cults in the South Pacific?'

'Those deluded tribes in New Guinea who thought the military transport planes of World War Two were flown by gods?'

'Exactly. Not only in New Guinea, but in the islands all around it; and the Cult started in the nineteenth century, when the first European traders arrived. The local people saw wonderful cargoes coming off the ships, and later off the aircraft. They wanted things like that for themselves and began to believe that the gods would send miraculous cargoes if everyone prayed hard. Their ancient way of life was completely disrupted by the Cargo Cult.'

'You think that extraterrestrials would want to be careful not to touch off a similar reaction among Earthlings?'

'If they're intelligent and have our best interests at heart.'

'But the aliens have already disrupted our culture to a certain extent with the flying-saucer flaps . . .'

'Not really, Roger. They've shown their ships to us so that we'll get used to the idea of an interstellar civilization. To prepare us for the day they actually *do* land.'

'Do you think it'll be soon?'

She hesitated. 'You may know that my group has been coming to these mountains for a number of years now, trying to make contact with the visitors. Mental contact. This year, for the first time, I think we may have been successful.'

I did my best to hide my scepticism. Darling, if you want to believe it, then let it be so! I made suitably encouraging comments while she described the experience, which struck me as a patent case of wishful thinking.

'I intend to write it up for the magazine, of course,' she said in conclusion, 'and I'd like to do an article on your encounter, too, Roger.'

I registered bourgeois alarm. 'I'd rather you didn't, Elaine. I've never told anyone about it – only you. And you're different from anyone I've ever met.'

'So are you, Roger.' She smiled and extended her hand as she rose from her chair. God! Had the gambit failed after all? My coercive faculty seemed paralysed. She said, 'Of course I'll keep your story in confidence if you want me to. Do look over my little magazine, though. And if you change your mind —'

'Must you go so soon?' I asked inanely.

The silver eyes twinkled. 'Well – we could go upstairs and dance if you like. The rest of the Aetherians were too tired after our mountain expedition, but I feel exhilarated. Would you like to take me dancing, Roger?'

My mind gave a triumphant shout. I bowed over her

hand, summoning suavity from God knows where. 'Enchanté, chère Madame.'

'You're French!' She was delighted.

'Only a Franco-American,' I admitted. 'Even Canadians make fun of our low accent, and our Yankee neighbours secretly envy our savoir faire – while calling us frogs behind our backs.'

'There are frogs who are princes in disguise. Are you one of those?'

Elaine, my beloved, I am indeed! And if my courage doesn't fail me, you may see the fantasy's fulfillment this very night . . .

So we laugh, and we mount the stairs, and we sweep arm in arm into the glittering ballroom while a hundred pairs of eyes watch. The orchestra of the famous old resort has instructions to intersperse contemporary music with a generous leavening of romantic oldies, so we hold each other close as we dance to 'Fly Me to the Moon' and 'Where or When'. With her in my arms I am no longer a lowly Assistant Convention Manager presuming above my station but a dark and debonair hero with a Mysterious Secret, squiring the most lovely woman in the room. The other dancers sense the psychomagnetism. We become the centre of attention, the golden couple wrapped in uncanny glamour. Our human race still does not recognize the existence of the higher mental faculties – but it can't help *feeling* them.

Elaine and I dance and smile and begin to open our minds to one another. Charily I lift the curtains hiding her emotions, using a gentle redactive probe, the type I instinctively developed when working with baby Denis. The floating thought-patterns are easily accessible. She has loved before and she has tasted ashes. The coolness is a symptom of unfulfillment and self-doubt. She is idealistic but retains a healthy sense of humour. She is really afraid that her pleasant and affluent world will end in a storm of radioactive fallout.

The musical beat becomes more modern, more compelling, and frankly sexual. Our bodies move to the explicit, angular rhythms, no longer daring to touch. But our minds approach conjunction now and I cannot help communicating my heat to her. It is accepted.

Finally, without a word, she leads me from the ballroom. We take the elevator to her luxurious suite overlooking the moonlit mountain range. We kiss at last and her mouth is velvety and cool, eager to receive my fire, pathetically hopeful of returning it. I hear my mindspeech shouting words of love and desire – and she gasps as her lips break away.

'Roger . . . my dear, it's so strange, but — '

I know. I know. Don't be afraid.

Aloud, I whisper, 'You heard a telepathic message from outer space and it didn't frighten you. Will you be frightened if I tell you why you were able to hear that alien message?'

Subconsciously, she already knows.

I hold her more tightly, kissing her brow, her cheeks, her upturned fragrant throat. My flooding passion is channelled into the ultraspeech and breaks through the barrier of her latency.

Elaine! Don't be afraid. I love you and I'll help you. Your mind-powers have lain dormant all your life but they're coming alive now. And here's the funny thing, my darling – I've been dormant, too, in a different way, until you came.

Roger? . . . *Roger!*

See? It's all true. True and wonderful. Now I'll help you, and later you'll help me.

She bespeaks me, tentatively at first, in clotted emotion-fuzzed utterances that gradually assume coherence. Then she becomes excited to the point of hysteria and I must constantly inject reassuring redactive impulses. When she calms I kiss her bare shoulder, her arms, the palms of her chilled hands. My PK finds the pins that hold her hair knotted. I release it and she cries out:

Roger? ReallyTRUE? Really HAPPEN? GodGodGod! You&I *minds communicate* . . .

Yes. Special minds. I love you.

Slowly, I undress her. I close the blinds with my PK, leaving only a slender beam of moonlight to illuminate her body. The blood sings in me and I must restrain myself. I say to her:

There are people who are born with extraordinary types of minds. I'm one. So are you. There are a few others that I know about. There must be many more. You've heard of extrasensory perception . . .

She moans in mingled fear and ecstasy, holding out her arms to me. 'Come,' she begs. 'Don't tell me any more. I can't bear it. Just love me.'

I am naked myself now, and – yes, a little afraid. I have had so many unfulfilled fantasies about the experience that lies ahead of us, so many dreams. I know what the perfection ought to be, and now I face the challenge of having to create it not only for myself, but also for her – because up until now, my poor Elaine has, like me, known only an empty release.

But she must not be frightened. I say, 'Please close your eyes, chérie. Trust me.'

My brain and body burn, and I am ready. As in the familiar dream I feel myself hovering above her. I enfold her in my arms, lift her without effort, and enter. Her coolness is shocked by my fever and she cries out. Her eyes open but now we can see only each other. The motion is mutual and quite perfect, for we are suspended together in a bright rapture that endures and swells while our minds seem to fuse. I have ignited her at last. When fulfillment comes and my own brain seems to shatter I feel her faint for the joy of it. Turning in the air, I support her, then let myself descend. We rest together for a long time and I thank God for her. We will stay together for ever like this, sharing mind and body, banishing all fear . . .

She awoke with her head on my chest. I was stroking her hair.

'I've never – never — ' She was unable to continue.

'Was it good?'

'I wanted you very much, Roger. Now I know why. Does – does the extrasensory thing account for it?'

'That, and my being something of a frog prince.'

She laughed giddily and began moving her body in gentle

rhythm, without urgency. 'You amazing man. I actually felt as though we were floating – doing it in midair.'

I was coming alive again slowly. 'I had to wait so long. And then, when I finally found you, I wasn't sure I could . . . the way I had dreamed it. But it happened. At last.'

She lifted her head and regarded me with astonished eyes. My mental sight caressed every plane of her face. Before she could ask the question I closed her lips with mine.

'You couldn't be!' she whispered when she finally broke free.

It was my turn to laugh. 'I warned you I had been dormant, waiting patiently on my lily pad for a complaisant princess. A veritable virgin frog.'

'I don't believe you. Is it some religious thing, then? No normal man — '

My coercion silenced her. I opened my mind and showed her the truth. To my amazement, she began to weep.

'My poor, darling Roger. Oh, my dear. And if we hadn't found each other — ?'

'I don't know. As you saw, my first experience with love ended rather badly. I was mistaken about the depth of her feeling because she was unable to open her mind to me. I couldn't risk that again. Do you understand?'

'And you're sure about me.' It was a statement.

'You went to the heart of the matter when you started to tell me that I wasn't normal. Of course I'm not. Luckily for me, neither are you. That's why you're going to marry me.' I was grinning at her in the moonlight and my fingers traced tickling pathways up and down the luscious curve of her spine.

She said, 'Oh, no!'

'You won't marry me?'

'Of course I will, fool.' She clung to me. 'I meant – perhaps we shouldn't do it again quite so soon. You destroyed me. Do you realize that?'

I gave a sinister chuckle. 'The prince is not to be denied. He has princely prerogatives – et un boute-joie princier!'

'But I don't know whether I can *live* through it a second

160

time tonight!' Even as she made false protest, she was encouraging my renaissance. 'If they find my poor little dead body in here tomorrow, you'll be the prime suspect. Think of your embarrassment when the prosecutor demands that you produce the weapon in court! Think of the vulgar sensationalism, the requests for autographs – aah!'

Shush.

Oh my darling oh Roger.

Have no fear. If you're really concerned, this time we'll do it on the bed.

Elaine rented a house in Bretton Woods and transferred the one-woman editorial office of her little magazine to its front bedroom. We made good use of the other one all throughout that enchanted summer and planned to marry in November, when her divorce action would be finalized. In those years the Catholic Church was ambivalent in its recognition of such marriages, and sexual liaisons such as ours were considered to be sinful; but I was ready to defy a regiment of archangels for Elaine's sake, and the guilt that must accompany the violation of one's principles was banished to the deepest part of my unconscious. Only those of you, reading this, who are yourselves operant metapsychics can understand the inevitability of our sexual merging, our excitement at the increasingly profound bonding that we experienced – the soul-mating that lovers have sought and celebrated throughout all the ages. Even though Elaine never attained full operancy in relation to other minds, she did become fully consonant with me. We spoke to each other without words, knew each other's moods and needs through telepathic interchange, shared sensations, even reinforced each other's ecstatic submersion. You lovers in the Unity would no doubt think our efforts pitifully naive and maladroit; but we thought ourselves in wonderland. Elaine's previous partners, most especially her insensitive husband, had failed to arouse her; her inhibitions had restrained her from any attempt at remedy. But when she was with me there was no need for any crass éclaircissement. I *knew* her from the very begin-

161

ning. It was the most amazing part of our love, and it also precipitated the ending because I was not wise enough to know the hazards of entering another's most private place while utterly disarmed.

The four short months with Elaine were the happiest time of my life. Without her I would become a hollow thing – a mere spectator when I was not a puppet. Looking back, I can see that our separation helped bring the great scheme to fruition; but whether the Lylmik engineered it deliberately or whether they simply took advantage of our little tragedy must remain an unanswered question. The Ghost surely knows, but it is silent, just as heaven was silent when I prayed for the strength of character that might have carried me beyond fury and pride to the forgiveness that would be so easy to give now, nearly 140 years too late . . .

But let me tell the story quickly. First, the happy memories:

Champagne picnics and love on an old Hudson's Bay blanket in the deep woods beside Devil's Elbow Brook.

A moonlit tennis game played in the middle of the night on a court at the White Mountain Hotel – and all the staff knowing about Elaine and me, and not daring to say a word because she was Somebody.

Pub-crawling with her in lowest Montréal on a Canadian holiday weekend, and defending her honour in a riot of psychokinetically smashed glassware when she was insulted by canaille even more drunk than we were.

Going down to Boston together, staying at the Ritz-Carlton, sitting on the grass for open-air Pops concerts, messing around the market, and never but *never* eating baked beans.

Taking jaunts to the Donovan family's summer home at Rye where she tried to teach me to sail, then browsing for antiques among the tourist-trappy little coast villages until it was time to finish the day with a clambake or lobster-broil and love on the beach.

Sitting petrified beside her as she drove her red Porsche like a demon through the Maine woods, playing tag with highballing log trucks going eighty-six miles an hour.

Lovemaking on a stormy afternoon in my ancient Volkswagen stalled in the middle of a Vermont covered bridge.

Lovemaking in a meadow above her house at Concord, while monarch butterflies reeled around us, driven berserk by the aetheric vibes.

Love in a misty forest cascade during an August heat wave.

Love in my hotel office at noon behind locked doors.

Love on a twilit picnic table, interrupted by voyeur bears.

Mad psychokinetic love in thirty-three postural variations.

Love after a quarrel.

Hilarious love.

Marathon love.

Tired, comfortable love.

And towards the end, a desperate love that did hold fear and doubt at bay for a little while . . .

There are memories of another type altogether, which I must deal with more briskly:

One of the most disquieting was my realization that she would never be able to overcome the mental blockages causing her latency. She could converse telepathically with me, and Denis could 'hear' her as well as probe her memories; but she was never functionally operant with others except when she was experiencing extraordinary psychic stress. Elaine's mind thus seemed to belong to me almost by default, and I felt the first stirrings of real guilt: we were *not* one mind but two, and to pretend otherwise was to court disaster.

She was able to keep very few things secret from me. This gave me numerous opportunities to learn how to mask from her my own reactions of shock or chagrin — as, for instance, when I found out just how wealthy she really was. She cheerfully made plans for my gainful employment in Donovan Enterprises 'after you give up your tedious little job at the hotel'. She had all kinds of ideas on how I might capitalize on my metapsychic talents (and how Denis could go far if we only liberated him from the clutches of the Jesuits). She wanted to expand *Visitant* magazine into a rallying vehicle for as-yet-undiscovered superminds. When

I balked at these and similar enthusiasms she was hurt, resentful and unrepentently calculating.

Elaine's loyalty was ardent. Nevertheless she was unable to disguise her disappointment when I was less than a success at a meeting with her brother the eminent Congressman, her other brother the wheeler-dealer land developer, and her sister the Back Bay socialite do-gooder. Elaine plainly regretted my lower-class origins, my lack of appreciation for the cosmological bullshit espoused by her Aetherian clique, and my persistently old-fashioned religious faith – which wasn't at all like the trendy version of Catholicism made socially acceptable by the Kennedy clan.

I introduced Elaine to the Remillards at a disastrous Fourth of July barbecue in Berlin thrown by Cousin Gerard. Poor Elaine! Her clothes were too chic, her manners too high-bred, and the covered dish she contributed to the rustic buffet too haute cuisine. She compounded the debacle by speaking elegant Parisian French to old Onc' Louie and the other Canuck elders, and by admitting that her family were Irish Protestants. The only Remillards who weren't scandalized were little Denis and my brother Don. Don was, if anything, too damned friendly towards her. She assured me that there was no telepathic communication between the two of them; but I recalled his coercive exploits of yesteryear and couldn't help feeling doubts at the same time that I cursed myself for being a jealous fool.

Later that summer, when we would briefly visit Don and Sunny to pick up or drop off Denis, whom we often took on outings, Elaine was distant or even covertly antagonistic towards my brother. At the same time she claimed to pity him and pressed me to 'see that he got help' in combating his alcoholism. I knew that any effort on my part would be worse than useless and refused to interfere – which provoked one of our few serious quarrels. Another took place in early September, when I took Denis back to Brebeuf Academy and revealed his metapsychic abilities to Father Jared Ellsworth, as the Ghost had instructed me to do. Elaine was irrationally convinced that the Jesuits would 'exploit' Denis in some nameless way. I assured her that

Ellsworth had reacted with sympathy and equanimity to the revelation (he had even deduced some of the boy's mental talents already); but Elaine persisted in her fretting over Denis, and her attitude towards him was so oddly coloured and tortuous that I was unable to make sense of it until long after the end.

The end. God, how I remember it.

It was late in October on a day when the New Hampshire hills were purple and scarlet with the autumn climacteric. We had gone on a season-end pilgrimage to the Great Stone Face, just she and I, and finished up at a secluded country inn near Franconia. It was one of those terminally quaint establishments that still draw Galactic tourists to New England, featuring squeaky floors, crooked walls, and a pleasant clutter of colonial American artifacts, many of which were for sale at ridiculous prices. The food and drink were splendid and the proprietors discreet. After our meal we retired to a gabled bedroom suite and nestled side by side on a sofa with lumpy cushions, watching sparks from a birchwood fire fly up the chimney while rain tapped gently on the roof.

We had been talking about our wedding plans and sipping a rare Aszu Tokay that the host reserved for well-heeled cognoscenti. It was to be a simple civil ceremony down in Concord, with one of her distinguished Donovan uncles officiating. Later we would have a small supper 'for the wedding party only', which effectively meant no Remillards except me. I listened to her with only half an ear, drowsy from the wine.

And then Elaine told me she was pregnant.

I recall a thunderous sound. It may have come from the storm outside the inn, or it may have been purely mental, my psychic screens crashing into place. I remember a fixed-frame vision of my hand, frozen in the act of reaching for the decanter. I can still hear Elaine's voice prattling on about how she was so glad it had happened, how she had always wanted children while her ex-husband had not, how our child was certain to be a paragon of 'astromental' achievement, perhaps even more brilliant than Denis.

Incapable of speech or even a rational thought, I sat

gripped by a grand refusal. It could not be. She had not said it. I think I prayed like a child, entreating God to cancel this thing, to save my love and my life. I would repeat the same futile supplications later through the bleak winter months as I tried in. vain to conquer myself and return to her; but always love would be obliterated as it was at that hellish moment, wiped out by a blast of volcanic rage and fatally wounded pride.

Of course I knew who the father was.

I finally turned my face to her, and I know I was without expression, my howling despair inaudible beyond the closet of my skill. Elaine cowered back against the cushions, shrinking from the exhalation of pain and menace.

'Roger, what is it?'

Her mind was, as always, completely open to me. And now that her thoughts concentrated on the certainty of the life growing within her, I could perceive a complex skein of memories woven about the embryonic node. The confirmation would be there.

I knew I should leave those memories of hers untouched. It was the only forlorn hope left to me. I must not look into the secret place but seal it for ever, pretend that the child's father was someone else. Anyone else.

The secret places. All rational beings have them and guard them – not only for their own sakes but for those of others. Who but God would love us if all the secret places of our minds lay exposed? I knew how to conceal my own heart of darkness; it is one of the first things an operant metapsychic learns, whether he is bootstrap or preceptor-trained. Only a few poor souls remain vulnerable always, trapped in the shadow-country between latency and conscious control of their high mental powers. Elaine was one. Open. Without secrets.

'Roger,' she pleaded. 'Answer me. For God's sake, darling, what's the matter?'

Don't look. She loves you, not him. To look would be a sin – against her and against yourself. You aren't a truth-seeker, you're a fool. Don't look. Don't look.

I looked. Our love had been sinful, and I must be punished.

She was calm as I lifted my barriers at last, showing her the incontrovertible fact of my own sterility, and the theft of her secret, and what made her betrayal impossible to forgive.

'If it had been anyone but him,' I said. 'Anyone. But, you see, I wouldn't be able to live with it.'

She looked me full in the face. 'Once. It happened once – that first time you took me to meet your family, at that silly Fourth of July barbecue. It was madness. I don't know what came over me. It happened before I realized – without my wanting it.'

No secret place. Poor Elaine. You *had* wanted it.

I saw the entire episode etched in her memory and knew I'd see it for ever. Don focusing the full force of his coercion, her fascination and willing surrender, Don laughing as he took her by the rockets' red glare, kindling in her a stupendous series of orgasms like chain lightning. And his child.

'I can't live with it,' I told her.

'Once, Roger. Only once. And now I hate him.'

No secrets at all . . . Anyone but him. Damn the mindpowers. Damn him! But never her.

'Roger, I love you. I know how much this must hurt. I *feel* the hurt. But I honestly thought the child was yours . . . that the thing with your brother was a piece of idiocy better left forgotten.' She tried to smile, showed me a glowing mental image. 'You love little Denis. He's Don's child.'

'I couldn't help it. Denis is different. Sunny was different.'

'I'm only fifteen weeks gone. I could — '

'No!'

She nodded. 'Yes, I see. It wouldn't make any difference, would it? It would make matters worse.'

I let the wretched contents of my mind seep out: The child *will* be brilliant. Don's mental faculties are far more impressive than mine, in spite of his flaws. As you know. Goodbye, Elaine.

'Roger, I love you. For the love of God, don't do this!'

I must. I love you I will always love you but I must.

I walked to the door and opened it. Aloud, I said, 'I'm going to take your Porsche back to the White Mountain

Hotel. In the morning, I'll send one of our drivers back here with it. There are a few things I must get from the house in Bretton Woods, but I should be out of it before noon. I'll leave my key.'

'You *fool*,' she said.

'Yes.'

I went out and softly closed the door after me.

Elaine married Stanton Latimer, a prominent Concord attorney, that November. He gave her child, Annarita, his name and they were a happy family until his death in 1992. The distractions of motherhood – and the decline in flying-saucer sightings after 1975 – led Elaine to abandon *Visitant*. She turned her leadership talents to environmental activism and campaigned against acid rain. In time she decided that she had imagined the more improbable facets of our liaison.

Annarita Latimer grew up to be an actress of vibrant and unforgettable presence who had a triumphant, tempestuous career. Like her mother, she was a powerful suboperant. Annarita's third husband was Bernard Kendall, the astrophysicist, who sired her only child, the fully operant Teresa – known to historians of the Galactic Milieu as the mother of Marc Remillard and Jack the Bodiless.

21

Supervisory Cruiser Noumenon [Lyl 1–0000]
10 May 1975

The Simb shuttle saucer made its ingress into the immense Lylmik vessel in the manner of a lentil being swallowed by a whale, and the four senior members of the Earth Oversight Authority gathered in the shuttle's airlock to watch the curious docking manoeuvres.

'I hate coming aboard Lylmik spacecraft. One is so likely to become overstimulated.' The Gi representative, RipRip Muml, whiffled its plumage in a gesture of libido suppression and sealed off four of its eight sensory circuits.

'Strange that the Supervisory Body should want to meet with us here in Earth orbit instead of simply transmitting its instructions mentally.'

The Simb magnate, Lashi Ala Adassti, watched the scene outside the viewport with rapt fascination. In spite of her high position in the Oversight organization, she had never before been invited to visit a Lylmik cruiser. 'I've given up trying to fathom the motives of the Supervisors, especially those relating to *this* perverse little planet . . . Sacred Truth and Beauty! Will you look what's happening out there in the parking bay?'

'An interesting spectacle, but hardly unnerving,' remarked the Krondaku, Rola'eroo.

'I've seen it a dozen or so times myself.' The Poltroyan magnate shook his head. 'But it still rattles me. It's as though we were being digested!'

The saucer rested on a kind of animated turf, pearly tendrils that rippled in peristaltic waves as they propelled the small spacecraft slowly along. A few metres away, on either side of the shuttle's path, plantlike excrescences apparently made of luminous jelly were sprouting up with graceful regularity; they unfurled pallid leafy ribbons and undulated in a questing fashion in the direction of the passing ship. Some of the larger plants 'fruited', producing crystalline structures that opened to discharge glittering powder that swirled around the shuttle viewports like saffron smoke. Behind these pseudo-organisms were rising much taller ones that resembled glassy tree-ferns and opalescent feather-palms. These soon formed an impenetrable jungle alongside the saucer, a bright corridor with purple obscurity lying ahead. The smaller ribbon-bearers became more and more numerous and their appendages reached out to caress the moving vessel's sides. It was like sailing underwater through a twisting tunnel alive with glowing albino kelp.

'By their spacecraft ye shall know them,' the poetical Gi murmured. 'Ours are preposterous and ramshackle, and their operation is so circumscribed by the reproductive habits of our crews that no other entities dare ride in them. Krondak ships are bleakly functional and those of the

Poltroyans cozy and baroque, while Simbiari craft like this one we are riding in are paragons of high technology. But how can one classify the Lylmik ships?'

'Peculiar,' suggested Rola'eroo, 'like the race that produced them.'

The others laughed uneasily.

The Poltroyan, a dapper little humanoid wearing heavily bejewelled robes, shared his meditation. 'We never really see the Lylmik, even though they must inhabit forms that are manifestations of the matter-energy lattices. They are not pure mind, as some have speculated – and yet they enjoy a mentality unfathomably above our own. They will tell us very little of their history – nothing of their nature. They are infallibly kind. Their zeal in furthering the evolution of the Galactic Mind is formidable, but they often seem capricious. Their logic is not our logic. As RipRip Muml has noted, this ship of theirs is an embodiment of the Lylmik enigma: it is lush, extravagant, playful. Certain of our xenologists have speculated that the enormous cruisers are themselves aspects of Lylmik life, symbionts of the minds they transport. We know that these beings are the Galaxy's most ancient coadunate race, but their actual age and their origin remain a mystery. Our Poltroyan folklore says that the Lylmik home-star Nodyt was once a dying red giant, which the population rejuvenated into a G3 by a metapsychic infusion of fresh hydrogen sixty million years ago. But such a feat is beyond Milieu science, contradicting the Universal Field Theory.'

'Our legends,' the Krondak monster said, 'are even more absurd. They suggest that the Lylmik are survivors of the Big Bang – that they date from the previous universe. A totally ridiculous notion.'

'No sillier than ours,' said RipRip Muml. 'The more simple-minded Gi believe that the Lylmik are angels – pseudocorporeal messengers of the Cosmic All. An unlikely hypothesis, but not inappropriate for mentors of our Galactic Mind.'

An impatient frown had been deepening on Lashi Ala's emerald features. 'We Simbiari don't tell fairy-tales about the Lylmik. We accept their guidance at the same time as we resent their arrogant condescension. Look how determined they are to give these Earthlings favoured treatment. The planet is a Lylmik pet! And yet the Supervisory Body seems blithely ignorant about just how unready for Intervention Earth is. How many times during the Thirty-Year Surveillance have we Simbiari been obliged to save the barbarians from *accidentally* touching off an atomic war? How many more times will we have to rescue the planetary ass during the upcoming pre-Intervention phase? All of us know that there is no way this world's Mind can achieve full coadunation prior to Intervention. Earth will be admitted to the Milieu in advance of its psychosocial maturation! Sheer lunacy!'

The Krondaku remained stolid. 'Should the Earth Mind deliberately opt for nuclear warfare during the next forty years, you know that the Intervention will be cancelled. Furthermore, Intervention is contingent upon a certain minimal metaconcerted action by human operants. If they cannot rise above egocentrism to the lowest rung of mental solidarity, not even the Lylmik can force the Milieu to accept them.'

Lashi gave a disillusioned grunt. 'No other potentially emergent planet ever got such special treatment.'

'The Lylmik always have reasons for their actions,' the Poltroyan said, 'incomprehensible though they may be to us lesser minds. If the Earthlings are destined to be great metapsychic prodigies, as the Lylmik maintain, then the risk of early intervention will be justified.'

'You can talk, Falto,' Lashi Ala shot back. 'Your people haven't been saddled with the bulk of the planetary surveillance and manifestation as we Simbiari have. Why the Lylmik didn't appoint you smug little mauve pricks as prime contractors for Earth, I'll never know! You *like* humans.'

Rola'eroo came as close to chuckling as his phlegmatic race was capable. 'Perhaps that is the very reason why Poltroy was not given the proctorship. Despite certain imputations of favouritism, I am convinced that the Lylmik desire a fair and just evaluation of humanity. And this' — he offered a magisterial nod to Lashi Ala — 'the citizens of the Simbiari Polity will conscientiously provide.'

'Oh, well, of course,' she muttered.

RipRip Muml gave a delicate shudder. 'Thanks be to the Tranquil Infinite that *we* have been spared close contact with Earth. Its artistic productions are exquisite, but the reverberations of violence and suffering are a sore trial to truly sensitive minds.'

'I've noticed,' said Lashi sweetly, 'that you Gi are too sensitive for any number of tedious but necessary assignments.'

The great yellow eyes blinked in innocent reproach.

Falto the Poltroyan interposed diplomatically. 'We all do the jobs we're best suited for, given the mind-set of the planet under evaluation.'

'And with a race as bumptious as humanity, you Simbiari end up carrying the can!' RipRip gave its phallus a cheerful flourish.

Lashi responded with simple dignity. 'We know very well that our people are still imperfectly Unified – and I did not mean to imply that we regretted our first assignment as prime contractor to an emerging Mind. On the contrary, we are honoured by the Milieu's mandate.' She hesitated, a troubled expression crossing her now glistening face. 'But the Oversight Authority concedes that Earth is an anomaly. It seems counter to all logic, therefore, that the Concilium should assign its proctorship to us, the most junior Polity in the Milieu. Surely this difficult and barbaric world would fare better under the more sympathetic guidance of Poltroy – or, even better, under the stern direction that the Krondaku vouchsafed to Gi, Poltroyans and Simbiari alike.'

The Krondak magnate's mind-tone was detached and serene. 'My race has proctored more than seventeen thousand planetary Minds since the Lylmik raised us to Unity. Only you three survived to coadunation and membership in the Milieu.'

'*We've* never had a winner in seventy-two tries,' the Poltroyan admitted, 'and we're still smarting over the Yanalon fiasco. A tough-minded Simb primacy might have saved that world ... Don't sell your abilities short, Lashi Ala Adassti.'

'You mustn't feel downhearted or put-upon,' the

hermaphrodite added kindly. 'Think how the Unity will rejoice if you succeed! We Gi will never enjoy such a triumph. We're too frivolous and sex-obsessed ever to be appointed planetary proctors. No newborn coadunate Mind will ever call us its foster-parents – and we are the poorer thereby.'

A harmonious chord of chimes sounded in the mental ears of the four magnates. Outside the viewports the iridescent glow intensified. The shuttle-craft was approaching the terminus of the overgrown tunnel, an iris gateway of yellow metal that opened slowly like the expanding pupil of a great golden eye.

Welcome. And high thoughts to you, most beloved colleagues. Please debark and join us in the hospitality chamber.

The shuttle had halted at the gateway. Rola'eroo extended a tentacle and activated the hatch mechanism, admitting a billow of warm, superoxygenated atmosphere to the airlock. The four entities toddled, strode, stalked and slithered down the integral gangway, crossed a short expanse of anemonoid turf flanked by crystal foliage, and entered the Lylmik sanctum. The gate shut behind them.

It was rather dim inside, comfortably so after the brilliant part of the ship they had just traversed. The walls and flooring were gently corrugated, transparent, and seemed to be holding back an encompassing volume of bubbly liquid that swirled slowly in ever-changing eddies of blue and green. In the centre of the room was a crescent-shaped table with three seats for the Gi, the Poltroyan and the Simb – and a squatting spot for the ponderous Krondaku. Besides the furniture, which was austere in design and made of the warm yellow metal, the room contained only a low dais about three metres square, formed by slight exaggerations of the floor ribbing.

The Earth Oversight Authority took their places and waited. Lashi Ala betrayed her apprehension by smearing the table surface with dabs of ichor from her perspiring hands. She tucked them into the sleeves of her uniform, where there were blotting pads, and buffed away the smears with her elbows. The other three Overseers tactfully averted their eyes and veiled their brains.

Above the dais there appeared a small atmospheric maelstrom.

Our heartfelt felicitations to you, dear colleagues, upon the successful completion of Earth's first phase of intensified overt manifestation.

In metaconcert, the Authority responded: We are gratified that the Supervisory Body approves, and herewith present a digest of data relevant to progress in coadunation of the World Mind. [Display.]

The maelstrom was enlarging, spinning in a plane perpendicular to the dais, and five distinct whorls were condensing out of it.

How interesting that the outbreaks of metapsychic operancy among the humans are so widely scattered. Even though the genes for high mental function are present in all racial groups, one notes that its phenotypic expression crops out with special vigour among certain Celtic and Oriental populations.

This has been allowed for in ethnodynamic equations. The sorting factors have a fascinating Darwinian aspect, in that those groups subject to great environmental — as opposed to social — stress tend to manifest the metapsychic traits most strongly. Thus the Georgian, Alpine, Hebridean and Eastern Canadian Celts tend to become operant more rapidly than their more numerous Irish and French congeners. The same is true of the Asian irruptive locus, with the North Siberian, Mongol and Hokkaido groups most noteworthy, together with the isolated fractions flourishing in Tibet and Finland. Unfortunately, the Australian aboriginal locus has become nearly extinct, as have the Kalahari and Pigmy concentrations in Africa. The Nilotic group trembles on the brink due to severe social disruption. In any case, these southern populations are now almost too small to be viable reservoirs of operant genotypes.

Tragic. But as we know, operancy must be combined with ethnic dynamism if coadunation of the Mind is to be achieved.

And on Earth, dynamism is largely a Northern function, due to the complex interaction of stress factors.

'Northern hyperfertility isn't to be sneezed at, either,'

murmured the Poltroyan, ex-concert. 'Which is why I put my money on the Canucks in the operancy sweepstakes.'

The other three Overseers flinched at the effrontery of their small colleague, but the Lylmik seemed amused.

You are most perceptive, Faltonin-Virminonin! It is indeed from that group, especially the northeastern Franco-Americans, that we expect the largest numbers of natural operants to be born during this critical pre-Intervention phase of proctorship.

The five atmospheric vortices had now assumed a decidedly material aspect. The Gi and the Krondaku, being the most ultrasensitive members of the metaconcert, realized with some excitement that the Supervisors were about to do them the unusual honour of assuming astral bodies – or, at least, astral heads. The news ignited the entire Authority, especially Lashi Ala, who had never experienced a Lylmik vis-à-vis encounter.

They asked: Is it your wish, then, that we devise plans for the special encouragement of these Franco-American operants?

By no means. This is a task reserved for others.

Others? . . . What others?

But before the Oversight Authority could pursue this puzzle further, they were completely distracted by the apparition unfolding before them.

Above the dais now floated five heads. Perhaps in consideration of the Poltroyan, Gi and Simb representatives, who had largely humanoid features, the heads each developed two eyes and a single smiling mouth. Their psychocreative flesh was roseate with no trace of hair, feathering, scales, or other epidermal outgrowth. The eyes of the central head were grey; those of the four surrounding heads were a brilliant aquamarine green. The Lylmik had no necks, but from their occipital regions trailed multiple ectoplasmic filaments like pale gauzy scarves stirring in a light breeze. Strangely, each of the different Authority magnates thought that the heads were supremely beautiful. Even those who had seen this manifestation of the Lylmik before felt that they could look into those eyes for ever without tiring; and poor Lashi Ala, meeting them for the first time, was reduced to bewitched helplessness.

'I am Noetic Concordance,' said the uppermost head.

'I am Eupathic Impulse,' said the lowest.

'I am Homologous Trend,' said the right-hand head.

'I am Asymptotic Essence,' said the one on the left.

The central head, which radiated the most overwhelming power of all, had the softest voice. 'And I am Atoning Unifex. We of the Supervisory Body embrace you and your organization. We thank you for what you have done, and charge you to carry on your assigned tasks in spite of discouragements, doubts and difficulties. It is known to us that the small planet we are orbiting at this moment occupies a critical place in the probability lattices. From it may emerge a Mind that will exceed all others in metapsychic potential. It is known to us that this Mind will be capable of destroying our beloved Galactic Milieu. It is further known to us that this Mind will also be capable of magnifying the Milieu immensely, accelerating the Unification of all the inhabited star-systems. For this reason we have directed this extraordinary attempt at Intervention. It involves a great risk. But all evolutionary leaps are hazardous, and without risk-taking there can only be stagnation, the triumph of entropy, and eventual death. Do you understand this, colleagues?'

We understand.

'Mental potential is not actualization. The human race must reach an acceptable level of operancy largely through its own efforts. We can guide, but we cannot force evolution of the Mind. Thus there still exists the possibility that this rising operant population may founder – either through internal or external calamity. There exists another possibility, fortunately diminishing, that the entire world may perish in a suicidal conflict. So Intervention is not certain. But we shall work towards it . . . you in your way and we in ours, full of trust.'

We understand.

'Go now and initiate the next Oversight phase. From time to time we will lend special assistance.'

We do not understand, but we acquiesce willingly.

The central head nodded. The eyes of all five were ablaze with irresistible psychic energy. The heads began melting away to ectoplasmic vapour, but the eyes remained to focus Unifying power.

Join with us, said the Supervisors, and the minds of the Overseers rushed into the joyous light.

A long time later, when the four awoke in their shuttle-craft, they instinctively came together to gaze out of a viewport at the blue planet rolling below.

'Incredible,' said the Krondaku.

'What an experience!' Lashi Ala was still in a state of near-total bemusement. 'I agree – it was quite incredible.'

The Gi shook its head, gently corrective. 'While Unity with the Lylmik is memorable, it is not the matter that Rola'eroo Mobak finds difficult to believe.'

'Certainly not,' the monster growled. 'It's what they *said*.'

The Poltroyan pursed lavender lips and hoisted a single eyebrow in unspoken query.

'The head in the middle.' RipRip Muml amplified its speech with a remembered vision. 'It said that the Lylmik were going to assist us. That's even *more* unprecedented than their original veto of the Concilium pull-out vote!'

Rola'eroo said, 'You will also recall that the Lylmik Supervisors told us that we were not to attempt positive reinforcement of the Franco-American operant group . . . that the task would be undertaken by others.'

Both Poltroyan eyebrows shot up and the ruby optics bulged. 'Love's Oath! You can't mean it!'

'I conclude that certain human operants are to be shepherded by the Lylmik themselves,' Rola'eroo asserted. 'By these aloof beings who scarcely ever condescend to participate in the Concilium deliberations, who tantalize us and confuse us when they are not vexing us with their mystical vagary.'

'There was nothing vague,' Lashi said, 'about that crew we met today. That central head was downright blunt.'

'Most uncharacteristic,' the Krondaku said. 'We must ponder the implications strenuously.'

The Gi had turned to the port and contemplated the blue planet with a certain foreboding. Its irrepressible

177

genitalia were blanched and subdued. 'Earthlings! Do you know – I'm beginning to be quite afraid of them.'

'Nonsense!' said Lashi Ala stoutly. 'We Simbiari know humanity better than any of you. They don't scare *us*.'

The three other entities exchanged thoughts of sudden, shared comprehension.

Part II
The Disclosure

1

New York City, Earth
21 February 1978

The flight from Chicago had been over an hour late, and helicopter shuttle service between Kennedy and Manhattan had been disrupted by the same fog that had delayed the airplane. The car-rental counter was mobbed, but here Kieran O'Connor's coercion expedited procurement of a Cadillac limousine. He and Arnold Pakkala, his executive assistant, took the front seat while Jase Cassidy and Adam Grondin got into the back. Then they were off in a squeal of expensive rubber, with the minds of Cassidy and Grondin clearing the way and Pakkala driving like the battle-trained Chicago commuter that he was.

Kieran closed his burning eyes and dreamed while the big black automobile roared up the Van Wyck and Long Island expressways in defiance of the speed limit. It negotiated the snarl of the Queens-Midtown Tunnel magically and bulldozed its way down 42nd Street. Other vehicles seemed to melt out of its way as it streaked up Avenue of the Americas, ignored by patrolling NYPD cruisers. It turned left on to West 57th against the lights, zigzagged from lane to lane amidst traffic apparently frozen in place, and plunged into the whorl of Columbus Circle like a black shark invading a sluggish shoal of prey species. Here, with vehicles coming at it from six directions, the limousine faced its keenest challenge. The targeting eyes of Cassidy and Grondin flicked to and fro and their minds shouted silent commands to the other drivers: *You stop! You go right! You move left lane! Up the kerb bike! Out of the way walkers! Go! Stop! Gangway!* Enchanted buses froze at the kerb or lumbered aside, private cars seemed to cower as they yielded; take-out-food delivery boys on bicycles and pedestrians scattered like pigeons before a hawk; even the pugnacious Manhattan taxis were demoralized and swerved out of the limousine's charmed path with tyres screeching and brake lights flashing scarlet alarm.

Arnold Pakkala guided the Cadillac with fluid precision

through the chaos, ran a red light for the seventeenth time that night, and floored the accelerator when he attained the comparatively unimpeded reach of Central Park West.

Adam Grondin said: Kennedy to Central Park 34 minutes. Beautiful Arnie.

Jase Cassidy said: Time to make it. Chief still asleep?

Pakkala said: Until I tell him to wake up.

A map image of New York City seemed to hover in his peripheral vision off to the right, among the lamplit bare trees of the park. He spotted a police cruiser, but Adam and Jase had already fuzzed the minds of the two officers inside. They knew they couldn't possibly have seen a Caddy doing seventy northbound, and turned their attention to a doorman walking three poodles who was suspiciously unencumbered by a pooper-scooper.

Pakkala said: Only a few blocks more.

The limousine charged across 65th Street on the fag end of the amber light, then hung a left on to 66th virtually riding the rims. For the last time Cassidy and Grondin exerted their coercive powers to stop the modest flow of vehicles on Columbus. The Cadillac took the final corner smoothly, decelerated, and drove up the ramp in front of the Lincoln Center for the Performing Arts. A touch of power brakes brought it to a sedate halt.

Cassidy and Grondin relaxed their overstrained brains with audible groans of relief. Arnold Pakkala's face had gone rigid in the wan light from the instrument panel. Still gripping the steering wheel, he let his head fall back against the padded rest. His eyes closed. The other two men flinched at the orgasmic discharge that energized the interior of the car for an instant, setting their own nerves afire with sympathetic vibration. Seconds later Pakkala was sitting ramrod-straight again, not one white hair out of place, stripping off his leather driving gloves with small, neat motions.

'Jesus, Arnie, I *wish* you wouldn't do that.' Grondin ripped open a pack of Marlboros with shaking hands and coaxed one out.

Cassidy wiped his florid face with a handkerchief.

'Wouldn't that be a helluva thing for the chief to wake up to? The fallout from your stupid come!'

Pakkala ignored that. 'Mr O'Connor may continue to sleep until I make certain that our subjects are actually inside, in their box. If our informants erred – or if they lied – other plans will have to be made.'

'Well, get cracking, dammit,' Cassidy snapped. 'Don't just sit around here getting your rocks off.'

Pakkala's face went rigid again. He seemed to be studying the hub of the steering wheel with blind eyes. Tiny flakes of snow sifted down and melted to pinpoint droplets when they struck the warm windshield. The engine idled soundlessly and Kieran O'Connor exhaled a deep, sighing breath that was almost a sob.

Grondin sucked cigarette smoke fiercely. 'Poor bastard.'

Cassidy said, 'He'll be all right. Just so long as those two dago butchers are in there where we can get at 'em.'

Nodding at Pakkala, Grondin said, 'Arnie'll find out. Umpteen thousand people in there, but Arnie'll find 'em if they're inside. Helluva head, old Arnie, even if he has his weird moments.'

'I still think this is the wrong place for a hit, though,' Cassidy said. 'I know the chief has to do it before any of the New York crowd expect him to act. But to do it *here* . . .'

Both men looked across Lincoln Plaza, where the five tall arches forming the façade of the Metropolitan Opera House enclosed a scene of festive splendour. They were more than ninety feet high and panelled in transparent glass from top to bottom, framing the four tiers of the house and the golden vaults of the ceiling. Colossal murals by Marc Chagall blazed on either side of a grand double staircase of white marble, carpeted in red. The walls were crimson velvet or gleaming stone, set off by twinkling sconces. In the central arch hung the famous starburst chandeliers, the largest at the top and the smaller satellites offset beneath it like a cluster of crystal galaxies. Rising bright against the black sky of winter, the opera house looked like the open door into a fantasy world, rather than the designated site of a double execution.

Tonight's house was a sellout, a benefit performance of

La Favorita by Donizetti. The performance was a new and lavish one featuring the superstars Luciano Pavarotti, Shirley Verrett and Sherrill Milnes, a rare treat for aficionados of Italian opera. Among the most devoted of these was a certain New York City business leader named Guido 'Big Guy' Montedoro. On most opening nights he was to be found in his regular box with his wife, his grown children and the spouses of the latter. Tonight, however, his companions were all male. Seated at the rear of the box were four trusted associates of the Montedoro Family, whose rented tuxedos bulged slightly under the arms. In front, next to Don Guido himself, was the honoured guest of the evening, Vicenzu Falcone. Don Vicenzu, an old friend of the Big Guy and a fellow music-lover, was being fêted on the occasion of his parole from the federal prison at Lewisburg, Pennsylvania, where he had been serving time for tax evasion. He was accompanied by his deputy, Mike LoPresti, who had kept the Brooklyn narcotics pipeline running more or less efficiently while his superior was hors de combat. LoPresti's brother-in-law, Joseph 'Joe Porks' Porcaro, the Falcone enforcer, was also in attendance. It was this same Porcaro who had gone to Chicago three days earlier to execute a contract on the upstart young consigliere of the Chicago Outfit, whose far-reaching activities had encroached once too often upon certain business interests of the boys from Brooklyn.

Porcaro, following LoPresti's orders, had trailed his intended victim to the posh Oakbrook shopping complex in the western suburbs of Chicago. He had smiled as the counsellor took pains to park his brand new Mercedes 450SL at some distance from other cars, lest their careless drivers open doors against its immaculate flanks and ding the paint job. When the consigliere went away, Porcaro wired a small bomb to the Mercedes, drove to O'Hare Airport, and was home in Brooklyn in time for a supper of linguini with white clam sauce.

Unfortunately for him – and for Underboss LoPresti, who had ordered the hit on his own authority without consulting Don Vicenzu – the Camastra Family's legal adviser had come to Oakbrook to pick up his wife and children, who had spent the morning shopping with the wife's mother. The young parents and their daughters, aged two and three, had approached the booby-trapped automobile together. But then Shannon, the three-year-old, decided that she had to go to the bathroom. Scolding her just a little, her father took her to a nearby department store while the mother and younger child waited in the car.

It was a cold and blustery February day, and only natural that Rosemary Camastra O'Connor should start the engine of the Mercedes to get the heater going.

[Fireflower!]

Wake up Mr O'Connor.

[Fireflower!] The dark hallway in the dingy flat in Southie with the emanations from the sickroom hitting him fresh again so that he nearly puked with the pain before he could shut it out *Kier Kier my baby are you back did you pray did you* . . .

Wake up. It's all right. We're at the Opera House.

[Fireflower!] Mom calling in her broken-glass-edge voice the voice only he could hear crying and dying clinging obstinately to her agony and to him *Kier Kier you did receive Holy Communion didn't you Kier you didn't sneak breakfast again did you oh you know you have to pray hard I can't so you must and then there'll be a miracle* . . .

Wake up sir. Open your eyes.

[Fireflower!] The hands dry as newspaper the fingernails blue and broken one hand gripping the tarnished silver-filigree rosary and the other tangled in his old sweater pulling him closer and him fighting to raise a higher and higher wall between the two of them and she calling out to the awful Irish God she loved the one who tortured *Kier Kier he tests the ones he loves best he loves us I love you Kier pray for the miracle pray Jesus it stops Jesus stop it please stop it Kier stop it* . . .

Mr O'Connor! Wake up!

[Fireflower!] Yes Mom I'll stop it even if damned God won't I know how . . . I know how . . . was it so easy? Blue eyes gone wide and black and empty pain gone mind gone are you really gone? And the boy screams [fireflower!] and

185

the grown man screams [fireflower!] and it expands in thunder under Illinois clouds as grey as Mom's fluffy hair on the coffin's cheap satin pillow and the coffin will have to be closed you understand Mr O'Connor wake up Mr O'Connor wake up!

Kieran opened his eyes.

Arnold Pakkala was there, and Adam Grondin, and Jase Cassidy. The loyal ones, the ones he had salvaged and bonded to him, the ones like him: hurt through their own fault, ever hurting.

He asked Arnold: Are Porcaro and LoPresti inside?

'Yes, sir,' Pakkala said out loud. 'Everything is exactly as Koenig and Matucci told us it would be. The two subjects are here with the dons. There are no women. Four button-men are inside the box and two are on watch outside. The intermission between the Third and Fourth Acts is about to begin. You and Adam and Jason can mingle readily with the crowd.'

Kieran unfastened his seat belt and removed his hat, his white silk scarf, and his dark-blue cashmere overcoat. Grondin and Cassidy hastily followed his example. All three of them were dressed in black-tie formal evening wear. 'Go around to Sixty-fifth Street, by the Juilliard School,' Kieran told Arnold. 'There's a tunnel on the lower level that goes under the plaza to the stage door. We'll meet you there afterwards.'

'Yes, sir. Good luck!'

Cassidy and Grondin were already out on the pavement, heading for the broad steps; but Kieran paused, half in and half out of the limousine, and smiled at his executive assistant. A mental picture hovered between them: a drunken derelict being kicked to death by a vicious punk in a Chicago alley, uttering a last telepathic cry for help.

'Luck, Arnold? You of all people should know better than to say that. People like us make our own luck.'

Kieran stepped out of the car and slammed the door. The Cadillac's headlights came on like some great animal opening its eyes. Arnold Pakkala raised his hand and said: I'll be waiting.

Kieran nodded. He stood there in spite of the arctic wind

knifing through his clothing, until the limousine disappeared around the corner. Yes, we make our own luck. We make our own reality, and when the bill comes due we pay cash on the barrelhead. Arnold and Jase and Adam didn't quite understand that yet, but they would, and so would the others when Kieran found them and bound them.

The Opera House began to shimmer. Thousands of people were pouring from the auditorium and the balconies on to the grand staircase for intermission. Cassidy and Grondin waited patiently, silhouetted against the brilliance.

[Fireflower.]

All right, Kier said to them. This is what I want you to do.

The performance was running long, and Montedoro and Falcone decided to spend this final intermission relaxing in their box, rather than attempt another sortie into the high-society crush out on the Grand Tier lobby. Three of the bodyguard were given permission to take a smoke break and Joe Porks was sent for a magnum of champagne. Mike LoPresti, whose musical tastes ran more towards cabaret singers than divas, appeased his boredom by using the binoculars to inspect the décolletages of the elegant ladies down on the main floor.

The two dons made favourable comments about the rousing curtain-closer ensemble that had ended Act Three. *La Favorita*, they agreed, was somewhat of a potboiler – which explained why the Met hadn't mounted a production since Caruso in 1905 – but it did have some soaring melodies, and Pavarotti was in splendid voice. Vicenzu Falcone was old-fashioned enough to express regret that the heroine was being portrayed by a black soprano.

Montedoro shrugged. 'At least she's not fat, and she's got a great legato. So if her colour bugs you, close your eyes during the duets.'

'Look, Guido, I don't mind a chocolate Carmen or Aïda – but there oughta be limits. When I was in stir I saw Price do *Tosca* on *Live from the Met* and it was fuckin' grotesque! What next? A Jap Rigoletto? It's all the fault of that damn Kraut, Bing. He squanders a bundle building this house, and we got trick chandeliers, no privacy, everything open like a goddam goldfish tank – and the singers gotta blast out their voiceboxes to fill the thing. The old Met was better.'

'Nothing stays the same for ever, Vince. Us old farts gotta change with the changing times.'

'Sez you! You're only sixty-seven and you don't have arteries sludged up like a Jersey backwater at low tide.' Falcone lowered his voice and began to speak in Sicilian dialect. 'And you don't have a US attorney standing on your testicles, ready to defy God and the Madonna and the Bill of Rights in order to make certain that you die in prison. Piccolomini, that head of a prick! Do you know why he pursues me? He intends to run for senator, and I am to provide him with his ticket to Washington. Illegal wiretaps, suborned witnesses, planted evidence – he doesn't care how he incriminates one. You had better guard your own precious arse, friend Guido.'

'I always have,' Montedoro said in English. The perfect acoustics of the auditorium filled the place with white noise during the interval, so the conversation between the two dons was inaudible even to LoPresti and the single remaining bodyguard, who were only a few feet away. Nevertheless, the man whom the newspapers called Boss of Bosses leaned very close to his old friend and spoke in the tongue of secrecy. 'Do you think that I'm blind to the government conspiracy against Our Thing? I saw it coming years ago, when that shitter-of-wisdom Robert Kennedy declared war on us. For this very reason, my own Family has diversified, distanced itself from the less savoury sources of income. The Montedoro Borgata is legitimate, Vicenzu! Well – very nearly so. My sons, Pasquale and Paolo, have more three-piece suits on their payroll than a Wall Street brokerage. You don't find cunting zealots like Piccolomini poking into *our* affairs. Not when they can spend their time more profitably pursuing the greatest importer of heroin and cocaine on the East Coast.'

'Perhaps I should peddle pizza?' Falcone growled.

Montedoro chuckled. 'Why not? See here – I know that your gross profits are tremendous, rising with each passing month. But you are having difficulty laundering the money. And some of your impatient young men complain that their share is slow in filtering down to them. I happen to know that the Sortino Borgata has the same problem, and there are rumours about Calcare's operation, too. It is the unprecedented quantity of money – the drug money – so inconvenient! But there are new methods of handling this embarrassment of riches, Vicenzu – tricks of modern finance.'

'Hah! You suggest that we hand the money over to you for safekeeping, my dear old friend?'

'Suppose,' Montedoro said softly, 'that we revive the Commission? Suppose that the Five Families work together instead of at cross-purposes? The Commission was a good idea – only ahead of its time. But now, with this massive influx of dirty money that must be invested if it is not to be pissed away in bankers' percentages, we need to unify to survive.'

'Oh, shit,' said Falcone in English. 'Now you're startin' to sound just like that Chicago asshole, Camastra.'

A troubled look crossed Montedoro's face. 'Al Camastra phoned me last night. He knew we'd be getting together. How did he know that, Vince? . . . And what Al had to say worried me.'

The door at the back of the box opened and Joe Porks came in, a tray of empty flute glasses in his hands and a big bottle of champagne tucked under one arm. He nodded deferentially to the dons and went over to LoPresti. The two whispered together. LoPresti, scowling, headed for the door while Joe Porks undid the cork wire on the magnum. There was a juicy *pop*. Joe began to pour.

Falcone was distracted by the actions of his minions. There was a creeping sensation behind his stiffly starched collar, which seemed suddenly to constrict his windpipe. He ran a finger behind the collar and grunted to clear his throat. 'Camastra! He always means trouble. Him and that smartass Irish consigliere of his. What kinda crap was he shovelin' this time?'

Before Montedoro could answer, the door to the box opened again. LoPresti stood there, his face grey and drawn, and behind him were three men in evening clothes.

The quartet edged inside and the door closed. The lone soldier on guard duty started up from his seat, groping in his armpit, and then crumpled to the floor with a muffled crash. He twitched and lay still.

'Jesus Christ,' said Joe Porks. His fingers tightened on the champagne bottle.

'Don't even think of trying it, Porcaro,' said one of the shadow men behind LoPresti. 'Take his piece, Mike.'

The two dons gaped. LoPresti stepped over to his enforcer, who seemed to be paralysed, and removed a .38 Detective Special from his shoulder holster. Joe Porks stood like a battered mannequin in an After Six display window, a full glass of bubbly in one hand and the big bottle in the other. Sweat poured down his forehead and his acne-pitted cheeks.

Falcone lurched to his feet to confront his Underboss. 'Mike, what the fuck's going on here?'

LoPresti's mouth worked as if he were trying to overcome a spasm of lockjaw. There were tears of rage in his eyes. He handed the revolver to one of the men behind him and then went to a seat beside Falcone and slowly lowered himself into it.

The shortest of the three intruders now stepped forward into the light. He was a man in his mid-thirties whose dark hair grew in a widow's peak, and his face wore one of the most compelling and terrifying expressions that the two dons could remember having seen during their unquiet lives.

Montedoro remained seated. 'A visitor from Chicago,' he said in a neutral tone. 'O'Connor, isn't it?'

Yes.

'Al Camastra mentioned your name when we spoke on the phone last night. Do you intend to kill Vince and me?'

No. But I will explain certain matters to you.

Montedoro nodded. His glance took in the sagging LoPresti and motionless Joe Porks, who was teetering a bit with the champagne but didn't spill a drop.

May we sit down? The intermission is nearly over.

Montedoro inclined his head graciously.

Your associates whom we met outside are resting in the men's lounge. They'll probably feel much better after a good night's sleep. The fellow on the floor will require prompt hospitalization. Porcaro and LoPresti, however, will receive their treatment from me.

O'Connor's two companions had gone to Joe Porks and relieved him of his burdens. They guided him to the fourth seat at the front of the box near to LoPresti and sat him down, then retired again to the shadows. The five-minute-warning chime sounded. People began returning to their seats in the boxes to the right and left. They paid no attention to the mobsters and their uninvited guests.

'He's talking,' Falcone whispered, his eyes bulging with terror, 'but he *ain't* talking.'

Montedoro was staring at Kieran with shrewd speculation. 'So you're Camastra's edge. No wonder he made you. No wonder he raised you to consigliere.'

'I have other talents as well, Don Guido. If you help reorganize the Commission and put it into efficient operation, you may benefit from my unique abilities yourself. And so may Don Vicenzu, and other businessmen of honour.' *But first we must settle another matter.*

Falcone said hesitantly, 'It wasn't me ordered the hit, O'Connor. You know that, don't you? You're a counsellor. Untouchable. But LoPresti was burned because you undercut us on the bidding last year for the Montréal Connection. That was a pipeline he sweat blood to bring in, and the froggies were all ready to deal – until you convinced 'em otherwise.' He gave a weak laugh. 'Maybe now we know *how* you convinced 'em.'

'I'm not a miracle-worker,' Kieran said. 'My . . . influence isn't long-lasting and it certainly doesn't extend over distances. What I offered Montréal was a better deal and safer conditions of transfer, using the Saint Lawrence Seaway. No danger of hijacking, no payoffs to cops or customs, and payment direct to Switzerland. Chapelle explained all that to LoPresti. It was a simple business matter, Don Vicenzu, but your man chose to treat it as a personal affront. He's stupid and shortsighted and vindictive, and so is his animal, Porcaro.'

'I agree,' said Falcone.

The lights in the Opera House were dimming and the

patrons settled down. Applause greeted Maestro López-Cobos as he entered the pit and motioned for the players in the orchestra to rise.

Then there will be peace between Chicago and the Falcone Family, Don Vicenzu?

The don spoke in a harsh whisper. 'I swear it. I swear it.'

And you are a witness to this, Don Guido?

'I am,' said Montedoro.

The hall had become very dark. The conductor raised his baton and the pianissimo notes of an organ began the overture to Act Four of *La Favorita*. LoPresti and Porcaro sat beside Falcone with only the rise and fall of their shirt-fronts signalling life, apparently held in a trance by the two associates of O'Connor who were glaring at the backs of their necks. Kieran rose to his feet and put his right hand on Porcaro's head and his left on LoPresti's. The paralysed men started violently and O'Connor himself suppressed a groan.

This . . . is not revenge, you understand. Only simple justice. A restoration of order. Don Guido, your men should be able to cope with the disposal of this pair without too much difficulty. It will be an educational experience for them. We will send them in on our way out.

And then O'Connor and the two men with him were gone, and the gold brocade curtain opened on the handsome Ming Cho Lee set of a monastery courtyard in Spain. The stage illumination lit the faces of the audience. Falcone was aware of a faint, peculiar odour. He leaned over and saw that the eye sockets of his henchmen had become streaming wells of dark fluid, and that neither man was breathing even though they both sat very straight in their luxurious chairs.

2

Alma-Ata, Kazakh SSR, Earth
10 July 1979

He was the most self-effacing member of the delegation of Indian parapsychology scholars visiting Kazakh State University, and afterwards many staff members at the Bioenergetics Institute (including the Director) denied that he had been there at all. But the truth was that he had been the one who arranged for the tour in the first place, as a pretext for meeting Yuri and Tamara.

The visitors had seen nothing of the laboratory where the young biophysicist and his wife worked, since it was under the Cosmic security classification. Instead they toured the Kirlian facility, where scanning devices purported to monitor the nonphysical aura of living things. Although one or two of the delegates asked indiscreet questions about corona discharge effects and water vapour, most were suitably impressed. In the afternoon there was a tea, presided over by the Director of the Institute, where the delegates were given the opportunity to mingle with the various project supervisors and a few of the percipient subjects whose psychic powers were under analysis. Yuri and Tamara were there, introduced simply as 'biocommunications specialists'. They said very little and slipped away early, and forgot about the group of Indian scholars almost at once. Their attention was fully occupied by the matter of Abdizhamil Simonov. There were rumours that Andropov himself was taking a personal interest in the KGB's inquiry into the mind-controller's sudden death.

That evening, as Tamara was putting little Valery and Ilya to bed, Yuri received a phone call from the Director.

'A distinguished member of the Indian Paraphysics Association tour group has asked for a personal meeting with you and your wife.' The Director's voice was strained and overly formal. 'He was told that such an appointment would be difficult to arrange, since it would have to be approved by Moscow. This did not deter him. He . . .

193

prevailed upon me to phone the Comrade Academician himself with the request. It was approved.'

Yuri could only say, 'How unusual!'

'You will meet this Dr Urgyen Bhotia in the main lobby of the Hotel Kazakhstan as soon as possible. He is a Tibetan resident of Darjeeling, and he wishes to speak to you about certain studies he has made that are relevant to your work. Show him every courtesy.' Before Yuri could respond, the Director hung up.

Tamara came out of the children's bedroom with lifted brows.

He transferred the amazing gist of the conversation to her in an instant, adding: I have no idea what this is all about but we are going to have to see this guru and postpone our discussion with Alla and Mukan until later tonight I'll call them while you get Natasha to babysit.

When everything was arranged, they took a bus across town to the soaring new hotel on Lenin Avenue, where only the most distinguished visitors were housed. No sooner had they come into the air-conditioned lobby than the strangely influential Tibetan was there bowing. He was a short, sturdy man with very brown skin, dressed in crisply pressed trekker's garb.

'Dr Gawrys and Madame Gawrys-Sakhvadze, I am Urgyen Bhotia. I thank you profoundly for coming here, and apologize for causing you inconvenience. I hope you will forgive my summoning you in such a precipitate manner, but I have waited nearly five years for this moment.' *Shall we stroll outside in the cool of the evening?*

Yuri froze in the act of shaking hands. Tamara said: I think that would be wise. Have you taken the cable car up Koktyube Hill?

Not yet but I hear it provides a marvellous view of the city.

Yuri said: You *know* us and our work? How can this be?

The Tibetan laughed and said, 'This is not my first visit to your lovely city of Alma-Ata, but it is my first opportunity to enjoy it with all my physical senses! Let us walk.'

He casually took an arm of each of them when they were outside and guided them across Abai Avenue into the gardens of the Lenin Palace of Culture as though he were the host and they the visitors. The fountains were lit with the coming of dusk and the spray from them was cooling and welcome. A heavy scent of flowers arose from the formal gardens and Urgyen paused to admire them.

'So many lush growing things in this splendid, modern city! The aether sings with vitality.' He might have been any age from forty to sixty. His head was shaved and his cheeks were such a bright red that they might have been rouged. His teeth were very white and perfect and his eyes, almost hidden in a mass of deep creases when he smiled, were an unusual hazel colour.

Tamara said, 'It is clear that you are one of the adept – unlike your colleagues. You will please tell us how you came to know of our psychic faculties and of our work, since both are closely guarded state secrets.'

'I know you,' the Tibetan said, 'because I have been blessed with an ability to perceive the bioplasma of the brightest ones across great distances. My vision extends only throughout Asia. But for more than twenty years now, since leaving Tibet, I have studied the soul manifestation by means of what you would call remote-viewing. I saw the two of you for the first time in 1974, when you were newly come to Alma-Ata, a double mind-star more brilliant than any I had found before. Since then I have watched, I rejoiced in the birth of your two brilliantly ensouled sons, and now I anticipate with you the coming of your third child, a daughter.'

'It *is* a girl?' Tamara exclaimed.

'Most assuredly.' Urgyen searched the faces of the young couple, ruefully acknowledging the mental barricades they had erected against him. 'Please do not be afraid of me. My only wish is to help you at this very difficult time, when you two and the many immature minds under your care find yourselves at a moral crossroads.'

'You say you have watched us,' Yuri stated. 'How close has your astral scrutiny been? Have you read our minds?'

'You know from your own remote-viewing studies that such a thing is impossible. Nor can I read them now unless you freely give access. Nevertheless, I am aware of the temptations bedevilling you and the dangers that you face. I asked myself and the Compassionate Lord if it was my duty to advise you.'

'And what,' Yuri inquired coldly, 'did your heavenly oracle say?'

'I was helped to understand that, in spite of certain inhumane actions you have abetted, you are both persons of goodwill. You have rejected the false joy of the great determinism that hands over the individual conscience to a group and evades personal responsibility. You know you are free, and you know you will have to make choices. Too many people of your nation deny this difficult truth. They do not understand that the human mind must cultivate both soul and spirit if it is to be integral.'

'You will have to explain that,' Yuri said.

They walked on, across the palace concourse and into trees where cicadas were beginning to buzz.

Urgyen said, 'A month ago there was a meeting of leaders in Vienna. The President of the United States and the Soviet President Leonid Brezhnev signed a strategic arms limitation treaty. At one of the their conferences, which took place in the Soviet embassy in Vienna, a person from your Bioenergetics Institute named Simonov exerted coercive and mind-altering force upon the American President, throwing him into a state of confusion and irrationality that still persists . . . The Chairman of your KGB was so elated by Simonov's success that he made arrangements to send the man to Washington, where he would be able to exert his inimical influence upon other American leaders, as ordered. The plan was aborted when Simonov dropped dead while jogging on the university campus.'

'An autopsy showed that his heart was enlarged and weakened,' Yuri said. 'It is a disability that often accompanies great psychic exertion. I myself am under a physician's care for similar symptoms.'

'Exactly,' said Urgyen sadly.

They walked in silence. Ahead was the brightly lit funicular station, the goal of many other evening strollers.

Tamara said, 'Abdizhamil Simonov was a tribal shaman before he was recruited to the Institute, a petty and vicious man who resisted all our efforts to dissuade him from cooperating in Andropov's scheme. He was half mad, a menace to world peace. The KGB thought they could control him, but we knew they could not.'

Urgyen nodded. 'There was also Ryrik Volzhsky, a strong coercer and an incorrigible corrupter of children. You have in your special programme at the Institute more than sixty youthful psychics. When Volzhsky persuaded your Director to assign him to the pedagogical staff, both of you admonished him to restrain himself. He laughed. Two days later he was found drowned in the Bolshaya Alma-Atinka River.'

'The normals can only agonize in their impotence when confronted by evil,' Yuri said. 'They can only utter foolish curses or wish the destruction of the wicked. We are more fortunate.'

'The soul would say so, but not the spirit,' said the Tibetan.

They came to the ticket office, where Yuri paid. Then the three of them got into one of the crowded red-and-yellow cablecars. The other holidaymakers made room for pregnant Tamara near the window, and a moment later they were soaring up the hillside, suspended in the clear air, with the discussion now relegated to telepathy.

Yuri said: So you presume to judge me and castigate me with your pious Eastern word-play . . . Soul and spirit! Talk instead of life and death! Talk of a pair of fearful children become the toys of power-corrupted old men who would use marvellous mind-powers as weapons rather than dedicate them to the good of humanity!

Urgyen said: But if you kill even in a cause that seems just are you any better than your oppressors?

Tamara said: We regretted the deaths bitterly. Yuri acted only after serious reflection.

Urgyen said: In Tibet in the eleventh century the poet Milarepa had mental powers like yours. He was able to strike his enemies dead from afar. But only after he renounced his usurpation of god-power did he become a saint.

Yuri said: We aren't saints. We are only persons wanting

to survive. Yes I killed and because I am a Pole and a Catholic I was tormented and I wish there had been another way but there was not. Once I was timid little Jerzy snatched from my parents in Lodz bullied and cajoled into mental slavery thinking there was no helping it. Then came Tamara! In Leningrad the scientists studied us and tested us and the military men tried to convince us that our duty was unquestioning loyalty and service to the state. But Tamara knew better and helped me to know also. Her dear father was exiled because he dared to protest and publicize the GRU's treatment of us and of other psychics.

Urgyen said: Your unhappy memories are clear to me . . . and I see what you are reluctant to state directly: that even then you thought it necessary to kill . . .

Yuri said: Why can't you understand!

Tamara said: There was a cold-blooded brute the chief of the GRU. Yes he was the first. He would have locked us away treated us as equipment rather than human beings to further his ambition. We were to be his secret weapon to spy with remote-vision on Chairman Andropov of the KGB. When our enemy died the GRU lost control of the psychic-study programme. Andropov and Brezhnev became fervent believers in the mind-powers, coopted the project and promised us and the other adepts that we would now be treated as honoured Soviet citizens. It was 1974. Six months after Papa's exile. I was 16 and Jerzy/Yuri 22. We were given permission to marry and sent to Alma-Ata.

Yuri said: We expected a barbarous outpost in Central Asia with camel caravans and fierce nomads and bazaars. Imagine our surprise at this green new city with the great university where we could study as well as be studied.

Urgyen said: You have acquired knowledge but not wisdom.

Yuri said: Gawno!

Tamara said: Urgyen Bhotia we are not Indians or Tibetans. Our soul does not flinch at the prospect of violence because our people have survived for centuries in violent lands enduring persecution. We know we face grave choices but we have made glorious plans and we are determined to see them carried out. This means defending ourselves if necessary. Yuri and I are the most powerful of all the minds assembled here in the pilot bioenergetics programme. We teach the young ones remote-viewing and convince them to hide their true ability from the KGB evaluators. The programme thus seems to progress very slowly. But the children understand that their minds set them apart that they must work for all the world not only for the Soviet Union.

Urgyen said: If you are the teachers it is that much more important that you reform your erring consciences.

'Here we are at the top of the hill,' Yuri said. 'Come, let us enjoy the view!'

There was an observation platform and a restaurant at the terminus of the cableway, and the other passengers disembarked laughing and exclaiming at the beauty of the panorama. To the north, lost in purple haze, were the steppes of the Virgin Lands, turned into fields and orchards by irrigation. The multicoloured lights of the great city were just beginning to twinkle on while the last sunset glow illuminated the eastern foothills. Behind Koktyube, to the south, was the Zailiysky Ala-Tau, a heavily wooded outlier of the high Tien Shan. China lay only three hundred kilometres beyond.

They stood at the railing, looking out over Alma-Ata. Tamara said, 'The city's name means Father of Apples. There are orchards everywhere, and vineyards. We have come to love this place. At the university, we are trusted. We say the proper things and are circumspect in the use of our higher mind-powers. We can do so much good, Urgyen . . . and someday when other persons like us in other parts of the world are able to reveal themselves and work openly, we will also. Then we will for ever renounce the self-defensive violence that we have been forced to resort to. I swear it.'

'You know there are many others, many minds with these powers,' Urgyen said. 'But do you know that there is a World Mind, of which you and I and the others, whether highly empowered or lowly, partake?'

'We know there is the Great Soul,' Tamara said. 'My many-times-great-grandfather told me of it when I was a child. Now we would call it the Conscious Field of Humanity. Some persons call it God.'

'It is not God,' said the Tibetan. 'God is spirit and cannot be infected by evil. But the World Soul can . . . and this is why I came to plead with you.'

Yuri cried: Soul! Spirit! Tell us plainly what you mean!

'I will try,' said the Tibetan. 'Years ago, when I was a monk called Urgyen Rimpoche and practised my mind-powers proudly, I thought I was one blessed by the gods, a living miracle who had the right to command heaven. I was young! In the turmoil that my poor country suffered during the Chinese invasion of the 1950s, my attempts to coerce divinity and repel the invaders were futile. Our little monastery was utterly demolished and we were beaten and called parasites by the Red soldiers. Of course, they were right . . . I had confused soul with spirit. So had my brother monks who had prospered and enjoyed prestige by cele-brating my talents. Along with many of my countrymen, I fled to India. After suffering much and losing my psychic abilities because of self-doubts, I began to acquire wisdom. The first thing I took to heart was the realization that the soul and its powers are not supernatural. They are no miracle. They are part of the natural human heritage and all people have them in greater or lesser degree.'

'We have also come to that conclusion,' said Tamara.

Urgyen said, 'The soul is neither physical nor spiritual. But it is still part of matter's realm, born with certain coalescences of matter and energy. Even atoms have a minute portion of soul! Higher organisms have much more. And there is a World Soul — '

'Do you speak of a World Mind?' Yuri asked.

'No, no. That comes later, with the infusion of spirit! But let me go on . . . The soul feels but it cannot know. It is — as most thinkers have recognized — feminine: life-giving, as patient and enduring as planet Earth whose soul-essence is part of each one of us. Living things form a hierarchy of soul, first tropistic, then sentient. Plants and animals. In us, souls dream and imagine and fantasize and create. They remember and they fear. They are basically passive and amoral. When the soul is properly entuned, its powers may move matter and change it. Sometimes the human soul swells large and begets ultrasenses, or a coercive will, or mental control of matter and energy, or the reorganization of dysfunctioning mind or body that we call healing.'

'Tell us how mind relates to soul,' Yuri demanded.

'Only in thinking creatures is the soul infused with spirit, making a mind.'

'And spirit is what?' Tamara asked.

'It does not belong to the realm of matter. We may call it divine, but it is of a different order of reality. It enkindles the intellect, orders all things in our minds, impels us upward as flames rise. It is masculine: impregnating and driving, engendering discipline, truth, wisdom and law. It makes thinking creatures yearn towards a higher reality, what I would call the face of God. It knows good and evil. It strives to unite in love with other minds and to form the World Mind. But it can be debased. Its impulse towards increasing organization can be crippled, even halted.'

They said: We do not understand. Especially we do not understand why you say WE threaten your World Mind.

'Look around you,' Urgyen invited. 'You see the terraced mountains with their forests and orchards, and you see a modern city. The mountains were upthrust ages ago, and slowly they are being worn down. The trees and other plant-life spring up from seed and grow – but when growth stops, they will die. The city of Alma-Ata is only the latest of many human settlements in the Valley of the Seven Rivers. Others flourished for a time, but when they stopped growing, they died. Growth! Evolution if you like, with life and mind organizing itself at ever-higher levels! If Mind does not grow, it will also die. My dear Tamara and Yuri, you are the vanguard of the planetary Mind, together with the others like you. It is so simple: you must be better than those who came before because spirit must grow as well as soul in the evolving World Mind. Without growth, there can only be death. If you, the leading shoots of your growing species, become corrupt, you will tend to corrupt the entire Mind.'

Yuri exclaimed: You would have us submit tamely to our enemies? Die rather than kill in self-defence?

Yes.

Tamara said: You want us to be like Mahatma Gandhi. But our system of values says we have a right to kill mortal enemies.

True . . . and yet your Avatar allowed his enemies to kill him.

Yuri said: We are not martyrs! We have a great plan and it requires living leaders. You yourself said it: We are the vanguard we can lead the world to peace!

Never if you kill to prevail. Never if you use the mind-powers that way. Think! What was hard in the beginning becomes more and more easy. Think! The once stricken conscience becomes dulled. Think! Who are you going to lead? Your peers? What of the lesser minds? What if they fear you and will not follow? Will you coerce and kill? Think of your children watching you and learning. Think.

Tamara said: Urgyen your message is hard to hear harder to accept. I don't know if I can accept it. But I do believe it . . .

Her husband rounded on her. 'How can you? After all we have suffered together – how can you?'

She placed her hand on her swollen body. Inside, the foetus leapt. 'I think it has to do with motherhood,' she said.

Urgyen nodded and smiled. 'Yes. And fatherhood.'

Yuri looked from one to the other in confusion. Both of their minds were open to him, showing. But he still could not understand.

3

Supervisory Cruiser Noumenon [Lyl 1–0000]
10 July 1979

'The former lama shows a coadunate sensitivity rare among humans,' said Eupathic Impulse. 'How gratifying.'

'He typifies an abhorrence of violence found mainly among Easterners of the Buddhist persuasion,' Homologous Trend said, 'and among the English. The trait is, as one has noted, regrettably uncommon.'

'Making the coadunation of the World Mind that much more unlikely,' Asymptotic Essence said.

'In the unlikelihood is the greatest glory,' said the poet, Noetic Concordance.

'All very well for one to look on the bright side of a situation that's hopeless,' Impulse said.

'One supposes that it was inevitable that perverse operants, such as the lamentable O'Connor, would use their higher mind-powers aggressively and for personal gain,' Trend observed. 'Such flawed personalities, are, after all, outside of the mainstream of mental evolution. But one regrets most deeply that a pivotal operant such as Yuri Gawrys, so estimable in other respects, has seen fit to use his metafaculties to kill.'

'The temptation was overwhelming to one of his mind-set,' Essence said.

'One fears he does not represent an isolated case,' Impulse added. 'On the contrary, he is probably typical, given that the most dynamic of the irrupting operant minds share the moral view of the West, not the East. Even Yuri's mate Tamara, inculcated with gentleness and true coadunate principles during her formative years, and assenting intellectually to the truth of the Tibetan's admonition, will undoubtedly succumb to the use of violence under extreme provocation. Human females will kill to defend their children even as they counsel them to embrace peace.'

Noetic Concordance radiated sorrow. 'Then the Tibetan's warning was in vain?'

'One may hope,' Trend said, 'that his message will have a positive influence upon other human minds at a more favourable point in mental evolution.'

'Strange,' Asymptotic Essence mused, 'that the lama should have so fortuitously conceived this advanced insight, and gone counter to his naturally retiring disposition to deliver it to Yuri and Tamara. If one had not noted the Tibetan's indubitably authentic mental signature, one might be forgiven for suspecting that he was none other than Unifex, masquerading again in human guise.'

'Indeed one might!' Concordance agreed.

'Now there is an oddity,' Eupathic Impulse remarked. 'That It should take pleasure in simply walking among the lower life-forms!'

'It empathizes so closely with them,' said Concordance. 'Should one be surprised when It assumes their physical form?'

'Yes,' Impulse said shortly. 'Krondaku may do so routinely, but it violates dignity and custom for a Lylmik to take on the material aspect of a client race.'

'One is being a bit stuffy,' Trend suggested.

'And one should remember,' Concordance appended, 'that It is in love.'

'It is in New Hampshire even now,' said Essence, 'having completed Its contemplation of the supernova in the Soulpto Group that threatened to irradiate the planet of the Shoridai. It saved them by interposing a gas-cloud – then sped back to Earth when It perceived an urgent necessity to harangue its slow-witted catspaw.'

'*That* one,' said Impulse darkly. 'He would have used the powers to kill also, if he had not been restrained. The very agent of Unifex – a reprobate!'

Noetic Concordance's mind smiled. 'Oh, I don't know. He rather grows on one.'

4

From the Memoirs of
Rogatien Remillard

Milieu biographies of my nephew Denis have covered the latter years of his childhood in considerable detail, thanks not only to his diaries but also to the reminiscences of his teachers and fellow students. For this reason I intend to highlight only a few incidents from that time.

First, let me correct a persistent error. Denis was never seriously endangered by Pentagon or CIA zealots seeking to utilize his talents for intelligence gathering or experiments in 'psychotronic' aggression. Other young operants *did* suffer from the compulsory enlistment attempts of official (and highly unofficial) groups; but Denis went unharassed, thanks to his Jesuit protectors at Brebeuf Academy and later to the Dartmouth Coterie, who formed an ad hoc Praetorian Guard as well as a circle of intimate friends during Denis's college years.

One story I must tell deals with the way Denis finally made contact with the Coterie and his other early operant associates, using a method so crude that he was too embarrassed even to mention it when he became a respected academic. His biographers assume that he instinctively used the declamatory mode of farspeech, calling out in a generalized fashion. They seem to think that when his developing powers reached an adequate level, numbers of isolated operants automatically responded.

The truth is otherwise – and much more droll.

After our encounter with Elaine Harrington, Denis was firmly convinced of the existence of other operants, and he made many attempts to contact them via telepathy. Working together, the boy and I checked out his 'broadcast range' by the simple expedient of having him bespeak me as I travelled to prearranged New England locales. Although intervening mountain ranges tended to block or interfere with his mental messages, as did the sun and electrical storms, we discovered that Denis could farspeak me reliably over a distance of more than a hundred kilometres. When he operated out of Brebeuf near Concord in central New Hampshire, as he usually did, he could theoretically blanket our own state, plus Vermont, Massachusetts, Rhode Island, and most of Connecticut – as well as a fair-sized chunk of Maine and those parts of upper New York that weren't shielded by the Adirondacks. Our record long-distance exchange during his school years covered 166 kilometres, between Brebeuf and East Hampton, Long Island, where I visited friends in 1977.

Nevertheless, in spite of his success in farspeaking me, Denis had no luck at all in contacting other telepaths using a generalized broad-spectrum hail. His mental CQs remained futile howls into an aetheric rain-barrel, messages lacking addresses, until that day in 1978 when we first tried the seriocomic tactic I dubbed Operation Witch Hazel.

It was in November, when Denis was eleven and in his final term of study at the academy. I had come down on a delicate and rather sticky mission: to break the bad news to Fathers Ellsworth and Dubois that their prize prodigy would not, after all, be matriculating at Georgetown University next year as they had hoped – and quite taken for granted. Denis himself had no objections to attending the Jesuit institution. It had a fine medical school and its faculty, secretly briefed by my nephew's clerical mentors, was quite willing to accommodate a twelve-year-old genius with a supernormal psyche.

But the Ghost had other ideas.

My interview with the good fathers was an uncomfortable one. Following the Ghost's suggestion, I told Ellsworth and Dubois that Georgetown, being situated in Washington DC, was too susceptible to infiltration by government agents or other parties who might take an unhealthy interest in Denis's talents. (This manoeuvre of mine was undoubtedly the source of later rumours that Denis was actually pursued by unscrupulous psychological-warfare specialists.) The priests were deeply disappointed when I told them that I had already arranged for Denis to enter Dartmouth College, a venerable Ivy League school in western New Hampshire. My arguments in favour of Dartmouth must have had a paranoid flavour – and even worse, smacked of ingratitude after the special pains taken by the Brebeuf faculty in the first five years of the boy's education. The two priests tried hard to change my mind; but I had my orders, and so I prevailed. With Don's total abdication of responsibility, I was Denis's de facto guardian and the decision was mine to make. In the end, I cheered them up. Dartmouth was a small college but it did have a school of medicine sympathetic to the concept of metapsychic research. It was nearby, in the beautiful town of Hanover on the Connecticut River. It had been founded in 1769 and numbered among its alumni such luminaries as Daniel Webster and Dr Seuss. Above all, because of its quixotic and individualistic atmosphere, it was about the last place in the world likely to be infiltrated by the CIA, the lackeys of the military-industrial establishment – or the KGB. So the matter was settled.

With the Ellsworth-Dubois ordeal behind me, I was glad to escape by taking Denis for a stroll into the grey and leafless woodland adjacent to the Brebeuf campus. The clouds hung low and there was a smell of snow in the air. Early frosts had withered the low-growing plant-life. Fragile rinds of ice crusted the puddles along the path. The boy and I walked for an hour or so, discussing Dartmouth and making plans to visit it over the upcoming Thanksgiving vacation. Then the conversation turned to a vexatious old topic: Denis's continuing futile attempts to farspeak other telepaths.

'I've been thinking over the *theory* of telepathic communication,' the boy said. 'Trying to discover why you and I can farspeak over long distances – while I have no luck when I call out to others.' He detoured so as to walk through a deep drift of maple leaves, kicking them into the air with childish satisfaction. 'The first possibility – and the most rotten! – is that there simply aren't any receptive minds within my telepathic radius. I just can't believe that. I *feel* them out there! They're probably unaware of their powers for the most part, but some of them might have a gut conviction that they're different from the rank and file of humanity . . . Now the second possibility: The minds are there but they don't hear me for some reason. I have to find out why my transmissions don't reach them even though I can farspeak you.'

Little chickadees, lingering tardily in the woods before their annual withdrawal to town and farmyard during fast winter, sang as we crunched along. I said, 'The problem might simply be that your closet telepaths aren't listening! Look how we ignore the sounds made by these birds while we concentrate on each other's voices.'

'That's a good point. The unknowns out there aren't expecting a telepathic message. They don't think such things are possible. So when farspeech inadvertently reaches them, they may not recognize it for what it is. They could think it was a daydream, or some notion cooked up by their own brains, or even a ghost or something.'

'Mm,' I said.

'If they were seriously expecting a farspoken message it would be entirely different. You know that our own headskeds were carefully planned. We were both alert and waiting at the time we'd arranged to communicate – and I knew where you would be. It didn't matter that your mind has a relatively puny receptive faculty — '

'Thank you very much!'

His solemn little face broke into a grin. 'Nothing personal. Your mind is a weak telepathic transmitter and you're not a very sensitive receiver. But my mind makes up for it. I put out a high-powered signal that you can read, and I listen for you with an ultrasensitive mental antenna. Theoretically, I should be able to bespeak other weak or untrained telepaths – if only they knew enough to listen to me.'

His mind flashed a farcical display advertisement:

TELEPATHS OF THE WORLD!
TUNE IN YOUR MENTAL EARS
WITHOUT FAIL
NEXT TUESDAY, 8:00 P.M. EST
FOR AN IMPORTANT ANNOUNCEMENT!

He added aloud, 'Of course we'd never dare do it. And even if we did, the very people we wanted most to reach would ignore it completely.'

'Eventually there will be a public acknowledgement,' I said. 'You *will* be able to discuss the powers openly someday . . .'

He nodded. 'When I'm grown up, and I have my research facility and a suitable aura of academic respectability.' The irony on his young face was almost tragic. 'But it's so tempting to take a short cut!'

'You're talking like a child.'

He wryly agreed. Then he gave me a sidelong look. 'You've saved me from making a lot of mistakes, Uncle Rogi. I'm just beginning to understand that. And the way you got me away from Papa – to this school, where I'd be safe and able to grow. Now this business of going to Dartmouth instead of Georgetown. I trust your judgement and you know I'd never try to probe your motivation. But I hope that someday . . .'

All I said was, 'At the proper time.'

He sighed. We walked along in vocal and mental silence for several minutes, and then he returned to our previous topic of discussion.

'I've thought of another reason why my farspeech might not reach other telepaths; signal incompatible with receiver. The AM/FM thing.'

'Could be,' I agreed. 'Our voices can whisper, talk, yell, sing. Why shouldn't there be different modes of telepathic output?'

'I believe there must be at least two. You know, when we're home in Berlin, how you and I can bespeak each other without Papa or Victor listening in? That's a sort of private mode. But there's a public mode, too – the way we farspeak when the message comes to you and me and Papa and Victor all at once.'

He stopped walking, frowned, and cogitated. Then he said, 'What if that private kind of telepathy is the most efficient kind? What if it's coherent farspeech, say, sort of like a laser beam of light! Public mode might be more like a streetlamp – casting light in all directions but only illuminating a small, nearby area. You need a tight beam for lighting up faraway objectives. Maybe thoughts need to be beamed, too.'

'Makes sense.'

His face went gloomy. 'But if that's true, then my random telepathic calls can never work. I don't know how I aim the beam . . . I suppose I recognize your mind-pattern and tune to it in some instinctive way when we go private, or when we do long-distance farspeaking. But how will I ever find out the mental signatures of unknown telepaths?' He was thinking hard, and in a moment he brightened. 'I bet they'd hear me if I spoke in public mode right up close to them! Then I wouldn't need any signature. After all, I heard Elaine okay when she was half a mile away on Mount Washington that first time, and later she could hear me when we were a couple hundred yards apart. Funny, though. I never seemed to be able to go private with her.'

I let that one lie. 'You can hardly travel all over the country farshouting in crowds, hoping to scratch up other telepaths. It would be prohibitively expensive, slow, and boring beyond belief.'

'There ought to be another ultrasense for locating people,' the boy growled. 'A seekersense.'

We were going downhill, towards a little brook. The low ground had moisture-loving red dogwoods and occasional small thickets of witch hazel. The clouds opened briefly, letting a shaft of sunlight lance down, and from a distance it seemed that the leafless branches were wrapped in a yellow haze. Then I realized that the witch hazel shrubs were in bloom. I pointed out the phenomenon mentally to Denis. It was a small bit of botanical sorcery repeated every late fall in the New England woods.

'Weird old witch hazel,' Denis said. 'No wonder the early folks thought it was magic.'

'That's why they used it for dowsing, I guess. You can find water by divining with just about any kind of wooden rod, or even a piece of wire. But the experts say that nothing works quite so well as a branch of witch hazel. I remember reading about one dowser who could find water just by moving a forked witch hazel stick over a *map*.'

'It's your mind that does the finding,' the boy said absently. 'The stick probably just helps you to focus the —' He broke off abruptly. His eyes met mine and we found ourselves mind-shouting in unison:

Seekersense!

'The guy really used a map?' Denis whispered.

I nodded. 'Found water on the island of Bermuda, as I recall. From here in the States.'

'It's a cockamamie idea. Totally bananas. To think that I might be able to dowse out telepaths with a forked stick and a road map.'

'Only,' I said pointedly; 'if you believe you can. But it can't hurt to try. I have a large-scale Delorme Atlas of New Hampshire in my Volvo . . .'

'Even if I did manage to find people, we'd still have to

drive to the place where they were so I could send out a public-type hail. We'd still have to do some hunting.'

'It can be managed,' I told him, 'Provided you don't turn up eight hundred prospects.' I reached into my pocket for my trusty penknife, and led the giggling boy into a witch hazel thicket to select a suitable forked stick.

I only saw a water dowsing operation once, and that was on television back in the '50s when I was just a kid. The programme was one of those down-around-home local documentaries that were common then, and featured a famous 'water-witch' from Hancock in the southern part of the state. I remember being disappointed, after the narrator's exciting build-up, when the witch turned out to be a balding elderly man with a lantern-jawed Yankee face and eyeglasses framed in black plastic. His clothes were unexceptional and his manner laconic – until he took up his forked stick.

In the experiment, a fifty-five-gallon drum full of water had been buried six feet deep in a freshly ploughed area of field. The witch held his Y-shaped divining rod by the two short arms and extended the thing ahead of him as he slowly walked up and down the furrows. The camera showed close-ups of his face, staring at the ground with rapt attention, eyes wide behind the eyeglass lenses, sweat beading his forehead. Then the camera pulled back and we saw the witch plodding towards us, stick outstretched.

And the point of the stick suddenly dipped down.

There didn't seem to have been any causative movement of the old man's hands: the stick just revolved a bit and pointed to an area near the witch's feet. The tiniest glimmer of a smile crossed his lips. He backed up, let the stick rise, then walked over the spot once again. A dip. He approached the spot from the sides. As if with a life of its own, the stick turned down perpendicular to the earth.

'I reckon she's there,' said the witch.

Two sturdy fellows with shovels stepped forward and the soft dirt began to fly. In a few minutes the drum lay revealed in an open pit; its bung was removed and water gurgled from it. The witch allowed as how he could find water 'mebbe eighty per cent of the time'. He was the fourth generation of his family to have the gift and apparently the last. His children and grandchildren, he said, lacked confidence. Then he added, 'But there ain't much call for water-witching nowadays anyhow. Folks feel a little foolish about it. They'd rather call in a geologist – nevvamind he hands 'em a whoppin' bill for his services, so long's he's *scientific*. But the old way still works . . .'

It worked for Denis, too – but only after six months of self-training. I watched him mind-hunting many times, first using the atlas, later poring over a series of aerial photos I'd purchased for him at the cost of an arm and a leg. I had very little seekersense myself (youthful experiments in imitation of the water-witch had proved that), but it was possible for me to share the boy's search by means of our mental rapport. He would sit at a table in a species of trance, the forked twig moving slowly over the surface of the map, and what passed through his mind was almost magical.

We have all flown in aircraft at night and looked down on the scattered jewel-lights that mark towns and settlements. The higher one is, the more indistinct the luminous splotch; but descend, and the individual streetlamps and lighted windows and slowly moving ground-cars become clearly visible. Denis's seeking looked rather like a night flight, when seen by my mind's eye. When he first began to hunt he sensed only bright fuzzy masses that signified concentrations of ordinary mentation: thinking people. But in time he learned to sharpen his focus, to sort the sapient blur into a sparkling collection of separate minds. They were multicoloured, bright and dim, large and small. Just as a dowser for water or minerals visualizes the object of his search, then directs his higher senses to find it, so Denis conjured up the quintessence of 'operant' mental energy and went hunting for it during a variant of the classic out-of-body experience.

The first operants he viewed, in a targeting operation, were his father and his brother Victor in Berlin. Initially it was hard for him to avoid the instinctive use of their mental signatures; but when he had conquered this technical glitch he was able to see the adult mind and the child only as tiny beacons of higher function, distinct in the miasma of normally talented thought. Don's younger children, who numbered six at that time, glowed dim and latent – a tragedy that Denis and I would understand fully only years later. But Don was a fitful variable star and nine-year-old Victor burned like a baleful ember hiding in a half-extinguished campfire.

Denis never farspoke them, never hinted to them what kind of a search he was engaged in. 'It wouldn't be good for them to know,' he told me in that sober, young-old way of his. And of course he was right.

The patient search for kindred spirits began to pay off in June 1979, when he finally located Glenn Dalembert's mind in the congestion of metropolitan Manchester. We set off on a frantic ground-search then, me driving the Volvo and Denis, entranced, sitting beside me with his finger hovering over a tattered aerial survey sheet. (By then he had been able to discard the witch hazel wand, to his manifest relief.) Panic set in when it became evident that our target was on its way *out* of Manchester. A wild chase on the southbound lanes of the turnpike followed, and once we almost lost Glenn; but we bagged him at long last in a hilarious and touching scene at Benson's Wild Animal Park, where he had a summer job coercing elephants in a small circus. The young man reacted to our telepathic revelations with equanimity and took an instant shine to Denis. The boy was stunned to learn that his newfound metapsychic ally was an undergraduate at Dartmouth. Glenn Dalembert became the first member of the now-famed Coterie and would become a champion of metapsychic rights during the dark pre-Intervention years.

A few weeks after finding Glenn, Denis tracked down the second Coterie stalwart, Sally Doyle, in her home at Troy. She was a minor celebrity in her hometown because of a knack for finding lost persons and things. She had graduated valedictorian of her high school class that year, and in the fall (quelle surprise!) she was to enter Dartmouth. Once again Denis was astonished at the coincidence. I, as you might imagine, remained unruffled.

We located only two other operants that summer. One was an elderly invalid, Odette Kleinfelter, whom we nearly frightened into cardiac arrest with our telepathic greeting – and hastily disqualified from recruitment. The other contactee was a Nashua girl a year younger than Denis. When we confronted her, she fixed Denis with a redoubtable glare and snapped: 'I suppose you think you're pretty smart!' Except for her metapsychic gifts, which we did not fully appreciate at that time, she seemed a bright but unexceptional child with that streak of mulish stubbornness that occasionally characterizes Franco-American females. Denis was leery of her, and for some years she would remain on the periphery of the growing body of young operants. In 1979 there was no hint of the girl's future role in the metapsychic drama. Her name was Lucille Cartier, and one day she would become Denis's closest colleague, his wife, and the mother of the Seven Founding Magnates of the Human Polity of the Concilium. But that was far in the future, and I will reserve Lucille's story until a later point in this narrative.

That fall, shepherded by Glenn Dalembert and Sally Doyle, Denis entered Dartmouth College. His seekersense quickly pinpointed three other suboperants among the student body, who were gathered into the Coterie through telepathic rapport. Two of these, a senior named Mitch Losier and a sophomore named Colette Roy, had been entirely unaware of their psychic talents until close contact with Denis brought about an accelerated floraison. The third, Tukwila Barnes, was a Puyallup tribesman from Washington state. At the time of Denis's matriculation Tukwila was a seventeen-year-old junior in the college's premed programme, a genius well aware of his talent for hands-on healing and soul-travel who was wise enough not to acknowledge his unorthodox skills publicly. He was a wary mind-screener who completely eluded Denis's dowsing, and only revealed himself after observing the activities of the Coterie for more than six months.

As Denis devoured the undergraduate curriculum in three hectic terms, he found time to ferret out three more operants whom he induced to enrol at Dartmouth. Gerard Tremblay was a happy-go-lucky worker in a Vermont granite quarry, nineteen years old, with no idea that he was a suboperant telepath. Gordon McAllister, the only one of the Coterie who would choose physics over psychology or psychiatry, was twenty-six and operating the family potato farm in Maine when he was tapped. He had always known that he was a bit fey, but out of filial piety had repressed his psychic tendencies as frivolous and unPresbyterian. The final, and oldest, Coterie member was Eric Boutin, who had worked for nearly ten years as the service manager in a Ford dealership in Manchester before Denis discovered him. Boutin's boss wept unashamedly when the most uncanny diagnostician of auto malfunction in the state of New Hampshire enrolled as a Dartmouth freshman at the age of thirty.

Denis received his Bachelor of Arts degree in June of 1980, applauded by me, his Coterie, his mother, and a goodly contingent of Remillard relations. Don did not attend. In 1983, when Denis was a mature and self-possessed sixteen, he was awarded an MD from Dartmouth Medical School. This time I escorted to the ceremony not only Sunny but also eight of her children – including the infant, Pauline. Twenty-four other Remillards made the journey to Hanover to celebrate the triumph of the family prodigy. Don, however, suffered a diplomatic attack of flu and remained in Berlin, attended by the adolescent Victor. They were not greatly missed.

Although Denis (as well as his Coterie) kept his extraordinary psychic powers under wraps during his study years, he continued to give his associates informal training. Mitch Losier, a methodical type who quickly became a seekersense adept, continued to trace other suboperants. Many of these were enticed to Dartmouth and eventually helped form the first North American operant nucleus. Denis served his three years' residency in psychiatry at the Mental Health Center associated with the college, and simultaneously took PhD degrees in psychology and mathematics (the latter in the field of cybernetics). His intellectual precocity had attracted considerable public attention, of course, and certain anonymous benefactors helped to finance the first small ESP research facility that he set up and supervised as a postdoctoral fellow.

For the next three years Denis worked with numbers of operant and suboperant metapsychics in this modest little laboratory. Members of his Coterie contrived to join him as they completed their own studies and residencies, sacrificing financial security for the advancement of mental science. During this time of metapsychic pioneering Denis published half a dozen cautious papers and skirted the morass of premature publicity that might have fatally tainted his image. Persistent media snoops – and there were some – were summarily dealt with by the mettlesome Boutin and McAllister, the designated enforcers of the Coterie. More subtle attempts at probing were sidetracked by certain persons high in the administration of the Dartmouth Medical School, who realized what a unique talent the college was harbouring.

As rumours of remarkable psychic activities at Dartmouth strengthened, hard-nosed investigators attempted an end run around Denis by importuning his father. Don was then attempting to operate a small logging business, having been fired from the mill for intractable alcoholism. The sensation-seekers were discouraged by bilingual curses and the menaces of Victor, who was by then a hulking youth with a notably malevolent demeanour. Denis had made many attempts to bring Victor into his own circle of young operants, but without success. Victor's coercive faculty had come on strong, together with a raging jealousy of his older brother. He wanted nothing to do with higher education or metapsychic experimentation. Eventually he dropped out of high school and joined Don in the woods.

In 1989, having established himself as one of the premier psychic researchers in the country, Dr Denis Remillard was admitted to the Dartmouth Medical School faculty as a research associate with the rank of Associate Professor of Psychiatry (Parapsychology). He was by that time twenty-three years old, almost totally alienated from his father and brother Victor, and committed to the work that would occupy him for the rest of his life . . . until his great mind was lost to humanity and the rest of the Galactic Milieu in the prelude to the Metapsychic Rebellion.

5

Alma-Ata, Kazakh SSR, Earth
18 January 1984

Only old Pyotr Sakhvadze noticed the earthquake.

The rest of the spectators and the crowd of ice skaters in Medeo Stadium were completely oblivious. Any faint seismic whisper would have been drowned out by the loud-speakers playing the waltz from *Yevgeniy Onyegin* and the shouting of the children. It is true that the side walls of the gaily ornamented yurta warming tents out on the ice swayed a little, and their horsehair tassels danced; but that might just as easily have been caused by a stray gust from the Zailiyskiy Ala-Tau intruding for a moment into the ice-rink's sheltered bowl.

But Pyotr knew better.

He was newly come to the Central Asian metropolis of Alma-Ata to live with his daughter Tamara and his son-in-law Yuri Gawrys and their three children, after nearly ten years of exile in Ulan-Ude, ministering to the mental-health needs of the Buryat Mongols. On this winter after-noon he was performing grandfatherly duties, shepherding Valery, Ilya and Anna – who were nine, seven and four years of age – on a skating outing at Medeo. Pyotr had nearly begged off going because of the sick headache that had plagued him for the past two days; but the youngsters would have been very disappointed, and he wanted so much for them to learn to love him that he pretended he felt better. He drove them in Tamara's red Zhiguli up to the big alpine sports complex in the foothills south of the city. Medeo's rink was world-class, and so cleverly sited that even in midwinter one could usually skate in comfort without bundling up. The three children had joined the throng out on the ice, leaving Pyotr to watch from a front row of the stands.

He had huddled there nursing his headache in silent misery for nearly two hours, feeling cold in spite of the tatty fur greatcoat and shapka he had brought from Siberia. He sipped mint tea from an insulated bottle, felt very sorry for himself, and wondered if he had made a serious mistake allowing his daughter to 'rescue' him from exile. Ulan-Ude wasn't the Russian Riviera like Sochi; but the Mongols were a vigorous and good-humoured lot and the psychic dabblings of their shamans were strictly apolitical . . . unlike those of Tamara and her high-strung Polish husband.

The headache grew worse, nauseating him with the pain. At last, when it seemed his poor head would explode, his eyes began to play tricks on him. The sunset-tinged snowy slopes that overhung the stadium started to shimmer, throwing off aurora-like beams of an unnatural green colour, and the bare rock areas were haloed with eerie violet. He felt the slight vibration of the earth tremor through the sensitive base of his spine and at the same time a lance of white agony seared his vision. He groaned out loud and tottered in his seat, nearly spilling the bottle of tea.

And then, a miracle!

His head cleared and was free of pain. The strange aura effect cut off abruptly. His muzzy brain snapped into a keen state of cognition. An earthquake! Yes! And accompanied by the same mental phenomena he had experienced twice before, in 1966 at the disastrous psychiatric conference in Tashkent, and just last year in Siberia, when a minor temblor had rocked the Lake Baikal basin.

It could not be a coincidence. It was a species of extra-sense! And he shouted:

You see, children? I am one of you after all! This proves that I, too, have the soul-power!

Dizziness overcame him and he lost track of reality until he heard the anxious voice of Valery, his oldest grandson.

'Dedushka? Are you feeling all right? We . . . we heard you cry out.'

Pyotr was aware of the cheerful music again, and he saw the two boys and their little sister standing in front of him in their bright jackets and knit hats with pompoms. Their breath was coming in quick cloudy puffs and their dark eyes were wide with astonishment. A couple of adult skaters had also stopped because of the evident concern of the children, and a sturdy woman in a blue speed-suit asked, 'Any problem here, comrade?'

'No, I'm fine,' Pyotr forced himself to say, giving a chuckle that was nearly giddy. 'I nodded off and nearly slid out of my seat. Silly of me.'

The adults paid no more attention to him but his grandchildren crowded closer. Pyotr could sense the swift telepathic exchange passing between Valery and Ilya. Their faces were distant, almost frightening in their maturity. But little Anna reached out to him with mittened hands, smiling, her cheeks as shiny as the Aport apples for which Alma-Ata was famous.

'Your head feels better now, doesn't it, Dedushka?'

He squeezed her hands gently. 'Much better, little angel. In fact – I think I have made a wonderful discovery!'

Ilya was almost accusing. 'We heard your mind shout to us. There was a strange image, too.'

'Didn't you feel the ground tremble while you were skating?' Pyotr asked. 'There was a small earthquake – and I perceived it with both my body and my mind!'

'I didn't feel anything, Grandfather,' Valery said.

'Are you sure you didn't imagine it?' Ilya said.

Anna piped shyly, 'I think I felt it, Dedushka. Was it sort of bright, and deep-down?'

'Yes, exactly!' Pyotr swept up the child, skates and all, and kissed her resoundingly. Then he crouched with a serious expression and told the three of them, 'I detected the faint preliminaries to the earth tremor with some kind of an extrasense, and the actual shock, the discharge of seismic energy, was translated into a visual phenomenon. It's just as the village elder Seliac said more than twenty years ago: I, too, have the soul! I am one of you! A true extrasensor!'

The children stared at him blankly. Their minds shared

subliminal comments that were as incomprehensible to Pyotr as the twittering of bats.

'Don't you see?' the old man said desperately. 'My terrible headache was part of it, and I saw coloured auras around the rocks as well. The important point is, I've had this type of experience before just prior to earthquakes, but I never realized its significance. Now I'm positive! Yes! It must be some new kind of psychic power – different from the telepathy or psychokinesis or out-of-body travel that your parents study at the Bioenergetics Institute. We must go home at once and tell them about it! It will be a wonderful surprise, and now perhaps they won't feel I'm such a useless burden — '

'You aren't a burden, Grandfather,' Valery said, but his smile was remote.

'Do we have to go home?' Ilya's mouth turned down at the corners. 'You said we'd stay until eighteen hours. I want to skate some more. *I* didn't feel any earthquake.'

Valery gave him a poke.

Anna threw her arms around Pyotr's legs and peered up at him. 'I know you have the soul, Dedushka. Never mind what *they* think.'

A coldness crept over Pyotr. The colourful whirl of skaters was growing shadowy as dusk fell, and the music now seemed harsh. All of a sudden the great banks of stadium floodlights flashed on, nearly blinding him with their reflection off the ice. Could he have imagined the entire episode? Was it only the wish-fulfillment of a septuagenarian fool? Or – more ominously – might he have suffered a small stroke? (The symptoms were suggestive, even to a rusty psychiatrist like himself.)

'There was a small earthquake,' he said firmly. It was real, my children! Believe me don't shut me out read it in my memories accept my mind-opening accept me . . .

They stood in a row looking at him, opaque – even the dear little Anna – seeming to weigh him among themselves. He tried to relax. He tried with all his heart to love them and not fear them, this new generation for whom he had suffered so much, whose freedom he had championed at the cost of his own liberty and professional advancement.

It had been rather easy to do when the truly alien young minds were yet unborn, when there were only Tamara and Yuri (then called Jerzy) and a handful of other frightened, gifted ones in danger of exploitation by the military and the GRU fanatics under Kolinsky. Pyotr had demanded that they be treated as Soviet citizens, not guinea pigs; and through his international professional contacts he had publicized some of the dubious directions that psychic research was taking in his country during the late 1960s and '70s. He had sounded warnings – and he had been silenced. But things changed for the better.

The children stared. Anna smiled first, and then Valery, and finally Ilya, who said:

'Yes, let's go home and tell Mama and Papa.'

'Zamechatel'no!' Pyotr whispered, lowering his head so they would not see his tears. Then they all trooped down to the cloakroom.

When they arrived at the big apartment in the new university quarter of Alma-Ata, the children ran down the hall ahead of Pyotr and burst into the kitchen where Tamara and Yuri were preparing dinner together, as was their custom when Yuri did not feel too exhausted after work. The unmistakable aroma of homemade kielbasa permeated the room, and Tamara was just lifting kachapuri, delectable Georgian cheese tarts, from the oven. With a great deal of shouting and jumping up and down, the children announced their grandfather's claim to a new psychic power. Anna still maintained that she had felt the tremor and experienced the terrestrial aura effect 'just like Dedushka'.

'Oh, I don't think she did,' the old man protested. 'Perhaps it was all my imagination after all.' He wilted under the barrage of juvenile protest and lifted his hands helplessly. 'Now I scarcely know myself whether or not it really happened.'

Yuri untied his apron after covering the simmering kettle of sausage and cabbage. 'Come along with me, Papa. We'll leave these Red Indians for Tamara to pacify and find something to steady your nerves.'

They went into the young biophysicist's cozy, messy little study and closed the door. Pyotr sank into an overstuffed lounge chair while his son-in-law poured brandy into a large glass from a leather-bound bottle.

'Not so much, Yuri! You mustn't waste it on a deluded old fool.'

'Drink. Then we'll find out what you've been up to.' Gawrys sat down at his desk and shoved aside dog-eared publications and stacks of correspondence. He formed his thin fingers into a steeple and studied the bluish nails, his pallid features in repose and his hair falling lankly over his high forehead. He took none of the brandy.

'What we really ought to do,' Pyotr mumbled, his face in the glass, 'is check with the university to see whether or not there was a small earthquake at about four-thirty this afternoon.'

'Tamara is attending to it.'

'Oh. Of course.' Even after living with them for more than two weeks, he never ceased to be amazed by the domestic interaction of practising telepaths. Pyotr took a hefty swig of the brandy. It was Georgian, not Kazakh, mellow and earthy. Pyotr sighed. 'It really happened, you know.'

'A psychic response to seismic activity is not unknown to science,' Yuri remarked. 'Other persons have described similar experiences.'

'Then it may be that I *am* a genuine extrasensor?' The old man half rose from his chair in his eagerness.

Yuri Gawrys lifted his eyes. They were dark blue, like the lapis lazuli stones Pyotr remembered inset in the silver knife-scabbard of Seliac Eshba, the patriarch of Verkh-nyaya Bzyb. 'Would you like to tell me about the other times you sensed impending earthquakes?'

'It happened twice before. The first was in 1966, before I got into trouble fending the jackals off from Tamara. There was a conference on mental health in Tashkent, in April.'

'Yes . . . a great quake devastated the city then.'

'When I arrived at the airport I began to suffer the same kind of headache, the same vision of ghostly luminosity playing about the earth's surface. And when the first shock occurred, my symptoms vanished. But there was so much confusion in the aftermath – our hotel was damaged, you see – that I never made the connection. Then last year in Ulan-Ude there was a rather small tremor. I read about it the next day in the newspaper and wondered a bit, but at the time I was distracted. It was December, when you suffered your second heart attack, and — '

'Yes, Papa, yes.' Yuri made an impatient gesture. 'You are very lucky to be a sturdy Georgian rather than a Polack with an unfortunate history of cardiac insufficiency. And there is so much work yet to be done . . . especially now, when we are about to enter into a new, positive phase of psychic research at the university.'

Pyotr's jaw dropped. 'But the KGB-sponsored programmes of bioenergetic weaponry! Surely you will remain locked into them indefinitely — '

'Andropov is dying,' said Yuri. 'He will not last another month. And when he goes, so will the KGB's stranglehold on our work. He was the one, together with Fleet Admiral Gorshkov, who originally saw aggressive potential in psychic faculties. While Andropov headed the KGB, he took a personal interest in the guidance of psychic research in the Soviet Union. You know, of course, that Secretary Brezhnev was himself treated by a psychic healer, and was completely in accord with Andropov's mind-war schemes.'

Pyotr nodded.

'When Andropov finally took over as Party Secretary he was already deathly ill. His grip on us slowly loosened. The awful days of summer 1979, when Simonov and others of his perverted ilk violated the American President's mind during the SALT II signings in Vienna, will not soon come again.' Yuri Gawrys's smile was terrible. 'We have weeded our mental garden at Kazakh State University's Institute of Bioenergetics. The job was a long one, but it is complete. The last poisonous growth was uprooted only last December. By me, personally.'

'Radi Boga! Your heart attack — '

'We all have a certain price to pay, Pyotr Sergeyevich. You have paid yours and I, mine. For the soul.'

'What will happen when Andropov goes?' asked the psychiatrist.

'There will be a holding action by the old guard, a caretaker put in place while young Gorbachev and Romanov fight their duel. Whichever wins, we will be safe. They are both well-educated technocrats who have no patience with . . . the unconventional. They will forcibly retire Admiral Gorshkov and we shall probably find that our funding is drastically reduced. It is laser and particle-beam research that will get the rubles now.'

'But — ' Pyotr hesitated.

'Shall I read your thought?' Yuri inquired, smiling gently now. 'This cutback will actually benefit us. The essential work – the gathering together of the psychically gifted here at the Institute – has already been done. We may deplore that these young people were taken from their families, as Tamara and I were, but in the larger view it is all for the best. Now that our minds are linked, we will always remain in contact with one another. The garden, Papa! The garden will grow.'

The old man sipped his brandy, unable to respond. After a few minutes the door opened and Tamara came in, buxom and radiant, her bright auburn hair struggling out of its confining chignon.

'I have spoken to Akhmet Ismailov at the Geophysical Observatory. At precisely eighteen-twenty-eight hours there was a minor earth tremor measuring two point four on the Richter Scale. Its epicentre was about thirty kilometres south of Medeo, in the Zailiyskiy Ala-Tau.'

'Ah!' cried Pyotr. 'I am one of you! I *am*!'

Tamara kissed the top of his head, where a few sand-coloured hairs still grew. 'Of course you are. You would be even if your head were stuffed with sawdust, instead of wise old brains that may be very valuable to our work.'

'You really think that I can help you, daughter? You aren't simply humouring me?'

Tamara laughed. 'Alma-Ata is in a zone of seismic instability. We have minor tremors often, and an occasional large one. Our buildings are specially engineered for safety. If you live here with us, Papa, your extrasense may get more of a workout than you would like. You may end up wishing that you were back in Ulan-Ude, shrinking Mongolian nut-cases! . . . Now please wash up for dinner.'

When Pyotr had gone out, Tamara said to her husband. 'The faculty is of a certain theoretical interest, and it will help Papa to adjust to us. He was afraid, you know.'

Yuri got up from his chair. 'I told him – obliquely, but he understood – about our Black Frost.'

'Was that wise?'

'He had to know that our group is trustworthy, and that we are not without means of self-defence. I spoke only of my own role in the terminations.'

'There must be no more of them! We must find other ways!'

'Hush.' He took both her hands and pressed them to his cool lips. 'We will find other ways. But above all, we must survive, my darling. Otherwise, the plan will not succeed and it will all have been for nothing.'

'The soul,' she whispered. 'The poor soul of our people. Why must it have this terrible dark side? But it has always been so. We progress only through violence, never through reasoning and love.'

'The normals of our nation will have to be taught to love us. It will not be an easy lesson. The plan that we have worked so hard on promises a way, but it cannot be put into force for many years yet. I do not have those years. It will be up to you to be strong. To defend all your mind-children from those who would destroy or pervert them. This Alma-Ata group must survive and link up with the others in other nations, with the World Soul, Tamara. Until then, the children must endure in a wilderness, defended by a valiant mother.' He looked down at her, full of pity. She was twenty-six.

'I will try to find peaceful ways,' she said. 'If they fail, then I will do as you have taught me.'

6

Excerpts from:

Address given by Yasuhiro Nakasone,
Prime Minister of Japan, at the
General Assembly of the United Nations

United Nations, New York, Earth

23 October 1985

At the time the United Nations Charter was signed in San Francisco on 26 June 1945, Japan was waging a desperate and lonely war against over forty-odd Allied countries. Since the end of that war, Japan has profoundly regretted the ultranationalism and militarism it unleashed, and the untold suffering the war inflicted upon peoples around the world and, indeed, upon its own people.

As the only people ever to have experienced the devastation of the atomic bomb, in Hiroshima and Nagasaki, the Japanese people have steadfastly called for the elimination of nuclear weapons. Nuclear energy should be used exclusively for peaceful purposes; it must never again be employed as a means of destruction.

We believe that all living things – humans, animals, trees, grasses – are essentially brothers and sisters, [and yet] our generation is recklessly destroying the natural environment which has evolved over the course of millions of years and is essential for our survival. Our soil, water, air, flora and fauna are being subjected to the most barbaric attacks since the Earth was created. This folly can only be suicidal.

Man is born by the grace of the great universe:

> Afar and above the dark and endless sky,
> the Milky Way runs
> towards the place I come from.

7

Hanover, New Hampshire, Earth
19 September 1987

The Saturday afternoon was classic autumnal Ivy League, with a clear blue sky above broad-leaved trees that were just beginning to ignite in their fall colours. Lucille Cartier was glad to be back at Dartmouth, glad that Doctor Bill had agreed to resume counselling her, happiest of all that the damn dreams had gone away with her return to the campus, and that there was as yet no sign of subversive mental influence from Remillard's Coterie.

She bicycled to her shrink session, going the long way around Occom Pond and approaching the Mental Health Center via Maynard Street. She arrived with ten minutes to spare, dismounted in a shady spot by the main entrance, and took slow, deep breaths.

I am not resisting therapy. It will help me. I need help and welcome it. I am glad to be here . . .

She lifted her eyes, looked across Maynard, across the big Hitchcock Hospital parking lot, across busy College Street. And there it was, not five hundred feet away, an old grey saltbox building that hulked among spindly birches and dark evergreens like a haunted house out of a Stephen King novel, its windows blank-eyed and sinister.

You won't put me off! I'm not afraid of you. To hell with you and your Coterie. I defy you!

Recklessly, she hopped back on her bicycle and zoomed across the road to stand in the very forecourt of 45 College Street. There were only two cars parked beside the saltbox – Glenn Dalembert's old Mustang with the odd-coloured door, and a spiffy new Lincoln with Massachusetts plates, no doubt belonging to some visitor.

You see? I'm back. You couldn't scare me away. I don't need you and I won't let you harass me. You can't recruit me against my will like you did Donna Chan and Dane Gwaltney. I'll live my own life, thank you very much . . . and I'll integrate my freak brain without surrendering to any mind-worm collective!

The saltbox building was utterly still, without telepathic response. And then Lucille realized that she had been using *his* private wave-length, what the mind-worms called a 'mental signature', perceptible to him alone. Obviously, he wasn't even here today. Her gesture of defiance was futile.

Or was it? She felt quite a bit better inside! For good measure, she gave Dr Denis Remillard's laboratory the finger, and then she rode her bicycle back to Maynard Street, parked it in the Mental Health Center rack, and went inside to keep her appointment.

DR SAMPSON: I'm very glad you decided to resume therapy, Lucille. I presume this means that you've decided to remain at Dartmouth rather than transfer to Rivier College for your senior year.

LUCILLE: Yes. That idea turned out to be a mistake, Doctor Bill.

SAMPSON: Would you like to tell me why you changed your mind?

LUCILLE: We — you and I — didn't seem to be getting anywhere with the therapy last term. And I was miserable here anyway, worrying about Mom having to cope with Dad all by herself besides teaching at the high school. I thought I'd solve that problem and help my own feelings of anxiety and guilt by simply going back home. I could day-hop to Rivier and complete my degree, and help Mom with Dad and the housework just like before. When I went back to Nashua for the summer break I felt pretty good for a few weeks . . . but then the old shit started all over again.

SAMPSON: The anxiety and insomnia?

LUCILLE: [laughs] Don't I wish that was all! . . . Look, Doctor Bill, I've got a confession to make. I haven't been completely honest with you. I didn't tell you all my symptoms.

SAMPSON: Why not?

LUCILLE: I was afraid to. If the college found out, they'd want to bounce me.

SAMPSON: [mildly] You know our relationship is confidential.

LUCILLE: Even so . . . it's so weird, you see. And it would

interest — never mind. I didn't think I had to mention it because I hadn't *had* the thing for a long time. Not since I was thirteen, bucking the puberty blues.

SAMPSON: Would you like to tell me about it now?

LUCILLE: I've got to. It's back. Going home again, living with my parents this summer, triggered it. I didn't say anything to them — they would have been scared to death, like they were the other time. You're my only hope now, you see. I won't go to Remillard! I *won't*!

SAMPSON: [nonplussed] Denis Remillard? Of the parapsychology lab?

LUCILLE: It's his fault it's come back! Damn him and his meddling! If he had only let me alone —

SAMPSON: [making a note on his pad] Lucille . . . Stop for a moment and relax. Then let's try to concentrate on this mysterious symptom you neglected to mention.

LUCILLE: All right. It goes back to when I was thirteen. The attacks of creepiness, nerves, anxiety — they really began then. And I also had nightmares. And then . . . the house burned down. I did it.

SAMPSON: You deliberately started the fire?

LUCILLE: No, no! I didn't mean to! But . . . it was a time when I was feeling all mixed up. Nobody understood me, that kind of adolescent bullshit, but something else, too. They really *didn't* understand! I couldn't talk to them . . . Dad was just starting to come down with the sclerosis thing and he was — was hard to live with. I was so sorry for him and wanted to help, but he was so angry all the time and didn't want me around him. Then I started to have these nightmares about fire. I was Joan of Arc and they were lighting the pyre and I was all noble and forgave them and the flames came roaring up to swallow me and my skin would burn and even my bones and I'd be nothing but clean bright sparks flying up to heaven *if only I wouldn't be afraid*. But I was afraid. So the flames hurt horribly because I wasn't Saint Joan at all, and I'd wake up yelling and get the whole house in an uproar, Mom and Dad and my kid brother Mike. It was awful. It was even worse the time I woke up and found my bedroom wall was all in flames.

SAMPSON: Good God! . . . I'm sorry. Go on.

LUCILLE: I got out the door and woke Mom and Mike and we got Dad into his wheelchair and made it outside safely. But by the time the fire department came, the house was too far gone to save much. Dad's piano burned. It was a Steinway grand he'd got years ago, before he was ever married, when he was going to be a concert pianist and studied at the New England Conservatory in Boston. It cost thousands of dollars and he kept it even when he gave up his classical ambitions. Then, when he got sick and couldn't do lounge gigs or even give lessons any more he wanted to sell it, to help out the family. But Mom wouldn't let him. He loved that piano more than anything. And I burned it.

SAMPSON: But you said you didn't start the fire deliberately. Why do you blame yourself?

LUCILLE: My room was right next to the one where the piano was. The fire started in the wall – the firemen could tell. I hadn't been smoking or anything dumb like that, but the whole wall near my bed and the piano on the other side of it somehow caught fire.

SAMPSON: An electrical short.

LUCILLE: There was no outlet on that wall, and only an ordinary lamp near the piano . . . Later on, they thought I might have walked in my sleep and lit a match. I told them it was my fault, you see. That I did it. But I didn't dare explain how! I dreamed that fire. The dream became more and more real . . . and finally, it *was* real.

SAMPSON: What do you mean by that?

LUCILLE: I did it with my mind. My unconscious. I'm one of them – the freaks that Remillard tests over at the parapsychology lab. He hunted me out long before he came to Dartmouth, when I was eleven. Later on, he and his Coterie wanted me to come here to school. I didn't want to, but there was the scholarship and my folks put on the pressure. I came when I was sixteen, and then Remillard really shifted into high gear. I should be grateful all to hell to assist the boy genius in his researches, even if I could only do a little telepathy when the moon was right, and melt ice cubes and jiggle tables. Dumb, useless things! I told him no. He kept on bugging me for three years, though, and so did his mind-worm clique! I told him all I wanted to do was live a normal life, study a legitimate science like biochemistry instead of waste time on occult nonsense. And I will!

SAMPSON: Excuse me, Lucille. You're an intelligent young woman. Don't you see any contradiction in what you've been saying?

LUCILLE: Remillard and his people give me the creeps — and I won't be experimented upon!

SAMPSON: I understand that. You want help. But why do you think I'm the one who can give it to you — rather than Remillard?

LUCILLE: It's a psychiatric problem. It really has nothing to do with parapsychology except — in its manifestation.

SAMPSON: You are convinced that this incendiary faculty is a genuine paranormal phenomenon?

LUCILLE: [laughs] There's even a name for it in folklore: fire-raising. Look it up in any compendium of witchcraft. You'll find true stories about people who start fires without any equipment — produce it out of thin air. Some of them even manage to burn themselves to death.

SAMPSON: You only did this once, when you were thirteen?

LUCILLE: I'm . . . not sure. We had other house-fires, small ones, when I was younger. There always seemed to be a natural explanation.

SAMPSON: The piano burning might have had one. A freak lightning strike, for example.

LUCILLE: It was me! My resentment of poor Dad. He only had time for his illness and the damn piano and never any time for me . . .

SAMPSON: Let's suppose your self-analysis is correct. Why do you think you're playing with fire again now, at this particular time?

LUCILLE: *I don't know!* That's why I came to you in the first place, when Denis Remillard's badgering got me so edgy last February and I couldn't sleep or study. I thought you'd just prescribe some Valium, but instead you got me into this analysis that didn't seem to help at all.

SAMPSON: You never spoke to me about being harassed by Remillard or his people.

LUCILLE: I didn't want you to know. I thought . . . oh, *hell*. Now you do know. Can't you help me? What if the fire nightmares start up here at Dartmouth like they did at home this summer?

SAMPSON: They haven't yet?

LUCILLE: No.

SAMPSON: You suffered from anxiety and depression here at school last spring, and yet the really serious warning from your unconscious only came to you when you tried to return home. Does that suggest anything to you?

LUCILLE: I had to come back here. To *you*. That's what my mind was telling me.

SAMPSON: Are you sure?

LUCILLE: Yes.

SAMPSON: I want to help you, Lucille. You must believe me. But you do understand that your analysis presents unique problems. All humans carry within their unconscious a load of destructive wishes left over from early childhood. You've studied psychology. You know what I mean. The mother takes the nipple from the hungry baby's mouth and it becomes enraged. A little child is punished for being naughty and wishes its parents were dead. We all had feelings like this once and we repressed them, and sometimes the guilt or something similar resurfaces in later life to give us psychic pain. But a toddler is too weak to murder its parents. And an adult who still unconsciously resents her father's neglect will not normally harm him physically. The unconscious may rage, but unless the person is psychotic it remains outwardly impotent and must find other outlets for its revenge.

LUCILLE: But my unconscious isn't impotent . . .

SAMPSON: Evidently not. And one might ask whether your *conscious* mind is similarly empowered.

LUCILLE: God. What am I going to do?

SAMPSON: The only useful answers in psychoanalysis are the ones you see clearly for yourself. I can guide you, but I can't force you to set your deep fears aside . . . And you *are* afraid of your paranormal powers, Lucille. You'd like them to go away so you can be just like normal people —

LUCILLE: Yes. Yes!

SAMPSON: But it seems quite likely that the powers won't go away. So we'll have to predicate our coping strategy on that supposition, won't we?

LUCILLE: [hotly] I know exactly what you're leading up to! And it has nothing to do with mind reading, *Remillard!*

SAMPSON: I haven't had too much professional contact with him, but there are those on the Medical School faculty who think highly of his work. For all his youth, he's a meticulous researcher. His test subjects aren't treated like mental patients, you know. Most of them seem to be Dartmouth students like yourself —

LUCILLE: And just *why* have so many of these psychic freaks come here? Why did I come? There was the scholarship offer, of course – but I felt an unnatural compulsion, too!

SAMPSON: [patiently] Is it necessarily bad to want to associate with others who share your unusual mental faculties?

LUCILLE: [despairingly] But I don't want them . . . I only want to stop burning . . . to be happy . . . to have someone understand me and love me.

SAMPSON: Your unconscious wants you to be happy, too. It wants you to face your dilemma honestly instead of running away from it. The unconscious isn't a demon, Lucille. It's only you.

LUCILLE: [after a silence] I suppose so.

SAMPSON: No one can force you to participate in Dr Remillard's experiments, Lucille. But you must ask yourself: Might your fear of him be irrational?

LUCILLE: I don't know. I'm all mixed up. My head feels so feverish and my throat is so dry. Can I get some water?

SAMPSON: Today's session is almost over . . . I have a suggestion. Let me find out some specifics of Remillard's research. Let me ask him – without mentioning you – about the general state of mental health among his subjects. Surely some of them must have experienced conflicts similar to yours. When I get more information, we can begin working out your coping strategy.

LUCILLE: But not with him.

SAMPSON: Not if you don't want to.

LUCILLE: He'll want me to join his group. He'll coerce me.

SAMPSON: [laughing] Over my dead body! And I played middle line-backer for the Big Green in '56!

LUCILLE: [admiringly] It figures. And you have the perfect name.

SAMPSON: Uh . . . well, that was long ago and far away. But you can rest assured that no one will coerce you into anything. Now, our time is up for today. Can you come again at the same time next Wednesday?

LUCILLE: Will the Center authorize more than one free therapy session a week for me? I mean, I can't afford —

SAMPSON: That's all right. Your case is unusual. As a matter of fact, it's the most unusual one I've ever encountered . . . But you will sleep with a fire extinguisher nearby, won't you?

LUCILLE: Yes, Doctor Bill. Goodbye.

SAMPSON: Goodbye, Lucille.

8

Berlin, New Hampshire, Earth
20 May 1989

Don Remillard didn't go to the Blue Ox on Saturday nights much any more, it being a lot cheaper to drink at home. But with Sunny waiting tables on the late shift at the Androscoggin Kitchen this week and Victor gone up to Pittsburg on some mystery errand, the younger brats would be running wild around the place. He'd end up belting a couple of them for sure, and then there'd be a row when Sunny got back – and God knows he had enough trouble with her already.

So he went down to the Ox, settled in at his usual spot on the far end of the bar, and started working through his quota of Seagram's. A few of his old buddies greeted him, but none stuck around to interfere seriously with his drinking. Little by little the place filled up and the tunes played by the jukebox got louder. By ten o'clock Don was almost deafened by the music and the racket made by the roistering mill-hands and loggers and their exuberant ladies. He had downed enough whisky to be more or less skunk-bit and incapable – and it hadn't done a damn bit of good.

He could still hear the obscene voices inside his head. The goddam telepaths. The ones who were out to get him.

Just look at that pathetic fucker! Can't hardly hold a glass without it sloppin' over. Eyes like poached eggs in ketchup! Skritch-jawed and grubby and wearin' a week-old shirt.

Crazy as an outhouse rat, too. Brains so pickled his power's petered away t'zilch. Won't be long now, he won't be able to shut us out. We'll nail him!

May not have to bother, he screws up again like he did today. You see the way he tried to clear the throat of the whole-tree hog he let jam up?

Hell, yes. Goddam jeezly bar-toad almost got chopped to red-flannel hash! . . . Hey, stupid! Finish the job next time. Do us all a favour!

Do Victor a favour. What's he need a drunken old fart like you on the operation?

'I taught him everything, dammit. Everything.'

Pig's ass. Kid got the outfit percolatin' despite you.

Yeah. That's right!

'I taught him everything! How to use his powers. Never woulda done it without me. Green kid! Shit – I *made* that kid.'

You made him what he is.

Whatever that is! Haw haw haw . . .

'Damn right . . . damn right. You tell 'im that.'

Hey, Vic! How long you gonna put up with your drag-ass old man? How long you gonna let the old stumblebum bollix up your show? Listen, Vic. Bright kid like you don't hafta put up with shit like he pulls. Lookit today. Feedin' the new Omark the wrong kinda stems. Coulda broke the christly rig! Family loyalty can be mighty expensive. Take our advice. Tie a can to the old asshole. Hire somebody who knows what he's doin'!

I'm considering it . . .

'The hell you are!' Don muttered viciously.

Old Ducky Duquette, who was nursing a bottle of

Labatt's a little way down the bar, looked at him with an expression of mild surprise.

Haw haw haw! You think Vic wouldn't get rid of you? Think again!

Tell him, Vic. Tell him why you went up to Pittsburg tonight. Tell him!

. . . I'm putting it up to Howie Durant to come in with us. He's an experienced hand with whole-tree chippers.

Way to go, Vic! Demote the old man to brush-piler. Better yet, get him off the operation altogether. He's an accident waitin' to happen, drinkin' on the job the way he does.

Maybe the sooner the accident happens, the better!

Wipe him out yourself, kid. Tip him over the edge. You don't hafta wait for us. Be our guest!

. . . It might be for the best. Easy enough to rig an accident with programmed incitement. His defences are negligible now and his farspeech no longer has the range to alert Denis or Uncle Rogi.

That's right, Vic. Be just another logging fatality. Happens all the time.

Don slammed his shot glass down on the bar and yelled, 'Oh no you don't, punk! I'll fry your fuckin' brains out first!'

Ralph Pelletier, the Ox's owner, who was tending bar as usual, called out over the din, 'Anything wrong down there?'

Don forced a big grin and shook his head. 'All I need's another double, double-quick!' He waved his glass.

Pelletier brought the bottle and poured. Don downed the whisky and immediately demanded more. The tavern-keeper said quietly, 'You've had about enough for tonight, Don. Finish this and then give your liver a rest.'

'Don't need your lectures, bonhomme. Just your booze. Un p'tit coup.' Don tossed money on to the mahogany. The bills fell into a puddle of spilled liquor.

Pelletier scooped them up with a grimace of distaste. 'Drink up and go home, Don. You hear what I'm saying?' He filled the double shot glass again. 'I mean it. Hors d'ici.' He went away.

Don mouthed silent curses after him. Pelly wanted to get rid of him. *Everybody* wanted to get rid of him! He sipped

236

from the glass and groaned. All around him the Blue Ox patrons laughed and the voices inside his head recited fresh indecencies.

Ducky Duquette edged closer, a tentative smile of sympathy creasing his weathered old chops. 'Ça va, Don? Had a rough week?'

Don could only laugh helplessly.

'Trouble out at the chantier, maybe? The logging outfit has growing pains?'

The mental voices chortled at the joke. Don pressed knuckles to his temples until pain submerged them, then lifted his glass with a trembling hand. 'My damn kid's gettin' too big for his fuckin' britches. Throwing his weight around.'

'Ah!' Ducky looked wise. 'Such a clever boy, your Victor. But perhaps impatient? That's the way of the young. Still, he's doing very well, isn't he? I heard about the big new contract he landed with Saint William. Amazing that they accepted the bid of such a youthful entrepreneur, eh?'

'Fuckin' fantastic,' Don muttered.

'You can be proud, Don. What sons! First Denis le Miro-bolant – and now Victor, with his own logging company at the age of nineteen.'

'And I'm such a lucky bastard, Ducky. I get to work for my own wiseacre kid! I taught him everything. And now he wants to kick me out.' His face lit up in a sour smile. 'But he won't get away with it. I know where a few bodies are buried . . . like how a shoestring operation like his is able to field so much expensive rolling stock.'

Fold your face, you drunken blabbermouth!

Vic – you gonna let him keep this up?

Ducky had gone wary. He lowered his voice. 'Tell you the truth, Don, there *has* been some talk. Lot of people wondered how Vic could afford that new Omark chip machine so soon after getting the second feller-buncher. Equipment like that don't grow on trees.'

'Lemme tell you something, Ducky.' Don draped an arm around the old man's neck and spoke in a coarse whisper. 'Any ol' wood rat knows that logging machinery does, too, grow on trees. All you hafta do is know what trees to look under. And when.'

Will you shut up, you peasoupin' lush?

He's gonna squeal, Vic. Don't say we didn't warn you. It's his fuckin' conscience, see. Confession's good for the soul, he thinks. Go ahead and confess, Don – we got the final absolution all ready!

We'll show him what happens to finks! . . . Give him to us, Vic. Come on! What're you waitin' for – a posse of county mounties goin' over your stuff with a magnifying glass and an electronic sniffer?

Don tittered. 'Wouldn't find diddly. Got every damn ID number and beeper-trace fixed. Told you my Vic was smart. And I taught him everything.' The injustice of it all overwhelmed him and his voice broke. 'Everything, Ducky. Not just the mind-powers but the business, too. Vic was nothin' but a high school punk when they pink-slipped me at the mill. It was my idea to go into the woods and start cuttin' pulp-wood.'

And you'd still be a low-bore stump-jumper operatin' with two chain saws and a pick-em-up if it wasn't for Vic!

You taught him? He taught you!

Who coerced the first big contract? Who rounded up the gear? Who found the right men, the ones who know how to keep zipped lips? Who keeps the whole show chargin' ahead in the black? Not you, you washed-up alcoholic cuntlapper.

'No gratitude,' Don moaned. 'From any of my children.'

Ducky blinked and began drawing away. 'Tough luck . . .'

'I know what Vic's planning,' Don shouted. 'But he won't get away with it! None of 'em will!' Heads were turning and he felt the pressure of hostile eyes delving after his dangerous secrets. Could the patrons of the Blue Ox hear the taunting voices too? No – of course not! They were only in his head. They were only imaginary! What was wrong with Ducky, then, looking so shit-scared? . . . God! How much had he blabbed 'Where the hell you think you're going?' Don grabbed Ducky by the front of the shirt. The old fellow yelped and pulled back, and his bottle of beer tipped and burbled onto the bar.

Ralph Pelletier, his expression thunderous, called, 'Goddammit, Don – what'd I tell you?'

238

He knows! They all know! They'll tell Vic! Tell the cops!
You spilled your guts just fine this time, fink!

Don shook Duquette until his dentures rattled. 'You won't tell! I never said anything about Vic's equipment. You hear me?'

'He's crazy! He's crazy!' Ducky gibbered, hanging in Don's grip limp as a spawned-out salmon.

Choke the lyin' sonuvabitch! Shut him up!

Lute Soderstrom, who stood six-six and had once punched a hole in the radiator of a Kenwhopper, stepped up behind Don and took hold of his arms. A couple of other Blue Ox habitués pried Ducky loose.

Don's howl was agonized. 'You won't get away with it! You're all in it together, aren't you? All working with Vic and the others to finish me off!'

'Ease him outside,' Pelletier said.

The jukebox was pounding a raucous dirt-rock tune. Women squealed and men shouted jocose advice to Lute as he wrestled his burden towards the door.

'They're waiting for me out there!' Don screamed. 'Waiting with Vic!' He tried to coerce the Swede: hopeless. He tried to trip Lute up by knocking over chairs or tables with his psychokinesis: he hadn't a glimmer. He was impotent. He was nothing. A carousel of light and noise and pain spun around him, slowly dissolving to black, and the jeering mental voices receded to a far distance. Don was a dead weight in Lute's powerful arms as they came out into the soft May night.

Lute dragged him around back to the Ox's dark parking lot, picked him up bodily, and dumped him on to a folded tarp in the bed of a little Nissan 4 x 4. 'You gonna be okay, Don.' He spoke soothingly. 'You stay here, get a little air, maybe sleep. I come back in just a little bit and drive you home, okay?'

Fais un gros dodo, ordure! Haw haw haw . . .

Don made an inarticulate noise. Lute nodded and went off.

You can't stay here.
You dassn't go to sleep!
Vic knows what you said. You gotta get outa here!

'Je suis fichu,' Don mumbled. 'Pas de couilles . . . mon crâne . . . ah, Jésus . . .'

Pretty late in the game to be calling on him, *shithead.*

He can't help you. Nobody can. Nobody cares what happens to you, you drunken freak. Nobody!

Nobody . . . nobody . . . nobody . . .

'You're wrong.' The words were slurred, tainted with the bile that had risen in his throat. He clutched at the side of the pickup's cargo bed, summoned strength, and heaved himself up and over. Then he lay on his face in the dirt for a long time, stunned.

Something crawled across the back of his neck and he opened his eyes, lifted his head, and grinned at the Nissan's left rear wheel. His senses were reeling but he was no longer a man without hope. The voices were wrong! Somebody did care. Somebody who would help him, who would even fend off Victor . . .

'Merci, mon Seigneur. Merci, doux Jésus!'

He struggled to his feet, fighting off nausea. His head seemed to be in the grip of iron tongs and he had to lean against the side of the Nissan until the pain subsided and he could see. He peered about anxiously among the parked cars and trucks for signs of the enemy. Nobody was there. Not *yet*. They were waiting for Vic, and it'd take the kid time to get back to Berlin from Pittsburg, sixty miles away via two-lane blacktop.

When he was steady he thumbed his wristwatch. The lighted read-out showed just a little past eleven. She'd have to work until one on Saturday and it was only a mile to walk, along well-lit Main Street and then Riverside Drive. She had her car. He could sit in it and wait, get coffee and sober up. It would be all right.

Pulling himself together, he shuffled on to the sidewalk and came around to the front of the tavern. The music and laughter were louder than ever. They'd forgotten all about him. Lamenting the callousness of it all, he set off north on Main, heading for the Androscoggin Kitchen restaurant and Sunny.

Don went to the take-out window and ordered a large black

coffee from Marcie Stroup, and asked her to have Sunny bring it to the car.

'Gee, Don, I dunno.' The girl eyed him dubiously. He was a filthy mess, reeking of alcohol, and he had caused scenes before at the Kitchen that had nearly cost Sunny her job.

'Please, Marcie. I'm not here to make trouble. It's really important. Tell Sunny that.'

The girl finally said, 'Okay,' and went off. He shambled over to Sunny's battered '81 Escort that was parked at the far side of the big paved lot, and got in on the driver's side after opening the door with his own key. The Andy K was bursting at the seams on this fine spring night. The lot was jammed with vehicles coming in and out and cruisers stopping for take-outs. The place was far too brightly lit for those murdering bastards to chance coming after him, so he leaned back and closed his eyes, feeling safe for the moment. The long walk had helped to clear his brain but his head ached worse than ever. It didn't matter. He welcomed the pain because it kept the voices at bay. Not that he really cared about their taunting any more. They couldn't touch him without Vic's say-so, and Sunny would take care of *him*.

'Don?' She was standing beside the open window, face drawn with worry and shadowed by the overhead illumination of the vapour lamps. She held a large container of coffee. The loving concern that radiated from her mind struck him like a sword in the heart. Poor Sunny. She was only forty-one, and she was old. Like him. He had put her through so much.

He smiled crookedly. 'Come sit with me.'

She handed him the coffee. 'Don, you know I can't. We're busy. I only came because Marcie said — '

His mind took hold of hers in an old familiar way, like a hand slipping into a glove. 'It's important. Just for a few minutes.'

She sighed and came around to open the passenger door, then slid in beside him. 'What is it?' Apprehension made her voice unsteady. She still had one hand on the door handle.

He downed a gulp of steaming liquid. 'I was at the Ox tonight. Making a nickel-plated jackass outa myself.'

She turned away miserably. 'Oh, Don. If only you — '

He interrupted her. 'Listen. I made up my mind! If you just help me, I'll give up drinking for good. I'll do what you been asking me to do.'

She looked at him, incredulous. 'You'll go to Denis? Let him check you into the detox clinic at Project Cork?'

Don gritted his teeth. Even the mention of the quaintly titled but nationally famous institute for alcoholism study at Dartmouth got his back up. Project Cork! Enough to make a grown man puke. But locked away in its stern sanctuary with Denis's powerful mind to shield him, no enemy would ever be able to get hold of him. Not Victor. Not the fiends of his own engendering.

'I'll go to Denis,' Don vowed. 'Tonight, if you like. Call him up and tell him I'm on my way.'

Tears filled Sunny's eyes. 'You really mean it this time?'

'I swear to God!' His eyes shifted. Was that something moving in the trees beyond the edge of the lot? Were they out there, listening? Don set the coffee on the dashboard and clasped his wife's hand. 'But I gotta go *now*, I need help now, Sunny. You understand?'

'You're in no condition to drive that far. I'll call Denis, and then when Victor comes home he can — '

'No!' Don seized her by the shoulders. Her eyes dilated with fear and he hastened to say, 'Victor's gonna be gone God knows how long. I can't wait! I've gotta go now or never!'

She took a resolute breath, detached his hands. 'I'll drive you myself. I'll call Denis and ask him to meet us on the road.'

'Good idea! Then you won't have to leave the kids alone too long.' He gulped more coffee and thought hard. 'We'll take Route 2. Ask Denis to meet us at the Saint Johnsburg Rest Area on I–91. Go call him, Sunny. Hurry.'

She stared at him, searching. 'You're sure?'

His mind cried: Sunny for the love of God *help me*!

She opened the car door and slipped out. 'I'll be right back.' Then she was hurrying towards the gaudy lights of the restaurant and he was alone, limp with reaction and relief. He reached over, locked the right-hand door, and rolled its window fully closed. He secured his own side as well. The car was stuffy and the windshield partly fogged by coffee vapour, but he was safe. His mind seemed to slip in and out of gear, focusing on one menace after another. Victor. The hostile voices. His brother Rogi, that back-biting weasel. Even Denis, remote, ice-hearted, intolerant of a hard-working father's human weakness . . . God, how he dreaded having to submit to Denis! He knew he'd have to come clean – tell Denis about the voices and the way they'd drawn Victor into the conspiracy, maybe even tell about the stolen equipment that had triggered the whole fuck-up in the first place. Denis would despise him more than ever! But he'd have to stand by his father nonetheless. Sunny would see to it. Wonderful Sunny . . .

And then Don caught sight of the black customized Chevy van. It was poised in the turn lane out on Route 16, signals blinking, waiting for a break in the heavy northbound traffic so it could enter the parking lot.

He's finally here.

It's about time!

Over here, Vic! Over here!

'No,' Don whispered. 'No, God.'

At least four other cars were trying to get out of that exit. The van was momentarily blocked. Sunny! . . . But she was probably still on the telephone. Could he make a break for the restaurant? It was too damn far away. The van would surely cut him off before he made it to the door —

And now it was making the turn to enter!

Frantically, Don switched on the ignition of the Escort. There was another way out, a dirt track that bumped over waste-ground. He floored the pedal and went ripping down a lane of parked vehicles. He clung to the wheel as his car careened over the rutted track and on to the highway. He swerved to avoid being rear-ended by a furiously honking station wagon, jinked on to the shoulder, then regained control. In the rearview mirror, he saw the black Chevy van trapped in the restaurant lot by a tangle of cars in front of it and behind it.

Vic! Vic! He's gettin' away!
In your mom's car. Northbound!

Don laughed at them. He checked the fuel gauge: nearly full. The traffic was heavy in both directions. Victor's farsight was lousy and his coercion didn't reach beyond a stone's throw. He could lose the kid in the maze of logging roads up the Androscoggin River beyond Milan, then double back and pick up Sunny.

You'll never get away!
We'll keep Vic on your trail!
You're finished, sucker.
Give up. We'll help Vic nail you!

Don was laughing so hard he nearly choked. 'You're not real! You can't hurt me! Go to hell!'

Oncoming cars were blinking their brights at him. He panicked for a moment, then realized that he was driving with only the parking lights on. Giggling, he flicked the headlight switch. Then he settled down and sped north along the river road toward the deep woods.

Sunny wept in Victor's arms, sitting beside him on the front seat of the black van. 'He was still very drunk. He's sure to have an accident! Victor, what are we going to do? How will we ever find him?'

He held her tightly. 'Hush, Maman. Let me think . . . There's Denis. He could try using his seekersense on Papa.'

She broke away and cried, 'Yes, of course! Hurry and telephone! He may not have left Hanover yet.'

The young man sprinted for the front door of the restaurant, dodging departing diners. Sunny sat with her face buried in her hands, trying to summon from latency the telepathic power she had used so long ago when her eldest son was a baby:

Denis stay home. Don't leave home yet. Stay Denis stay . . .

After an interminable time, Victor returned, alight with triumph. 'Caught him! He was on the way to the car, but he dropped his keys – and then he heard the phone ringing and came back.'

244

'Oh, thank God. And he'll – he'll search? And tell you where to find your father?'

Victor started the engine of the van. 'Denis will track Papa down, then call me at home. He said there may be some difficulty because Papa's aura tends to be suppressed by the alcohol. But you're not to worry. We'll find him. And now I'm taking you home.'

'But I'll have to speak to Mr Lovett first,' Sunny protested. 'He'll be furious — '

'I've already spoken to him.' Victor's smile was invincibly reassuring. 'He's not furious, he understands it's a family emergency. It's going to be all right, Maman.' He took a tissue from the console dispenser and wiped her tears, then bent and kissed her cheek with warm lips.

Sunny felt herself relaxing, giving over volition to this tall, masterful son who was so like the strong, youthful Don she had married twenty-three years ago. She said, 'I know how hard it's been for you lately, Victor. You're bitter. I understand why. But you must help your father, if only for my sake.'

The black van was moving slowly forward. Victor gripped the wheel and stared straight ahead. 'Just leave everything to me,' he said. 'Now fasten your seat belt and we'll go home.'

An excruciating thirst, a tight bladder and a skull-piercing chorus of woodland birds woke Don.

His rheum-clogged eyelids opened with reluctance to misty dawn. Every joint above the waist ached and every joint below was numb. His brain was swollen too large for its fragile bony case and was on the imminent verge of exploding. He cursed, invoked a compassionate God, and asked himself aloud where the hell he had ended up *this* time.

It was the usual Saturday night blackout. The usual Sunday morning hangover. But he was in Sunny's car, not his own. What the hell? . . . Oh, yeah. His heap was in the shop. He must have taken hers.

The windows of the Escort were curtained in condensation. He rubbed a clear space and tried to focus his bleary eyes. There were giant shapes around him, yellow and blue, with jointed arms held rakishly akimbo. The nose of the little car was snuggled up to the flank of a monster machine. Another, even larger, confronted him with threatening insectile jaws. On its back was a cab bearing the legend:

REMCO PULPWOOD LTD., BERLIN, N.H.

Don cursed anew, then fell back into the seat. The thing with the jaws was Victor's new feller-buncher, a self-propelled tree harvester capable of shearing two-foot trunks in a single bite. Grouped around it were other pieces of heavy equipment: the hydraulic boom loader, the whole-tree chipper he usually operated, the tree-length delimber, the second feller-buncher looming out of thick mist.

He was out in the forest at their logging site up the Dead Diamond River. He was hiding from Victor.

He remembered very little of the previous night. His last clear recollection was when he passed through the town of Errol thirty miles north of Berlin after a nightmare flight through the back country around Cambridge Mountain. Goaded by the voices, he had been afraid to return to Sunny at the restaurant. Instead he had decided to head west and work his way down to Hanover and Dartmouth via the roads along the New Hampshire–Vermont border.

But somehow he hadn't. Obviously he'd driven north out of Errol instead of west. God knew what had impelled him to come to the family logging operation . . .

He opened the car door and just managed to catch himself before falling out. The shack! There was water there, the white-gas stove and coffee makings, maybe a few Pepperidge Farm cookies left in Victor's private stash, maybe a half bottle of brandy in the first-aid box. Scorning the Sanikan, he relieved himself against one of the tyres of the Omark tree-chipper that had nearly taken his arm off yesterday. That'd show the bastard!

He was fumbling with the padlock on the shack when he heard the sound of an automobile engine.

Terror-stricken, he froze – only to be spotlighted by twin beams that stabbed suddenly out of the fog. The approaching vehicle was dark and blocky. The KC spots mounted on the roof glared at him but no other lights showed at all. It was Victor's black van.

Don heard his son's mind-voice:

Hold it right there, Papa.

The coercive grip and the light held him like a hypnotized moth. The van stopped about twenty yards away and Victor got out.

Don said: They sent you here, didn't they! They told you how to find me! They turned you against me – after I did everything for you!

Victor said: You imagined them. The voices. You're sick. You've been sick for years. Your mind wasn't strong enough to adapt.

Don said: Don't come near me! I know what you're planning. You heard me shooting my mouth off in the Ox!

Victor said: Yes. You wanted me to.

Don said: You're as loony as I am! Why the hell would I want you to hear me call you – to hear me — '

Victor said: To hear you call me a thief?

Don said: You are dammit you are! I taught you everything – but I never taught you that. *They* did.

Victor said: You're pathetic. No use to anyone. You hate yourself so much you want to die. But you're too much of a coward to kick off like a man, so you try to drink yourself to death.

Don said: You're all against me Rogi Denis you we're all freaks together but you shut me out of your minds left me alone to suffer left me alone with *them*.

Victor said: They're you, Papa.

Don said: Bastardsonuvabitchfuckingcocksuckerbrat . . .

Victor said: The voices are you. All the filth. All the accusations. All the threats. The mutation broke you, Papa. You're one of evolution's throwaways and it's time for you to go. You really are too dangerous now, and Denis will be here soon. Neither one of us could get a fix on you until you woke up, you know. Fortunately for me, he drives cautiously on dirt logging roads. Unfortunately for you . . .

Don said: What – what are you going to do?

Victor said: What you want me to do. It'll be an accident. A drunken man playing suicidal games.

The dark silhouette disappeared as the blinding yellow lights shut off. Don crouched in the shack doorway, rubbing his eyes. He saw Victor get into the van and drive away. In his mind, the terrible voices spoke together:

Now.

The big diesel engine of the new feller-buncher coughed into life. Its shear, mounted on a twenty-six-foot knuckle boom, lifted into the air with a hiss of hydraulics. Then the whole rig came lumbering towards him on caterpillar treads, the grab-arms and the blades that could sever a two-foot tree trunk in a single bite held open at the height of a man's chest. The machine's cab was empty. Before Don turned to flee, screaming, he saw the control levers moving by themselves and heard silent laughter.

9

*From the Memoirs of
Rogatien Remillard*

Since that Sunday promised to be a hectic one, with two convention banquets and a fund-raiser dinner-dance scheduled at the hotel, I went to the 6:30 A.M. Mass at the little church in Bretton Woods. It was a rustic place, dimmed by stained glass windows in abstract patterns. Hikers, golfers and other resort employees like myself made up most of the somnolent, thinly scattered congregation. I arrived a few minutes late, so I slipped into a rear pew back in a dark corner. For this reason it was not immediately noticed when I died with my brother.

It happened during the sermon. My mind was wandering and I had become aware of an increasing sense of unease, only partly dulled by my semiwakeful state. The foreboding may have been an aspect of precognition; but I had no real intimation of catastrophe until I abruptly lost my hearing. I saw Father Ingram's lips move but no longer heard his voice. In place of the background noises of shifting bodies, coughs and rustling prayer booklets there was a great hush, hollow and portentous. I snapped into alertness.

248

Then came an appalling noise, a deep grinding rumble laced with a more shrill, undulating sound, like brasses wailing in dissonance or howls from a chorus of lacerated throats. It built to a thunderous crescendo as though the earth itself were being rent open beneath me. I was immobilized by shock. I remember wondering why the priest was oblivious to the tumult, why the other worshippers kept their seats instead of leaping up in panic, why the church roof remained firm when by rights it should have been tumbling down around my ears.

Any notion I had of being caught in an earthquake was disabused when I went blind. At the same time it seemed that a band of red-hot metal clamped about my breast and squeezed, stopping my heart and breath in an explosion of agony. I thought: a coronary! But I was only forty-four, in perfect health – and hadn't the Family Ghost told me that I had a long life ahead of me? Lord, it's a *mistake* . . .

The shattering racket and the pain cut off simultaneously. My body seemed immersed in a thick and swirling medium. All around me was darkness, a liquefied void that was neither air nor water. Then I realized that the black wasn't empty at all; pictures were flashing in it, appearing and disappearing with subliminal rapidity almost like single-frame cinema projections displayed on dozens of small screens encircling me. I recognized early childhood scenes with Tante Lorraine and the young cousins, school days, Don and I blowing out candles on a joint birthday cake, Onc' Louie walloping the pair of us for some transgression, Christmas caroling in deep snow, fishing in the river, an embarrassing freshman high school dance. The vignettes whirled faster and faster and I realized at last that they were memories, the accelerating replay of a life.

But not my life. Don's.

For the first time I experienced real fear in place of stunned astonishment. The riot of images was acquiring a full sensory and emotional input and I seemed caught in an insane mélange of sights, sounds, tastes, smells, visceral and tactile sensations. My mental voice cried Don's name and I heard him babbling an incoherent, furious reply.

All of the remembered scenes were showing *me*. And the emotional transfer revealed that my twin brother despised and hated me to the very depths of his being.

Why, Donnie, why?

The only reply was rage. The visions were drenched in it. I seemed to be at the centre of a psychic tornado with Don's mind flailing at me from every scene, hurt and degraded. His wife, his children, his friends flickered past, all wounded by his soul-sickness, all diminished, their attempts to help him rejected until it was too late. And he blamed it all on me.

But I don't understand why!

I felt myself standing firm in the centre of the vortex while he whirled, helpless, remembering the very worst of it: his rejection of Denis, his corruption of Victor, the torment he had heaped on Sunny and the other children during the years of alcoholism, his seduction of Elaine in a calculated desire to hurt and humiliate me. To my amazement I saw that he was desperately sorry for all those things, and had been for years. What lingered was the source of the sins, his abiding hatred of me. In the final scene of his life he punished himself for it, but the action was one of severance and not remorse.

Donnie, I don't know why you hate me. But it's all right. I've never hated you.

He said: You should have.

He controlled the machine with his own psychokinesis. I screamed, begging him not to do it, but of course it had already happened. The blades that cut him in half cut him free of me at last.

I opened my eyes. Bill Saladino, the limping old church usher, was nudging me with the collection basket and grinning. I fished inside my jacket for the envelope and dropped it in. Bill winked at me tolerantly and stumped away, carrying the little basket of offerings up to the altar to be blessed.

Don's funeral was a big one, attended by scores of Remillards together with nearly two hundred others who had grown up or worked with him. He looked fit and handsome in his casket after the local croque-mort performed his duty; and the eulogy delivered at his burial Mass proclaimed God's unsearchable ways as well as his compassion for the brokenhearted, to which category Don indubitably belonged. There was a good deal of sotto voce reference to 'blessed release', and the pious aunts reassured one another that alcoholism was a disease one simply couldn't help. Sunny, supported by husky Victor at her left elbow and the slight but commanding Denis at her right, bore up well. Her eight younger children stood about her dry-eyed at the gravesite while the cousins and aunts and female neighbours wept.

The official verdict on Don was death by misadventure. Denis and Victor had driven their cars simultaneously into the logging site just as the runaway feller-buncher, with Don's severed body still held in its grab-arms, struck a large stump with one of its tracks and tipped over into a ravine. The resulting mangle, and a double dose of coercion aimed at the green-faced investigating deputies, made plausible to anyone but an experienced logger the final report on Don's demise. One of the witnesses, at least, was of unimpeachable reputation.

Denis and I were at the same motel, and the morning after the funeral we breakfasted together. He would be staying to help Sunny wind up Don's affairs while I was heading back to the White Mountain Resort and the pre-Memorial Day rush. The coffee shop was crowded and noisy, but noise is immaterial when the conversation is largely mind-to-mind. The pair of us might have been father and son: a gaunt older man in a good summer worsted three-piece, thumbing through the *Wall Street Journal*, and a vaguely undergraduate-looking youth in a navy-blue jogging outfit whose extraordinary eyes were blanked out by dark glasses.

Denis lifted the plastic pot. 'More coffee? I think I've solved the mystery of my young siblings' nonoperancy.

I said, 'Half a cup, maybe.' Victor's certainly at the bottom of it — and maybe Don, too. It's impossible that not a single one should have inherited telepathic ability, given the fact that your mother has occasionally shown flashes of the talent. Jeanette and Laurette were telepathic as infants but then seemed to lose it. I'm not sure about the others —

'Sugar?' It was the same with the other six. They were born with higher faculties but had them deliberately suppressed by aversion-conditioning: mental punishment. I got hold of the youngest, Pauline, who's seven. She was vulnerable through grief and shock and it was easy for me to – to – I suppose you'd call it hypnotize – render her receptive to my command that she regress to babyhood and describe her impressions of Victor and Papa. It was clear what had been done. Poor little Paulie! But Papa had nothing to do with it, thank God. It was all Victor.

The ruthless young bastard! . . . But how was it possible? He would have had to suppress the babies when he was still just a kid himself! How old was he when the girl twins were born? Four? And then Jackie and Yvonne and the boy twins coming bang-bang-bang and George just after you bachelored at Dartmouth in '80 that'd make Vic ten – and he would've been twelve when Paulie arrived my God my God no innocent kid could do such an evil thing —

[Detachment.] I'll have to show you some of my juvenile psychiatric case histories. He could do it, all right. Nothing is more self-centred than a toddler. Why do you think some of them have tantrums? They want the world to turn around them. Most children outgrow that mind-set and discover altruism. It's useful for survival, actually. But there are exceptions: sociopaths. Vic certainly seems to fit the profile. At first he acted to secure his position as Papa's favourite. Later, his motives would have become more complex. Power-oriented. You see the way he's going. He's an uneducated man, just as Papa was. A shallow thinker with a stunted conscience and tremendous drive and over-weening conceit. Papa had those attributes, too, but he lacked self-confidence because he was afraid of his psychic powers. Also, he'd been inculcated with moral values from earliest childhood, which Vic hadn't, and guilt warred with egoism, leading to ultimate destruction. Vic is a much tougher nut than poor Papa. Even without higher faculties he'd be something to reckon with. I have a feeling that being a pulpwood tycoon is only the beginning of his ambition . . .

'Want to pass me a little more strawberry jam? Thanks.' What the devil are we going to do?

He mind-screens like the Chase Manhattan Bank vault. I can't see into him and I can't budge him a millimetre with coercion. I'm virtually certain he's used his powers in shady ways for self-aggrandizement. Those logging contracts, for instance, and the big bank loan for capitalization of the company. Pure coercion. And there are rumours that at least two pieces of his equipment were acquired via moonlight requisition. Watchmen and guard dogs are no problem for an operator like Vic. (They wouldn't be to me!) And God knows enough logging gear gets stolen by purely *normal* thieves . . .

'Interesting article here in the *Journal*. Want a look? Seems Senator Piccolomini's narcotics bill has a good chance of passing.'

Do you mean to say there's nothing we can do to stop that young freebooter?

'Let's see. Hey – bad news for the pot smugglers!' Getting legal proof of his wrongdoing would be very difficult. And what's to prevent him from coercing a jury even if we did get the goods on him? A Homo superior criminal has the odds in his favour. And if one tries to counter him using his own weapons . . . well, you saw what happened to Papa.

I exclaimed out loud, 'Doux Jésus – you can't be serious! I told you the way it was. I shared it!'

But I was *there*. With Victor. He's a terrific screener, but he let the triumph leak. I was standing there spewing my guts out and he was crowing! . . . Papa was a morbid and self-hating man, like most alcoholics, but that night he'd been scared into asking for help for the first time. He wasn't sunk in despair, he was reaching for a way out. Taking a first step on to a very shaky bridge across a black canyon. And somebody cut that bridge somebody sabotaged his newborn hope somebody planted a powerful coercive incitement to suicide that reinforced his own underlying tendency toward death: *Victor!* He knows I know. He knows I can't do a thing about it.

Can Victor . . . hurt you?

No more than Papa could. [Concern.] But I'm not so sure about you, Uncle Rogi. Your mind is pretty transparent, especially about emotion-charged matters. Your sharing of Papa's death . . . if Victor found out, he might think you were a threat. I've been considering ways to protect you.

I pushed away my plate. 'I don't think I'll finish these hot cakes after all. Waitress! Will you give us our cheque, please?' *Christ Denis what a crock of shit maybe Don was right after all powers cursed —*

A long time ago you said that what you'd really like to do is open a bookstore in a quiet college town.

. . . You're right. I'd almost forgotten.

You're a topflight convention manager. You could probably get a job in hotel management somewhere else in the country. But Hanover really needs an antiquarian bookshop, and if you were there you wouldn't be *alone.* There are nearly forty of us working at Dartmouth now, research assistants and subjects in my lab. You could help us. And I'm certain we could protect you.

'Somehow,' I said, smiling, 'I don't think I'd be in serious danger here. I have a strong belief in guardian . . . angels.'

'Don't be a fool!' Even through the dark glasses I could see Denis's eyes blaze and feel the searing force of his mind that took hold of me like a puppy. He released me instantly as I reacted with fear and astonishment. His mental speech was anguished:

I should have been able to save Papa from Vic! I ran away from the situation at home shut out what I knew was happening did it to survive and because I believed my work more important than my biological father's life but I *should* have saved him *should* have loved him and didn't and I'll always blame myself always feel him dying dying lost in despair and I won't lose *you* the same way damn you Rogi can't you understand? . . . One day I'll find a way to checkmate Vic. Until then the powers *are* cursed and perhaps we are too but I'll find a way to redeem us and if that isn't megalomania I don't know what it is maybe I'm crazier than Vic and more futile than Papa but I must go ahead. I must! Please help please understand please know who you are to me why I need you . . .

'Denis,' I said, reaching across the table. 'Tu es mon vrai fils.'

Tears were streaming from behind his dark glasses. At my touch he lifted his chin and the drops of moisture vanished. 'That's creativity,' he said softly in response to my start. 'A psychic power we've just begun to investigate, perhaps the capstone for all the rest. Let me show you, Uncle Rogi. Join us.'

Love and a sudden inexplicable revulsion warred behind my mental barricade. Prudence dictated that I safeguard myself from Victor. But as for becoming closely involved with Denis and his crowd of youthful operants . . . no. By no means.

The waitress handed me the check. I calculated the tip and fished in my wallet for bills. Denis and I headed for the cashier.

You must come with me to Hanover! His coercion was poised. Ordinarily, I could fend him off readily (as I had been able to fend off Donnie and Victor) but there was a chance that if I drove him to extremes he might feel compelled to bludgeon me down. For my own good. I couldn't let that happen.

So I smiled over my shoulder at him.

'I think,' said I, 'that I'll call the shop The Eloquent Page.'

10

Supervisory Cruiser Noumenon [Lyl 1–0000]
26 April 1990

Four Lylmik minds watched from their invisible vessel as the last civilian evacuees from the American space station boarded the commercial shuttle Hinode Maru. The smaller

American orbiters were still mated to the station's half-completed drive-unit while their crews completed the demolition arrangements.

The vector of the meteoroid that had struck the manned satellite might have been calculated with diabolical precision. The impact had killed the orbital velocity needed to keep the structure circling the Earth at its temporary altitude of five hundred kilometres, as well as killing six workers. The twenty-three other persons aboard the station survived because of the airlock system connecting the 'Tinkertoy' units. These had suffered only minimal damage; but the power-plant that might have restored the velocity of the station was unfinished, and kicking such a huge satellite back into orbit by means of auxiliaries would have taken more booster engines than the Western world, Japan and China possessed. The addition of Soviet boosters would have sufficed to save the station. However, in addition to its multinational commercial facilities, research labs and astronomical observatory, the American station had also included a module with functioning military surveillance apparatus. The Soviets had declined to assist in the salvage; and now the elaborate station, only a few months short of completion, travelled a rapidly decaying orbit that doomed it. Rather than await the inevitable reentry and fall to Earth, the United States had decided, for strategic and safety reasons, to blow it up.

'The waste, the dashed hoped,' Noetic Concordance mused. 'The discrepancy between the promise of this great station and its abortion, brought about by a mere chunk of nickel-iron coated with ice . . . The situation is fraught with nuance. I shall compose a poem.'

'You'd better wait until I finish analysing the disruption of the probability lattices,' Homologous Trend warned. 'This event may have a truly nodal significance.'

'Then perhaps I'd better plan an elegy.'

'A dirty limerick, rather,' Eupathic Impulse suggested, 'dedicated to the low-orbit proponents at NASA. If they'd been satisfied to build a smaller station at high orbit, as the Soviets did, a hundred meteor hits couldn't have knocked it down. But this close-in structure *was* more economical –

assuming that no large object disrupted its delicately maintained low orbit during construction. One concedes that the odds were all in the Americans' favour! But, let's see:

The engineers trusted to luck,
Since they wanted more bang for the buck . . .'

'*Please,*' Homologous Trend admonished.

Asymptotic Essence said, 'I think I perceive some sources of your anxiety, Trend. The new détente between the United States and the Soviet Union is lamentably fragile. In spite of their joint Martian Exploration Project, the ancient political dichotomy persists. The loss of this American station will be viewed by the strategists of both nations as a disruption of military parity.'

'Oh, well, of course,' Eupathic Impulse conceded. 'One need only analyse the psychological dynamics at work. The Americans knew that their space station was immensely superior to the Soviet one from a standpoint of technological sophistication, and it was also to be a showcase of international goodwill. This made the Americans chockful of condescending magnanimity. (They love being grandfather to the world even more than we Lylmik do!) The Soviet-American Mars expedition was intended to be only the beginning of a new era of scientific, economic and cultural intercourse between these two powers. Now, however, the Americans stand humiliated. The impetus towards camaraderie in outer space is disrupted. Worse, the Soviets will have a strategic advantage – at least until the Americans put up a new space station. (Two years? Three? The American economy is already strained.) One hopes that Trend's computation does not point towards the death of détente, but one must also keep in mind that we are dealing with ethical primitives.'

'Logically,' Essence said, 'the Americans should not feel threatened. There are any number of robot surveillance satellites that can be co-opted as backup spy-eyes – and Omega knows both nations still have parity in nuclear weaponry. But the space station was a symbol of national pride as well as security, and the Soviets will certainly exult over the disaster while the Americans will feel naked to hostile scrutiny. And when has human warfare ever been logically motivated?'

'Listen to this,' Noetic Concordance broke in. 'An experimental apostrophe, but having possibilities: *O Meteor! Frost-cauled detritus of primordial cataclysm, fatal vagrant . . .*'

'One detects a soupçon of bathos,' said Asymptotic Essence with regret.

Eupathic Impulse was less charitable. 'You certainly can't use the meteor as the subject of the poem. It was a Pi-Puppid. How can one possibly compose an elegy on a Pi-Puppid? Now if the thing had belonged to a meteoric cloud having more intrinsic grandeur – say, if it had been a Beta-Taurid or even an Ursid — '

'I have the revised probability analysis,' Homologous Trend declared, displaying it without further ado.

Asymptotic Essence voiced the mutual dismay. 'A threat to the Intervention Scheme? Surely not!'

'Beyond a doubt,' Homologous Trend affirmed, 'if one carries the proleptic analysis to the eighteenth differential, as I have done. The cuspidal locus results from my injection of the character of the American President. His background and his marketing genius link him inescapably to the destiny of the (at base) commercial orientation of the failed space station. Now his bellicose, jingoistic opponents will prevail. The next American station will be austere – and entirely military. With the dire consequences that you see in my projection of events for the next twenty years.'

Eupathic Impulse strove for neutrality of tone and failed. 'One might ask why the Supervisory Body failed to investigate the critical nodality of the space station earlier – and why we didn't take steps to protect the precious thing?'

'In the first case,' Trend said, 'it is the responsibility of Atoning Unifex, acting with us in Quincunx, to define situations susceptible to such investigation. In the second case, overt protection would have violated the Scheme as it stands: Shielding the space station against meteoroids of consequent mass would require use of a sigma-field (which the Earthlings would surely have detected with their radio-telescope array); or else a preprogrammed hyperspatial matter trap (which as we know is unacceptably hazardous in a solar system having significant casual interplanetary traffic); or else we should have had to deploy a guardian vessel authorised to zap, deflect, grab, or otherwise dispose of intrusive space flotsam (which would grossly contravene the Oversight Directives).'

'Well, now what?' Eupathic Impulse asked.

Trend said, 'The event requires contemplation by all five entities of the Lylmik Supervisory Body, acting in the aforesaid Quincunx.'

'Anyone know where It is today?' Asymptotic Essence asked.

Noetic Concordance shrugged mentally. 'Either extragalactic or lurking about that college again. We'd better call.'

The four combined in metaconcert: Unifex!

One responds.

[Situational image] + [probability analysis].

Serene preoccupation. *Oh, yes. The collision was today, wasn't it?*

Reproach. One might have shared one's prescience.

Well, I didn't exactly use prescience . . . but I do apologize. There is no need for concern or action on your part with respect to this situation.

One disputes the probability analysis of Homologous Trend?!

Not at all. I plan to cope with the matter personally.

! [Forbearance.] Indirectly, one presumes, rather than through rescue of the space station.

Oh, yes. The station's nodality hinges upon its use in weaponry surveillance. I shall simply render the entire concept of spy-eye satellites obsolete. Metapsychically. The planetary Mind has already evolved the capability. Bifurcation is imminent. I do not violate the planetary Will in this but, as it were, anticipate the determination.

One of your esteemed Remillards?

No. The Scottish connection has been working on this particular speciality. Given a gentle nudge, there should be a satisfactory manifestation within the critical time-period, restoring the original coefficients of the sexternion and putting our Intervention Scheme back on the rails.

Comprehension. Most gratifying – and ingenious.

I really should have contemplated the matter with you prior to the space-station disaster, however, in order to have spared you needless distress. My absent-mindedness is getting to be a scandal. I become rapt in nostalgia, to say nothing of my joy in the unfolding of the metapsychic World Mind at long last . . . Now you must excuse me.

'Gone again,' Asymptotic Essence said. 'Ah, well.'

'One notes how confident It remains,' Homologous Trend remarked.

Noetic Concordance said, 'It has a unique perspective.'

'One hopes,' Eupathic Impulse added astringently, 'that It knows something we don't know about these contentious larvae, validating Its confidence in them . . .'

'The probabilities are in Its favour,' Homologous Trend said, 'as one might expect.'

The four entities shared certain ironic retrospections. Then they waited. Eventually, Eupathic Impulse said, 'There goes the destruct signal for the space station.'

'O Fireball!' declaimed Noetic Concordance. 'O perished pride of rigid circumstance — '

The other three Lylmik settled back to study the spectacle while the poet's mind continued its commemoration.

11

Chicago, Illinois, Earth
2 May 1990

He had completed the mental exercises that he was accustomed to perform at the start of each business day, and now Kieran O'Connor stood in front of the floor-to-ceiling window of his office and let his mind range out. His aerie was on the 104th floor of the Congress Tower, Chicago's most prestigious new office building, and from its vantage point he could oversee thousands of lesser structures, hives of concentrated mental energy that invigorated his creative mind-powers at the same time that they stimulated his hunger. Kieran had known other great cities — Boston, where he was born in poverty and educated in Harvard's affluence; Manhattan, where he had apprenticed in a law firm having a sizeable Sicilian fraction among its well-heeled clientèle – but the effete and tradition-bound East was an unsuitable home base for a unique upstart such as himself. Instinctively he had come to the dynamic heartland of North America, to this city notorious for its cavalier misprision and polymorphous get-up-and-go. Chicago was the perfect place for him; its commerce was thriving, its politics dishevelled, and its morals overripe. It was a coercer's town with bioenergies that matched Kieran's own, not suffering fools but welcoming bullies with open arms – a bottomless wellspring of novelty, hustle and clout.

From his high place Kieran looked out across a bristling forest of skyscrapers, a grid of crowded streets, green bordering parklands along the Lake Michigan shore that flaunted lush tints of spring. Countless cars ant-streamed along the multiple lanes of the Outer Drive. The lake waters beyond were a rich iris-purple, paling to silver along the eastern horizon. Outside the breakwater was a dancing sailboat. On a whim, he zeroed in on it and was rewarded with the ultrasensory impressions of two people making love. He smiled and lingered over the emanations momentarily, not with a voyeur's vulgar need but in dispassionate reminiscence. He had other pleasures now; still, the resonances were good . . .

A chime sounded, pulling him back to reality.

He turned away from the window and went to his enormous desk. The polished surface mirrored a single yellow daisy in a black vase and a photograph in an ebony frame – Rosemary holding the infant Kathleen, little Shannon in a white pinafore clinging to her mother's skirts. Rosemary and Kathleen would never grow older, but Shannon was a moody fifteen-year-old now, resisting initiation into her father's world. The phase would pass; Kieran was sure of it.

The chime sounded again.

Kieran touched one of a line of golden squares inset into the rosewood desk-top. A compact communication unit lifted into ready position. Arnold Pakkala looked out of the screen with his deceptively distant expression. His colourless eyes seemed to study a potted fig tree behind Kieran's right shoulder.

'Good morning, Arnold.'

'Good morning, Mr O'Connor. You'll be interested to know that Grondin has checked out and approved two more California recruits. They'll be flying in to the corporate training facility next week.'

'Excellent.'

'Mr Finster is standing by on the Washington land-line. However, I must also advise you that Mr Camastra's car has just entered the Tower parking garage. He must have taken an early flight from Kansas City.'

'Hmm. He'll be in a stew so we won't keep him waiting. Let me know as soon as he gets up to the office. There's time for the Finster call, I think. Put him through, full-sanitary scramble.'

'Right away, sir.'

The communicator screeen displayed a sequence of security codes punched up by Kieran's executive assistant. Eventually these dissolved into a close-up of Fabian (The Fabulous) Finster, whose engaging smile featured two large upper incisors separated by a comical gap: chipmunk teeth. Most people were so captivated by that droll grin that they failed to take note of the icy green eyes above it. When Fabian Finster had earned his living as a bottom-of-the-bill mentalist in Nevada casino shows, he had enhanced his naturally striking appearance with neo-zoot suits trimmed in blinking LEDs. Now that he was one of the confidential agents of Kieran O'Connor, Finster strove for a more conservative image and had taken to Italian silk suitings and striped ties, with nary a trace of glitz. But the show-biz aura still clung to him, and he still performed occasionally to keep up a front, even though most of his time was now occupied by more serious and lucrative activities.

Kieran said, 'We'll have to make this quick today, Fabby. Did you wrap up Senator Scrope?'

'Tighter than a rattlesnake's ass, chief. You should have seen his face when I mentioned the number of his secret Icelandic bank account . . . Our pipeline into the Armed

Services Committee is now secure. Damn good thing, too. Reading politicians' minds is like snorkelling in a sewer. Shit galore – but you got one helluva time finding the one piece you really need before you drown in the utterly extraneous.'

Kieran laughed. 'Congratulations on doing a super job. I suppose you're worn out with the effort now and ready for a quiet gig at the Hotel Bora Bora.'

The mentalist's grin widened. 'I can read your mind all the way from here . . . almost. You got something interesting cooking, I wouldn't mind giving it a spin. Provided I don't have to stay in Washington. After digging in the brains of these politicos for six months, I'm fed to the teeth. Really makes a guy appreciate the lucid crumminess of the Mob mind.'

'What I have for you is an excavation with a good deal more class. How would you like to go Ivy League, Fabby? Do a little investigating for me at Dartmouth College up in New Hampshire?'

'Ah hah. You want me to sniff around that ESP project!'

'So you've heard of it.'

'I even read the new book by that Dartmouth prof that hit *The New York Times* best-seller list. It took me two weeks – what with having to look up all the big words – and I'm still not sure the guy said what I think he said.'

Kieran's tone was incisive. 'I had no idea that parapsychology research was being taken so seriously by legitimate institutions. Jason Cassidy and Viola Northcutt are looking into the work being done at Stanford on the West Coast, but I want you to find out what this man Denis Remillard is up to – especially what practical applications of the higher mental powers might lie behind the theoretical considerations set forth in his book.'

'You mean, is the guy up to anything dangerous to *us* – or is he just blue-skying around?'

'Precisely. Remillard's book is a very unlikely best seller. It's difficult to read and its conclusions are veiled to the point of deliberate obscurantism. He almost seems to be bending over backwards to make his data appear prosaic. Of course he couldn't squelch the inherent sensationalism of the topic completely, even with the pages of dry statistics and the academic jargon. His experimental verification of telepathy and psychokinesis is one of the hottest scientific stories of the century. But I have a feeling that Remillard is holding back. I want to know what other psychic experimentation might be going on at Dartmouth that the good doctor has decided not to publicize . . . for prudence's sake.'

'Jeez,' mused The Fabulous Finster. 'If certain parties start taking mind reading and animal magnetism seriously, what's going to happen to our *edge*?'

'Work me up a complete dossier on Denis Remillard. Get as much information as you can on his close associates as well. I'm particularly interested in how many adept mentalists he's recruited for his research. How powerful they are. How committed.'

'You want me to turn head-hunter if I turn up any live ones?'

'Use the utmost discretion, Fabby.' Kieran's eyes rested for a moment on the photo of the late Rosemary Camastra O'Connor and the two lovely children. 'This is a dangerous game. The government may have infiltrated the Dartmouth project – or even foreign agents. Remillard's book hints at a worldwide network of cooperating psychic laboratories beginning to achieve significant results after years of fumbling and marking time. I want to know if there's any truth in that idea, or if it's only wishful thinking.'

'I get the picture.'

'One last thing. If Remillard or any of his people show the least hint of being able to probe *your* mind, get out of there fast and cover your tracks.'

'I understand,' came the cheerful reply. 'Not to worry, chief. I won't screw up. I've noticed how people who cross you seem to get these weird cerebral haemorrhages . . .'

'Senator Scrope's wrap-up nets you a cool Bahama million, Fabby. The payoff on Remillard's organization could be even bigger. Goodbye.'

Kieran touched a golden square, breaking the scrambler patch. The screen went dark. Almost immediately, another square inset on the desk began blinking red.

Kieran keyed the intercom. 'I'll see Mr Camastra at

once, Arnold.' He recessed the com-unit into the desk, performed a brief Yoga transmutation designed to lift his coercive energies to the highest level, and sat back to await the arrival of his mafioso father-in-law.

'You heard, Kier? You heard? *He didn't veto!* I got the word from Lassiter in Washington on the car-phone just as we exited the Kennedy!'

Big Al Camastra stormed into the room. His cyanotic lips trembled in fury and a small driblet of saliva trailed from the corner of his mouth. The two bodyguards accompanying Chicago's Boss wore expressions of apprehension.

'I heard, Al. I've been expecting this.' Kieran came around his desk, solicitous, as Carlo and Frankie helped Big Al settle his bulky body into the office's largest leather armchair.

Al raved, 'That yellow-belly bastard! That fink! He's just gonna hold the bill until tomorrow without signing it, then it automatically goes into law even without his signature.'

Kieran nodded. 'The President wants the law but he didn't want to give public affront to its opponents.'

'What the hell kinda religious man is he? Goin' against the Catholic Bishops and the Council of Churches and the NAACP and the fuckin' PTA, for chrissake? They all lobbied for the veto. We all knew he'd *have* to veto! How could he do this? God – you know what this means? It's Repeal all over again!'

'Boss, take it easy,' Carlo pleaded. 'Your bionic ticker . . . you gotta calm down!'

'A drink!' Big Al roared. 'Kier, gimme a drink.'

'Al, you shouldn't,' whined Frankie, catching Kieran's eye and shaking his head frantically. 'The doc in K.C. said — '

Kieran O'Connor lifted one hand in peremptory dismissal. The two bodyguards stiffened and their eyes glazed. Both of them turned, completely docile, and left the room – oblivious to the fact that Big Al had enjoined them only five minutes earlier not to leave him alone with Kieran O'Connor under any circumstances.

The don had forgotten his own order. He was leaning back in the chair, one puffed and blotchy hand over his eyes, muttering imprecations. Kieran busied himself at an antique sideboard where cut-glass decanters sparkled in the sunlight. 'A little Marsala won't hurt you, Poppa. I'll have some, too. It's a nice virginale that DeLaurenti discovered and sent in to New York on the Concorde last week. If you like it, I'll have a couple of cases sent out to River Forest.'

Kieran took one of the filled glasses and wrapped the old man's tremulous fingers around it. He let healing psychic impulses flow from his body to Camastra's through the momentary flesh contact. 'Salute, Poppa. To your health.' Kieran lifted his own glass and sipped.

A bitter smile cracked Big Al's pallid features. 'My health! Madonna puttana, you should have seen those vultures giving me the eye in Kansas City, wondering if I'd drop dead right in front of 'em so's they could call off the Commission meeting and the vote!'

'The flight back has tired you out. You should have gone home to rest instead of coming downtown directly from O'Hare. Everything will work out fine. The Commission did as we expected. I won't have to exert mental pressure on them directly.' He raised his glass to the old man again and returned to his seat behind the desk.

Big Al watched him with hooded eyes. At forty-six, Kieran O'Connor was still youthful, his dark hair only slightly silvered at the temples and at the distinctive widow's peak above his wide forehead. With his olive skin and dark brown eyes Kieran looked more Italian than Irish – but he *wasn't*, and that should have stalled him in the consigliere niche permanently, no matter whose daughter he had married. Big Al still didn't quite fathom why it hadn't.

'The Commission voted you your seat,' Camastra told Kieran. 'You're the Acting, as of today, and they give tentative approval for you to take over when I retire. But we're not outa the woods yet. Falcone and his dinosaur faction keep harping on tradition, bitching because you're not a paisan'. They're willing to give you respect – but not to the point of joining your new financial consortium.'

Kieran made an airy gesture. 'Patsy Montedoro's influence will keep the younger dons on our side, and the Vegas and West Coast people are solid. Let Falcone and his pigheaded conservatives stew in their own juice for another year. Their racketeering and gambling interests have been on a long slide for over a decade – and now that the Piccolomini legislation is on the books, they're caught by the shorts. The end of Prohibition was a Sunday-school picnic compared to the legalization of marijuana and cocaine, and the decriminalization of other drugs.'

Big Al shook his jowls in bewilderment. 'How could the President do it? Every piss-poor tobacco farmer in Dixie will be planting pot or coca trees. Little old ladies'll grow opium poppies in window boxes! We'll have a country fulla junkies.' He gulped his wine.

Kieran got up and refilled the don's glass. 'No we won't, Poppa. The other provisions of the Piccolomini Law will see to that. The educational campaigns against all forms of chemical abuse ... the compulsory treatment or confinement of hard-narc addicts ... the capital penalties for outlaw dealing. What the government has done is to say: "Okay, you low uneducated trash, you unemployables, you losers, you cheap thrill-seekers. Go ahead and smoke yourself into a stupor if you want to – and pay Uncle Sam tax on each joint. Or snort till your nose falls off – but don't bother nice people while you're doing it, or we lock you up and throw away the key. And don't commit a crime under the influence, or recruit underage users, or peddle shit illegally – or you die." It's a very simple, sensible solution to a nasty problem, Al. The Treasury will recover revenue lost from the declining sales of tobacco and hard liquour, the streets will be cleared of criminals supporting their habit, and the big bad Mafia will have the financial floor cut out from under it once and for all.'

'It's indecent,' Big Al said. 'Sell cheap pot and crack and kids are gonna get it. I don't give a damn about the adult addicts. Let 'em turn their brains to stronzolo! But the little kids . . .'

Kieran resumed his seat with a shrug. 'The bleeding-heart liberals and the church people and the social workers tried to tell the President and Congress that. And so did we, of course.'

Al stared morosely into his wine. 'Thirty per cent. We lose thirty per cent of our income just like that with the legalization – and we're the most diversified of the Families! New York, Boston, Florida, New Orleans – they're gonna drop fifty per cent at least. And California — !'

'The Outfit will have a lean year or two. But those Families who go into my venture-capital pool will eventually end up richer than ever. Chicago is leading the wave of the future, Poppa, and my consortium will provide the impetus for a whole new profit structure. We'll survive, and so will the Families who follow us.'

'Follow *you*.' Blood-webbed eyes burned for an instant with the old antagonism and fear; but then came a fatalistic little laugh. 'What else could they do but follow you, stregone? Sorcerer!'

Kieran's expression was earnest, his coercive faculty working at max. 'Al, we can't keep running a two-hundred-billion-dollar business like a gang of nineteenth-century banditti – squabbling over a shrinking pie, eliminating rivals by shooting them and stuffing their bodies in car trunks. Times have changed. In two years, human beings will be walking on Mars. All financial transactions will be fully computerized. Most of the old rackets will be as dead as the peddling of narcotics. Sure, the Mob is rich. But you know what they say about money: if you just sit on it, it might as well be toilet paper.'

'Yeah, yeah,' the don said wearily. 'We gotta invest. I know.'

'Invest properly, Al, so that the money makes more money. That's what I've been doing as your consigliere – and what I'll continue to do when I'm Boss.'

'Boss of Bosses,' Camastra muttered.

Kieran did not seem to hear. 'In addition to our legitimate investment corporation for the Organization funds, we now have our own small tank of sharks to work with – three of them, all under my thumb and without the slightest off-colour taint to attract Justice Department bloodhounds. We own Clayburgh Acquisitions, Giddings & Metz, and

Fredonia International. They're takeover artists, Al, the kind of outfits that specialize in the leveraged buy-outs of troubled or vulnerable companies. So far, our little pets have confined themselves to modest raids of the loot-'em-and-dump-'em type. But now I'm ready to give them the go-ahead for some real action. Once the capital pool is ready, we're going after the biggest money there is.'

'What, for God's sake?'

'We'll begin with small defence contractors – the ones whose stock took a dive during the late-lamented détente. With the space-station disaster and hawkish noises starting up again in Congress, those defence companies will come back like gangbusters. When we're ready to tackle a biggie, there's McGuigan-Duncan Aerospace, the firm that almost crashed when their Zap-Star orbiting mirror weapon was axed by the Pentagon economizers. I have a strong hunch that by 1993 – when we have a new President and the Mars Project is recognized for the useless PR stunt that it is – this country will wake up and realize how far ahead of us the Russians are in the space arms race. Then those Zap-Stars may get a new lease on life.'

Big Al had gone the colour of chalk. 'You think there's gonna be a *war*?'

'Of course not. Only a fresh defence initiative. Once we've wrapped up McGuigan, we can go after G-Dyn Cumberland, the submarine builders. And Con Electric is shakey with the Japanese and Chinese undercutting their domestic products – but they were the fourth largest defence contractor in the country during the 1980s, and the Pentagon certainly won't buy missile parts from Asia.'

'Madonna puttana! You really mean it!' Big Al's glass fell without a sound to the thick beige carpet. Inside his thoracic cavity, the pacemaker adjusted his heartbeat in response to the elevated level of adrenalinemia.

Kieran was patient. 'History has shown that there is no greater potential for profit than in a suitably stimulated military-industrial complex – and the stimulation is imminent. The Soviets don't really want war and neither do we. But both countries are bound to slide back into the Cold War groove in response to internal tensions. We have our high unemployment and monumental national debt. They have their eternal food and consumer-goods shortages, and Slavic angst.'

'What if you guess wrong about a defence build-up? What if this US-Russian Mars Project makes us all buddy-buddy with the damn Reds and the disarmament thing gets into high gear?'

'Then it would be Goodbye, Daddy Warbucks.' Kieran waved one hand dismissively. 'But we won't let that happen. We'll protect our investment.'

Big Al stared at his son-in-law with the unaccepting disbelief of a man confronting an impending natural disaster – an avalanche descending, a looming tornado funnel – and then his face cleared and he began to laugh uproariously. 'Jesus!' he wheezed. 'Jesus H. Christ! Wait till that cazzomatto Falcone gets a loada *this* action!'

Kieran touched a golden square. Immediately the door to the outer office opened and his executive assistant appeared.

'Yes, sir?' Arnold Pakkala inquired. His mind added: The two hoods are sitting quietly biting their fingernails, and you have a conference call coming up at ten-thirty with Mr Giddings and Mr Metz in Houston, and then an early luncheon with General Baumgartner.

'Mr Camastra is ready to leave now, Arnold. Would you ask Carlo and Frankie to step in?' Kieran stood in front of Big Al with an outstretched hand and a cordial smile. 'Thanks a lot for stopping by, Poppa. Betty Carolyn invited me to bring Shannon to your place tomorrow for dinner, so I'll see you then. If you feel up to it, we can talk over this new financial business in more detail.'

Supported by his bodyguards, Big Al surged to his feet. 'Sure. We'll talk tomorrow.' He was still chuckling but his eyes refused to meet those of the new Acting Boss of Chicago. 'You can bring the two cases of Marsala. It's real good stuff. See you, Kier.'

Kieran O'Connor turned to the window to look out again over the luminous lake. The sailboat with the lovers was gone. He focused his farsense on a big cabin cruiser moving up the river towards the Michigan Avenue Bridge.

Arnold said: Ten-thirty. Shall I set up the call to Houston?

One person in the cruiser was telling another person a scandalous anecdote about the Illinois Attorney General and a certain labour official.

Kieran said: Give me five minutes to meditate and clear my mind. Then bring on the sharks.

12

Milan, New Hampshire, Earth
16 August 1990

It was the worst psychic stakeout in his experience, from beginning to end, bar none.

The damn tippy little rented johnboat! Essential to his night bass fisherman cover, it was dismayingly low in the water, its aluminium hull clanked at his slightest movement, and it stunk from decaying salt-pork bait trapped down under the duckboards.

The damn hot, muggy night! Not a breath of fresh air stirred over the small lake ringed with summer cottages, and after four hours of surveillance, he was sopping wet with sweat and cramped all to hell.

The damn fucking bugs! They really were – mating, that is – and doing it all over *him*. Perhaps it was the seductive stench, or the little boat might just have provided a convenient rendezvous out there in the middle of the lake. Whatever . . . aquatic insects by the hundreds, gossamer-winged and mostly connubially linked, fluttered, crept and copulated in and about the anchored johnboat. Any shift in posture by the boat's occupant produced a cellophanish crunch.

The damn fish! Smallmouth bass, gourmandizing on the besotted bugs, leapt explosively out of the water at unnerving intervals. If he had been a genuine angler, the sight of the noble lunkers would have warmed his heart. But Fabian Finster was a city-bred, sports-hating sophisticate who preferred his fish filleted, gently grilled and served with lemon-butter sauce. Periodically, when the feeding frenzy in the waters around him disturbed his concentration to un unbearable degree, he would break off the surveillance, muster his coercive faculty, and blast both predators and prey. The fish would hightail it into the depths and the bugs would faint, fall into the lake and drown. All would be serene for ten minutes or so, until a new swarm of insects arrived and the fish pulled themselves together again.

The real corker, however, the brain-bender supremo of that enchanted evening, was a technical surveillance problem: the subjects were speaking – and thinking telepathically – in *French*. He had encountered this in his nightclub days, too, and learned to fake translations by cracking the linguistic formulation of the thought and extracting its purely imaginal content. (*Ha ha, ugly gringo! Read my mind! Tell me I have six thousand-dollar bills in my money-clip!*) But translating more than a phrase or two of a foreign language was a bitch of a job for a mentalist – analogous to eyestrain. The intense concentration required would leave him physically and mentally pooped, by no means a healthy state for a guy in the espionage and extortion racket. Add to the French translation grief an uncanny premonition of disaster that no psychic could afford to ignore, and Finster decided he had been very unwise to accept the Remillard assignment, no matter how much loot Kieran O'Connor dangled as bait.

Bait!

SCRAM! FUCK OFF! FUCK ELSEWHERE!

Momentarily alone again in the starlight, Finster sighed.

His troubles had started at the beginning of the assignment, when he'd tackled the kid professor, Denis Remillard. Denis was a truly boffo screener of his private thoughts, nobody to mess with. Any probe attempt by Finster would not only have been detected – but its source would have been pinpointed. So he'd settled for crumbs, bits of 'public' telepathy Remillard addressed to his friends and associates. Denis spoke only English and his subvocal thoughts were also couched in that language. But what thoughts! The prof

272

ratiocinated on such a rarefied level that poor Finster was totally out of his league, lost in a labyrinth of symbolic logic, gestalts, alatory subintellections and other horrors. If Denis was working on anything potentially threatening (or useful) to the O'Connor enterprises, it would take a better brain than Finster's to prove it at this stage. He had suggested, and his Boss had concurred upon, a more indirect course of investigation. Finster would leave Denis and his Coterie alone until there were hints of more than theoretical activity, and concentrate his efforts on the young genius's many relatives. One or more of them might provide useful leverage material for future action against the Dartmouth group.

It was when Finster began surveillance of Denis's uncle, who acted in loco parentis to the professor and worked at a big resort in the White Mountains, that culture shock struck. Like most persons who considered themselves one-hundred-per-cent Americans at that time, Fabian Finster was completely ignorant of the French-speaking minority population of New England. Uncle Roger was a harmless fellow who spoke fluent Yankee – but his thoughts were an untidy mélange of French and English. Sorting them out had consumed a tedious month, during which Finster stayed as a guest at the resort during the high season, eating too many gourmet meals. But there had been a payoff: Uncle Roger was preparing to leave his job because he was afraid! Afraid of Denis's younger brother, Victor, the black sheep of the family.

Bingo.

Finster had zeroed in on Victor immediately, and discovered that the twenty-year-old man was not only a telepath but a powerful coercer as well – certainly stronger than his older brother and perhaps even more compelling than Kieran O'Connor himself. Furthermore, he was a crook, using a legitimate business as a front in much the same way that Kieran did, only on a vastly smaller scale.

O'Connor was very interested.

Finster was instructed to study Victor and his operation, using the utmost caution. He was always to stay out of coercive range, which they pegged at a hundred yards to be on the safe side, more than twice Kieran's sphere of psychic influence. He was to eavesdrop both electronically and telepathically, being especially alert for useful dirt. Each night Finster would fast-transmit the tape of the day's data to Chicago via scrambled land-line, and there would follow consultation and fresh orders from the Boss.

For three weeks, Finster had shadowed the young pulp-wood entrepreneur in and around his home base of Berlin, New Hampshire. It soon became apparent that the shady aspects of Victor's operation were expertly papered over; there was no immediate prospect of blackmailing him. He had no wife, girlfriend, boyfriend or significant other susceptible to outside menaces. (He shared support of his widowed mother and younger siblings with Denis, but seemed to have no real love for any of them.) His financing was tightly secured in two local banks and a third in Manchester. He had logging contracts in both New Hampshire and Maine, and seemed ready to expand into Vermont as well – as soon as he could pin down the appropriate persons to coerce. Given Victor's apparently invulnerable setup, Kieran O'Connor decided he had two options at the present time: He could let Victor be, as he had Denis, filing him for future reference; or he could invite the young man into his own criminal coalition.

Finster was now completing the feasibility study for the latter alternative . . . and it was looking dimmer and dimmer. In Finster's judgement, Victor Remillard was not only a mental badass, he was probably a nutter to boot. His French-English thoughts were often chaotic, indecipherable. There were dark hints of no less than three murders perpetrated within the last year, together with an indeterminate number of psychic and/or physical assaults. He dreamed of monsters, and most of them had his own face. He hated Denis, and only some deep-lying inhibition constrained him from doing violence to the older brother he both envied and despised.

Fabian Finster had long cherished a salutary fear of Kieran O'Connor; but he had decided that he was even more afraid of Victor Remillard. When he finished up for the night, Finster intended to pass on to the Boss his own urgently negative vote regarding any alliance with Victor. On the contrary, the Mob might give serious consideration to putting out a contract on this kid before he spread his web any wider . . .

Sweaty, pest-ridden and disquieted, Fabian (The Fabulous) Finster resolutely stayed on the job, whispering a simultaneous translation and running commentary into a bug-smeared Toshiba microcorder hung on a lanyard around his neck. Meanwhile, on the screened porch of his lakeside summer cabin, Victor Remillard drank cold beer and went about the business of recruiting fresh heads for his growing coven of psychic henchmen. He was concluding an interview with a middle-aged Canadian telepath of dubious moral fibre who had driven down that day from Montréal in a brand-new Alfa Spider.

'Now the two of 'em just sit there chewing things over . . . Now Vic offers the guy another bottle of Hibernia Dunkel Weizen from the refrigerator on the porch (Jesus!) . . . Now Vic says out loud in Frog, "I agree that a merger of our two groups might be advantageous, Roe-bear, but it must be on my terms. I will make the machine march – be the boss." And Fortyay says, "For sure, Vic. No – uh – hassle. I have seen for myself who you are and what you are." And he takes a fast slug of suds, trying to be brave. And Vic leans towards him and smiles just a little and thinks: "Is it that you are *certain* your four playmates will accept my direction? Without making any doubts? I am not playing kids' games, Roe-bear. I am going to shock the gallery" – dammit! he means score big – "with this mental thing. My Remco pulpwood operation is just – uh – for starters. I'm going to be a big vegetable" – shit! – "big shot and make more millions" – wait, that means *billions* – "than you can count. So will the people who work with me. But you will have to do things my way. Do you understand, Roe-bear? No one makes the cunt with me – uh – fucks around with me and manages cheap – uh – gets away with it." And the other guy says out loud: "Good blood, Vic! I told you, anything you say!" And his brain is dripping blue funk like a colander, and he thinks: "You know why we're anxious to join up with you. Who else knows the music – the angles – of this mind business like you? Up in Kaybeck, me and Armang and Donyel and the rest have been just – uh – spinning our wheels, fooling around with small-beer scams. We know we gotta come South to get where the real – uh – action is. And that means joining your outfit. Why do you think I made my proposition regular?" He means above-board. "Drill in my head all you want. Drill in the boys' heads. you'll see we aren't – uh – bullshitting." And Vic is all charm now. He says, like: "Swell!" They both laugh. The thought-patterns are formless friendly – only underneath Roe-bear is still trying not to wet his pants and Vic's sub-basement has a gleam like *your* steel tiger-pit, Boss . . .'

Finister hit the pause button of the recorder and shifted position. Inky ripples spread out in circles from the john-boat. The water was now littered with insect bodies and the bass, sated, had retired for the night. Finster prayed that soon Victor would, too.

He whispered a few more translations and comments as the young man led his visitor down the front steps of the cabin and walked with him to the Alfa Romeo. A next meeting was set up, to include the other members of the Canadian gang. Then the Spider's headlamps flashed on, making two paths of wavering light on the lake that stopped short of Finster's boat. The car backed, turned and drove off along the shore road.

Victor Remillard's mind was strangely aglow. He stretch-ed, yawned, then walked down the path to the small dock in front of the cabin, where he stood looking out over the lake with his arms folded.

Finster's boat began to move slowly towards him, drag-ging its sash-weight anchor.

'Oh, shit,' muttered the mind reader, 'Shit a *brick*.'

He lunged for the three-horse outboard mounted at the stern and yanked the starting cord, producing pathetic burbling sounds. He yanked again and got a few apologetic pops. Cursing, he fumbled the small oars into their locks and flailed desperately at the water while the boat picked up speed, moving in the opposite direction.

'Turn me loose, dammit!' There were other cabins on

the shore, some with lights. He yelled: 'Help! Help! . . .' But his voice died away to a croak, lost in the summer chorale of frogs, crickets and katydids.

Nothing left to do! The tall silhouette at the end of the dock was barely ten yards away. Finster ripped buttons from his soggy sportshirt to get at the .357 magnum Colt Python in its underarm holster. He lifted the gun with both hands and tried to aim, but the Colt seemed to have a life of its own and the blood-hot metal fought to squirm out of his grip, and when he clung to it, it became heavy as the lead sash-weight anchor and tried to break his wrists, and then he saw that the barrel was pointed at his right knee-cap and his finger was tightening on the trigger, and he screamed and flung the thing sideways and it fell overboard and Vic laughed.

I'll jump out! his mind howled. And I can't swim but I'd rather drown —

He was drowning.

Drowning in his own vomit that had flooded up his throat and into his windpipe. He made a terrible noise as he crashed against the low aluminium gunwale, his head and upper body hanging over the side, his eyes wide open beneath the dead-black water. And the mental voice:

Don't be any more stupid than you've already been. Not until we have a chance to talk.

Talk? . . .

He was sitting upright, wet only with his own perspiration, and the boat glided smoothly up to the dock and stopped. A hand was extended to help him climb out.

He looked up. The zillions of stars in the summer sky outlined a tall, good-looking young man with dark curly hair. His mind was a simmering blur.

'Talk?' Finster repeated out loud, a wan chipmunk grin trembling on his lips.

'Come up to the cabin,' Victor told him curtly, and turned his back to lead the way off the dock. When the mind reader hesitated, something seemed to clamp his heart with red-hot pincers, making his knees buckle; but in a split second the pain was gone and he stood upright again, and the damn frog growled over his shoulder, 'Grouille-toi, merdaillon!'

Finster needed no translation. In fact, he was inclined to agree with Victor's rude assessment of him. It was the royal screw-up of his life – what was left of it – and he was a certain goner. Once this realization came, Fabian Finster's spirits paradoxically lifted.

'Sit there,' Victor ordered, when they came through the screen door on to the cabin porch. Finster lowered himself into a wicker chair with cretonne cushions. Did he dare ask for a beer?

Something awful lit up behind Victor's eyes. 'I could squeeze your brain like a grapefruit, Finster. I could force you to tell me everything you know about the ones who sent you to spy on me, then kick your ass out of here with nothing but scrambled eggs left inside your skull. I've already done that to a couple of snoopers. One was a Russian – can you believe it? – offering me three hundred grand to get him into my brother's laboratory. I took his money very gladly and he disappeared without a trace. The woods are lovely, dark and deep, Finster. You could go the same way . . . or maybe not. You've got a certain familiar smell about you.'

And he lifted his mind-screen to give the barest glimpse of reprieve.

'All *right*!' Finster shouted, breaking into a guffaw of relief. 'I dig what you're thinking, amigo! Do I ever!'

'Oh, yeah?' Victor's voice was like ice, and the tantalizing image the mind reader had grasped so desperately did a chameleon shift and faded to imminent doom. Finster sat up straight, waiting for it.

But Victor was smiling. 'You're not one of my brother's stooges. You're not from the government. You're not a Red. Your mind's spread open like a planked salmon, Finster. I know exactly what you are.'

'I'm a crook, Victor,' Finster said. 'Just like you. And I'm here following orders from another crook – who is definitely *not* just like you. He's big. Maybe the biggest, pretty soon. You reading my mind?'

'Better than you know. Tell Kieran O'Connor exactly

what I say, Finster . . . Stay away from me. If your people try to interfere with me, I'll send them back to O'Connor's office in Chicago to die, right in front of his fancy desk. But you also tell him that I have certain plans. If he lets me alone, here in my home territory, maybe the day will come when the two of us have things to say to each other. It won't be soon. But when one of us *really* needs the other, I'll talk to him . . . Do you think you can remember my exact words, Finster?'

The mind reader shrugged, hooked one thumb around the lanyard that hung from his neck, and pulled out the Toshiba microcorder. 'You're on the record, Mr Remillard.'

' 'Then get out of here.' Victor turned away, heading for the interior of the cabin.

'No beer?' Finster ventured.

'No beer.'

'Figures,' Finster said. He went out the screen door, closed it very carefully, and headed for the dock.

13

From the Memoirs of
Rogatien Remillard

As a bookseller, I have noted a curious thing: There are certain scientific books of epochal importance, titles recognized by every educated citizen in the Galactic Milieu, that nevertheless languish unread by modern people. One thinks of Darwin's *Origin of Species*, Freud's *Interpretation of Dreams*, Wegener's *Origin of the Continents and Oceans*, Wiener's *Cybernetics*, and other works that provoked controversy in their day – only to subside into banality once their contents had passed the test of time and merged with the common body of human knowledge.

Denis Remillard's towering work, *Metapsychology*, is another that suffered this ironic fate. Now, 121 years after its publication, only a few scientific historians bother to read it. But I remember the uproar attending the book's appearance early in 1990, when it sold nearly 250,000 copies in hardback format during its first year and became the common coin of TV talk shows and articles in the popular press – an amazing performance for a highly technical work, bristling with statistics, written in a dignified and daunting style. *Metapsychology* presented for the first time an integrated scheme encompassing all forms of mental activity, normal and supranormal, with an emphasis upon mind's interrelation to matter and energy. In a detailed and elegant series of experiments, scrupulously verified, Denis demonstrated how the so-called higher mind functions are inherent in the mental processes of *all* human beings. He showed how every mind contains, in some measure, powers both ordinary and extraordinary. His keystone theory explained the unusual activities of psychic adepts in terms of operant metafunction, and the deficiencies of 'normal' people as an aspect of metapsychic latency – where operation of the higher powers was either inhibited by psychological factors or precluded by a limited talent.

Metapsychology provoked intense discussion – and a certain dismay – within the scientific establishment, since it presented hard evidence that the higher mental functions were genuine phenomena and not merely dubious conjecture. Psychic researchers (and there were many besides Denis), after enduring decades of condescending tolerance or out-and-out ridicule from their conservative peers, basked in a new and unprecedented atmosphere of respect as they found themselves courted by the media, by sundry government agencies, and by commercial exploiters scenting a new growth industry that might eventually rival aerospace or genetic technology. Numbers of hitherto clandestine operants 'came out of the closet' as a result of Denis's book and became involved in serious research projects. There were also legions of quacks – astrologers, tea-leaf readers, spoon-benders and practitioners of black magic – who enjoyed a brief heyday riding the coattails of the legitimate metapsychic movement. The public was entertained for months by debates and squabbles among the mixed bag of opposing psychic factions.

Denis himself remained largely aloof from the altercations his book had spawned, distancing himself from popular journalists, television interviewers, and other purveyors of mass titillation. He had not yet publicly revealed that he himself was one of the principal subjects of his experiments, nor were other operant workers at his Dartmouth laboratory identified by name to nonprofessional investigators. Attempts to make an instant celebrity of the author of *Metapsychology* were doomed by Denis's humourless and erudite manner, his penchant for quoting statistics, and his total lack of 'colourful' personality traits. Media snoops found lean pickings at the scene of his researches, a drab old saltbox on College Street in Hanover, across from the Hitchcock Hospital parking lot. The metapsychology lab's personnel was loyal and close-mouthed, giving superficial cooperation to reporters and interested VIPs while making certain that no really sensational data came under outside scrutiny.

Fortunately for the disappointed newsmongers, there were plenty of less diffident psychic researchers at other institutions who were more than eager to fill the metapsychic publicity gap. These basked in the limelight and hastened to publish their own researches — as well as their critiques of Denis's magnum opus. Since most ordinary people have a gut belief in the higher mental powers, the public at large reacted positively to the opening of the new Metapsychic Frontier. There were surprisingly few commentators, in those early days, who envisioned any problem in having an elite population of operants living and working among 'normal' humanity . . .

Late in 1990 when the Mind Wars scandal broke and it was revealed that the Defense Department of the United States had attempted to pressure psychic researchers into undertaking classified projects, public opinion experienced its first anti-meta shift. But this was destined to be swept away in the fresh furore that came the following year, when Professor James Somerled MacGregor of Edinburgh University revealed to a stunned world the first truly practical application of mind-power. MacGregor's demonstration was a total vindication of Denis's theories. It was also responsible for opening a rift in the human race that not even the Great Intervention would heal completely.

To digress momentarily from the earthshaking to the jejune, I must note that 1990 was also the year that I started my bookshop, The Eloquent Page. Nowadays the place has quasi-shrine status, but I continue to resist attempts by various busybody groups to institutionalize it. The shop persists under the original proprietor at its address of 68 South Main Street, Hanover, New Hampshire. For the sake of Galactic tourists, I have a section devoted to works by and about famous Remillards. (I even have for sale a few fragile copies of the first edition of *Metapsychology*, exorbitantly priced. Inquiries are invited.) However, my stock in trade remains, as always, one of the largest collections of rare science fiction, fantasy and horror books in New England. My shelves hold no modern liquid-crystal bookplaques; every volume is printed on paper – and a goodly percentage of them are still sturdy enough to be read. I welcome browsers of all races, even Simbiari, provided they utilize the plass gloves I keep available and refrain from dripping green mucus on the stock.

The choice of the bookshop premises was not mine. I had initially decided to rent a place farther north on Main Street, closer to the Dartmouth campus, where there was much heavier foot traffic and where my business instincts assured me that trade would be brisk. This intention, however, was thwarted by an old acquaintance.

I remember the sunny autumn day that the rental agent, Mrs Mallory, took me on a round of inspection. Even though I had already expressed my preference, the lady insisted on showing me one last vacant property.

'It's such a pretty place, Mr Remillard,' she told me, 'the corner shop on the ground floor of the historic Gates House building across from the post office. A marvellous example of the Late Federal style, absolutely the ideal ambience for a bookshop! The premises are a tad smaller than the location down by the Hanover Inn – but so much more evocative. And there's a lovely large apartment available on the third floor.'

I agreed to look the place over, and it was everything she had promised. The apartment, in fact, was virtually perfect. The store itself, however, seemed far too small for the type of establishment I was then contemplating, a combination of used books and current hardbound and paperback volumes. I told Mrs Mallory that I found it charming but unsuitable.

'Oh, dear! I really thought you'd like it.' She gestured at the old beamed ceiling, the frowsty little nooks at the rear. 'The atmosphere of antiquity – can't you feel it?' And then she smiled conspiratorially and said in a lowered voice, 'It's even *haunted*.'

I paused in my inspection of the bay display window, polite incredulity on my face. 'Interesting. I'm sure having a ghost in one's bookshop would be quite a novelty, especially since I plan to specialize in fantastic literature. But I'm afraid the place really is too small, and too far from the campus to attract much evening trade — '

And then I felt it. Without conscious volition, I had let my seekersense range out, the weak divination faculty I had been practising under Denis's tutelage with a view towards guarding myself from intrusions by Victor or other undesirables. I had managed to learn how to detect the distinctive bioenergetic aura of fairly strong operants, such as Denis, Sally Doyle or Glenn Dalembert – provided that they were within a radius of ten metres or so and not shielded by thick masonry or some other barrier.

And now, scanning this old frame building's empty corner premises, I farsensed the presence. I stood rooted to the spot, sweat starting out on my forehead.

Mrs Mallory was chattering on: ' . . . and if you're sure you'll need more space, we might talk to the owner, since the little coffee shop next door might not renew its lease and it might be possible to double the square footage available . . .'

I seemed to hear someone say: Tell her you'll take it.

Who's there? my mind cried. Whothehell *is* that?

'I beg your pardon?' said Mrs Mallory.

I shook my head. *It was in the back room.*

'I know!' she exclaimed brightly. 'I'll just let you stay and look the place over at your leisure, both the store and the apartment, and you can drop in at my office later with the keys and let me know what you've decided.'

'That will be fine,' I said. The sound of my voice was distant, dimmed by my concentration on the detecting ultrasense. *It was coming out of the back room into the main part of the shop.* Mrs Mallory said something else and then went out, closing the street door firmly behind her. Dust motes eddied in the brilliant sunbeams shining through the display window. As I began slowly to turn around for the confrontation, an idiotic extraneous thought flickered across my mind: In late afternoon, I would have to make some provision so that the strong sunlight would not fade the books.

There's an awning. All you have to do is lower it.

'Bordel de dieu!' I spun around, exerting my farsense to the utmost, and detected an all-too-familiar aura. It had no form, nor was there anyone visible in the shadowed rear of the shop.

The Family Ghost said: It's been a long time, Rogi. But I had to be certain that you took this place and not the other.

'Ah, la vache! I might have known . . .' I stood with one hand braced against the wall, laughing with relief. 'So you've been haunting this shop, have you?'

The previous tenant was a trifle reluctant to vacate and I had to insure that the lease would be available. Sometimes it's perplexing, trying to determine precisely which occasions require my personal attention. My overview of the probability lattices is by no means omniscient, and after such a long time my other faculty is unreliable.

'So! You've made up my mind for me and I'm to be forced to rent this place even though it's too small. Is that it? My poor little Eloquent Page and I will go broke just to satisfy your ineffable whim.'

Nonsense. You'll do well enough if you stock antiquarian books and forget about the cheap ephemera. The clientèle will seek out your establishment and pay suitably high prices for collector's items, and you can also do mail-order business . . . Be that as it may, it is not your destiny to achieve commercial prosperity.

'Well, thanks all to hell for the good news! As if my morale isn't low enough, changing careers at the age of forty-five and playing lab-rat for one nephew while another contemplates offing my ass.'

Victor is otherwise occupied. You need not worry about him.

'Oh, yes? Well, you'd better keep him in line!'

I may not influence him or the other Remillards directly. It would violate the integrity of the lattices. You are my agent, Rogi, because you *have* been influenced. You must live and work here, in this place that is appropriate, only two blocks away from the house at 15 East South Street.

I was totally mystified. 'Who lives there?'

At the present time, no one who need concern you.

I snarled, 'Oh, no you don't!' and pointed a determined finger at the volume of air that seemed to radiate the aura of le Fantôme Familier. 'I'm not standing still for any more of your mysterious directives from Mount Sinai! You cut the crap and give me a damn good reason why I should rent this shop instead of the other one − or find yourself another patsy.'

There was a cryptic silence. Then:

Come with me.

The front door opened and I was firmly impelled out on to the pavement. I heard the locks click. A couple of coeds sitting at a sidewalk table in front of the little restaurant next door eyed me curiously. I let the Ghost shepherd me around the corner. It said:

Walk east on South Street.

All right all right! I said rebelliously. For Godsake don't make a public spectacle out of me!

I − or perhaps I should say we − walked along the quiet side street. It was only two blocks long, and near Main Street were a few commercial structures and widely separated old homes converted into offices and apartments. There was very little traffic and only sporadic bits of sidewalk, so I strolled along the edge of the street, past landscaped parking lots and mellow frame residences, and crossed Currier Place. There stood the Hanover public library, a modernistic pile of red brick, concrete, and glass-wall framed in enough greenery to allow it to blend unobtrusively with the more classic buildings around it. Immediately east of the library was a large white clapboard house with dark green shutters, a modest portico, and third-floor dormers, set well forward on a thickly wooded lot that sloped towards a deep ravine in the rear. On a weedy and unkempt lawn lay an abandoned tricycle. A football and a yellow Tonka Toy bulldozer decorated the porch, along with a sleeping Maine Coon cat that resembled a rummage-sale fur piece. Two hydrangea bushes flanking the steps still carried pink papery blooms. No people were in evidence.

I stood under a scraggly diseased elm and stared at the house that would one day be famed throughout the galaxy as the Old Remillard Home. The Ghost said: You will note its convenient proximity to the bookshop.

I didn't say anything.

The Ghost went on: Six years from now, Denis will buy this house for his family. Many years later it will be Paul's home —

'Paul?' I said out loud. 'Who the devil is Paul?'

Denis and Lucille's youngest son. Marc and Jon's father. The Man Who Sold New Hampshire. The first human to serve on the Galactic Concilium.

Starlings were yammering up in the elm and the golden autumn sun heated the asphalt pavement and gave a faint pungency to the air. The pleasant old house – as solid and homely a piece of New Hampshire architecture as one could imagine – seemed to be drowsing in the late-afternoon calm of this little college town. I looked at it stupidly while my mind took hold of what the Ghost had said and tried to digest its import. The 'galactic' bit was too bizarre to penetrate at first, so I seized on a more down-to-earth improbability.

'Lucille? Marry Denis? You've got to be kidding.'

It will happen.

'Admitted, she's one of his most talented psychic subjects. But the two of them are hopelessly incompatible

– fire and ice. Besides, I happen to know that she's in love with Bill Sampson, a clinical psychiatrist at Hitchcock. It's an open secret that they'll marry as soon as her analysis is complete and there's no ethical conflict.'

The Ghost said: Lucille and Denis must marry and produce offspring. Both of them carry supravital alleles for high metafunction.

'Tu parles d'une idée à la con! They don't even *like* each other. And what about poor old Sampson?'

An unavoidable casualty of Earth's mental evolution. His wounded heart will recover. The deflation of the Cartier-Sampson liaison will be one of your most critical tasks in the months ahead. When Lucille is free, she will naturally gravitate to Denis, her metapsychic peer, and the genetic advantage of their union will become self-evident to her. If it is not, you can discreetly press the point.

'Me? *Me?*' I was sandbagged by the casual arrogance of the Ghost. 'You think this girl's some kind of computer I can reprogramme?'

You'll find a way to work things out. You *must*. Sampson is hopelessly latent, an unsuitable mate for this young woman who is so highly endowed with the creative metafunction. It is unfortunately true that she and Denis have clashing temperaments, but this is not an insuperable barrier to a fruitful marriage. Lucille will be an ideal professional partner for Denis as well. Her drive and indomitable common sense will counter his tendency to brood and vacillate. There will be continuing tension between them, especially in the later years. It is then that your own supportive role – and your fortuitous proximity – will be most advantageous.

'I'm your mole, you mean! Put into position for continuous meddling with people who aren't even born yet – isn't that it?' I pulled myself together. Although the street seemed to be deserted, it would hardly do for local residents to look out of their windows and discover a middle-aged loufoque haranguing an elm tree. I walked on to the east, where the street curved into Sanborn Road and the wooded precincts of the Catholic church.

Sternly, I addressed the Ghost in mental speech: I see

very well the role you intend for me. I am to be your agent provocateur, interfering with upcoming generations of Remillards like some evil genius in a goddam Russian novel!

Nonsense. Your influence will be entirely beneficial. You will be needed. Your qualms are understandable, but they will fade as the importance of your mental nurturing manifests itself.

If I refuse the commission — ?

I cannot coerce you. If your compensatory influence is to be effective, it must be freely given. The unborn Remillards needing your help are not ordinary human beings, however, and your sacrifices on their behalf will have far-ranging consequences.

How . . . far?

Rogi, vieux pote, I have already said it – but you refused to accept the implication. And so I will be explicit, so that you will know exactly what is at stake. You are a member of a remarkable family: one that will one day be the most important on Earth. Denis and Lucille's children and grandchildren are destined to become magnates – leaders, that is – of the Human Polity of the Concilium of the Galactic Milieu.

'C'est du tonnerre!' I cried, aghast, and my mind asked the halting question: Are you telling me that we . . . the planet Earth . . . will become part of a galactic organization *within my lifetime*?

There was a furious honking and a sarcastic voice that called, 'Howsabout it, Charley? You gonna stand in the street till you grow roots?'

I snapped out of my daze to see a laundry van two feet away from me in the middle of Sanborn Road. There must have been something in my face that turned the young driver's impatience to concern. 'Hey – you feeling all right?'

I lifted one hand and hastened on to the sidewalk. 'I'm OK. Sorry about that.'

The driver eyed me uncertainly, then shrugged and drove on.

The Ghost said: My dear blockhead.

You, the entity who reads this, will doubtless think the

same of me. Had not the Ghost told me long ago that it was a being from another star, that its intentions were benevolent and our family was of crucial importance? A man possessed of the least modicum of imagination might have deduced *some* design behind these uncanny manoeuvrings – always supposing that the spectral puppet-master was real and not the perverted manifestation of my own unconscious.

I made an attempt to gather my scattered wits. 'When will this . . . invasion of extraterrestrials happen?'

Never! Rogi, you are a prize idiot! Le roi des cons! Why should we invade your silly little world? The starry universe is our domain and our cherished responsibility, and we come to a world only when we are called.

'Elaine and her people called you,' I muttered bitterly. I reverted to mental speech when I noticed a workman cutting the lawn of the church across the street. Why didn't you respond to Elaine's appeal, mon fantôme? All her people asked was that you bring us the blessings of your galactic civilization before we're destroyed in a nuclear holocaust. Wasn't that a good enough reason for you to bestow your cosmic CARE packages on Earth?

The Milieu does not dare to contact a developing world until the planetary Mind attains a certain maturity. Premature intervention would be hazardous.

To *whom?*

To the planet . . . and to the Milieu.

Well, don't cut it too fine! Détente's on a fast track to hell again and every other tin-pot nation in the Third World seems to have an atomic bomb ready to defend its honour. You wait too long and your flying saucers might land in a radioactive slag heap!

The likelihood of a small nation detonating a nuclear weapon is unfortunately high. But the prospect of full-scale nuclear war between the great powers is infinitesimal at the present time. The danger seems destined to escalate with the passage of time, but my prolepsis indicates that the Great Intervention will almost certainly take place before your civilization destroys itself.

Well – when *do* you land, for chrissake?

When there is worldwide recognition of the higher faculties of the mind, and when those faculties are used harmoniously by a certain minimal number of humans.

Are you talking about the kind of thing Denis is working on?

Denis and many others. Metapsychic operancy is the key to lasting peace and goodwill among disparate entities – human and nonhuman. To know the mind of another intimately is to understand, to respect, and ultimately to love.

Then all of the citizens of your Galactic Milieu have the higher mental powers – telepathy and psychokinesis and all that?

The spectrum varies from race to race and from individual to individual. But all Milieu minds share telepathic communication and our leadership enjoys formidable insight. In matters of gravity there can be no duplicity among us, no misunderstanding, no irrational fear or suspicion.

No wars?

We have never experienced interplanetary aggression. Our Milieu is far from perfect, but its citizens are secure from exploitation and institutionalized injustice. No individual or faction may flout the will of the Concilium. Every citizen-entity works towards universal betterment at the same time that it is encouraged to fulfil its personal potential. Ultimately, the goal of our people is to obtain that mental Unity towards which all finite life aims.

'Grand dieu,' I whispered. 'Ça, c'est la meillure!' Without thinking, I had turned left on to Lebanon, a major thoroughfare. My heart soared like that of a six-year-old on Christmas morning. I had thrust aside all my doubts as to the authenticity of the Ghost. If it was a figment, its delusions were comforting ones. I asked:

How many planets belong to this Milieu?

Thousands. Our present coadunate population includes some two hundred thousand million entities – but only five races. This is a very young galaxy. Eventually, all thinking beings within it who survive the perilous ascent of technology's ladder will find Unity with us. My own race, which was the first to attain coadunation (the mental state leading to Unity) has the honour and the duty of guiding other peoples into our grand fellowship of the Mind. Nearly a quarter of a million juvenile races are currently under observation, and six thousand of those have a high civilization ... but you humans are the only candidates approaching induction.

Jesus Christ! when I tell Denis —

You will tell no one, least of all Denis. These revelations are for your own encouragement, given because you demanded of me good reasons for your continuing cooperation.

Denis deserves to know!

He would be distracted from his great work. He must go on his own way for now, assisted by you in secret. His trials – and there will be many – will be *his* incentive.

God, you're a cold-blooded bastard! Suppose I tell him in spite of you?

Denis would not believe you. You are being very silly, Rogi. Your obtuseness wearies me.

'Sometimes,' I whispered with a certain malicious satisfaction, 'I get pretty sick of me, too! Poor Ghost. You picked a weak reed for your galactic shuffleboard game.'

There was a spectral chuckle: I myself have had my own ups and downs ... but here we are in front of the real-estate office. Mrs Mallory awaits your decision on the bookshop rental.

I felt in my hip pocket for the two keys she had given me, one for the Gates House store and one for the apartment upstairs. The two pieces of brass were cool in my hand. God knew what they would unlock in my future.

The Ghost said: I have a small token for you. Look in the gutter.

I did, and there among the leaves and pebbles and gum wrappers was a gleam of red. I picked up a dusty little key ring. At the end of its short silvery chain was a novelty fob, a red glass marble of the type we kids used to call 'clearies', enclosed in a wire cage.

Well? asked the Ghost.

Don't rush me, dammit! I said. Then I opened the office door and went in to sign the lease on my haunted bookshop.

14

Hanover, New Hampshire, Earth
22 December 1990

The test chamber was heavily insulated against sound, temperature change, and extraneous electromagnetic radiation. Its air was filtered and its lighting dim and blue, which latter turned the ruddy colour of the kitten's fur to grizzled grey and its amber eyes to smoky topaz. In the ceiling were video and ciné cameras, radiation detectors, and other environmental monitors, focused on the cat and on Lucille Cartier. The young woman, wired with body-function electrodes, sat in a chair at one end of a heavy marble balance table. The kitten perched opposite her on the table top; the twin EEG transmitters mounted near the inner base of its ears were only two millimetres in diameter and almost completely concealed by the fur. On the table between Lucille and the cat was the ceramic platform of a hermetically sealed, ultrasensitive recording electrobalance. It looked rather like a medium-sized cheeseboard with a glass dome cover.

Vigdis Skaugstad's telepathic voice said: Ready Lucille?

Lucille said: Steady&Ready. Minou too.

The kitten said: [Play?]

Lucille said: Soon now wait be good.

Vigdis said: Systems running scale hot GO.

A white baby spot flashed on, illuminating the glass-covered balance plate. Simultaneously the blue lighting faded away, leaving most of the room in darkness. Lucille began to hum monotonously. She was still only imperfectly operant in creativity and the music helped to suppress her insistent left brain and induce the necessary lowering of the intercerebral gradient. She stared at the dazzling balance plate, trying not to 'will' too forcefully, urging the primal power that resided in her unconscious mind to flow towards the controlling conscious. In this way primitive humanity had summoned its gods, worked its magic, achieved transcendence, even compelled reality: by bridging unconscious and conscious, right brain and left, in this subtle, quasi-instinctual way that had been all but lost with the advent of the conquering word. Verbalization, a left-brain function, had given birth to human civilization – but at a price. The ancient creative powers were repressed, and lived on mainly in the archetypal guise of muses, those flashes of artistic inspiration or illuminating insight that welled up from the soul's depths almost without volition. And the old magical aspects of creativity, the ability to direct not only the 'mental' dynamic fields but also the fields generating space, time, matter and energy, were relegated to the dreamworld in most individuals.

It had been so for Lucille Cartier until four months earlier. Then, bowing at last to the counsel of her analyst, she had agreed to undertake training at the Dartmouth Metapsychology Laboratory that would raise her latent mind-powers to operancy. 'The faculties are part of you,' Dr Bill Sampson had told her, 'and you'll have to accept the fact. And learn to control them – or they'll control you.'

So she had come at last to the grey saltbox building. To her great relief, Denis Remillard had assigned her a congenial and nonthreatening mentor. Vigdis Skaugstad was a visiting research fellow from the University of Oslo, a specialist in psychocreativity. She was thirty-six, pug-nosed and rosy, with very long flaxen hair that she braided and wound about her head in a coronet. Vigdis's own psychic talents were unexceptional, but she was a gifted teacher; and her tact and empathy had led Lucille to over-come most of her deep-seated repugnance towards the research programme – if not her dislike of its young director. Working with Vigdis, Lucille had learned telepathy very easily. This most verbal of the higher powers quickly assumes a 'hard-wired' status in the brain of a talented person, as do most of the related ultrasenses. But Lucille's other significant faculty, creativity, had required a tedious, almost Zenlike regimen to raise it to the operant level. It was still far from reliable. Lucille took training exercises almost every day from Vigdis, and at the same time worked towards her doctorate in psychology. Thus far she had sedulously avoided socializing with other operants, except for an occasional lunch with Vigdis.

The laboratory cats, on the other hand, were her dear friends.

The animals were used in many different experiments, especially those involving telepathy, a feline long suit. Lucille's special affinity with the cats had at first provoked jokes among the staff about witches and their familiars; but the joshing had cut off in short order when Lucille seemed to establish a genuine mental linkage with one particular kitten, leading to an apparent creativity manifestation that was having its first controlled test today.

'Ooh, Minou,' Lucille crooned aloud. And to the cat: Let's do it baby you and me let's do it together again . . . together Minou!

The kitten's large ears swivelled and its pupils widened as it stared fixedly at the shielded balance platform. It saw the image in Lucille's mind and it knew what she was trying to accomplish.

So it helped.

'Minou, Minou, ooh-ooh,' sang Lucille.

The little animal's whiskers cocked forwards in anticipation. It uttered a barely audible trilling sound, the hunting call of the Abyssinian breed, and its black-tipped tail twitched. Except for its relatively large ears and eyes, its conformation and colour were almost exactly those of a miniature puma.

'Ooh-ooh-ooh.' Here it comes kitty here it comes . . .

The insubstantial image, brought forth from Lucille's memory.

[Amplified by kittenish predatory lust. Oh, fun!]

A smudgy cloud had begun to form above the centre of the ceramic balance pan. It was ovoid, smaller than an egg, with a pointed anterior and a humped posterior.

'Ooh!'

[JumpjumpNOW!]

Impatiently, the kitten darted forward and batted the glass dome. The psychocreative image shimmered as woman and cat faltered in their mental conjunction, then sharpened as they drew together again.

'Ooh-ooh, naughty Minou, not yet wait until we're through.' Good baby yes work with me sit still help MAKE

IT keep it under the glass don't let it get away until it's *here* stay stay work with me . . .

[Mouse!]

Yes.

[MOUSE!]

The form was still translucent, in the early stage of materialization that Vigdis Skaugstad had called 'ectoplasmic Silly Putty'. But the mousy shape was entirely plausible and becoming more detailed with passing seconds. Snaky little tail. Jet-bead eyes. Tiny ears and whiskers – shadowy, yet, but placed where they belonged. (And how many patient hours had Lucille spent beside the cage in the critter room of the Gilman Biomedical Center, commiting those anatomical details to memory so that her mind's eye and creativity function would be able to resummon them whenever she commanded it . . .)

The illusion became opaque. It settled on to the ceramic balance platform beneath the glass dome. It had four feet with claws, a fur-clothed body that shone sleek under the bright spotlight.

[Warmth of MOUSE smell of MOUSE twitchy allure of MOUSE!]

The kitten crouched, waggling its rump, stamping its hind feet in preparation for the spring —

'Nooh-ooh, ooh-ooh.' Not yet Minou not yet wait baby you can't get at it under the glass wait soon soon . . .

Abruptly, the read-out on the electro-balance went from zero to 0.061 μg. The mouse simulacrum began to move, its eyes sparkling and its nose sniffing. It scuttled obliquely off the pan and went through the thick lead glass of the dome cover, heading for the table edge.

The kitten sprang.

Squeee!

[Gotcha!]

The psychocreative mouse vanished.

Lucille Cartier sat back in her chair and sighed, while the room lighting brightened to normal incandescent and the Abyssinian kitten bounded about, searching for its elusive prey. The test-chamber door opened and Vigdis Skaugstad came in, all smiles.

'Wonderful, Lucille! Did you notice the mass gain?'

'Not really. I was too busy making the mouse squeal. Minou is so disappointed if it doesn't.' Lucille reached into the pocket of her flannel skirt and took out a little ball with a bell in it, which she threw to the kitten. Her face was weary and her mind dark.

Vigdis began to disconnect the body-function monitors that had been pasted to the human subject. The kitten abandoned the ball to mount an attack on the dangling electrodes.

'No no, kitty,' Vigdis scolded. 'Behave yourself – or maybe next time we wire *you*.'

'Minou wouldn't cooperate then,' Lucille said, disentangling the small paws. 'She won't perform unless the experiment is fun. I should be so lucky.'

'It was hard on you?' Vigdis's kind, china-blue eyes were surprised. 'But you said doing the materialization was always an amusement for the two of you – and your heart and respiration level were not significantly elevated during the activity.'

Lucille shrugged. 'But now we aren't just playing. The mouse isn't just a pounce toy, it's an experiment with the data all recorded for analysis.'

'But the experiment was a great success!' Vigdis protested. 'And not just the materialization – although it was the best you have ever done – but the fact of the metaconcert! This is our first experimental confirmation of two minds working as one. Your EEG and the cat's were like music, Lucille! I shall write a paper: "Evidence of Mental Synergy in a Human-Animal Psychocreative Metaconcert." '

'That's a new term, isn't it? Metaconcert?'

'Denis coined it. So much more stylish than mind-meld or tandem-think or psi-combo or those other barbarisms you Americans are so fond of, don't you think?'

Lucille only grunted. She stood up, transferring the kitten to her shoulder.

Vigdis said, 'We shall have to repeat the experiment, and similar ones. Eventually, we will want to try the metaconcert with you and a powerful human operant, such as Denis.'

At the door, Lucille whirled around. 'Not on your life!'

'But he would be the best,' Vigdis said, gently reproving.

'Not him. Anybody but him!'

'Oh, my dear. If there were only some way I could help you to overcome your antagonism towards Denis. It was all a misunderstanding, your earlier feeling that he was trying to force you to participate — '

'I have the greatest respect for Professor Remillard,' Lucille said, heading out into the hall. 'He's brilliant, and his new book is a masterpiece, and he's had the good taste to let me alone during most of my work here. Let's keep things that way . . . Now I'll take Minou home, and then I'm off to finish my Christmas shopping.'

Vigdis followed as Lucille headed for the Cat House, an opulently furnished playroom where the resident animals ran free. 'Lucille, I'm sorry but there is something you must do first. I didn't want to upset you before the run, but it is very important that you speak to Denis before you leave for the Christmas break. He is waiting for you in the coffee room.'

Oh *Vigdis*!

Lucille you must. Please.

'If he has any more friendly admonitions about Bill, I'm going to be awfully pissed, holiday season or not!' Lucille stormed. 'I've had enough flak from my family without Denis adding his contribution.'

'The conference has nothing to do with Dr Sampson. It is an entirely different matter.'

'Good,' said Lucille shortly. Then she relented at Vigdis's hurt reaction to her asperity and apologized. 'Don't take me seriously. I'm still tensed up over the experiment . . . Did I tell you Bill wanted to give me a diamond for Christmas? His late mother's ring. But I refused. As long as I'm still his patient, there mustn't be even a hint of – of our commitment. But the analysis is nearly complete.'

She opened the Cat House door and bent down to put Minou inside. The place harboured five Maine Coon cats, three Siamese, and two other Abyssinian kittens, all breeds noted for metapsychic precocity. The animals lounged on carpeted ledges and shelves, peered from padded lairs, slept in baskets, clambered up feline gymnastic equipment, and lurked amid a well-chewed jungle of potted plants. Minou ignored the lot and made a beeline for the feeding station.

'Is it your family's disapproval of Dr Sampson that makes you so downhearted?' Vigdis asked, bending to scratch the head of a Siamese that had come to caress her ankles.

'They're being very pigheaded, and it's so damned unfair! I thought they'd be happy when I told them Bill wanted me to marry him.'

'A psychiatrist and his patient,' Vigdis murmured. 'There are ethical considerations — '

'To hell with that! And that's not what's bugging Mom and Dad. They don't want me to marry *anyone*.' They don't understand they only know their own stupid fear and Bill the doctor was supposed to cure me of it exorcise it make me normal like them and instead he *loved* it loved *me* and they can't stand that it proves them wrong and proves me good and lovable and them wicked because they hate and fear me and they'll be sorry Bill and I will make them feel so small so ashamed make them burn with shame burn burnburn *BURN WITH SHAME* —

The cats shrieked.

As if some switch had been thrown, the room exploded in a clamour of tormented kitten squeals, full-throated Siamese yowls, and the lynx-roars of frenzied Coon cats. The women dashed out of the hall and slammed the door.

'Uff da!' said Vigdis.

Lucille had gone white. 'I'm so sorry! The poor little things! God – will I ever get this thing under control?'

Vigdis put an arm about the trembling girl. 'It's all right. Your creativity was energized inadvertently. You must expect that to happen sometimes when you are tired or stressed. The cats were not harmed, only frightened.'

Lucille repeated dully, 'I'm sorry. I'm sorry.' Sorry my mind is perverse sorry my folks don't like Bill sorry they fear me *does Bill*? sorry they don't love me but just let *him* love me —

Lucille be strong. You want to be loved of course so do we all.

I think . . . he may be afraid too.

Yes. He may. You must face that. Your Bill is a normal. *He understands!*

He is twice your age an experienced clinician yes he very likely does understand and I am sure he loves you very much even if he is also afraid. But normal! Oh Lucille my child I should tell you . . . but how can I? Your parents may have known in their hearts loved you more than you realized . . . but how can I tell you how —

What?

Lucille . . . I loved a normal man. We married before my faculties became operant under the tutelage of Professor MacGregor but then afterwards the difference the terrible difference I did not want to believe what the wisest operants warned me about I knew my love would be strong enough but in the end Egil divorced me the price paid for becoming operant is permanent alienation from normal human attachments.

I don't believe it!

It is true.

It can't be . . . the way you said. Bill loves me! He knows exactly what I am and he loves me.

He cannot know you. Your mind is closed to him. Your true self will always be unknown and you can only love him rejecting lying —

'No!' Lucille said aloud.

The cats had fallen silent and the old building creaked in the blustering wind. Somewhere in an empty office a telephone rang five times before being switched to the answering machine.

Vigdis said, 'It's getting late – nearly six. I must go back to the test chamber and finish up.' Her mind had veiled itself, withdrawn from the younger woman's defiance. 'Please don't forget to meet with Denis before you leave.'

Vigdis hurried away and Lucille stood there for several minutes, seething with resentment, before going downstairs to the room on the main floor that had once been the kitchen of the saltbox and now served as a coffee room for the research staff. It had been furnished with cast-off furniture. To honour the holiday season, there was an eighteen-inch spruce tree decorated with multicoloured LEDs sitting on an old lab cart in front of the window.

As Lucille entered the room, Denis Remillard turned away from the coffee machine near the Christmas tree, holding two steaming cups. Of course he must have known exactly when she would arrive . . .

'Good evening, Professor Remillard,' she said stiffly. 'Dr Skaugstad said you wanted to see me.'

'Sugar?' Denis lifted one of the cups. 'The half-and-half is all gone, I'm afraid.'

'Black is fine.' As if you didn't know!

As always, his mind was fathomless below its socially correct overlay. He was dressed for the weather in a red buffalo-plaid shirt, corduroy pants, and Maine hunting shoes from Bean's – an incongruously boyish bête noire who held out the coffee mug to her with a noncommittal smile. His awful blue eyes were averted, watching the snow outside the window.

'They say we'll get another eight inches before tomorrow. It'll be rough for travel.'

Lucille said, 'Yes.'

'I'm glad that your creativity run was successful. The implications of the mass pickup on the simulacrum are almost more intriguing than the metaconcert effect.'

'Vigdis has staked out the metaconcert paper,' Lucille said sweetly. 'That leaves the mass gain for yours.'

Denis nodded, still looking out the window. 'You might be interested in an article in the current issue of *Nature*. A man at Cambridge has suggested a mechanism for the psychophysical energy transfer, based on the new dynamic-field theory of Xiong Ping-yung.'

'No doubt the Chinese Einstein will connect us mind-freaks to the real universe in due time, and the Triple-A-S will heave a great sigh of relief. But if you don't mind, I'll give the six-dimensional math and lattice-construct theory a miss for now. Too many other things to think about.' She set her coffee down, untasted. 'Just what was it you wanted to discuss with me, Professor?'

'A certain problem has come to light.' Denis spoke slowly, keeping his tone casual. 'At parapsychology establishments in California, New York, Virginia and Pennsylvania, workers have been approached and offered enormous salaries as an inducement to join a secret unit being formed at the Psychological Warfare School of the Army Research and Development Center at Aberdeen, Maryland. Persons who declined – and we believe most did decline – were then subject to great pressure by the Army representatives. In several cases, the pressure amounted to virtual blackmail. The more polite decliners were urged to set up a psychic-research data pipeline to the Pentagon. The military is particularly interested in the areas of excorporeal excursion, long-distance coercion, and the psychocreative manipulation of electrical and electronic energy.'

'The bastards!' Lucille exclaimed. 'It's the atomic weapons thing all over again! Whether we like it or not, we're going to be used — '

We are not.

She gaped at him. He turned from the window so that his eyes caught hers for an instant like a cobra mesmerizing a rabbit. An instant later he lowered his gaze and she was left floundering.

He said, 'The human mind is not a docile piece of machinery, Lucille – especially not the mind of an operant metapsychic. Perhaps some time in the future we operants may learn to disguise our thoughts so thoroughly that we can deceive one another readily in moral matters – but that time hasn't come yet. Any operant sympathetic to this insane Mind Wars concept will be expelled from our research projects. Sent to Coventry. Thank God the point is moot thus far.'

'You're positive nobody's gone over?'

'Nearly so. However, if certain overzealous Pentagon types discover just how close we really are to psychic breakthroughs of global importance, they may resort to more dangerous tactics. The advent of excorporeal excursion alone will turn foreign policy on its ear . . . So we won't be able to remain passive in the face of this threat. The people at Stanford are going to blow the whistle on the dirty recruitment tactics – especially the attempted extortion. When the scandal breaks, public and Congressional outrage will dig the grave for the Army's Mind Wars scheme.'

'And then they'll leave us alone?'

'I'm afraid not. I'm certain that the military will continue to try to penetrate our research groups for intelligence purposes. But I'm determined that this will *not* happen here at Dartmouth, where so many strong operants are concentrated. So far, we seem to be secure. Very few normals outside of the college administration are aware of what we actually do, and I've examined all of our workers and operant subjects without finding a single person who was suborned by Pentagon head-hunters. That is – I've examined everyone except you.'

'Well, nobody's tried to buy me or dragoon me. God help them if they tried!'

'I have to be sure of that,' said Denis.

'You – what?'

The eyes took hold of her again.

'I must be quite certain.'

He set his coffee mug down beside the little Christmas tree and closed the distance between them. His psychic barricade, that wall of impregnable black ice, was dissolving now and she could see for the first time a hint of the mentality that lay behind. It was even worse than she had feared. The coercion was impossible to resist, as cold and impersonal as the northeast wind driving the blizzard. What a fool she had been to think that he had tried to coerce her before! He'd done nothing – only *talked*, exerted ordinary persuasive force. She had been left free, then, to make her own choice.

Now there was no choice.

Dissolving, berating herself, helpless before his invasion, she could only watch as he posed the questions and read the replies her mind passively delivered up. Humiliated, too supine even to rage, she found herself suddenly alone; and her only memory was of a mind-voice, as unexpected as a razor cut:

Thank you Lucille. All of us thank you. We're very glad that you are one of us . . .

The window drew her like a magnet. She pressed her nose against the frosty pane and looked out into tumultuous white. The snow-bleared red of his Toyota's taillights shone at the exit of the parking lot and then disappeared.

She was all alone in the laboratory building. A curl of vapour arose from her neglected coffee cup, sitting beside the empty one Denis Remillard had left behind. The Christmas tree blinked against the backdrop of the storm.

One of them.

Am I one of them?

Lucille turned out the room lights, leaving the little tree lit, and went upstairs to make her peace with the cats before going to supper.

15

Edinburgh, Scotland, Earth
11 April 1991

A classic Scotch mist fell on the tenements and closes of Old Town, rendering the quaint streetlighting even more inadequate than usual, but the two persons who stalked Professor James Somerled MacGregor had no difficulty at all keeping track of him. His gangly figure was a blazing beacon to the psychosensitive as he tramped through the murk, haloed by a raging crimson aura lanced with occasional fresh bursts of white indignation. His subvocal thoughts, more often than not, were broadcast heedlessly on the declamatory mode.

Two million quid! The bloody cheek of it!

Oh, aye! He'd been expecting something like this to happen once the EE work reached the critical transition from theoretic to practical. He'd alerted the other metapsychology research establishments actively studying the function to keep a sharp watch for attempts at subversion. And now this! The low, furacious skites hadn't made their move in America or India or West Germany – they'd tried it *here*, in Scotland, on his very own patch that he'd taken such pains to secure!

Of course loyal Nigel had told the CIA where to stuff their fewking proposition. Whereupon the spooks had piled insult upon insult by telling him that he couldn't hope for a better offer from MI5, who were hamstrung by recent budget cuts. Then they'd hinted that he would enjoy life a lot more in a nice Maryland condominium than in a guarded compound in the Negev Desert or a GRU facility on the outskirts of beautiful metropolitan Semipalatinsk!

Small wonder that Nigel's creative metafaculty had run slightly amok at that point, setting the Yanks' attaché cases on fire and prompting their hasty withdrawal. Nigel had bespoken his boss at once, and he and Jamie had held a council of war in Nigel's Canongate rooms, with the windows open to disperse the stench of scorched cordovan, and tumblers of Laphroaig to calm their righteous ire. Now that the security of the Edinburgh Parapsychology Unit was compromised, there seemed little hope that they could continue on the cautious schedule of action championed by Denis Remillard and Tamara Sakhvadze and the other operant conservatives, who advocated delaying the public announcement of EE capability until there were at least a thousand adept practitioners scattered around the world. This move on Nigel by the CIA meant that other intelligence agencies would soon be homing in on the EE workers. Once the world militarists became aware of the advanced state of EE, they might risk a neutralization scheme of draconian scope in order to preserve the strategic status quo.

The only thing for it was to do a media demonstration just as soon as possible.

Once the news was out, the risks would be diminished – if not quite eliminated. World opinion would help safeguard the adepts from any blatant pogrom or conscription attempt. Yes . . . that was the only way to go. There'd be resistance from Tamara and Denis to overcome. Their timetable had been carefully reasoned. And Denis would certainly balk at participation in a demonstration, since he'd stuck his neck out so far in the publication of *Metapsychology*. Right, then – Jamie would gladly put his own cock on the block. They'd do the media demo right here at Edinburgh University. Probably take until autumn to set it up. Meanwhile, they'd all have to take precautions, just as young Alana Shaunavon had urged that very afternoon. Curious, her having that premonition of danger . . .

As Jamie squelched along, cogitating, he was oblivious of other pedestrians on the High Street. There weren't many, since it was nearly one in the morning and the mist was thickening to drizzle. Normally, he would have taken a bus from Nigel's place to his own home a mile away in the northern New Town, but he'd wanted to give his anger a chance to cool, besides mulling over what would have to be done next. Set up safeguards for his own people in the morning. Then excurse to America and tackle Denis. Or should he do that as soon as he got home? What time was it in bloody New Hampshire, anyhow? . . .

He was just short of North Bridge when the two superimposed mental images struck him like a physical blow.

Alana!

And the Unknown.

. . . Alana Shaunavon, his most talented EE adept, shivering with her witch-green eyes full of apprehension after a perfectly harmless jaunt to Tokyo, gripping the arms of the barber's chair white-knuckled and confessing that she'd had a flash of dire foreboding. Impending disaster. He'd reassured her, then forgotten the matter until Nigel Weinstein alerted him to the attempted subversion. And now Alana's face sprang to Jamie's mind again – from his memory or from somewhere else – projecting a second warning . . .

. . . that was savagely blotted out by the mental override of the Unknown. A man, physically present nearby, strongly operant.

Turn right MacGregor into the next close.

The compulsion was irresistibly exerted. The intent was murderous.

Jamie was both stunned and incredulous. An *operant* enemy? But that was impossible! Both Denis and Tamara had flatly assured him that their governments had no operant agents. Denis had checked Langley many times with his seekersense and Tamara had subjected the files of both the KGB and GRU to remote-view scrutiny.

'Who's there?' Jamie called. And then telepathically: *What do you want? Where are you?*

Come in here under the archway.

Helpless, Jamie turned off the High Street into the entry of the close, one of those narrow urban canyons peculiar to Edinburgh's Old Town that gave access to the warrens of tenement blocks. The corridor was nearly pitch-dark in the mist. Jamie had no penetrating clairvoyance that would spotlight the way, no dowsing ability that might identify the mentality coercing him. He stumbled on irregular pavement and nearly took a header, then managed to orient himself by looking up at the sky, which shone a faint golden grey above the silhouetted roofs and chimney pots.

'Who are you?' Jamie demanded. *American? Russian? Sassenach?!*

Keep walking.

His footsteps splashed and echoed in a narrow alleyway. He came out into a broader courtyard where there was a bit of fuzzy illumination from a building on the right and saw an insubstantial figure, standing still.

Come closer to me.

What the devil do you want?

Let's just get this over with.

Jamie battled the coercion, reeling like a drunken man, but his betraying legs carried him on towards the waiting Unknown. He tried to shout out loud, but his vocal cords now seemed paralysed. Strangely, he was not afraid, only more than ever furious. First Nigel – now him!

The Unknown held a narrow tube, no larger than a biro, with a faint metallic gleam. He pointed this at Jamie.

Closer, Closer.

Don't be a bloody fool! Jamie's mind shouted. *You won't stop EE by killing me . . .*

In retrospect, Jamie was never quite sure what happened next. Strong arms suddenly grasped him from behind and hauled him off his feet. He got his voice back and uttered a bellow that rang up and down the close. The Unknown swore out loud, crouched, and thrust out the cylinder. Jamie heard a sharp hiss. Then he was wrenched violently to one side by the person who had seized him and fell in a heap on to the slippery stones, striking his head. Roman candles popped in the vault of his skull and he heard running footsteps receding into the distance.

'How're you doing, man? Did he hurt you?'

Dim flame of butane cigarette-lighter. Deep-set eyes and touselled fair hair glistened in the drizzle. A burly man wearing a duffel coat, bending over him. A wry but friendly smile.

'I think I'm all right,' Jamie said. 'Bit of a bump.'

His rescuer nodded, extended a big hand, and helped Jamie climb to his feet. Although he was not young he was built like a stevedore, and he topped Jamie's six feet three inches. He held the lighter high, and its blue flame gave a surprising amount of light.

'Your friend the mugger seems to have run off. Did he get your wallet?'

'No.' Jamie used his handkerchief to dry his wet hands and explored the lump on his head with caution. 'Thanks very much for your help.'

'Good thing I happened along. Now and again I use this close as a short cut. Want me to hunt up a policeman?'

'No . . . it wouldn't do much good, would it? As you said, he's gone. I'd rather go home.'

'Whatever you say.' The lighter snapped off. 'But take my advice and stick to lighted streets after this. Better yet, take a taxi. You'll find one back there on the High Street.'

'Yes, well — '

The man in the duffel coat started off in the direction taken by the fleeing Unknown, calling over his shoulder with conventional good humour, 'Get along now. We'd really hate to lose you.'

'A suggestive remark, that,' Jean commented.

'And with that he was off.' Jamie drew her more tightly against him, the palms of his hands enclosing her breasts as though they were talismans through which the healing magic flowed. 'And it's only now, when I'm able to think clearly, that I realize how odd it was that he was able to see that I was in mortal danger. It's not as though the operant mugger had a gun or a knife. There was only the wee tube thing there in the dark. *I* was certain it'd be the death of me because the bugger's mind assured me of the fact – but how did my Good Samaritan know?'

Tell me the answer, said his wife's mind.

My rescuer was an operant too he must have been and that means . . . of course, it's only logical that there should be others but good God that they should be *watching us*!

'You aren't inconspicuous,' she said, laughing softly. 'As you said, it's logical.'

They lay together, naked before the fire, on a rug she'd made herself of pieced black and white Islay sheepskins. When he had come home, raging with worry and fear, she had closed her mind to him and not permitted him to tell the story until she had administered the great sovereign remedy there in the dark library, their private sanctum. Then she'd listened calmly.

He said, 'We'll have to work out some ways to guard ourselves, until the public demonstration can be arranged. All of the EE adepts will be at risk. Aside from the mysterious assassin, there are the government agents lurking about. The CIA for certain – and if the two who talked to Nigel are to be believed, there are Russians and Israelis and even British agents to worry about . . .'

'You think they might try kidnapping if other recruitment tactics fail?'

'It's a possibility,' he said sombrely.

She kissed his wrist lightly. 'What you must do then is steal a march on the lot of them. For Whitehall, a preview of coming attractions, demonstrating how an EE adept would react to involuntary sequestration by going out of body and raising a hue and cry among his colleagues. For the Yanks, a suggestion that Whitehall pass on the good word, with a judicious warning against poaching. For the others, a more devious approach. You and your colleagues will have to descend to cloak-and-daggering. Excurse into the appropriate embassies in London – and perhaps in

Paris as well – and find out whether there are any nefarious schemes being planned against you. If there are, take the aforementioned steps.'

Jamie gave a delighted laugh. 'Damn, but you're a cool one!'

She grabbed him by his Dundrearies and pulled his face close. 'Only because I don't think the intelligence people want to harm you. They don't know enough about you yet, my dear, for that. But your mystery man, the operant mugger, is something else altogether. He frightens me, and I have no notion at all how you can protect yourself from a person like that. He came from nowhere and vanished back into it. You know nothing of his motives. He may even have been a madman — '

'No,' said Jamie. 'He was sane.'

'Then perhaps he's been frightened off by the other one. We can pray that it's so. And you can follow your rescuer's advice and take care not to travel in lonely places.'

'Not while I'm in my body, at least,' he said, and he kissed her lips, and they lay together for a few minutes more watching the fire die, and then went off to bed.

16

Zürich, Switzerland, Earth
5 September 1991

The eleven men and one woman who constituted the PRD, the banking regulatory board of Switzerland, watched without emotion as the confidential agent known as Otto Maurer showed his videotape of the photographed documents that verified the nature of Dr James Somerled MacGregor's researches.

'It is now confirmed beyond a doubt,' Maurer said, 'that the psychic procedure for remote clairvoyant viewing is reliably practised by no less than thirty individuals connected with the Parapsychology Unit at Edinburgh University, plus an undetermined number of other persons in other parts of the world who have made use of the mental programming techniques for this – uh – talent, as perfected by Professor MacGregor and his associates. Pursuant to my instructions, I have assembled other documentation from the Psychology Department, the Astronomy Department, and the Office of Media Relations for the Medical School of the University of Edinburgh. This material confirms that on or about twenty-two October of this year, MacGregor will hold a briefing for world media announcing . . . *and demonstrating* this psychic espionage technique.'

The twelve banking directors uttered varied cries of dismay. Maurer lowered his head in a momentary gesture of commiseration, then said, 'It is needless to belabour the obvious. MacGregor's researches effectively write "finis" to the confidentiality of the Swiss banking system. Additionally, widespread utilization of psychic espionage will trigger chaos in every stock market, commodity exchange and financial institution throughout the world, opening virtually any transaction to the danger of public scrutiny . . . This concludes my report, Messieurs and Madame, and I await your questions and instructions.'

The woman asked, 'This MacGregor – has he any radical political affiliation? Is he a Red? An anarchist? Or simply an ivory-tower academic unaware of the potentially disastrous consequences of his actions?'

'He is none of these things, Madame Boudry. MacGregor is a Scot and a fierce idealist. It is military secrecy he seeks to demolish by introducing this psychic spy technique, thinking thereby to preclude the possibility of nuclear war. The collapse of the world financial structure would seem to him a small price to pay for peace.'

There was an appalled silence.

A stout, placid-looking man asked, 'You have explored avenues of – of influence that might deter him from his demonstration?'

Maurer nodded. 'I have, Herr Gimel, but without conspicuous success. He is fearless, in spite of an attempt upon his life last April and intensive surveillance by a number of state security agencies. He would be affronted by any attempt at bribery. His position at the university is impregnable, and his professional status is beyond reproach so there is no chance of his work being discredited before or after the fact.'

'His personal life?' Gimel inquired.

Maurer spoke in English. 'Squeaky clean.'

The bankers chuckled bitterly. A frail, ill-looking man with burning eyes leaned towards the agent and quavered, 'Are you telling us that there is no way of stopping this man?'

'No licit way, Herr Reichenbach.'

The invalid clasped the edge of the mahogany table with skeletal hands. 'Maurer! You will have to think about this matter urgently. It is of paramount importance to us, to your country's continuing prosperity. Find a way to stop this demonstration – or, failing that, a way to delay it. MacGregor himself is the key to the problem! Do you understand me?'

'I'm not sure, Herr Reichenbach . . .'

'It is privacy that this psychic madman threatens. A fundamental right of humanity! This thing you have shown us, this technique of spying, is a nightmare out of George Orwell that any right-thinking person would repudiate with horror. You say MacGregor hopes for peace. I say MacGregor is the greatest menace civilization has ever known. Think of it. Psychic overseers scrutinizing every action of business, politics, even our personal lives. Think of it!'

Maurer's eyes swept around the board-room table. The other eleven PRD members were nodding their heads in solemn affirmation.

'Do something,' old Reichenbach whispered. 'Think very carefully, then do something.'

17

From the Memoirs of
Rogatien Remillard

That first year of mine in Hanover was very difficult. There is inevitably a lot of hard work involved in getting a new business off the ground, and my Eloquent Page bookshop was strictly a one-man operation. Early in 1991 I travelled a lot, hitting sales and thrift shops and jobbers all over New England as I gathered the basic stock of used fantasy and science-fiction titles that were to be my speciality. I ordered new books as well – not only fiction but also science nonfiction of the type that I thought might appeal to my hoped-for clientèle. When spring came and the shop was pretty well filled I opened the doors to walk-in customers and began to prepare catalogues for the mail-order trade. Denis and his Coterie were faithful patrons. They even sent their student subjects along through subtle application of the coercer's art.

My nephew was always urging me to participate in this or that experiment at his lab, but I invariably declined. The place crawled with earnest young students, all gung ho for the advancement of metapsychology, who made me feel like a scapegrace fogey when I refused to share their enthusiasm. And then there was the Coterie. Except for Sally Doyle, who was earthy and nonjudgemental, and her husband Tater McAllister, who had a wacko sense of humour in spite of being a theoretical physicist, the Coterie did not consist of folks I would have freely chosen as drinking buddies. They were fanatically loyal to Denis and his goals and did not suffer the heretical mutterings of the Great Man's uncle with equanimity. My reluctance to sacrifice myself on the altar of mental science was viewed as semitreasonable by Denis's chief associate, Glenn Dalembert, by Losier and Tremblay, who ran the main operancy test programme, and by the mystic medicine man, Tukwila Barnes. Colette Roy, Dalembert's wife, reacted to my negativism with the perky hopefulness of a camp counsellor confronting a recalcitrant eight-year-old. But she moved me not a whit more than did Eric Boutin, the strapping ex-mechanic, whose toothy grin did not quite conceal his itch to whip me into tiptop mental shape, for my own good as well as the good of the cause.

'No thanks,' said I, not giving a flying fuck that I was thereby letting the side down. I would not accept operancy training. I would not let them measure my overall PsiQ. I would not even submit to a simple assay of my meta-faculties. (Researchers now tended to classify the mind-powers under the headings of Ultrasenses, Coercivity, Psychokinesis, Creativity and Healing – later broadened to Redaction.)

Maybe someday, I said, lying in my teeth. But not now.

The publicity splash generated by the publication of Denis's book finally petered out, to my relief, and the media abandoned Hanover to cover more newsworthy events such as the Mars Mission, the African plague, and the never-ending Middle Eastern terrorist attacks. The mysterious researches of my nephew became strictly stale potatoes, journalistically speaking – until the Edinburgh bombshell exploded late in October.

Denis knew it was coming. In spring, MacGregor had tried to enlist the cooperation of the Dartmouth group, in addition to that of the Stanford team, for his upcoming demonstration. Denis turned him down flat, and he tried to convince the Scot to postpone the press conference – or at least make the EE demonstration a private one for a select group of United Nations representatives. I only found out what was in the wind by accident, when Denis let anxiety over what he felt was a premature disclosure leak into the vestibule of his mind, where I picked it up – and was aghast. If MacGregor and his people came out into the open with a demonstration of their powers, linked to a patently political proposal, other metapsychics would also feel constrained to do so. Denis's group, beyond a doubt! They would acknowledge their operancy in support of the idealist proposal of their fellow researchers, and when they did my own protective colouration would be destroyed.

MacGregor had confided to Denis his reasons for deciding to go ahead; but Denis did not at that time reveal those reasons to me. I only saw that my nephew had apparently caved in to the pressure exerted by his older colleague and had abandoned a carefully orchestrated scheme that would have revealed the existence of operant minds to the world only after a period of careful preparation.

Instead, it was to be: Voilà! Like us or lump us.

I was as furious with Denis as I was frightened for myself. We had a flaming row over the matter that led to our first serious estrangement. I cursed myself for ever coming to Hanover, where it was inevitable that I would be drawn into whatever ruckus attended Denis. My original reason for coming, Denis's fear that Victor might try to harm me, now seemed to be without foundation. I had seen Victor only at the Christmas and Easter family gatherings, and he had been distantly cordial. It looked as though the real danger to me, ironically enough, was going to be Denis himself! And I was trapped. All my money was invested in the bookshop and it was too late to set it up elsewhere. I would have to stay in Hanover.

However, I distanced myself from Denis and the other operants almost completely from April, when the Edinburgh matter came to a head, to October. Swaddled in midlife depression, I overworked, trying to distract myself and force my infant business into the black. I stayed open until midnight. I wrote reams of letters to speciality collectors proffering my wares and inquiring about rarities. I went to conventions of science-fiction and fantasy fans and peddled my stuff, making friends and contacts who would be invaluable in later years. I nearly managed to forget what I was. A mental freak? Not I, folks! I'm only a humble bookseller. But if you're into the occult, I might have just the title you're looking for . . .

It was Don who put an end to the charade.

Throughout the early fall, as my anxiety about the upcoming EE demonstration increased, I slept very badly. I would awake stiff with terror, my pyjamas and pillow soaked with sweat, but unable for the life of me to remember the content of the nightmare. Then October came and the hills flagged their scarlet warning of approaching winter, and the petunias in the decorative tubs out on the sidewalks died with the first touch of frost. In the misty dawn, when I lay in bed in that odd state between sleep and full wakefulness, I began to feel again the familiar touch of my dead brother's mind. He had wanted so desperately to be free of me . . . but now, without me, he was lost.

I tried to blot out my irrational fantasies in the time-honoured family fashion, just as Don and even Onc' Louie had done before me. Sometimes the drinking helped. As a side effect I suffered a drastic 'psi decline' (for few things are as detrimental to the metafaculties as over-indulgence in alcohol), and this brought reproaches from Denis, along with tiresome offers of help. I refused, even though I was quite aware that I needed some sort of therapy. Somehow I had conceived the notion that to seek psychiatric help would be to 'give in' to Don. I told myself that he was only a memory. He was dead, prayed over by the Church, buried in consecrated ground. Thoughts of him could hurt me only if I let them – and I would not! In time I would conquer him and the fears we had shared. Time would heal me.

But the bad dreams and the depression and the feeling of hovering doom that the French-speaking call malheur only sharpened as the day of the Edinburgh press conference drew nearer. I could no longer get to sleep at all without drinking myself into insensibility. A certainty took hold of me that I would end as Don had, a suicide, and damned. In earlier years I might have prayed. I still went through the arid formalities of religious practice, but only to ward off additions to my already intolerable spiritual burden. My prayers had the thin comfort of habit, but lacked the trust in divine mercy that compels the probability lattices . . .

One day, rummaging through a recently arrived shipment of used books, I came upon a title that I remembered Elaine burbling over, a study of yogic techniques. I had smiled when she told me how the book had 'helped her resolution of the death-space'. (Death had been the furthest thing from my mind in those days!) The exercises she had described seemed to be mumbo jumbo, Eastern balderdash. But now in my extremity I took the book up to my untidy apartment and devoured it in a single reading. The states promised to the adept seemed analogous to the 'astronomical consciousness' of Odd John, that supreme detachment that had made both the conquest of the universe and death become irrelevant to him.

So I tried.

Unfortunately, I was not very good at the meditations. They were too inwardly directed, too chilling to the sanguine Franco soul. Still I blundered on, for if the yogic exercises failed as the alcohol had failed, what hope was there? The inevitable day would arrive, and the exposure, and then I would be drawn along with all the rest of them to the inevitable end.

At the start of his research, Denis had told me that there was only one assured way that operants could escape the Odd John Effect, the potentially fatal dichotomy between Homo superior and the less favoured mass of humanity. It lay in giving the 'normals' hope that someday they – or their children or their children's children – might also attain the higher mind-powers. Much of the current work at Dartmouth was directed towards this end, and it was to be the subject of Denis's next book. Other research groups in other parts of the world were also studying the problem, trying to bridge the gap, to demonstrate that metafaculties were a universal fact of human nature.

Given time, these preparatory efforts might have defused the normals' perfectly rational fear of us. But there was no time.

18

Edinburgh, Scotland, Earth
22 October 1991

His mental alarm clock woke Jamie MacGregor at precisely 4:00 A.M., and he began the most memorable day of his life with a queasy stomach and aching sinuses. The first could be attributed to stage fright and a lingering anxiety over the spooks, who might still be entertaining notions of kidnapping him before he let the EE cat out of the bag. The second was evidence that his prayer for just one more day of beautiful October weather had gone unanswered; the low-pressure trough that had lurked coyly above the Orkneys for the past week now sat astride Britain, charging the atmosphere with inimical ions. That might mean that the demonstration could be adversely affected. Under laboratory conditions the matter could easily be remedied through artificial neg-ion generation – but any such fiddle was out of the question during the public experiments, where the EE faculty had at least to *seem* invincible.

Ah, well. If Nigel or Alana experienced problems he would simply step into the breach himself, and professional modesty be hanged.

It was still very dark. Lying there beside Jean, whose mind cycled in the serene delta waves of deepest sleep, Jamie MacGregor addressed the first order of business: banishing the sinus headache. He relaxed, adjusted his breathing, then summoned a picture of the front of his own skull in cutaway. He let gentle insinuation become a firm command: *Decrease histamine production shrink membranes inhibit mucus secretion initiate sinus drainage LET THERE BE NO PAIN.*

It happened.

He savoured relief for a few moments, listening to the faint ticking of sleet against the windowpanes and his wife's gentle snores. Her strongest faculty was the healing, and she had taught it to him and to their two children and to numbers of their colleagues at university. The gift was widespread among Celts and many Scots possessed it suboperantly, with its practice requiring only strong will power and never a modicum of doubt. It did not seem to matter whether or not the healer's perception of the ailment's source was scientifically accurate. Experiments with their own young Katie and David had proved that – and Jamie had to smile as he recalled certain bizarre visualizations by the children. Yet if a person sincerely believed that tiny demons with hammers were the true source of sinusitis, wishing the evil creatures dead would work a cure just as surely as his own explicit redactive commands had done . . .

Outside in Dalmond Crescent an automobile engine whirred to a reluctant start and settled into a rough idle. The car did not drive off and Jamie's uneasy stomach reasserted itself. Damn them! Who was it this time? He cursed his inability to identify individual auras at a distance. Those lucky enough to possess the faculty, seeker-sense adepts such as Denis Remillard or the Tibetan Urgyen Bhotia, who headed up the Darjeeling establishment, did not have to fear being stalked or ambushed by human predators. But Jamie was blind to mental signatures. There was only one way he would be able to find out which foreign agent or British spook had spent a dreary night on station outside his house and now suffered predawn demoralization that required the comfort of a car's heater.

Jamie let his mind go out of body.

He seemed to ascend through the bedroom ceiling, through the loft, through the roof. He hovered above leafless trees tossing in the wind and streetlamps glimmering on the dark granite paving setts. One of the autos parked along the crescent, a Jaguar XJS HE, had twin plumes of vapour rising from it. Jamie swooped down to peer inside and saw Sergei Arkhipov, the London KGB resident, wiping his streaming nose with a sodden handkerchief before sucking a tot from his nearly depleted flask. The stereo was playing 'Fingal's Cave'. This solitary vigil by an agent of Arkhipov's high rank undoubtedly meant that the Russians had finally ruled out a kidnap attempt, even as the Americans had. Sergei was probably standing by only to make certain that no other faction – especially the GRU, Soviet military intelligence – got reckless.

Were there other spooks about? Jamie rose high again and began to search for signs of the Yanks or MI5; but the other parked cars on the street and in the adjacent mews were empty, and the only wakeful persons in the neighbourhood besides himself and Arkhipov were Mrs Farnsworth and her fretful infant and old Hamish Ferguson, insomniac again, watching *Deep Throat* on his VCR.

318

Jamie's upset stomach responded now to self-redaction and he returned briefly to his own body to prepare for the principal excorporeal excursion. Jean, sensing his tension, half woke and sent out a little nonverbal query. He told her: No no it's nothing sleep lass sleep not quite time to rise for the Big Day . . .

Then he was off again through the freezing dark, a soul that would girdle the globe before returning to its physical anchorage. But first, before crossing the Atlantic, he'd stop at Islay, for Gran.

Storm winds out of the northwest smote the shoulder of the island squarely, shoving mountainous waves into Sanaigmore Bay. The farmsteading in its hollow seemed to crouch like a patient, sturdy beast, back to the gale. To Jamie's mind's eye, refined by the EE faculty as it never was during short-distance attempts at clairvoyance, the Hebridean darkness was as lucid as day, except that there were no colours and the lack of shadows gave the scene a peculiar flatness. The area lights that usually lit the farmyard at night were out and the house looked unilluminated as well, alarming Jamie. But when he glided down and came close he saw the glow of a paraffin lamp through the kitchen window and a smoky thread blasted horizontally from the chimney of the ancient, peat-burning hearth. His older brother Colin and his wife Jean and their grown son Johnnie, who worked the farm now, were still abed, enjoying the last precious half hour of rest. But Gran was up getting breakfast, as was her custom. He heard her humming as she put another peat on the fire and stirred the porridge.

Jamie said: Gran it's me.

Dear laddie you took the time to come! said she.

For your blessing now that we're ready to show our secret to the world . . . I see your electricity's gone out in the storm.

Aye and the fancy cooker and the lights and the closed-circuit telly to the barn and all the other modern thingamajiks useless until Colin wakes and starts the Honda generator but he and Jean and Johnnie will wake to hot food naetheless I cooked over peat for fifty years and I don't mind doing it now it's a comfort to know the old ways still have their worth.

. . . And now some of the oldest of all to be new again Gran.

Affection! To think I'd live to see it! Eighty-one years but not even my Sight gave me a hint of how it would *really* be and I'm so proud so proud.

Well I still have misgivings. If only we could have waited until there were more as adept at the soul-travel as Nigel Alana and I.

No you could *not* wait not with Them skulking about Godbethankit you've been unmolested you must get it into the open then you'll all be safe.

If the demonstration succeeds.

Now stop that. What have I taught you man and boy for thirty-nine years but that doubt's the mind's poison causing the powers to sicken and wane? Shame on ye!

I expect it's all this science that's spoiled me.

Laughter. Now don't be afraid. I See that your showing will bring about a new world and it's Mother Shipton's joke you see: *The world then to an end shall come in Nineteen Hundred and Ninety-One*.

! So that explains *that* . . . still I wish I had the Sight like you and Alana and your confidence. When I remember what happened back in April my narrow escape I still get a cald grue if it hadn't been for that big chap who came along by chance —

So it was chance was it!

Ah Gran.

Ah Jamie. Stop fashing yourself laddie just do what you've prepared yourself and Nigel and Alana for don't think of the cold world watching with its mechanical moonlet eyes pretend it's the first soul-trip just like long years ago a natural thing if a wonder an old thing cherished in spite of doubts and oppression and now it's time we showed it proudly and how will you like being a famous man my own wee Jamie?

You're a cruel old woman to laugh at me when I'm all in a flaughter but I love you. Now charmbless me in the

Gaelic for I must be off to California and the Antipodes to make sure that all's ready.

Very well: Cuirim cumerih dhia umid sluagh dall tharrid do vho gach gabhadh sosgeul dhia na grais o mullach gu lar unid ga ghradhich na fire thu i na millidh na mhuaih thu . . . I put the protection of God around you a host over you to protect you from every danger the gospel of the God of Grace from top to ground over you may the men love you and the women do you no harm.

Amen! Thank you dear Gran goodbye.

Farewell Jamie my own heart.

As he waited with the throng of journalists to be admitted to the auditorium of the University of Edinburgh's George Square Theatre, Fabian (The Fabulous) Finster amused himself by ferreting out others like himself who had crashed the event with forged credentials.

The exercise was not difficult. All intelligence operatives live their waking hours wrapped in a miasma of hair-trigger vigilance and subacute anxiety. A sensitive like Finster perceived this 'loud' mind-tone as easily as if a neon sign were being worn on the forehead of the emanator. So far, he had spotted spooks from France, East and West Germany, Britain's domestic intelligence service MI5, the Israeli Mossad, the CIA, and (rather strangely) the Swiss Banking Regulatory Bureau PRD. Four Soviet GRU agents were among the sizable press corps from TASS. There was also a lone KGB man playing a clandestine game whom Finster had contrived to stand next to. This Russian was a squat, fair-haired man with a nasty head cold and rumpled clothing. He wore a lapel badge identifying him as s. HANNULA — HELSINGEN SANOMAT.

There was a flutter of action near the theatre's main entrance.

'Look at that!' Finster exclaimed to the counterfeit Finn. 'They're going to let the TV crews into the hall ahead of the working press! It happens every goddam time.'

A rumble of indignation went up from the less favoured media representatives. Their protests were partly appeased when some two dozen young people wearing University of

Edinburgh Psychology Department sweat shirts came out of a side door and began passing out press kits.

The alleged Hannula growled, 'Now maybe we will get a clue about the kind of circus these academic publicity-hounds are planning.'

Considerately, he handed one of the thick information packets to the little squirrel-faced American next to him, whose ID badge read: J. SMITH — SEATTLE POST-INTELLI-GENCER. As the Soviet agent opened his own packet he was thinking:

But surely it cannot be significant EE breakthrough not coming from here this oldfashioned ridiculous place they couldnot have kept data secure most likely merely another crude stunt suchas MacGregor described literature but if demonstration not crucial then why CIA crablice pursuing him&associates try lure to America HolyMother what awful stuffed head fever perhaps I come down pneumonia this prickish Scottish dampness at least GRU donkey-fuckers aborted lunatic scheme kidnap MacGregor conscript into RedArmy psiresearch overcome KGB advantage Alma-Ata . . .

Finster studied his press kit for a few minutes, then asked the KGB man, 'Is there much interest in psychic phenomena in Finland?'

'Oh, yes. That kind of thing is part of the national tradition. We Finns have been accused of practising witch-craft by Swedes and other superstitious people from time immemorial.' He sneezed and cursed and made use of a stained handkerchief.

'Gesundheit,' Finster told him cheerfully. (He was getting very good with other languages.) 'How about your neighbours to the east? Would you call the Russians superstitious?'

'Hah! They are perhaps the worst of all.' Hannula became very absorbed in the handout material.

'Not much useful stuff here,' Finster noted. 'Will you look at this, for chrissake? *A History of the British Society for Psychical Research, 1882 to Present*. Did my editor send me halfway around the world for that kinda shit? And this bio-sheet on MacGregor is hardly anything except summaries

322

of the guy's publications. How's this for a grabber? "EEG Beta Activity Correlates Among Six Subjects During Short-Range Excorporeal Excursions". Jeez!'

The Soviet agent managed a perfunctory chuckle. He thought:

Shortrange it *must* be shortrange source New Hampshire assured us remoteviewing still unreliable but if so *why* Americans offer so much money Weinstein *who* try assassinate MacGregor April *when* idiots allow us enter hall begin sodding demonstration?

'Any minute now,' Finster said absently, still studying the press-kit material. 'Say – here's a choice bit. Did you know that MacGregor's official title here at Edinburgh University is "Holder of the Arthur Koestler Chair of Parapsychology"? This Koestler was a famous writer, an ex-Commie who wrote about the abuse of power in the Red Bloc. When he died he left a pile of money to found this psychic professorship. Wouldn't it send up the Russkies if MacGregor has discovered something big? We all know the Reds have been trying to develop Mind Wars stuff for twenty, thirty years. Lately, there've been rumours that they're close to succeeding.'

Hannula was blank-faced. 'I have heard nothing about that.'

Finster flashed his chipmunk grin. 'I'll just bet you haven't.' He folded the information packet lengthwise and tucked it into the Louis Vuitton shoulder bag that contained the tools of his trade – audiovisual microcorder, cellular telephone with data terminal, and the seasoned reporter's indispensable steno pad with three Bic pens. Only the most careful scrutiny would have revealed the illegal comsat-scrambler hookup on the phone and the needle-gun charged with deadly ricin concealed within the Bic Clic with the silver cap.

'Look!' Hannula cried. 'Something happens!'

The doors of the auditorium were opening at last. A ragged cheer arose from the media people waiting in the lobby and the mob surged forward in a body. Finster called out to Hannula, 'Stick with me, buddy! I always get a good seat!' And somehow the throng did part minimally to let the dapper little American pass through. The KGB agent hastened to follow, and the two of them raced down the centre aisle and plopped breathlessly into seats in the third row. 'What'd I tell you?' Finster bragged. 'Best seats in the house.'

Hannula groped beneath his own rump. He extracted a placard that said: RESERVED TIME MAGAZINE. Consternation creased his brow.

'Relax,' Finster told him. He took the Russian's sign, together with one from his own seat that said: RESERVED CORRIERE DELLA SERA, and tore both sheets to bits. Reporters milling about in search of their proper places were open-mouthed. Finster's eyes swept over them. 'We have a perfect right to sit any place we want. Versteh'? Capisce? Pigez? You dig?'

The other journalists looked away, suddenly absorbed in their own affairs.

The hall was jammed with more than a thousand people, and some of those lurking about the fringes were plain-clothes police officers. Finster pretended to jot down items on his notepad as he relocated the other spooks. Only the CIA, masquerading as an SNN Steadicam team, and the TASS crew were more advantageously placed than Finster and his Soviet acquaintance. The Brits were clustered fifth row far left. Both sets of Germans were way in back with the luckless standees – who now included a distinguished Italian science editor and a hopping-mad *Time* stringer. The Israeli agent and the lady from the Direction Générale de la Sécurité Extérieure were side by side, chatting chummily. But what had become of the Swiss bankers' spy? Ah. Somehow he had wormed his way to the very front of the theatre, to the area between the seats and the platform edge, where he stood focusing his Hasselblad in the midst of a crush of television technicians. The fellow's mind was wrapped in feverish excitement, but because of the distance, it was impossible for Finster to sift out coherent thoughts. Obscurely troubled, Finster frowned.

'Ah,' breathed Hannula. 'It is about to start.'

A white-haired woman in a heather-coloured suit had come out on to the platform and stood expectantly, holding a cordless microphone at the ready. Behind her was a simple small table with another microphone, and a wooden chair. Hung upstage against a curtain backdrop was an impressive GPD video screen that measured four metres by five. It had been flashing enigmatic test patterns while the audience settled down, but now it had gone blank except for the digital time display in the lower right-hand corner that indicated 09:58. No other apparatus was in evidence.

Ready-lights on the TV cameras surrounding the platform began to wink on like wolves' eyes glittering in fireshine. Technical directors muttered into headsets, giving last-minute instructions to their colleagues who manned a great gaggle of satellite-transmission vans massed outside on George Square and Buccleuch Place. A few still-cameras clicked and buzzed prematurely and print-media people whispered establishing remarks into their microcorders. At precisely ten o'clock, the university spokeswoman cleared her throat.

'Good morning, ladies and gentlemen. I am Eloise Watson, the director of media relations for the Medical School of the University of Edinburgh. We would like to welcome you to this special demonstration and press conference organized on behalf of the Parapsychology Unit of the Department of Psychology. Immediately after the demonstration, questions will be accepted from the floor. We must ask that you hold all queries until then. And now, without further ado, let me present the man you have been waiting to meet – James Somerled MacGregor, Koestler Professor of Parapsychology.'

She withdrew, and from the wings shambled a tall and loose-jointed figure. His jacket and trousers of oatmeal tweed were baggy and nondescript, but he had compensated somewhat for their drabness with a waistcoat cut from the scarlet MacGregor tartan. Still-cameras snapped and whirred and TV lenses zoomed in for close-ups of a lean and wild-eyed face. MacGregor's beaky nose and thin lips were framed with extravagant Dundreary whiskers of vivid auburn. His hair, unkempt and collar-length, was also red. He clutched a sensitive dish-tipped microphone with big bony hands, holding it up as though it were the hilt of a Highlander's claymore presented in defiant salute. When he spoke his voice was gruff, with the barest hint of a lilting western accent.

'What we're going to show you today is a thing that people of a certain mind have been doing for hundreds of years – perhaps even thousands. I learned it myself from my grandmother in the Isles, and I've managed to teach it to numbers of my colleagues. You'll be meeting some of them today. The phenomenon has been called out-of-body experience, remote-viewing, astral projection, even soul-travel. Lately, psychic researchers have taken to calling it excorporeal excursion or EE. I'll stick to those initials during the demonstration for the sake of simplicity, but you journalists can call it anything you like – just so long as you *don't* call it magic.'

There were scattered laughs and murmurs.

Jamie's fierce, dark eyes glowered and the audience fell silent. 'EE isn't magic! It's as real as radio or television or space flight! . . . But I didn't invite you here today to argue its authenticity. I'm going to show it to you.'

He half turned, indicating the huge video screen at the rear of the platform. 'With the kind assistance of the University's Astronomy Department and the GTE Corporation, we have arranged for several live television transmissions to be beamed exclusively to this theatre from other locations. I will be able to speak directly to the persons you will see, using this microphone – but they won't see me. All they will receive from me is an audio signal, like a telephone call . . . Now I think we're ready to begin.'

At a gesture from MacGregor, a balding, bearded man in his forties came on stage, saluted the audience with a wave, and seated himself at the table. Jamie said, 'I'd like to introduce my old friend and colleague of twenty years, Nigel Weinstein, Associate Professor of Parapsychology here at the University. He will explain his role in a few minutes. But first – may I have the California transmission, please?'

A colour picture flashed on to the screen. A smartly dressed woman and an elderly man sat in easy chairs before a low glass table. Opposite was a long settee and behind them potted plants and a window that appeared to overlook moonlit waters spanned by an enormous suspension bridge. City lights starred the surrounding hills. The display in the corner of the screen now read. SAN FRANCISCO USA 02:05.

The woman said, 'Good morning, Professor MacGregor – and all of you members of the world media there in Edinburgh, Scotland! I'm Sylvia Albert and I host the Late-Late Talk Show here on KGO-TV, San Francisco. We're coming to you live via satellite in a special closed transmission that was arranged at the personal request of Dr Lucius J. Kemp of Stanford University. Dr Kemp is no doubt well known to you all as a distinguished brain researcher and a Nobel Laureate in Medicine . . . Will you tell us, Dr Kemp, why you're participating in this demonstration?'

Kemp had been staring at his clasped hands. Now he nodded very slowly several times. 'Numbers of my colleagues at Stanford have been involved in parapsychology research for some twenty-three years. I've watched their progress with great interest, even though my own work involves a different area of study – one that you might say is more conventional.'

He looked directly into the camera and levelled an index finger at his viewers on the other side of the world. '*You* might say! I say parapsychology is as respectable as any other branch of psychiatry. Now I study brain cells, things you can see and touch and measure. But the brain is a peculiar piece of matter that houses the mind – which we scientists most definitely *cannot* see or touch, and which we are only incompetently able to measure. The nature of mind, and its capabilities, are still nearly as mysterious as outer space. It wasn't too many years ago that the majority of educated people – scientists especially – dismissed parapsychology as nonsense. Things aren't that way today, but there are still sceptics in the scientific establishment who will try to assure you that paranormal psychic phenomena are either nonexistent or else freakish effects without practical value. I am not one of those scientists . . .'

The screen in the Edinburgh lecture theatre was now filled with the Nobel Laureate's face, copper-brown skin stretched over high cheekbones, black eyes narrowed with the intensity of his emotion, a few drops of perspiration trickling from the snowy wool of his hair on to his broad forehead. Then he flashed a brilliant smile.

'Because of that, the parapsychology researchers at Stanford nailed me! They asked for my help with this experiment, and they got it. That's why I'm here in the wee hours of the morning along with Miss Albert and the director and crew of her show and the three impartial witnesses we've asked to assist us.'

The camera pulled back again and the talk-show hostess rapidly explained how the experiment was going to work. The three witnesses had each been asked to bring a small card with a picture or a few lines of writing. The subject of the card was to be known only to them, and they had sealed it inside three successive envelopes. The witnesses now waited in the TV studio's green room, where guests assembled before being taken on stage for their interviews. There were no cameras in the green room and the monitor there had been disconnected.

Now Jamie MacGregor asked, 'Miss Albert, is it true that there is no means of outside communication in this green room? No telephones or radio equipment?'

'None whatsoever,' she said.

'Very good. I want to be sure that the journalists with us here in Edinburgh understand that. Go on, Lucius. Tell us what your own part in the experiment will be.'

'I'll wait,' Kemp said, 'until you tell me that your colleague, Dr Weinstein, is ready to undertake a remote-viewing of those cards the three witnesses have hidden away on their persons. When you give me the word, I'll go to the green room and stand in the doorway. I'll ask the witnesses to take out the envelopes and hold them up, unopened, for two minutes. After that they'll accompany me back here to the cameras, envelopes still unopened. And then we'll see, won't we?' He smiled.

'Aye, we certainly will,' Jamie said. 'Thank you, Lucius.'

The audience in the theatre let out a collective sigh. Seats creaked as many of them hunched forward. Jamie was holding a whispered colloquy with Nigel. The KGB agent turned to Finster and whispered, 'If this works – great God, the repercussions!'

'You can say that again,' the Mafia's man agreed. 'In Finnish.'

Nigel picked up his own microphone. He was still seated at the table, while Jamie had withdrawn to the left side of the platform.

'I'm afraid,' Weinstein said, his expression mischievous, 'that your worst suspicions are about to be confirmed. I'm going into a trance.'

Tension-relieving laughter.

'Usually we do this EE business in a soundproofed room to avoid distraction. We relax in a kind of glorified barber's chair equipped with monitoring gadgets that tell what our brains and bods are up to while our minds go soaring through the blue empyrean . . . but that wouldn't do today. We want you to see how *ordinary* EE can be. But I warn you – don't cough or drop your pencils or crack chewing gum while I'm off, or I just might crumble to dust before your eyes like Dracula in the sunlight.'

More laughter. Then total silence.

Nigel had closed his eyes and was breathing slowly and deeply. Up on the giant video screen the American scientist and the talk-show hostess waited.

'Ready,' said Nigel in a flat voice.

Jamie spoke into his microphone. 'You may go to the green room now, Lucius.'

The California camera followed Kemp into the studio wings, where he vanished amidst a clutter of equipment. Then it swivelled back to Sylvia Albert and held. Twenty-six seconds clicked by on the digital display.

Nigel's eyes opened. 'Got it,' he said simply.

Jamie went to the platform edge. 'Would one of you be so kind as to pass up a sheet of paper and something to write with?'

A BBC technical director thrust up a yellow sheet and a pencil. Jamie nodded his thanks and passed them on to Nigel, who scribbled energetically for a few minutes. Then he gave the sheet back to Jamie, who returned it to the

BBC man, saying, 'Hold on to that. We'll want you to read it shortly.'

Almost nine thousand kilometres away, the two minutes having passed, Dr Kemp was returning to the talk-show set leading two women and a man. The newcomers sat down at the glass table and placed their sealed envelopes in front of them.

Sylvia Albert said, 'May I present our guinea pigs! Lola McCafferty Lopez, Assistant District Attorney for San Francisco County; Maureen Sedgewick, Associate Editor of the *San Francisco Chronicle*; and Rabbi Milton Green of the B'nai B'rith Hillel Foundation of the University of California at Berkeley . . . Now, will you tell us what results you have, Professor MacGregor?'

Jamie leaned down to the BBC crewman. 'Sir, would you please read out what Dr Weinstein wrote?' He reversed his microphone so that the tiny parabolic receiving dish at its tip was aimed at the technician.

'First card,' came the man's voice clearly. 'From a Monopoly game: GO DIRECTLY TO JAIL, DO NOT COLLECT $200.'

The audience roared as on the screen, the attorney ripped open her multiple envelopes and showed the card. The cartoon face peering through bars loomed in an extreme close-up.

'Second card,' the BBC man read. 'Handwritten quote from Shakespeare: "To be, or not to be: that is the question".'

The Edinburgh audience was murmuring loudly. As the California camera zoomed in for the second confirmation the noise swelled to a clamour. Jamie lifted his arms. 'Please! There's still Rabbi Green's card.'

The BBC man read, 'Picture postcard of planet Earth taken from space with handwritten note on back: "Let there be light".'

Instead, there was bedlam.

The false reporter from the *Helsingen Sanomat* covered his face with his hands and groaned, 'Yob tvoyu mat'!' Finster appended, 'In spades, tovarishch.'

While the hubbub quieted, Jamie gave brief thanks to

the California participants and the screen blanked out. Almost immediately it was replaced by a new image, a stark newsroom desk backed by a station logo: TV–3 AUCKLAND. A comfortably homely man and a blond young woman with an abstracted Mona Lisa smile sat close together at one end of the desk. The time was 20:18.

'Good evening, Professor MacGregor! Ron Wiggins here, with your graduate student Miss Alana Shaunavon, who flew in on Air New Zealand SST from London earlier today. Alana, tell us just a little bit about yourself.'

'I'm a doctoral candidate in parapsychology at Edinburgh University, where I work with Professor Jamie MacGregor. There are thirty-two of us at the Unit, in various stages of training for EE – excorporeal excursion. I was chosen to come here and attempt to view a message written by a member of the audience there at the Edinburgh press conference.'

Ron Wiggins gave a worldly chuckle. 'Well, we'll give it a fair go! . . . And here to keep a sharp eye on things are Bill Drummond of the *Auckland Star*, Melanie Te Wiata of the *New Zealand Herald*, and Les Seymour of the *Wellington Evening Post*.'

The camera panned over the scribes, who sat at the opposite end of the desk, looking aloof. Wiggins said, 'As I understand it, Alana will leave her body here in Kiwi Land and attempt to project herself more than eighteen thousand kilometres to Scotland — '

'Excuse me,' the girl interrupted firmly. The close-up showed eyes of a magnetic emerald green. Her voice was low and cajoling as she contradicted Wiggins. 'It's really not like that, you know. Subjectively, I may feel as though I were travelling, but I don't – any more than we travel when we dream. Current metapsychic theory holds that the EE experience is a type of sensory response, like long-distance sight. Farsight. But it's not mystical, and my mind certainly doesn't leave my body.'

'Mm,' Wiggins said. 'Be that as it may, let me assure our witnesses here and overseas that we have no electronic means of viewing events there at the Edinburgh press conference. Furthermore, we aren't broadcasting this transmission to our national audience. It's a coded impulse beamed solely to Scotland via satellite. We are recording here for a later presentation, however, in conjunction with the material we expect to receive from our people on the scene in Edinburgh . . . And now, Alana, are you ready to begin?'

'Yes.'

Jamie spoke once again to the BBC man who had read Nigel's results aloud: 'Sir, will you please select a colleague in your immediate vicinity to write our sample message for Alana?'

'Right,' said the Beeb technician. 'How about this Swiss bloke over here with the Hasselblad?'

There was a brief wrangle when the Swiss seemed reluctant to cooperate, apparently perturbed when camera lenses were aimed in his direction by the TV crews of several dozen nations.

Fabian Finster felt the skin along his spine tingle with the same uneasy premonition he had experienced earlier. He whispered to the KGB agent, 'You know anything about that guy? Otto Maurer, his badge says, photographer for the *Neue Züricher Zeitung* . . . but I have reasons to doubt that he's legit.'

'He would not have been admitted without a computerized credential check. He is surely a bona fide journalist. As legitimate as you or I.'

'Idi v zhopu,' scoffed The Fabulous Finster. The thunderstruck Russian gaped at him.

Meanwhile, the Swiss had evidently complied with the request to pen a brief message. Jamie MacGregor was saying, 'Thank you, Herr Maurer. Now if you will place the sheet of paper on the floor, face down. None of the people around you have seen what you've written? . . . Good. You must try not to think of it, either. EE seems to be an ultrasense quite distinct from telepathy. It also seems inconsequential what position the target object may be in, or what barriers of matter may lie between the target and the percipient. What we seek to demonstrate is that EE makes it possible for trained persons to remotely view virtually anything in any part of the world.'

A wave of incredulous exclamations swept the hall. Somebody called out, 'But if that's true, it means —'

'Please!' Jamie held up his hand again. 'Let us have the demonstration first, then the questions.'

'I have already read the paper,' came the amplified voice of Alana Shaunavon. Her young face was enormous on the screen, the brilliant green eyes fixed, wide open, blinking slowly. 'He has written a verse in German:

Die Gedanken sind frei,
Wer kann sie erraten?
Sie fliegen vorbei
Wie nächtliche Schatten.
Kein Mensch kann sie wissen,
Kein Jäger erschiessen.
Es bleibet dabei: die Gedanken sind frei.

I can translate it rather freely: "Thoughts are free, who can discover them? They fly past like shadows of the night. No one can know them, no hunter can shoot them down. When all's said and done, thoughts — " *My God, look out! His camera! It's a weapon!*'

A wild fracas broke out on the floor and there were shouts as the Swiss attempted vainly to rush away. But too many bodies and too much equipment hemmed him in and he went down, tackled by two intrepid Canadian Broadcasting Corporation telecasters. The lethal Hasselblad was wrestled away and smashed by a soundman of the Fuji Network. Plainclothes police officers materialized and camera crews leapt about balletically recording the capture.

As Maurer was being hauled away, he screamed, 'Fools! Crétins! Er hat Sie alles beschissen! Don't you know what's going on here? What this MacGregor has done? Um Gottes Willen . . . Pandora's box . . . ruin . . . chaos . . . anarchy . . . Weltgetümmel . . .'

The uproar subsided slowly. Jamie spoke into his microphone and the screen was wiped clear of the New Zealand transmission. There was a burst of video clutter and then the simple advisory:

OVERSEAS TELEPHONE MESSAGE READY
AUDIO SIGNAL ONLY

'Jamie? Jamie? I could not wait!' A woman's voice, speaking heavily accented English, came through a hiss of interference. 'I saw everything – but then I became so excited that I lost the sight! Tell me – is everything all right?'

The confusion subsided and the attention of the crowd of newspeople was drawn once again to the platform. Jamie MacGregor tugged at one of his Dundreary cheek-whiskers. His expression was resigned. 'All is quite well for the moment, lass. But I think this wee carfuffle's only the beginning of what we'll be seeing anon.'

'Yes, that's true . . . Are you ready for me to speak? I must not waste any time. We may be cut off at any moment if my little bypass of the monitored circuitry is traced.'

Jamie said, 'Just wait for a moment, while I ask our Edinburgh University communications people to show the journalists in our audience where this telephone call is coming from.'

The loudspeakers trilled a brief electronic aria and the video display printed an advisory:

ORIGINATING: 68–23–79 ALMA-ATA USSR
VIA SKS-8 + EUS-02 GTE/BT 4-3

The female voice said, 'I am Tamara Petrovna Sakhvadze, Deputy Director of the Institute for Bioenergetic Studies at Kazakh State University, and a member of the Kazakh Academy of Sciences.'

'Nevozmozhno!' A pained whisper escaped the false Hannula. Others in the lecture theatre seemed equally unbelieving and they sprang to their feet shouting questions.

'Silence!' Jamie roared. Then he spoke gently into the microphone. 'Tell us why you've joined the demonstration today, Tamara Petrovna.'

'I am a person who loves my country and its people. I am also a scientist, dedicated to discovering truth. And finally, I am the mother of three small children whose minds are just beginning to flower. I have worked in the field of parapsychology since 1968, when I was only a young child. My late husband, Dr Yuri Gawrys, was my close associate. Like Jamie MacGregor, I have specialized in the phenomenon of excorporeal excursion, along with clairvoyance and certain other metafaculties. On several occasions, I have . . . met with Jamie and with certain other scientists in other parts of the world. When Jamie told me he was determined to demonstrate EE, I agreed with his decision. The work we are doing here in Alma-Ata falls under the highest security classification, and this telephone call is a technical violation of Soviet law. And yet I make it with the full consent of every one of my colleagues here at the Institute, in the interests of all humanity.

'You people, listening to my words being beamed to you via many satellites, try to understand! You Americans, especially, listen! The whole world will benefit from what we do today. To my fellow citizens of the Soviet Union who hear me, I say: Eto novoye otkrytiye prinesyot polzu vsyemu chelovyechestvu! An extraordinary door is opening, and from behind it shines a light that does away with all state secrets. There can be no more clandestine weapons research, no surprise military actions, no first-strike capability. The people of the Soviet Union need no longer fear attack by the USA, and Americans need no longer fear us. We can now work to resolve our differences without the threat of accidental or deliberate nuclear war. Our children can look into the future with hope again. My children can . . . and Jamie's . . . and yours.'

The voice paused, and the immediate response of those listening was like the upsurge of a tremendous rising wind, wordless, laden with emotional energy. But before the sound wave could crest, Jamie cried out, 'Wait! Let her finish!'

She said, 'I was there with you, a witness to one man's despair. I saw his violent reaction when he realized what changes we must expect when the higher mind-powers come into common use. He was afraid. He warned of Pandora's box, and perhaps his warning is justified. "Die Gedanken sind frei" . . . thoughts are free, but with freedom comes responsibility. There will be great difficulties to overcome if we are not to exchange one kind of danger for another. But the door is opened and nothing can close it!

A new age of the mind has dawned on our planet and all of us must enter into it. We must face this terrible new enlightenment courageously, together. As a first step . . . I invite you, my dear Jamie, and all of the scientists in the world who study the higher mind-powers to come to a meeting – the First Congress on Metapsychology. I invite the journalists of the world also. Come to Alma-Ata next year, in September when the fragrance of ripening apples fills our lovely city. Come and let us take the first step towards mir miru – a world at peace.'

'Tamara, my lass, we'll be there,' said Jamie MacGregor. Then he bowed his head to the tumult of shouting that erupted in the theatre and waited patiently until order was restored and he could begin answering the questions.

After the press conference was long over, two foreigners with press ID badges still pinned to their raincoats sat together in Greyfriars Bobby's Bar, making steady inroads on a bottle of the Macallan. The astonishing news had spread like wildfire and the place was packed, rocking with song and jollification as students and other celebrators marked the arrival of the new age of the mind with an impromptu ceilidh that showed signs of escalating into a riot.

'I never knew "Comin' Through the Rye" had words like that.' The Fabulous Finster was slightly scandalized.

'Hah,' said the KGB man. 'You should hear the unexpurgated version of "For A' That". Or "Duncan Gray". Or "Green Grow the Rashes, O!" Yes, the Scottish hero poet, Robert Burns, wrote very earthy songs. We are very fond of him in my country. He was truly of the proletariat.' He brought his glass down on to the tiny table with a thud and carolled in a raspy basso:

'Green grow the rashes, O!
Green grow the rashes, O!
The lassies they hae wimble-bores,
The widows they hae gashes, O!'

The patrons gave a yell of approval. Somebody with an accordion tried to drag the Russian from his seat; but he shook his head violently, red-rimmed eyes gone wide, and croaked, 'No! I will not sing! I cannot sing!'

Nobody took it amiss. Usquebalian dejection is no novelty in an Edinburgh pub. The musical gilravagers directed their attention elsewhere and Finster refilled his companion's glass. 'Drink up, Sergei, old hoss. I know why you're feeling low. To tell the truth, I'm a trifle shook up myself. Talk about a bombshell! My Boss back home'll be farting flames. Yours, too, I betcha.'

The Russian agent tossed down the dram and began to pour another. 'You are talking nonsense. And my name is Sami, not Sergei.'

Finster shrugged. He reached out, clamping the other man's hand tightly to the bottle, and leaned very close. His face was so friendly, so droll. With that gap between the large front teeth, the face seemed like that of a saucy squirrel in a cartoon show for children. Who could feel threatened by a squirrel?

'Tell me honestly, Sergei. Do you think that dame in Alma-Ata will be able to pull it off? The open-door psychic congress? Or has she bought herself and her bunch a quick ticket to the Gulag?'

It was not a comical squirrel asking such questions. It was not even a reporter from Seattle, USA. Who was it? Why was it so necessary to answer this funny little man?

'She was devilishly clever. Deputy Director Sakhvadze . . . just like a damned Georgian . . . knowing our countries still officially embrace détente . . . and *we* must uphold noble world-image . . . next year Diamond Jubilee Revolution! . . . Sakhvadze all but confess she and her cohorts are involved in Mind Wars research . . . just as your scientists are also, belka! . . . What a joke on both our countries . . . we must fulfil the world's expectations of us now, like it or not . . . Die Gedanken sind frei und wir stehen bis zum Hals in der Scheisse . . .'

The squirrel did not seem willing to believe this. 'Do you mean your government is going to let her get away with it?'

The tipsy KGB man laughed, then blew his nose resoundingly. Finster's coercion was no longer needed.

'Little squirrel, she has *already* got away with it. In that lecture hall were perhaps forty television cameras, trained on MacGregor and his video screen. Sakhvadze's words and their origination were broadcast live to our people as well as to the rest of the world. We cannot claim her message was a hoax because its source in Alma-Ata can be verified easily by the computers of British Telecom. Doubtless this verification will also be trumpeted to the world via the free satellite transmissions . . . Oh, yes! The lovely Tamara Petrovna has caught both the Soviet and American governments by the balls, and she is on a downhill slide. The Cold War is over, thanks to the Scottish Professor. You and I are washed up, Amerikanskiy. You are not CIA — but whatever you are, you are finished. The soul-travellers and the mind readers will expose the most closely guarded secrets of our two nations as easily as cracking hazelnuts. There is nothing left for us but to become friends . . . just as Robert Burns wished. Yes, little squirrel! The proletarian poet of Scotland was a great prophet! Do you know what he said?

For a' that, and a' that,
It's comin' yet, for a' that!
That man and man the world o'er
Shall brothers be for a' that.'

'Sure,' Finster agreed, smiling. 'Sure, Sergei. One for all, and all for one. At least until we get rid of our mutual enemies.'

19

*From the Memoirs of
Rogatien Remillard*

When the live telecast from Edinburgh ended at 7:00 A.M. Eastern Time I was in a state of near-mortal funk. I downed a neat tumblerful of Canadian Club sitting there in my armchair in front of the blank television screen while my brain kept replaying that scene of the crazed Swiss photographer screeching his Cassandra warning as the Scottish police hauled him away.

Pandora's box! Oh, yes, indeed. It was opening wide to an amazed and fascinated world, and what was inside was *us*.

I had to call Denis. I told myself it was to find out what plans he and his people had. On my first three tries, his home phone was busy; then I only got his answering machine. I called the lab and reached Glenn Dalembert, who had come in early to make a videotape of the Scottish demonstration.

'Yeah, I got detailed for the scut-work while everybody else watched the big show in comfort at home. This afternoon we'll do a replay for the full Medical School faculty, together with learned commentary by yours truly and homegrown EE talent displays by Colette and Tucker. With Denis gone, I'll be in charge. Want a freebie ticket?'

'Denis has gone where?' I demanded.

'Down to West Lebanon. They're sending an Air Force chopper to shuttle him to Burlington International where the Washington flight will be held for him — '

I cut Glenn off. '*They?* D'you mean those Mind Wars bastards roped Denis in after all?'

My nephew's associate gave a strained laugh. 'Oh, no. Nothing so picayune as the Army or the CIA this time. The President himself called Denis at home right after the telecast. Seems he read the book and was very impressed, and now he's pegged Denis as the guy most likely to give him the straight poop about the authenticity of MacGregor's blockbuster.'

'Oh, shit,' I groaned. My nephew – the Kissinger of metapsychic realpolitik! He would be asked to help recruit American operants for MacGregor's noble scheme. He would certainly reveal his own operancy. Or would he?

Glenn had turned solicitous. 'Roger, is there something wrong?'

'Everything's wrong.'

'Listen – come to the faculty meeting and we'll talk. Better yet, join Colette and me for lunch — '

'No thanks. You folks have a good time at the show-and-tell. I'll be just fine.' I hung up, then took the phone off the hook.

Denis. He was the only one who could help. I could try to reach him at the airport by telephone . . . but that was no good. I wouldn't be able to *say* what was wrong . . .

Farspeak him, then. Make the appeal mind-to-mind.

I slouched over to the bedroom window and stood there in my pyjamas and grubby old terry-cloth robe trying to marshal my booze-addled wits. It was not going to be easy to attract Denis's attention with the all-important telepathic 'hail'. My mind was weakened and Denis would surely be preoccupied with the enormity of MacGregor's gamble and by the upcoming Oval Office meeting. Furthermore, the bulk of Crafts Hill lay between me and the West Lebanon Regional Airport, four miles south of Hanover. I would have to muster up sufficient strength to 'flow' my mental shout around the hill and puncture my nephew's brown study. Once alerted, he would have no difficulty tuning in to my puny thought-beam.

But how was I going to manage that initial hail?

An idea slowly formed. One of my yogic exercises featured a spiral focusing of body energies spinning centripetally in towards the heart, which certain psychic authorities proposed as the vital centre of the modern human being. This so-called in-spiralling chakra meditation had tended to promote feelings of comfort and power even in my beleaguered soul. I could do it. The reverse form of the exercise, the out-spiral, had carried a cautionary note for novices. It was alleged to have more drastic effects in the focusing of energies and was more difficult to control. Since additional psychic trauma was the last thing I had needed during the awful summer and fall, up until now I had given this particular form of meditation a firm miss. But it might just offer me my best shot at reaching Denis.

I assumed the appropriate posture, one I had dubbed 'Leonardo's X-Man', still standing there at the window. I closed my eyes, shielded myself from external stimuli as best I could, and concentrated on the region of my heart. Far more than a mere blood-pump, the heart is also a gland whose secretions help in the regulation of the entire body. I tried to visualize it as the focus of my being, a receptacle of life-force and love. When there was a distinct knot of warmth behind my lower breastbone, I coaxed it out to begin a slow, tight, flattened curve. It moved to the left and downward, traversing my solar plexus. Gaining strength and speed, it spiralled smoothly up to the branching of the trachea and the thymal remnant, then arced left within the body's frontal plane. It dived down through my spleen, illuminated the suprarenals, and swung back up towards the thyroid in my throat – for the first time passing outside my body as the spiral widened. A long curve brought the still-meagre ball of energy to the root of my spine, where lay the chakra that yogic tradition deemed one of the most vital. I felt a great influx of fresh power enlarge and accelerate the ball. It swung upwards, seemed to blaze behind my closed eyes, and began its final swift circuit through the elbow of my extended left arm, through my left and right knees, through my right elbow. I was waiting as it flew towards the crown of my head and branded it with the impress of a single mental signature, adding a dollop of heavenly appeal as a sop to the faith of my fathers. Then I hurled it away from me, that cri de coeur véritable:

DENIS!

Simultaneous with the farspoken hail came a terrific neural ignition, part orgasm and part high-voltage shock. My body convulsed and I fell heavily to the floor.

[Images: Full-colour 3–D Denis face stunned. Air Force helicopter open door blades windmill tearing fog fabric coloured runway lights yellow Toyota Land Cruiser.]

???GoodGodUncleRogi??? What'sWRONG?

. . . sorry . . . trying hard get your attention . . .

! You almost blasted me off my feet whatinhell you upto I suppose Glenn told you WhiteHouse summons . . . !!! . . . HOW DID YOU DO THAT?

[Image drenched in sheepishness.] Outspiral chakra Leonardo's X with cyclotronic kundalini embellishment . . . worked a little better than expected . . .

Fuckingidiot! Don't you know that could be dangerous?

Yes.

Acute anxiety. Dammit bon sang d'imbécile you leave thatstuff alone until we go over it together I really *mean* what I say!

Yesyesyes but had to reach you had to . . . [image].

Concern. EdinburghDemo provoked fear? Explain.

[Concatenated images.]

Uncle Rogi . . . what you need I can't do at a distance. But you must believe me when I tell you it will be all right. *[Airman beckons inside chopper Denis nods ducks blades scurries into aircraft door shuts airman orders seat belt signals pilot upup and away.]*

Denis . . . what President want?

You can probably guess: my analysis assessment Scottelecast. Legit? Practicable solution armsrace? Howmany EEops potential US/USSR/Scotland/Elsewhere? When online? Anychance Russ have jump on us already emplace their Psi-Eye?

Psi-Eye!

Prexyname ever the GreatSalesman. Fortunately can tell him Russ EEprogramme controlled by Tamara [kiss!] she deceived Politburo re her project readiness so not emplaced. Russ, EEops all peaceniks group purged of GRU/KGB/opportunist/fanatic heads last decade. Now Russ operants tend antiestablishment because 'elitist phenom operancy' remains suspect under Marxist dogmatism. Tamara will see to honest observer team setup. There will be no war.

That was never my worry. Too selfish . . .

Then?

[Projected image: Screaming figure waving camera disappears beneath bodycrush hauled up handcuffed dragged away.] Pandora's box ruin chaos anarchy and worse OUR EXPOSURE OURS DENIS!

Difficult days yes there will have to be economic summits global cooperation in many other psychaffected areas —

You don't understand yet what I'm driving at! We will be pawns manipulated hated the coercers willbe offered power over others —

This won't happen. Do you think we haven't anticipated

such a thing? It was dealt with in the longrange plan that had to be scrapped but we will preserve our freedom and dignity. President wants set up MetaBrain Trust. Public. Plan for best use other operant faculties besides EE goodof-country goodofworld. Guess who invited to be chairman?

! You had to write that goddam book.

Relax. My forte research not administration. I'll decline with humblethanks let Brawley of Stanford or The Astronaut sit in Washington metahotseat.

How can you not listen when 900-lb canary sings?

Laughter. Now you know why I had no photo on bookjacket *Metapsychology*. All President has to do is take look at me [image] would YOU entrust Third Millennium diplomacy to halfbaked egghead twerp? . . . I'm safe plan propose myself special adviser sortof GrandYoungMan metapsychology.

Denis . . . are you going to tell him that you're operant?

Yes. I'm sorry Uncle Rogi . . . for your sake. But soonerorlater we have to come out with it.

Despair. Later. Much later.

Yes . . . I argued Jamie MacGregor pleaded caution wanted postpone until operants numerous more organized for selfpreservation and my training normals → operancy proved feasible. But MacGregor cited increasing peril globalwar . . . and another factor. He said: We are all members humanrace survive or perish together no Homo-sapiens vs Homosuperior only Homoterrestris. Earth Man.

Resignation. Bitterness. Still terrible gamble Godsake nobody seriously believes Russ planning launch WorldWarIII —

That was not deciding factor. I told you there was something else. Someone tried to kill Jamie in April. He was afraid his whole group endangered so decided to go to ground do demo soonest. His attacker not KGB/GRU/CIA/XXX. *He was another powerful operant.*

Jésus Christ.

Man coerced Jamie into darkalley physique metarendered fuzzy aimed tubething at paralysed Jamie apologetic implacability just then muscleman in duffelcoat came scared off assailant was not affected coercion nextday Jamie examined alley found needle later analysed coated deadly poison ricin favourite assassins no other clue attacker . . . or rescuer. Damn worrying.

Operant crooks in Scotland! So New Hampshire doesn't have monopoly afterall. [Familiar image quickly erased.]

Jamie says coercive ability assassin formidable. Disguising of appearance interesting jibes with my current-studies creativity —

The mysterious power to cloud men's minds. The Shadow knows! . . . Or are you too young to know that nonsense?

I've heard classic radiotapes. But apparently attacker not really invisible or passerby might not have saved Jamie. Affair peculiar. If not metagovernmentagent (impossible we would *know*) then who?

Wild card. Odd John had one. Psychometa.

Jamie positive attacker sane.

You intend tell President metavillains atlarge?

Will mention possibility. But this minor compared to prospect end nucleardeterrent.

MacGregor figure he's safe now?

He thinks now Psi-Eye scheme revealed danger minimal. Actually Swiss Bank Agentfakephotographer had best motive for offing Jamie. Perhaps metassassin another of theirs. Governments not only ones with valuable secrets.

Be sure you tell President that. Eventually we'll need bodyguards and they come expensive.

Hogwash.

Pauvre innocent! Go go carry out great mission pray Goodness triumphs . . . Were other academiclights also summoned President?

He said no. Maybe later.

Hah. So that's wayofit. By time you return Dartmouth you famous inspiteofself President will see to it whetherornot you agree head BrainTrust.

Humour. It was the book. Talking heads come&go but if you write book you are AUTHORity.

Laughter. Easing.

. . . Uncle Rogi we're approaching Burlington Inter-national. Please try not to worry. When I get home you must let me try to help you. (Yes yes I know how could I not tu es mon père!) Other Remillards all over US&Canada will find selves in your position after I exit metacloset. Most of them will cheerfully admit they haven't a metafaculty to save their lives. You can too. But it would be best if you didn't conceal your powers. Best for you for all operants as well. We must hurry day when operancy commonplace as musical/artistic/intellectual talent similarly unthreat to normals – damn! – there I go we're just as *normal* as they are aren't we?

Pour sûr.[?]

Nonoperants will realize in time that they have nothing to fear from us.

But they do.

Oh Uncle Rogi.

. . . and we have even more to fear from them. We're outnumbered.

Exasperation. If you spent some time with us at the lab you'd know we're finding ways to . . . neutralize . . . antagonists. Peaceful ways. You and your oneman stand! You don't have to face this alone can't you see the only way is through solidarity even nonoperants know a lonemind is doomed there must be two or three or more loving for Love to heal and initiate transcendence please please monpère don't shut us out —

We'll discuss later. Smallthing compared momentous events demanding your attention. You must not be distracted.

We are landing . . . Please Uncle Rogi please join us. [Guile.] You will ease my mind.

Will think over carefully. Bon voyage et bonne chance mon fils.

I stood looking out of the window. Outside, the morning mist was burning away and the streetlights had gone out. I was hungry, very nearly cheerful, but still perversely determined to best my inner demons in single combat. I would certainly have to find out just what self-defensive manoeuvres Denis and his people had discovered, but as to joining with them – letting Denis into the secret parts of my mind – it was impossible. A Franco father cannot stand naked before his son.

As I stared at the passing cars below and the students hurrying up Main Street towards their early classes a mundane thought stole into my skull. If the presidential favour did confer fresh notoriety upon my nephew, there would surely be a great new demand for copies of *Metapsychology*. If I called the jobbers in Boston with a rush order, I could get a leg up on the competition at the big Dartmouth Bookstore down the street. And when Denis returned, I might prevail on him to do a signing session. He had never autographed copies of his book before, but he might agree to help me out.

Just as I was turning away from the window my eyes focused upon the glass itself. I swore mildly. Some damn kid with a BB-gun must have been taking pot shots at squirrels. There was a small hole neatly drilled in one of the upper panes. But it was a strange hole, lacking the typical halo crater produced by the impact of a missile, and there were no cracks radiating from it. It was about a quarter of an inch in diameter and the edges were not sharp, but smooth. Perplexed, I studied the tiny opening, which was above my eye level. Then I went to a drawer in the kitchen and got a tape measure.

The hole was six feet two inches above the floor, my exact height in bare feet. I felt a blob of warmth begin to form again behind my ribs. Wondering, I touched the top of my head.

Surely not. But on the other hand . . .

Denis would no doubt be eager to test it. Should I agree? Why not, provided the rest of my mind was left inviolate? I chuckled at the thought of the consternation this 'mind-zap' power would provoke among the academics. Nothing in any of my readings on parapsychology had prepared me for an effect such as this, nor had there been any mention of it in the lengthy catalogue of higher mental phenomena in Denis's book. Not only was my zapping new, it was also fraught with possibility . . .

How d'you like *them* apples, Donnie? Maybe you better rest in peace if you know what's good for you, mon frérot!

I went to the telephone. It was after 8:30 and the book jobber in Boston would be open. I decided to triple the order I had originally decided upon. Denis would beef about the autograph session, but he'd cooperate.

Now I was certain of it.

20

Alma-Ata, Kazakh SSR, Earth
24 October 1991

Any other General Secretary would have commanded her immediate presence in Moscow before a Star Chamber tribunal. It was a mark of this man's populist style, and his shrewdness in dealing with the often nonconformist scientific element, that he came to her. He dismissed his hovering aides, sat casually in front of her desk in the small corner office of the Institute for Bioenergetic Studies at Kazakh State University, and chatted about the weather.

Tamara served him tea without hurrying. Afterwards she did not resume her normal seat behind the desk but pulled up a side chair next to him. They could both look out of the window and see the high Tien Shan's white rampart in the south. The day was brilliant, but the first storm of the season was forecast for tomorrow. He would decline the proferred hospitality of the Kazakh Party Secretary and fly back to Moscow tonight.

'And tell the comrades of the Politburo your elucidation of the Edinburgh Demonstration,' he concluded, sipping the tea. 'Delicious.'

'I have prepared a précis of our work on excorporeal excursion.' She smiled winsomely, a plump, dark-eyed woman whose shining red hair was worn in a tidy knot, and indicated a sealed portfolio on the desk. 'It also contains recommendations for the speedy establishment of a corps of psychic observers. I will be honoured to cooperate in its deployment, of course.'

He eyed her over the rim of the tea glass. 'Of course. I daresay we couldn't do without you . . .'

She shrugged. 'I know my people and their capabilities. This EE business is often more of an art than a science. You understand that the operants will require congenial working conditions in order to do their work properly. They are loyal Soviet citizens – you have my word of honour on it – but fully committed to peace.'

The General Secretary sighed. 'This is going to be difficult.'

'For us,' she said, 'it has been difficult for twenty-five years.'

The General Secretary finished his tea and took up the portfolio. Unsealing it, he leafed through the papers. After a few minutes of silence, he said, 'You were not at all surprised to see me come here, Comrade Doctor.'

'I confess that I was curious about the reaction of the Politburo to the Edinburgh Demonstration, as were all of my people. We did not think you would panic, but we had to be sure.'

'Radi Boga! You spied on us!'

'And on the American President and his advisers, and on the leaders of the People's Republic of China, and on the Pope.'

'The Pope?' The General Secretary was taken aback. 'What did *he* do?'

'He wept, Mikhail Semyonovich.'

'And so did Comrade Dankov of the KGB,' the Secretary muttered. 'You will be interested to know – if you don't already – that the ever-vigilant comrades on Dzerzhinsky Square were foreskinned to a marked degree at your personal participation in the Edinburgh Demonstration. Dankov demanded the immediate liquidation of you and your entire cadre of wizards. It seems you have deceived your KGB sponsors rather spectacularly.'

'It was a matter of survival . . .'

'As you know, Dankov was made to see reason. There was greater difficulty with the Defence Council. Marshal Kumylzhensky pushed for a pre-emptive nuclear strike.

348

This is still a serious option if we do not have a competent EE inspection team to balance that in the West.'

'We have sixty-eight EE adepts, most with global faculties. It is an adequate number. The combined EE adepts of the West number more than eighty – over thirty in Britain, perhaps forty-five in the USA. There are also scattered groups of neutralist percipients in other countries. Their numbers will grow, as will our own.'

The little office was becoming chilly with the close of day, but the General Secretary's balding head had a gleam of sweat. 'The militarist lunatics were voted down resoundingly for now. The Politburo knows that the present euphoric mood of our people would never countenance a first strike – no more than it would allow the psychics to be harmed. The people demand – demand! – that MacGregor's proposal be implemented.'

'There was dancing in the streets of Alma-Ata,' Tamara said.

'And in Moscow. And everywhere throughout the Soviet Union! By allowing them to view that telecast – and we are investigating *that*, too! – we have indeed opened the door to a new age. But that age may not be golden, as you and your idealistic associates hope, Tamara Petrovna. You know that I have been striving for years now to upgrade our faltering economy, to instill a new spirit of industry and progress into our people, to control military adventurism, to fight the ingrained corruption, the laziness, the despair infecting our youth . . . And now, suddenly, there is this! Our enemies all around us will be thwarted in aggression by the psychic observers. The people will expect drastic disarmament initiatives. They will believe that reductions in our huge defence budget will bring about improved domestic conditions. For a while, they will wait patiently for this to come about. Perhaps they will wait as long as a decade, distracted by our travels to Mars and other wonders. But then . . .'

'I read your subvocal thoughts, Comrade General Secretary. We are not a unified nation. Discipline and right order have up until now been preserved among our disparate ethnic elements primarily through the Great

Russian bureaucracy, and the people's determination to stand fast and defend the Motherland against the common enemy.'

Smoothly, he took up the skein of his own thoughts again. 'But without that enemy to distract us, the masses will look more critically at the kind of life they live – at the inefficiencies of our system, at the often unjust decrees of the central power structure, at our economy based upon obsolete philosophic principles that falls further and further behind the other industrialized nations of the world . . . Look into your crystal ball, Tamara Petrovna, you and your psychic colleagues with your shining dream of peace for the future! Will we have that peace in the Soviet Union? Will we be able to adapt fast enough to avoid catastrophe?'

She turned her face away abruptly, lips tightening. 'I don't know. Sometimes I *do* see the future. And far away . . . years from now . . . there is a great change, a time of expanding horizons, when our people will help to colonize the stars as we now seek to colonize Mars . . . But the near future? I do not see that, Comrade General Secretary. Thank God I do not. The job of guiding our nation through the last perilous years of this twentieth century is yours, not mine – and I also thank God for that. Now take the portfolio with the details of the psychic-oversight scheme, and do what you must.'

'While you watch,' he said.

She rose from her chair, turning her back on him, and looked out at the gleaming mountains. 'While the world watches.'

21

From the Memoirs of
Rogatien Remillard

The specifics of the EE monitoring plan were promptly delivered to both Washington and Moscow, and a Summit was scheduled. The much-battered Strategic Arms Limitation Treaty was dusted off, updated and promised to an exultant world as a Christmas present.

In the United States, the emplacement of Psi-Eye was considered a fait accompli by the general public – and the White House did nothing to discourage the impression, nor did the Soviets. Most people were happy to believe that vigilant American EE adepts (inevitably dubbed pEEps) had settled in on the job immediately following the Scottish telecast. There were 'Big Brother Is Watching You' jokes and voyeuristic editorial cartoons, however, and a tentative panic on Wall Street that was quashed by the President in a brilliant personal appeal. Some nay-sayers recalled the madman who had tried to shoot MacGregor with a camera-gun, whose identity was released to the press by the British only after a question had been raised in Parliament. By and large, however, the United States reacted with happy exuberance to the Psi-Eye scheme. It was seen as a virtually foolproof reprieve from nuclear doomsday. The identities (and the numbers) of the pEEps were kept secret, of course; but everyone knew that they were en garde night and day, keeping a mind's eye out for potential Kremlin button-pushers – at the same time that their noble Russian opposite numbers scrutinized the US Joint Chiefs sulking impotently in the Pentagon war-room.

In actuality, neither the American nor the Soviet authorities achieved a working psychic monitoring effort for nearly three months, until early 1992. There were endless niggling details to be resolved, the most critical of which was: Where do you look? As in the classic BEWARE OF THE DOG sign ploy, however, the mere proclamation of Psi-Eye was as good as its actuality. Neither of the superpowers was willing to risk being caught out trying to steal a march on the other – and although the Americans and Soviets might have had doubts about each other's Psi-Eye capability, they had none whatsoever about Scotland's. At the close of the Edinburgh Demonstration, Jamie MacGregor had remarked offhandedly that the University's independent psychic surveillance team of thirty-two EE adepts was already at work, and would be issuing regular press releases of selected US and Soviet military secrets. The team's revelations were far from sensational; they were not intended to be. But they did provide a continual reminder to the world that excorporeal excursion was a reality, and inspired the two superpowers to get on with the right stuff. Both the Soviet Union and the United States behaved with unblemished probity throughout the Summit talks, the SALT signing and ratification, and the initiation of nuclear disarmament. The threats to world peace came from entirely different directions.

Here in the United States, a groundswell from burdened taxpayers called for an immediate halt to military spending. The few remaining Congressional hawks, the fundamentalist Red-haters, and the as yet insignificant numbers of meta-sceptics had their objections steamrollered into oblivion. The President, shrewd as ever in his reponse to consumer demand, hailed Tamara Sakhvadze's call for a World Congress on Metapsychology, and then proposed that the United States host a sister international conference on shared high technology. The Soviet General Secretary said that his nation would eagerly participate in both meetings. Then he suggested that Professor Jamie MacGregor be nominated for the Nobel Peace Prize.

My nephew Denis was closeted with the President for nearly a week, briefing him on virtually every aspect of current metapsychic research. He also testified before the House Committee on Science and Technology, the Senate Armed Services Committee, and a full meeting of the Cabinet. He would accept only an advisory appointment to the Presidential Commission on Metapsychology, but promised to consult with the Meta Brain Trust on a regular basis.

Figuratively crowned with laurel and trailed by belling newshounds, Denis returned to Dartmouth intending to get back to his researches. It was a vain hope. Post-Edinburgh and post-Washington, he and his little establishment became very big news indeed. Now prestigious foundations stampeded to Dartmouth's door, proffering endowments; and these, unlike the tainted Pentagon grants that Denis had helped to discredit during the Mind Wars scandal, were accepted 'for the good of Dartmouth College and for the advancement of metapsychology as a whole'.

There would be no more dodging of the media, either. Submitting to the inevitable, Denis put his associate Gerard Tremblay in charge of the lab's public affairs. At that time, the vivacious former granite-quarryman was thirty-one years old and had taken his MD just three years earlier. In spite of his Franco heritage, he was the member of the Coterie that I liked least. He was a fiery, good-looking fellow with intense presence; but I had always thought him a bit of a brown-nose, suspecting that his obsequious manner might be compensation for an unconscious envy of my nephew. My suspicions were to be eventually confirmed. But until he precipitated the disastrous Coercer Flap during President Baumgartner's second term, Tremblay did an outstanding job coping with the media, with curious politicians, and with the many national and international organizations that suddenly focused their attention on the shoestring research establishment at 45 College Street, Hanover, New Hampshire.

Tremblay's first PR triumph took place in November 1991, with the interview of Denis by the investigative news programme *60 Minutes*. CBS was prepared to devote the entire hour-long telecast to metapsychology's Wunderkind. The interview would be combined with a tour of the Dartmouth facility and would show the actual testing of operant subjects, who would remain anonymous. Denis's lab was a prime media target because it had always remained off-limits to journalists during the blizzard of publicity attending the publication of *Metapsychology*. Heaven only knows what kind of Frankenstein shenanigans the *60 Minutes* people hoped to uncover. As it happened, the programme was destined to be nearly as memorable as MacGregor's Edinburgh shocker . . . only this time *I* was there, doing my thing in front of the network cameras, and daring the world to make something of it.

22

Excerpts from the CBS-TV:
Public Affairs Programme 60 Minutes
17 November 1991

FADE IN
BG STILL SHOT (MATTE) EXT DARTMOUTH
RESEARCH FACILITY A picturesque, rather dilapidated
three-storey New England saltbox building, dark grey;
resembling a barn on side of wooded hill, it looms almost
ominously above a stretch of rain-wet pavement and is
framed by bare-branched trees. In FG of MATTE stands
reporter CARLOS MORENO, whose hard-hitting questions, mobile woolly-bear eyebrows, and divergent squint
have often provoked unexpectedly revealing responses from
even the most guarded interviewees.
TITLE AND CREDIT ROLL

SUPERMINDS AMONG US?
Produced by Jeananne Lancaster
CARLOS MORENO
(addressing viewers)

Tonight we conclude our special three-week investigation
of the startling new developments in psychic research by
meeting a scientist who is acknowledged throughout the
world to be one of the most influential in the field. He
heads this laboratory at Dartmouth College in New
Hampshire . . . a place that has been, up until now,
completely off-limits to reporters. *60 Minutes* will be
taking you inside this deceptively modest building, the
workplace of the man who was described by the President
of the United States as 'the most awesome person I have
ever met, an authentic supermind' . . . But first, let's
meet him in a more conventional setting . . .

INT BOOKSHOP
Begin with ECU of DENIS REMILLARD, with downcast
eyes; then SLOW REVERSE ZOOM to a FULL SHOT of
him sitting at table in ELOQUENT PAGE BOOKSHOP
signing volumes for a crowd of CUSTOMERS who include

students in Dartmouth sweat shirts, professional types, working-class types, retirees. Remillard is slight of physique, blondish, with a pleasant, shy smile. He wears tweed jacket with shirt and tie, exchanges inaudible comments with his fans during MORENO VOICE OVER.

MORENO (VOICE OVER)

Denis Remillard looks more like a graduate student than an Associate Professor of Psychiatry at an Ivy League school. He is only twenty-four years old and he has always shunned publicity – even after his book, *Metapsychology*, leaped to Number One on national best-seller lists last year. Unlike the other psychic researchers we've interviewed during this series, Denis Remillard doesn't concentrate on narrow areas of mind-study. Instead, he's a theoretician who has tried to fit the puzzling higher mental powers into a larger context.

CU REMILLARD

REMILLARD

I think my book was a success because people are very open to new ideas now. Things that our grandparents would have called absurd – like travelling to Mars – are reality. But the New Physics shows us that even *reality itself* isn't what common sense says it ought to be!

(quizzical boyish grin, eyes averted)

The universe isn't just space and time, matter and energy. You have to fit *life* into a valid Universal Field Theory – and *mind* as well. That's basically what my book is all about. Theoretical physicists and life-scientists have known for quite a while that the old view of the universe as a kind of supermachine just doesn't work. It doesn't explain the natural phenomena we experience, and it especially doesn't explain the higher mind-powers, which have never fitted into a conventional biophysical format.

INT BOOKSHOP – CLOSE SHOT MORENO Remillard and his fans visible in BG as CAMERA MOVES BACK.

(addressing viewers)

MORENO

As he autographs copies of his book here in Hanover, New Hampshire, in a little shop owned by his Uncle Roger, Denis Remillard hardly seems to fulfil one's expectation of a world-renowned psychologist – much less a supermind. But he was the first person summoned to be a presidential consultant on psychic affairs following the sensational Edinburgh Demonstration. He declined the chairmanship of the President's recently organized blue-ribbon Advisory Commission on Metapsychology . . . But he *has* agreed to head the American delegation to Alma-Ata in the Soviet Union, where researchers from dozens of nations will meet next year to discuss the practical applications of mind-power . . . And last week, Remillard's lab was singled out for a ten-million-dollar grant from the Vangelder Foundation. The allocation has been earmarked for an investigation into ways whereby ordinary people – people like you and me – might some day be able to learn the amazing mental feats that Denis Remillard has studied and written about . . . feats that *he himself* performs.

MEDIUM SHOT – REMILLARD, UNCLE ROGER, FEMALE FAN

Remillard's CONVERSATION with his Uncle, who brought over a fresh supply of books for autographing, and the young Female Fan is audible at LOW VOLUME under MORENO V.O.

MORENO (V.O.)

Yes . . . it's true. Vouched for by no less an authority than the President of the United States. Not only is Professor Denis Remillard a distinguished psychic researcher, but he also possesses extraordinary mind-powers himself!

REMILLARD

(looks up from book to Fan)
Well, it's not the kind of thing one brags about or shows off in bars. But . . . yes, I am what we call metapsychically operant.

FEMALE FAN

(hesitantly)

Do you mean . . . you can *read my mind*?

REMILLARD

(laughs)

Certainly not. Not unless you deliberately try to project a thought-sequence at me. However, I *am* aware of the general emotional tenor of your mind. That you're not hostile, for instance. That you're fascinated by the idea of higher mind-powers.

FAN

Oh, I am! It would be marvellous to do things like soul-travelling or telepathy or that mind-over-matter thing . . . whatchacallit?

REMILLARD

Psychokinesis.

FAN

That's it. Just imagine being able to go to Las Vegas and *clean up*!

The rest of the CUSTOMERS laugh and murmur at this.

REMILLARD

(patiently)

But I can't, you know. Even if I were dishonest enough to try to manipulate slot machines or dice or a roulette wheel with my mind — how long would it take the casino owners to catch on? I'd be tossed out on my ear . . . at the very least.

More laughs and murmurs from CUSTOMERS.

FAN

But . . . then what *good* are the powers?

REMILLARD

You might ask Professor Jamie MacGregor that . . . Actually, I find my own metafaculties most useful in conducting experiments. I can compare my own reactions to those of the test subjects in psychokinesis training, for example.

FAN

(interrupts, gushing)
Ooh, Professor, do you suppose — ? I mean, would it be an awful imposition if you *showed us*? I mean, I've seen it done on TV by those Russians, but to see you do it *live* . . .

CUSTOMERS

(ad lib exclamations)
Hey! . . . Wow! . . . Would you? . . . Super! . . . Please!

REMILLARD

(indulgently)
And Mr Carlos Moreno told you to ask me – right?

FAN

Uh . . . I'd really appreciate it.

CU REMILLARD looking sardonically into camera. For the first time we see that his eyes are effulgent blue, almost glowing within their deep orbits.

REMILLARD

Your camera crew is quite ready? . . . Well, PK is one of the least significant metafaculties, so I guess I don't mind doing a small demonstration. After all, we can't let the Scots and the Russians garner all the kudos . . . Why don't I use these copies of my book?

MEDIUM SHOT. Remillard takes a volume, turns it so that front cover faces camera. He balances book precariously on one corner of its cover, takes hands away, and leaves book poised sur la pointe.

Now it's impossible to balance a book like this, right? Defies the law of gravity.

He balances another book on top of the first, also on its corner. The books do not tremble or totter; they are rock-solid.

And if we balance another book on that . . . and then a third . . . and then a fourth . . .

He does so.

. . . You know I must be either holding the books up

with mind-power, or else I'm some kind of a [BLEEP]ing magician. And if I then extract the bottom book . . .

He does so, leaving the three upper books hanging in thin air.

. . . and the top trio remains there, then you have to be positive that something rather out of the ordinary is going on.

CUSTOMERS

(ad lib exclamations, applause)

How about that! . . . Sheesh! . . . Eat your heart out, Houdini!

Remillard shrugs. The three books in the air tumble to the table with a clatter. His UNCLE ROGER, the bookshop owner, a beanpole with greying hair and a youthful face, steps forward looking humorously indignant. Camera CLOSES ON HIM.

UNCLE ROGER

Is that any way to treat books? All you have to do is write them. I have to sell them!

He extends his hands and beckons solicitously. All four books fly off the table to him. He grasps them and forms them into neat stack.

CUSTOMERS

(ad lib shouts, a feminine squeal)

God! . . . Holy [BLEEP]! . . . You see that? . . . Sonuvagun!

UNCLE ROGER

You didn't know? Sorry. My nephew should have told you that it runs in the family.

[SCRIPT PAGES OMITTED]

TWO SHOT – STEADICAM FOLLOWING MORENO AND REMILLARD

Emerging from TELEPATHY EVALUATION CHAMBER, they walk down HALLWAY towards Remillard's OFFICE, continuing conversation begun in chamber.

REMILLARD

Only persons who already possess strong latencies for metafunctions can reasonably expect to develop into operants after training. It's like any other kind of talent: singing, for example. One must first be born with a proper set of vocal cords. Then the person might become a talented amateur without training. Usually, however, the voice must be trained. The singer practises for years, and with luck a great singer might result. But nobody can make an opera singer out of a person who lacks the right vocal cords, or who is tone-deaf. And you can't make a really competent vocalist out of someone who hates to sing, or who suffers from terminal stage fright. . . . It's a similar thing when you work to raise a latent metafunction to operancy. Some will fail to make it, and some – we hope! – will sing at the Met.

MORENO

(frowning)

Then all human beings don't have the potential for developing these higher mind-powers?

REMILLARD

Of course not – any more than all people can become great opera singers. This is why my proposal to test all Americans for latent mind-powers is so important. The powers are a national resource. We must discover who among our citizens have the potential for becoming operant – then give them proper training.

MORENO

Sort of like the Astronaut Programme?

REMILLARD

Yes . . . but enrolling both children and adults. Let me try to clarify the concept of latency for you. Our studies have shown that everyone is metapsychically latent to a certain extent. The strength of the latency may vary from power to power. Dick may be strongly latent in telepathy and weak in the healing faculty, while Jane is just the opposite. With hard work, we may make an operant telepath of Dick and an operant healer of Jane. But their weaker latencies may never amount to anything.

MORENO

Suppose I was a latent telepath. Could you make me operant?

REMILLARD

Maybe. Keep in mind that there's no hard and fast line between latency and operancy, though. Maybe you're a natural – what we call a suboperant. All you need is a bit of practise and you're able to broadcast telepathically to the Moon. But suppose your potential is weak. We might train you till your skull warps – but discover that your operant telepathic radius is only half a metre in diameter. Or you can only broadcast at night when the sun's ionization of the atmosphere is minimal, and even then only when you're completely relaxed and rested. You'd be an operant, technically speaking, but your metafaculty wouldn't be very useful. Except possibly for pillow talk.

MORENO

(smiles briefly)

You mention factors that can inhibit operancy, like ionization. Does this mean that there are ways to screen out telepaths – or stop them from using their powers?

REMILLARD

We're only beginning to discover ways to do this. It's very hard to foil the ultrasenses, such as excorporeal excursion and telepathy, that don't seem to require much expenditure of psychic energy. Things like psychokinesis, on the other hand, can be rather easily frustrated by external factors. And *internal*, subjective factors can be even more inhibitory.

TRACK INTO REMILLARD'S OFFICE

Angle favouring door as Remillard ushers Moreno inside. The office furniture is old, academic-shabby. Extensive wall bookcases overflowing with books and papers. Computer terminal. Wall hologram of human brain. Painting of Mount Washington, New Hampshire. And everywhere –

on desk, shelves, brackets, floor – PLANTS growing luxuriantly.

MORENO

(looking around)
Quite a conservatory you have here, Professor. You must have a green thumb.

REMILLARD

(examining droopy plant on desk)
Actually, it's more like a green mind, I guess. Now this poor little Paphiopedilum really needs mental TLC, so I keep it close by and let it share my aura as well as the occasional healing thought.

He sits down and motions Moreno to a seat.

MORENO

(puzzled)
Your aura?

REMILLARD

(seeming vaguely annoyed with himself)
The bioenergetic field that surrounds my body – and that of every other living thing. Plants included.

MORENO

(nods, as if suddenly recalling)
It seems to me I've read that certain people can even *see* the aura that surrounds others . . . Can you see auras?

REMILLARD

Yes. If I concentrate on it.

MORENO

What do auras look like? What does *mine* look like?
CU REMILLARD
He is cupping his hands about the sick orchid plant and staring at it with mild intensity.

REMILLARD

Auras look something like glowing, coloured halos that pulse and change. Healthy plants usually have a golden halo. Animals and people have more varied colours.

Operants have halos that look bright to another operant who concentrates on viewing them. Since you're latent, Mr Moreno, your aura is quite faint. It's reddish, shot through with flashes of violet.

MORENO (V.O.)

Does the colour of a person's aura have any significance?

REMILLARD

We haven't worked out precise correlations yet. The individual aural colouration tends to vary according to mood, health and the kind of mental activity being engaged in.

MORENO (V.O.)

Any particular significance to my red and purple?

REMILLARD

(looking blandly into camera)
I'd prefer not to comment on that today.

TWO SHOT – MORENO AND REMILLARD
Favouring Remillard and taking in the striking hologram of the brain.

MORENO

(in brisk mood switch)
We were discussing things that can inhibit the operation of the higher mind-powers ... I suppose things like liquor, drugs, fatigue, illness – they'd all have an adverse effect on operancy, wouldn't they?

REMILLARD

Oh, yes. If anything, the higher faculties are even more sensitive to such things than the lower ones. But there are all kinds of other factors that can diminish one's operancy as well. For example, what the lay person calls mental blocks.

MORENO

Can you clarify?

REMILLARD

Let's take a more common mind function like memory.

We've all experienced forgetfulness. Suppose I'm sitting next to a lady at a dinner party and I can't remember her name. Now why is that? Am I eighty-seven years old – in which case my forgetfulness is to be expected? No, I'm young and compos mentis. But no matter how much I exert my will power, I just can't remember. A psychoanalyst might come up with any number of reasons why. Perhaps the lady is an old flame who jilted me many years ago. Perhaps her name is the same as that of my Internal Revenue Service auditor! Or perhaps the problem is simply a very difficult foreign name that I failed to concentrate on when the lady and I were introduced. Any one of those rather subtle factors could inhibit memory. Metafunctions can be inhibited similarly.

MORENO

How about emotions? Anger, say. Or fear. If a person with strong metafunctions was afraid of the reactions others might have – afraid of hostility – could that make his powers go latent?

REMILLARD

It's possible. A strongly hostile or sceptical group of observers can also inhibit displays of metafunction.

MORENO

Have *you* ever experienced a diminishing of your own mind-powers because of emotional influences?

REMILLARD

(hesitating)

No. If anything, the adrenalin released by my body in response to such emotions would tend to reinforce my metafaculties. But then, I've been using the powers all my life, from the time I was an infant. When we begin training small children to operancy, we'll probably find that their higher faculties will remain usefully operant under all but the most extreme inhibitory conditions. After all – you yourself are seldom too shocked to speak. Or to see or hear. Or even to react in an emergency.

CU MORENO

MORENO

This testing and training programme you advocate. Some people might say it had certain dangers. We'd be setting up a kind of élite mind-corps, wouldn't we? One that might eventually feel justified in seeking political power on the basis of their superior mentality.

TWO SHOT

REMILLARD

I don't think there's any danger of that.

MORENO

Oh? . . . Do you mean these operants would think politics was beneath them?

REMILLARD

(impatiently)

Certainly not. But there are so many other jobs to do that operants would find more satisfying. Einstein didn't run for President, you know.

CU MORENO

MORENO

(suddenly)

Do you, as a powerful operant, feel superior to normal people?

CU REMILLARD

REMILLARD

(again looking at plant, frowning)

The way you've phrased that question is somewhat inimical. Does a concert violinist feel superior to the audience? Does a mathematician feel superior to a cordon-bleu chef? Does a librarian with an eidetic memory feel superior to an absent-minded professor who won a Nobel Prize?

(lifts eyes and speaks deliberately)

Mr Moreno, we all do things we know are wrong . . . like harbour prejudices to boost our insecure egos. One can suffer from shaky self-esteem no matter how well educated or how poorly educated one happens to be. Even television journalists can show bias for or against people they interview . . . I don't *think* that I look down upon persons without operant metafunctions. I'd be a fool if I did. I have certain talents, yes. But I lack so many others! I can't play the violin or sing or even cook very well. I'm not good at drawing pictures or playing tennis. I'm a terrible driver because I'm always off in the clouds instead of paying attention to traffic. I tend to shilly-shally around instead of making decisions promptly. So I would be an integral idiot to think of myself as a superior being . . . and I don't know of any other operants who think that way. If they do exist, I hope I never meet up with them.

CU MORENO

MORENO

How about the flip side of that question, then? Do you ever feel threatened by nonoperants?

TWO SHOT – REMILLARD FAVOURED

REMILLARD

When I was much younger I kept my mind-powers completely under wraps because I didn't want others to know I was different. I wanted to be just like everyone else. You've interviewed a number of other operants for your television series, so you know that such protective colouration activity is the usual thing for youngsters who grow up with self-taught metafunctions. Minorities who seem to be a threat to majorities make the adaptations they must in order to survive.

MORENO

Then you admit that operant psychics *can* pose a threat to normals!

REMILLARD

(calmly)

I said *seem to*. Persons who are different from others in marked ways are often perceived as threatening. But it doesn't have to be that way. That's what civilization is supposed to be all about – resolving differences maturely, not acting like bands of frightened children. The gap between operant and nonoperant is only the latest that modern society has faced. We also have technology gaps, economic gaps, cultural gaps, the generation gap, and even a sexual gap. You can refuse to cross the gap and throw rocks at each other, or you can cooperate to build a bridge to mutual betterment.

INTERCUT STOCK SHOTS – MONTAGE

Riotous scenes at London and Tokyo stock exchanges; mobs besiege banks at Geneva and Zurich; Monte Carlo Casino with sign: RELÂCHE/GESCHLOSSEN/CLOSED UNTIL FURTHER NOTICE; *Time* magazine cover: DEFENCE STOCK DEBACLE; newspaper headlines: RUSSIA DUMPS GOLD, OIL LEASE CHAOS, COCA-COLA FORMULA REVEALED, OFFSHORE TAX REFUGES SELF-DESTRUCT; *Newsweek* magazine cover: WHO WILL WATCH THE WATCHERS?

MORENO (V.O.)

But we've seen the turmoil that rocked the world stock and commodity markets following the Edinburgh Demonstration. And you must know that certain financiers and businesses that depend upon secrecy for their operations look upon telepathy and excorporeal excursion as deadly menaces. Other very serious problems are just beginning to crop up. Operants aren't numerous enough yet to pose much of a threat to society or to the global economy, but what about the future, when the superminds you propose to train begin to invade every walk of life?

TWO SHOT

REMILLARD

Operants aren't invaders from outer space, Mr Moreno. We're only people. Citizens, not superbeings. We want just about the same things that you want – a peaceful and prosperous world for ourselves and our children, satisfying work, freedom from prejudice and oppression, a bit of fun now and then, someone to love . . . This invasion of yours: Do you realize you could be talking about your own children or grandchildren? Our preliminary studies seem to show that the human race has reached a critical point in evolution. Our gene pool is throwing up increasing numbers of individuals with the potential for becoming what you call a supermind.

MORENO

(looking slightly shaken)
My children?

REMILLARD

Or those of your cousins and uncles and aunts . . . or neighbours, or co-workers. In years to come, all humans will be born operant! But that's a long way off, and we poor souls are going to have to endure life in the transition zone during the foreseeable future. I won't minimize the fact that we may have a tough time. Adjustments will have to be made. But all throughout human history society has had to confront revolutions that overturned the old order. In the Stone Age, metal was a threat! The first automobiles frightened the horses and doomed the buggy-whip makers. But what one group sees as a threat, another group may hail as a blessing. Not to belabour the point . . . but did you notice that the latest issue of the *Bulletin of the Atomic Scientists* has turned back the hands of its doomsday clock from two minutes before midnight to half past eleven?

MORENO

(permitting himself a wintry smile)
Is that how you operants see yourselves, Professor? As the saviours of humanity?

CU REMILLARD

REMILLARD

(sighs, fingering the plant)
Sometimes I wonder whether we might be the first scattered spores of the evolving World Mind . . . and then again, we might be only evolutionary dead ends, the mental equivalents of those fossil Irish elk with the six-foot antlers that were gorgeous to look at but losers in the survival game.

He looks at the plant, which seems noticeably perkier. Opening a desk decanter, he pours a bit of water into the pot.

MORENO (V.O.)

(incredulously)

A *World Mind?* You mean, some kind of superstate, like the Marxists envisioned? Operancy will lead to that?

TWO SHOT

REMILLARD

(laughs heartily)

No, no. Not a bit of it! No chance of our evolving into a metapsychic beehive. Humanity's individuality is its strength. But, you see . . . with the telepathy, especially, you have the potential for vastly increased empathy: mind-to-mind socialization on a level above any we've ever known . . . And it would be such a logical and elegant survival response, the World Mind. A perfect counterpoint to our increasingly dangerous technical advances.

MORENO

I still don't understand.

INTERCUT MYXOMYCETES NATURAL HISTORY SEQUENCE – paralleling Remillard's VOICE OVER.

REMILLARD (V.O.)

Perhaps an analogy will help. There's a peculiar group of living things called Myxomycetes – or, to give them their more prosaic name, slime moulds. A slime mould is either an animal that acts like a plant, or a plant that acts like an animal. Officially, it's a type of fungus. But it's capable of independent movement, like an animal. In its usual form, the slime mould is like a tiny amoeba, flowing here and there on the forest floor engulfing and eating bacteria and other microscopic goodies. It eats, it grows, and in time it splits like a genuine amoeba into two individuals. In a favourable forest environment there will be thousands or even millions of these little single-celled eaters going about their individual business . . . But sometimes, the food supply gives out. Perhaps the forest dries up in a prolonged drought. In some way the individual cells seem to realize that it's 'unite or die' time. They begin to come together. First they form blobs

369

and then rivulets of slime. These flow towards a central point and combine into a multicelled mass of jelly that becomes a real *organism*, sometimes more than thirty centimetres in diameter . . . and it creeps along the ground. Some creeping slime moulds look like pancakes of dusty jelly and some look like slugs, leaving a trail of slime behind. The organism may travel for two weeks, looking for a more favourable place to live. When it stops migrating it changes shape again – often to a thing like a knob at the end of a stalk. In time the knob splits open and releases a cloud of dusty spores that fly through the air. Eventually the spores come to earth, where warmth and moisture turn them into amoebalike individuals again. They take up their old life – until the next time things get rough and Unity becomes imperative . . .

TWO SHOT – REMILLARD AND MORENO – STEADICAM FOLLOWING –

We discover them as they are approaching the exit of the RESEARCH FACILITY. Moreno is leaving.

MORENO

And you really believe that human minds will have to come together in somewhat the same way in order to survive?

REMILLARD

The idea seems very natural to a telepath, Mr Moreno. It's only a higher form of socialization, after all. To a tribe of primitives living at the clan level, the notion of a complex democratic society seems hopelessly bizarre. But primitives transplanted into industrial nations have often adapted very successfully. Think of some of the Southeast Asian hill folk who came to America in the 1970s and '80s. A World Mind is quite plausible to operants, and of course it would include nonoperant minds as well.

MORENO

I don't see how!

REMILLARD

Neither do I . . . at the moment. But that's the payoff

that some of us metapsychic theoreticians envision. A society of the mind evolving towards harmony and mutualism that still lets individuals retain their freedom. That's one of the topics we'll be discussing in Alma-Ata next year, at the First World Congress on Metapsychology. We'll deal with practicalities first, but then the universe is the limit! It may take a few thousand years to accomplish a World Mind, but I like to think of the meeting there in Kazakhstan as the first little blob of amoebas flowing together into a true organism. The creature is still tiny and not very effectual . . . but it'll grow.

CUT TO MORENO CU – AGAINST PROGRAMME LOGO (MATTE)

MORENO
(addressing viewers)

Denis Remillard's vision is an amazing one – but then he is an amazing man. Perhaps, as the President said, a supermind. Right now there are at most a few hundred others like him scattered around the world. But tomorrow, and next year, and in the twenty-first century fast approaching, those superminds among us will multiply. And as they do, they'll change the world. How they change it remains to be seen . . . I'm Carlos Moreno for *60 Minutes*.

FADE TO COMMERCIAL BREAK

23

From the Memoirs of
Rogatien Remillard

Why had I done it?

What perverse compulsion had led me to top my nephew's display of psychokinesis with one of my own, thus revealing my most closely guarded secret on a television programme beamed around the globe?

Oh yes, I had been more than a little drunk at the time,

having given in to the need to fortify myself against the invasion of my bookshop by Carlos Moreno and his squad of muckrakers. But to show my power so flippantly, with such cornball insouciance! I had to be cracking up.

After the fatal taping session in the shop, when we had all had our giggle and it occurred to me what a piece of lunacy I had perpetrated, I went on a towering binge. I missed the actual *60 Minutes* telecast that took place on Sunday, three days later, as well as the debriefing party afterwards that was given at the Metapsychology Lab, where Denis and his Coterie celebrated having thrown their bonnets over the windmill. Apparently only one person missed me, out of all that supposedly psychosensitive lot, and wondered where I had disappeared to, and figured things out, and had the compassion to come and ring the bell to my apartment and shout telepathically until I was roused from my stupour and coerced into opening the door . . .

Lucille.

'I knew it!' she exclaimed, pushing inside. 'I just knew you'd done something stupid. Look at you! Roger, what are you *doing* to yourself?'

'Good question,' I mumbled, grinning down at her. But my drunken insolence quailed in the face of her terrible charity. I must have looked like a sodden scarecrow, half conscious and filthy; but she had helped tend her invalid father for years and had no trouble at all coping with me. She forced me to take a shower, dressed me in clean pyjamas, and pummelled my brain until I swallowed a vitamin-laden milkshake. Then she put me to bed. When I woke up ten hours later she was still there, dozing in a chair in the parlour, and my hurrah's nest of an apartment was now spotless and my entire stock of booze had been poured down the drain.

With my head throbbing like a calliope at full steam and my knees a-wobble, I looked in hung-over wonderment at the sleeping young woman, trying to think why she, of all people, had come to my rescue.

Her eyes opened. They were brown and very stern, and I couldn't help remembering how she had sent Denis and me packing when we had first dowsed her out eleven years earlier.

'Why?' she said quietly, echoing my telepathic question. 'Because I know just what came over you when Denis did his thing and you knew the jig was up. Poor old Roger.'

She stretched, then got up from the chair and looked at her wristwatch. 'Quarter to eight. I have a seminar at nine this morning, but there's time to scramble some eggs.' She headed for my kitchen.

'What d'you mean you know?' I croaked, shuffling after. '*I* don't even know! And what the hell right do you have coming up here and interfering with me? Don't tell me the fuckin' Ghost sent you!'

She began to crack eggs. The sound was like axe-blows against my tortured eardrums. I lurched and her coercion reached out and coolly tipped me into a kitchen chair. I let out a groan and caught my head before it bounced on the freshly polished maple table top. A few moments later she was shoving a cup of coffee under my nose.

'Microwaved instant, but strong enough to etch glass,' she said. 'Drink.' Coercion locked on, stifling my instinctive refusal. I drank. Then she produced a nauseously aromatic plate of eggs with buttered toast. My guts cringed at the loathsome prospect.

'Eat.'

'I can't — '

YES YOU CAN.

Bereft of will power, I dug in. Lucille sat down opposite me and sipped tea, keeping the compulsion firm by maintaining eye contact. She was not a pretty woman but her face had that high-coloured attractiveness indicative of a formidable character. Her dark hair was cut in a simple pageboy with the bangs just touching thick, straight brows. She wore a scarlet turtleneck sweater and jeans, and her hands were raw, the once polished fingernails damaged from the heavy housecleaning chores she had undertaken on my behalf.

As my stomach filled and my aching head deflated to a size approximating normality, I felt ashamed of my surly ingratitude and more than ever mystified that she should have been the one to think of me. She had been an occasional customer at the bookshop, showing a rather regrettable penchant for fantasy books featuring dragons. Her mind had always closed primly at my avuncular jests and resisted my attempts to put her on to a more sophisticated style of escapist literature. Lucille knew what she liked and stuck to it with Franco stubbornness. She was not even a full-fledged member of the Coterie, but only one of the more talented experimental subjects – a mere student – which made her assertion that she understood my mental state all the more improbable.

'But I do understand,' she said, reading my subvocalizations. 'You and I are really quite a bit alike. Both of us are still trying to adapt, asking questions about ourselves that desperately need answers.'

I glared at the nervy little chit, mopping my plate with the last of the toast. Her coercion slid aside as I managed to prop my mental barricade into position.

She only smiled. 'There's a person who's helped me to find some answers, Roger. I think he could help you, too. I'm going to come back here this afternoon at three o'clock and take you along with me to meet him.'

'No, you aren't,' said I. 'Don't think that I'm not grateful to you for shovelling me up and putting this place back in order after my lost weekend – but I'm quite all right now. I don't need any help from your friend. And don't think you can force me. You'll find I'm not nearly so susceptible to coercion when I'm compos mentis.'

She leaned towards me earnestly. 'I wouldn't coerce you to come. That wouldn't be any use. But you must, Roger! You know that you're seriously in need of help. Everybody knows.'

I laughed. 'So I'm the talk of the town, am I? A disgrace and an embarrassment, sans doute, to my nephew the distinguished supermind! And which one of his brilliant young colleagues have you pegged to drag the black sheep out of his alcoholic wilderness?'

'None of the Coterie. I want you to talk to my own analyst, Dr Bill Sampson. He isn't an operant at all. But he has more insight – more caring competence – than that whole damned labful of superior metapsychic pricks. Denis included.'

Oh my God. I squeezed my crusty eyelids shut.

She babbled on. 'When I felt how deeply afraid you were there in the bookshop, with the TV people closing in and Denis put in the position of having to demonstrate his PK, I was just appalled. Then you *defied* it! I knew right then that I'd have to do something to help you. Take you to Bill. He helped me lick my dragons and he can help you —'

Lightning struck.

Now I knew why I had made that lunatic gesture in front of the TV cameras, why I had berated myself so that her mind's ear overheard, why I had admitted her to my squalid sanctum, asking if my own special dragon had sent her.

It had.

Poor little kindhearted Lucille! Let me reinforce my mind-screen, hiding from you the blaze of certainty. It had been more than a year ago that I was admonished to break up your love affair with Dr Bill Sampson, and I put the notion completely out of my mind. But synchronicity is not so easily denied . . . and here we are, and there the inevitability awaits us.

Once again I am not a man but a tool. And how is the dirty deed to be done? (Neither she nor Sampson are fools, and any blatant action, such as reporting the prima facie breach of doctor-patient ethics, would tend to solidify their liaison rather than sever it.) No, I would have to be both subtle and direct.

All that is really necessary is to show old Sampson the truth.

The psychiatrist is a normal, but he is clearly enthralled by the metapsychic phenomenon in his beloved. Show him how he has played the romantic hero, rescuing a malleable young Andromeda from the mental rock where she chained herself as dragon-meat. The princess is tender and grateful now; but her chains can be taken up and worn again at any time – and they can be stretched to fit two minds as easily as one when reality inevitably intrudes on the glamour. Then she will destroy the mortal lover as well as herself, surrendering to her dragon's fire . . .

Does he think that love will transcend? Then show him what operancy really means – what a mature operant can do – what *she* will be able to do some day! Now, blinded and gentled, she shrinks from prying into the deeper layers of his mind. But pry she will, and she'll find the petty, cruel, and unworthy thoughts that flit through every human mind, no matter how loving, and in her hurt she'll fling them into his face. Show him how easily it's done! And then coerce him. Show how his darling will be capable of violating his sovereign will, should the mood come upon her. Show him the PK! Give him just a hint of the healing faculty's flip side! And then the clincher. Project the image that every operant, even the most noble, holds deep in his heart when he compares himself to lowly normals. Show him Odd John's truth.

'*I was living in a world of phantoms, or animated masks. No one seemed really alive. I had a queer notion that if I pricked any of you there would be no bleeding but only a gush of wind . . .* '

Learn the truth, Dr Bill Sampson. Then find a normal woman to love and leave Lucille Cartier to her metapsychic destiny. Learn the easy way, from somebody who learned the hard way.

'Roger,' Lucille said. 'Please come with me this afternoon. It will all be for the best.'

'I hope so,' I told her. 'God, I hope so.'

24

Supervisory Cruiser Noumenon [Lyl 1–0000]
4 June 1992

When the fanatics successfully smuggled the second of the Armageddon devices into place, and that place was the Israeli nuclear weaponry works at Dimona, the portents were such that Homologous Trend felt impelled to consult with its three fellow entities.

'One must admit,' Trend told the others, 'that my anatomization of the probability lattices is somewhat disorderly – but that's Earth for you. However, the resultant inevitably leads to still another global crisis capable of disrupting the planetary sexternion – and Intervention.'

'One's sensibilities churn,' Eupathic Impulse said, upon viewing the analysis. 'From this one locus proceed conflicts not only in the Middle East, but also in South Africa, Uzbekistan and India.'

'One is chagrined,' Asymptotic Essence said, 'given the worldwide flowering of goodwill after the Scottish Demonstration, to note that the group instigating the atrocity stubbornly persists in its ancient tribal hostility mode. Other Earth populations at higher and lower levels of sociopolitical organization experienced positive transformational nuances as a result of MacGregor's ploy. What's wrong with this bunch?'

'Status Three indigenes,' Noetic Concordance observed sadly, 'are a perverse and difficult lot, more likely to stall in metapsychic development than other classifications. Status Threes vest authority in puppet rulers dominated by a powerful priestly caste. The intellectual establishment is subservient, and upward mobility of individuals is limited according to their profession of orthodoxy. The higher mind-powers – even elementary creativity – tend to be repressed, except insofar as they serve the narrow religious objective. The mind-set is intolerant, reactionary, xenophobic, and more than a little silly. Fanaticism is a prime activator of psychoenergies and the view of consequents is minimal. Even this impending catastrophe is seen by the perpetrators as a glorification of the All.'

Eupathic Impulse said, 'One has a sneaking suspicion that this particular terrorist group wants to get its licks in before the inspection teams of the UN Nuclear Nonproliferation Agency include persons adept in farsensing.'

Trend waved all this thought-embroidery aside. 'You three agree with my dire prognosis. Do you also agree that the gravity of the situation demands that we summon Atoning Unifex for a contemplation?'

'One regrets having to disturb It,' Concordance said.

'But if Earth is to be spared this profound trauma, overt action will have to be taken.'

Asymptotic Essence permitted itself the barest hint of vexation. 'Another deliberate skew of the noögenetic curvature? That will make three inside of fourteen months, including the rescue of MacGregor from the Mafia hit-man and the augmentation of the Alma-Ata group's coercion of the Soviet TV net. How long must we keep this up? If Earth's Mind were treated in a normal manner, it would never achieve coadunation!'

Eupathic Impulse was inclined to agree. 'Intervention in due season is one thing: continued interference with significant nodalities on the evolving mental lattices is quite another. If it were any entity save Unifex commanding this most atypical wet-nursing, one might have the most serious misgivings.'

'One of the most notable incongruities is our own physical presence here,' Noetic Concordance reminded the others. 'One questions why the Supervisory Body does not simply work through the Agent Polities, who are more than a little scandalized by our participation.'

'One may question,' Eupathic Impulse noted wryly, 'but one doesn't necessarily get straight answers.'

Homologous Trend said, 'One *must* trust Unifex.'

Eupathic Impulse said, 'If It would only share Its prescience!'

Noetic Concordance said, 'Of all our vague and absent-minded Lylmik race, It is the most terribly preoccupied. And weary. One intuits that It would transfer the burden of Galactic mentorship and submerge Itself in the Cosmic All in a trice, were It not faithful to some great overriding dynamic — '

'Which It declines to share,' Impulse said.

'We must trust It,' Trend reiterated, 'as we have since the dawn of the Milieu, when It selected us four from all the eager Lylmik after manifesting the Protocol of Unification. Unifex *has* shared . . . as much as It has been able to do so. You know our racial Mind's limitation as well as its strengths. We are ancient and tending towards stagnation, conservative and over-fond of the mystical lifestyle. Unifex's great vision of a Galactic Mind was able to electrify us, to send us beyond the Twenty-One Worlds in search of other, immature Minds that we might shepherd towards coadunation. Towards Unity. *That*, if you will, was the great outrage Unifex committed: the initiation of the Milieu. You younger entities have let the memory of it slip away in your earnest contemplation of present anomalies.'

'Yes,' the three admitted. For some time they filled their minds with the Milieu's essence and drifted, serene.

But Trend recalled them. 'The two Armageddon devices are in place. Action, if it is to be taken, must be taken soon. Let us summon Unifex.'

They called in metaconcert.

And It was there with them, glowing in the liquid-crystal films of the star-cruiser's innermost heart, emanating its familiar emotional mix of affection and crotchety longanimity.

The Quincunx formed. The problem was set forth.

Unifex told them: 'One may take no preventive action. This awful event happens . . . as it must and as it has.'

'May we ask why?'

'To unite the World Mind more fully in pain, as it has failed to unite in joy during the past seven months of premature celebration. This calamity is only one in the ultimate educative series leading towards the climax: pain upon pain lesson upon lesson ordeal upon ordeal.'

'We suggest, in all respect, that the teaching process might be less radical. As you saw from your contemplation of the problem as formulated, there is a distinct probability that the United States and the Soviet Union will abandon their newborn rapprochement and be drawn into a fresh posture of hostility. The operant human minds will no longer be viewed as an assurance for peace, but rather as a hindrance to necessary war!'

'Nevertheless, we will not forestall the detonation of the Armageddon devices.' Unifex's mind-voice was sorrowful, but It declined to reveal the thought-processes – proleptic or otherwise – that had led to Its judgement.

The four subsidiary Lylmik entities came as close to outright dissent as they had ever done in the two-million-year life of the Quincunx. 'We suggest that it may be unloving of you to fob us off on this grave matter without resolving some aspect of the paradox. Do you base your decisions upon analysis of the probability lattices, as we do, or are you privy to some recondite data-source that influences your special treatment of the planet Earth?'

'I may not tell you that . . . What I may tell you is that the lessons to be learned by the Earthlings must be learned most especially by the operant minds. It is these, not their contentious latent brethren, who must mature in Light if there is to be an Intervention. The majority of the operants must decide freely that their mind-powers must never be used aggressively. Never. Not even in a cause that their intellects perceive as good. And because this truth is counter to one of the deepest imperatives of human psychology, its apprehension will be attained only at a fearful price . . . a price that will not be fully paid until *after the Intervention.*'

The four were aghast.

Unifex said, 'O my friends, I admit that I have not been sufficiently forthcoming since our Earth visitation began. I admit that I have reserved data and allowed myself to be submerged in perplexity. But I have forgotten so much and the chasm between the human mind and our own is so vast . . . You are aware that Earth's nodalities are more critical to the future of the Milieu than those of any other world – and yet our own role in its mental evolution remains unclear to me. Often I must act through feeling rather than through logic! This world, unlike the worlds of the Krondaku, Gi, Poltroyans and Simbiari, does not occupy a place clearly defined in the larger reality. I have been able to penetrate its mystery only partially myself, by processes outside of intellection. So I can only beg you to bear with me . . . and in return, I shall offer you a species of metaphor. If you attend to it, certain aspects of the Earthly paradox may be clarified.'

'We are eager to experience your metaphor.'

'Very well,' said Unifex. 'We five will contemplate it together, but as individuals and without any metapsychic penetration of the human participants in the drama. We will empathize with the Earthlings to the fullest, and view the spectacle as much on their simple level as is possible for us. Please accompany me mentally now to Japan, where a baseball game is about to be played . . .'

It was the final contest of an exhibition series: the first East-West Championship ever organized, and one of numerous goodwill enterprises that had been undertaken in various parts of the world in the joyous aftermath of the Edinburgh Demonstration. For a few brief months, the planet had given itself over to a carnival of hope, reacting to decades of nuclear anxiety. There had been festivals of music and dance and drama and poetry, and there were seminars of knowledge sharing, and there were games. Seven countries had participated in the baseball series, and now it had all come down to a last championship game between the mighty New York Mets and the formidable Hiroshima Carp. The teams were tied at three games apiece in the seven-game series.

The players, clad in colourful close-fitting suits, enacted the deceptively simple contest before an audience of more than 150,000 fans, who had packed the vast Hiroshima Yakyujo to the topmost tier. Those who viewed the game on television numbered nearly a billion – some twenty per cent of the global population – and included many who, like the fascinated Lylmik, were more interested in the symbolic than the sporting aspect of this particular match-up.

It was a multilayered event: physical, psychological, mathematical. There was even an elusive musical element in its alternation of violent action with intervals of pregnant ennui. Atoning Unifex imparted to Its fellow entities an instantaneous knowledge of the rules, the attributes and eccentricities of the players, and the strategic theories employed by the team managers during the previous games of the series.

'There are actually a number of metaphors being manifested here,' Unifex said. 'As we watch, let us also synthesise and strive to apply the essential wisdom to the larger reality.'

Then the game began, and for more than two hours the exotic beings were caught up in the symbolic conflict. The game was closely fought until the seventh inning, when the Mets leaped ahead, 4–2. They kept their lead through the bottom of the ninth, and the Carp came to bat for the last time facing a make-or-break situation.

The Mets pitcher, the celebrated Zeke O'Toole, was no longer in the flush of youth and obviously tiring, but it was out of the question that he should be replaced. Instead, he adopted an excessively cautious technique designed to frustrate and anger the opposition. He posed, ruminated, and eyeballed the Carp players on deck and the waiting batter in an insolent and intimidating manner. The tactic resulted in two strikeouts, and wails of dismay arose from the Carp partisans in the stadium. Their desolation was transformed into fresh hope, however, when the next batter hit a single, and the one after him doubled.

'Now the climax of the drama approaches,' Atoning Unifex said. 'The next scheduled batter is the Carp pitcher, an untalented ball-walloper who will undoubtedly be replaced by a pinch hitter. Yes. Here comes Kenji "Shoeless Ken" Katsuyama, a redoubtable but somewhat erratic man in the clutch situation. The Carp manager takes a monumental gamble sending him in. If this massively muscled young slugger can connect with the ball, he may very well hit it into the hyperspatial matrix! He would score himself on a home run, and bring in the men on second and third, winning the game for the Carp. To avoid this outcome, one might expect the wily veteran pitcher, O'Toole, to give this dangerous rival a walk to first base. This might set up a double play if the men on base attempt to steal, wiping the Carp out and winning it for the Mets. Or, even if a single Carp should score on the walk, it seems virtually certain that the unagile Katsuyama would be tagged for the third out on a subsequent play, also giving victory to the Mets. Another possibility, more perilous for the Mets, is that with Ken taking first on a walk and the bases loaded, the next batter up might put the Carp into an advantageous scoring position. O'Toole and Katsuyama are both in what humans call the hot seat.'

'The Japanese fans certainly do not concede defeat,' Noetic Concordance remarked.

'See how they plead for a home run,' said Eupathic Impulse, 'exerting all their collective coercion! What a pity the metafaculty has such a large suboperative component.'

Homologous Trend displayed statistics on the powerful young batter's past performance. 'This Shoeless One does not seem to know the meaning of the term "strike zone". One notes that he has been known to flail away at bean balls. This may influence O'Toole's style of play.'

'The batter is impatient with the dilatory tactics of the elderly pitcher,' Asymptotic Essence said. 'The men on second and third base hold back, wary of the American's reputation as a butcher of base-stealers.'

Zeke O'Toole was dawdling conspicuously on the mound, but he was given the benefit of the doubt by the Japanese plate umpire. Meanwhile, Katsuyama glowered, pawed the earth, and gripped his Mizuno bat in a strangle hold.

Atoning Unifex said, 'Play ball, you dragass Irish grandstander!'

Now the catcher was sidling to the right, obviously expecting a waste pitch thrown wide. O'Toole shook his head minimally. A split second later he hurled a sizzling knuckleball high and inside, barely crossing a corner of the plate.

Strike one.

There were more delays. O'Toole sketched a series of cryptic signals, then finally threw one very wide for ball one. Katsuyama stomped about, twirling his bat and grimacing. He took his stance and waited. And waited. When the pitch came, curving and slow, he swung heroically. He missed.

Strike two.

The Lylmik were aware of Shoeless Ken's mounting fury. He stood in a kind of sumo crouch while a fastball came zinging in, deliberately wide, for ball two.

O'Toole chewed his cud of spruce gum, nonchalantly cupped the return behind his back, swivelled his head to spear the men on base with his pale and ornery eye, then seemed to bow his head in prayer. The fans hooted and screamed but the complaisant umpire merely waited. At last the pitcher wound up and delivered wide and junky for ball three.

'This is called a full count,' Unifex said. 'One notes that the veteran O'Toole remains cool while Katsuyama is livid.'

The men on base were ranging out desperately. O'Toole wasted no time but wound up with barely legal celerity and threw a wide pitchout to the waiting catcher. It was intended to be a fourth ball, walking Katsuyama and nailing the man creeping along the base line towards home plate, but it barely scraped the edge of the strike zone and . . .

Kwoing!

Crowding the plate, uttering a martial shout, Shoeless Ken swung his bat in a flattened arc at that hopelessly wide pitch. The connection came perilously close to the bat's tip; but so heroic was the swing that the ball took off like a blurry white meteor into the remotest coign of left field, topping the fence. A tsunami of ecstatic sound engulfed Katsuyama as he ceremonially encircled the bases. He bowed to the crowd. Then he bowed to Zeke O'Toole, who still stood on the pitcher's mound with folded arms.

The huge electronic display posted the final score:

HIROSHIMA CARP 5

NEW YORK METS 4

HIROSHIMA CARP WIN PLANET SERIES

4 GAMES TO 3

In the Lylmik cruiser invisibly orbiting Earth, the supervising entities studied the baseball game in its totality, frozen in the spatiotemporal lattices like a fixed specimen on a slide, viewed under a microscope at extreme magnification.

'One observes the obvious historical parallel,' said Homologous Trend. 'The old antagonism ritualized.'

Asymptotic Essence said, 'One notes that, in sharing this

sublimation with their fellow humans, the two powerful nations speed coadunation of the World Mind.'

Eupathic Impulse said, 'One perceives that you, Unifex, knew the outcome and educational potential of this obscure contest before it began. This reinforces my own hypothesis of a great Proleptic Peculiarity in the planet's sexternion — nodally determined by yourself!'

The poet, Noetic Concordance, was silent for some time. Its contribution, when it finally came, was almost tentative. 'One observes that the American sports fans in the stadium cheered the Carp victory even more fervently than did the Japanese . . .'

Atoning Unifex let Its mind-smile embrace the four. 'Well done. Hold the collection of metaphors deep in your hearts. Return to it from time to time to assist your contemplation of Earth. And tomorrow when the atomic bombs destroy Tel Aviv and Dimona, mourn with humanity. But remember that the probability lattices are not certainties. They can be moved by fervent acts of will. Both love and evolution act in an elitist way. And now, farewell.'

Part III
The Intervention

1

From the Memoirs of
Rogatien Remillard

Paul Remillard, my grandnephew, made an observation during his first address to the Galactic Concilium in 2052, when Earth's long proctoring by the Simbiari finally ended and human magnates were admitted at last to the Milieu's governing body.

'There are two prices that must inevitably be paid by the operant mind. The first is a reluctant but certain alienation from the latent members of one's race – and its consequent is pain. The second price is less obvious, an obligation of the higher mind to love and serve those minds who stand a step beneath on evolution's ladder. Only when this second price is freely and selflessly paid is there alleviation from the pain of the first . . .'

By the time Paul bespoke those words, he was merely uttering a truism that operant human beings had recognized (and debated) for more than sixty years. It was foreshadowed in Tamara Sakhvadze's keynote speech before the First Congress on Metapsychology in Alma-Ata in September 1992, where vigorous exception was taken to it by certain factions. It was formally codified after the Intervention in the ethical formulae imparted to all student operants by their Milieu-trained teachers, but not fully subscribed to by the Human Polity until our recalcitrant race instigated the Metapsychic Rebellion in 2083, learning its lesson at last as it nearly destroyed the Milieu that had prematurely welcomed Earth into its benevolent confederation.

You reading this who are immersed in the Unity take the principle for granted. It is as old as noblesse oblige or Luke 12:48. As for the operant minds who denied or tried to evade their duty to serve, they are all dead or reformed except me. For a long time I thought I was tolerated as a harmless cautionary example – the last Rebel, the sole surviving metapsychic maverick, neither a 'normal' human mind nor an operant integrated into the Milieu's Unity. I believed, like other Remillards, that I had been allowed to persist in my unregeneracy because of my famous family and because I was no menace, my refusal having been grounded in bloody-minded stubbornness rather than malice or arrogance.

But now, as I approach the climax of this first volume of my memoirs, I am inclined to revise my modest evaluation of myself. Perhaps there *is* a deeper purpose in my relegation to the sidelines in la grande danse. I do bring, after all, a unique perspective to these memoirs. This may be the reason why I have been compelled – by something – to write them.

The rain seemed interminable during the summer of 1992, not only in my own section of New England but also in much of the rest of the Northern Hemisphere, as if the sky itself were obliged to share in the universal sorrow following the Armageddon strike. There was the human tragedy, the half million dead and more than two million others rendered homeless, and the suffering of the injured that would extend over so many years. But there was also the symbolic loss: The land holy to Jews, Christians and Muslims was debarred to us for uncountable years beneath its pall of radioactivity.

The devices exploded in Tel Aviv and Dimona by the Islamic Holy War terrorist group had been crude, with a yield of about ten kilotons apiece. The fallout was intensified by the incineration of the Israeli nuclear weapons stockpile in the Dimona blast; and it was debris from this that spread northward in a wide swath, heavily contaminating both Jerusalem and Amman and rendering some forty thousand square kilometres of Israel and Jordan uninhabitable for the foreseeable future.

In the early days of that summer of lamentation, when the rain was poisoned and the whole world was shocked into incredulity, the magnitude of the disaster almost lifted it out of the political realm. Human beings of all races and all religious faiths mourned. A massive multinational relief effort mobilized while church bells tolled, mosques overflowed with bereaved Muslims, and Jews around the world sang Kaddish – not only for the dead and for lost Jerusalem, but for the dashed dream of peace.

'We could not watch everywhere,' the EE adepts said. 'There are too few of us, and the Armageddon strike was completely unexpected.'

True; but there was still an irrational undercurrent feeling of betrayal. The miraculous 'happy ending' of the metapsychic coming had proved a hollow mockery. Not only had the operants failed to prevent the calamity, but they were not even able to help locate the perpetrators. It was more than a year later that ordinary UN investigators cooperating with Interpol traced the members of the Iranian clique that had planted the bombs and brought them to trial. The psychotic Pakistani technician who had sold them the plutonium had long since blown his brains out.

After six weeks, the airborne radioactivity was almost entirely dissipated and the summer rains were clean again. Over most of the planet, the deadly isotopes were spread very thinly, and they sank with the rain into the soil or drifted to the bottom of the sea. Earth recovered, as it had from Hiroshima and Nagasaki. But the Holy Land was ruined. With the farmlands contaminated by the heaviest fallout and livestock dead or scattered, the rural population that had escaped immediate injury fled in panic to the nearest unaffected cities, triggering food riots and the collapse of law and order. The Jordanian government disintegrated almost immediately. Israeli officials set up an emergency capital at Haifa and vowed that the nation would survive; but by August, expert consensus held that the economy of the Jewish homeland, always fragile, had this time suffered a mortal blow. Surviving middle-class and professional Israelis began a growing exodus to the United States, Canada and South Africa. Some Oriental Jews and Arab Christians resettled in Morocco. Upperclass Muslims and others with foreign bank accounts readily found haven. But the bulk of the displaced Muslim population faced an uncertain fate. Armageddon had killed more Jews, but it had left far greater numbers of Muslims homeless because of the fallout pattern. Few Christian nations were inclined to offer them asylum because the refugees were associated in the popular mind with the cause of the Islamic terrorists, and because a vengeful minority proclaimed their intention of escalating Armageddon into a full-scale jihad. Responding to popular opinion, the politicians of Europe, the Americas and the Pacific Basin concluded that the refugees would be 'unassimilable', a social and economic liability. Dar al-Islam countered proudly that it would take care of its own. However, when the speechmaking ended, it appeared that only Iran was eager to welcome large numbers of immigrants. Other Islamic countries were willing to open their doors to small numbers of homeless; but the oil glut and overpopulation had already strained their economies, and they feared the political consequences of an influx of indigents.

The displaced Muslims were notably reluctant to put themselves at the mercy of the fanatical Shiite regime in Iran. Most of them were Sunnis, of a more moderate religious persuasion then the Iranians, and they were appalled that the Ayatollah had proclaimed Armageddon to be justified under shari'ah, the traditional Islamic law. Furthermore, the refugees suspected (quite rightly) that they would be required to show loyalty to their new country by fighting in the long-standing war between Iran and Iraq. A few hundred fiery young men accepted the Ayatollah's invitation. The rest of the 1.5 million men, women and children remained encamped in squalid 'receiving centres' in Arabia and the Sinai, subsisting on charity, until China announced its remarkable proposal. When this was approved, the great airlift began early in September. By the end of the year the last of the displaced families were resettled in remote 'Lands of Promise' in Xinjiang. Red Crescent and Red Cross inspectors reported that the refugees were made welcome by their co-religionists, the Uigurs, Kirghiz, Uzbeks, Tadjiks and Kazakhs, who had lived in that part of China from time immemorial; they worked on collective farms in the oases and the irrigated deserts and adapted well – until Central Asia blew up in the course of the Soviet Civil War, and only the Intervention saved the Xinjiang population from becoming cannon fodder in the projected Chinese invasion of Kazakhstan.

The Intervention also restored Jerusalem to the human race as a city of pilgrimage. Milieu science decontaminated the Holy Land and thousands of the original inhabitants elected to return. However, since the Milieu statutes forbade any form of theocratic government, neither Israel nor Jordan were ever reborn. Palestine became the first territory governed solely by the Human Polity of the Milieu (successor to the United Nations) under mandate of the Simbiari Proctorship and the Galactic Concilium.

The rain was torrential on 21 September 1992, the last Monday of the summer, which turned out to be a very memorable day at my bookshop.

The excitement began when I unpacked a box of paperbacks I had purchased as part of a job lot at an estate sale in Woodstock the previous weekend. The spines visible at the top showed mostly science-fiction and mystery titles dating from the 1950s, and I'd bought three boxes for thirty dollars. I figured I would at least recoup my investment, since I had already spotted a moderately rare collectible, *The Green Girl* by Jack Williamson. As I sorted through the rest of that box I also uncovered a halfway decent first edition of *The Chinese Parrot*, a Charlie Chan mystery that I knew would fetch at least fifteen from a Dartmouth physics professor of the same name. I began to whistle cheerily, even though the storm was lashing the streets and the wind roared like a typhoon. There probably wouldn't be a customer all day – but who cared? I could catch up on my sorting.

Then I reached the very bottom of the box. I saw a soiled manila envelope marked SAVE THIS!!! in a pencil scrawl. There was a small book inside. I pried the corroded clasp open, let the envelope's contents slither out on to my worktable, and gasped. There lay Ray Bradbury's *Fahrenheit 451*, from the limited Ballantine 1953 edition of two hundred copies, signed by the author. The white asbestos binding was spotless.

With the utmost care, I edged the precious volume on

to a sheet of clean wrapping paper and carried it to my office at the rear of the shop. Setting the treasure reverently aside, I sat down at my computer and summoned the current paperback collectors' price guide, my fingers shaking as I tapped the keys. The screen showed the going rate for my rarity. Even in VG condition, it would sell for no less than six thousand dollars. And my copy was mint.

I chortled and hit the keys again for the Worldwide PB Want List, and a moment later began to scrutinize the small group of well-heeled bibliophiles who presently coveted my nonincendiary little gem; a Texas fantasy foundation; a doctor in Bel Air; a Bradbury completist in Waukegan, Illinois; the Countess of Arundel, a keen collector of dystopias; the Library of the University of Taiwan; and (hottest prospect of all) a certain wealthy horror writer in Bangor, Maine, who had just recently begun to snap up rare Bradburiana. Did I dare to start the bidding at ten thou? Would it be worthwhile to invite the Maine Monstermeister to inspect the book, so that I could try reading his mind to see what the traffic might bear? And to think I'd acquired the thing for a piddling thirty dollars!

And you should be ashamed of yourself.

I looked up with a start. Coming towards me from the front of my shop was Lucille Cartier, followed by another woman. I erected my mental barrier with haste, stepped outside the office and closed the door, and gave the pair a professional smile.

'Well, hello, Lucille. It's been quite some time.'

'Five months.' *You'd really take advantage of a poor unsuspecting widow who didn't realize how valuable that book was?*

Don't be ridiculous. The rule is caveat vendor, and I'm as ethical as any other book dealer. 'Have you been keeping busy with that new PhD of yours?'

'Fairly busy.' *But not nearly as busy as you espèce de canardier!*

'Is there some way I can help you?' *And what's that crack supposed to mean?*

For starters you can BUTT OUT of my relationship

with Bill Sampson! 'I'd like to have you meet my co-worker, Dr Ume Kimura. She's a visiting fellow at Dartmouth from the University of Tokyo, here under the auspices of the Japanese Society for Parapsychology.'

'Enchanté, Dr Kimura.' I abruptly terminated my telepathic colloquy with Lucille, which was straying close to dangerous waters. It was very easy for me to concentrate all my attention on the Oriental newcomer, who really *was* enchanting. She was older than Lucille, and exquisitely soignée, with a complexion like translucent porcelain and delicately tinted lips. A black wool beret dotted with raindrops was pulled down at a saucy angle above her exceptionally large eyes, which had black feathery lashes and little of the epicanthic fold. She wore a trenchcoat of silvery leather with a wide belt that emphasized her tiny waist, and a high-necked black sweater. Her mind was densely screened in a manner that gave a new dimension to inscrutability.

Lucille said briskly, 'Ume and I are colleagues in a new project that will investigate the psychoenergetic manifestations of creativity — '

'Working with Denis?' I cut in, raising my eyebrows in exaggerated surprise.

'Of course working with Denis,' Lucille snapped. 'We've been associated with the Metapsychic Lab since the beginning of the summer term.'

'I haven't seen him much lately,' I said. 'He seems to be spending most of his time in Washington since Alma-Ata. Were you and Dr Kimura able to attend the big congress?'

'Oh, yes!' exclaimed the delectable Ume, her eyes sparkling and her mind all aglow with a spill of happy reminiscence. 'It was a most profound experience – more than three thousand metapsychic researchers, and over a third of them operant in greater or lesser degree! So many interesting papers and discussions! So much warmth and rapport!'

'So much talking and cautious telepathic chitchat,' Lucille said. 'So much political pussyfooting.'

'It was a good beginning,' Ume insisted. 'Next year, in Palo Alto, the Metapsychic Congress will meet for the second time with a much expanded agenda – especially in the matter of education, the training of new operants. That must be our most urgent goal.'

I frowned, remembering the media furore that had greeted the final resolution at Alma-Ata, proposed by Denis and seconded by Tamara and passed by a large majority of the Congress. Both Lucille and Ume picked up on my scepticism.

'Denis was absolutely right to push through the resolution calling for metapsychic testing of all people,' Lucille said. 'I can't understand the objections! We have very reliable mental assay techniques now. You'd think that after Armageddon, the necessity of finding and training all potential operants would be obvious.'

'A pity,' I said, 'that Denis's resolution didn't specify voluntary testing.'

'Oh, for heaven's sake,' Lucille said. 'We have to test *everyone*. That stands to reason.'

I shrugged. 'For an intelligent woman, you're really very naive.'

Ume looked at me with perplexity. 'You really believe that this will be a problem in the United States, Mr Remillard? Such a universal testing programme is quite acceptable in Japan, I assure you.'

'It'll be a problem,' I said. 'A big one. I'd be glad to explain the ins and outs of the independent Yankee psyche to you over lunch, Dr Kimura.' My mind was still well guarded, but Ume's mental veil thinned then for just an instant, giving me an unexpected glimpse of something very encouraging indeed.

Her lashes lowered demurely. 'That would be delightful. Lucille and I thank you very much.'

So much for my tête-à-tête hopes! I gritted my teeth in frustration – and then had to jack up the strength of my mental shield against the renewed and insidious coercion of Lucille, who was now grinning heartlessly at my discomfiture.

She said, 'You're *so* closely attuned to the social and political implications of operancy, aren't you, Roger? I can't wait to hear your opinions on the subject. But before we go to lunch, let me tell you why we came here today. I mentioned that Ume and I have a creativity project. We're studying persons who seem to be able to exert a metapsychic influence on energy — or even generate energy mentally. Denis said that you apparently experienced such a psychocreative manifestation right after the Edinburgh Demonstration. As I understand it, you inadvertently conjured up some form of radiant energy and melted a small hole in a window.'

'A Kundalini zap,' I said.

'Denis recommended very strongly that we check with you on your experience. I was told that it took place when you were under unusual conditions of stress.' All the time she was speaking, the damn girl was skittering slyly all over my mind, giving little prods with some incisive faculty quite different from coercion. I found out later it was an aspect of the redactive function, a primitive mind-ream. As she crept and poked, her telepathy hectored me on my intimate mode: What have you been saying to Bill? WHAT you sneaky undermining ratfink sale mouchard? What did you tell him cafardeur?

I said, 'I was shit-scared when I zapped the window, if you call that stress.'

Ume giggled.

Lucille said: Tu vieux saolard! Ingrat! Calomniateur! Allez — déballe! Foutu alcoolique!

I said: Nice to know you haven't completely abandoned your French heritage kiddo but I'm not really an alcoholic you know only an alcohol *abuser* as an experimental psychologist you should watch those fine distinctions!

The insults flew like bats out of hell, but her outward cool never wavered. She said, 'Roger, we'd like you to participate in a series of simple experiments. An hour a day over the next eight weeks would provide us with ample data to begin with. Now that you've concluded your therapy with Dr Sampson, we can hope that your creative potential has been somewhat restored. The energy-projecting faculty is extremely rare. You'd be advancing our understanding of psychocreativity greatly by working with us.' WHAT HAVE YOU TOLD BILL ABOUT ME?

'I'll think it over.' Nothing he didn't already suspect.

Suspect? *Suspect?*

She was still on the intimate mode, smiling on the outside and raging on the inside, with enough antagonism slopping over now into the general telepathic spectrum for Ume to catch. The Japanese woman blinked in astonishment.

Lucille said suddenly, 'And if you don't mind, we'd also like to take your zapped windowpane for analysis.'

I have to hand it to her: She almost got me. I let out a guffaw at the incongruity of the request . . . and at that instant she shot a sharply honed and extremely powerful version of the coercive-redactive thrust right between my eyes. It was a zinger worthy of Denis himself (and I discovered later that he'd taught her the technique) and it rolled me back on my heels. If I hadn't been expecting her to try something, that probe might have turned my mind inside out like a shucked sock. But Lucille hadn't really had a close view of my mental machinery in more than a year, not since the time she'd played Good Sam after the *60 Minutes* taping. If I'd cracked, she'd have gotten the whole story – Ghost and all. But I didn't crack.

I said, 'You see? I *am* feeling much better. Old Sampson's a topnotch shrink. I never really thanked you properly for introducing me to him, Lucille. I owe you. You want my zapped windowpane? You got it! But I think you'd better find another experimental subject for your creativity project – for both our sakes, and maybe for Sampson's, too.'

'That wouldn't help. It's too late!' And then she burst into tears, and turned around and rushed out of the bookshop, slamming the door so violently that the little bell came off its bracket and fell to the floor.

'Bon dieu de merde,' I said.

Ume and I looked at each other. How much did she know?

'I know more than I should, perhaps,' she whispered, her huge dark eyes sad. 'Lucille is my very dear friend, and she has told me that her relationship with Dr Bill Sampson is faltering badly. She believes that you are somehow responsible. Are you, Mr Remillard?'

What Lucille's coercion had failed at, Ume's empathy accomplished. 'Yes,' I admitted wretchedly.

'Why?' Ume was calm.

'I won't explain my motives to you, Dr Kimura. It was for Lucille's own good. Sampson's, too.'

'They are wrong for each other,' she said, averting her gaze. 'It was very obvious to all of us. Nevertheless, we did not feel we had the right to meddle in the lives of the two lovers. Lucille knew of the general disapproval of the operant group. It seemed only to strengthen her feeling towards Bill.'

'I know.' I went up the middle aisle to the front of the shop, bent and picked up the fallen door-chime, and hung it back in place. The rain was letting up a bit.

'You felt that you did have a right to interfere?' Ume asked.

I turned. 'What I did was necessary. Lucille's badly hurt and I'm sorry. But I did have the right to interfere.'

'Tell me only one thing. In your swaying of Bill's feelings – did you lie about Lucille?'

'No.' I dropped my barriers just for an instant so she could see that I had told the truth.

Slowly, Ume nodded. 'Now I understand why she put off so long approaching you about our project, even though Denis was very anxious for us to include you in it. Today she suddenly insisted that we come here. She had been upset about Bill for more than a week. He seems to have . . . spoken to her just after our return from Alma-Ata.'

It figured. News about the extraordinary discussions there opened a lot of people's eyes to the seamier potentialities at large in the metapsychic wonderland. There was the hitherto underreported coercive function, for one thing, and the ominous implications of the mental testing programme. I'd been doing my own special number on Sampson over a period of some eight months, and the success of my subversion had been signalled when he finally punched me in the nose. Fortunately, it happened outside of office hours. When I broke off my counselling sessions in mid-July Sampson had been fully primed to doubt and fear his operant young fiancée. Alma-Ata had sparked the blowup, and now it looked like my Ghostly mission was nearly accomplished. Shit . . .

Ume put a gloved hand on the sleeve of my old tweed jacket. 'Please. There is still the project. You will not wish to work with Lucille, but would you consider working with me? The creativity studies are most important. I myself have manifested a modest projection of actinic radiation, as have certain others working in the Soviet Union. But no one has ever channelled psychoenergies in a coherent beam of great strength, as you seem to have done. Let me show you the theoretical correlation between physical and psychic energies presently being postulated by workers at Cambridge and at MIT.' Would you open your mind a bit please? Thank you —

Voilà! The limpid thought-construct flashed to me inside of a split second. It was abstract as all hell and fiendishly complex – but I understood! Her transmission was to ordinary telepathic speech as a Turbo Nissan XX3TT ground-car is to a bicycle. Not that I would be able to explain the concept verbally to anyone else; but I *would* be able to remember it and project its symbolic content.

'I'll be damned,' I said appreciatively. 'Is that one of your new educative techniques? The ones you use in operant training?'

'Oh, yes. It is called bilateral transfer. One coordinates the output of the brain hemispheres. I would be happy to teach you this and any of the other preceptive techniques that interested you, if you would only agree to the experiments.'

'I'm tempted.' Oh, was I. And working with her in the lab wasn't even the half of it . . .

The winsome academic turned up her charm rheostat. I was aware that it was merely another aspect of coercion, her will acting to master mine, but what a difference from Lucille's effort! Ume said, 'We would respect your desire for noninvolvement with the operant community, Mr Remillard. There would be no pressure.'

'Call me Roger.'

'And Lucille will present no problem for you. I shall

have a discreet word with Denis. He can assign her to other creativity studies.'

'All right, Dr Kimura, under those conditions, I agree.'

'Please call me Ume.' Her expression was very earnest. 'I think we will be able to work together very compatibly, Roger. And now, shall we talk about things further while we share a nice Dutch lunch?'

'I hope I won't disappoint you,' I whispered. 'Once I was rather good at this, but it's been a very long time.'

'I can sense the latent power. It only needs to be reawakened. Sadness and repressed violence have clogged the flow of ambrosial energies.'

'Violence? Ume, I'm the most harmless guy in the world.'

'No, you are not. Your great reservoir of psychocreativity remains sealed up within you, and this puts you in peril, for if these energies are not used in creation, inevitably they destroy. The font of creativity lies within all human souls; in women, it is very often never channelled to the conscious level, but rather fruits instinctively in childbearing and maternal nurture. A very few men are also creative nurturers. But most – and certain women – must guide their creativity deliberately into the exterior reality by intellectual action. They must build – work. Unchannelled creativity is very dangerous and readily turns to destructiveness. The creation process is painful. One may be strongly tempted to evade it, since its joy is largely postponed until the creation is complete – and then the satisfaction is intense and lasting. Destruction brings pleasure, too, dark and addictive and nonintellectual. For the destroyer, however, process is all; he must continue, lest darkness catch up with him and he come at the end to the hell he has deliberately prepared for himself.'

'Donnie . . .'

'Hush, Roger. Do not think of your poor brother now. This is a time for you to think of yourself, and of me.'

Ume and I saw each other perfectly in the dark. Her aura was a rich blue, warmer close to her body and scintillating gold at the halo's edge. I glowed a flickering and shadowed citron, with an outer aureole of dim violet. My root chakra had a faint, hopeful carmine radiance, signifying that the spirit was willing while the flesh was weak.

'Don't worry. We are going to take a long time,' Ume said. Her lips brushed my forehead, cheeks and mouth as she spoke. 'This is a very old way in my part of the world. In the West, it has been called carezza. It is unappreciated because of the impatience of occidental lovers, who seek explosive release rather than immersion in a pool of enduring light.'

Her lips had taken on the golden glow now, and so had her eyes. The outermost precincts of both our minds had opened so that we could synchronize the pleasure; but in spite of what she revealed to me of her life, the real identity of Ume stayed that night and for ever apart from me . . . as I remained hidden from her. She had brought me to the small rented house on the Ruddsboro Road where she lived alone. It was sparsely furnished, almost ascetic, with many oddly shaped ceramic vases holding arrangements of leafless branches and dried grasses and bare, gnarled roots. The rain still fell. A brook outside the bedroom window rushed over its bed of granite boulders, filling the place with pervasive thunder. Ume had been straightforward about the sexual attraction, and I in turn was honest about my abaissement du niveau psychique. Sampson's psychoanalysis really hadn't helped me all that much spiritually, aside from bolstering my courage and putting me more or less on the track towards sobriety. I'd confessed to Ume that I was very dubious about coming up with anything useful in the creativity experiments. She had countered with suggestions for a rather different style of therapy. I had doubts about that, too, but she only smiled wisely.

'We will begin very slowly and proceed very slowly,' she said, kissing my shoulders, stroking my inert arms in the lightest possible manner with the tips of her fingernails. 'You must not speak. Try not even to think. Simply rest in me. Resist arousal. My mind will speak to you and my body will share its creativity. You will discover things about me and I will familiarize myself with you. There will be feedback and a very slow increase of energetic potential.

Very slow. Now sit here among the cushions and take me to you gently . . .'

This is Ume:

. . . A frail, strange child. The oldest of three daughters. Her home is in the city of Sapporo on Hokkaido, the rugged northern-most island of Japan. Her mother, once a school-teacher, now cares for the family. Her father is a photographer whose business never seems to prosper. Both parents are descended from the Ainu, the aboriginal inhabitants of the island. The heritage shames the husband and wife and they never speak of it. The oldest daughter, with her betraying fair skin and exotic eyes and the slight waviness of her silken hair, is a reproach. She is not the favoured child.

. . . A little girl of six. Her father takes close-up photographs of her face for an advertising assignment. The child is obedient but impatient with sitting still. She wishes ardently to run out of the stuffy room to play with the little girl next door. This other child's face, distorted but recognizable, appears on three successive negatives of a film roll, in place of Ume's own.

. . . The father is astounded. He experiments and the miracle happens again. He begins to realize what must be happening. 'Ume!' he cries. 'Dear girl! You must do this again!'

. . . The child is eager to please him, to feel his love and admiration. She cooperates in her father's experiments for weeks. It is learned that she can imprint film not only while it is in the camera, but also when it is outside it – provided the film is not exposed to normal light. In the beginning her 'thoughtographic' images vary greatly in clarity, depending upon whether she is summoning them from her imagination or 'reading' them directly from her surroundings or from a book. Her best pictures are made with Polaroid film. All she has to do is stare into the lens and think about a subject while her father clicks the shutter. He makes many photos of Ume's thoughts. He praises her lavishly and dreams of the millions of yen the family will make when little Ume enters show business.

. . . The father's father learns of the marvel. He comes

from the Ainu settlement to the city and studies the little girl. 'She is possessed of an ancient demon,' he says. 'She will bring bad luck.' The father is scornful. He has found a book. It tells how thought photos were produced by a psychic researcher named Tomokichi Fukura in a remarkable series of experiments between 1910 and 1913. Another book, translated from English, tells how the American physician Jule Eisenbud obtained psychic photos from a hotel worker named Ted Serios. Serios also stared into a Polaroid camera. Most of his images were fuzzy and eventually his rare talent faded away. But the talent of little Ume does not. The more she practises, the better her results. Her pictures are now superbly sharp. She can do both colour and black-and-white.

. . . The great opportunity comes at last. The girl will appear on a television show featuring local amateur performers. She and her father have prepared for a whole year. But when she comes on stage before a live audience, she is devastated by sudden shyness. Her performance is a fiasco. A week later her father is killed by falling in front of a subway train in the main Ohdori station of Sapporo.

. . . The televised failure has one good result. It brings the little girl to the attention of Dr Reiko Sasaki, a respected parapsychologist. This woman becomes a second mother to the girl. The real mother is only too glad to relinquish care of her. Under Dr Sasaki's kind tutelage, Ume again produces thought photos. She also shows evidence of being telepathic. Helped by the good doctor, the girl receives a fine education, becomes Dr Sasaki's assistant, and cooperates in research that shows how her thought photos are made.

. . . Unconsciously, Ume directs photons to impinge upon a selected area of photo-emulsion, creating concrete images of her thoughts. She can affect emulsion even when it is heavily shielded. Many careful experiments prove that the photons are not derived from existing sources of light. Either Ume's mind excites the emulsion atoms or air atoms to a point where photons are emitted, or else she creates the photons ex nihilo – out of another aspect of the Greater

Reality, as proponents of the new Universal Field Theory would say.

... The strange and lonely little girl is now a woman, pursuing her own goals. Dear Dr Sasaki is gone, and so is the girl's mother. Her two sisters do not have her metapsychic talent. Ume writes to them, and to her nieces and nephews. Sometimes there are answers.

Then Ume sang a poem:

Autumn light painting
shadow patterns bright and dark;
my mind reflects them.

Now her entire face was bathed in golden radiance, and her breasts became autumn moons, and her sex a mystery of midnight blue that I saluted as she sank down, enclosing me. Her hands seemed to weave a luminous fabric around about us, an auroral chamber that rippled in the remote sounds from the cascading stream outside.

She pressed her fingertips to my nipples, my breastbone and my throat. My aura there kindled into lotuslike flames, no longer sickly but rose-gold and shimmering. Her fingers traced mystical patterns on my back, and I saw with my mind how the skin retained the cool blazing designs, and how they blossomed and became more intricate all by themselves after her hands had passed on.

I began to waken. The penetration was very slow, a hesitant growth after a long, parched dormancy. She arched her body back and brought the fire-limning fingers over my shoulders. I kissed the golden roses of her breasts, reverently pressed lips and tongue to the aural mandala burning above her heart. It was incredibly sweet, and as I drank from it it throbbed and expanded, and became invested with rainbow colours. A blue brillance now poured from her hands, becoming golden as it gushed over my lower limbs. She rose up, freeing me, and I groaned in protest.

Trust me! We have so long a time ...

I kissed all of her turning body, now clothed in astral fire. There were pulsating symmetries of blue-white with aureate coronas at her mons, her navel, her heart and her throat. Both breasts were blinding stars. I was fully potent again myself, burning crimson and gold. *Please!* I besought her. *Let me return!* But she only lifted my arms, that had hung helplessly at my sides, and delineated the pathway of every nerve with scarlet epidermal radiance.

I wanted to crush her, to devour her, to impale her on the incandescent blade and burn her to ashes. *No*, she said. *No. Wait my dear one wait.*

Tears of frustrated fury scalded my face. I was enveloped in a thundering inferno with her coolness flickering madly out of reach. And then she guided the star-fires to my eyes . . . and into my mind burst the most beautiful thing I had ever known, a psychocreative lotus-form revolving and ever-changing in a thousand glorious variations. A new rare energy spread from my loins, up my spine, and suffused my trunk and limbs. She was suspended in the flower's heart, her body golden and her hair and blazing écu azure. I enfolded her at last and she descended. I penetrated her so profoundly that it seemed I would pierce her heart, and there we stayed rapt together in contemplation of our own many-coloured splendour. There was never a culminating orgasm as such, but we shared joy that persisted without cloying as we elaborated upon the beautiful thing flowering between us, our personal creation. Whatever it was, we had made it together, and we worshipped it for hour after hour until we seemed to pass effortlessly into dreams, separated, but still conjoined in the memory of that fantastic night's work.

We woke the next morning contented, at peace, and the best of friends.

Ume and I were never lovers in the conventional sense. We never lived for each other or felt a need for permanent commitment. We were more like two musicians coming together in a duet of perfect harmony, delighting in a work of art that neither of us could have created alone. Sometimes sex was a part of it, and sometimes not. Coitus was always sublimed in the service of creativity – and since what we made was abstract, vanishing as music vanishes, it was probably not a true creature of love. But it was marvellous and it did us both good.

Ume's experimental work with me at the Metapsychology Lab, on the other hand, was a failure. Under controlled conditions, I could not generate the least attoerg of detectable energy anywhere in the electro-magnetic spectrum – let alone produce a coherent laserlike beam. The out-spiral yoga technique only left me with top-of-the-skull headaches. (The in-spiral, on the other hand, was a great adjunct to carezza!) I spent far too much time messing around in the lab during the eight weeks of experimentation than I should have, and at the end of it I was dismissed from the creativity project as a nonstarter and my zapped windowpane was relegated to some forgotten storage cabinet.

Denis told me, 'There's an off chance your creative function might become operant with practise, but I don't hold out much hope. Our educative techniques are most successful with youthful subjects. You're forty-seven and your metafunctions are encrusted with a lifetime's accumulation of neurotic dross. The more psychoenergetic powers will probably always remain latent, except possibly under conditions of great mental stress.'

'No big thing,' I said, glad of having escaped guinea-pig status. 'I can live very well without it.'

I was wrong about that. But then I've been wrong about a lot of things throughout my chequered career.

Lucille Cartier and Bill Sampson endured a stormy severance. In time – and most likely thanks to Ume's subliminal reassurances – Lucille came to understand that I had not acted maliciously. I was more to be pitied than censured, and she decided to forgive me. The peace pact was sealed during the Christmas season of 1992, when she presented me with what she said was a much-needed addition to my bookshop; a dark and shaggy Maine Coon kitten to chase mice, keep me company in morose moments, and lend the place tone.

The kitten became the first Marcel LaPlume. By the time

I discovered that he was not only telepathic but coercive as well, I was too used to him to give him up.

2

Excerpts from:

Final Conversation between
Captain, Orbiter Module and
Surface Exploration Team

Joint Soviet-American Mars Expedition

Noctis Labyrinthus, Mars

2 November 1992

GAVRILOV: What is your position now, Volodya?

KLUCHNIKOV: We are 32 metres [garble] top of the fog is perhaps 20 metres below us. It is not stable as it was yesterday but is rising as sunlight [garble] the fissure and melts [garble].

GAVRILOV: Say again, Volodya. You are breaking up.

KLUCHNIKOV: We're 32 metres down the canyon wall. Descent is easy, Top of fog bank 20 metres below but rising. Today fog bank is rising. Do you copy, Andrei?

GAVRILOV: Roger on the copy. Fog rising . . . I am scanning the other fissures of the Labyrinth of Night. Fog is filling most of them. Perhaps the small dust storm yesterday provided condensation nuclei. Is the fog hampering your operation?

KLUCHNIKOV: Not yet . . . Are you receiving any video yet, Andrei?

GAVRILOV: Negative on the video signal. Wayne, you had better give that fancy American camera a good kick.

STURGIS: Listen, I been pounding on this sucker ever since we went over the rim and she started cutting out [garble] seals on the housing when we bumped her. But if it's something else, like maybe a glitch in the power supply, I can likely fix [garble] to put our money on the ciné camera today. She's doing fine, so we'll have the record. Tough luck about your travelogue, Andrei.

GAVRILOV: [laughs] Well, you fellows will just have to give me a word-picture of your descent into Night's Labyrinth. Be sure to let me know at once if you see green men with four arms.

STURGIS: Hey, you betcha. Ol' Tars Tarkas himself creeping up out of the mist [garble] but red layers of rock. We're taking regular samples. It's sedimentary and a fast eyeball scan shows no evidence of macrofossils. There's a sizable dyke of blackish igneous rock a few hundred metres to the east of us. On our way back up we'll work our way over and grab a specimen.

KLUCHNIKOV: Wayne, do you see how the dust in the crevices is not so dry and fluffy any more? It is more like coarse sand. I will take some . . . under the surface it begins to firm up even more. The outcroppings have that spongy look even more down here than on the surface. They are something like orange coral, but there is no coral structure. No regularity indicative of life.

STURGIS: Hey . . . you know? Hey.

KLUCHNIKOV: What?

STURGIS: Over here. Like a little, shallow cave. Does that look like a puddle of ice to you?

KLUCHNIKOV: It does. Sheltered [garble] from yesterday. There is no dust on it. I will chip some out.

STURGIS: Oh-oh. Here comes the fog.

KLUCHNIKOV: Helmet lamps.

STURGIS: Aye-aye, Commander . . . Helps a little. No problem climbing down [garble] goddam crunchy sand. And some of the outcroppings have sharp edges. But outside of that [garble].

KLUCHNIKOV: Wayne, do not descend so quickly. I cannot see you.

STURGIS: Sorry, Volodya, I wanted to . . . the damnedest thing. You got me in sight now?

KLUCHNIKOV: Yes. This fog, ulcers to its soul, is getting thicker than clotted cream and —

STURGIS: Hey. Hey. I don't believe this. Put your headlamp to a rock. Look. Just look.

KLUCHNIKOV: The rocks look wet.

GAVRILOV: Say again, Exploration Team? You found *wet rocks*?

STURGIS: It looks like a thin coating of ice on the rocky outcropping, with liquid water in a film on the surface. I'm taking a sample.

KLUCHNIKOV: Fog . . . it is the fog. Look— the porous rocks are all getting this – this icy rind. And if we go lower . . .

STURGIS: Now you wait for *me*.

KLUCHNIKOV: Usrat'sa mozhno . . . This is incredible.

STURGIS: Sheesh. Oh, wow.

GAVRILOV: What is it? What have you found? What do you see?

KLUCHNIKOV: Down here there is plenty of light, you understand, but the fog turns everything to an orange haze . . . and the rocks have a glistening coating. It is much darker than the ice. In my helmet lamp it is sometimes dark blue-green, sometimes brown. Yey bogu. It changes before my eyes.

STURGIS: It's alive.

GAVRILOV: You think you have found Martian *life*?

STURGIS: Well, it's not like any chemical reaction *I* ever saw . . . but then I'm only a geologist. What this stuff is starting to look like is a gelatinous marine growth. It's swelling very slowly. It must be frozen – what's the ambient, Volodya? – but there's this glistening film of what sure as hell looks like liquid at the surface.

KLUCHNIKOV: The ambient temperature is minus seventeen Celsius.

STURGIS: Jeez – that's warm. There must be a thermal vent at the bottom of the fissure. That was one of the hypotheses about this damn Labyrinth, with the craters all connected by wormholes . . .

GAVRILOV: Life. Life on Mars. What a magnificent achievement for the Diamond Anniversary of the Revolution.

STURGIS: And Colombus sailed the ocean blue . . . 500 years ago, comrades. One for America, too.

GAVRILOV: Of course. Of course. This is wonderful.

STURGIS: Right where we half expected to find it: down in

the cracks . . . We're taking samples. Damn. That's tough. The pick ain't gonna do her, Volodya.

KLUCHNIKOV: Let us see what [garble] diamond-bit drill?

STURGIS: Yeah, that might work. Stuff's like some incredibly tough plastic. Resilient. But it'd have to be, right? To live in this godforsaken place . . . Ah. You got that micro-sabresaw handy?

KLUCHNIKOV: Here. Yes . . . That looks like it will do it. I think I'll [garble] you get the specimen packed. Here, connect the life line [garble] another ten metres or so further down I want to check out the temperature and take an atmospheric [garble] stay here much longer.

GAVRILOV: Are you descending further, Volodya? You are garbled.

KLUCHNIKOV: The outcroppings inter[garble] . . . reconnoitre a bit farther . . . [garble] on the rocks. Not amorphous, like the other, but with a kind of jellyfish radial symmetry. Like a thick pancake perhaps fifteen [garble] and two, three centimetres thick.

STURGIS: Jee-*zuss*. It's – it's corroding the stainless steel baseplate.

KLUCHNIKOV: Fantastic . . . [garbled] . . . that stupid specimen, Wayne. Get your arse down here and *look*.

STURGIS: Oxidizing the thing like a house afire . . . What the hell is it? God – I think the blade's going. And the drill bit —

KLUCHNIKOV: . . . are quite beautiful, with flowing structures of ultramarine blue that engulf and seem to eat the green-brown [garble] . . . with a light of their own. Like lucite lanterns.

GAVRILOV: Volodya. Commander Kluchnikov, come in. Your transmission is breaking up and fading badly.

KLUCHNIKOV: It is a fairyland. The beauty. Wayne, come down.

STURGIS: Goddammit, Volodya, will you quit [garble] so sure this stuff can't get at *us*. It could be dangerous. The acids or whatever that I released when I [garble] a fuckin' vanadium-steel blade to a rusty nubbin. Do you hear me? Commander?

KLUCHNIKOV: I am coming. You will not believe [garble] right off the rock.

GAVRILOV: Exploration Team, this is Orbiter. Come in, please. Come in Exploration Team.

KLUCHNIKOV: Zakroy ebalo, Andryusha. We are too busy to [garble] life-forms of exquisite beauty. They are hard, but resilient, and some of them are biolu[garble] of them right off its rock and into my collection bag.

STURGIS: Listen . . . listen, Volodya. Get up here fast, hear me? Don't touch those things. Anything that can live in this awful place —

KLUCHNIKOV: Now, then. What ails you, little [garble] so active. How did you [garble? scream?] . . .

STURGIS: Volodya.

GAVRILOV: Vova. Commander. Vladimir Maksimovich.

STURGIS: I'm coming. I'm coming . . .

GAVRILOV: The thing, Wayne. The thing he picked up. The Martian.

STURGIS: Hey. You okay, Commander? . . . oh . . . oh, no. No.

GAVRILOV: Wayne, what's happened?

STURGIS: . . . [garble] . . . not a user-friendly world. No. Tell 'em that, Andrei. Any place but Mars! Oh, Jesus. I can still [garble] fly in blue amber dissolving [garble? scream?] . . . on my suit like little drops of blue soup. Growing. Primordial soup is blue-green, Andrei [garble] . . . love you dear Ruth . . . [garble] . . .

TRANSMISSION ENDS

3

Du Page County, Illinois, Earth
20 January 1993

As the chairman of the Republican National Committee came slowly to the point, Keiran O'Connor's attention wandered — and thus it was that he heard the unaccountable mental voice.

Desiccated embryos returned to water . . . floating in aloof sadness . . .

'Even though some people may think it premature to consider such a matter at this early date, let me assure you that the Nominating Committee of the Republican Party does not,' Jason Cassidy said. 'We suffered a devastating defeat in November. The incumbent beat our ass into the dust. He's riding high on the platform of economic prosperity that the Democrats stole from us, and he's managed to convince the voters that the metapsychic peace initiative and the disarmament programme are both personal triumphs.'

Floating in the lustrous sea . . . letting their dry blood reconstitute . . . plumping out, regaining form . . .

Do any of the rest of you hear that voice? Keiran demanded.

Four of the five men sitting around the fireplace with him on that bitterly cold night strained their farsense, listening. The other man, Brigadier General Lloyd A. Baumgartner, USAF (Ret.), only sipped his Drambuie and stared at the Aubusson carpet in front of Keiran O'Connor's hearth. He wondered, in a subvocalization that was clearly perceptible to the telepaths, just when the National Committee Chairman would get to the point and offer him the 1996 Republican presidential nomination.

Jason Cassidy said, 'There was a time when candidates were picked in smoke-filled rooms at the nominating convention itself. Later, primaries influenced the nomination and presidential aspirants began their campaign a year in advance.' I hear absolutely zilch Kier.

Len Windham said: I don't get anything but the subvocals of our male Cinderella impatient for his glass-slipper fitting. Would you look at that noble profile? Holy Gary Cooper! And the silver cowlick will be a political cartoonist's delight.

Neville Garrett said: I don't detect anybody.

Arnold Pakkala said: Nor do I . . . The domestic staff was given the night free as you ordered. There is no one in the house except the six of us.

'Today,' Cassidy droned on, 'the presidential nominating

413

process is infinitely more complex and requires long-range strategic thinking. The National Committee has been working on that strategy ever since our November defeat, in consultation with Mr Windham and Mr Garrett, our Party poll and media specialists, and certain senior advisers.'

Like Mr Moneybags Kieran O'Connor! General Baumgartner said to himself. And now it's all perfectly clear. Why he acquired McGuigan-Duncan Aerospace and kept me on as CEO in spite of the losses I'd incurred in the Zap-Star debacle. Why his media flunky Garrett was so interested in my glory days as a Moonwalker —

And now the embryonic music starts . . . peeps and squeaks and fidgets and flowing bloodhum . . . a song of rebirth from death . . .

Kieran said: Scan the entire house and grounds Arnold. I can still hear the voice and now there's some damn music carrying over.

Yes sir.

Cassidy said, 'The '96 presidential race is going to be even tougher for us than the '92 campaign. A two-term incumbent, one of the most popular presidents in history, will be able to pick his own nominee – and we know that nominee will be Senator Piccolomini.'

Another self-righteous Guinea prick, thought the General.

'We could, of course, stick with our Republican candidate of last fall.'

If you want to lose again, the General thought. The goddam quarterback really knows how to lose with style!

'However,' the Chairman went on, 'Piccolomini will be a hard nut to crack because of the success of his antinarcotics programme, because of his close ties with the incumbent, and because of his undeniable personal magnetism.'

So, thought the General, you can't run your bought-and-paid-for Minority Leader, Senator Scrope. He's smart but he's a nerd, and putting him up against Piccolomini would be peeing into the wind.

'We've studied a number of prospects, only to conclude that most of them do not project a suitable image. The Party will be developing a new platform for '96 in response to what we see as gathering threats to our national economy and security. The candidate we seek must exemplify that platform. He must be a man of authority, of proven courage, in tune with conservative patriotic values. A man who will confront the disasters that our experts foresee with a forthrightness unclouded by pseudoliberal globalism.'

General Baumgartner straightened and frowned at the Republican Chairman. 'Disasters? What kind of disasters, Jase?'

He was answered by Kieran O'Connor. 'By the end of this year our Middle Eastern oil supplies will be entirely cut off by escalating Islamic wars in the Persian Gulf and Arabia. Our re-elected Democratic President and the Democrat-controlled Congress will not dare send in American military forces. They have boasted that theirs is the Party of Peace. An American military action in support of the oil industry would be unthinkable.' Arnold. Listen!

Sea creatures . . . holothurian and crustaceans sad and glad . . . singing and dancing in bloody water . . . a funeral dance and a birth dance . . .

Pakkala said: I detect no intruder anywhere within the perimeter of the estate. There is an aurora borealis tonight and you have been hypersensitive lately. Perhaps there is some metapsychic phenomenon operating analogous to the skip of AM radio waves —

Kieran said: No. Never mind Arnold.

'Our analysts,' Cassidy said, 'believe that the world is on the brink of another serious energy shortage. Thermonuclear power is still two decades away. Without that Persian Gulf oil, a major depression will affect all industrialized nations. The Third World will be pushed to the brink of anarchy. Africa is certain to blow up and Pakistan is on the verge of an armed confrontation with India.'

Are they right? Baumgartner asked himself. If they are, America is heading for the biggest mess since World War II – and whoever the president is, he'll find himself in the same shoes Harry Truman wore when he had to decide whether to invade Japan or drop the bomb . . . Christ! No magical mystery metawhoozis finagling can keep America safe from *this* crock of shit! Only strong leadership by a real man – somebody people could be sure wasn't trading the country off for some pie-in-the-sky utopia scheme hatched by Commies and loopy Scotch professors and fortunetelling freaks.

A dance . . . a water dance with embryos . . . I've been gestating it for more than six weeks now ever since we knew Nonno was dying . . . .

Kieran said: Oh Christ!

The ballet is a tribute to his memory . . . so much more tasteful than the usual gangland obsequies . . . I want you to share it . . . If you like it I may finish my performance alive Daddy . . .

'The turn of the century,' Cassidy said solemnly, 'may turn out to be the most dangerous period in American history.'

And one, thought the General, in which certain industries stand to make an unconscionable amount of money – especially if they own the White House. As if they could control *me* the way they do that sleazy little douche bag Scrope! O'Connor and Cassidy and the rest of their cabal think I'd play along . . . be manipulated like poor old Ike. Just let me get into that Oval Office!

'Events may accelerate,' Cassidy went on, 'so as to give us a good shot at winning even in 1996 if we present a candidate with a powerful, take-charge image. A man who knows his own mind.'

General Baumgartner said, 'You know those mentalist freaks – those metapsychics in the Psi-Eye programme – could be real trouble if they got into the political arena.'

'We do know that,' Kieran O'Connor said. 'Party strategists have been examining the metapsychic movement very carefully. Those people represent a menace to American liberty, General. We'd expect our presidential candidate to come down hard on any suggestion that metapsychics participate directly in government.'

'Fuckin' A!' the General affirmed. The others chuckled.

Daddy it's for you . . . it's for Nonno . . . I won't go to his funeral tommorrow but I will mourn him in the dance . . . and you . . . and me . . .

Kieran said: Shannon!

Arnold Pakkala said: Sir – your *daughter?*

Kieran said: The goddam voice. It's her she's here screening herself threatening I think she may know —

Pakkala said: Where is she? I'll take care of it.

Kieran said: NO. I must. We'll have to finish this – *Jase*! Wind up the pitch and then get him out of here! Neville you and Len take him to your place. Jase and Arnie will help you wrap him up . . .

'Our pollsters and analysts are eighty-six per cent certain that there will be a Republican president in the White House by the year 2000,' Cassidy said. 'The odds are longer for '96, but worth the push. The National Committee has designated a unanimous choice for the perfect candidate. That man is you, General Baumgartner.'

'Gentlemen,' said the General, 'I'm – I'm really overwhelmed.'

Escaping from his guests in the library, Kieran hurried to the nearby butler's pantry, where there was a master monitor-intercom unit. He tapped 16 and the screen lit, giving a long overhead view of the indoor swimming pool located on the mansion's lower level. The chamber was dark except for what appeared to be underwater illumination of a concentrated cobalt blue. A shape suspended within the light gyrated rhythmically. From a small loud-speaker of the intercom came the nervous, deformed sound of Erik Satie's *Embryons Desséchés* being played on a synthesizer. Kieran tapped the code that would turn on the main room lights and the underwater lamps of the natatorium. Nothing happened.

'Shannon?'

Kieran spoke calmly into the mike. At the same time he manipulated the zoom control of the monitoring camera to magnify the image of the swimmer. She was eighteen but looked more like a twelve-year-old. Her legs were long and beautifully shaped but the rest of the body was angular, the breasts small and flat, the hips boyishly narrow. She was wearing a chaste white maillot. Her long hair swirled in an inky cloud, its normal bright Titian red masked by the Cerenkov blue of her visible psychic aura. From her extended wrists curled other diaphanous filaments that her hands seemed to caress and weave as she undulated in the submarine ballet she had dedicated to her dead grandfather.

Her wrists were cut, trailing streamers of blood.

'Shannon, I'm watching. Do you hear me?'

I hear, Daddy! Holothurian larvae clinging to their purring, grotesque parent . . . break away break away, babies! . . . go free if you can and celebrate spineless triumph . . . be sure to hide from the light!

'Shannon, come out of the water.' *Come out.* COME OUT.

He exerted his full coercion while the zany electronic music tinkled and trilled. Sweat had broken out on his brow and he found that he was holding his breath, commanding her to hold hers. But the range was too great for his compulsion to take hold of her. He felt, to his horror, a reciprocal mind-clutch and a gentle warning:

No . . . I must finish this dance . . . come down and watch me properly, Daddy. Your creatures have gone away now . . . come and share mine with me . . . I'll help you . . . THE HOLOTHURIAN SPINS A WEB LIKE MOIST PURPLE SILK —

'Damn you!' Lashing out violently, he broke her mental shackle and erected a defensive barrier. She only laughed. The blue light was fading with the end of the first embryonic song. A ruddy glow introduced the second.

This is the dance of the edriophthalma, a crustacean with sessile eyes . . . of a mournful disposition, it lives in retirement from the world in a hole drilled in a cliff . . . Nonno! Dear Grandpa Al do you want me with you shall I retire behind my film of red water with my mind's eye turned inward?

'Shannon – for God's sake!'

The music was a lugubrious parody of a funeral march. The swimmer's limbs folded tight against her body and she became a fetal ball, pinkly throbbing, floating some six feet below the surface of the water. A measured stream of silver bubbles, flattened like coins, tumbled upward from her emptying lungs.

Kieran stormed through the formal dining room into the main hall and ran to the elevator. As he punched G and the door whisked shut, he felt a hot pounding begin in his chest. There was an irresistible urge to inhale, pressure on his eardrums, a scarlet fog seeping into his peripheral vision, a deadly stirring in his loins. God damn the little bitch! He'd delayed the bonding too long —

The elevator door opened. Kieran staggered along a passage walled with thermopane windows that cast wan light on the snowy landscape outside. The great house had been built into the east side of a hill and even now, in the dead of winter's night, the metropolis over forty miles distant lit the sky like false dawn.

This is the third and final song . . . the lively podophthalma have eyes on mobile stalks . . . they are skillful and tireless hunters but they must be cautious – their own flesh is good to eat! . . . Eat or be eaten, Nonno. You lived in such a world and so will I twice over . . . if I choose to . . .

Jolly galloping music and a vision of a slender form darting zigzag through black water, leaving twin trails of golden blood behind. Kieran ran sluggishly, as though he himself were under water. It was impossible for him to breathe, harder and harder to move. He passed the exercise room and the spa and finally came to the open door of the natatorium. It was dark inside and there was a strong smell of chlorine. The synthesizer music filled the tiled chamber with clanging echoes. His mind screamed.

Shannon!

Deep in the pool was an upright, spindle-shaped violet glow. It brightened abruptly, then shot up like a submarine missile breaking the surface with a great splash and a dazzling burst of white light. A parody of a symphonic finale blasted from the overhead speakers. Erik Satie's jocose treatment of marine life was coming to an end, and so was the sinister water ballet of Kieran O'Connor's daughter.

He was finally able to haul in a gasping breath. His eyesight cleared and he stabbed at the control panel on the wall beside him. Normal incandescent light flooded the room and the only sound was the slap of wavelets against the sides of the Olympic-sized pool. Above the middle of the water a girl in a white tank suit floated on her back, eyes closed, hair fanned out like strands of algae, arms extended cruciform. She was smiling.

To Nonno. To my Grandfather on the day of his entombment. With love from Shannon.

'Come out,' Kieran told her.

Descending, she swam, using a vigorous backstroke. She climbed the ladder and stood looking up at him, pale and shivering, with tiny drops of water winking at the ends of her eyelashes. Her mind shone bright and it was impervious to either probing or coercion.

'I hope you liked my dance, Daddy. It was for you, too.'

He took hold of her hands and raised them, studying the wrists. The cuts were not deep and she had not severed the tendons, but there was a steady flow of blood that mixed with the water of her dripping body to make a pinkish puddle on the travertine floor. He released her, turned, and walked out the door. 'We can fix you up in the gym. Let's go.'

She followed with complete docility. The trainer's cubicle in the elaborately equipped exercise room provided hydrogen peroxide, antibiotic ointment, and bandages. He sat her on the massage table and wrapped her in a voluminous towel before tending her wounds, closing the lips of the cuts deftly with butterfly tapes and finishing up with gauze and temporary cuffs of waterproof plastic wrap.

'Now you can take a hot shower without spoiling my first-aid job.' His voice was gentle.

'Thank you, Daddy.' She eyed him askance. 'You won't make me go to the doctor for stitches, will you? I can heal myself easily enough. But I had to have . . . the effect.'

'You had to scare the living shit out of me,' he told her in a level tone, turning to rinse his hands of her blood.

'Have it your own way.'

'How did you get out here from Rosary at this time of night?'

'I took Tippie Bethune's car and just drove out, then hid the car in Goldman's orchard and walked up our driveway. You were all so busy with your low politicking that it was easy to fudge your minds and sneak inside. I sang only for you. Don't you know about the intimate mode of farspeech? You can aim it at only one person.'

So she knew about his plans for Baumgartner! 'There'll

be hell to pay when the college authorities find out you skipped.'

She shrugged. 'I'll take my shower now.'

When she was gone, Kieran took several damp towels and went to clean up the gory traces she had left on the floor. The members of his domestic staff were well-paid psychics, bonded to him and utterly loyal; but he did not want them to know about this escapade. It was extreme — even for Shannon.

He said to her: You ought to examine your unconscious motivation for this piece of adolescent idiocy. The guilt you feel because of who/what you/we are is irrational. Seeking punishment to atone for my/your/Al's imaginary wickedness is also irrational. Attempting to dissociate yourself from me/Family/yourmentalheritage is not only irrational but futile. There is no rebirth for us. We are.

He put back the first-aid supplies, then lay down on the Panasonic Shiatsu lounger and turned it on. Timed waves of vibration soothed away some of the stress. It was nearly one in the morning. Big Al's funeral was today. She'd loved the old bandit deeply. She didn't think it a bit hypocritical that he had confessed a lifetime of sins on his deathbed and expired with the Viaticum on his parched tongue.

Damn her! She *would* have followed Al tonight if he hadn't given in to her and begged . . . The suicide attempt was his own fault. It was the culmination of a lot of things — mainly his own neglect of her developing mind-powers. She'd grown up pathologically shy, introverted. There'd been suicidal hints that he had tried to laugh off. The Edinburgh telecast had been traumatic, intensifying her brooding. And now Big Al's death, and her growing realization of her father's extraordinary ambition. She would have to be bonded. The alternative was probably a descent into madness or self-destruction.

But to bond his own daughter . . .

She was mind-humming a reprise of the crustacean dirge as she took her shower. The musical parody was superimposed incongruously upon an image of Queen of Heaven Mausoleum, a fulsome monument to Italian-American piety that would, come daylight, receive the mortal remains of Aldo Camastra.

Keiran said: Shannon? Do you know why so many of your Grandfather's people prefer tombs in a place like Queen of Heaven rather than ordinary burial in the ground?

I never thought about it, Daddy.

Back in the Old Country, cemeteries may be more than a thousand years old. Space in the earth is at a premium. When a new grave is dug they may find old bones. The bones are taken up and put into a kind of storage place called an ossuary, all mixed up higgledy-piggledy with the bones of other skeletons.

How awful!

The only bodies sure to be left undisturbed are those interred in aboveground tombs or in mausoleums. That ancient fear of not being left to lie in peace lingers in tradition even here in America. Tradition can be a powerful motivator. Many kinds of tradition.

. . . Oh, I *know* the twisted justification that Al and the others in the Outfit subscribed to, Daddy — the old story about the simple peasants resisting tyranny in Sicily, then later on using the Thing as a steppingstone to power and wealth in this country. But it's different for you! You're no persecuted immigrant. You have mental powers that you could use to help all humanity, just as the organized meta-psychics around the world are doing. But you won't join them, will you, Daddy! You'd rather get rich and then take over the country with your Mental Mafia.

Is that how you see it?

'That's how it is!'

Shannon came out of the spa wearing a white velour sweat suit, with her hair bound up in a towel. Revulsion and frustrated love radiated from her but her voice remained measured. 'You're worse than Big Al ever was, Daddy, because you came deliberately into the Outfit. He and the others had their Family tradition, but you joined them because you'd analysed the possibilities in cold blood. And you've done very well, transferring the Mob assets into legitimate business and covering your tracks. You're

Big Al's son-in-law but nobody holds it against you — especially after your mind exerts its special charm.'

Kieran laughed.

'Will bossing President Baumgartner be power enough for you, Daddy? Or are you bucking for Boss of the World?'

'You could be my little Crown Princess,' he said.

She folded her bandaged arms and looked down on him lying in the chair. 'No,' she replied with cool dignity. 'The embryo dance helped me decide. I'm leaving here, getting out of Rosary College and transferring to Dartmouth. I'll ask that Professor Remillard to accept me in his psychic Peace Corps thing. I won't do anything to hurt you, but I won't stay with you any more. I've been very silly and naive, thinking it was natural for us to — to be above normal people. The Edinburgh Demonstration was like some kind of miracle, opening my eyes. That wonderful Russian woman and her vision! And then Denis Remillard explaining his educational plan for all people with metapsychic talents — '

'He's very good on television,' Kieran admitted. 'Very nearly as charming a coercer as your depraved old Dad . . . but also an idealist with no notion of the way the normal world actually works. He and the rest of them are in for a rude awakening, you know.'

'No, I *don't* know!' Shannon flared. 'Suppose you tell me.'

Kieran got up from the lounger and regarded her with concern. She had begun to shiver again and her lips were blue. He wondered how much blood she had lost. 'If you're really interested, I'll explain it to you. But not down here. I could use some coffee and brandy right now, and so could you.'

He headed for the door and she trailed after. 'I know you think I'm only a child,' she said as they approached the elevator. 'Maybe I am, but you can't expect me to accept this — this scheming of yours without questioning it!'

'Be sure you ask the right questions. You've led a very sheltered, pampered life up until now, thanks to the loyalty of Bayard and Louisa. Not all of us have been so lucky. I wasn't. Neither were Jason or Arnold, or Adam or Lillian or Ken or Neville, or most of the other people you so glibly designate my Mental Mafia. I wanted to spare you the horror stories. It seems I made a mistake, denying you the history of the persecuted minority we all belong to.'

The elevator door closed as Kieran pressed 3.

Shannon said, 'When I saw MacGregor and his people do the Edinburgh Demonstration, I was just devastated. There they were, doing their thing just as though it were – natural. And I thought: It doesn't have to be Daddy's way, hiding the powers, using them selfishly. I could come out in the open! When more and more operant people began to reveal themselves I got so excited I thought I would die. I wanted to confess what I was, too! But I was afraid . . .'

'For a good reason.'

Her eyes were pleading. 'We're different, but not so very different. The normals have been so grateful about the Psi-Eye programme. The sensible ones support the metapsychic testing plan, too. The opposition is just from fundamentalist fanatics and people without the education to appreciate the good we can do. When the normals learn more about what operancy really means — '

'They will try to kill us,' Kieran said.

Shannon stared at him, speechless, and in that split second of appalled vulnerability absorbed the details of the peril that he projected. Then they were at the third floor of the mansion and emerged into a part of the house that had always been officially barred to her (although she had snooped through most of it when Kieran was out of town). Here were the self-contained guest suites for certain visitors; the antiseptic sanctum that housed the awesome mainframe computer with its huge data bank, connected by dedicated fibre optics to corporate headquarters in downtown Chicago; the satellite receiving station; the mysterious 'recovery room' that was occupied from time to time by certain Mental Mafia recruits; and – most tantalizing of all – a locked room referred to in hushed tones by the household staff as the Command Post and by Kieran as 'my study'. Shannon had never been inside it. Few people other than Kieran himself and Arnold Pakkala had.

They stood now in front of its door, armour-plated steel without a knob or latch. Kieran pressed his right hand against an inset golden plate. There was a complex clicking sound and a single electronic chime. 'Open up,' Kieran commanded, and the door slid silently aside, admitting them.

Shannon uttered a low cry of astonishment.

Her father smiled. 'Do you like my study? I do, very much. You may come here as often as you like from now on. I'll reprogramme the door. But please don't attempt to operate any of the equipment until I've given you proper instruction. I can begin that now, if you like.'

'Oh, *yes*.'

'Sit there while I make our coffee.' He opened a taboret and took out a Chambord. 'I amuse myself by thinking of this room as the high-tech equivalent of the kingdoms of the world that Satan showed to Jesus from the pinnacle of the temple. If I *were* the Earth Boss, I could certainly supervise things very nicely from right here ... Kona or Naviera?'

'Kona,' she whispered. She sat on the edge of a maroon leather settee, looking very young. Her mental barriers had fallen completely. Kieran came to her, unwound the turban from her head, smoothed the damp hair, and kissed her crown. As he did so he slipped a subliminal command into the exposed psyche that would prevent voluntary closure until he released her. It was a thing he had learned to do instinctively when he bonded the first hurt minds to himself – how long ago? – before her birth.

Daddy I feel very strange.

Relax dear baby.

He handed her the steaming coffee with a splash of fine cognac, feeling his energies begin to mount. He had feared there might be an insuperable inhibition, but there was not. So, he thought, we think we know ourselves, but we don't! Perhaps all devoted fathers keep the thing repressed in the unconscious. It was as true an instinct as the other, so closely related, that bound mind to mind in perfect loyalty. He wondered if anyone else among the operants had discovered it. He thought not. The hierogamy was an old mystery that repelled the overcivilized mind, dying with the old Celtic and Greek votaries . . .

'Are you comfortable now, Shannon?'

Her smile was dreamy. 'Yes. The coffee is good.'

'Drink it all.' He slipped off his Shetland cardigan, folded it, then unknotted the blue silk scarf he wore at the open neck of his shirt.

'I thought the coffee would wake me up. But now I feel very sleepy.' The dark lashes fluttered. She set her empty cup aside and relaxed against the cushions.

'You can spend the night here,' Kieran said. 'I often do. It's the one place I know that I'm completely safe. The windows are armoured glass and the entire room is a self-contained little fortress. Secure.'

Shannon's eyes had closed. 'It's snowing. I can see the snowflakes with my mind, blowing in the cold wind. Whenever I do that I feel so lonely.' Her face was as white as the soft velour suit she wore.

'You aren't going to be lonely. You'll be part of our group now.' Would she remember? The others hadn't — except Arnold, whose love had been strong enough to overcome the posthypnotic suggestion. You won't remember, he told the deepest part of her soul. Not unless you want to.

'I feel cold again,' she murmured. 'A little.'

'Let me warm you,' he said, and touched the switch that would turn off the lights and blind the machines.

Shannon remembered.

4

Edinburgh, Scotland, Earth
7 April 1994

When the girl came with the sandwiches, Jamie and Jean and Nigel fell to with the usual voracious appetite of the EE adept, but Alana Shaunavon didn't even seem to notice the plate in front of her. She stared out of the pub window at the statue of the wee dog, faithful and melancholy in the rain. A hardy Japanese tourist focused his camera on it, took the shot, and hurried off along Candlemaker Row. Two nurses huddled under a single umbrella came into the pub for lunch, and an old man in a black trench coat moved slowly in the direction of the churchyard gate. He had a plastic carrier bag.

Alana sighed, lifted the teapot, and poured a bit into her cup. It had gone cold.

'Here now, we can't have that,' Nigel said. He took the pot in both hands, squinted at it with keen determination, and grinned when steam spurted out of the spout.

'What a useful talent,' Jean MacGregor observed. 'With you around the house, one wouldn't even need a micro-wave. Or an electric blanket.'

Nigel filled Alana's cup. 'So I've told this lovely lady many a time to no avail.'

Alana smiled absently. 'You want a wife, luv, and I'm not the marrying kind.'

'Piffle,' said Nigel. 'I won't give up, you know. Drink your tea and eat your sandwich. You'll need your strength for this afternoon's outing. It's Dallas again. Sibley and Atoka think the Super-Stealth skin formulation may be hidden there in a fabricating subcontractor's place.'

'How dreary.' Alana took one bite of sandwich and one sip of tea. 'We've wasted five months haring about after this silly ferrite coating process. Why couldn't the bloody stubborn Yanks simply hand the thing over to the Russians instead of daring us and Tamara's people to find it? There's so much more important work we could be doing.'

'They're testing,' Jamie said. 'Measuring our capabilities and our resolution, and making a classic American "Don't Tread on Me" gesture. You can bet that the formulation is in a lead box walled up in a reinforced vault surrounded by an electrified grid in the midst of an alligator pond . . . but we'll find it, whatever the rigamarole, and we'll send copies to Washington and Moscow via diplomatic pouch and tell the world press we've done it. Then we'll chalk up another triumph for globalism and wait for the next confrontation.'

'Neither side really cares about the radar-invisible gunk,' Alana complained. 'It's only a matter of scoring off each other. They may've thrown away their nuclear arms, but it seems they're just as determined to dominate the world as they ever were – and our metapsychic peace initiative is nothing but a referee in the charade.'

'Did you really expect an instant Golden Age, my lass?' Jamie's smile was ironic.

'I hoped it would be better than this,' Alana admitted, looking out the window again. The old man in the black raincoat was consulting a small book and gazing about. 'We don't have the spectre of nuclear war between superpowers anymore, but the old East-West antagonism and suspicion are still there, and the little countries cling to their eternal squabbles. There's war in Arabia and war in Kashmir and war in Botswana and war in Bolivia . . .'

'And I'll never pray at the Wailing Wall,' Nigel said, 'and your tea is getting cold again, and what is so fascinating about that old chap lurking about out there?'

Alana said, 'It's odd. He's subvocalizing both the words and tune of "Amazing Grace". I can tell he's in a great state of emotional agitation, and one would normally be able to read his thoughts like a hoarding under those conditions – but because of the hymn-singing I can't get a glimmer. I wonder if the poor old thing is lost?'

'A kind of normal's thought-screen, is it?' Jean asked. 'How interesting. Do you know, I think our young Katie and David may have cottoned on to that one! There've been times when I've noticed television commercials and theme songs and other nonsense cycling over and over in their sly little brains when they were obviously up to some deviltry.'

'We'd better hope the technique doesn't catch on in diplomatic circles,' Nigel said.

'According to Denis Remillard,' Jamie said, 'it already has. But fortunately, not too many normals are able to keep it up for any length of time . . . I forgot to mention that Denis popped over via EE very early this morning. He had some important news. Dartmouth is establishing a Department of Metapsychology with some whacking great grants that've fallen down the chimney, and Denis is being promoted to full professor and will head the thing up.'

'Lucky sod,' groaned Nigel. 'And here we are with the University casting about for ways to put us under the UK Civil Service! Can't you just see our metapsychic peace initiative tucked tidily away in Whitehall?' And he sang, in an excruciating fruity tenor:

> 'But the privilege and pleasure
> That we treasure without measure
Is to run on little errands for the Ministers of State!'

'Denis had some bad news, too.' Jamie spoke in a lower tone. 'The bill for universal metapsychic testing of all American children died in committee. The Civil Liberties Union and the Bible-thumpers carried the day. Now the testing is to be done on a strictly voluntary basis. There was some demand that the names of the participants and the results of the metapsychic assay be made a matter of public record, but Denis is fairly certain that meta-supporters in Washington can shoot that one down by invoking the famous American right to privacy. I asked Denis if he senses any serious groundswell of antimeta sentiment building, but he thinks not. More like a blasé attitude on the part of the normals, he said – taking the mental marvels for granted the way they do space travel.'

'We were all heroes,' Nigel declaimed, 'right up until the last nukes in North Dakota and Skovorodino were dismantled! But what have we done for humanity lately?' He lifted his beer in a mock toast.

'Denis's new book is about due,' Jamie added. 'He's calling it *The Evolution of Mind*. He said it may shake people up. I hope the lad hasn't said anything too reckless. Sometimes he strikes me as a bit toplofty, and I don't think that would sit well with the American public. Your Yank-on-the-street tends to follow egalitarianism right out the window, pretending that people really are all created equal and deserving of equal treament across the board. It doesn't work out that way in actuality, of course – but God help the fellow who advocates any elitist scheme.' He chomped up the remains of his sandwich and took a deep draft of Arrol's.

'We, on the other hand,' Nigel said, 'just love an aristocrat.'

'Speak for yourself, you kosher Sassenach!' said Jean with spirit.

A number of colourful racial slurs were exchanged in good humour, and then all of them but Alana concentrated on food and drink. She persisted in her abstraction until she suddenly said:

'Will Denis's new book have an explanation for precognition?'

'Have you had a skry, then?' Jean's face was troubled. 'Not another warning?'

'Not exactly,' Alana said. 'No firm premonition, only a kind of feeling. Just now.'

Nigel regarded the young woman with a pretence of exasperation. 'She's facing her weird again, that's what. So she can get out of the excursion to Dallas.'

'It's no joke,' Jean admonished him. 'Not to anyone born and reared in the Highlands. Our own little Katie's had the Sight – and I don't mind telling you it scares me. The other metafunctions are only extensions and elaborations of our normal mind-powers, after all. But precognition seems supernatural somehow . . .' She turned again to Alana. 'Your feeling: was it for good or ill?'

'I – I don't know. I've never felt anything like it. It wasn't frightening. No vision, no notion of an event impending. Perhaps just the opposite.' She gave a small laugh and once again turned to the window. The old man was stooped over, rummaging in his carrier bag while the rain beat on his exposed neck. 'He's still singing the hymn,' Alana noted softly. 'Still upset. Perhaps it's *his* precognition.'

'Funny you should ask about the theoretical aspect of the Sight,' Nigel said. 'I was defending the crystal-ball effect as a legitimate metafunction to Littlefield and Schneider just the other day. It has to be a warping of the temporal lattices producing a wormhole in the continuum through the agency of the seer's own coercion. In theory, one could catch glimpses of the future or the past quite as readily as contemporaneous remote-viewings in the here and now. It's a matter of willing – coercing – a momentary plication of time rather than space.'

'But how,' Alana said slowly, 'can you explain the *unpremeditated* glimpse of the future? The vision one doesn't ask for?'

Nigel looked uncomfortable. He swirled the last of his beer in the bottom of the glass. 'It's hard to explain that through dynamic-field theory, I admit. You see, the temporal nodalities that we call "events" require instigating forces. Causes, if you like. But if the unexpected premonition doesn't originate in the coercivity of the seer, we must ask just what the source of the coercive vector is. It could be another person. It could be the collective unconscious of humanity, if you want to accept Urgyen Bhotia's theory.'

'Or it could simply be angels,' said Jamie MacGregor.

Alana started. 'Oh, you're putting me on!'

He was rummaging in his notecase for the Parapsychology Unit's credit card. Discovering it at last, he waved it at the barmaid. 'If you eliminate the coercivity of the seer as the instigator of Sight, and eliminate the coercivity of other *people* – using the term in its broadest sense to mean "sapient entities inhabiting our physical universe" – then you are left with an enigma. An extradimensional genetrix. An initiating force outside the eighteen generative dynamic fields, but nevertheless congruent to the three matrix fields.'

The barmaid took Jamie's card away. Her face had an old-fashioned expression.

'Are you speaking of God?' Alana asked.

'Not necessarily,' said Jamie. 'The Universal Field Theory doesn't define God, or the Cosmic All, or the Omega, or whatever. But if such an entity exists outside our physical universe, then it must have a method of relating to that universe. Denis Remillard believes in God and suggests that an integral sexternion – or a whole gaggle of them – operates between the All and the dimensional construct we call the physical universe. He says the sexternions already have a perfectly good name in religious tradition: angels! Word means messenger.' He signed the credit-card slip with a flourish and pocketed his copy.

Alana peered at him with suspicion. 'Do you mean to say you *really* believe second sight is instigated by angels?'

Jamie shrugged. They were all rising from the table and going after their raincoats. 'I didn't say that. I said it was a theory, and one of Remillard's to boot. You can think as you like, lass.'

'Do you still feel fey?' Jean asked Alana solicitously. 'You're dreadfully pale and you didn't eat a thing.'

'It's a blank,' the girl whispered. She tried to smile. 'There doesn't seem to be anything beyond.'

'Take my arm,' Nigel urged her.

Alana's eyes slid away. 'I'd really rather not. Please, Nigel.'

'No problem,' he said easily, and held the door open.

The two women went out into the rain.

By the churchyard gate, the elderly man was now kneeling on the pavement, rooting in the plastic carrier bag and muttering. He had lost his hat and the rain soaked his thin white hair and ran down his furrowed cheeks. He looked up wildly and froze as he saw Alana.

There shalt not be found among you any one that useth divination, or an enchanter, or a witch! For all that do these things are an abomination unto the Lord: and because of these abominations the Lord thy God doth drive them out from before thee!

Alana stopped as the cry flooded her mind and tried to crowd Jean back into the pub doorway with her body, but she was not quick enough; the machine pistol that the old man pulled from his bag spat five sudden gouts of yellow fire and woke thundering echoes up and down the ancient street. Alana crumpled, her face turned scarlet and formless, dead before she reached the ground. Jean took only one bullet, but that was in the neck, and she fell back into Jamie's arms with her life fountaining on to the rain-darkened granite pavement.

The old man shouted: 'Thou shalt not suffer a witch to live!' He threw down his weapon and darted into the Greyfriars churchyard.

Jamie went to his knees with Jean clasped to his breast, hearing her mind say what her voice was unable to utter:

Katie and David . . . love them. . . . continue the work . . .

He bent and kissed her, with the rational part of his brain assuring him that this could not be happening. Not to her. Not to them. Their life together had been absurdly perfect, an idyll throughout the thirteen years of their marriage and professional collaboration and the rearing of their joy-bedight offspring. This sort of ending was impossible.

Jean said: I'm always with you.

He kissed her again, and was aware of a terrible howling sound. Then, shockingly, he was almost bowled over by a plunging shape and knew it was Nigel, gone after the madman, screaming at the top of his lungs.

Jean said: He mustn't. Stop him.

When Jamie continued to cling to her, she mustered up a last coercive impulse.

Go before it's too late!

He lowered her carefully to the stones. People were pushing out of the pub, babbling and shouting. Several cars had stopped and their occupants looked out, horror-stricken. Jamie dodged pedestrians and pounded through the churchyard entrance. Beneath one of the venerable trees just softening in spring leaf was a fierce orange blaze. Nigel stood over it, his scholarly face as implacable as the marble death's-heads that decorated the seventeenth-century tombs on either hand. A man writhed in the midst of the fire, making a shrill keening sound.

Jamie ripped off his coat to blanket the flames, rolling the burning man on the wet turf. Suddenly, without a word, Nigel leapt on to Jamie's back and clawed at his eyes. Jamie levered himself upright, got a grip on the wrists of the smaller man, and pried the hands away from his face. Redness tinged the vision of one eye.

'No, Nigel! For God's sake!'

'Let the swine burn!' Nigel sank his teeth into Jamie's right hand. Agonized, Jamie lifted Nigel bodily and flung him headfirst against the trunk of the tree. He fell, groaning feebly, and Jamie turned again to the smouldering body beneath the raincoat.

There were people running about the churchyard now and a sound of approaching police cars. The flames seemed to be out. Jamie pulled a fold of fabric aside and saw the charred features of the fanatic – hawklike nose, bold brow-arches of Caledonian bone, lantern jaw – a face very much like his own. The eyes in their lidless sockets seemed to retain an uncompromising gleam and the mouth, distorted by the rictus of violent death, might have been triumphantly grinning.

Jamie let the cloth drop back. He got up and limped over to Nigel, who appeared to be embracing the tree as he attempted to haul himself upright. One sleeve of his coat was torn and his bald pate was purpled with a massive contusion. Jamie extended his left hand to his colleague and pulled him to his feet. Nigel reciprocated by binding Jamie's bitten hand with a handkerchief.

Police officers came and led them away, and then there was an interval during which they were asked the same questions over and over again with irritating persistence. Dr Nigel Weinstein was arrested and charged with culpable homicide. Later he was released on his own recognizance to attend the Third Metapsychic Congress, which was held that year in Edinburgh. He did not present a paper.

In February 1995 Weinstein was aquitted when the Scottish jury brought in a verdict of 'Not Proven'. By then, however, with the worldwide publicity given the trial, the damage had been done.

5

Survey Vessel
Krak Rona'al [Kron 466-010111]

Sector 14: Star 14-893-042 [Landa]:
Planet 4 [Assawompset]

Galactic Year: La Prime 1-357-627
[8 August 1994]

The monstrous Krondaku are a race fabled throughout the Galactic Milieu for their ancient wisdom, their merciless objectivity, and their composure. But there is another aspect to the great tentacled invertebrates that other polities (except the Lylmik) do not suspect.

At thōse rare times when they can be certain of being unobserved by exotic minds, the Krondaku are given to fooling around.

The mated pairs, especially, in conditions of absolute privacy, will cast aside all decorum and circumspection and for a brief interval submerge themselves completely in sensory input. They revel, they wallow, they become intoxicated voluptuaries – drinking in, above all, the supernal pla'akst sensation engendered by their ponderous amours. Only the Gi, those paragons of concupiscence, have a greater capacity for pla'akst than dallying Krondaku. When the passionate interlude ends, its memory lingers on and suffuses the normal Krondak phlegmatism with sunniness. For a while, the terrible monsters are awash with uncharacteristic bonhomie.

It was in just such a mood that two senior Krondak planetologists approached the Landa solar system in the 14th Sector.

Comparator Dota'efoo Alk'ai and her mate, Attestor Luma'eroo Tok, had received a most unusual assignment from the Sector Base on Molakar [Tau Ceti-2]. They were to go themselves, without the usual support crew consisting of a mixed bag of Milieu races, and perform an update assessment on the fourth Landa planet, which they had surveyed many Galactic millenaries ago. Once a promising prospect for colonization, the world had suffered the misfortune of being within a critical distance of supernova 14-322-931B-S2. As this dying star exploded, it launched a relativisitc blast wave of high-energy particles, x-rays and gamma rays in all directions. For several centuries, the normal background cosmic radiation flux through the Landa system increased by a factor of nearly five thousand, with cataclysmic effects upon the biota of the single habitable world. The blast wave had swept past Landa exactly two Galactic millenaries ago [5476 Earth years]. The 14th Sector Survey Authority decided it was now time to find out if the irradiated fourth planet had simmered down, and if it was still potentially colonizable. A full-scale resurvey was not required. Experienced fieldworkers such as Dota'-efoo and Luma'eroo would be able to decide rather quickly whether or not the world was a write-off.

The Landa solar system lay on the outer fringe of the Orion Arm of the Galaxy, some 6360 light-years from Molakar. Travelling at its usual brisk displacement factor of 370, the starship of the two Krondak planetologists required 17.19 subjective Galactic days to make the trip, which was executed in eighteen consecutive hyperspatial catenaries. Twice each day, as the ship entered and left subspace by means of its upsilon-field superluminal translator, the two entities within experienced a brief moment of horrific pain, which they bore with Krondak stoicism. But in between the translations, when they were alone together in the grey limbo of the hyperspatial subuniverse, that most remote of nonlocations, the couple felt free to doff their dour racial façade and romp. They had not had a honeymoon in more than five millenaries, and its glow stayed with them as they neared the journey's end and climbed reluctantly out of the connubial vat of glycerin, imidazolidinyl urea, and iso-yohimbine.

The terminal break through the superficies was due any minute. They headed for the survey craft's control room slithering side by side, settled into their squatting pads, and waited. A small cyan indicator on the instrumentation panel flashed on as the translator mechanism spun the upsilon-field gateway. The viewport showed only quasi-dimensional grey negation . . . and then there was a unique swimming snap, a *zang* attended by incredible agony, a *zung*, and relief. They had returned to normal space, in the vicinity of the Landa system.

The smallish G1 sun was of modest mass and luminosity, unassociated with solar companions. It shone golden-yellow, exhibiting minimal flare activity and an attractive 'butterfly' corona with pearly equatorial streamers and polar plumes. Five of its family of fourteen planets were immediately visible to the multiple Krondak oculi, but all of them were gas-giants of no interest to colonization evaluators.

Luma'eroo shut down the overdrive mechanism and fired

up the subluminal gravo-magnetic propulsion generators. He switched the ship's navigation unit from automatic to tentacular. A crawling network of faint violet fire, the rho-field, now clothed the outer hull of the dull-black spheroid. Under Luma'eroo's pilotage, it went full inertialess and proceeded to the fourth planet, moving at a sizable percentage of the speed of light. The ship took up station in a geosynchronous orbit a few hundred thousand kilometres above a bluish-green, cloud-swirled world.

'I wish thou wouldst not hot-dog, Tok.' Dota'efoo's admonition had overtones of fond languor; the after-effects of the recent debauch were still very much with her.

'The sooner we get this evaluation over with, the sooner we can begin the trip back to Molakar.' Luma'eroo's primary eyes retained a misty periwinkle colour and his integument was flushed with the telltale rosy blotches of fulfillment. 'This mission is hardly likely to end positively, Alk'ai, given the proximity of the poor planet to the supernova.'

'I daresay thou art right,' Dota'efoo said, stroking his warty dorsal prominence with absent-minded affection as she stared out the main viewport. 'Just look. The cloud cover has deteriorated to only about fifty per cent and there are polar ice caps now. The atmospheric ozone layer must have been zapped to a green frazzle. All-in-All pity the life-forms! . . .'

'I'm going to call up a précis of our last survey. It's been a long time — and thanks to thee, O alluring source of hyperhedonia, my mnemonic faculties are just the least bit unresponsive.' He flicked a request to the computer and the abbreviated data flashed into both their minds:

EVALUATION SUMMARY — 14-893-042-4

This eminently habitable world is a typical small metallolithoid with an equatorial radius of [5902 km] and a mean density of [5.462 gm/cm^3]. It has a nickel-iron core and is internally heated by natural radioactivity. The dipolar magnetic field is classed 06:2:05:9. Planet Four is attended by three interlocked moons: A is a coreless lithoid giant with a diameter 0.22 and a mass 0.01 that of the primary; B and C are lithoid midgets scarcely 1/1000th as massive as A, orbiting at the equilateral points of the giant. Planet Four has an axial tilt of 19.35 degrees and a nearly circular orbit around its sun. Its year is equivalent to 611.3 Galactic days and its day 93 time units. The planetary albedo is 39.7 per cent.

The atmosphere of Planet Four is generally within acceptable parameters for Milieu races: 22.15 per cent oxygen, 0.05 per cent carbon dioxide, and 77.23 per cent nitrogen, with the balance consisting of noble gases, hydrogen, ozone, miscellaneous trace gases, miscellaneous suspended particulates, and varying amounts of dihydrogen oxide vapour. Clouds formed of the latter shroud about 62 per cent of the planetary surface.

Land areas comprise 19 per cent of Planet Four, and 81 per cent is covered with dihydrogen oxide oceans with an average salinity of 3.03 per cent. Nearly 20 per cent of the hydrosphere is epicontinental and very shallow. There are many freshwater lakes of small area. The lithosphere has a Class 4 motile-plate structure with a basaltic abyssal sea-floor and granitic continents. Two continents are of moderate size and five are much smaller. There are myriads of continental-class islands and many extensive island-arcs at oceanic plate boundaries. Continental mountain ranges have formed adjacent to the active subduction zones of the two principal land masses, and some of their peaks exceed [6000 m] in height. The continents also feature eroded highland remnants of earlier cycles of continental drift. There is moderate vulcanism in the island-arcs, along mid-oceanic ridges, and in the subduction ranges.

Planet Four has a generally warm and humid maritime climate, lacking polar or continental glaciation. Tropical conditions prevail in the equatorial belt, with full-summer temperatures exceeding [40°C] and no winter. The midlatitude continental temperature range is: summer – above [40°C]; winter – above [10°C]. Island temperatures are generally lower than continent in summer and higher in winter. One small continent near the North Pole has a summer maximum temperature of [23°C] and a winter minimum of [-5°C]. There is only one small desert, in the rain-shadow of the coast range at the equatorial region of the largest continent.

Life-forms of Planet Four are C-H-O-N-S-Fe proteinoid, predominantly aerobic. Both the oceans and the land harbour large populations of protist and multicellular autotrophs. There are some 690,000 species of photoautotrophic, chemoautotrophic and mixotrophic plants – with green photoautotrophs making up the majority of micro- and macroflora. About 60 per cent of the energy they bind is taken up by heterotrophic life-forms. Heterotrophs include some 2,000,000 species of protists, plants and animals – marine, amphibian, terrestrial and semiaerial. Most of the animals and about half of the protists and plants are mobile. Higher species of animals display homeostasis, bilateral symmetry, disexuality, and endoskeletal body structure, with increasing cephalization in the more highly evolved species. The most advanced lifeform is a presapient ovoviviparous semierect terrestrial biped with a brain classification of 67:3:462. It is stalled in its cephalic evolution by a low birth rate and the presence in its ecosystem of six major predators, two of them aerial.

PRELIMINARY PLANETOLOGICAL RATING:
Suited for colonization, with optional ecological modification to the Fifth Degree.

WEIGHTED RACIAL COMPATIBILITY PERCENTAGE:
Simb: 89. Gi: 80. Poltroyan: 48. Krondak: 13.

'Well,' Dota'efoo noted sadly, 'even a quick visual scan shows that the place was severely damaged. The cloud cover's down to about fifty per cent. The climate has cooled to the ice-age stage, and the concomitant lowering of sea level has exposed nearly all of the continental shelves. The greater percentage of the islands has merged into dry land.'

'So much for Gi colonization. Without plenty of island trysting sites, their reproductive psychology packs up and the eggs are sterile.' Luma'eroo activated a battery of monitoring devices at the same time that he sent the craft plunging out of orbit. When the black spheroid reached the planetary tropopause it came to an abrupt halt, hovering in the deep-blue sky while thin jet-stream winds hummed around it. 'At least the magnetosphere has recovered to its normal value. Reversed, though.'

'I was afraid of that. Is the ozone layer rebuilt?'

'To within normal parameters for the G1 sun.' He twiddled with the radiation-monitoring unit, which was overdue for a refit. 'Albedo's down to twenty-eight overall. UV and solar wind penetration to surface within normal range. Ditto the cosmic radiation.'

Dota'efoo studied the atmosphere analysis. 'Oxygen is down by a full two per cent, and nitrogen is up one. Carbon dioxide has gone from .05 to .03 . . . And just look at the biotic differentiation read-out! We've lost nearly half of the plant species and an even larger percentage of the animals to hard radiation overdose, UV exposure, or general niche deterioration.'

'It could have been worse, Alk'ai, and the place *was* perhaps overspeciated. Residual populations have probably expanded to fill most of the vacant niches – to say nothing of the successful mutations. The grosser supernova damage to the biota seems to have healed.'

'But the world is still ruined.'

He blinked his primary optics in doleful agreement. 'It is no longer libidinously stimulating enough for the Gi and it is now too cold and dry for the Simbiari. It remains too warm, too deficient in oxygen partial-pressure, and too gravity-strong for us Krondaku. That leaves only the Poltroyans as potential colonizers – but the place is probably too warm for them as well, except in the circumpolar regions.'

'And don't forget, we'd also have to do ecological modification of a high degree to accommodate our little mauve brethren. This planet never did have enough sulphur springs or useful species of purple anaerobic photosynthesizers for their tastes.'

'Too true,' he agreed. 'Shall we bother doing a surface recon? Or wouldst thou prefer that we simply mark it for a dead loss and minimize the insult to our freshly heightened sensibilities?'

She hesitated. 'I would like to descend, Tok – if thou wouldst indulge me. We did spend so much time on the original survey. Besides, it's fitting to give it the utmost benefit of the doubt.'

'I agree.' Disdaining the instrumentation, he did a fast metapsychic farscan of the largest continent, which projected some distance into the North Temperate Zone. This part of the world, which had the most landmass, was at the onset of winter; but there was as yet no snow on the ground and the vegetation was still adequately lush. 'Let us visit the eastern coast of the major continent, Alk'ai.

There is a great river now traversing the old continental shelf and a rather interesting embayment.'

'Very well.'

The survey vessel plummeted towards the planetary surface in a straight line, shielded by its rho-field from the constraints of gravity-inertia and by a temporary sigma-field from atmospheric ablation. The region Luma'eroo had selected was just at the terminator, and so they landed just as the sun was going down behind low hills, painting a dancing golden pathway across the indigo waters of the windswept bay. There was abundant plant-life. On the hills and on the exposed headland where the ship rested were stands of trees with sturdy ligneous stems and deep-green aciform leaves. Other species of trees in the lowlands on either side of the river showed the beginning of chlorophyll degeneration in their obviously deciduous foliage, which was stained in startling coppery, xanthic and rubineous hues.

The Krondaku emerged carefully from the ship and moved with difficulty in the gravitational field that was nearly twice their racial optimum. They slithered over a ground cover of low-growing anthophytes. Some were dried out; others, still green, bore star-shaped pink, yellow or white sexual organs. The air tasted of terpineol, geranyl acetate, coumarin and phenylethyl alcohol. There was also a distinctive chloride-iodide exudation from the marine organisms at the rocky margin of the sea. An offshore breeze made a rustling sound as it passed through the needle-leaf trees, and waves crashed on the seaward side of the headland. Up in one of the trees, an invisible creature voiced a complex warbling ululation having a frequency between two thousand and four thousand cycles per second. Small white-winged animals in a ragged V-formation flew low over the bay waves, heading towards the open sea.

The two tentacled monsters contemplated the scene for some time, utilizing both their conventional senses and their ultrafaculties. The sun set and the cloudless sky turned from yellow to aquamarine to purple, studded with the first bright stars. The major moon, in its full phase, came up over the blackening eastern sea like a great disc of refulgent amber. One of the twin moonlets was also in view, shining modestly silver through the silhouetted branches of a nearby tree.

'Ruined.' Dota'efoo spoke with emphatic finality. 'In its present state, the planet is patently unfit for colonization by any of the coadunate races of the Milieu.'

'It's hopeless,' Luma'eroo agreed. 'Ecological engineering up to the Tenth Degree wouldn't even begin to put it back into shape.' He ruminated for a few moments more. 'Strange . . . it rather reminds me of *their* world.' And he projected an oafish racial image that had become a notorious target of low humour among less charitable Simbiari and Poltroyan planetologists.

'By the All-Penetrant – I do believe thou art correct. Shall we go back inside the ship and check the correlates?'

'With pleasure. My plasm aches from this burdensome gravity.'

The two Krondaku reboarded and went again to the control room, where the computer confirmed Luma'eroo's hunch. The weighted compatibility percentage was an amazing 98.

'And so, in the most unlikely event that they are admitted to the Milieu, our poor little orphan planet would undoubtedly be among the first worlds to be colonized by *them*.' Dota'efoo called up some additional data. 'Here is a noteworthy item. They recently sent an exploration team to their most hospitable neighbour planet – a dusty red frigid-desert hulk with an exiguous atmosphere. They are also constructing orbiting habitats in a futile effort to siphon off their excess population.'

'Idiots. Why don't they simply limit procreation?'

'It is contrary to the prevailing ethic of certain racial segments, and others are too ignorant to appreciate the reproductive predicament of their planet. Thou must understand, Tok, that these people are even more fecund than the Poltroyans, and this poses technical difficulties for practical contraception as well as motivational ones. Their principal means of population control are famine, abortion, a high infant death-rate among Class Two indigenes, and war.'

'Those amazing humans!' Luma'eroo lifted four tentacles in a gesture of puzzlement. 'If the Lylmik are truly intent upon foisting them upon the Milieu, we are in for some interesting times. I think we may someday be grateful, Alk'ai, that there are numbers of solar systems on the far side of the Galaxy that await our personal scrutiny.'

His mate allowed a barely perceptible risibility to enter her mind-tone. 'And yet, they do have a certain reckless courage. Imagine a race of their classification seriously attempting to colonize a nearly airless, frigid-desert planet . . . or worse, artificial satellites!'

'It surpasses understanding.'

Dota'efoo summoned a last modicum of data from the computer. 'If Earthlings *are* accepted into the Milieu, their overpopulation problem will become an asset overnight. As of now, we have 782 ecologically compatible planets within a 20,000-light-year radius of their home world all surveyed and ready for settlement.' She flicked a dismissive tentacle at the viewport, with its moonlit seascape framed by ever-green trees. 'And this place makes 783.'

'Frightening. They'd very likely overrun the Galaxy in a few millenaries . . .'

Dota'efoo shuddered. 'Let's get out of here.'

Her mate activated the rho-field generator to full intertia-less and sent the survey vessel screaming into interplanetary space.

6

From the Memoirs of
Rogatien Remillard

On the face of it, there was nothing suspicious about the accidental deaths of my three nieces.

The twins Jeanette and Laurette, who were twenty-one, and their sister Jacqueline, two years younger, were driving home from a ski weekend in North Conway early in January 1995 when their new RX-11 went out of control on the icy highway, crashed, and burned. Denis flew back from Edinburgh, where he had been called as an expert witness for the defence in the sensational trial of Dr Nigel Weinstein. Once again he and Victor supported their widowed mother through the ordeal of an old-fashioned Franco–American veillée, funeral Mass, and cortège to the family plot in the cemetery outside Berlin, where the girls were buried next to their father.

Sunny was not just grief-stricken, she was devastated. Both Denis and I detected nuances of irrationality beneath the stuporous anguish that cloaked her mind, but neither of us recognized the fear. Denis had to return to Scotland immediately. He urged me to stay in Berlin for the week following the funeral to make a closer assessment of his mother's mental health. When I told him that Sunny seemed in the grip of a morbid depression, he asked a colleague from the Department of Metapsychology, Colette Roy, to come to Berlin for consultation with the Remillard family physician. Dr Roy, Glenn Dalembert's wife, had been studying the abnormal psychology of operants and was the best redactive prober (outside of Denis) working at that time at Dartmouth. Her examination of Sunny was inconclusive and she urged that I bring Sunny to Hanover for a further evaluation at the Hitchcock Clinic. Sunny adamantly refused to go. She said she would not leave the other five children, who ranged in age from thirteen to eighteen, even when Victor offered to pay for a full-time housekeeper. The terrible anxiety that Sunny displayed at the suggestion that she leave her rather fractious adolescent brood was diagnosed by Dr Roy as just another symptom of the depression; but in this Colette was mistaken. Sunny, the mother of two metapsychic giants, had managed for all her latency to screen her innermost thoughts with a thoroughness none of us dreamed possible.

When Denis returned to New Hampshire after Weinstein's acquittal and pleaded with her, Sunny finally agreed to a two-week course of treatment at Hitchcock, with monthly outpatient checkups to follow. She also said she would accept domestic help in the big house on Sweden Street that Denis and Victor had bought for her four years earlier. Victor interviewed and rejected a parade of Berlin applicants, and eventually hired one Mme Rachel Fortier of Montréal, an amazonian femme de charge who came with the highest references and eye-popping salary requirements. Sunny accepted the housekeeper with apparent goodwill, and by the second week in February things seemed to be going back to normal.

So I went to a science-fiction convention.

Every year since 1991 I had attended Boskone, a sedate gathering of fantasy buffs, writers, artists, booksellers and academics. Those unfamiliar with such meetings may get a hint of the general atmosphere when I say that I, a known operant and close relative of one of the most famous metapsychic personalities in the country, was looked upon as nothing out of the ordinary by the convention-goers. I was just another bookseller, not to be mentioned in the same breath with genuine celebrities such as the best-selling author of *Tessaract One*, the producer of the *Gnomeworld* video series, or the first artist to do on-the-spot lunar landscapes.

Sometimes at these conventions I shared a table in the dealers' room with a fellow bookseller, offering middling rarities and telling all comers about the much greater trove of goodies to be found at my shop in Hanover. Sometimes I just circulated and perused the other dealers' wares for likely items, or bought a few pieces of artwork, or attended the more bibliophilic panel discussions, or sat in on readings by my favourite authors. I scarcely ever bothered with the endless round of parties that was a feature of convention nights, preferring in earlier years to do my serious drinking in solitude. The only festivity I attended was the combination masquerade and meet-the-lions bash that traditionally took place on Friday evening. There one might legitimately scrape up acquaintance with notables, so as later to be in a favourable position to offer them modest sums for their hand-corrected proofs, typescripts (a surprising number of science-fiction writers still refused to process their words), autographed first editions, or literary curiosa of a marketable sort.

Boskone XXXII was held at the Seraton-Boston. When the dealers' room opened on Friday the tenth I made my rounds of the tables and greeted old friends and acquaintances among the hucksters. The antiquarian pickings seemed leaner than in other years and the prices higher. Very few new books were now being published in the hardcover format; even first editions from the big houses were issued mostly as large paperbacks. Regular paperbacks, on the other hand, proliferated like fleas on a spaniel in August in response to the reading explosion of the '90s. Desktop printing technology had given rise to a host of cottage publishers of every stripe – fantasy not excluded – and limited collector's editions of every Tom, Dick or Mary with even the most tenuous claim to fame crowded the good old stuff off the tables.

I did manage to find firsts of the G&D *Fury* by Henry Kuttner, and a fine copy of the remarkable science-fantasy *World D* in the London Sheed & Ward edition of 1935.

As I dickered for the latter with a bookseller acquaintance, Larry Palmira, I became aware of a strange hostility in his manner. At first his subvocalizations were too indistinct to decipher; but as we settled on a final price somewhat higher than I had hoped for, I heard him say:

And you won't coerce ME into going a buck lower dammitall so go try your mental flimflam on some other nebbish!

I signed the credit-card slip and gave it to him smiling. He bagged my book and said, 'Always great to do business with you, Roj. Drop in when you're in Cambridge.'

'I'll do that, Larry,' said I, and walked away thinking hard.

I decided to test my suspicions and stopped at the booth of another dealer friend, Fidelity Swift, pretending interest in a Berkley paperback first of *Odd John*, ludicrously overpriced at twenty-five dollars. She let me beat her down a little. Then I looked her in the eye and murmured, 'Come on, Fee, gimme a break. You better be nice to me, kiddo. You know what they say about not getting a metapsychic pissed . . .'

'No,' she laughed. 'What do they say?' In her mind was a fearsome image: Nero's garden lit by human torches.

I thought: Merde dans sa coquille! And said, 'Damned

if I can remember. Double sawbuck, last offer. Cash on the barrelhead.'

'Sold!' Relief gushed out of her like blood from a cut artery. The nightmare picture faded but her deep disquiet was now obvious.

I handed over the money and took my prize, saying goodbye while I broadcast the most benignant vibes I could conjure up, superimposed upon an image of her that shaved off thirty pounds and ten years and arrayed her plain features in idealized sexuality.

'See you around, Roger,' she breathed, all apprehension swept away. I winked and hurried out of the dealers' room.

The trial. The goddam Scottish trial!

Weinstein had been extremely lucky to win the famous 'Not Proven' verdict permissible under Scots law. The lunatic clergyman he had incinerated was unarmed, and witnesses had testified that the old man had offered no threat or resistance when Weinstein ran him down. Only some fancy psychiatric footwork about diminished responsibility due to temporary derangement and Denis's testimony about the inadvertent projections of creative flame exemplified by 'Subject C' and documented in his laboratory (Lucille's identity was disclosed only to the judge) brought about Weinstein's acquittal. Even then there were dark editorials about 'persons of special privilege' flouting the common law of humanity. The Metapsychic Congress, held four months before the trial, had attempted to anticipate and disarm public apprehension by pointing out that only a minuscule percentage of operants possessed mental faculties that could be classified as threatening to ordinary mortals. There were more reassurances later. How many normals, given Weinstein's provocation, might not have been carried away as he was to the point of violence? In the United States, Weinstein's immolation of the mad murderer became the most hotly argued case since a quiet electronics technician had shot four aggressive young muggers on a New York subway back in the '80s. Behind the rational argumentation and scholarly disputations on the dark side of the unconscious lurked something uglier and more atavistic. The man who had slain Jean MacGregor and

Alana Shaunavon had denounced them as witches, and quoted the Bible as justification. Of *course* intelligent modern people understood that metapsychic powers were a natural consequent of human evolution. There was nothing devilish or black-magical about them. But on the other hand . . .

There was a simple remedy for the irrational fear of a single individual. I had worked it myself on Fidelity Swift. But it was a temporary thing, like a clever actor making an audience believe in a character being portrayed. We operants would be able to disarm the fear of some of the normals some of the time – for a little while. But how would we convince them of our amity over the long haul?

Sunk in the old malheur, I went up to my room to stash the book purchases before going to supper. As I came back into the corridor I was reminded by the number of costumed figures prowling about that the masquerade and meet-the-pros party was in full swing down in the hotel's grand ballroom. There would be music and drinks and conviviality, and such a mob scene that nobody would bother thinking twice about my sinister mental attributes.

The down-elevator door opened to reveal a chamber jammed with exotic fun-seekers. I spotted a squad of youths dressed in medieval battle-gear, a nubile lass with flaming hair and a four-foot 'peace-bonded' sword, wearing what seemed to be a bikini of silver poker chips, a Darkoverian mother with two Darkoverian moppets, a statuesque black woman in a white satin evening gown with a little white dragon perched on her shoulder, a stoutish middle-aged gent clad in a conservative suit whose mundane appearance was belied only by the propeller beanie on his head, and a large ape sporting emerald fur and illuminated eyeballs, who had neglected to use a personal deodorant.

'No room! No room!' chorused this bunch as I made to enter the elevator. The ape opened its mechanically augmented white-tusked jaws and stuck its carunculated tongue out at me.

But there is, occasionally, justice in this world. I speared the smelly ape with my most potent coercive impulse and commanded: 'Out!' It complied like a lamb and I took its place to universal plaudits. We made a nonstop trip to the ballroom level.

The party had attracted nearly two thousand people. Perhaps half were in fancy dress. A live band played things like 'Can You Read My Mind?', 'Rocket Man', 'Annapurna Saucer Trip', Darius Brubeck's 'Earthrise', and John Williams's 'Theme from *Gnomeworld*'. In between sets the convention Toastmaster introduced the artists and writers present, and a spotlight tried to pick designated stars out of the crush. There were also parades of the more spectacularly costumed fans across the stage. Those who were particularly beautiful, humorous or technically awesome received warm ovations.

I headed immediately for the nearest open bar. By the time I had downed three Scotches, I felt considerably cheered. I had repinned my convention badge so that my name was mostly obscured by the lapel of my suit coat. Five attractive ladies (and one flamboyantly gorgeous transvestite, whose gender I detected too late to worry about) danced with me. I introduced myself to the convention Guest of Honour, a tottering nonagenarian survivor of the Golden Age, and by dint of the most gentle coercion and a speedily fetched raspberry seltzer got him to personally inscribe a copy of Boskone's commemorative edition of his early short stories.

And then I withdrew to the sidelines for a breather . . . and had my first shock of the evening when I saw Elaine.

Even though she was now over fifty, she was still breathtaking. Her tall slender figure was clad in a long gown of some lightweight metal mesh that flowed from her neck to the floor like molten gold. Her arms, shoulders, and back were bare. The dress's collar was a wide, upstanding band of gold adorned with stones like blazing orange topazes. She had a single heavy bracelet of the same jewels. Her hair was blond now, piled high on her head in an intricate coiffure of stiffly arranged ringlets sparked with gold glints. She was dancing with Dracula.

I gulped down the dregs of my latest Scotch and pressed towards the dance floor. Poor Drac didn't have a prayer in the face of my coercion. For some reason the band was playing a melodic standard, 'Old Cape Cod'. Elaine stood there among the other dancers, dismayed by the abrupt retreat of her caped and befanged escort, not yet noticing me. I do not recall what my thoughts were. Perhaps seeing her after so many years had drained my brain of everything except the irresistible compulsion to be near her again.

I took her into my arms and we picked up the beat. She stared up at me, wordless. Her mind said: Roger!

'Voulez-vous m'accorder cette danse, Madame?'

'No! . . . Yes.' Oh, my God.

'May I compliment you on your dress. It's much too chic to be a costume.' How appropriate that we should meet again at a bal travesti. Do you come to Boskone often?

'No,' she said. 'This is my first time. My daughter thought I'd find it amusing. She's – she's a rabid science-fiction fan.'

Your daughter . . . Don's daughter . . . she would be twenty. May I ask her name?

'Annarita Latimer. She's there, costumed as Red Sonja.' My eyes followed her mental indication and I was surprised to see the strapping redheaded wench in the silver-dollar bikini. She was too far away for me to scrutinize her directly for operancy, and I am unable to detect operant auras in lighted places. So I simply asked, 'Did she inherit the mind-powers?'

'I – I think so.' She won't let me in, Roger. There's a barrier, like a shining wall of black glass. One doesn't notice it except at very close range . . .

That explained my failure to spot her operancy in the elevator.

'What does Annarita do?' I asked easily. 'Is she going to college?'

'She's at Yale Drama School. I think she'll be a very good actress.'

'Sans doute,' I murmured. 'And your husband?'

The music was ending. We applauded, and then the MC took up the microphone to announce the costume prizes. I led Elaine to the edge of the dance floor, where Dracula waited, glowering.

Her mind told me hurriedly: Stanton died three years

ago Roger now I am married to *him*. 'Gil, darling! Let me introduce you to a very dear old friend of mine, Roger Remillard. Roger, this is my husband, Gilbert Anderson.' The Third, she appended telepathically.

Dracula shook hands with me as though I were Van Helsing. His features, blandly handsome aside from the well-fitted orthodontic fangs, wore a pensive, well-bred little frown. 'Remillard . . . Remillard. You wouldn't by any chance be related to — '

'It's really a very common Franco–American name,' I said. 'Thanks for letting me dance with Elaine. We haven't seen each other in years. Are you enjoying the convention?'

He uttered some hearty inconsequentialities, deftly extracted from me my modest means of earning a living, and decided I was no threat after all. 'Maybe we can get together for lunch or something later on this weekend.'

'Great idea. Let's try to do that,' I replied with equally false enthusiasm, simultaneously reassuring Elaine that I was out of it. I asked her: What is he? Upper management? Stockbroker?

She said: VP and chief corporate legal officer.

I said: It figures given the fangs.

And then I pretended to see someone across the crowded room that I had to speak to, so I bid the pair of them adieu. Fleeing, I told her: You are more lovely than ever be happy chèrie and never never have anything to do with metapsychic operants . . .

Then I hurried out of the ballroom, wretched again, and sought a dark corner to lose myself in. I found it in one of the hotel cocktail lounges. Hunched on a stool at the bar, I ordered a double vodka on the rocks. When I had finished it my brain was as incapable of telepathic reception as any normal's.

And so he had to tap me on the shoulder to get my attention.

I peered groggily at the intruder standing behind me. It was a tall young man with dark curly hair wearing a Flying Tiger jacket, haloed by a fierce neon-red aura. Victor said, 'I might have known I'd find you here getting sloshed. On y va!'

He took hold of my arm firmly and seized my mind in a grip like a pit bull's. I saw stars and lurched against him. A rude rummaging was going on in my head, punctuated with offhand thrusts of pain. I was unable to speak. Victor whispered urgently in French, trying to get me out of the bar, but my feet weren't moving. Then something inside my skull seemed to crumple and I moaned out loud and began to walk, biddable as any zombie.

'That's better,' said Victor. He steered me towards the elevators. 'You're all checked out. We'll go up to your room and pick up your things.'

'What . . . what the hell?' I protested.

The elevator was crowded with noisy conventioneers. Victor pressed the button for my floor. I didn't know what kind of mischief he had wrought in my brain, but I was sobering rapidly and was once again able to understand mental speech. I also had a hideous headache.

He said: We're driving north Uncle Rogi up to Berlin Maman needs you and I'm taking you to her.

I said: Sunny? . . . Dieu is she all right what's happened is it serious have you called Denis —

Shut up Uncle Rogi. There is no crisis. When I said Maman needed you I was speaking generally. She needs you if she is to get well and I am to be freed from Denis's meddling.

The elevator door opened and we got out. My head was swollen with lava and the corridor rolled from side to side like a skiff caught in the trough of storm waves. Victor held me up, inserted the coded plastic key-card into the slot of my room door, and thrust me brutally inside. I staggered to the bed and collapsed on it. Muttering obscenities, my nephew relaxed his hold on me and went into the bathroom to gather my things.

Going horizontal must have helped my brain by increasing its blood supply and I regained a measure of self-control. What the devil was going on? What did Victor really want?

He came out of the john carrying my pyjamas and a pouch of toiletries. 'What I want is a simple matter, Uncle Rogi. Maman has been very upset for quite some time. She has . . . suffered from disturbing fantasies. About me.' He went to the closet and pulled out my seat bag and two-suiter and began to stuff my clothing into them. 'Her problems have affected my younger brothers and sisters. Interfered with my plans for their future. It didn't matter so much when they were just kids, but now that they are approaching an age when they can be useful to me, I can no longer permit Maman to indulge herself by undermining my influence over them. I was very disappointed at having to write off the girls.'

Slowly, I sat up. He had his back to me as he emptied a drawer of some *Operator 5* magazines I had intended to sell.

He said, 'I urged Maman to go to Hanover, to put herself under Denis's care in long-term resident therapy. It would have been the ideal solution. As you know, she refused to leave the younger ones in my charge. She suspects, you see – as she came to suspect in the case of Papa.'

'So you *were* responsible for Don's death.'

Victor zipped up the cases with great efficiency, got my parka from the closet, and tossed it to me. 'Papa killed himself, as we all know. He was a pathetic, self-destructive sot. So are you, Uncle Rogi, but you are much more intelligent and I think your death wish is probably as spineless as the rest of your character.' He opened the outer door. 'Let's go.'

I had no choice. His coercion scooped me off the bed like a back-hoe. I teetered along after him with terrible speculations oozing out of my mind. As we waited for the elevator I asked him:

Why did you kill the girls?

He shrugged. 'Ces garces, elles étaient chaudes lapines.' Their rebellion took the form of promiscuity. It was disgusting. I had hoped for alliances with some of my associates. It is an excellent way of cementing loyalties you see but these sistersluts balked. They took my gifts made promises then did as they pleased. Coercion as you know has its limits. Perhaps I was too domineering during their early adolescence and fear made them reckless. At any rate

453

it was not working and they were behaving scandalously bringing the family into disrepute. I will not have that.

'Mon zob!' I sneered – then nearly screamed out loud as he fetched my mind a blinding wallop.

Watch yourself Uncle Rogi . . . So you find my yearnings after bourgeois respectability amusing do you? You weren't impressed by the progress of Remco Pulp and Chemicals? Perhaps you don't realize how far along I've come in the business world. Small wonder when we hardly ever see one another except at funerals. That will change.

The elevator arrived and we got in. I was so tightly controlled that I couldn't blink without the young bastard's permission. But he couldn't keep me coerced for ever . . .

He said: No. And that's the problem overall. With Maman and the family and even with my notorious older brother! Unlike you Uncle Rogi I have ambitions. And they will require the close cooperation of others whose loyalty I can count upon. Yvonne is eighteen and compliant. She is not nearly so good-looking as her late older sisters but she has youth and my associate Robert Fortier will find her acceptable. Pauline unfortunately is still too young but she will mature.

Good God you're scheming up a fucking dynasty —

Tu l'as dit bouffi!

The elevator reached the lobby and disgorged us. Victor handed the two bags to me, deposited the card-key in the box at the desk, and thriftily had a clerk validate his parking ticket. Then we headed for the lower-level elevators. For the first time I began to realize what a desperate situation I was in. I still didn't entirely understand why he wanted me, but want me he did. He could coerce me into doing any number of things and lock me up incommunicado in the interim without Denis suspecting anything. Denis was, after all, distracted by matters of global importance; erratic behaviour by his black-sheep uncle was only to be expected.

We descended into the bowels of the great hotel. The lowest parking level, where Victor had had to park his Porsche because of the convention crowd, was quiet, very

454

cold, and virtually deserted. He drew me along in his wake as he strode to the sports car.

We'll take the interstates up to Hanover. Tomorrow we can begin making arrangements for your move. By the time Denis gets wind of it you'll be settled in Berlin and they'll be reading the banns at Saint Anne's.

The banns! . . .

Of course. Don't you understand Uncle Rogi? You're going to marry Maman and relieve Denis's anxieties about her and help make certain that my surviving brothers and sisters remain under my control. And I'll find other uses for you too as time goes on.

'No!' I yelled. And from some mental reservoir I called up the power to snap his coercive lead. I flung the two bags at his head. He ducked and they skidded across the polished white hood of the car. He struck back at me and it was as though twin ice picks had been driven into my ears. I shrieked and almost fell, then recovered with a heroic act of will and tried to run. A mental thunderbolt struck me between the shoulder blades and seemed to sever my spine. I sprawled headlong, still screaming, and in seconds he was on me.

'Ferme ça, vieux dindon! Arrête de déconner!' Victor knelt on my chest and grabbed me by the hair. His eyes were like paired heliarc torches and I knew he could fry my grey matter and turn me into a drooling idiot if he chose . . . but he didn't want to go that far. He needed me and so he hesitated with his psychocreative lobotomy, and I saw my last chance. The knot of fire ignited behind my breastbone and stark terror and prayer accelerated it into an out-spiral: around and around and around. Victor's blazing eyes dimmed with surprise and then alarm. He let go of my head and flinched, so that the ball of energy I shot at him did not strike his face but glanced along the edge of his skull just above the hairline, cauterizing a shallow furrow in scalp and bone.

He howled and fell off me. In desperation I rolled under a nearby Winnebago camper with my nerves on fire from the psychozap and most of my muscles turned to Jell-O. I knew I was a goner. I could hear Victor scrambling on the pavement and reviling me in French and English.

And then he dropped like he'd been brained with a sledgehammer.

I lay there in semidarkness, smelling the Winnie's chassis lubrication and a burnt-pork stench. Victor was utterly still except for slow, stertorous breathing.

There were measured footsteps approaching: Klok . . . klok . . . klok . . . the sound amplified by the dank concrete walls and pillars of the underground garage, that haunt of lurking urban menace. I felt my neck-hairs prickle and my guts go loose. I couldn't see the aura of the approaching operant because it was deliberately being suppressed; but I could feel it, like the horrid quavering of the nerves when you stand under high-voltage power lines.

My view of him was cut off by the rows of parked cars until he came up to where Victor lay. I saw sturdy Timberland high-tops with red wool socks and black chinos stuffed into them. Arms enclosed in down mackinaw sleeves reached down to grasp Victor, taking the back of his belt in one massive hand and the collar of his jacket in the other. My nephew's body ascended out of view. The booted feet plodded to the Porsche and I heard a heavy thud, as if some vandal had desecrated the expensive vehicle by plonking a duffel bag full of books on to the roof. The car door opened and there was a softer thud. The door slammed.

The feet approached the Winnie and my two travel bags were set down next to it. The aetheric tension had dissipated and I felt enveloped in blessed relief.

A telepathic voice said: Victor will think you did it. That was quite a commendable mental effort of yours. It provided a neat cover-up for my necessary obtrusion.

Is that you?

Who else? . . . I don't think you'll have to worry about interference from Victor for a few years now. He'll give you up as a bad job and try to find other ways to cope with his family problems.

But Sunny —

You've probably saved her life. To say nothing of your

own. Once the two of you were married, Victor would have felt free to activate his unconscious oedipal retribution fantasy, wiping out his mother's threat to his ambitions.

I don't understand.

Then I suggest you reread *Hamlet*. But not on a dark and stormy night . . . Au 'voir, cher Rogi. Until the next time.

I began to squirm out from under the camper. The booted feet walked away, their sound dispersed by the serried ranks of parked vehicles. By the time I was able to stand up, the underground garage was silent again. I could see Victor, unconscious, slumped behind the wheel of the Porsche.

Eh bien, Rogi, you long streak of piss. Saved again! Or is your psychocreativity more inventive than you suspect?

I picked up my bags. My suit was filthy and I had no doubt that my face was, too; but front-desk personnel are inured to such things during science-fiction conventions. No explanations would be required. All I had to do was say that I had changed my mind about checking out.

I went to the elevator and pressed the Up button. The damned thing took for ever to arrive.

7

Concord, New Hampshire, Earth
13 May 1995

JARED ELLSWORTH, S.J.: Denis! Wonderful to see you again. Sit down! Sit down! What has it been – ten years?

DENIS REMILLARD: Twelve. When I got my MD.

ELLSWORTH: And a lot of water's gone over the dam since then, hasn't it? Brebeuf Academy is very proud of you, Denis. I shouldn't admit this, but we haven't been exactly diffident about letting endowment prospects know that you were one of our early alumni.

REMILLARD: Oh, that's perfectly all right, Jared. It makes me feel less guilty about not doing more for the Academy myself.

ELLSWORTH: Nonsense. We've appreciated your generous contributions. You'll be glad to know that Brebeuf's gimmick has been copied in other parts of the world. Now there are a dozen or so other free schools for the gifted children of low-income families. But I haven't heard that any of them harboured a really wild talent like you! Merely normal geniuses. [Laughs.]

REMILLARD: You might be interested to know that the operant population has about the same IQ spread as the normal. Just as many dummies among us as smartasses.

ELLSWORTH: That could lead to problems.

REMILLARD: It has. We don't talk about it very much publicly. A German team just completed a study, a meta-psychic assay of prisoners and inmates of institutions for the criminally insane. A disproportionate percentage of the incarcerated con men and bunco artists show traits of suboperancy in the coercive and telepathic modes. The percentage of psychopaths with operant traits is also higher than expected.

ELLSWORTH: [whistles] Any theories about that?

REMILLARD: The psychos might have kept their sanity if their fragile minds hadn't been burdened with the additional load of operant function – with all the stress that entails. Mental evolution is bound to leave a lot of maladaptive souls fallen by the wayside. The operant crooks who kept their marbles adapted – but the wrong way. They used the mind-powers opportunistically. It's a big temptation, even among the high-minded. The less intelligent metacriminals got caught, probably not even realizing that they had the powers. They thought the mind reading was just keen insight and the coercion a gonzo personality. The more intelligent operant crooks would still be at large, of course. No doubt highly regarded by their beneficiaries and damned by their enemies as financial wizards . . .

ELLSWORTH: It makes you wonder about the charismatic leaders of sleazy cults. And certain great and magnetic villains of history such as Hitler and Stalin.

REMILLARD: Some day, when we know more about the geno-types for operancy, there'll be some fascinating research done. But today, we're more concerned about this – this lower stratum of operants for pragmatic reasons.

ELLSWORTH: Mm'm. I can imagine. Bound to be baddies among you, of course, as in any other human population. But it's a thing not too many normals thought about prior to Dr Weinstein's trial – not that he could be classed among your common or garden variety of delinquent. [Takes out a pipe and begins to pack it with tobacco.] The criminal operant will pose tricky legal problems. I suppose the really powerful ones would be able to coerce juries and witnesses as well as read the minds of the prosecuting attorneys.

REMILLARD: Probably. But the real difficulty isn't in the courtroom antics. After all, the authorities can always do as the Scottish Lord of Justiciary did in the Weinstein case: bring in a watchdog operant as an amicus curiae to be on the lookout for mental hanky-panky. No . . . the problem is going to be getting the goods on operant crooks in the first place. Superior metacriminals would be able to cover their tracks in any number of mind-bending ways. Posthypnotic suggestion, for instance. This has great limitations and probably wouldn't work at all in blatant cases like first-degree murder in front of witnesses, but it might very well succeed in less emotionally charged crimes. Frauds and conspiracies and other kinds of white-collar shenanigans. You're no doubt aware that the financial world is still in an uproar over its theoretical loss of transaction secrecy. Objectively, the financiers know that the chance of a crooked operant spying on them is close to zero. *Now*. But what about later, as operants become more numerous? The global economy is in a much shakier condition than most people realize due to the impact of operancy. Not many economic analysts have written about the matter. They're afraid of making the situation worse. It was bad enough when all they had to worry about was Psi-Eye investigations of KGB and CIA bank accounts in Switzerland. This new recognition of potential operant criminality has thrown them into a real swivet. And there's no remedy yet. We'll have to wait until more operants are trained for oversight work – and are willing to take it on. It's not going to be the most popular career choice among idealistic young heads.

ELLSWORTH: Thought police! Good heavens, what an idea.

REMILLARD: [laughs hollowly] You should see my hate mail! The common folk aren't quite so sure any more that operants belong to the League of Superheroes. Have you ever watched that Alabama TV evangelist, Brother Ernest? According to him, we're nothing less than the vanguard of Antichrist, the mystery of iniquity, with all power and signs and lying wonders . . . and the Last Judgement is only five years away! It's to laugh — until you realize how many viewers the man has. And there are other antioperant movements poking their noses out of the woodwork. That outfit in Spain, Los Hijos de la Tierra, the Sons of Earth. And the Muslim fundamentalists are fully convinced we're the agents of El Shaitan. You know, Jared, operancy will bring about a profound social revolution during the Third Millennium — but only if we operants manage to survive the Second! There's a real possibility that militant normals might opt for the easy way out of the dilemma we pose . . .

ELLSWORTH: [waving out a match and snorting smoke] Don't give me that eschatological bullshit! Defeatism? From somebody who had the finest Jebbie education lavished on him? [Gestures to photo portrait of Teilhard de Chardin by Karsh of Ottawa.] From somebody who sopped up Papa Pierre's nostalgie de l'unité and global consciousness and optimistic expectation of Omega like a thirsty young sponge? Don't talk poppycock! You swelled heads are a challenge for us normals, but we're going to work it out. This isn't the Dark Ages, and the hysterical fools don't rule.

REMILLARD: No. Thank God, they don't. You'll have to make allowances for me, Jared. I'm afraid I've always had a tendency to fall into negativism and intellectual agonizing when the going gets tough. That's more or less why I came to see you.

ELLSWORTH: And here I thought it was to atone for your shameful neglect of your old teacher all these years.

REMILLARD: I need a very specialized kind of moral advice.

None of the ethicists at Dartmouth had the foggiest notion of what I was talking about. Their counsel was worthless.

ELLSWORTH: Was it really! Oh, the arrogance of the intellectual elite. Nobody has problems like *you* have problems. I always think of John von Neumann on his deathbed, deciding to convert. Is he thinking humbly about making his peace? Is he awed at the imminence of the Infinite? No. He says, 'Get me a *smart* priest.'

REMILLARD: [smiling] So they brought him a Jesuit, of course.

ELLSWORTH: [sighs] I'll bet it still cost him an extra half hour in purgatory. But never mind that. What's *your* bitch?

REMILLARD: There are two of them, Jared, with both universal and particular application. The first goes under the seal of confession.

ELLSWORTH: Uh-*huh*.

REMILLARD: It concerns a matter we've already touched on. Suppose I know the identity of a metapsychic criminal. But the way I found this person out was by mental intrusion: reading the secret thoughts. A deliberate violation of which our crook was unaware.

ELLSWORTH: This is your great moral dilemma? Same thing as stealing a letter that incriminates. The theft is wrong.

REMILLARD: I acknowledge the guilt. That's not the problem. If it was a letter I stole, I could send it to somebody in authority who could take action. When you steal thoughts things aren't so easy.

ELLSWORTH: No.

REMILLARD: Aside from my reading this person's mind and discovering the general fact of wrongdoing, there is no proof whatsoever of the person's guilt. He was not fantasizing, because I can see the effects of his crimes quite clearly. But the perpetrator is ordinarily an excellent screener − you know about that? okay − and most probably no other honest operant person has the least inkling what he has been up to. There is no corroborating evidence of crime, nothing that would stand up in a court of law. Some of the things he's done wouldn't even fall under our present criminal code. For instance, there's no law against mind-to-mind mayhem; at most, our courts would view it as simple or aggravated assault, with the injury not provable. So what am I going to do?

ELLSWORTH: [expels smoke slowly] Neat.

REMILLARD: I thought you'd like it. Objectively, that is. It's Shit City when you're on the inside looking out.

ELLSWORTH: This metapsychic monster of depravity. He's intimately known to you? I mean, you're close enough so that there's absolutely no possibility that you've misunderstood the situation?

REMILLARD: The person is a relative.

ELLSWORTH: Uh-*huh*. And we are dealing with very serious moral matters?

REMILLARD: The most serious.

ELLSWORTH: Obviously, you can't haul this person down to your local police station and – uh – turn his mind inside out.

REMILLARD: Obviously not. First, he would probably kill me if I tried it. Secondly, even if I did succeed in wringing a confession out of him – say with the help of operant friends – it would be inadmissible evidence. In the United States, one may not be forced to incriminate oneself.

ELLSWORTH: The only logical recourse is to try to nail him with some evidence that's concrete. Do as the government snoops do: use the illegally obtained information to scratch up other stuff that *will* hold up in court. You understand – hem! – that I'm not advising you to do anything sinful.

REMILLARD: But . . . I couldn't.

ELLSWORTH: You couldn't, or you wouldn't? Do you mean you're too busy to see justice done? You've got *other* things to do?

REMILLARD: [doggedly] Yes. I have duties. Obligations to the metapsychic operant community. To evolving humanity as a whole. To find evidence against this one miserable bastard might be impossible. There might not be any. Searching for it could alert him and endanger me. Endanger my work.

ELLSWORTH: You seriously believe he'd try to kill you?

REMILLARD: Or do me grave mental damage.

ELLSWORTH: You are never morally obligated to put yourself in danger in order to do good. Caritas non obligat cum tanto incommodo. One can assume such an obligation freely, as officers of the law do, but a private individual does not have such a duty.

REMILLARD: [sighs] I thought not.

ELLSWORTH: On the other hand, Christ told us we're blessed when we give up our life for our friends. It is the ultimate magnification of love. Of course, he was propounding a behavioural ideal . . . The valiant thing is not always the prudent thing. As you say, you have your work, and it is undoubtedly important.

REMILLARD: I – I can't just stand by and let him get away with what he's done! He may do it again.

ELLSWORTH: You could be patient. Bide your time and watch.

REMILLARD: I'm so distracted by other things. This is . . . so small compared to the other problems I have to deal with. So damned personal. I pushed it aside earlier when all I had were suspicions, and that was wrong. My negligence cost lives. Now that I'm certain about him, there doesn't seem to be anything I can *do*.

ELLSWORTH: You think you're the only one who ever faced this? It's old, Denis! Old as the human race. Listen to King David: 'Be not vexed over evildoers. Trust in the Lord and do good. Commit to the Lord your way; trust in him and he will act. He will make justice dawn for you like the sun; bright as the noonday shall be your vindication.'

REMILLARD: This evildoer is my brother.

ELLSWORTH: Oh, son.

REMILLARD: It may be my fault he's like this. I never liked him. I never tried to show him that what he was doing was wrong. When I was a kid, I was relieved to get away from home and come here, away from him. When I was a grown man I still avoided him, even though I knew he had deliberately suppressed the mind-powers of my other young brothers and sisters. I was afraid. I still am.

ELLSWORTH: You should get your siblings away from his influence.

REMILLARD: I tried. Only one of them is legally an adult, and she won't come. He's mesmerized her. The others . . . I tried to convince my mother to come away with them. I know she wanted to, but she still refused. He's influenced her, too. I can't force them.

ELLSWORTH: Then you've done all you can for now. Keep working on your mother and the older sister but don't do anything to endanger them . . . You really do think there's further danger from this brother of yours?

REMILLARD: I suspect that he's killed certain individuals who were a threat to his business. I know for a certainty that he killed three of my sisters who defied him.

ELLSWORTH: Oh, my God. If I was in your shoes, I expect I'd go for the sonuvabitch with a shotgun and a bag of rifled slugs.

REMILLARD: No, you wouldn't. Neither would I. That's the hell of it . . . All right, Jared, let's table this one. All I can do is follow your advice and wait. Now this second problem is by no means as grave, so let's discuss it ex confessio —

ELLSWORTH: Don't you want your absolution?

REMILLARD: Oh . . . I didn't really think of this dialogue as an actual confession. I only put you under the seal to protect you from any hazardous obligation you might otherwise have felt constrained to assume.

ELLSWORTH: The mention of grace embarrasses the learned psychiatrist! It never occurs to you to accept the forgiveness of Christ. You're like millions of other educated Catholics, Denis. You've kept the sense of guilt but not the sense of sin, and absolution without *solution* looks like a cop-out to you. It seems too damned easy.

REMILLARD: Maybe.

ELLSWORTH: But that's what grace is all about. It's a gift and a mystery. We're allowed to take it if we're sorry — even if we can't undo the evil we've done. A psychiatrist tries to offer solutions to guilt, but very often, as in your case, there *are* no solutions. That's where we priests have the advantage. We can channel the grace even if you feel you don't deserve it.

REMILLARD: [laughs softly] A spatiotemporal sexternion.

ELLSWORTH: Say *what*?

REMILLARD: God can be coerced. Never mind. It's just a dynamic-field-theory in-joke.

ELLSWORTH: You want the absolution or not? For the neglect and the violation.

REMILLARD: Lay it on me.

ELLSWORTH: [Prays in a low voice and gestures.] All right, what's the second problem?

REMILLARD: Do I have an obligation to reproduce? To have offspring?

ELLSWORTH: You're *serious*?

REMILLARD: It's been pointed out to me – by my busybody Uncle Rogi, as well as by an esteemed Soviet colleague named Tamara Sakhvadze – that inasmuch as I'm going to be twenty-eight years old next week, I should marry and father children in order to propagate my undeniably superior genes.

ELLSWORTH: Uh – the idea doesn't appeal to you?

REMILLARD: Not really. I've always been much more interested in intellectual stimulation than sex. The occasional biological urge distracted me, but it was easily squelched. I've never felt passionately attracted to a woman – or to a man, either. Frankly, the whole sexual thing seems rather a nuisance. You squander so much energy in it that could be devoted to more productive pursuits. God knows, I don't seem to have enough hours in the day for the work that has to be done!

ELLSWORTH: The Jews of the Old Testament were given the solemn duty to increase and multiply. But this part of the Old Law wasn't carried over into the New. No one is obliged to procreate now.

REMILLARD: Two persons whose opinion I value highly think otherwise. One is Tamara, who is a Neo-Marxist. The other is Urgyen Bhotia, who was a Tibetan lama and now professes an idealistic humanism.

ELLSWORTH: I can see why both of them might believe as they do. The good of society, as opposed to that of the individual, is paramount in both their faiths. Christianity – and Western civilization as a whole – gives the individual sovereignty in reproductive matters. On the other hand, having disposed of obligation, let us proceed to the more delicate matter of the most perfect choice . . . Let me ask you a question that's cheeky but not impertinent: Just how special *are* you?

REMILLARD: My metapsychic armamentarium has been rather painstakingly assayed. It was compared with that of known metapsychics all over the world in a study just completed by the University of Tokyo. My higher faculties exceed those of everyone else by several orders of magnitude. I am fertile, and there's a reasonable expectation that I would pass my alleles for powerful metafunction on to my offspring – particularly if my mate were highly endowed mentally herself.

ELLSWORTH: [breaks off in coughing fit and sets pipe aside] Well! In general, one might compare your case to that of certain royal alliances in the old days. When marriages were made for beneficial political considerations. Peace-making and the like. I recall that Queen Jadwiga of Poland was deeply in love with a certain prince but married Jagiello, the Grand Duke of Lithuania, in order to unite the two countries, bring the pagan Lithuanians to Christianity, and save her kingdom from the threat of the Teutonic Knights. Her act was self-sacrificing – the more perfect choice. She had no moral obligation to do it, though.

REMILLARD: And what about me? I'm a free man, not a goddam optimal phenotype!

ELLSWORTH: You have a right to your individuality. If marriage is repugnant, you may certainly remain single. On the other hand —

REMILLARD: Well?

ELLSWORTH: Your preference for the solitary life may be selfish. Even unhealthy. You were always too cerebral as a boy, and now – forgive me – you've grown up to be a rather atypical man.

REMILLARD: Tamara and Glenn Dalembert say I'm a cold fish. Urgyen says I have an unfortunate proclivity for the inward-trending spirituality of the East, which is contrary to the loving globalism that must characterize those in the forefront of mental evolution.

ELLSWORTH: Good heavens . . . I wonder if your lama has read Teilhard?

REMILLARD: It wouldn't surprise me a damn bit.

ELLSWORTH: I won't belabour an obvious point. But much is expected of those to whom much is given. In the matter of the more perfect choice. And there is the love. Your Tibetan friend was right about that. I'm sure you feel that you love humanity in the abstract, Denis. Your sense of duty testifies to it. But a person like you . . . you need to know love in the concrete sense as well. Marriage and family life are the most usual pathway to love's fulfillment. But if you are certain it would be impossible for you —

REMILLARD: I'm — I'm not certain.

ELLSWORTH: Perhaps you're only afraid.

REMILLARD: My uncle, the matchmaker, has even suggested a woman he felt would be the perfect mate. She's a colleague of mine at Dartmouth. I laughed at him, of course. But then I checked out her assay, and it was amazing how her metafunctions were strong in areas where my own are weakest. Psychocreativity, for example. She's a brilliant woman. She's my temperamental opposite, however, and — and sexually experienced, whereas I am not.

ELLSWORTH: Oh. Does the poor girl have any notion that you're considering her as the royal consort in this grand eugenic scheme?

REMILLARD: Certainly not. I did the analysis with complete objectivity and discussed it with my closest colleague, who concurred as to the young woman's suitability. My — my larger obligations to evolving humanity were also a subject of discussion. My genes. There is an undeniable tendency of evolution to proceed in jumps, rather than small, gradual increments. And I'm one of the jumps.

ELLSWORTH: Are you, by George! Denis, there's something terribly surreal about this conversation. You aren't a set of privileged gonads and this young woman you evaluated is not a mere source of superior ova. You can't ask her to marry you if you don't love her.

REMILLARD: Why not? Arranged marriages have been the rule among most human societies from time immemorial. She would have to agree, of course. But I presume that she would see the genetic advantages of our union as readily as my other colleagues did.

467

ELLSWORTH: Denis! Listen to me. You're not prize cattle. You'll have to live and work together and raise children.

REMILLARD: I don't know why one couldn't research marriage just like any other subject. There have been intensive studies of the psychodynamics of stable, mutually satisfying conjugal relationships. The most questionable factor would be Lucille's sexual sophistication. We'd have to deal frankly with its potentially inhibitory influence upon my libido.

ELLSWORTH: Lucille! So she does have a name. And do you think she's attractive?

REMILLARD: [surprised] Well, yes. I guess she is, in a rather austere way. Funny – her character isn't austere at all. I think one might call her passionate. She has a temper, too. I'd have to – to modify some of my mannerisms. I'm kind of a snot, you know.

ELLSWORTH: [laughs] By all means, modify. Does Lucille like you at all?

REMILLARD: She used to actively depise me . . . I was a trifle tactless in urging her to join our group in the early days. We hit it off better now. She's accepted her own operancy, which was quite a problem for her when she was younger. She may still be somewhat afraid of me. I'd have to work on that.

ELLSWORTH: Denis – you've made your decision. Just let love be part of it.

REMILLARD: I'm sure we'll work very hard learning to love one another. The children will help. It'll be fascinating to analyse the penetrance of the various metapsychic traits in the offspring. And she and I would begin operant conditioning of the fetuses in utero, of course, and evaluate preceptorial techniques as we train the infants. It'll be the metapsychic equivalent of Piaget's research. Lucille should be fascinated.

ELLSWORTH: I'm going to pray my head off for your poor little kids. And for you and Lucille, too.

REMILLARD: Do better than that, Jared. Marry us. I'll let you know the date just as soon as Lucille and I work everything out. It shouldn't take long.

468

8

From the Memoirs of
Rogatien Remillard

On the face of it, their marriage should have been a disaster.

Decreed by inhuman entities from another star, sordidly abetted by me, arranged in a coolly rational agreement between two mature young persons who were not even faintly fond of one another, and undertaken for the sake of an abstraction, the union of Denis Remillard and Lucille Cartier, when judged by the sentimental criteria of the late twentieth century in the United States of America, was peculiar to the nth degree.

The media came breathlessly scurrying to chronicle what they hoped was the first great metapsychic affaire d'amour . . . only to have the principals dismiss all inquiry into the romantic aspects of their betrothal and dwell instead upon the heritability of mental traits. The eyes of the interviewers glazed over as the putative lovebirds discussed assortative mating, the differentiation between penetrance and expressivity on the one hand and dominance and epistasis on the other, and the uncertainty of positive eugenics. Confronted with such esoterica, gossip columnists and 'human interest' video scavengers beat a hasty retreat. A sedate article dealing with the genetic rationale of the Remillard–Cartier nuptials eventually appeared in *Nature*.

On 22 July 1995, Lucille and Denis were wed in Hanover's quaint fieldstone-Gothic Catholic church. The ceremony was attended in person by the families and colleagues of the couple, and viewed through excorporeal excursion by an undisclosed number of operants scattered throughout the globe. The bride wore a tailleur suit of pale blue linen and the groom a two-button lounge suit of navy summer worsted. They were attended by Dr Glenn Dalembert and Dr Ume Kimura. A wedding supper took place at the Hanover Inn, after which the bridal couple departed for a symposium on operant educational techniques being held in Brussels. The bride's diminutive bouquet of forget-me-nots and white mignonette was caught by Dr Gerard Tremblay, the Metapsychology Department's ingenious public-relations maven, and he married an operant colleague named Emilie Bouchard later that year.

When Denis and Lucille returned from their brief academic honeymoon, they lived for some months in the Dartmouth faculty apartments. Early in 1996, at my suggestion, they bought the big old house at 15 East South Street, near my bookshop. After furnishing it to their taste and organizing what they called a Preliminary Metapsychic Prenatal Curriculum, they began to make babies with the same competence that they brought to their experimental work. Philip was born in 1997 and Maurice in 1999. A stillbirth in 2001 was the occasion of great sorrow; but the couple assuaged their disappointment by doing a revision and update of the Prenatal Curriculum and the first outline for their joint opus, *Developmental Metapsychology*. The next child, Severin, was born in 2003; two years later came Anne, then another miscarriage, then Catherine in 2009 and Adrien in 2011 – at which point Denis and Lucille prematurely judged their reproductive duty to be completed. The six offspring were all metapsychic prodigies as well as healthy and scrappy Franco—American kids nurtured by parents who loved them dearly.

And loved each other.

Oh, yes. Denis had maintained all along that love could be learned if both parties were determined, and he was right. I never pried into their sex life – which one presumes they managed as efficiently as they did everything else – but I did spend many hours each month in their company and in that of their growing brood. They came to love each other devotedly as husband and wife, and each was the other's best friend – which is much rarer.

If I were asked to point out the principal factor leading to the success of their unorthodox union, I would say the *politeness*. From the beginning, they adhered to a self-imposed rule that they would always behave towards each other with care and consideration, as though one spouse were the honoured guest of the other. All disagreements would be debated logically, with as much heat as necessary, but without personal reproaches or fits of sulking. There would be no casual rudeness, no flippancy, no baiting or other psychological game-playing at the other's expense, and absolutely no taking the other person for granted. In the early part of their marriage, when they were still adapting, their relationship seemed to me to have a 'more charitable than thou' artificiality – even a comical Alphonse-and-Gaston aspect. After all, at this point in history one expected a certain breezy camaraderie between husband and wife. Yet here were these two highly idiosyncratic scientists – the one capable of freezing the ballocks of a brass baboon with his coercion, the other possessed of a temper that could literally set a house afire – conducting their domestic affairs in an atmosphere of courtly gentility that Queen Victoria might have thought a trifle extreme.

I called it weird; but then I had been brought up in the rough-and-tumble menage of Onc' Louie and Tante Lorraine. I was further amazed when Denis and Lucille carried their exquisite civility over into their relationship with their children. Later, I understood what a brilliant behavioural ploy the courtesy was. (And of course a highly structured family and social system has characterized the majority of human operants ever since the Intervention.) In a home where emotional nuances are almost continually broadcast by the minds of operant family members (shielding requiring effort and being an art only gradually learned by the young), there is a 'crowded' ambiance that demands individual restraint and a reserved manner of action. Ume Kimura explained to me that in Japan, which in those days had an enormous population crammed into a very small area, similar extremes of politeness prevailed. Etiquette, some wag has said, is just an effective way to keep people from killing each other. Strong operants such as Denis and Lucille knew instinctively that they would have to live by more formal rules than normals, and so would their children.

The politesse, far from putting walls between my nephew and his wife, smoothed what might otherwise have been a stormy or even calamitous first year of marriage. In the

471

beginning they had only professional respect for one another, a goal mutually agreed upon, and a listing of theoretically compatible character traits that Denis wryly dubbed 'Sonnet from the Portuguese, Computer-Enhanced'. They were telepaths, bound to attain the deepest knowledge of each other's virtues and flaws, and so for them there was no glamour-tinged first phase of wedded life, no seeing the Beloved Other as a marvel of perfection; conversely, there was no posthoneymoon letdown. Since they were both mature and motivated, they worked hard to modify grating mannerisms and habits, made allowances for irreconcilable frailties, and strove continually to bolster the ego of the partner. From this initial effort soon came an easing of friction, and also, I have no doubt, the intense pleasure of sexual mutuality – the same as Ume and I enjoyed during our time together.

Later, when Lucille and Denis began to really know one another, there was fondness – and still later, love. They never experienced the consuming thunderbolt that struck me when I first saw Elaine; nor could their love compare in intensity to Marc's helpless physical passion for Cyndia Muldowney, or Jon's consummate metapsychic union with Dorothea Macdonald, the woman known to Milieu historians as Illusio Diamond Mask. Instead, Denis and Lucille seemed to grow slowly together. Their minds plaited, remaining individual but each supporting and enhancing the other with shared strength – almost like the mythical red brier and white brier that entwined and grew in a straight dual trunk towards the sun, blooming in arboreal splendour rather than in a tangled thorny sprawl upon the earth, as lesser roses did.

Lucille was always the braver; Denis was wiser. He was glacially efficient and just; she was fervently high-minded, with a greater creative insight. In later life he was retiring and scholarly; she became the grande dame of metapsychic society, as brilliant (and controversial) as their last child, Paul, who was conceived after the Intervention and nurtured in utero on the exotic mental precepts of the Galactic Milieu.

Together, Denis and Lucille wrote six landmark studies

of human metapsychology. They were personally instrumental in bringing about the Intervention itself. Denis died as a martyr to Unity without really having known Unity. Lucille lives on in this Centennial Intervention Year, an honoured pioneer and formidable clan matriarch. Their legacy is enormous, but its undoubted culmination is in their descendants – justifying the great gamble they embarked upon back in 1995. Their children became the Seven Founding Magnates of the Human Polity. Among their grandchildren were Jon, who was called a saint by both exotic and human minds, and Marc, who was called the Angel of the Abyss.

And now there are two more generations – Marc's children, Hagen and Cloud, and their newborn offspring – all carrying the precious genes for superlative metafunction as well as self-rejuvenation – which Denis never dreamt of in his wildest fancies as he and Lucille exchanged their vows.

I dedicate this memoir to all Remillards, living and dead, and most especially to the one who is both.

9

New York City, Earth
6 November 1996

Kieran O'Connor was old enough to remember when presidential candidates made their victory or concession speeches on the day following the election. But here it was, only 11.45 P.M. at the General's campaign headquarters in San Francisco, and the race was decided already. The Republican candidate – Kieran O'Connor's candidate – had been defeated. But Kieran was well content.

The four quadrants of the Sony split screen on the wall of Warren Griffith's Manhattan townhouse switched from varied depictions of network pundits commenting on the 292 electoral votes safely in Democrat hands to a single image of a handsome, silver-haired man. CBS, NBC, ABC and SNN were opting to telecast Lloyd Baumgartner's concession speech live.

Kieran reached for the remote control. It lay between his stockinged feet on the littered cabriole cocktail table. When Kieran cancelled the mute, the measured accents of General Baumgartner filled the room. He delivered his brief announcement in perfect extempore style, his eyes unwavering as he looked directly into the cameras, his manner tranquil in defeat. He thanked the voters who had given him a majority of the popular vote and nearly carried him to an upset victory. He thanked the party that had chosen him as its standard-bearer, thanked his devoted campaign staff, and thanked his gentle-faced wife Nell, who stood at his right shoulder, smiling with tears in her eyes. Baumgartner did not say that he would be back in the running again for the fateful presidential race in the year 2000, but his partisans and political opponents alike took that fact for granted. His rival, Stephen Piccolomini, had won the presidency riding on the coattails of the retiring incumbent, but he had not rolled up the expected landslide; his margin was a precarious twelve electoral votes, and his party retained only a two-seat majority in the Senate.

'Next time,' muttered Warren Griffith. 'Next time you're in, General. And so are we.'

The speech ended to applause and the split screen showed pan shots as the network cameras swept over Baumgartner's campaign workers, who packed the ballroom of the famous old St Francis Hotel. Some of the people were weeping, but others stomped and cheered as if for a victory, and dozens of hand-lettered signs waved on high, proclaiming:

THE BEST IS YET TO COME!

When the vice-presidential candidate approached the lectern for his turn at the microphone, Kieran flicked the remote's instant-replay pad, programmed it for five minutes, and watched Baumgartner once again declare himself defeated. Then Kieran turned off the Sony and the wall-screen went back to being an excellent counterfeit of Fuseli's *The Nightmare*, 1781 version. Griffith, who was the chairman of Roggenfeld Acquisitions and one of Kieran's principal strategists, liked that LCD projection so much that he'd had it on for nearly six months. There had been jokes about it when Kieran and Viola Northcutt arrived early in the evening for the election-night vigil.

Now Griffith got up from his chair and said, 'We *still* deserve to celebrate!' He padded off into the kitchen and returned with a bottle of Pol Roger and three glasses. The two guests pretended to be surprised, just as socially proper telepaths all over the world did under similar circumstances. Griffith said, 'Our candidate did not lose. He merely didn't win emphatically enough.' Untwisting the wire, he eased out the cork and restrained the overflow with psychokinetic expertise. Then he made a respectful gesture to Kieran, calling for a toast.

Kieran O'Connor nodded and his severe features softened as he watched the bubbles rise. Catching an unvoiced hint, Warren Griffith flopped back into the wingback chair he had occupied throughout most of the evening. Viola Northcutt was curled up in the corner of the leather sofa opposite Kieran, unshod feet neatly tucked under her camel's-hair skirt. Somewhere in the townhouse an antique clock chimed three in quavery deadened tones.

I liked the placards that Baumgartner's people made, said Kieran. Let's drink to that: 'The best is yet to come'.

The others repeated his spoken words. Kieran sipped his champagne, but Griff and Viola tossed theirs down and went for refills.

'I'll hand it to the General,' Viola said. 'He was strong. A lot better than we ever dared hope.'

'That viewing-with-alarm speech fingering the Meta Brain Trusts's influence on the Democrats struck just the right note,' Griff said. 'Shot our boy up a good sixteen per cent in the polls. It was a gamble, but we really proved that America's love affair with the operant clique is just about kaput. Before this campaign, I doubt that one voter in a hundred knew what metacoercion was – or redactive probing either.'

'Neither did the General,' Northcutt put in with a cynical grin. She was a heavyset blonde woman in her late forties, one of Kieran's earliest recruits, who had become his best operant head-hunter. Viola had vetted all the presidential campaign personnel, both operant and normal, to make certain that only loyalists would be able to exert influence on Baumgartner. Even so, the General had proved less psychologically malleable than they had hoped.

'Before we lock Baumgartner in as our millennial candidate,' Kieran said, 'we're going to have to make certain that he had no suspicion that his mind was manipulated during this campaign. We may have pressed too hard when he balked at the anti-Soviet speech in October.'

Viola shrugged. 'Len and Neville felt it was important that the General express doubt about the Kremlin's commitment to peace. We had the posthypnotic suggestion done prudently. Doc Presteigne handled it when the General had gas for some root-canal work.'

'But it didn't work,' Kieran said. 'You forgot that Baumgartner was a warm chum of the cosmonauts back in the pre-Mars days. He sincerely believes that the Russians have abandoned their expansionist philosophy. You can't depend upon a posthyp to overcome a strong conviction any more than you can coerce over the long term.'

'How will we convince him, then?' Viola asked.

Kieran extracted his feet from among the mess of coffee cups, empty beer and seltzer bottles, and snack food that crowded the cocktail table. 'When the hard-liners on the Politburo take charge, Baumgartner won't need convincing.'

'Hard-liners?' exclaimed Griff. 'Take over *when?*'

Kieran poked through a platter of ravaged deli noshes until he found a whole-meal cracker with a hard-boiled egg slice and a shaving of lox. He dabbed it artistically with mustard. 'When the present General Secretary dies . . . and civil war breaks out in Uzbekistan.'

Viola and Griff stared at him. He showed them a mental schematic with a number of key elements blanked out.

'Jesus God,' whispered Griffith.

'It's nothing you two have to concern yourselves about for a while yet,' Kieran said. He popped the tidbit into his mouth and chewed it up, then downed the remainder of the champagne. 'What you *will* have to deal with is Baumgartner's immediate future. Griff, I want you to find him a sinecure position on one of our foundations – say the Irons-Conrad. I want him completely divorced from the military-industrial complex and big business in the public mind. Our lad is a political philosopher now, asking questions and providing answers.'

'Speaking of which,' Viola interposed, 'we still have that matter of Baumgartner possibly suspecting that he's being manipulated. It's going to be tricky doing a deep-scan without his cooperation, you know. We've never tried it on a person who wasn't being – actively recruited to the inner circle.'

'We've got to know,' Kieran insisted. 'Whatever it takes. It's imperative that Baumgartner have no inkling of our own operancy. He'll only carry conviction in the next phases of our political campaigning if he firmly believes that operants are dangerous – a threat to normal humanity.'

Viola was frowning as she thought. 'For a proper ream-job, the subject has to be rendered unconscious for something like thirty-six hours. No way to handle that without hospitalizing him. We'll have to come up with something that will satisfy him and the PR people. Nothing psychiatric. We don't want to risk an Eagleton fuck-up.'

'Eyes,' said Griffith. 'I had an uncle, had some kind of eye thing. Terrible headaches, then lost the sight of one eye. The docs fixed him, he was good as new.'

'Sounds usable,' Viola said. 'Presteigne would know what the ailment is and how to simulate the symptoms. Very likely both the headaches and the blindness can be voodooed – by Greta, maybe. Baumgartner won't suspect a thing when we bring in our own eye specialist . . .'

Kieran nodded. 'Work it out as soon as you can. I want to keep him newsworthy. I can see him doing lecture tours and hosting fund-raisers for the by-elections in '98. There are at least four Senate seats that could go Republican in the Bible Belt if we play our cards right and pick up on the antioperant sentiment building there.'

'It'll build a lot faster,' Viola muttered, 'once we get good old Señor Araña on line!'

Griffith said:?

Viola looked guiltily at Kieran, but he lifted a dismissive hand. 'I was going to tell Griff about it anyhow.'

'A step-up in the antioperant crusade?' Griffith asked.

'Exactly,' said Kieran. 'You know that my overriding concern is to insure that operants not loyal to us are banned from government service or political office. Even more important is to stir up grassroots sentiment against the metapsychic clique. I suppose you noticed the article in the *Times* this weekend about the Swiss banking group's plans to hire telepathic investigators.'

'No! God – if they do it, the Japanese'll be next. And next thing you know, the Justice Department or the Treasury'll want their own Metasnooper Corps, and our organization will be up the well-known excremental watercourse!'

'Not if I can help it,' said Kieran O' Connor. 'Fortunately, we still have a Republican-packed Supreme Court. Next year my people in Chicago will engineer a test case to get a ruling that any form of operant screening of employees by private corporations is an invasion of privacy and unconstitutional. That will lay the groundwork for further action . . . such as the efforts of Araña. Why don't you tell Griff why we happen to be in New York, Viola?'

She grinned as she fished her suede boots out from under the cocktail table and began to put them on. 'Our great and good buddy, The Fabulous Finster, has bagged us a very big fish indeed, and he is arriving tomorrow at Kennedy with this recruit figuratively tucked under his arm. The man's name is Carlos María Araña, and he is an unfrocked Dominican, late of Madrid, where the authorities were only too willing to be rid of him.'

'Araña?' Griffith blinked. 'Hey – didn't he start that fanatical antioperant movement in Spain? What was its name – Hijos de Putas?'

Viola Northcutt guffawed. 'Come on! Hijos de la *Tierra*, Griff. The Sons of Earth. Kier figured it was time for them to open a North American branch.' She stood up, stamped her feet the rest of the way into her footgear, and brushed the crumbs from her skirt. 'We're going to play off Araña's fanaticism against Baumgartner's reasoned opposition to operant influence. The Spaniard will play dirty and Baumgartner will deplore his intolerance. I mean, we don't really want to burn the confessed operants at the stake, do we? Not yet . . . Where'd you hide our coats, Griff? Kieran and I have to get back to our platonic little nest at the Plaza and get some sleep. Our cucaracha is coming in on Iberia's early flight tomorrow and poor Finster's going to need all the help he can get.'

Kieran stood up, yawned and laughed. 'Don't you worry about a thing, Vi. Fabby's tamed Señor Araña very thoroughly. It was a tough assignment – perhaps the toughest he's ever had to handle. But he's delivered the goods.'

'They don't call him Fabulous for nothing, eh?' Warren Griffith helped Viola on with her coat, then assisted Kieran. 'I wouldn't mind meeting this Finster, Kier. If it wouldn't compromise your security arrangments, of course.'

Kieran smiled. His mind touched that of his associate, giving both reassurance and warning. 'Maybe another time, Griff. Fabby will be dead beat, and I have other matters to discuss with him before he leaves for Moscow on Friday.'

Moscow! Kier don't tell me that's the way —

'I wouldn't dream of telling you, Griff. You're a man who thinks for himself. That's why you're part of my organization. I'll be getting in touch with you soon on the Petro-Pascua acquisition.'

But Kier the man's a moderate the first reasonable Russian leader we've ever dealt with you can't —

I can. Make no mistake about it Griff if it suits my purpose and it does I can. 'Thanks a lot for playing host. Don't bother to see us out. Vi and I can find our own way.'

10

Alma-Ata, Kazakh SSR, Earth
15 September 1997

A chill settled quickly over the plaza in front of the Lenin Palace of Culture once the sun dropped behind the parched hills. Yellow leaves, prematurely fallen in the great drought that had plagued Central Asia that year, were swirled by the sharp breeze around the dusty shoes of Colonel Sergei Arkhipov, who sat on a bench near the Abai monument, waiting.

From time to time as his ulcer gnawed, Sergei would slip an antacid tablet into his mouth. What he really needed was food, but he could not leave his post until the first afternoon session of the Sixth Congress on Metapsychology ended, and Donish furnished a report upon his fellow delegates' state of mind.

Finally, people began to emerge, hurrying down the palace steps as if eager for their own suppers. Most of the longbrains went off into the park on the left, on their way to the Kazakhstan Hotel where the foreigners were being lodged. Numbers of locals, heading for the buses, came straight down Abaya Prospekt and passed directly in front of Sergei's bench. One of these was a compact young man in a green windbreaker who carried a canvas briefcase. His hair and complexion were dark and he wore a squarish black skullcap with white embroidered designs on the sides.

Deliberately, Sergei projected a thought as this man approached: Move faster blackarsed longbrain my poor stomach is devouring itself I was sure you would stay in your fucking meeting all night.

'And good evening to you, Comrade Colonel!' The young KGB agent, Kamil Donish, smiled good-humouredly and sat down on the bench. 'An outstanding panel on psycho-energetic projection's more benign aspects went a bit overtime. There was this Italian, Franco Brixen, who reported that his people at the University of Torino have been able to inhibit the growth of malignant neoplasms in rats — '

'Tishe!' hissed Sergei irritably. 'What do I care about such trivia? Tell me the mood of the operant delegates —

their feelings on the matter of the Islamic riots, especially – so that I can pass the information on to the General Secretary's aides before his speech tonight.'

'They regret our use of extreme force. But you can hardly expect them to side with Muslim fanatics who label them allies of Satan.'

'Don't play your longbrain games with me, Kamil. I'm not feeling well and I want straight answers. Are the foreign operants satisfied that we have acted properly? Do they accept our reassurances that the uprisings were isolated occurrences, and that the situation is now under control?'

Kamil's black eyes flashed. 'Comrade Colonel, you remain obstinately a man of your time. Of course they don't! The whole world can see what is going on in Uzbekistan through the mental vision of their EE adepts. The only reason that the global news reports have downplayed the matter is that there is voluntary restraint being exercised by the operants themselves. They give their local journalists the bare details of our troubles, but without sensational embellishment that might inflame world opinion. The Soviet Union is being given the benefit of the doubt! Oh, yes – there are some bleeding-hearts among the delegates who deplore our killing of the so-called innocent bystanders during the storming of the Bukhara airfield. But most of the Congress attendees are politically sophisticated persons who realize the gravity of the situation – the danger of civil war. Most nations of the world are on our side, Comrade Colonel. They have no wish to see the Central Asian Republics explode like Iran and Pakistan.'

'But do they worry about their safety here in Alma-Ata?'

'Certainly not,' Kamil said. 'They know that the nearest fighting is more than a thousand air-kilometres away. They are also aware that this is a modern city, with a minimal number of Shiite fanatics among the populace. Operants who had any doubts about their personal welfare stayed at home. The majority accepted the assurances of Academician Tamara Gawrys-Sakhvadze that Alma-Ata welcomes them even more eagerly than it did in 1992. The Comrade General Secretary can make his little speech tonight without fear of any hostile response.'

'Well, that's a relief. You longbrains are all the Secretary's darlings – the showpiece of his much vaunted policy of Otkroveyinost'. If he got a cold reception from the foreign delegates at the Congress, certain persons in Moscow would be encouraged in their attempts to discredit him.' Sergei's mind showed an image of a tightrope-walker.

'Discredit him – and us.' Sombreness spread over Kamil's face. 'You are not part of the Twentieth Directorate, Comrade Colonel, but you are quite aware of our critical role in the New Soviet Openhearted Society that the Secretary has championed. All loyal citizens have rejoiced in the new freedom and the acceptance of personal responsibility for progress. But Otkroveyinost' would be impossible without the EE monitoring function of the KGB Twentieth.'

'Oh, you are all certified heroes,' Sergei agreed archly. 'Just do your job efficiently and pinpoint the terrorist reactionaries without at the same time scaring the simpleminded to death! Especially the Muslim simple-minded.'

'Some of my co-religionists are deficient in social consciousness,' Kamil admitted. 'This modern Age of the Mind had come too quickly for them to assimilate. According to the Prophet, magic is one of the Seven Ruinous Sins – and we operant metapsychics are accused of its practice. Furthermore, it is being said that the Last Days are upon the Earth, and our appearance is one of the signals thereof. The KGB's reliance upon EE monitors inflames the reactionaries and makes even loyal Muslim citizens fearful.'

'And so the powder keg at the southern belly of the USSR grows hotter each day – and I, for one, do not see any simple solution to the mess,' Sergei said. 'Thus far, the General Secretary has been lucky. The outbreaks have been small enough to be put down by the militia or by the KGB's own Border Regiments. But if the antioperant paranoia grows, the jihad movement may spread from the Shiites to the vast numbers of Sunni Muslims in Soviet Central Asia. Then nothing less than the Red Army will suffice to control the insurrection – and we will all be in a very deep arsehole.'

Sergei's imagination drew a portrait of Marshal Yegor Kumylzhensky, the hard-liner Minister of Defence and longtime Politburo opponent of the General Secretary. The figure had horns, wolfish teeth, and brandished a tactical missile as an erection.

Kamil giggled. 'You are getting very good at that for a shortbrain, Comrade Colonel. You should take the operancy exam again sometime.'

Sergei swore and spat on the pavement. A pretty young woman passing by frowned at the uncultured behaviour.

'She labels you a crude old fart,' Kamil whispered slyly.

'I can read her mind well enough,' Sergei growled. 'As for you, you are an insubordinate blackarse who would have been shot for speaking to your superior in such a way back in the old days.'

'Old days! If those old days still prevailed, you would be waiting for American missiles to blast your family instead of revelling in Japanese VCRs and North American movies and British silver-disc music and satellite-transmitted sports programmes from half the countries of the globe. Cheer up, Comrade Colonel. It's not such a bad brave new world! Who would ever have thought that the KGB would be applauded as good guys?'

Sergei shook his head and took another antacid tablet.

Chuckling, Kamil unsnapped his briefcase and took out a minicorder. 'Here are my hushaphone comments on the opening session of the Congress and the afternoon panels. There is really nothing extraordinary going on that the General Secretary need be concerned about. We operants are worried about our image worldwide, and about the unreliability of our techniques for detecting clever psychopaths among us. We are concerned about the US government's proposal to ban operants from seeking political office. The Congress is not, by and large, worrying about the status of operants in the Soviet Union. Our nation is looked upon by most of the delegates as a progressive place, ascending rapidly into high-tech prosperity after shelving an ill-considered political experiment. Our successful juvenile suboperant screening programme is admired, as are the new schools for accelerated EE and telepathic training. The Japanese think that their operant teaching techniques are superior. Perhaps they are. Tomorrow is education day and there should be lively discussion.'

'Fuck the lot of you and your discussions,' said Sergei wearily. 'All I care about is smooth sailing for the General Secretary's speech tonight – and then two weeks' rest cure in Sochi for my poor aching gut.'

Kamil Donish arose from the bench. 'Do svedanya, then, Comrade Colonel. I'll look for you in the audience tonight. Try to calm your tummy with some nice yogurt or rice pudding before you come, though. You don't want to make your sensitive longbrain neighbours uncomfortable.'

Sergei threw an obscene mental menu suggestion of his own after the departing young agent. It was blithely ignored. Longbrains! What an arrogant and nonconformist lot they were – more loyal to each other and their global clique of do-gooders than to any motherland! The General Secretary was taking a colossal risk, pinning his policy to them. By far the majority of Soviet longbrains were not even Slavs! Look at Kamil – a Tadzhik, one of the fast-breeding Asian groups that now outnumbered the true ethnic Russians. The Twentieth Directorate of the KGB and the academic metapsychic groups swarmed with black-arses, Caucasians and Mongoloid riffraff . . . but then, so did every other segment of Soviet society, operant or normal. What a hell of a world . . .

Not caring who overheard his dark thoughts, Colonel Sergei Arkhipov walked along Lenin Prospect to the Arman Café. He had only forty-five minutes to grab a bite to eat, and then he would have to go out to the Alma-Ata KGB HQ and liaise with the locals prior to the General Secretary's arrival at the air terminal. His opposite number had issued a supper invitation that Sergei had declined. He wanted to coddle his stomach in peace.

He peered into the café. There was a waiting line, of course, and many of the persons standing there wore the red and green delegate badges of the Sixth Congress on Metapsychology. Sergei pushed past them, ready to flash his KGB card, confident of being shown immediately to an empty table.

And so he was. But as he settled down with the menu he was astounded to see another man approach his table, grinning in a cocksure fashion, and pull out a chair.

Sergei opened his mouth to put the upstart in his place. It was a dapper little fellow, obviously a foreigner, whose badge read: J. SMITH — SIMON FRASER UNIV. — VANCOUVER. His two upper incisors were comically large, like those of a squirrel.

Sergei closed his mouth. He had to. J. Smith's coercion had taken control of him as though he were a wooden marionette.

'Hey there, Sergei! How you doing, old hoss?' The Fabulous Finster snapped his fingers and a waitress rushed over with another menu before he even drew his chair up to the table. 'Been a few years since we pub-crawled in Edinburgh, eh? We've got a whole lotta catching up to do . . . By the way, you heard the sad news from Tashkent? The Grand Mufti of Central Asia was assassinated. Terrible thing. The poor old guy's head burst into flame just as he was going into the Barak-Khana Mosque and the whole goddam city's gone ape. They think some perverted metapsychic operant musta been responsible. I couldn't get out fast enough this afternoon, I'll tell you. I was lucky to get a plane . . . Well! Enough of that. What d'you say we order, eh?'

'Yes. Certainly.' Sergei heard the voice coming from faraway. Surely, he thought, it could not be his own.

Dr Pyotr Sakhvadze regarded the enormous silver platter and its contents with undisguised consternation.

'But this is a great honour for you!' the mâitre d' insisted. His Kazakh moustachios bristled and he was slightly miffed. It was obvious that the kitchen staff of the big hotel had gone to considerable trouble to produce the special tribute. 'You are the aksakal, the Whitebeard of the Feast! You must carve the dish and distribute it to the other guests, who have ordered this traditional delicacy in celebration of your eighty-third birthday. Bon appétit!'

He placed the carving tools in front of Pyotr and withdrew, full of dignity. Most of the others at the table – his grandchildren, his daughter Tamara and her colleagues the Kizims, and the three foreign guests – were applauding and laughing. Telepathic jests crackled in the aether so energetically that Pyotr could almost (but not quite) understand them.

On the platter, the braised whole lamb's head seemed to stare at him with an air of jaunty mockery. One ear was up and the other down. Quail eggs stuffed with ripe olives formed its eyes, and it had a peeled ruby pomegranate in its mouth and a collar of lacy gold paper. The head perched upon a steaming bed of besbarmak, the famous Kazakh lamb and noodle stew. Pyotr, as designated aksakal, was not only expected to serve this outlandish culinary triumph, but he was also obliged to accompany each portion of head-meat with a suitable witticism.

'We operants only think we've got troubles,' Pyotr said to the lamb's head. 'You, in your position, you *know* you've got troubles.'

Everybody laughed and radiated sympathy except for his oldest grandson Valery, whom Pyotr had teased mercilessly last week for mooning over a young woman who would have nothing to do with him. Now innocence poured from Valya's mind like watered honey, but his close-set Polish blue eyes had a suspicious gleam. So! He was the one responsible for this, was he?

Pyotr cleared his throat and continued. 'I am only a decrepit psychiatrist, not a faciocephalic surgeon. If I were to serve this head, I fear I would do it so slowly that we would be here all evening and miss the distinguished speakers who will honour us with their presence later in the Palace of Culture. And so it is with pleasure – to say nothing of relief – that I delegate the carving of this pièce de résistance to the founder of the feast, Valery Yurievich, whose idea it was to honour me in this unusual way. It is the custom, I know, for the aksakal to cut off and present to a favoured guest that anatomical portion of meat most appropriate to his nature. But alas, I cannot give my grandson the part he deserves. The chef has cooked for us the wrong end of the sheep.'

He bowed and sat down to uproarious laughter and clapping. Valery had turned red to the tips of his ears.

Tamara, who sat at the foot of the table, addressed her son. 'I left the arrangements to you, and you play undergraduate pranks! Now how are we going to eat this monstrosity?'

The American, Denis Remillard, sitting on Pyotr's right, had his strange compelling glance fixed on the swinging doors of the restaurant kitchen. He said gently, 'Allow me.' And then there was a miracle. The two sturdy waitresses who had brought the besbarmak in the first place came out again, pushing a serving cart loaded with side dishes. After distributing these, they transferred the silver platter to the cart and began to carve and fill the plates of the dinner party with the besbarmak, which turned out to be delicious. Besides the meat stew with its diamond-shaped noodles, there were bowls of fragrant broth with floating herbs, feather-light rounds of bread, spicy palov, pickled mushrooms, melon rind, and a salad of cucumbers, tomatoes, scallions and exotic green stuff. The wine, which Valery had preselected with a good deal more seriousness, was a Château Latour that brought tears of rapture to Pyotr's eyes. He forgave his grandson, and Valery led the birthday toast; and then Pyotr proposed a toast to Denis, and Denis proposed a toast to the Sixth Congress, and Tamara proposed a toast to the Seventh, which would be held the following year in Boston.

'You must go with us there, Papa,' Tamara said to Pyotr. 'We will celebrate your birthday in the American style.'

'No feasts!' Pyotr pleaded.

'If you came up to New Hampshire,' said Denis, 'we could cook you a traditional ham and baked-bean supper with pumpkin pie and whipped cream.'

The old man leaned towards the American. Being unable to converse telepathically on the intimate mode, he simply whispered. 'I think it would be a great improvement over this boiled lamb's head. I am a Georgian, you see, and our cuisine is celebrated throughout the Soviet Union. My grandchildren have been barbarized by their residence in this way station of Marco Polo . . . My dear Professor, I am so grateful to you for salvaging the dinner. None of the others would have had the mind-power to coerce the waitresses over such a distance.'

'You must call me Denis. And it was my pleasure. But I think that any one of your grandchildren, had they thought of it, would have been able to do as I did.'

Valery, Ilya, and Anna protested: *Oh NO Professor!*

Pyotr did not hear, but the expressions on the young faces were eloquent enough. 'It's true. They are growing up to be mental bullies, all three, too clever by half. They are — are — oy! I don't know the English word for what they are!'

'Whippersnappers,' Denis offered.

Pyotr was delighted. 'Yes! They think the world will leap as they snap their marvellous mental whips. You must take care, Denis, that your own new baby son does not grow up so disrespectful of his shortbrained elders.'

'We attempted a simple form of ethical guidance even before the baby was born,' Denis said seriously. 'I'll be describing the new prenatal educational techniques that my wife Lucille and I devised for Philip in a paper I'm delivering tomorrow.'

There were expressions of interest from the other academics around the table. Urgyen Bhotia said, 'I find it fascinating that you would include ethics in your prenatal curriculum. Newborns are, of course, completely self-centred. And the infant human is egotistical in its evaluation of right and wrong.'

'When the infant is a normal, that's acceptable,' Denis said. 'It may even be acceptable for the weaker operants. But' — he shrugged — 'Lucille and I weren't sure just how strong-minded our offspring would be. You may have — er — read the article in *Nature*.'

Alla and Mukar Kizim, who were friends and close associates of Tamara at the university, exchanged meaningful looks. 'It is a matter that perplexed us as well,' Alla admitted. 'We have held off having children, wishing to give their young minds the best possible guidance both before and after birth. But I think we also were somewhat fearful of not being able to control them. There have been instances among our colleagues . . .'

'In America, too,' Denis said.

'I don't think we've had much trouble in Scotland,' said Jamie MacGregor. 'Even normal Celtic parents are coercers from the word go. You hardly find a spoiled brat among us.' He hesitated, then added, 'There are crazies, though. And *I* have a paper on that.'

'Children are very precious to our people,' Tamara said. 'It is always so in lands where nature is cruel and young life is vulnerable. It has been said by some psychologists that we have been too kind . . . that our children grow up lacking in initiative and inner strength because they were coddled. And when they become adults, and find how harsh life is, they either strike back and become cruel themselves or else bend dumbly to the yoke.'

'Each nation,' Urgyen said, 'has its own strength and weakness. The roots of both are in the relationship of parents and children. I think Denis's talk of ethical training for the infant mind will be among the most significant to be delivered at this Congress. It will be my pleasure to lead a symposium on operant-nonoperant moral relationships. In light of the Tashkent tragedy, the subject is appropriate.'

There was an uncomfortable silence. Finally, Annushka Gawrys said impulsively, 'It *couldn't* have been one of us who did that awful thing! It's not possible!'

Jamie MacGregor said, 'Lassie, I'm sorry. But it is possible. My dear friend Nigel Weinstein has had to retire from active metapsychic work just because it's possible.'

'It could have been a provocateur,' Tamara said. She switched to mental speech, even though it would exclude her father: *Our internal politics . . . you visitors see only the bright new face of the Soviet Union the Secretary's sweeping changes in the economy the unrestricted flow of information the new pride taken by workers inspired by Otkroveyinost' . . . but there is a faction in the Kremlin bitterly opposing the Secretary as a traitor to Marxist-Leninist ideology and they are allied with senior militarists who resent their drastic budget cuts and diminished power . . . Marshal Kumylzhensky aspires to head the*

Politburo himself and has deep hatred for Kirill Pazukhin Chairman KGB and General Secretary it is suspected that some of the Islamic rioting was fomented by agents Glavnoye Razvedyvatelnoye Upravleniye so as to discredit the Twentieth Directorate assassination of Grand Mufti would fit in with such a scheme . . .

Urgyen Bhotia was incredulous: This Marshal would toy with civil war just to bring down a political enemy? He would cause the death of thousands of citizens merely to consolidate his power in Moscow?

Mukar Kizim said: It is only non-Slavic people the black-arses like us who die.

Jamie MacGregor asked: What'll stop this fool Marshal?

Tamara said: He is 73 years old . . . But his lackey Vadim Terekhov head of the GRU is only 56 and a Politburo aspirant. The consensus is that the General Secretary himself a man loved and respected by almost all the proletariat is the greatest bulwark against the militarists and diehard Marxist ideologues.

Denis Remillard said: I hope he has good bodyguards . . . especially tonight.

Tamara said: Tonight the nine of us the strongest minds I am able to trust utterly will guard him.

The General Secretary was showing signs of winding down now. He had set aside his notes to address the Congress delegates less formally, and Finster whispered, 'It won't be long now. I hope those TV cameras stay on close-up for the big finale. We want this to be the zap seen round the world.'

Colonel Sergei Arkhipov was incapable of vocal response. He was a skull-prisoner, no longer in control of his own body and knowing he would soon die. Nevertheless he watched the Killer Squirrel's professional modus operandi with fascinated detachment through the windows of his own eye sockets; and from time to time he even asked mental questions, which his captor answered quite frankly.

At supper, the Squirrel had given a brief account of his life – the creepy child, the third-rate entertainer and drug addict, the obscene 'redemption' through bonding to the

American megalomaniac, the progression from psychic spy to blackmailing suborner to specialist in wet affairs . . . It appealed to Sergei's mordant Russian sense of humour that the Squirrel's master, the archcapitalist exploiter O'Connor, should be the great enemy of metapsychic globalism. And in Moscow the zealous Marxist ideologue Kumylzhensky shared the identical viewpoint! If this crucial mission of the Killer Squirrel succeeded, both O'Connor and Kumylzhensky would win. Everyone else would lose. Oh, it was rich.

Four other KGB agents stood there in the wings of stage right with Sergei and Fabian Finster, and all including the Squirrel wore on their lapels the golden shield with stylized sword and red star, surmounted by the black IX of the Ninth Directorate. It was the insignia of the unit assigned to the security of top Party leaders. To any casual observer backstage in the Lenin Palace of Culture, the men — including the rather undersized one in the flashy double-breasted glen plaid — were part of the General Secretary's bodyguard.

To the subordinate four, the Killer Squirrel was simply invisible. This was a most useful faculty for an assassin to have, but Finster had explained to Sergei that there were limitations. The mental exertion required to project the illusion increased with the cube of the distance from the operant's brain. Thus it was very easy to render oneself invisible (or psychically disguised) when close to a normal observer, but relatively difficult to manage when the observer was farther away. Finster was also limited by having to retain his coercive hold on Sergei himself. Effectively, this limited his invisibility radius to less than nine metres. Thus he could not simply walk out on to the palace stage and terminate the General Secretary without being detected. Nor could he fulfil the special purpose of his assignment by means of an ambush. It was O'Connor's plan to incite antioperant feeling by making the assassinations seem to be an operant conspiracy, and so Finster had to play a part.

Sergei had been very surprised to learn that Finster was armed. He assumed that the longbrain would kill with astral fire, generated by mind-power alone. As all the world knew, this was the way that the Scottish operant had worked. But no. The Squirrel had explained that he was quite impotent in the conjuring up of mental fire. It was a knack, and his talents ran along other lines. Nor could he kill by cooking brains or stopping hearts, lethal aptitudes possessed by his master, O'Connor, among others. Finster explained that these killing methods, while tidy and much more efficient than psychocreative flaming, would not have the propaganda impact of the latter. So Finster intended to use an ingenious infernal device to *simulate* astral fire, and the General Secretary would – as the Grand Mufti before him – seem to die from the assault of an operant terrorist.

Tell me something belkushka, Sergei asked now. Were you there in Edinburgh to kill Professor MacGregor?

Yes, said Finster. But not at the press conference. By then it was too late, and I only went to provide a firsthand account of the affair to my principal. I tried to kill MacGregor six times during the months preceding his announcement. Each time I failed. He was being guarded.

By his metapsychic compères?

No . . . By somebody else. It was worrying. I never told the Boss about that bit.

This Boss. Why do you serve him? Kill for him?

Irony. I love him.

Now do not balls about with me! Why?

Why do you work for the KGB?

At first I was patriotic. Then I enjoyed the power. Then I was stuck in the shit like everybody else. Then . . . [laughter] when we were *transformed* it was just a job. Just a job . . .

You don't enjoy it now that you're respectable cops?

No.

That's where we differ then Sergei. I've always liked my job! This assignment's the biggest kick yet.

Belkushka. Little killer squirrel.

Laughter.

Out in the auditorium, the delegates were laughing, too. There was a smattering of applause for a particularly well-chosen piece of comic relief delivered by the General Secretary as he approached the end of his speech.

Finster pinched off the KGB colonel's maundering thoughts and concentrated on the matter at hand. Behind the Commie leader, seated at a long table decorated with red bunting and bouquets of autumn flowers, were ten or a dozen people – high mucky-mucks of the Metapsychic Congress with a few odd spouses and older kids. One seat was empty. The head lady, after introducing the Comrade Secretary, had gone off into the left wings. She was a plump, auburn-haired woman with a distracted overcast to her well-guarded mind, but she did not project the dangerous vibes Finster had learned to beware of. Most of the others seated on the platform seemed similarly harmless: an old guru type, four assorted Russkies, Jamie MacGregor, a Russky couple, and three kids in their late teens or early twenties who had to be the offspring of Madame Chairperson. No threat in the lot, for all their vigilance. He'd take care of them with the mind-buster, his great projection of sensory confusion.

The only potential joker in the pack sat at the far end of the table. Unlike the others, he was dressed formally in a dinner jacket and had a cold, uptight little smile on his face. Oh, yeah. Give Denis Remillard a guitar and a mike, take away the chromalloy bear-trap mind, and you'd have a young John Denver! Talk about a monster in wimp's clothing . . . Remillard would have to be handled. He was at extreme coercion range and probably uncoercible anyway. So stick to the mind-buster, but thicken it to max between Remillard and the podium. Then? Would the prof try a hit? He wasn't a known antiaggression freak like MacGregor or Madame Sakhvadze. Fact was, he almost never demonstrated his faculties in public, or even talked about them. Which was bad.

All right, just go for it. Speed and surprise and *fwoosh* and then haul ass for dear life to the big ZIL ticking over outside the stage door of the palace.

Ready . . .

'You have changed the course of world history,' the General Secretary told the Metapsychic Congress. 'In six short years you have given fresh hope and a vision of a golden Third Millennium to all nations, large and small. Thanks to you – and to others who had the good sense to understand and implement your dream – we have seen the end of the suicidal arms race and the beginning of true globular social thinking. But let us not deceive ourselves. There are still grave problems confronting humanity in many parts of the world, and some of them pose as great a threat to civilization as the late, unlamented nuclear deterrent. There is a terrible plague in Africa. There is continued bloodshed and terrorism in parts of the Islamic world. There is hunger and suffering caused by extremes of weather. There is a growing shortage of energy. And, yes . . . there is even controversy over the proper role of operant persons in relation to the larger human community. We must confront these problems honestly and openly, and work together to solve them. We must never lose sight of the fact that we all belong to the human family. All of us share the wish that the future will bring to us and our children, peace, prosperity and mutual respect. I thank you. I thank you for *everything*.'

The delegates rose for a standing ovation and Finster turned to the four agents standing behind him. He held a silvery cylinder. The sounds it made were nearly inaudible and its needles coated with poison killed in a subtle way. The four agents, blinded and voiceless, crumpled slowly to the floor.

Sergei realized that he was next. A sudden spurt of adrenalin energized him, weakening Finster's coercive hold. Clumsily, Sergei fell against the killer and knocked the needle-gun to the floor. Finster's arm scythed out and he broke Sergei's neck with a single karate chop. Then a swift-moving foot crushed Sergei's larynx.

Paralysed and silenced, but with his mind free, Sergei watched Finster take up a huge bouquet of red roses from a folding table near the proscenium arch. Out on the stage, the General Secretary was bowing and smiling. He waved to the continuing thunder of applause. Finster approached, his mind radiating homage and loyalty, and the leader of the Soviet Union held out his hands to accept the flowers.

Sergei's lips moved. He managed a small, useless sound. His eyes caught sight of Academician Sakhvadze in the opposite wings and he *thought* at her. She started as though electrically shocked and hesitated. Fool! Sergei raged. He thought at the American – but, ah! Holy Mother! A mind-numbing surge of sensation smote him, obliterating pain and darkening his vision. Was he dead? No, not yet! He saw a flash of brilliant orange and felt an unspoken shriek of disbelief. His nervous system – that fragment of it still precariously connected to his brain – shrank from another mental assault emanating not from one mind but from thousands.

Sergei seemed to hear two titanic voices shouting. *NO! NO! NO!* The formally dressed American and Tamara Petrovna had paid for their indecision and together they were trying to support a terrible headless figure. Cowards, Sergei told them. Cowards.

NO! NO! NO! the man and Tamara begged the raging audience. The anger and sorrow swelled into a vital thing, the minds of the delegation meshed spontaneously into metaconcert and focused on the hated target.

Something was running towards Sergei.

NO! NO! NO!

It was a man, brighter than the sun. A flaming angel come for him and his sins.

NO . . .

Not an angel. Only a small man enveloped in seething energy, and then tumbling bones glowing red-hot on the boards of the stage.

From each, Sergei thought, according to his abilities. To each according to his needs.

He closed his eyes for the last time, smiling.

11

Laconia, New Hampshire, Earth
7 February 1998

As the critical years of coadunating consciousness dawned for the indigenes of planet Earth, the Milieu stepped up its psychosocial surveillance. Ever larger numbers of field-workers went planetside to track firsthand the irruptions of operancy among different population groups, gathering data on the numbers of metapsychically talented children being born, the spectrum of the various functions, and their potential strength – given optimum nurture and education.

The results of these late studies were a source of both enthusiasm and anxiety among the exotic observers. It had been known even in Earthly prehistoric times that the race had an exceptional creative component to its Mind; but the most recent samplings had begun to show just how awesome human psychocreativity might eventually prove to be. Analysts among the Krondaku were finally able to verify what the Lylmik had cavalierly stated at the inception of the Intervention scheme: humanity's mental potential undoubtedly exceeded that of any other race in the galaxy – coadunate or noncoadunate. Whether the puerile Earthlings would survive to manifest the potential was as questionable a point as ever.

Exotic field-workers on Earth were usually Simbiari or Poltroyans, since they had the most humanoid form and so required the least expenditure of psychic effort in projecting illusory bodies. Often the Poltroyans did not even bother with mental disguise. They were a trifle short in stature compared to average humans, but with wigs, a dab of Pancake make-up to lighten their purplish-grey skin, and contact lenses over their ruby irises they could pass as natives among many Earth populations.

Fritiso-Prontinalin, who called himself Fred during his sojourn on Earth, and his colleague Vilianin-Tinamikadin, who was known as Willy, were young Poltroyan psycho-geomorphologists on their first assignment as xenosur-veyors. Their project, a rather tedious one that had them tending automated data accumulators in widely separated parts of the world, attempted to correlate operancy in the farsensory spectrum with long-term population residence in the proximity of granitic lithoforms. The hypothesis wasn't working out too well in any sampling area except New Hampshire – and here the correlates were so high that the two researchers suspected a fudging factor. Discouraged and very much in need of a break, they decided to drive down to Laconia from their secret base camp in Waterville Valley and take a holiday. Primed for a weekend of alien thrills, they joined the crowd that had packed Laconia for the annual World Championship Sled-Dog Derby.

The sky was heavily overcast and the temperature hovered around the freezing point of a saline solution – glorious weather for Poltroyans, who generally hail from wintry planets – and Fred and Willy mingled happily with the mob. In recent weeks they had done extensive fieldwork in Norway, and they had brought souvenirs with them to New Hampshire – distinctive Samish 'caps of the four winds' – which they wore to cover their bald mauve skulls. Otherwise their garb was ordinary American winter gear, comfortable enough but skimpy and drab when compared to the gem-studded fish-fur parkas and mukluks of their home world. They told curious natives that they were Lapps. This helped to explain away their shortness and also made them some quick friends, since many of the mushers and fans were of Scandinavian descent.

On Saturday morning Fred and Willy caught the first round of Husky-drawn sled races in the hard-charging sprint classification. When their favourite dog-team did poorly, they went around afterwards to offer condolences to the driver, a petite lavender-eyed blonde named Marcie Nyberg who reminded them very much of certain girls they had left behind them.

She was quite ready to commiserate. 'Just my luck! I didn't bring the right kind of wax for the runners, and none of the places in Laconia stock it. It's called Totally Mean Extra Green. I don't suppose you guys ever heard of it.'

'Well, no,' Fred admitted. 'In Norway we use another kind.'

But Willy was rummaging in the kangaroo pouch of his

anorak and murmuring, 'Wait a minute! Wait a minute!' And then, triumphantly, he pulled out a flat container of pinkish metal with a soft pad at one end. 'Marcie, you're not going to believe this, but I remembered that I had this defrictionizer stowed away in here from the last time I was on – from *Norway*. I think it would be just the thing for snow conditions today. Please try it.'

Marcie examined the container dubiously. 'Gee, I never saw this kind of wax before. Is this writing on the side? I thought Norwegians used the same alphabet as we do — '

Hastily, Willy said, 'That's Samish. You know, the Lapp language. The stuff is simple to use. You just stroke it on, using the pad end. It's not like crayon wax. It's – it's new.'

Marcie grinned. 'Okay, Willy. I'll give it a try this afternoon. Thanks a whole bunch.'

She had to tend to her dogs' feet then, so the Poltroyans said goodbye and went to watch a weight-pulling event. Malamute dogs, much more massive than the rangy Huskies, strained eagerly to move sledges loaded with weights up to a ton per animal. Fred and Willy were overwhelmed at the strength of the furry quadrupeds – and especially interested to note that the handler of the heavy-weight Grand Prize winner had unconsciously exercised a telepathic rapport with his dog, aiding its performance.

When the contest was over, Fred went to the man and offered hearty congratulations. But when he offhandedly added a remark about telepathic encouragement, the musher let loose a blast of profanity that nearly took off the Poltroyan's quaint four-cornered cap.

'Use telepathy? Me? You accusing me of being one of them goddam cheating *heads*? Well, lemme tell you, pipsqueak, I run my dogs honest, and any guy that says different can taste a knuckle sandwich!'

He was a black-browed bruiser with a stubbly jaw and the number 22 pinned to his down jacket. Several other dog-handlers crowded around, looking none too friendly, and the prize-winning Malamute took a lunge at Willy with its lips curled back from enormous teeth. Fortunately, its owner had a good grip on its chain.

Fred quickly apologized. 'I'm sorry! I didn't understand!

We're visitors from Norway, you see. We didn't know that – er – that kind of thing was considered improper here.'

The animosity of the bystanders dwindled and Number 22 seemed slightly mollified. 'Well . . . so long as you're foreigners and don't know better, I won't take offence. But you better watch it, fella. Calling somebody a head won't make you any friends in this part of the US and A.'

'No, sirree,' the others chimed in. 'Damn tootin'!'

Number 22 squinted at the Poltroyans in suspicion. 'You two wouldn't be heads yourself, would you?'

'Oh, my, no,' Willy said. 'We're Samish. You know – Laplanders. The people who used to herd reindeer.'

'Reindeer!' humphed Number 22. 'Mighta known.'

'Oh, we're very interested in dogs, too,' Fred said. 'Ours are called Spitz. They're something like small Huskies.'

The Malamute handler was patently unenthusiastic and his dog, a huge grey and white creature with black eyes, continued to growl. 'You see this?' The musher indicated a big round button pinned beside the cloth square with the numerals 22. 'You wanta stay outa trouble, you better know what it means.'

Fred and Willy took a closer look. The button was a depiction of Earth as seen from space, a blue disk splashed with white. 'It's very attractive,' Fred said.

The man gave an unpleasant laugh. 'It means I'm one of the Sons of Earth, shorty. A normal human being, and proud of it! You ever heard of us?'

'Yes,' said Willy, keeping a neutral expression.

'Well, then you know where I'm comin' from. As far's I'm concerned, God made this Earth for normal human folks – not for freako heads who break the laws of nature and try to lord it over the rest of us like they're some kind of fuckin' master race.'

'Yeah!' members of the crowd affirmed. 'You said it, Jer! Damn right on!'

Number 22 slackened the dog chain a fraction and the Malamute reared. 'I don't know what goes on in Norway, but in *this* country we're gonna make sure that real people stay in charge of things – not freaks. You get what I'm saying?'

'Oh, yes,' said Fred, backing away. There were quite a few of the big blue buttons being worn by the crowd. Neither Poltroyan had taken any note of them before.

'Well, thanks for explaining,' Willy said. 'And congratulations again on winning the Golden Bone. You've got a really fine dog there.' And with that, Fred and Willy fled, hurried along by hostile and contemptuous aetheric vibrations. They stopped near a refreshment stand to catch their breaths.

'Half-masticated lumpukit!' Fred swore. 'That was a nasty one.'

'The buttons must be a new fad here in America. I certainly don't recall seeing them in New Hampshire last year at the ski jumps. It seems to me that the Sons of Earth were still a disreputable fringe movement then. Membership was quite furtive.'

'Not any more.' Fred was looking about. 'Love's Oath – every third or fourth person seems to be wearing one of those buttons. We'll have to send notification to the Oversight Authority.'

'They're probably aware of the situation. But we'll do it.'

It was almost time for the next heat of sprints that Marcie was scheduled to participate in, so the Poltroyans decided to get something to eat and go cheer on their new friend. Willy dug in his pocket for a credit card and ordered two hot dogs with sauerkraut and mustard and two Classic Cokes. Then the exotics wandered over to the racecourse, sipping and munching. The beverage's alkaloid was invigorating even if it wasn't quite sweet enough, so they tossed in three or four maple-sugar candies to saccharify it. The delicious sulphur taste of the shredded hot vegetable mingled nicely with the speckled buff condiment's bite. Too bad that the proteinoid was too highly nitrified for really safe metabolization – but an occasional treat wouldn't kill them.

When the heats began they forgot the unpleasant incident with the Sons of Earth and revelled in the excitement of the racing. Dogs howled, mushers yelled, the spectators cheered on their favourites, and a diamond-dust snow sifted down on everything. It was glorious! And when the final times were posted, Marcie and her team had won.

Fred and Willy ran to her, shouting their congratulations.

'Your wax! Your wax!' She swept the pair of them into her arms like a mother embracing her children. 'The wax made all the difference! I love you guys, do you know that?'

She was covered with crusted rime thrown up by the galloping dogs, and one could almost forget she was the wrong colour and chromosomally incompatible. Fred and Willy pressed lips with her because that was what her mind told them she wanted. Then she brushed herself off and untied the vivid Day-Glo racing vest with her number, 16, and pulled it over her head.

On the jacket underneath was a big blue button.

Marcie was bubbling over as she began to load her dogs into her truck. 'Listen, you guys. Tonight there's a Musher's Ball with beer and chili and a live band. I want you to come. My treat! You can meet the whole gang and tell them about the crazy wax and the whole Laplander thingypop!'

'We'd love to,' Fred said sadly.

'But we really have to go now,' Willy concluded. 'Please keep the wax. I wish I had more, but – it's in short supply.'

Marcie's face fell. 'Oh, guys. What a shame you can't come. Maybe you could catch me later? The Adirondack's two weeks off — '

'We're finishing our work in the States very soon,' Fred said.

'We're really sorry,' Willy added.

'Well,' Marcie said, 'it was awfully nice knowing you. I'll always remember you two.'

The Poltroyans turned and walked away. All around were mushers tinkering with sleds or adjusting harnesses and traces. The loudspeakers announced the start of another event and the dogs began to yelp, eager to be off and away.

'Let's go home,' Fred said.

'I wish we *could*,' Willy muttered.

'Oh, you know what I mean,' said Fred.

Together, they headed for the place where they had left their car.

12

*From the Memoirs of
Rogatien Remillard*

We were not yet pariahs, only suspect.

The terrible murder and instant retribution that had taken place in Alma-Ata were played and replayed on the television screens of the world. The implications – perceived almost instinctively by every normal person – were argued in heat and in cold blood, but then rationalized away because humanity was not yet prepared to turn upon and repudiate the operants.

After an investigation that took more than a year, Soviet forensic scientists, assisted by experts from many other countries, determined that the assassinations of the General Secretary and the Grand Mufti were not accomplished by psychocreative energy at all, but by a chemical explosive device that was almost but not quite without traceless residue. That the agent provocateur had been operant himself was verified by the testimony of the delegate-witnesses there in the Lenin Palace of Culture, particularly those who had been on stage. The killer had used a quasi-hypnotic technique to stun and confuse those close to the General Secretary. Only Denis and Tamara had been able to resist the mind-paralysis; but they could not prevent the murder.

The killer's true identity was never discovered. His image was shown distinctly on the tapes of the video cameras recording the event; but the face was obscured by the large bouquet of flowers at first, and then by the minature explosion. He had turned away as he started to flee, again hiding his face from the cameras, and his subsequent cremation obliterated any other clues to his identity.

The cremation, not the murder of the Soviet leader, was what really gave the world pause.

After months of hedging, a special investigatory committee of 'blue-ribbon' metapsychologists called by the United Nations issued a lengthy analysis of the so-called Retributory Incident. Its findings can be compactly summarized:

1. The assassin of the Soviet General Secretary met his death through a process of incineration by psychoenergetic projection.

2. The energy projected came from the brains of the operant delegates who had just witnessed the assassination.

3. The energy was focused and amplified by means of a manoeuvre known as 'metapsychic concert', in which numbers of operant brains act as one synergistically, the whole being capable of an output greater than the sum of the parts.

4. It was not possible to calculate with total accuracy the amount of energy focused upon the assassin, since its characteristics were anomalous. (For example, there were no auditory manifestations as there had been when the General Secretary's head was vapourized by the explosive device.) Furthermore, it was not possible to calculate the percentage of psychoenergy generated by individual delegates.

5. The metafaculty of psychocreativity, which may generate energy, is at present poorly understood. Except for the Weinstein case, there is no previous record of a fatality resulting from the projection of psychic energy. Metapsychic concert is also poorly understood. Its manifestation has been experimentally verified by magnetoencephalography; but in no instance have researchers ever encountered an effect even remotely approaching the magnitude of the Retributory Incident.

6. In the opinion of the investigatory committee, the Incident was the result of an unconscious velleity on the part of the delegate-minds, without true volition. In lay language, the delegates were so shocked and angered by the General Secretary's murder that their mutual loathing of the perpetrator generated the blast that killed him.

7. On the advice of the committee, no action at law against the delegate-perpetrators was contemplated by the Soviet judiciary. It was felt that the principle of diminished responsibility applied to their actions in view of the heinousness of the crime they had just witnessed.

8. Repetitions of Retributory Incidents could not be ruled out, given similar provocatory circumstances.

9. The committee recommended strongly that legal scholars, ethicists and moral theologians address themselves to the unique problems of culpability devolving upon metapsychic operancy. The ancient question of whether the law should take the will for the deed would have to be reopened when, ipso facto, the will *was* the deed.

Debate over the philosophical and legal implications of operancy would beget an avalanche of articles, monographs and books off and on over the next fifteen years, until the topic received its ultimate resolution in the Intervention. Of course Denis did not serve on the investigating committee. (The fact of his nonparticipation in the destructive metaconcert was proved when the Simbiari Proctorship reopened the inquiry into the Incident in 2017, at Denis's insistence.) Lucille, who had not attended the Sixth Congress because of her confinement with her first son, Philip, *did* serve. It should be noted that she laid open her personal psychocreative case history to assist the committee in its deliberations, an action that required great courage at the time. Fortunately for her, the committee decided that it was not necessary to include that history in the public record.

You, the entity reading these memoirs, should not get the impression that reaction to the Retributory Incident was as reasoned and high-minded as this chapter may have thus far implied. On the contrary, there was a royal rumpus kicked up in the United States, where the media hashed and rehashed the affair ad nauseam, bringing the term 'psychozap' into slang usage, together with the pejorative 'head', applied to operants — which was perversely embraced by us and later used as an innocent appellation. As the Third Millennium approached, cranks and fanatics of every sort crept out of the woodwork – most notably the Sons of Earth movement, which claimed worldwide adherents by 1999 and succeeded in disrupting part of the Eighth Metapsychic Congress in London.

The Great California Earthquake gave new life to the prophecies of Nostradamus. Never mind that the prophet's dating for the quake was so ambiguous that it might have referred to any century following the sixteenth with the locale of the seismic disaster unspecified. Two other pertinent quatrains from Nostradamus were dusted off and presented to the gullible as portents of things to come:

L'an mil neuf cens nonante neuf sept mois,
Du ceil viendra un grand Roi deffraieur.
Resusciter le grand Roi d'Angolmois.
Avant que Mars regner par bonheur.

Apres grand troche humaine plus grande s'appreste,
Le grand moteur des Siecles renouvelle.
Pluie, sang, laict, famine, fer et peste
Au feu ciel veu courant longue estincelle.

Which can be roughly translated:

In the seventh month of the year 1999,
A great King of Terror will come.
He will revive the great King of the Mongols.
Before that Mars will run riot.

After great human suffering, even greater comes,
When the great motive power of the Centuries is renewed.
Rain, blood, milk, famine, iron [war] and disease
In the heavens is seen a fire, a long flow of sparks.

The hysterical could equate the new, bellicose leader of the Soviet Union, Marshal Kumylzhensky, with the King of Terror. By a long stretch of the imagination, the new Genghis Khan could be seen in the insurrections flaring up in Soviet Central Asia. (No one yet had any inkling that the Chinese were watching the accelerating dissolution of the USSR with keen interest.) The continued fighting throughout the Islamic world was certainly a source of suffering, and the crazy weather that had rotted the crops in some parts of the world while parching others also seemed to fit. As to the milk, there remained the legacy of the Armageddon fallout, poisoning both milk and 'blood' in a wide swathe of the Middle East and the Balkans for seven years now. The fateful Seventh Month of 1999 came and went without any signal disaster; but in August, the total eclipse of the sun that was visible in Europe, the most embattled regions of the Middle East, and the Indian subcontinent wreaked havoc among the superstitious, who were certain that the end of the world had come. After that crisis had passed, there was another to be endured on 11 November, when Earth passed through the great Leonid meteor 'storm', a Nostradamic fiery flow of sparks if there ever was one. But once again Earth abided, the day of wrath was unaccountably postponed, and the eschatologists went back to their original prediction of doomsday at the actual turn of the Millennium.

Sadly enough, certain of the Remillards did meet their end during those days. Their tragedy went virtually unnoticed because of the gaudier events that Milieu historians have concentrated on; but I will tell it here as part of the family chronicle.

In the months following the Alma-Ata affair, Denis brooded over the misuse of operant metafaculties. He discussed this subject at length with both Tamara Sakhvadze and Urgyen Bhotia, and was convinced that resolute pacifism was the only ethical course open to persons with higher mind-powers. There remained, however, the odious problem of Victor. Denis had told Lucille what he knew and what he suspected about his younger brother, and she was simultaneously outraged and wary. Lucille was particularly concerned for Sunny and the nonoperant siblings left under Victor's influence, and pressed Denis to do something to help them, even if it meant a direct confrontation that might end in violence. But Denis refused, countering her reproaches with both logic and his espousal of the superChristian ethic. No course short of engineering Victor's demise was likely to resolve the terrible stalemate – and Denis would not kill his brother in cold blood even to save the lives of his mother and the others.

Denis stood by, apparently impotent, while his younger twin brothers Louis and Leon, who turned twenty-one in 1999, were brainwashed by Victor and joined him in Remco Industries as nonoperant factotums. Both young men were ruthless and intelligent, and they were also completely trustworthy, unlike many of Victor's operant associates. That left only George, who was nineteen, and Pauline, two years younger, still living with Sunny. George was an unprepossessing young man, very unassertive, who was studying computer technology under Victor's orders. I had always thought him a poor stick. Paulie, the youngest of Don and Sunny's big brood, was an exquisite creature. Except for her dark eyes, she was the image of her mother as a young woman – and when I saw her that year at the family Easter get-together, suddenly matured into radiant femininity, my heart stood still.

Their older sister Yvonne had been married in 1996 to the middle-aged operant crook Robert Fortier, whose sinister mother still acted as Sunny's nominal housekeeper, all the while contriving to dominate her utterly. Over the years, by use of ingenious metapsychic variants on old-fashioned racketeering, Victor and Fortier had converted Remco into an international operation that now owned not only pulpwood harvesting companies but a large paper mill in New Brunswick, a chemical plant in Maine, and other forest-product industries in cities scattered across upper New England and southeastern Canada. Having succeeded so well in his first dynastic play, Victor now decided to attempt a much more audacious variation on the theme.

One of my nephew's underhanded acquisitions was a small genetic-engineering firm in Burlington, Vermont. This outfit had perfected and patented a bacterial organism called a lignin degrader, that broke down (i.e., 'ate') a common waste product of the pulpwood industry, converting it into a host of valuable chemicals that had heretofore been obtained from increasingly scarce petroleum. The process utilizing the superior bug was very nearly ready to be put into production, and it was going to be a gold mine; but Victor's Remco Industries faced a dilemma well known to medium-sized corporations – it did not have enough capital to develop a lignin-chemistry company of its own, which would reap huge profits. Rather, it would have to license the process to giant petrochemical conglomerates and settle for a much smaller piece of the pie.

Naturally, Victor balked at this. The golden bug and its principal nurturer had been stolen from a famous Michigan university at considerable risk to Victor's own hide, and he had invested a good deal of money in the perfecting of the process. Having won game and set, as it were, he wasn't going to let outsiders rob him of the match.

There was only one font of finance he felt he could safely approach for additional capitalization, a money source that had earlier approached *him*, only to be repulsed. Now, Victor decided, the time was ripe for reconsideration. And so he made a telephone call to Kieran O'Connor's Chicago office, waited patiently while his name was passed from buffer zone to buffer zone in the corporate hierarchy until it reached the Boss of Bosses, and then made his proposition.

A merger, to their mutual profit. To seal the deal, Victor would marry Shannon O'Connor and Kieran would take Pauline Remillard.

O'Connor laughed his head off at the raw Franco chutzpah of it all. It was *primitive*. It was damn near Sicilian! Still, Kieran had kept his eye on Victor over the years and had been impressed. At the callow age of twenty-nine, Victor was worth upward of sixty-two million dollars — peanuts when compared to Kieran's own empire, but not too shabby when you remembered that the kid had started out with nothing but his drunken daddy, a '74 Chevy pickup truck, and two Jonsered chain saws boosted from a local logging-equipment supplier. And this lignin-gobbling bacterium had possibilities. Kieran's facile mind hatched a scenario in which the process could be used as a fulcrum in a scheme to corner the world's energy supply. As for Victor himself, he would either have to be made an ally or eliminated. The dynastic link-up opened the way for either option.

After their telephone conversation had gone on for some ten minutes, Kieran told Victor that he was inclined to accept the proposition. There were, however, two small matters that would have to be clarified. First, did Victor have his sister Pauline under complete control, as Kieran did Shannon? . . . and was she really beautiful and unsophisticated?

Of course!

Kieran hoped that was true, because they couldn't coerce the girl permanently. The second matter was more delicate. Kieran did not want Pauline as his wife or mistress. He would possess her only once (for reasons not explained to Victor), and after that she would be married to Kieran's close associate Warren Griffith, who had recently lost his third wife under tragic circumstances. There was, however, this thing about Griff. He was brilliant, both in coercive talent and business acumen, but he had special personal needs. Pauline, as his wife, would live in a ménage à trois, and the third party was a young man of rather stern disposition. Did Victor understand?

Different strokes for different folks, Victor said. But Kieran would have to make *damn* certain that Paulie didn't end up like the third wife.

Kieran would see to it personally.

Then there was no problem.

And so this decidedly curious arrangement was agreed upon. But Victor made the mistake of explaining the situation very carefully to Pauline while she was under his coercive hold. He talked to her for three hours one late October afternoon when the sky was clear and the trees were in full colour on the hillsides surrounding Berlin, and then he left her in the back yard of Sunny's big house on Sweden Street, sitting on a rustic bench under an incandescent maple tree. When her brother George came home that day from computer college, she asked him to take her for a ride in his car along the Androscoggin River, and while they drove she told him without any emotion at all (for that was the way Vic's brainwashing affected the forcibly latentized) what was in store for her.

George thought about it in his nerdish way. And he thought about his own future as a superhacker under Vic's mental thumb, and his older brother Denis's apparent inability to help any of them. Then he told Paulie not to worry. They drove up to Dave's Gun Shop in Milan, where George bought a handsome Marlin 120 shotgun with a twenty-six-inch barrel and a genuine American walnut stock and forend, all hand-chequered, because George didn't want to wind things up in a sleazy way. After that they found a nice spot where Paulie could watch the river and the trees reflected in it and not notice a thing. There was string in the glove compartment that George tied cleverly around the trigger and guard of the gun to take care of himself.

Vic knew at once when they died and so did I; but for some reason he did not receive the farspoken truth of the affair that was transmitted to me in the split second of George's final agony. Instead, Victor went to the car and found the note, which he destroyed before calling the State Police to report the double tragedy. He was mad as hell. Kieran O'Connor took the news more calmly and said that he would think things over, and doubtless something could be worked out between them after all. He promised to get back to Victor early next year, after the Millennial hysteria cooled and the financial world returned to normal.

Sunny's link to reality that had become insupportable was shattered by this final trauma. She smiled a great deal at the double funeral and said that Don and the five dead children spoke to her from heaven, saying she would soon be joining them. Victor now had no objection to her going to Hanover to live, so Sunny spent her last months in the pleasant house on East South Street with Denis and Lucille, rocking newborn Maurice and reading storybooks to little Philip.

I saw her nearly every day. She remembered who I was when I would address her as Marie-Madeleine, as I had done when we first met in the Berlin Public Library thirty-eight years earlier. We often spoke about those days. At other times, her drifting mind perceived young Maurice as baby Denis, and she and I would re-enact some of the simple metapsychic teaching games I had devised so long ago. Such charades soothed her even as they tortured me, but at any rate they did not last long. She died the next spring, in March, impatient for the flowers to bloom.

13

Mount Washington, New Hampshire, Earth
31 December 1999

There was the question of where to spend the Turn of the
Millennium . . . Her father was going to an opulent masked
ball in Vienna where the international set was prepared to
outdo the twilight of Byzantium, and he invited her to
accompany him. She declined. It wasn't her style to waltz
away the fateful hours in the company of tipsy financiers
and diamond-crusted media stars, and then at midnight
link arms to sing 'Brüderlein und Schwesterlein' and 'Auld
Lang Syne', awash in sentimental tears and vintage
champagne.

No. She wanted something different . . . just in case the
world did end, as the crazies kept predicting. Something
incomparably dramatic.

Kieran laughed indulgently, but then went all serious
and reminded her that she would have to be with him in
Zürich without fail on Monday January 3 for the signing
session establishing their new European satellite consortium, in which she was a nominal officer. Perhaps, he
suggested offhandedly, she could spend the holiday
weekend skiing. She would be welcome to use Darmstad-
ter's chalet at Gstaad, since he and his family would be
going to the ball.

She thought about that. She was a superb skier, and her
operancy gave her unusual talents that added zest to the
sport. But she would not go to Gstaad. For one thing, her
father had suggested it. For another, it was crowded and
artificial and she might meet people she knew. Her fancy
painted a very different picture of the Millennial Eve: a
precipitate slope of powder snow, virgin in the moonlight,
and herself flying downhill, a streaming torch in her hand,
into the blackness below. Yes!

And then she had another great idea. The perfect place
– and an appropriate companion.

She telephoned him and invited him to be her guest in
the Bugaboos. He did ski, didn't he?

'Yes,' he said.

'Then let me send the family Learjet for you and we can meet in Banff. Our chopper and a private guide will be waiting. We'll have to see one another eventually. Why not do it this way, without him even knowing?'

'He doesn't know?'

'He's in Europe. That's why I'm . . . free.'

There was a pause on the other end of the line, and then he said, 'If you'd like something really climactic, an even bigger thrill — '

'Bigger than skiing the *Bugaboos*?'

He told her what he had in mind and this time it was her turn to hesitate. 'Is it possible?'

'If you're black diamond . . . and if you have some PK, it's quite possible. I've done it twice.'

'I suppose it's illegal or something.'

'Oh, yes, definitely.' He laughed.

'Tell me where to meet you!' she demanded.

And so he had; and early the next morning she had driven out to DuPage County Airport and taken the Lear herself. It took her a little over two hours to get to North Conway, New Hampshire, from northern Illinois, since she had to detour around some bad weather over Buffalo. But when she touched down at White Mountain Airport she found bright sunshine, fresh powder, and a throng of like-minded ski nuts overflowing the resort town, all determined to await Gabriel's trump schussing their brains out. There were no rental cars to be had, but she coerced the young man at the Hertz office into giving her the keys of his own nifty little BMW sports coupe. Then she drove north to Wildcat Mountain, where she spent what was left of the day and the early evening warming up her muscles on the rather modest slopes of Upper Lynx and Lower Catapult, all the while eyeing the real challenge that loomed to the west, dazzling in its deepest snow-cover in decades.

Could they get up there without a chopper? He'd said they could, in spite of the fact that it was deadly dangerous as well as prohibited. That, of course, made it perfect.

Along about seven she was ravenous so she drove down to Jackson, to a well-known country inn on the Thorn Hill

512

Road. There she dined alone on lobster bisque, a salad of spinach, endive and red onions with mustard-vinaigrette dressing, veal scallops with black mushrooms and cognac sauce, potatoes rösti, and steamed baby green beans. She drank a single glass of a fine Souveraine California Cabernet and left the rest (to the scandal of the host), and finished with a pumpkin-pecan tartlet and a pony of calvados.

Then it was time to meet Victor Remillard.

Following his instructions, she drove to the deserted parking lot of the Mount Washington Carriage Road. Its gate was open and she turned off her headlights and went in, following a ploughed track through very deep snow that was sometimes drifted higher than the roof of her car. The sky to the south had a warm glow from the lighted slopes at Wildcat, three kilometres away, but aside from that the only illumination was from starlight. The moon, four days past its full, had not yet risen above the eastern heights. Near a deserted ticket-taker's shack was a cleared space where a peculiar vehicle was parked. It looked like a boxy van precariously perched above four very wide tractor treads. She parked beside it and studied it with fascination.

Only a few minutes passed before he came, driving a big four-wheeler that he slewed around smartly, throwing up a plume of snow that glittered under the stars. He parked a few metres away, then got out and came crunching towards her. Pulling up her hood and slipping on her gloves, she stepped out of the BMW and went to meet him.

Shannon O'Connor I presume.
Victor Remillard . . . I know.
Hey good screen!
And yours.
Lots to hide?
Haven't you?
Touché.
Pas du tout.
Ready fun?
Believe it.
Good sky.
No wind.

Headwall powder!
Super!
PK OK?
?? Yes. ??
Homing.
Not in SnoGo?
UP only. DOWN XC.
Oo!
Treeslalom.
Ace hi!
Mogulbomber?
Yo!
Aerials too?
Only 720 Möebius!

Sure you can drive this thing?
Marchons!   No hands babe!
Ready when you are.   I'm *valuable*.
Épatant!   To Papa!
Mg fusees!!   Not you?
Torches X 2?   We'll see.
Wired for stereo.   **LET'S GO!**
Hardhat?
And deepvision
Nightvision?

!Hotdog hotdamn hotdog hotdamn hotdog!
    !Hotdog!

So they were off in a roar of monster twin diesels, charging
up the famous road leading to the summit of Mount Washington. But they weren't going to the top; they were going
by ingenious and unlawful routes to the lip of the Headwall
of Tuckerman Ravine, a steep glacial cirque that had been
scooped into the southeastern flank of the peak during the
past ice age. The ravine was a natural trap for snow blasted
off the Presidential Range by the hurricane winds of the
region. In this final winter of the Second Millennium, one
of the coldest and stormiest in decades, the vast bowl of
Tuckerman Ravine was filled with snow more than twenty-
five metres deep. People normally skied Tuckerman in the
spring, when most of the snow in the country surrounding
it had melted and it was possible to hike up through the
woods from Pinkham Notch to the Hermit Lake camping
shelters on the ravine floor. The only way to get to the
Headwall from Hermit was to slog with your skis on your
back – up and up and up. At the rim of the declivity – if
you got that far on the fifty-five-degree slope – you skied
down. The great challenge was to schuss, to ski straight to
the bottom. The feat had last been accomplished by Toni
Matt in 1939. Once down the Headwall, it was possible to
take the precipitous Sherburne Ski Trail back to the Notch
and the highway. In the dead of winter, however, nobody
skied Tuckerman Ravine. The powder was bottomless and

the scene magnificent, but the upper reaches of the mountain were off-limits to the public. It was deadly up there, with some of the fiercest winter weather on Earth.

But not on that New Millennium's Eve.

'Did you lay on the Sno-Crawler just for me?' Shannon asked.

'Not on your life. It belongs to the contractor who services the weather observatory and the TV and microwave transmitters on the summit. During the winter the Carriage Road is closed halfway up and unploughed. Once a week this crawler goes up with supplies and the relief crew.'

'And you can just hop into the thing and make free with it whenever you fancy a little jaunt?'

He laughed. 'Not by a damn sight. But I have my methods.'

They sat side by side in bucket seats, strapped in with sturdy web harnesses. Shannon had erected her heaviest mental screen, the dual-layer one with the false substrate that she used to defeat her father's probing. Victor had made a perfunctory stab at it during their initial encounter, then backed off; but she could still feel the searing power of him, like a searchlight held at steady focus against a window blind; and when they had faced each other in the dark parking lot she had seen his ghostly aura – vermilion laced with steely flashes of blue, the colours of potency and danger.

Inside the surging vehicle, studying the electronic displays on its console, Victor Remillard hardly seemed to be the black mental menace her father had described. His bare head was a mass of tight dark curls. He wore a one-piece Thermatron ski-suit with all the high-tech options – temperature control, spot massage, com-unit, stereo sound-surround and locator beacon – ready for anything. (But *she* wore her old red North Face jacket and pants with the Ski Patrol patch from Snowbird! One up.)

She said, 'My father's off in Vienna, where the Third Millennium has already come. He and his plutocratic friends are at a fancy-dress ball like the last act of some Strauss operetta. Next week he takes control of the Dione satellite-engineering consortium – the one that's to build the European section of Zap-Star.'

'Nice for him.'

'I'm to be its nominal CEO.'

'Nice for you.'

'Daddy expects me to be a figurehead.' She smiled, letting just a bit of her supposed scheme to seize control of the consortium seep beneath the margin of her outermost screen. Victor jumped on it, just as she knew he would, and crashed the frangible barrier for a thorough scan of what lay behind. He was sure that he'd laid her mind wide open – just as her father was always sure. But Shannon's true self was secure behind the secondary shield, letting the intruder see only what she permitted him to; and as Victor sorted through what he believed were the plans and dreams of Kieran O'Connor's daughter, he himself lay vulnerable to her . . . and she entered softly.

God – he was strong! By no means as intelligent and demonic as her father, and with ambitions predictably narrow in scope. But what a coercer, and what brutal unformed creativity was there, waiting only to be moulded and directed! He would do. Oh, yes, he would do.

She finished her lightning penetration long before his scan was complete. He had noticed nothing, and when he finally withdrew, smiling in a patronizing way at her callow scheme to rule the consortium, she simulated dismay at the mental violation and then pretended to sulk.

'You'll have to do a lot better than that if you expect to put one over on your old man.'

She let him wait, repaired outer barrier back in place, and then said, 'I suppose you could think of a better plan.'

'I might.' His eyes were fixed on the snow-depth-and-density monitor and he throttled back. They had passed the dark bulk of the shuttered Halfway House and come into the open. There were great drifts blocking the way now, some of them six metres high. Victor studied their contour and composition and the nature of the rocky terrain buried beneath them, then geared down to clamber over. An unsecured boot-bag tumbled towards the rear of the cabin as they ascended a steep incline, zigzagged, then came back more or less to horizontal and proceeded up the invisible road.

Shannon said, 'Nicely done . . . So my little plots interest you, do they? I thought you wanted to form an alliance with my father. You could report my contemplated subversion to him, you know, and score.'

'Perhaps I'm playing an altogether different game. Just like you.'

The powerful headlights of the Sno-Crawler lit a hairpin section of the way that doubled back along a precipice skirting the Great Gulf, another big cirque on the north side of the mountain. They had passed above the tree line now, but rime-coated scrub decorated the crags and sparkled as though it were coated with sugar. Victor accelerated, conquered a small avalanche fall, and headed up the icy Five-Mile Grade, an exposed section that had been swept clear of loose snow by the nor'easter winds. Tonight the air was still. Victor punched a control button deploying the tread spikes and the crawler chewed its way upwards.

Shannon said, 'My father thinks he has control of my mind. My loyalties. From the very beginning, he's used this – this technique to bond his associates to him irrevocably.'

'It's pretty obvious the technique didn't work on you.'

'It does when I'm with him. Then I'm like all the others, under his spell . . . Even at other times I can *belong* to him. When I'm lonely and afraid of myself and everything else and want it all to end, then I'm caught in his vision of the Absolute, and I know Daddy's way is the only way that makes sense . . . But then he loosens his hold. Perhaps he's too caught up in other things to bother with the little satellite minds orbiting him and worshipping . . . And I remember how he bound me. The fire racing up my spine and exploding my senses and burning my resistance to ashes. It should have taken – the bonding. But it didn't, not fully. I think Daddy may have been inhibited because I was his daughter, and his will didn't finalize the personality conjunction. It took me a long time to remember. To know why my own world had died along with the honest love – daughter's love – I had felt for him. Now, when I love him, he's not my father. When I'm myself, and I know who he is and what he did to me, I hate him.'

The sudden explosion of approval – of kinship – that escaped him was a profound shock to her and a revelation. He said, 'Hate. That's your antidote. Mine, too. But I've known it for ever.'

She had the ski gloves in her lap and she pulled each finger carefully, straightening it, before rolling the gloves and tucking them into her jacket. 'He'll try to bond you, too. It's the only way he'll allow operants to be associated with him.'

Victor let out a harsh bark of laughter. 'Y a pas de danger! . . . Or as you micks might say – in a pig's eye! I'd like to see him break into my skull — '

'He doesn't. That's not his way at all. He makes us love him. With those who aren't – aren't naturally inclined to accept him, he uses a hypnagogic drug to weaken their psychic defences, then seduces them. If the person recognizes what's being done, he kills them. He's killed one hundred and eighty-three natural operants and bonded forty-six. He finds most suitable ones when they commit certain crimes. Scams. Conspiracies. There's a kind of suboperant signature that he recognizes. The people themselves don't realize that they have the powers. In the seduction, he shows them what they can be, with his help. It's wonderful. That's why we'll do anything for him, commit any atrocity. The man who assassinated the Russian Premier and the Grand Mufti of Central Asia was one of his. Daddy has a lot of reasons for wanting to foment war. His Zap-Star satellite defence system needs concrete global villains as targets – not just scattered groups of Islamic hotheads.'

'He's got it right,' Victor conceded. His knuckles tightened on the wheel as the vehicle entered the Cutoff Track, bypassing another notch that was full of deeply drifted snow. 'He's done a damn good job consolidating power. My operation is small potatoes in comparison. But it won't stay that way.'

'If you oppose him directly,' Shannon said, 'he'll kill you. If you try to join him, you'll end as I have. Bound.'

He was silent for several minutes, guiding the big machine through a chaos of compacted white ice blocks. Despite the strut suspension that dampened the worst of the lurching, the cabin bounced and tilted and flung its occupants against their seat harnesses like rag dolls until they finally exited the Cutoff and came back on to the buried Carriage Road proper.

Victor said, 'They all want to bind us, Shannon. Starting with our parents, of course, at the very beginning. They say they love us and then make conditions. They try to hold us back, to keep us from climbing above their own puny level. They want to live through us – on us! – like some kind of psychic vampires. That's what love is. At least your father's version makes no bones about it.'

'I never thought about it that way.'

'Well, *start*. Your unconscious mind knew and you started to hate and you started to free yourself. I've always hated them all and I've never been bound. I take the little empty ones and use them, and crush the mind-fucking lovers. I'll crush your father someday, and my brother Denis, who's even worse.'

'Daddy'll get you if you let him near you. I know what your scheme is. You think you can marry me and hold him off long enough to take what he has. But you won't be able to help yourself. I can sense it in your soul. The – the attraction. Daddy wouldn't have to drug you. You'd find him irresistible.'

He was scowling, punching up snow-depth read-outs as the vehicle crept through looming blue-white corridors. 'Maybe I'd bond him to *me*! Suppose you tell me just how he works it.'

Shannon opened her mind instead and showed him.

Merde et contremerde! Loathing spilled from Victor's mind before he sealed off.

She said: The bliss of it and the welcome pain are long gone and now the Absolute is formless and dry and all that drives me is the need to bring him down to take the power away and have him *know* that I did and for that I need your cooperation.

Victor swore again in French. He superimposed the

snow-condition analogue on the true-terrain display and discovered that the blip of the crawler was off-course. Somewhere they had missed the Alpine Garden Link just above the Six-Mile Post of the road. It was only a simple hiker's track cutting in a southerly direction across the windswept upper shoulder of the mountain. The crawler reversed, growled slowly backward in its own tread-prints. The headlights withdrawing made the snow-plastered crags seem weirdly artificial, like stage sets fading out.

Shannon said: You *must* help me. I warned you in time. I saved you from him.

Shut up! Let me think!

He saw the way on the right, rough as hell but open, along a gentle slope below Nelson Crag. He began to smile, retracted the ice-spikes, and deployed the flanges. The Sno-Crawler roared as he gunned the engine. 'Only two kilometres left to go . . . Tell me: how much is your old man really worth?'

'I don't know. I doubt that he does. He controls more than a hundred big corporations, a TV network, two airlines, a major oil company, five big aerospace contractors – and that's only in North America. He has links to conglomerates in Europe, Japan and Korea.'

'What about this political thing? Does he really control the Republican Party?'

'Not the whole thing. That'd be impossible – even for him. He does own four Senators and nineteen Representatives from key states. The politicians aren't operants, of course. Some are bought and paid for, some know they're the tools of special interest but don't realize that their strings are pulled by Daddy, and a few believe they've managed to retain their integrity even though they've accepted Daddy's help. Like the President of the United States.'

'President Piccolomini? My ass!'

'President *Baumgartner*. He'll win the Millennial election next fall. Daddy's troupe of media consultants and PR hotshots and political-action committee fronts have it all worked out. Baumgartner is a forceful spokesman for law and order. He's hawkish on the Arab countries that have cut off our petroleum supplies and he's wary of Russia and China. He's willing to accept Daddy's antioperant strategy in order to exploit the backlash against President Pic. You know how antsy the normals have been getting, worrying about operants turning into thought police and that kind of malarky. The Sons of Earth thing was started deliberately in this country by Daddy's agents just to work up tensions for the upcoming election.'

'Your old man is antioperant? I don't get it.'

'Daddy sees Pic's Brain Trust and all the public-spirited operants as a personal threat. And they are Victor. If there is ever any organized metapsychic education programme in this country and operants become numerous and powerful, Daddy is bound to be exposed as an operant himself. A maverick one. He'll be ruined. Not financially – he's beyond that. But his edge will be lost. His source of power.'

They drove on and on, over a surface that was now much smoother, tumbled granite rubble almost completely buried in deep, crusted snow, and wind-scoured slabs of rock that had been planed by the ice-age glaciers. In the hollows and in the lee of the occasional crag were drifts. Glittering spicules of ice danced in the crawler's headlights. On their left, the whiteness fell away to black and they began to skirt the top of Tuckerman Ravine at last. They could see the Headwall itself, a precipitous apron of untouched silver under the waning moon, which had risen above the crest of Wildcat and Carter Dome.

Victor decelerated, changed course to avoid a dangerous cornice of snow, then headed for the rim again. A moment later they stopped. He cut the engine and extinguished the exterior and interior illumination. Side by side, still imprisoned in their harnesses, they sat looking over the drop-off. There were sparkling strings and clusters of tiny building lights in the Wildcat Ski Area and along Pinkham Notch, where houses and roadside establishments lined the highway. Only a few cars and trucks were abroad. Most of the drivers had evidently found some congenial place to wait the Millennium out.

Victor unfastened his straps and hers. They went into the back of the cab to put on their ski boots and other equipment. Shannon unpacked the flares and checked her wristwatch. It was four minutes until midnight. Together, they climbed on to a rippled ice crust, carrying their skis. Victor had left the keys of the crawler in the ignition and now he slammed the door shut without locking it.

'Are you just going to leave the thing here?' she asked.

He gestured towards the summit. The antenna complex and other small structures were barely visible against a velvet sky dusted with incredible numbers of stars. In one of the buildings shone a little yellow light.

'Somebody from the weather station will put on fangy showshoes and come down for the machine in the morning. It's a good thing the weather's calm. Some of the windblasts across this rock pile could blow our little ten-ton ice-buggy clear to Massachusetts.'

They bent to their bindings and put on hard hats with heated visors. Neither had poles. Psychokinetics, whose minds are able to exert motive power affecting their own bodies, rarely have need of them.

Shannon peeled the wrapper from her magnesium flare, activated the ignitor, and held the smoky white light aloft. In an instant it cleared and blazed brightly. Over to the east, fireworks were exploding above Wildcat's slopes and a river of golden luminescence had begun to flow downhill. The new year had arrived and skiing torchbearers celebrated the unabated progress of time.

Shannon said, 'Happy New Millennium, Victor.'

He lifted his unwrapped cylinder. The tip lit with a loud concussion, activated by his own psychocreativity. 'Happy postponement of doom, Shannon. For a little while, anyway.'

She said: Will you help me? Not merely to kill him you understand he must be taken down at the peak of his hopes when he thinks the black Absolute is within his grasp.

When?

It's years away . . . but I'll let you know. Go your own way for now never act to threaten Daddy directly and you'll be safe from him. He's afraid of you at the same time that he's attracted. He'll wait. I have a plan of my own worked out. I'll explain it at the bottom of the slope after the schuss going back through the woods . . .

All right.

They manoeuvred to the lip of the chasm. The descent was not vertical, it only seemed to be – a perfect expanse of powder, unimaginably deep, fresh and clean.

GO.

Their minds pushed them off. They were on their way, flares held high, trailing twin plumes of nebulous white like a pair of comets on straight parallel paths into the dark.

14

Stockholm, Sweden, Earth
10 December 2003

Trumpets played a fanfare and the orchestra began the national anthem. Queen Victoria Ingrid and her entourage entered the assembly hall of the Konserthuset and the audience, including Lucille Remillard and Gerard Tremblay up in the loges, rose to its feet. The ceremony had begun and the honours would be bestowed, too late to do any good.

Lucille's dark-green velvet gown was heavy, and she adjusted its folds unobtrusively with her PK. The metafaculty also served to hoist the tops of the wretched long white gloves, which persisted in slithering unmodishly down towards her elbows. Her feet, crushed into high-heeled pumps, ached in spite of her distrait attempts at self-redaction and so did her full breasts, deprived of baby Severin's milking for this one day of vain celebration. Some of her discomfort must have been evident, for Gerry Tremblay took her left arm to steady her, projecting his usual solicitude.

Oh Gerry never mind I'm all *right.*

None of your bitching darling I can tell when I'm needed your faithful esquire at your service m'lady Prop-Ups & Resuscitations Our Specialty.

Will you at *least* stay on the intimate mode or do you

want every meta in the place to know the laureate's wife has sore feet and bursting boobs? There! Her Majesty's seated and down we go . . . *aah*.

Pauvre de toi.

Oh shut up . . . Goodness what a lot of diamonds! And furs do you suppose that's a *sable* it must be good grief what a difference from the ceremony for Jamie and Tamara at Oslo last year so friendly and modest —

— excepting the bomb scare!

Oh for heaven's sake you know what I mean even the King was as friendly and downtoearth as anyone but *this* crowd LordLord ostentation to the eyeballs I've never seen anything like – mate-moi ça! Can those be real emeralds let me deepsee . . . goodGod they are I see the inclusions and they're like *walnuts*!

There goes the brass section again darling afraid we'll have to rise again for the entrance of the heroes —

'No, madame and monsieur,' came a whispered voice. 'That will not be necessary.'

Lucille turned in surprise. The seat on her right, which had been empty during the entrance of the Queen of Sweden, was now occupied by a distinguished-looking older man in white tie.

'This time,' he continued softly, 'only the Queen rises to honour the laureates as they enter. On this night, you see, they are mental royalty. Her equals.'

'How charming,' Lucille murmured. The music swelled as the laureates, paired with members of the Swedish institutions who had voted them the honour, entered the auditorium. To Lucille, the scene was unreal: the gilded hall with its statuary, rich drapery, sconces and flags, the young Monarch in her sparkling white dress and tiara, standing at stage left giving anachronistic homage, and, above all – her husband. Yes, there was Denis, looking insignificant beside the Valkyrie splendour of a female professor of psychiatry of the Karolinska Institute, who would introduce and laud him. She scarcely noticed the other honourees of the evening; but behind them were seated rows of laureates from years past – including Jamie MacGregor and Tamara Sakhvadze, who had received the Peace Prize in 2002. Lucille would never have intruded her mind upon Denis at that moment; but she did not hesitate to call out to Tamara and Jamie on their intimate modes. Both looked up towards the loges where relatives of the laureates and other dignitaries were seated. Tamara smiled and projected understanding and comfort. Jamie projected an image of a winking eye and a species of mental cartoon, in which a rather tatty figure with a Nobel medallion hung about its neck sat on a snowy street corner proferring a beggar's cup; behind it was a sign: BROTHER, CAN YOU SPARE A GRANT?

The laureates and the others bowed their heads respectfully to the Queen and took their seats as the music played on, and then there was applause, and the Nobel Foundation chairman approached the lectern to give his salutatory address.

The man beside Lucille said, 'It is an occasion for metapsychic operants to celebrate, is it not? There is your supremely talented husband, finally receiving the recognition he has long deserved, and his two great colleagues among the previously honoured laureates, and the Prize in physics goes to Professor Xiong Ping-yung, for his formulation of the new Universal Field Theory incorporating life and mind into the mathematical fabric of the universe.'

'And he's probably asking, just like we are,' Gerry Tremblay put in, 'whether anyone but a handful of academics and this overdressed Swedish mob scene cares.'

The old gentleman chuckled quietly. 'Things are that bad in your country?'

'And in most others,' Lucille said. 'It's a grand gesture being made here tonight, but one would appreciate it more if the pickets outside the Concert House went away.'

'My country is a free one, as is yours, madame. But very many of us welcome you wholeheartedly.' He bent minimally over her hand. 'I am Dr M. A. Paulson of the Karolinska. You are known to all, Madame la Doctoresse, and also the famous Dr Tremblay.'

'Not so famous as some,' Gerry said, with a light laugh.

'It is well known that you are an eminent colleague of the Remillards, Doctor. Your own researches into coercivity are a foundation-stone upon which other researchers have erected many a scholarly edifice. Including tonight's Laureate in Medicine. Professor Remillard has been unstinting in his praise for your work, and his debt to you.'

'We're members of the same team,' Tremblay said. 'Everything I am, I owe to Denis.' His eyes were on the platform. 'I'm the one who feels honoured that he was able to make use of my findings.'

Lucille said, 'Gerry and Professor Glenn Dalembert have worked with my husband almost from the beginning, Dr Paulson. And there've been many other colleagues at Dartmouth making their own invaluable contributions to the field of metapsychology.' She smiled. 'Even I.'

'But the synthesis,' Paulson whispered. 'That is always the critical matter, is it not? So many workers, all adding their share to the growing body of knowledge – and then the one brilliant mind fashions of the bits and pieces a coherent whole.'

'That's Denis, all right,' said Gerry Tremblay. 'And tonight he's finally being honoured for it. It's a scandal that it's taken this long.'

'Some of us on the Committee think so, too, Dr Tremblay,' the Swedish scientist said. 'But the Karolinska, especially, is a most conservative body. We do not honour persons for a single discovery so much as for a continuing career of excellence.'

'Oh, come on!' said Gerry archly. 'It's all politics, and you know it. Denis's seminal work was *Metapsychology*, and that was published thirteen years ago. Since then he's just been elaborating on the theme. We all know why you waited so long, even though he's been nominated a dozen times – and we know why the Norwegians took ten years to cough up the Peace Prize for Jamie and Tamara. *They're* the real scandal. Everybody in the whole damn world knows they deserved to get the Nobel years ago, but the petty politicians hesitated to set a precedent by honouring superior mentalities. That's been Denis's problem, too – and even old Xiong's. He's been plugging away at his theory for damn near twenty years out there in Wuhan University. He was even nominated in 1988! But when the operants acknowledged their powers publicly, he did, too.

Just a bit of telepathy and creativity, hardly enough to bother about when the rest of his brain – the conventional part – has Einstein beat six ways from Sunday. But that was enough to put your Royal Academy of Science in a snit, wasn't it? Old Professor Xiong wasn't playing fair – he was a superbrain!'

Heads were turning as Tremblay's passionate whispering became more and more audible. The elderly Swede listened with his head bowed. A burst of applause signalled the end of the Nobel Chairman's address and Gerry sat back, lips tight. Lucille's gloved hand stole over the armrest and squeezed Gerry's hand.

Simmer down Don Quixote . . .

And the Committee only coughed up the Prizes out of *guilt* now that the metas are being persecuted now that the normals have turned on us . . .

Gerry. You're off intimate again and there must be other metas in the audience. *Please.*

'What you have said is sadly true, Dr Tremblay,' Paulson admitted. 'But we have tried to make amends, as the Norwegian Nobel Committee did in the case of Professor MacGregor and Academician Sakhvadze. We are dismayed by the disgraceful enmity that operants have had to suffer. Much of it has been due to fear and misunderstanding. Can you believe that normal-minded persons of goodwill have come to appreciate your predicament more fully with the coming of public demonstrations of intolerance?'

'We would like to believe it,' Lucille said softly.

Down on the stage, a member of the Royal Academy of Science was proclaiming the merits of Xiong Ping-yung in Swedish. When he concluded his remarks, he addressed a few sentences of recapitulation in Chinese, addressing the old mathematician directly. Then the laureate rose from his seat, crossed the stage to the Queen, and bobbed his white head. Unlike most members of the glittering assembly, Xiong was dressed only in a simple black suit with a high collar. With their farsenses, Lucille and Gerry Tremblay could perceive the exchange of remarks between the laureate and the young Queen.

'I bow to you, Queen Victoria Ingrid, not as one who

kowtows to royalty, but to honour the beautiful living symbol of a great nation that has honoured me.'

The Queen shook his hand, a glint of humour in her eyes. 'I congratulate you, dear Professor Xiong. Here is your citation, and your medallion. Later, when you sit beside me at dinner in the Stadshuset, you must explain your Theory to me. If you can help me to make head or tail of it, I will gladly bow again to *you*.'

The old man laughed delightedly, made a second obeisance, and returned to his seat amid applause.

'In years gone by,' Dr Paulson whispered, 'the poor old chap would have had to go down off the stage via a flight of stairs to greet the monarch – then go up those stairs *backwards* in order to show the proper respect! Our late King Gustaf abolished the custom. We Swedes do progress, you see, but slowly. It is the same all over the world. Old ways make way for the new, but often only after precarious and tentative transitions.'

The winners of the Literature Prize and the Chemistry Prize were proclaimed, but Lucille watched and listened with a distracted mind. Paulson was right, of course. Right about the dangerous transition period. But could he also be right about the normals beginning to understand? The metapsychic backlash had only intensified since President Baumgartner took office. His abolition of the Brain Trust and sponsorship of the Benson Act prohibiting operants from seeking public office or serving on law-enforcement bodies was a savage piece of prejudice that the Supreme Court was debating even now. Of course the law was unconstitutional! It had to be . . .

Chin up Luce darling illegitimis non carborundum.

I'm sorry Gerry I know it's stupid of me to be brooding *here*.

The Nobel Prizes are going to give operants increased status you know help us to face down Baumgartner and the witch-burning yahoos the Court will rule in our favour it's got to we're citizens and the Benson Act is de facto disenfranchisement.

Of course it is. Why can't the normals get it through their heads that operancy is only relative? Its seeds are in every human mind! We can't go back to the Dark Ages operancy IS and it will continue to be. The trait has evolved and now it's becoming manifest in the population and you might as well try to outlaw brown eyes!

That's becoming plainer and plainer to them but they still hold the power and are afraid of losing it . . . And we're going to do something about that too.

? Gerry ? Is this another one of *her* great notions?

She has a name. You'll have to use it eventually when she becomes my wife I know you disapprove of her ideas but she's right the only way to avoid being oppressed is to have clout. Power.

. . . You are serious about her then.

Emilie agreed to a no-fault divorce last week. I didn't want to distract you or Denis with it. You were so excited about Stockholm. We're doing it as amicably as possible. Em will keep the house in Hanover and the kids and continue her part-time work at the Department. As for me . . . I didn't want to bother you with *that* either but I'll be leaving Dartmouth. Leaving academia. Shannon and I will be moving down to Cambridge. When the Benson Act is struck down, I'll run for Congress.

My God!

We operants have a lot to offer to normal society. But we're imbeciles if we sit by like pacifistic fools and let them set up the scaffolds. Massachusetts! Home of that old American custom burning witches! It's going to be our rallying point —

Another of Shannon O'Connor's ideas?

She's operant too . . . even if only a little bit.

Sometimes I wonder about that! . . . Gerry please don't present this to Denis as a fait accompli leave your options open for just a little while longer discuss it with him with Glenn and Sally and Mitch and the others we NEED you —

Not any more you don't. What I had to give Denis took. And good luck to him.

!! . . .

'I have the honour to present now our Nobel Laureate

in Medicine, Professor Denis Remillard of Dartmouth College in the United States of America.'

The elderly Swedish doctor was nudging her gently, breaking her out of her distraction and pointing to the glittering stage. Denis was advancing towards the Queen, bowing in the graceful Japanese fashion, from the waist, as Ume Kimura had taught him, speaking to Her Majesty with smiling lips and grave, shadowed eyes. He received the leather box with the medal and the portfolio containing the citation, bowed again, and returned to his place. Lucille applauded wildly, realizing that she hadn't farsensed a thing her husband had said to the Queen.

The ovation continued as the final honouree of the evening retired, and then a few brief words from the chairman closed the ceremony. The trumpets blared for the last time, the Queen withdrew, and the musicians played a sprightly Hugo Alfvén piece as a recessional for the laureates and the others on stage. Cars would be waiting outside to carry them, their relatives and other honoured guests to the gala dinner at the City Hall.

Lucille realized with a start that her cheeks were wet. 'Gerry, wait for me while I go to the powder room. I'm a mess.'

She fled, leaving Tremblay standing in the aisle behind the loges with Dr Paulson.

'Will you be going to the dinner?' Tremblay inquired politely.

'No, I have had quite enough excitement for tonight. I will bid you adieu, Doctor. But before I go, please accept a bit of advice from an old man.'

Gerry tried to look receptive.

'You feel in your heart that Denis Remillard wronged you by not granting you sufficient credit for your work. Whether he did or not is immaterial. Do not let your envy and disappointment drive you to a reckless course of action that may bring disaster upon you and all of your operant associates.'

'I don't know what the hell you're talking about,' Gerry laughed. 'And I'm afraid you don't either.'

'It is hard to work with genius. I really cannot blame

530

you for fleeing. You know that in the laboratory you will only be competent and so you turn the beacon of your ambition in another direction. Be careful. You think falsely that Remillard used you. He did not – but certain others will.'

Gerry Tremblay's face was immobile. He looked into the old man's grey eyes, probing with all his power, and met stone.

'I didn't think you'd change your mind,' Paulson said. 'But I thought I would make the try as long as I was here tonight anyway. It has been an evening to remember. Please give my fondest regards to Madame Remillard . . . and it may be some small consolation to you to know that even the great Xiong Ping-yung owes something of his monumental formulation to the thoughts of others. The germ of the Universal Field Theory was suggested to him by none other than I myself! But that was long ago and far away, and I have long since forgotten most of my higher mathematics. À bientôt, Dr Tremblay.' He walked off.

A nut, Gerry told himself. A salty old Swedish nut! He probably creeps out of the woodwork every year and makes a pest of himself at the Prize ceremony.

Forcing himself to believe this, he went off to find Lucille.

15

Chicago, Illinois, Earth
27 February 2004

KIERAN O'CONNOR: Come in, Gerry. I'm glad you could get here on such short notice. I wouldn't have torn you two lovebirds apart so soon after the honeymoon if it wasn't important . . . Shannon getting settled in the new place?
GERARD TREMBLAY: The house is crawling with interior decorators and carpet-layers. I'm glad to be out of the war zone for a little while.
O'CONNOR: Got your offices all set up in Cambridge?
TREMBLAY: Pretty well. Still trying to find the right staff.

O'CONNOR: Don't be in a rush. Where are you recruiting? My old Alma Mama, Harvard?

TREMBLAY: [laughs] I'm running as a Democrat, sir.

O'CONNOR: I understand there are still a *few* liberals lurking in the ivy . . . Sit down, for heaven's sake, man. And don't call me 'sir'. If you can't manage 'Dad', try Kier. How about a drink? Cheer the cockles on a cold afternoon.

TREMBLAY: Thank you . . . Kier. [Looks around in awed admiration.] My God, what a view from this office! On a clear day —

O'CONNOR: You can see Milwaukee. Less smog than there used to be. One good by-product of the energy shortage, at any rate . . . Scotch? Sherry? Campari?

TREMBLAY: Campari and soda would be fine.

O'CONNOR: Did you enjoy Nuku Hiva?

TREMBLAY: It was fantastic, sir – Kier. I don't have the EE faculty, you see, so I've never been able to indulge in mental globe trotting. Or the regular kind, either, on an Associate Professor's salary!

O'CONNOR: That'll change.

TREMBLAY: I'm looking forward to it.

O'CONNOR: No false pride, eh? That's a healthy sign.

TREMBLAY: Shannon and I understand each other. Her money will be a means to an end. An end that both of us feel is infinitely worthwhile.

O'CONNOR: That end of yours is the reason I asked you to come here to confer with me. We don't know one another very well yet, Gerry. That is . . . you don't know me. I've been interested in your political aspirations, and I'll confess that I watched you there in New Hampshire even before you and my little girl worked together on the Millennial Democratic presidential campaign. Both of you have made friends in the Party who'll do you a lot of good now that you've decided to seek office yourself.

TREMBLAY: I have Shannon's good advice to thank for any success I might have had as a campaign aide. And of course, she funded our caucus's effort. That took a lot of courage when the whole country knew *you* were for Baumgartner.

O'CONNOR: Shannon is a grown woman with a right to her

own opinions and political loyalties. Having metafaculties herself – even though they're very modest ones – she was very upset when Baumgartner's campaign took on an anti-operant stance. She broke with the Republican people here in Illinois over the issue and decided to go all-out for Kennedy. And what better state to do it in than New Hampshire?

TREMBLAY: It was great for a gesture. But to really *do* something in the political arena, one needs a state with a bigger population base.

O'CONNOR: [laughs] More clout! You don't have to tell me. I was born in Massachusetts. You made a wise change of domicile, Gerry, and I wish you good luck in your campaign . . . But wishes are a penny a peck, right? I want to help you in a concrete fashion as well. Not with money, because Shannon's got more than you need, but with people. I want you to accept the services of two of the finest political advisers in the country – Len Windham of Research/Market/Data, and Neville Garrett, whose agency handles media liaison for top people in both parties.

TREMBLAY: Kier . . . I don't know what to say!

O'CONNOR: Just say yes. They'll send people up to Cambridge tomorrow to begin coordinating your campaign.

TREMBLAY: Well, of course! My God, I never dreamed . . . a conservative like you . . . but *why?* It can't be because I'm your son-in-law. I'm not a fool . . .

O'CONNOR: Can't you read my mind, Gerry?

TREMBLAY: No, sir! For a normal, you're one of the most opaque mentalities I've ever run across. And we operants don't read minds with the facility that normals credit us with. That's just one of the myths – the misunderstandings that have got to be cleared up if this antioperant hysteria isn't to balloon into a national tragedy.

O'CONNOR: Exactly my own feeling. Partisan politics and fundamentalist bullshit shouldn't dictate national policy on an issue as sensitive as metapsychic operancy. Dammit – my own little girl is a *head!* I can't stand by while fanatical assholes call her and people like her freaks or servants of Satan! This is the United States of America, not some benighted camel-jockey theocracy run by ayatollahs! I was deeply disturbed by the antioperant position Baumgartner took in his last campaign and by his support of the Benson legislation. We can thank God that the Supreme Court tied a can to *that* piece of madness.

TREMBLAY: But Senator Benson has been one of your protégés for years —

O'CONNOR: No more, by Christ! Man's turned into some kind of religious nut in his old age. A senile Grey Eminence. I blame *him* for pushing the antioperant position on Baumgartner. I don't believe that the President sincerely espouses the vicious canards being circulated about you people. I think he's uninformed, and he's been influenced by bad advice.

TREMBLAY: His antioperant stance helped win him the Millennial election. Whether Baumgartner acted out of conviction or from expediency —

O'CONNOR: Yes, yes, I see what you're driving at. But what *I'm* trying to say is that Baumgartner's not a lost cause! Gerry, I don't believe Kennedy has a hope in hell of unseating the President this fall. We're going to have another four years of Baumgartner, for better or worse. But with you in the House of Representatives, you'll be in a legitimate position to counter the antioperants. Baumgartner's my friend. When I talk, he listens! I'll admit he hasn't been listening lately . . . but we have a good chance of changing that now that the Supreme Court has struck down the Benson Act. Baumgartner's no fool. He'll change if it seems polite to do so. Your job – our job! – is to upgrade the operant image so he'll be forced to repudiate the fanatics.

TREMBLAY: And bring back the Brain Trust?

O'CONNOR: Mm'mm . . . have to go slow on that, Gerry. The old Trust was dominated by academics who were totally out of touch with the prevailing mood of normal voters. There was an elitist smell to them that didn't sit well with the American psyche. It was ridiculous for Copeland to plump for Cabinet status for what was merely a presidential advisory commission. And downright suicidal for Ellen Morrison and those Stanford people to persist in lobbying for universal metapsychic testing when it was plain that the mind of the country was against it. Once the nuclear menace was out of the way, the Psi-Eye programme began to seem more of a threat than a benefit. *You* know! An American equivalent of the KGB's Twentieth Directorate . . .

TREMBLAY: When I'm elected, I'm going to push for programmes that will use operants in ways clearly beneficial to the normal majority. No elite corps . . . no thought police . . . concentrate on *good* powers . . . how about redaction, f'rinstance? Psychic healing works! But wha'd'you hear about it? Nothing. EE got all the funding . . . yeah, and now *none* of the meta programmes got funding . . . my field, coercivity . . . take delinquent kids and turn them around . . . funny . . . kind of dizzy . . .

O'CONNOR: Are you feeling all right, Gerry? You look a bit pale.

TREMBLAY: Maybe . . . maybe I'm coming down with a bug. Feel lightheaded.

O'CONNOR: And I called you halfway across the country when you belong in bed! Gerry, you should have told me.

TREMBLAY: Felt . . . felt all right this morning . . . funny . . .

O'CONNOR: Easy, my boy. Give me the glass. Good. Just relax. Close your eyes for a minute or two. Close your eyes. Rest. Rest, Gerry.

TREMBLAY: Rest . . .

O'CONNOR: Rest, Gerry. [Touches intercom.]

ARNOLD PAKKALA: Yes, sir?

O'CONNOR: Dr Tremblay and I will be here for a while longer, Arnold. But there's no need for you and the rest of the staff to wait.

PAKKALA: Whatever you say, sir.

O'CONNOR: [after an interval] Gerry. Can you hear me? No? *Can you hear me now Gerry?*

TREMBLAY: *Yes,*

O'CONNOR: *Good. Relax Gerry. Relax with your eyes closed. I'm going to turn off the lights and then I want you to open your eyes and look at me. Do you understand?*

TREMBLAY: *Yes . . . God! The colours the colours singing purple and gold sungold bittersweet cloud the liquid depths the colours and the perfume and the ambrosia O God . . .*

O'CONNOR: *Fly away into it Gerry let me lift you fly away.*

TREMBLAY: *BeautifulbeautifulGodsowonderfulamazing . . . God! J'ai besoin de toi . . .*

O'CONNOR: *Of course you need me and I need you. Fly Gerry. Fly.*

TREMBLAY: *Who are you what are you don't leave me . . .*

O'CONNOR: *Je suis ton papa ta maman ton amour ton extase!*

TREMBLAY: *Extase!*

O'CONNOR: *Look closely at me. Beyond the coloured light.*

TREMBLAY: *Bright too bright the light hurts my eyes Papa . . .*

O'CONNOR: *There my son close your poor pained eyes see how comforting the black. But I had to see all of you Gerry how special you are so much better than all the others the mind elaborated into full trained operancy sensitive and subtle an educated mind a psychologist with professional insight into secrets hidden from small minds yes my son my beautiful one you'll understand I'll have so much to show you and it will bring joy to you as you serve.*

TREMBLAY: *Papa why are you black now?*

O'CONNOR: *The Absolute is black and I reside there. When there was neither sun nor moon nor earth nor planets nor starry universe there was the dark and in it was calm and an end and there will be again.*

TREMBLAY: *Black the deep black the inaccessible black from which all things come and to which they go . . .*

O'CONNOR: *Yes! Clever son beautifulbrained son to see in the dark the form of the Formless the meaning of the enigma yes yes the source of life is death and all light finds its end in deep night in the negation of the Absolute.*

TREMBLAY: *God?*

O'CONNOR: *He is light we reject him and his burning.*

TREMBLAY: *No no no LIGHT CREATION LIFE GROWTH DIFFERENTIATION COMPLEXIFICATION MENTA-TION COADUNATION UNITY LIGHT . . .*

O'CONNOR: *A sham a joke a cruel hoax they lead only to pain. Creation groans! He is a God of pain we are born in it live in it die in it he wills it for all his creatures for all growth is pain inescapable. But there is a secret way I know a way I share with my beloved ones in a great antithesis! We do not create we destroy the dark is our birthright our Black Mother whose belly is a void that takes us in . . . dam dham nam tam tham dam dham nam pam pham . . . to consummation.*

TREMBLAY: *Papa Papa I don't understand I'm afraid of the dark!*

O'CONNOR: *Darkness is fearful only when viewed by the fleeing turn around accept it embrace it know it love it.*

TREMBLAY: *But how?*

O'CONNOR: *Make your own darkness behind closed eyes follow me along the Left-Hand Path an old neglected way but one that annihilates the corrupting Light the painful Light follow me into the Black and together we will know a moment of ineffable beauty the one perfect and final joy: leading all into the void.*

TREMBLAY: *I understand. It's true. I'm tired of pain. Show me. Papa show me . . .*

O'CONNOR: *Come.*

O'CONNOR . . . Gerry? Can you hear me, boy? Gerry?

TREMBLAY: God. Kier? What happened. Jesus, did I pass out?

O'CONNOR: Seems like it. How do you feel now?

TREMBLAY: A little woozy. But I think I'm okay. Dammit, there's this flu thing going around back East . . .

O'CONNOR: I'm going to take you out to the house and we'll have Doc Presteigne check you out.

TREMBLAY: Listen, I'm feeling okay. Really! . . . Now, this lobbying you wanted me to do on President Baumgartner. You realize that a freshman Congressman's influence on a President of the opposition party is going to be just about nil —

O'CONNOR: Not so. He's going to like you, Gerry. And listen to you! *He will do as you want as I want just as you will...*

TREMBLAY: You want me to coerce him.

O'CONNOR: That's an ugly word. *Persuade* him! . . . And the message you'll be getting across is a very important one. We were discussing it just before you dozed off on me, boy. Do you remember? We want Baumgartner to *keep pressing for antioperant legislation.* The Benson Act is dead, but we can lobby for other laws that will be in our best interests. Laws restricting operants. Who is in a better position to warn the country about operancy's dangers than you, Gerry? You've seen them conspiring to take power . . . You know what mischief ambitious or evil-minded heads are capable of . . . Don't you Gerry? *Don't you?*

TREMBLAY: Yes.

O'CONNOR: President Baumgartner has begun to get soft. We put him in the White House and now that he's a shoo-in for a second term the bastard's forgotten who his friends are! His mind is normal, but he's a tough nut, Gerry. He was an astronaut and a corporation president, you know. Nobody's patsy.

TREMBLAY: Your other people can no longer handle him . . .

O'CONNOR: So *you're* going to work on him. Subtly. Using posthypnotic suggestion and subliminal hints most of the time and saving direct coercion for critical situations. He must never have the remotest notion of what you're up to. You'll have to be artful in the presentation of your public persona as well. On the face of it, you'll be a liberal Democrat championing the rights of operant metapsychics and other minorities.

TREMBLAY: Yes.

O'CONNOR: *You see my overall plan, don't you Gerry? The rightness of it the brilliance the inevitability?*

TREMBLAY: *Yes yes oui oui mon cher Papa . . .*

O'CONNOR: Fine! Now let's get our coats. The rush-hour traffic on the East–West Freeway should be past now, and we'll have an easy trip out to the house. [Touches office-garage key-pad.] Frankie? You want to bring the Bentley around? Thanks a lot.

16

Washington, DC, Earth
20 January 2005

With her way cleared by the Secret Service bodyguard, Nell Baumgartner rushed into the Capitol Rotunda. To be late for her husband's second inauguration! Oh, please, God, she begged. Not that . . . And the *news!* How would Lloyd react? Should she tell him now or wait until after the swearing-in ceremony?

Agent Rasmussen, holding her arm, said, 'It's going to

be OK, Mrs Baumgartner. The Chief Justice is just coming up to the platform. You're going to make it.'

The huge white-marble chamber was chilly even though it was packed with people – members of Congress, White House staffers, influential Republicans, and personal friends and relatives of the First Couple. Outside a blizzard was raging, and so the inauguration was being held indoors for the first time since 1985. The blizzard had delayed the First Lady's dash from Reagan Jetport. She had landed in Washington only a half hour earlier after flying from the bedside of her two-year-old granddaughter, Amanda Denton.

The Marine Band finished playing as Agent Rasmussen and the First Lady reached the platform. She composed herself, took a deep breath, and smiled radiantly at her husband. His returning smile echoed relief. The child was going to be all right.

She was dimly aware of people standing close by – the Vice President and his wife; the Senate Majority Leader, Benjamin T. Scrope; the Speaker of the House, Elijah Scraggs Benson; and there was the Party Chairman, Jason Cassidy, and beside him their old friend and long-time supporter, Kieran O'Connor, with his daughter Shannon and his son-in-law Congressman Tremblay. Shannon Tremblay's eyes were wide with concern. Had she heard about little Amanda's crisis? Nell Baumgartner gave the young woman what she hoped was a reassuring wink. An instant later she forgot Shannon as a Bible was placed in her hands – the one she would hold while the President took his Oath of Office.

The Chief Justice of the Supreme Court stepped forward, her face solemn. The President placed his left hand upon the book, which was opened to Psalm 8, the prayer he had recited years ago when he first set foot on the Moon. He raised his right hand.

'I do solemnly swear that I will faithfully execute the Office of the President of the United States and will to the best of my ability preserve, protect and defend the Constitution of the United States.'

Then the band was playing, and he was moving to the

lectern where he would deliver the Inaugural Address, and she only had seconds to tell him, and she thought, *Should I?* And it seemed that a voice was warning her to forbear, to let it be . . . but she knew what was in the speech Lloyd was about to deliver and she could not let him go ahead without knowing —

The music was drawing to a close. Swiftly, she stepped up to him and touched his sleeve. He turned.

'Little Amanda is all right, Lloyd,' she whispered. 'The neurologists at Johns Hopkins say it isn't epilepsy at all. Lloyd – our granddaughter is going to be a metapsychic operant. It was the spontaneous breakthrough from latency that caused the convulsions.'

The President said only, 'They're certain?' And Nell nodded, then stepped back.

The music stopped. All eyes in the Rotunda were on the President. He folded the sheets of paper he had just moments before placed in front of the microphones, and put them into his inside breast pocket. 'My friends,' he began, 'the Inaugural Address I had prepared no longer seems appropriate. In order for you to understand why, I'm going to share with you some very startling news that my wife Nell has just brought to me . . .'

He paused, passing his hand across his forehead, and there were murmurs of amazement from the audience. But then he straightened and spoke resolutely for ten minutes, and at the end there was a shocked silence, and then subdued applause with a rising undercurrent of voices that the Marine Band finally drowned out with 'Hail to the Chief'.

Shannon O'Connor Tremblay said: Well Daddy?

And her father replied: It will be up to Gerry and he damn well better not let us down.

17

From the Memoirs of
Rogatien Remillard

Halloween 2007.

I have a zapshot here before me to jog my memories of that day. It shows three cunning little devils – my great-nephews Philip, Maurice and Severin, aged ten, eight and four at the time – costumed as imps for the holiday, in a blatant piece of typecasting, by their long-suffering nanny Ayeesha.

Thanks to Ghostly confidences, I knew at the time that the boys would grow up to be Founding Magnates of the Concilium. Thanks to Ghostly compassion, I did *not* know that one of them would perish in the Metapsychic Rebellion of 2083, fighting to extricate the human race from the Galactic Milieu . . . But that is another story that must wait to be told. I will write now of events that led to the Intervention, and my own peculiar role as a bit player in them . . .

All that day, my bookshop had been under siege by poltergeists, for by then Hanover crawled with the offspring of operant metapsychics. Every Halloween, in the old American tradition, local merchants endured an endless stream of costumed youngsters extorting treats, the donation of which was supposed to render one immune from tricks. In my youth, trick-or-treat escapades were tame: soaped windows, upset trash cans, demounted garden gates, toilet-paper festoons on shrubs and – in the case of notorious neighbourhood ogres – walks and porches defiled with smashed jack-o'-lanterns and rotten eggs. In the new Age of the Mind, however, Halloween had become the one day in the year when operant youngsters could release their inhibitions more or less with impunity. Reined in by parental coercion the rest of the time, the kids tended to go bananas once they put on their costumes and set out to pillage and plunder. By unwritten law the deviltry was restricted to those under the age of twelve, and no property was to be destroyed or rendered so befouled or bollixed as to require expensive repairs. Aside from that, the sky was the limit.

My bookshop, as I have mentioned, primarily suffered the onslaught of poltergeists. The books on the shelves would dance and tumble to the floor; the window displays (of expendable volumes) were in a perpetual state of manic frenzy; the little customer reading area in the front right-hand part of the store had chairs and ashtrays dancing and rag rugs curling and writhing on the floor. Poor Marcel LaPlume, my huge Maine Coon cat, had retreated to the basement storage room after being harassed one time too many by hailstorms of Cat Chow levitated from his dish and mind-generated static charges that set his fur crackling. I had a big bowl of Snickers candy bars as tribute to the invaders, but as often as not the operant children would thank me for the treat – then pull off the trick anyhow on their way out of the shop.

Another unwritten rule was that the depredations should cease by 2200 hours. My shop was not ordinarily open so late on weekdays, but only a madman would have closed up early on Halloween and left the premises unguarded. That year, as the evening of pranks came to a close, I wondered why I had not yet been visited by Denis and Lucille's children. As it drew on towards quarter to ten, I concluded that they were saving me until last, and had planned some particularly gross piece of mischief for poor old Uncle Rogi.

My farsense tingled. I looked up from the catalogue I had been perusing and caught a glimpse of disappearing horns and red grease-painted small faces outside. My deep-vision identified the lurkers and I braced myself.

The door opened by itself and the chime rang eerily. Three telepathic voices sang:

Did you ever think, as a hearse goes by,
That you might be the next to die?
They wrap you up in a long white sheet,
And bury you down about six feet deep!

Giggles, instantly squelched, came from the mind of four-year-old Sevvy. The songsters paused . . . and I saw coming in the door and inching along the polished floorboards a flood of white, slimy little things — hundreds of them — glistening as they looped and squirmed into my shop. And the inevitable chorus of the old children's song:

The worms crawl in! The worms crawl out!
The worms play pinochle in your mouth!
Your body turns a mossy green,
And pus runs out like thick ice cream!

The three juvenile devils, shepherding their obscene cohort, came bounding in, squealing and laughing.

Trick or treat Uncle Rogi!

The books danced a fandango. The drawer of my antique cash register flew open with a jangling crash and the bills and loose change fountained up, then rained down into the midst of the wriggling maggoty mass on the floor.

'Call them off!' I bellowed.

Promise to teach us dirty French!

'Jamais!'

The worms crawl in the worms crawl out . . .

'That does it,' I intoned ominously. 'There's only one way to deal with this situation.' I reached into my trouser pocket. 'Beware! Beware, all you alien invaders! Beware the power of the *Great Carbuncle*!'

I held up my key chain, with its dangling fob of a red-glass marble caught in the little metal cage. Using an old trick of creativity that had long delighted the children, I made the thing glow. At the same time, I smote the three young minds with my adult coercion, freezing them in the midst of their capers and cutting off the PK motive-power of the lolloping larvae.

The boys screamed. Their tongues protruded and their eyes bugged out of their grotesquely painted faces, and one after another they fell to the floor — at a safe distance from the now motionless mélange of icky lucre and nameless white things.

I waved the Great Carbuncle over the lot of them in a coup de grâce, then laughed and cancelled the coercion. The boys jumped up shrieking with mirth and I told them to wait while I loaded my still-video camera with a fresh floppy disk. They posed, grimacing, while I took their zapshot.

'Let's see it! Let's see it!' they shouted, and would have raced into the back room of the shop where the computer and video-printer were if I hadn't once again stopped them in their tracks.

'Who,' I demanded sternly, 'is going to clean up this disgusting mess?'

Little Severin grinned up at me winsomely. 'It's only cut-up spaghetti, Uncle Rogi. Didn't it make *great* worms?'

'Great,' I sighed, wondering how many of my fellow merchants on Main Street had been similarly victimized.

'Let's print the picture!' Philip said.

'Do it quick, Uncle Rogi,' Maury added. 'Mom'll kill us if we don't get home by twenty-two.'

I took a plastic sack and three pieces of cardboard out of my wrapping supplies. 'First you take these, and scoop up the worms and the money. When you get home tonight I expect you to sort the money out, wash it, and bring every nickel of it back to me tomorrow after school.'

The telephone rang. Admonishing the imps to get cracking, I answered. It was Denis, not wanting to trust my telepathy.

'We've had some bad news.' Immediately he added, 'Not any of the family. But I want you to come over to the house. This new development makes the damn Coercer Flap look like a practical joke.'

'The kids are here. I'll bring them.' I hung up. 'Leave that! Bas les pattes, kids, we're going home.'

Their minds caught my serious intent instantly and they changed from devils into obedient operant children. I turned off the shop lights and we hustled out and around the corner and down South Street a block and a half to the family home. There were only a few costumed children still abroad. We hurried past the library, where the collection of pumpkins carved by Hanover youngsters and displayed in the forecourt was a predictable shambles. I was surprised to see five cars parked in front of Denis and Lucille's place. As we tramped up the front steps the door opened and the nanny, Ayeesha Al-Joaly, who was strongly suboperant, shooed the children upstairs and indicated to me mentally that I should join the others in the living room.

Most of the Coterie was there. Glenn and his wife Colette, Sally and Tater McAllister, and big Eric Boutin, who had taken over as Denis's chief PR person with the defection of Gerry Tremblay, were gathered around a bound atlas open on the coffee table, talking in low voices. Denis, Tukwila Barnes and Mitch Losier were seated on dining-room chairs, side by side, with Lucille hovering behind them. All three were in a state of EE trance. The TV set on the wall had its audio turned off and the picture showed a murky aerial view of some city on a plain with a considerable mountain range in the background. Many of the city buildings were in flames and others, broken and devastated, poured out clouds of black smoke.

'My God, what's happened?' I cried.

Lucille hurried to me, her finger to her lips; mentally indicating the excorporeals who were obviously in the process of farsensing the disaster. She said:

Alma-Ata. And other places as well. It looks as though full-scale civil war has broken out in Soviet Central Asia, abetted by outsiders. They targeted Alma-Ata especially because of the operant educational facility at the university.

Tamara — ?

Safe! After the Congress in Montréal she and the three children and Pyotr stopped off on the way home to stay for a time with Jamie in Edinburgh . . . You knew that Tamara's middle son Ilya and Katie MacGregor announced their engagement last week?

No.

Well they did. And the pair made a trip to Islay to see Jamie's old grandmother who's 96 and they took their time because you know how grim things have been in Alma-Ata this year with the fighting so close by. They were to leave for home two days from now it's some kind of miracle that they escaped but the *others* the best of the Soviet academic operants the cream of the researchers oh Rogi the PEACE-MAKERS so many of them concentrated there the top minds God the university area is a fire-storm Tucker is scanning the situation but we're afraid we're so afraid . . .

What time is it in Alma-Ata?

Early morning. Everyone was on the commute in the streets students and teachers and all the university people the planes came from Peshawar in Pakistan over the high ranges Stealthed of course and Soviet Muslim sympathizers sabotaged phased-array radars in Pamirs and a key detector-satellite relay of course Moscow scrambled their interceptors but it was too late suicidal Muslim pilots screaming Din! Din! Din! certain they were on their way to Paradise —

Tukwila Barnes, the Native American who was probably the most talented EE adept in the Coterie, opened his eyes and made a small moaning sound. Lucille turned away from me and rushed to help him. He was ashen and trembling and his black eyes spilled tears. He began to twitch and flail his arms involuntarily then, as though he were falling into some kind of epileptic fit. I strode over and helped Lucille hold him while Colette Roy gave him a shot of something. When the medication hit him he crumpled, but he was a lightweight and I caught him easily and carried him to one of the couches. Somebody brought an afghan to cover him and Colette propped his head with cushions. We all stood there waiting for him to pull out of it. When he did, there was no need for him to speak. From his shocked mind poured images of holocaust, broadcast at an awful psychic amplification. From elsewhere in the house I heard the little Remillard boys shriek out loud and the baby, two-year-old Anne, begin a panicky wailing.

'Shit,' whispered Glenn Dalembert. He knelt beside Tucker and placed a hand on his forehead. He was the most powerful coercer in the group aside from Denis, and as he took hold of the EE adept's mind the cataract of nightmare sensations chopped off.

He said, 'Got him. Colette, you and Lucille see to the kids.'

Slowly, Barnes responded to the sedative. His eyes calmed and when he finally said, 'Okay,' Glen turned him loose. Sally Doyle proffered a glass of water. Tucker shook his head. 'Not now . . . might barf . . . God, I don't see how any of them could have escaped.'

'Did they drop nukes?' Eric Boutin asked.

Barnes shook his head. 'Conventional high explosives – but top-of-the-line. Alma's not *that* big a city. Eleven planes got through and it was enough. The university is just gone.'

Nobody said anything. Nobody even seemed to be thinking anything.

Finally, Glenn said to Tucker, 'Just lie there. We're still waiting for Denis and Mitch to get back. Denis is over-viewing and Mitch went to check out the Kremlin. Soviet news says that the whole goddam Central Asian region erupted in simultaneous armed revolt. They claim to be on top of things – but about twenty minutes ago CNN reported that there had been a big Iranian attack on the Soviet oil fields and refineries around Baku on the Caspian Sea.'

'Supported by a ground insurrection,' said Denis.

Everybody turned around.

He had risen from his chair, and although his face was pinched and pale and his eyes seemed to peer from deep inside his skull, he was in full control of both body and mind. He went to the fireplace, where a blaze had been kindled in honour of the holiday, and warmed his hands. Colourful gourds, pumpkins and corn dollies were displayed on the mantel.

'First I did a broad scan, roughly below the forty-fifth parallel,' Denis said. He watched the leaping flames. 'I tried to farsense massive stress emanations from among the normal populace. There seemed to be a dozen or more distinct foci between the Tien Shan and the Caspian: Alma-Ata, Frunze, Tashkent, Dushanbe . . . Let me see that atlas.' He went to the coffee table and bent over the map, stabbing with his finger. 'Here, here, here – all these cities east of Tashkent where the Uzbek revolt was concentrated. Up for grabs again.' He turned to another page showing the Caspian region. 'I did a closer scan in here, around Baku and up the west coast of the sea. This is the Azerbaid-zhan Republic, a tough bunch of Turks with a history of resistance to Moscow rule. What evidently happened was that a flight of B-1Ds from Tehran came in at near water-level and bombed hell out of Baku itself, its two big pipe-lines and the railroad and highway links to the west, and the other pipeline and refinery complex up the coast at

Makhachkala. The local insurgents simultaneously set off blasts in just about every refinery, pumping station and airfield from Makhachkala south to the Iranian border.'

'Christ,' said Tater McAllister. 'Coupled with the oil losses from the Uzbek fields, this new strike really puts the Soviets in deep shit.'

Denis said, 'The Azerbaidzhan region will be very hard for Moscow to pacify using ground forces. They've already sent in paratroops and gunboats from the naval base at Astrakhan on the Volga, but the Uzbek revolt left the Red Army short of reliable infantry and armour units. This new flare-up may be more than Kumylzhensky can handle without heavy air-strikes against the insurgent cities – or even the tactical use of neutron bombs . . .'

I said, 'The damn country's falling apart!'

'Not quite,' Denis said. 'It can cut its losses by abandoning the Central Asian republics and concentrating on regaining the really critical Azerbaidzhan region . . . It's only a matter of time, I'm afraid, before Moscow declares war on Iran and Pakistan.' He glanced at Mitch Losier, who was still sitting in his straight chair, lost in the EE aether. 'When Mitch gets back, he may have some information about that.'

Lucille and Colette returned from dealing with the children, and Denis flashed them a detailed recap of his discoveries. We all found places to sit down. (I was on the floor in a corner, keeping my mouth and mind shut now as became one who was only an honourary member of the Coterie.) Eric Boutin deftly served coffee and tea from the Krupps unit built into the low table. The conversation fragmented.

Lucille told Denis that the children had been calmed and a redactive wipe-job performed upon their trauma, which was fortunately shallow. Ayeesha had taken a tranquillizer and was saying her worry beads. Tukwila Barnes declared that he was famished and brought in the basket of candy treats that had been left in the front hallway to serve the neighbourhood urchins. Tater, Glenn and Colette discussed the latest developments in the Coercer Flap, starring the black sheep of the Coterie, Gerard Tremblay. The

Congressman from Massachusetts now stood charged with the crime of aggravated assault upon the President of the United States and interfering with a federal official in the performance of his official duties. Justice Department lawyers were wrangling over what other charges might apply in the case. Gerry had done the dirty deed on Monday. This was Wednesday. One might wonder what other surprises the week had in store . . .

And one would not have long to wait before finding out.

Mitch Losier coughed, opened his eyes, and sighed. He was the most solid and comfortable-looking of the Coterie, which ran to ectomorphic cerebral types. His tonsure of greying hair gave him the air of a kindly pastor or a country doctor. With the attention of the group now riveted on him – for he had excursed to Moscow – he stood up, stretched and went to the table to accept a cup of tea from Eric. He added sugar and then made his contribution to the roster of catastrophe.

'Moscow has declared war against each and every Islamic nation of the world. While reserving the right to retaliate in response to today's attacks, it will forbear force of arms temporarily and attempt to resolve the conflict through peaceful means, in consultation with the heads of state of Iran, Pakistan, Turkey and the Kashmiri Republic.'

'Thank God!' Lucille cried.

'That's the good news.' Mitch stirred his tea and sipped. 'The bad news is, that motherfucker Kumylzhensky has arrested every metapsychic operant in the Soviet Union. In the light of today's surprise strike, he feels their loyalty to the nation is deeply suspect. They are to be interrogated and held in custody until the state of internal emergency has passed, and then put on trial for treason.'

In those dark days, when even persons of goodwill were soul-burdened with the malign aetheric resonances of hatred, fear and suffering, there were many people in the United States who watched the disintegration of the Soviet Union with righteous triumphalism: the godless Commies had finally got what was coming to them. For the Sons of Earth movement, however, the Soviet misfortune had an ironic twist. To the Sons – who had very nearly become respectable among the American underclass by that time – all operants, including most especially the Soviets, were involved in a conspiracy to destroy religion, freedom and the sovereign rights of individuals. Yet here was the Red military dictator himself denouncing the superminds as 'the greatest menace the Communist Revolution has ever faced'. As Kumylzhensky thundered on about the alleged misdeeds of the Twentieth Directorate, it became evident to world observers that the KGB as a whole had been acting to bring about the downfall of Party and military right-wingers, and restore the impetus toward an open society in the Soviet Union that had been so tragically reversed following the death of Kumylzhensky's predecessor. Excorporeal excursions by outsiders into the cells of the purged operants revealed their motivation to the world. The EE adepts of dozens of nations became witnesses for the defence – at least in the forum of public opinion. Even the most naive and fearful normals eventually came to believe that the imprisoned Soviet operants had been a force for good, not evil.

In America, the hard-core membership of the Sons of Earth would eventually talk their way around this ideological paradox, but the movement had lost much of its momentum, along with any semblance of a moral base for its antioperant position. All over the world religious leaders – even some Muslims – made resounding statements in favour of operant civil rights. The Pope finally got around to issuing an encyclical, *Potestates Insolitae Mentis*, affirming that human metapsychic powers are a part of the natural order, by no means devilish, and as 'good' in the eyes of God as any other part of his creation – provided those powers are not abused.

It was a watershed time, even though we operants did not realize it. From then on, even in spite of the Coercer Flap and other operant high crimes and misdemeanours, the surge of blind antioperant prejudice began to decline. The reversal was not an overnight affair. Pockets of antioperant fanaticism remained in the United States and would be exploited on the very eve of the Intervention. But the majority of otherwise worthy people who had been infected by fear and the prejudice of ignorance slowly experienced a change of heart that would bear unexpected fruit just when the most valiant champions of operancy faced their darkest hour.

18

Baie Comeau, Québec, Earth
5 February 2008

'We have all waited a long time for this!' Victor Remillard was speaking his Yankee version of Canuckois into a loud-hailer. 'And it seemed as though the damned process was never going to work right, and some of us were tempted to abandon the project, and dump the holy bacteria and their dedicated keepers into the Saint-Laurent . . . I know *I* was tempted.'

The bundled-up audience of refinery workers and gaugers and tanker crew members yelled and whistled their appreciative unbelief, and their thoughts were plain to read: You, boss? Give up? Tu te fiches de nous! Don't try to kid us!

Victor gave a comical shrug and joined in the laughter. He was wearing an old mangy raccoon coat and a long knitted muffler and a white hard hat like those of the workers – only dirtier and more dented. Standing beside him, Shannon O'Connor could not have been more of a contrast, swathed in ankle-length arctic fox and holding an empty silver champagne bucket. It was her tanker waiting at dockside to take on the cargo.

'When we conquered the production problems, we disco-vered we had distribution problems,' Victor declaimed. 'And we solved that, too. And today this refinery of ours is ready to ship its first batch of lignin-derived gasohol fuel to energy-starved Europe!'

Everybody cheered.

'I know you're wondering why we're standing out here

freezing our pétards off, while inside the plant all those pampered germs are gobbling pulpwood in nice warm vats and shitting liquid gold. So I'll cut the speechmaking short and show you just what we've been waiting for – and what Mme Tremblay's tanker's been waiting for!'

There were more cheers while Shannon handed him the silver bucket in exchange for the hailer. Victor positioned the container under a huge flexible hose that had been jury-rigged for the occasion and yelled, 'Dupuis – open 'er up! But easy, for the love of God!'

The Chief Chemical Engineer of the facility, who was stationed at a redundant manual valve manifold outside the control shed, gripped a big wheel. He turned it a fraction of a centimetre and pinkish liquid dribbled into the champagne cooler. An acrid organic odour spread through the frigid air.

'Yo!' Victor hollered, and the flow ceased. He carried the bucket over to a venerable black Mercedes, his official vehicle during his supervisory visits to the Baie Comeau plant of Remco International. The car had been decorated in honour of the day's festivities with Canadian and American flags and bunches of multicoloured balloons. The manager of the refinery slipped a plastic funnel into the fuel tank. Victor poured the liquid to loud applause.

'And now, my friends – we come to the moment of truth! Have we really manufactured a revolutionary new fuel . . . or is it only bug pee after all?'

While the workers were laughing he slipped behind the wheel. The engine started with a roar, and the renewed cheers were drowned out when the tanker that towered above the pumping station sounded its great diaphone horn.

Everybody knew that the car had been all warmed up and primed to go, but the symbolism was all that counted. Victor jumped out, leaving the engine running, opened the other door for Shannon, and bowed her in during a final bout of clapping. Then they drove off the quay and the ceremony was over. The crowd dispersed and the hose-handling derrick on the ship lowered its cable to begin the cargo-loading process.

*

They drove out of town towards the new airport, for she would have to go directly to Washington to confer with the eminent criminal lawyers who were preparing Gerry's case. Victor slowed the Mercedes and pulled off the road into a deserted log-scaling yard where trees hid them from passing traffic. He stripped the decorations off the car, dumping the flags into the trunk and letting the helium-filled balloons waft away into the leaden sky. Then he got back in and they sat there.

'Why did your father let you do it?' he asked.

'He thinks he's fattening you for acquisition. He's been watching your situation very keenly in spite of the fireworks in Washington. The way you weathered the capital crunch – squeaked through without losing control of the process – impressed him no end. Beware of sharks trolling bait.'

'Just let him try . . . Is this scandal of your husband's some of your doing? Are you using him to set your father up?'

Shannon laughed, a throaty, appetite-laden sound. 'Why don't you read my mind?'

'I've done that already.'

He pulled her towards him and his icy lips and tongue possessed her hot mouth. Her white fox toque fell from her head and the long auburn hair flamed against the pale fur of her coat. His hand tightened, cupping her skull, and she moaned, her mind crying her need. Victor's other hand nearly encircled her neck. The fingertips against her upper spine seemed to be drawing energy from her supercharged pelvic nerves, draining —

No please Vic not that way damn you not that way let's try it for once my way please *please*!

No.

It's not love you fool there's no real loss no bonding why won't you there's nothing of *him* only me why not please oh do it —

I'll give you your pleasure I owe you that but in my own way . . .

Bastard! . . . Oh God how I hate you how I hate you . . .

Hold on to that. Guard it very carefully until you're ready to exchange him for me.

'At least he's human,' she wept aloud. 'But you . . .' She screamed then as the orgasms began, and was lost to warmth.

19

*From the Memoirs of
Rogatien Remillard*

Now I shall have to tell you about Gerry Tremblay, once a valued member of Denis's Coterie, whose spectacular disgrace was one of those backhanded blessings that seem to prove God's sense of humour.

The Pope's encyclical dealt frankly with the great sources of temptation that must accompany powerful operancy – a sinister fact of life that the American metapsychic establishment, in particular, had long tried to sweep under the rug. This ostrich attitude, a tendency to discount the possibility of disaster until it smacks you in the teeth, was probably quintessentially American. Even in the worst of times, we were a people who hoped for the best and believed that good intentions covered a multitude of sins. Because we were a young nation, because we skimmed the cream of the planetary Mind, and because our land was unarguably the richest and most fortunate on Earth, Americans had the arrogance of the golden adolescent upon whom fate smiles. We thought we were invincible as well as stronger and smarter than everyone else. We suffered a periodic comeuppance but bounced back as triumphalistic as ever. Even today, citizens of the Human Polity of the Galactic Milieu who are of American extraction tend to display a tiresome smugness about their heritage.

At the turn of the twenty-first century, the American metapsychic establishment shared the national flaw. It had deplored the Nigel Weinstein affair, but explained it away as a piece of temporary insanity. The atrocities of the Flaming Assassin were more patently criminal – but they, too, could be attributed to a madman. In other parts of the world, where there were fewer cultural inhibitions against the public avowal of operancy, there had been crimes committed in which metapsychic powers were used with obvious malice aforethought. In America – for reasons that became clear only after the Intervention – few such crimes were ever prosecuted; and none of them, until Tremblay's, had the aspect of a cause célèbre. American operant leaders had tended to sidestep the ethical aspects of their gifts and concentrate instead on the scientific and social applications of them. The few persons, such as Denis, who knew of the existence of evil and exploitative operants found themselves hamstrung by gaps in our legal system. American law, with its reverence for individual rights, makes no provision for the *mental* examination of suspected criminals. The very idea is contrary to the Fifth Amendment to the Constitution, which says that no person shall be compelled in a criminal case to be a witness against himself. However, if this principle holds, certain types of operant criminal activity can never be proved beyond a reasonable doubt. The Scottish jurors had come to this conclusion in the Weinstein case. It seems likely that Kieran O'Connor and Representative Gerard Tremblay (D-Mass.) counted upon escaping retribution in a similar manner when they conspired to coerce the President. O'Connor's role in the affair was never proved. Poor Gerry got what was coming to him – and forced a fundamental revision of operant ethics at the same time that he became the ultimate cause of Kieran O'Connor's undoing.

As I have stated earlier, I never really liked Gerry Tremblay. One might credit prescience or redactive insight – or perhaps just the old Franco instinct for smelling a rat. Psychoanalysts would doubtless point out that it was Gerry's deep-seated insecurity and envy that laid him wide open to O'Connor's peculiar brand of sorcery. He was certainly besotted with his wife Shannon, who pretended to mould Gerry to her father's specifications at the same time that she was planning the ruination of both of them.

After Gerry was elected to his first two-year term in 2004, he served on the House Special Committee on Metapsychic Affairs, where his unique position as the only operant congressman assured him of continuing publicity and growing influence. The stance he took was surprisingly conservative, dismaying the operant establishment. He helped kill a measure that would have set up federally funded training schools for operant children. In a speech that was widely televised, he pointed out that this very sort of programme – which was being followed in a number of liberal countries such as Japan, West Germany, Great Britain, the Netherlands and the Scandinavian nations – was leading to the formation of elite groups of operant children, the same kind of group that had tried and failed to take political control of the Soviet Union. While the Soviet operants had evidently worked on the side of the angels, could one assume that all operants would inevitably be so high-minded? Representative Tremblay, an operant himself, counselled great caution. He declared that Americans should remain aloof from any schemes that would distance operant youngsters from normals and foster unhealthy illusions of superiority. While he was not in favour of having obstacles put in the way of operant training per se, he hoped that it would always be seen as an adjunct to regular public or private schooling – with operant and normal children educated together. This was the American way, avouched the Gentleman from Massachusetts, and the *best* way – for the sake of the young operants themselves and the nation as a whole.

Gerry's speech was a smash, and he was well on the road to the big time. Progressive operants tried in vain to point out that federal funding of their programmes was vital. In those depressed times, the states had no tax revenues to spare for operant training; private facilities for operants, except at institutions such as Dartmouth, MIT, Stanford, and the Universities of Texas, Virginia and California-Davis, where there were long-standing Departments of Metapsychology – were too expensive for the majority of gifted children. Minds would be wasted, the operants warned.

Not so, replied Tremblay. In time, when the nation could afford it, Congress would reconsider funding a generalized operant education programme. But these were perilous days. America was threatened not only by unemployment, inflation and shortages, but also by the escalating Holy War of the fundamentalist Muslims, which now had spread further into Africa, India and the East Indies; and China had taken a mysterious turn towards isolationism that alarmed both its neighbours and the United States. Tremblay told his fellow operants to be patient – and to ask not what their country could do for them, but what they could do for their country.

As the agent of Kieran O'Connor, Gerry Tremblay was given two important assignments. The first was to influence both the President and Democratic members of Congress in favour of O'Connor's military-industrial contractors, especially those connected to the Zap-Star satellite defence system, the new ON–1 Space Habitat, and the proposed Lunar Base. Gerry was successful in this area because Baumgartner was committed to a strong military posture and to the American space programme, and liberal Democrats who favoured the latter could rather easily be made to see the high-tech side benefits of the former.

Gerry's second assignment was to discourage Baumgartner from granting special privileges to operants, thus denying a power base to the operant establishment. The defeat of the Operant Education Bill was a great start for Gerry . . . but immediately after that he realized that O'Connor's second mandate was a no-hoper.

The factor that disrupted the carefully laid scheme was a small one: the President's grandchild, Amanda Denton. Baumgartner's antioperant feelings, never too firmly grounded in personal conviction, were shaken by the religious leaders' statements on the matter – and then utterly shattered by the little girl. She was a resident in the White House, along with her parents and two older brothers. Ernie Denton, the husband of Baumgartner's only daughter, served as a presidential aide; and whenever the Chief Executive felt depressed, he'd send Ernie off to fetch Amanda. The child was both charming and good for what ailed the President. (She grew up to be a Grand Master Redactor, a superlative metapsychic healer.) And with Amanda cavorting about the Oval Office, Gerry Tremblay didn't have a prayer of reinstituting the antioperant mood that had characterized Baumgartner's first term.

This was a serious worry to O'Connor. In 2006, Gerry was re-elected to the House . . . but so were seven other operants from liberal states. Bills were introduced to reorganize and upgrade the EE Service of the Defence Department, which had been starved for funds during the past four years. The FBI, concerned that Islamic terrorists might once again target American cities, pressed for the recruitment of operant agents. There was a predictable outcry from conservatives; but such agents were widely used now in other countries and had proved effective – if unpopular.

And then came the greatest threat thus far to O'Connor's schemes. He had been grooming his creature, Senator Scrope, to run for president in 2008, since Baumgartner was restricted to two terms by the XXII Amendment to the Constitution. But the country now perceived the charismatic Baumgartner to be the Man on a White Horse who would save it from the maelstrom engulfing the rest of the world. In spite of all O'Connor's lobbying efforts, Congress passed a repeal of Article XXII in May 2007, and by the middle of October the necessary three-fourths of the state legislatures had ratified it. Baumgartner was free to run again, if he chose to do so. And if he did, the next four years boded ill for O'Connor and his secret operant cabal.

On 27 October, a delegation of the Republican National Committee (not including Chairman Cassidy, who had lost control of the organization) was scheduled to call on the President and formally request him to run for a third term. O'Connor's instructions to Gerry Tremblay were explicit. There could be no more subtlety. Gerry was the only O'Connor partisan with free access to the West Wing having the mental muscle for a full coercive thrust. He was to arrange for an appointment with the President immediately following that of the delegation, so he could station himself in the Oval Office's anteroom. From there he would eavesdrop telepathically, and at the critical moment compel the President to say that he believed the repeal of Article

XXII to be an unwise and dangerous move – and that under no circumstances would he run again.

It was a desperate scheme and it might have worked, for Baumgartner would have contradicted his own public image of firm decisiveness if he repudiated the statement – and to charge that he had been coerced would put him in an even worse position. He would know his mind had been tampered with; but he would not know who had done it – or when it might happen again – and O'Connor was certain that subliminal follow-up thrusts by Gerry over the next few weeks would demoralize him and force him to accept the inevitable. At worst, Baumgartner would seem to be suffering a nervous breakdown and his allegations of mental compulsion would be unprovable.

The day came. Gerry arrived early for his appointment and was shown into the anteroom to wait by a White House usher who fell victim to his more subtle coercive wiles. Gerry watched as another usher shepherded in the delegation, together with a single minicam video journalist who would record the historic moment. Gerry suffered a brief qualm when he recognized an operant among the delegates, Dr Beatrice Fairweather of the University of Virginia; but there seemed to be little danger of her detecting the coercive impulse. Her metafaculties were not strong, and she would have no reason to suspect that Baumgartner was being mentally manipulated.

The door to the Oval Office closed, leaving Gerry seated as close to it as he could get. Two oblivious aides worked at desks on the opposite side of the room. He exerted his farsenses and summoned a close-up image of the President.

There was a spate of greetings and preliminary chitchat, and then the delegation spokesman, the former Governor of Delaware, got to the heart of the matter:

'Mr President, we have brought to you a request of the most critical importance, dictated by the Republican Party and also by millions of American citizens who have flooded our offices with their letters, videograms, and phone calls. The Twenty-Second Amendment to the Constitution was repealed for one reason and for one reason only – so that you would not have to step down from the presidency at this time when our beleaguered nation needs your continuing guidance so desperately. So I put the question to you frankly. Will you accept the nomination in 2008?'

Gerry took hold of Lloyd Baumgartner's mind in that instant. He saw from the President's eyes, heard with the President's ears, spoke with the President's mouth and vocal cords.

'Ladies and gentlemen, this is an extraordinary honour that you offer me, and I want to assure you that over the past week I have been thinking and praying over it — '

WHAT ARE YOU DOING TO MY GRANDPA?

' — so that this decision I give you today represents my carefully considered judgement, what I believe will best serve the needs of our great nation. I must decline – I must decline — '

GRANDPA! GRANDPA! YOU LET GRANDPA OUT OF HIS HEAD!

Through the President's eyes, Gerry saw the door of the Oval Office fly open and Amanda, like a pinafore-clad avenging angel, dash directly towards the desk where her grandfather sat. Far behind her, out in the anteroom, Ernie Denton stood gaping at the enormity of his five-year-old daughter's presumption.

' — I must decline — '

Baumgartner was fighting the hold. And the damn child was slashing at him with all her raw infant strength. Gerry's sight of her and of all the others inside the office dimmed as the captive mind began to slip away.

Gerry lurched to his feet, knowing that if he could only manage eye contact with the President he could reassert control. The little girl screeched and pointed at him standing there in the doorway. The six members of the delegation and the goddam cameraman, too, turned to look at him. The child cried out loud:

'That's not Grandpa talking. That's *him*! He's inside Grandpa's head. Uncle Gerry is making Grandpa say things he doesn't want to say!'

The Secret Service men materialized out of nowhere, pinioning Gerry's arms. In a last-ditch effort, he forced Baumgartner to say, 'Decline . . . decline . . .'

Then the linkage broke. Dr Beatrice Fairweather, a little old lady with a kindly face, stepped up to Gerry and put her fingers on his forehead and opened his faltering mind like a sardine can.

'Oh, dear,' she said. 'I'm afraid the child is right.'

The President slumped back into his big leather chair. He said hoarsely, 'You bet your sweet ass she's right! Arrest that man!'

Gerry Tremblay relaxed then, and even managed a rueful little smile for the camera as the Secret Service agents led him away.

In July 2008 Tremblay went on trial. The evidence of Beatrice Fairweather was disallowed under the statutes prohibiting self-incrimination, but little Amanda Denton was a telling witness for the prosecution. Her testimony, together with that of the President, was sufficient to convict Representative Gerard Tremblay of aggravated assault and battery, and interfering with a federal official. A count of kidnapping was thrown out. Tremblay's appeal of the verdict eventually reached the Supreme Court, which upheld his conviction. He was impeached and expelled from the House of Representatives and served two years and six months of a concurrent three-to-twenty-five-year sentence.

In 2012, both houses of Congress passed the XXIX Amendment to the Constitution, which would permit defendants in criminal trials (operant or not) to be cross-examined mentally by a three-person group of forensic redactors – one for the defence, one for the prosecution, and one acting as amicus curiae. The Amendment was submitted to the state legislatures but had not been ratified by the requisite three-quarters of the United States by the time the Intervention took place.

Upon his parole in 2012, Gerry Tremblay became an officer in Roggenfeld Acquisitions, a firm specializing in the leveraged buy-outs of aerospace contractors. Five months after his release from prison, his wife Shannon presented him with a baby girl, Laura, who was destined for a spectacular role in the private life of a certain Magnate of the

Concilium forty years into the future. Tremblay complaisantly acknowledged Laura as his own.

He never learned – unlike his father-in-law, Kieran O'Connor – that it had been Shannon who sent little Amanda to visit her grandfather on 29 October 2007, and also arranged for Dr Fairweather to join the nominating delegation at the last moment.

20

Oversight Authority Vessel
Sada [Simb 220–0000]

Podkamennaya Tunguska Basin
USSR, Earth

20 June 2008

The huge Simbiari Authority flagship and its attendant fleet of twenty-six smaller observation vessels descended slowly and openly, in broad daylight, over the event site. By order of the Lylmik Supervisors, the commemoration was to be deliberately conspicuous, reminding the populace of this war-torn Earth nation of a truth they had once championed – that human beings were not alone in the starry universe.

On the bridge of the Sada, Captain Chassatam, his Executive Officer Madi Ala Assamochiss, and Senior Oversight Magnate Adassti watched the view-screen, which was in terrain-proper mode, as the wilderness of verdant bogs and conifer thickets drew closer and closer.

'Approaching stasis altitude,' said the Exec.

'Very well,' said Captain Chassatam. A fast farsight sweep told him that the formation was perfectly organized, and seconds later it hovered motionless some six hundred metres above the taiga. One level of his mind commanded the attention of all crews, while another signalled the Simbiari chaplain stationed in the topside bubble to organize and energize the solemn metaconcert aimed at coercing God.

O Source and Sustainer of Life! Our minds and the Mind of the Simbiari Polity in all the far-flung reaches of the Galaxy praise you this day at the site where your martyrs, the crew and survey personnel of the Observation Vessel Risstimi, did one hundred planetary orbits ago choose to sacrifice themselves rather than bring great harm upon the innocent people of a world placed under their care. Help us to understand and appreciate your martyrs' extraordinary act of love. Console the bereaved among us who lost kin and dear friends in the event. If it should be your will, give us the courage to emulate their selfless action freely and without fear, confident as they were confident that you will receive our undying minds in the Great Mind even as our bodies perish. We trust that you will welcome us one day as you welcomed them into your Divine Milieu of unending peace and light, love and joy. Praise to you, Author of the Universe and exemplar of perfect Unity! Praise throughout all space and time! We Simbiari say this with one Mind.

WE SAY IT!

'A chopper approaches from Vanavara,' the Exec noted, inserting its image into a corner of the view-screen. All three Simbiari scrutinized the tiny craft with their farsight and did a surface probe of the humans within. Lettering on the body of the helicopter indicated that it belonged to the local reindeer-herders' collective.

'I'd hoped for a higher-status set of eyewitnesses than this,' the Magnate said rather peevishly. She mopped green mucus from her face. As the senior personage present it had been her duty to express ritual sorrow during the prayer.

'They've closed down the air bases at Ust-Ilimisk and Tura,' the Captain said. 'They'll have to send jets from Krasnoyarsk.'

'Military observers always receive higher credibility ratings from Earthlings,' Magnate Adassti said. 'I hope they're not asleep at the switch down there at PVOS.'

The Exec said, 'The chopper carries a pilot and the local stringer for the Evenk People's Video Net. The journalist has remembered to load his camera and take off the lens cap, and he's framing a fair shot of the fleet.'

'Thanks be to sacred Truth and Beauty,' the Magnate sighed.

The small craft came whop-whopping over the spruces, following an erratic course. The Magnate turned her thoughts to higher things, reminiscing out loud in what she hoped was a comradely fashion.

'My sainted Auntie Bami Ala was among the Tunguska martyrs. I recall her clearly, even though I was a mere toddler when she left on her first exotic assignment. She was only a TechOne with the Taxonomical Service, but very keen at the thought of bringing Milieu enlightenment to a suboperant world. Dear Auntie . . . She showed me my first visuals of humans. I had to fight to keep from gagging at the first sight of them — those horrid dry skins, like Poltroyans only ranging in pigmentation from dusty black to fish-belly pink. She explained their strange physiology and shocked me to the toe-webs. No algae symbionts in the epidermis, so they were constantly eating and excreting through a hypertrophied gastrointestinal tract — even making a *ceremony* of foodtaking. And I had thought that the Gi were uncouth! Auntie told me about the primitive state of human technology and psychosocial development, and then scandalized me even more by admitting that the Lylmik had the highest hopes for Earth. But I'll tell you, Captain, that even now I can hardly imagine a more unlikely candidate-world for coadunation of the local Mind.'

'I don't know,' the Captain said. 'They may give us a run for the money in the high-tech field. Their rate of advancement has been little short of stupefying.' He waved a hand at the wealth of ingenious mechanisms that crowded the bridge of the Sada. 'Give humanity a few more decades and they'll have most of this. With their elaboration of the Universal Field Theory, they've been able to begin work on gravo-magnetic propulsion. And it's only a fluke that they haven't tamed fusion yet. Fooling around, wasting their resources on manned-satellite schemes. If they only knew that we have nearly eight hundred worlds for them!'

'Captain,' the Executive Officer warned, 'the exotic aircraft is venturing too close to the rho-field coronal zone. Shall I push it off?'

'Do so. We can't have the thing dropping out of the sky

like a zapped mosquito . . . That's better. Neat work with the pressor, Madi Ala. We'll give him just a few more minutes and then send him off. The emotional tone of the pilot is turning flaky.'

'The journalist must make an explicit record of our presence,' Magnate Adassti averred. 'The Lylmik were emphatic on that point.'

The Captain sipped carbonated water from his platinum flask with a certain air of disdain. 'Does the Supervisory Body *really* believe this manifestation will divert the Soviets from their internal conflicts? Frankly, with the way things are going down in Transcaucasia, I doubt that a mere fleet of starships over the Stony Tunguska will even make the evening news.'

'Vulgar cynicism is hardly called for, Captain.' The Magnate was somewhat starchy over his minor breach of decorum. Rehydrating oneself among equals or in informal situations was certainly acceptable. But the Captain had not even bothered to ask her permission before drinking, and the Executive Officer was a subordinate! Flight crews were a roughhewn lot, regrettably egalitarian.

The Captain only chuckled at her subliminal rebuke. 'It looks to me as though the Soviet Union is only a half skip away from complete disintegration. Cynicism seems quite justified.'

'Nonsense. The nation may be battered, but its economy and governmental structure are still basically intact. The reports of our presence here will be sent to Moscow and eventually disseminated throughout the planet. As to what good the manifestation will do . . . we can expect benefits to accrue over the long term.'

'Earth hasn't got a long term. If the Lylmik hold off Intervention much longer this whole Second Oversight Phase will be a wasted effort. We'll find ourselves with a suboperant world again! The normals are starting to kill off coadunating minds down there, you know.'

'Unfortunately, this is true,' the Magnate admitted. 'If only the imprisoned Soviet operants had embraced a pacifistic stance, as their colleagues in other countries advised them. Poor misguided ones! The military dictator in the

Kremlin was badly jolted by the mass escape attempt of the aggressively empowered adepts. Nearly fourteen hundred minds lost to the overall coadunation effort . . . I fear that an ethic of nonviolence is a tough bolus for many Earthling operants to swallow.'

'The bunch at Darjeeling stayed peaceful – until the Muslim mob tore them to pieces. On this planet, metapsychic operants may be in a no-win situation. It's happened on other worlds.'

'The Lylmik still hold out hope. On the other hand, the revised schema postulates that Intervention must occur within the next five years here, or it probably will not occur at all . . .'

'Captain, the helicopter is retreating,' said the Exec.

'Yes, Madi Ala, I see. The poor pilot's had enough. He's frightened nearly out of his mind. He didn't have nearly as much to drink today as the journalist.'

A telltale blinked an alert and the Exec said, 'Now we are being scanned in the infrared by a Soviet satellite surveillance system as well as by the phased arrays at Krasnoyarsk. Is this allowable?'

The Captain passed the buck to the Magnate, who said, 'Affirmative. But obscure any attempt at configuration fine-scan of the Sada by light-amplifiers. I don't want us to be too blatantly on the record. We'll remain in position for a few more minutes and let EuroSat ZS spot us on its next sweep. Three sightings should provide modest credibility and give the Earthlings something to think about besides killing one another.'

'Very well,' said the Captain. He was watching the view and slurping from his flask again, radiating overfamiliarity. 'You ever been landside in Siberia, Magnate Adassti?'

She gave up on any attempt to maintain a refined atmosphere and hauled out her own water supply, indicating to the Exec that she should also feel free to imbibe. 'No, most of my work here has been administrative. I have gone abroad during the past five orbits monitoring the Metapsychic Congresses . . . Montréal last year after they decided not to risk Moscow; Paris, Beijing, Edinburgh – all large cities. And before that I attended the session held in a quaint rural hostelry in Bretton Woods, New Hampshire. Bizarre! . . . I presume, Captain, from your reference to mosquitoes, that you yourself *have* visited Siberia.' She shuddered. The insects were insanely fond of Simbiari body fluids.

'I went down once, not long after the martyrdom. One of my academy mates crewed on the Risstimi. What a sight it was! The burnt trees just beneath the blast zone were standing upright, but all around them was this vast elliptical area of trunks smashed flat and radiating outward. Not a single Earthling was harmed. But if the crew of the Risstimi hadn't hung on to the failed control system mentally, the ship would have continued right across the continent and impacted on Saint Petersburg, where nearly two million people lived at the time.'

'Truth!' exclaimed the Exec. 'I didn't know there were that many.'

'I wonder if this damn planet will ever appreciate what we've done?' the Captain mused. 'Not just what the Risstimi crew did, but all the rest of it. Sixty thousand years of watching and guiding and cosseting, all the while praying that the silly clots wouldn't botch it.'

Magnate Adassti had a grim little smile on her emerald lips. 'If Intervention does take place and we undertake the proctorship, we'll make *sure* the Earthlings are properly grateful. Shaping up minds as barbarous as these for full Concilium participation is going to require heroic psycho-correctional measures. After what they've put us through — '

'Captain,' said the Exec. 'We have a wing of MiGs zeroing in on us from Krasnoyarsk.'

'It's about time,' the Magnate snapped.

The officer hesitated, then blurted out, 'Farsense Monitoring reports that the Soviets think we may be a Chinese secret weapon.'

'Chinese?' blared the Captain. '*Chinese?* Can't the flaming idiots recognize a flight of UFOs when they see one?'

Magnate Lashi Ala Adassti dripped green heedlessly over the shiny instrumentation console as she swallowed great gulps of charged water. 'Up the Cosmic All!' she blasphemed. 'The nincompoops!'

'So much for *that* brilliant Lylmik ploy,' the Captain told her. 'Your orders, Magnate?'

'Get us back into orbit and invisible. We'll be hearing from the Supervisory Body soon enough.'

21

From the Memoirs of
Rogatien Remillard

The flight of flying saucers detected over Siberia made a very minor news splash. The videotape of the event – which was sold to Western news agencies for an enormous sum by the Soviet government – was exquisitely detailed, so much so that it was deemed a masterpiece of special effects by the ciné wizards of Industrial Light and Magic. NASA analysts said that no spacecraft propulsion system known to science could account for the movement of the alleged saucers. They simply defied Newton's Laws of Motion. These adverse judgements, coupled with the suspicious date of the sighting, on the anniversary of the Tunguska meteorite fall, led most authorities to dismiss the tape as a hoax.

Over the next couple of years there were other saucer reports from different parts of the world – none quite so spectacular as the Siberian affair, but nevertheless impressive in the aggregate. Alas! The world was so preoccupied with mundane troubles that the notion of extraterrestrial visitors caused no excitement at all. So the saucers were back again? Big deal. So was the rain in Spain, the Dust Bowl in Oklahoma, and Killer Smog in London and Tokyo.

Feeling very low one dreary November evening in 2008 (I had just finished composing a long and querulous video-gram to Ume, who had moved back to Sapporo the previous summer), I sat in my apartment above the bookshop, reading and drinking. The book was an old favourite, a peerless historical novel by H. F. M. Prescott called *The Man on a Donkey*. The booze was Laphroaig, a lovely dusky malt that Jamie MacGregor had brought over on his last visit. Sleet rapped at the storm windows, the fire was low in the Franklin stove, and my stockinged feet rested on the warm shaggy belly of my cat Marcel, who was asleep on the claw-shredded ottoman.

The doorbell rang. It was after 2300. Reluctantly, I sent my farsight down into the street entryway, where I saw Denis. Setting the Prescott aside with a sigh, I extracted my feet from their cozy shelter and padded over to the buzzer.

Come up, I told my nephew. Is anything wrong?

Yes and no. I just want to talk to you if you don't mind. I am not quite blotto.

I'll redact you sober.

You do and I'll sic Marcel on you . . .

I opened the hall door and he came in, dripping.

'I walked from the lab,' he said, taking off his raincoat. 'What a rotten night.'

I got another tumbler, splashed in Scotch, and held it out to him. Denis rarely indulges, but it didn't take telepathy to know what he needed. He flopped down on the sofa, took a belt, and sighed.

'The President called me earlier today.'

'He should be feeling pretty high,' I opined. 'The landslide victory to end all landslides. He's got his third term – and probably a fourth and fifth if he wants them — '

'Uncle Rogi, do you remember when I was a kid, and just learning to do long-distance scanning? We didn't call it EE then. It was just mind-travelling.'

'Sure, I remember. You'd drag me along. Only way I ever got very far out of Coos County, mentally speaking.'

'What we were doing was a farsensory metaconcert, a mind-meld. I didn't know *that*, either. You know, it's a funny thing. I've never been able to go metaconcert with anyone except you and Lucille. Glenn says I'm too wary, too jealous of my mental autonomy to be a team thinker. Lucille thinks I may just be afraid to trust . . . Whatever it is, it's there. And I want to excurse tonight with a partner – someone who will magnify my own sight. Luce is out. Now that she's pregnant again I want to keep her as tranquil as possible.'

The implication was dire. 'And this EE's likely to be anything but, eh?'

'I tripped out myself earlier this evening, right after the President's call. He told me that the Secretary of Defence had the wind up over something his Psi-Eye people had spied. He asked me to check it out.'

I poured myself another finger of Scotch and downed it before Denis could stop me. 'What happened? A nuke on the Kremlin?'

'It's in China . . . whatever it is. I couldn't get any more of a handle on it than the Washington pEEps. That's why I need you. Minimal though your solitary output is, when it's yoked with mine I should experience a magnification up to threefold through synergistic augmentation.'

'Your humble servant,' I muttered. Minimal!

Denis dragged the ottoman over to the couch, displacing Marcel, who hissed bitterly at the imposition and slunk off to the kitchen. 'Sit here beside me. We can put our feet up and it'll be nearly as good as the barber-chairs at the lab. I suppose I should have asked you to come down there, but — '

'You knew I wouldn't, and it doesn't make a damn bit of difference where we do it.'

'No. It doesn't.'

The body contact was unfamiliar and disquieting. Good God, was I afraid of him? His mind was utterly silent. Wide open. Waiting. I closed my eyes and still saw the living room through mind-sight, but I made no move towards him. I turned the kitchen wall transparent and saw the cat opening the breadbox to steal an English muffin. I had forgotten to fill his food dish. I kept on going out through the house wall and saw the oddly unshadowed streets slick with freezing rain and cars going up and down Main Street with tyres and wiper blades crunching.

Denis said: Come.

I said: All right all right it's just been a hell of a long

time since you were in my skull and you were only a kid then and now tu es un gros bonnet the Biggest Mindshot of the lot and I *do* want to help you but what you ask of me ah Denis a Franco father cannot stand naked before his son —

No no it won't be like that metaconcert among adults isn't that kind of merging please don't worry. This will not be like your experiences with Ume or Elaine those were an altogether different type of mental intercourse believe me trust me I am only Denis the same little Denis et tu es mon vrai père! Ça va Uncle Rogi?

Ça va ça va mais allez-y doucement dammit!

He took me away . . .

I am not much of a head. I use telepathy without a qualm, of course, and do everyday things such as deep-scanning letters before opening them and tracking potentially light-fingered customers around the shop and anticipating the moves of idiot drivers. But the larger faculties I use grudgingly (except with the ladies!) and there is almost always a sense of uneasiness after the fact, as if I had indulged a secret vice. Excorporeal excursion is ordinarily very difficult for me. I can 'call' over fairly long distances, but to 'see' – much less use other ultrasenses – is an exhausting piece of work when it is not completely impossible. I had braced myself for the joint trip with Denis, expecting the usual exertion. But what a difference! I hardly know what to compare that mind-flight to. There are certain dreams, where one does not really fly but rather takes giant steps, one after the other, each one covering the proverbial seven leagues. Long ago, when I had eavesdropped on the mind of little Denis as he slowly scanned New Hampshire for other operants, I had seen on the eerie mindscape the jewel-like clusters of 'light' that mark the positions of living human brains – the latents glowing dimly, the operants blazing like tiny stars. There was something of this effect as Denis and I loped westward across the continent, each heroic bound covering a greater distance and attaining a greater height than the last, until at the Pacific Coast we soared up without pausing and described a vast arc above the mindless dark of the northern ocean. But *was* it mindless? There were none of the starlike concentrations, but there was something else: an intricate whispering coming not from below but from all around me, as if millions upon millions of infinitesimal voices were carrying on conversations – or even singing, since the sensation had a rhythmic pulsation to it, a tempo that was ever changing and yet somehow orchestrated . . .

It is the vital field of the world, Denis said. Life and Mind interacting. The biosphere forms a latticework that is entire but the noösphere the World Mind permeates it only imperfectly as yet and so the field is sensed by our minds only as a whisper.

I asked: When this World Mind finishes weaving itself together what will there be?

And my nephew said: A song.

We came to Japan and touched its shimmering arc. But there was no time for me to seek Ume, although I thought of it; and a moment later we were decelerating over China, flying low above the great Yangzi River basin, one of the most populous regions of the world. It was full daytime there, of course – and the minds blazed. The perception was overwhelming to me and I lost all sense of direction and differentiation; but Denis bore me onwards, his goal now in view, and in another instant we were poised above the metropolis of Wuhan and ready to get down to business.

Denis said: Now we must do the real metaconcert Uncle Rogi. The flight was only a peripheral linkage a kind of piggyback ride. What I want you to do now primarily is relax. We are going to fuse our wills so that we have a single purpose. That's what metaconcert is. ONE WILL one vector for the channelled faculty in this case the close inspection of a *thing* inside a small laboratory in a modest building of the university. When I ask it you must help me to penetrate using all the strength you have. Do you understand?

Yes.

You may feel yourself fainting don't be concerned I'll hold you the vision will be mine even if you fail but hold out as best you can for as long as you can.

Yes.

572

Now.

It seemed that the sun rose. What had been drab was fully coloured and what had been merely bright now became supersaturated with a brilliance that would be intolerable to physical eyes. At that time there were some six million people living in close proximity in the Wuhan tri-city area, and about ten thousand of them had some degree of operancy. Naturally most of these were concentrated in the university district, which lay east of the Yangzi near a small lake. We seemed to plummet out of the sky. Abruptly the mind-constellation effect was gone and we were *there*, wafting along a modernistic concourse where crowds of students and academics streamed in and out of buildings, rode bicycles, or lounged about under leafless trees soaking up a bit of late-autumn sunshine.

Denis knew where to go. We passed through the white-stone outer wall of a smallish structure, entered offices where people worked at computer terminals or shuffled papers, much as they do in any university, and then we reached the lab. There were three men and two women inside, and from the paraphernalia I knew at once that it was a metapsychology establishment. The so-called barber-chair, with its apparatus for measuring the brain activity of a 'performing' operant, was virtually identical to similar devices at Dartmouth. Around the chair on the bare concrete floor was a ring about three metres in diameter, studded with little gadgets all wired together, the whole attached by several heavy cables to a bank of equipment racks. Some of the front panels were demounted and electronic guts hung out, which the scientists tinkered with.

Denis said: When I was here earlier I examined this stuff and recorded the gross details of the circuitry. Now I want to try microscrutiny. Hang on to your hat Uncle Rogi. I'll try to be as quick as I can . . .

He zeroed in, and I felt as though my eyes were being torn out of my skull – but of course my physical eyes had nothing to do with the ultrasensory scan; the pain was somewhere in my nervous system where farsight impulses only partially belonging to the physical universe were being amplified in some terrible esoteric fashion by my nephew's supermind. The brightness was awful. In it detailed pictures of God knew what were flickering like flipped pages in an old-fashioned book. I saw them distorted, sometimes whole and then fragmented like jigsaw puzzles. They made no sense and the rapidity of the image-change was indescribably sickening. I think I was trying to scream. I know I yearned to let go of Denis, to stop the agony, but I'd promised. I'd promised . . .

It ended.

Somewhere, somehow I was weeping and racked with spasms. I knew that – and yet another part of my mind stood aside, upright and proud of itself for having successfully endured. The suffering faded and my farsight once again perceived the Chinese laboratory.

Denis said: That was very good. The test subject has arrived. I'm going to break concert for a moment and check her out.

The supernal vividness of the scene faded to a washed-out pastel. I saw that only one of the scientists in the room was an operant. His aura was a pale yellowish-green, like a firefly. And then the door opened and in came a young woman with an aura like a house afire, stuffing the last of a sweet rice cake into her mouth and licking her fingers. She wore a smart red leather jumpsuit and white boots with high heels, and greeted the scientific types in a bored fashion before plopping down in the barber-chair. One man hooked her up while the other researchers completed their equipment adjustment, closed the panels and went out – leaving the operant alone.

Denis re-established the metaconcert. Once again every detail of the place was extravagantly clear and I noticed for the first time a parabolic dish hanging above the operant's head. It looked something like a lamp reflector with a complex doodad at the centre.

In an adjacent control room, the crew was powering up. The operant leader gave a telepathic command and the test subject began to count steadily in declamatory farspeech. The brain-monitoring systems were all go.

On the count of ten a mirrored dome sprang into existence, hiding the woman in the chair from view. Simultaneously, her telepathic speech cut off. The dome was approximately hemispheric, shaped like the top half of an egg and apparently as slick as glass. It did not quite touch the hanging reflector, but the ring of small components on the floor had been swallowed.

Before I could express my astonishment, Denis said: One more push Uncle Rogi. The best that you can do . . . through the mirror surface!

Our conjoined minds thrust out, and this time I did lose consciousness, after enduring only the briefest flash of mortal agony. When I recovered my senses, I found I was sitting on the sofa in my apartment in Hanover, my head throbbing like the legendary ill-used hamster in the classic dirty joke. I heard the sound of retching in the bathroom and water running in the sink. After a few minutes Denis came out, towelling his wet hair and looking like the living dead.

'Did we get through the goddam thing?' I whispered.

'No,' said Denis.

'It was a mechanical mind-screen, wasn't it . . . The thing they said couldn't be made?'

'*I* never said it.' Denis went slowly to the coat closet and dragged out his Burberry. I had never seen him look so terrible, so vitiated. His emotions were totally concealed.

'D'you realize they can stop Psi-Eye with a thing like that?' I nattered. 'The Chinese can do anything they damn well please behind it and the EE monitors would never know! If *you* can't punch through it, then no meta on Earth can . . . Is there any way at all to open it up?'

'Destroy the generator,' Denis said. 'Aside from that – I don't know. We'll have to build our own and experiment.' He opened the outer door. 'Thank you again for your help, Uncle Rogi.'

'But we're back to square one!' I cried. 'The Chinese are paranoid about the Russians and vice versa. They'll start the arms race all over again or even pull a pre-emptive strike!'

'Good night,' my nephew said. The door closed.

I spat one obscenity after him on the declamatory farspeech mode and damned if Marcel didn't stroll out of the kitchen and eye me with sardonic humour. He leaped to the gate-leg table where the half-full bottle of Laphroaig still stood, and cocked his great whiskers at it.

'Best idea I've heard all night,' I told him; and I settled down to finish off the Scotch while the icy rain lashed the window and the cat took his place again at my feet.

22

New York City, Earth
4 March 2012

There were a handful of operants at the Sloan-Kettering Institute, so Dr Colwyn Presteigne had kept his mental shield at maximal strength during the entire three hours of the consultation. The strain – to say nothing of the emotional trauma resulting from the diagnosis – hit him in the taxi. He only regained consciousness at his destination, with the panicked cabbie yelling at him over the intercom and the doorman of the Plaza peering anxiously through the open door.

'Oh, for God's sake, it's all right,' Presteigne growled. 'I only dropped off to sleep for a moment.' He pushed his credit card through the slot in the armoured barrier. 'Take fifteen.'

'May I help you, Dr Presteigne?' The doorman solicitously raised his umbrella and extended a white-gloved hand.

'Never mind.' The physician retrieved his card, climbed out, and strode into the hotel. Arnold Pakkala was waiting in the lobby.

He said:?

Presteigne's features were set again in their habitual cast of thoughtful benevolence. His mind was impenetrable beneath the outermost social level. He said: Tell Kier I'm on my way up.

Arnold said: ???

Presteigne turned his back on the executive assistant and

576

headed for the elevator. He braced himself to resist any coercion; but Arnold only stood there trying without success to forestall the escape of inarticulate grief, then turned away towards the house phones.

Adam Grondin opened the door to the suite when the physician exited the elevator. More diffident than Arnold, he made no attempt to seek information. 'The Boss is in the sitting room.'

Presteigne nodded, slipped off his topcoat, and took the folder out of his briefcase. 'See that Kier's things are packed up. He'll have to go in right away.'

'Shit,' Grondin whispered. 'Shit shit shit . . .'

'Put a call through to Mrs Tremblay and ask her to wait on hold. I think he'll want to tell her himself.'

'Okay, Doc.'

Presteigne went into the sitting room and carefully closed the door behind him. Kieran was standing at the window in his dressing gown, his hands locked behind him.

'Sit down, Col. Take a drink. Don't bother to say it – just open wide.'

Mute, his vision blurring with tears, the physician obeyed.

Kieran O'Connor looked out over Central Park. Rags of mist infiltrated the budding trees. A policeman on horseback stopped at a bench where a vagrant lay covered with newspapers and began speaking into his walkie-talkie.

'It's interesting,' Kieran said, 'that it should have hit me this way. One could make an interesting case for divine retribution – if it weren't for the fact that I won't let this stop me.'

'But, Kier, it's metastasized. Both the lymphangiography and the bone isoenzyme tests show — '

'I don't *need* that much longer.'

'I've made arrangements to have you admitted immediately under a fictitious name — '

'No.'

'But you've got to!'

Kieran laughed. 'You doctors . . . so accustomed to controlling life-and-death decisions.' Don't be a fool Col what do I care for your damned palliatives your brain-weakening chemicals I've lived with pain all my life I'll accept this too and keep my power until the Black Mother takes me in and all the rest as well it's perfect it's even appropriate Her jest at my expense Her proof that I'm the one loved most just as She always said where's your faith where's your love I'll *redact* the damn thing fend it off mind over matter you know it can be done you know other operants have done it why not me?

Kier you don't assay that highly in the redactive metafaculty. Some minds are good at healing and some aren't and self-redaction is the least-understood aspect of the metahealing process all bound about with unconscious factors that can enhance or inhibit —

Kieran turned around, halting the doctor's expostulations with a gentle impulse. 'Enough, Col. I agreed to your tests because — because I was interested. I guess I always suspected something like this would happen as I got down to the wire. It's just another omen.'

'Without any sort of treatment the pain will become unbearable.'

'I can bear anything, for good reason.' *Except disloyalty* . . .

Presteigne lowered his head in capitulation. 'You're the Boss.' He hesitated. 'I asked Adam to put in a call to your daughter. I thought you'd want her to know. I'm sorry if I presumed.'

Kieran's face stiffened. A wraith-image of Shannon, strangely distorted, flickered across his adamantine mental screen. And then it was gone and he was smiling. 'Col, assuming your worst-case scenario — that any attempt at self-redaction on my part will be ineffective — how much longer will I be able to raise it?'

'If you're capable now it's some kind of fucking miracle! Please excuse the morbid pun.'

But Kieran was chuckling in appreciation. 'All right, that's plain as the proverbial pikestaff! I think the best thing to do then is to get back to Chicago. You go out and tell Shannon that all this was a false alarm. That I'm fine.'

Presteigne sighed. 'You're the Boss,' he said again.

Still laughing quietly, Kieran turned back to the window. 'Poor little girl. She'll be so relieved.'

23

Excerpts from:
The New York Times *'Science Times'*
1 May 2012

Sigma-Field Seen as the Key to Cheap and Reliable Fusion Power

Application also seen in development of mechanical mind-screen.

By BARBARA TRINH

Special to The New York Times

PRINCETON, N. J. – The long-awaited break-through in the development of small nuclear-fusion power systems was confirmed with the demonstration last week of MIPPFUG at Princeton University's Institute for Energy Research. MIPPFUG (the acronym stands for Miniature Proton-Proton Fusion Generator) differs from conventional fusion reactors in that it utilizes a 'bottle' formed out of a sigma-field to contain the intensely hot fusion reaction, rather than currents of electromagnetism.

For more than 50 years, scientists have been frustrated in attempts to tame fusion by the inherent limitations of the electro-magnetic confinement system, which requires massive radiation shielding and elaborate safety precautions. Fusion power-plants have remained uneconomical up until now not only because of their complexity, but also because a typical deuterium-tritium fusion plant produces only about one tenth the power of a nuclear fission reactor of the same size.

The new sigma-field confining system is fail-safe – unlike the magnetic one, which stores up enough energy to possibly destroy the reactor in a split second in case of a malfunction. The sigma-field system has the additional advantage of absorbing the gamma radiation produced in the proton-proton fusion process utilized in MIPPFUG. Where this absorbed radiation 'goes' is still one of the great mysteries of the booming new branch of science known as dynamic-field physics.

According to Dr George T. Vicks, who developed the sigma-field mechanism for the MIPPFUG project, the 'bottling' of fusion energy is only the first of what may eventually be a host of valuable applications of the sigma.

'A sigma is basically what the science-fiction writers like to call a force field,' Vicks says. 'It's a six-dimensional thing bound into the spatial dimensions of our space-time continuum. That sounds complicated – and it is! But you can understand rather easily what a sigma can do if you think of it as a kind of invisible wall. There are different kinds of sigmas. The one for MIPPFUG acts as a barrier to the enormous heat of nuclear fusion.'

Other types of sigma-fields, Vicks says, can block out other types of energy – or even matter.

'Some time in the future,' Vicks says, 'we'll be able to design sigmas that act as roofs or meteor-barriers or shields against radiation or weapons. A sigma-field might even make a good umbrella! It could form the basis for those tractor beams that science fiction has spaceships use to push or pull or grab things out in the void.'

An even more exotic application of sigma technology would be in the world's first effective mechanical thought-screen.

'So far,' says Carole McCarthy, an associate of Vicks at Princeton, 'no one has been able to come up with reliable barriers to telepathy or EE or other mental powers. This is because thought doesn't propagate in the four dimensions we call space-time, as sound and other forms of energy do. Mental impulses propagate in a six-dimensional entity we call the aether. The sigma-field, which also has six dimensions, might just be able to mesh with the aether in a way that would stop thought impulses cold.'

This type of thought-screen was suggested by the late Nobel Laureate, Xiong Ping-yung, shortly before his death in 2006. Xiong was honoured for formulating the Universal Field Theory, upon which sigma research is based. There has been increasing speculation in the West that China may be already working on such a device secretly, in connection with its increasingly defensive posture vis-à-vis the Soviet Union.

24

Du Page County, Illinois, Earth
4 August 2012

The muggy midwestern air hit Victor Remillard like a hot barber towel as the door of the Remco jet opened. Shannon Tremblay was waiting at the foot of the steps, her white cotton caftan billowing in the wind. Pregnancy became her, heightening her colour and adding needed flesh, but aside from these changes her condition did not show. Victor could not resist scanning the perfect tiny body of the fetal girl. It was only five months alive and even now its mind showed certain familial metapsychic traits. It was damned spooky.

Shannon felt his touch and laughed. 'Laura's going to be the clincher, you know. The factor to force Daddy to bring you into the organization — even without bonding. He's really very superstitious. She's an omen to him. A symbol. He may even think of her as a superior version of *me*, to be used . . .'

They hurried over the tarmac to the small airport's parking lot. The temperature must have been far over 40° Celsius and the sunlight was like blazing bars thrust through rising masses of purplish thunderheads.

'Have you told Gerry?' Victor asked.

'Of course. Why not? I think he may be relieved. Daddy was always pressuring us to have children . . . especially a girl. He was disappointed when nothing happened and blamed me, since there's no doubt that Gerry's fertile. Of course, you know why I wouldn't. Not until now. Laura will be *our* celebration, Victor — not Daddy's.'

Her black Ferrari Automa was running at high revs,

keeping cool. She touched the lock, opening both doors, and said, 'You drive. The guidance system is preset for most of the way.'

He nodded and slid on to the icy leather seat with a sense of relief. It had been difficult to control his sweat glands. He could handle either the heat or the fear-excitement reflex, but it was hell bucking both of them at once. He checked the routing on the dash map-display, put up the spoiler, and eased the Ferrari out of the lot on to the airport frontage road.

'When is Gerry due out?'

'Next week.'

'Is your old man going to stiff him?'

'Certainly not. Gerry's valuable, even if he's tainted.' Her lips quirked. 'He's valuable to us, too, so don't let me hear any more divorce bullshit. Not until we've won.'

'Suit yourself.' As they came on to the ramp for Route 64, he punched in the automatic guidance, took his hands from the wheel and his foot from the accelerator. Cruise control took over, merging them neatly with the eastbound traffic flow. On a second-class highway like 64, with only two pilot-stripped lanes in each direction, their speed was held down to 120 kph with no left-hand prioritizing; but in a few minutes they turned on to southbound 59, a three-laner, and the priority function of the guidance system began to communicate with transponders in other vehicles, sweeping them out of the Ferrari's way. They accelerated to 200 and in moments they were swinging on to the East-West Expressway and roaring towards Oakbrook, well spaced among the other privileged cars in the innermost of five eastbound lanes.

'I wish to hell we had pilot-strips in my neck of the woods,' Victor groused. 'It's still all manual in northern New Hampshire, except on the Interstates, and no priority speeding anywhere. New Hampshire doesn't believe in it.'

'Illinois is glad of the licensing fees – but then, they have a lot more bills to pay. We all know that New Hampshire keeps costs down by giving its welfare clients bus fare to Massachusetts.'

Victor chuckled. 'An old Yankee custom. No taxes, no frills, and devil take the hindmost.'

'He just may,' Shannon murmured, 'unless we're very, very careful. But I had to have you *see* what Daddy's got, Victor.'

The console beeped to warn them that they were approaching their exit and the termination of programmed cruising. Victor took the wheel again as they went on to the Midwest Road ramp. He had never been to Kieran O'Connor's mansion, but the blip on the dash-map showed the way. The Ferrari slowed to a sedate ninety and made its way through rolling wooded hills where white-painted paddock fencing or weathered split rails delineated the boundaries of large estates. They turned into an unmarked lane and went another half kilometre, then came to a halt before massive gateposts of red brick surmounted by bronze lanterns. Wrought-iron gates four metres high swung open when Shannon zapped them with a hand-held beamer. Victor saw that the thick bank of blooming shrub-roses surrounding the property had concealed an inner double barrier of chain link and electrified mesh. More fencing bordered the drive and behind it bull mastiffs and Dobermanns watched the Ferrari's progress with silent alertness. A short distance further along they came to another perimeter of charged chain link topped with razor-wire. On the other side of a reinforced steel gate was a guard kiosk with cameras, spotlights, windows of one-way glass, and several unobtrusive gun-ports. A rustic sign at the barrier said:

> WELCOME. STAY IN YOUR VEHICLE.
> OBEY INSTRUCTIONS PROMPTLY.

'Sweet shit,' muttered Victor.

Cameras swivelled, inspecting the car and its occupants. An electronic voice said: 'Good day. Please state your name and business.'

Shannon rolled down her window, leaned out and waved. 'It's me, guys! And a friend of mine. Call off the dragons.'

'Yes, *ma'am*,' said the loudspeaker. 'You may proceed to the house.' The gate opened and the tyre spikes that had protruded from the roadway sank back into metal receptacles. The Ferrari drove along a winding landscaped drive.

'God help the poor bastard who has to read the water meter,' Victor said.

'Don't be silly. That's all done remotely in Illinois.'

'Where does he hide the antiaircraft batteries?'

'In a wing of the stable.'

'You're serious?'

'Don't talk like a fool,' she snapped, 'or I may just regret bringing you out of the New Hampshire boondocks and stick with Gerry after all.'

Victor stomped on the brakes, turned, and seized her by her upper arms. Coercion smote her like a cannon shell and she cried out with hurt and rage. He ripped aside her outer mind-screen as if he were tearing paper and blasted her strong inner shield to painful shards that swirled like a dizzy kaleidoscope while she cowered, furious and delighted. He saw her true. Saw the hate for Kieran O'Connor overarching every other conviction in her soul and her need of *him* and him alone tightening the knot of purpose.

'Bitch,' he laughed, setting her free.

They drove on, and the house came into view. It was a modernistic pile with cantilevered balconies, built partly into the eastern side of a hill and heavily shrouded with gnarled white oaks and Scotch pines. Protruding from one part of the roof was a structure like a blind control tower surmounted by antenna arrays. Victor could see at least three other big steerable dishes lurking among the trees at the crest of the hill.

'Is that where it is?' Victor asked, mentally indicating the tower.

'Yes. He calls it his study. To the rest of us, it's the command post. In the beginning it was only a glorified communications and data-retrieval centre. Over the years Daddy kept modifying and adding to the equipment. He built a redundant control centre in the subbasement, too – and there are underground cables connecting his equipment with three commercial satellite uplinks, in case anything happens to the antennas here on the grounds.'

They pulled up to a side door and Victor switched off the engine. Shannon's window was still open. A hot wind smelling of roses and freshly sprinkled grass mingled with the last cool gasp of the Ferrari's air conditioning.

He said, 'Your father would have to be an idiot not to know that our relationship isn't a simple matter of business.'

'He knows,' she said calmly.

'He knows I'm here today?'

'I'm supposed to be converting you to his point of view. Since my little white body has thus far proved to be a less than irresistible inducement, I've been ordered to tempt you with more exotic thrills.'

Victor laughed. 'Let's get on with it.'

Inside, the mansion was silent and apparently deserted. Shannon explained that with her father out of town, the domestic staff did only routine housekeeping chores. The domestics, the security people and the ground keepers were all bonded operants who by temperament, intelligence or education were not suited to executive positions in O'Connor's organization. They lived in comfortable homes of their own in what was called The Village, in a distant corner of the estate. Shannon told Victor that some of the staff had belonged to the ménage for more than twenty years.

They went up in a big service elevator to the third floor and passed down a carpeted hallway. From the vantage point they could see the sky darkening as the storm approached.

'Let me explain the background of what you're going to see,' Shannon said. 'You know that Psi-Eye inspired the superpowers to end their nuclear arms race. But most of the small nations that had tactical nukes stashed away balked at giving them up – especially after Armageddon showed that the network of EE surveillance couldn't possibly prevent terrorist-type attacks by small forces. The little nations such as South Africa and India didn't give a hoot whether Psi-Eye publicized their arsenals or not. They rather welcomed letting their enemies know they were in a position to retaliate.'

'Especially after the Jihad got rolling in Asia and Africa,' Victor acknowledged. 'Can't say that I blame them.'

'Some defence analysts in America and the Soviet Union worried about the situation and proposed a worldwide cooperative satellite defence system. In the States, so long as the Democrats controlled Congress and the White House, there was talk but no action. The Russians got a system on the drawing boards when Pakistan and Iran started sponsoring revolts in their Central Asian republics – but their civil war broke out before they could carry the plan further.'

Outside the windows, the oak trees were showing the bottoms of their leaves in the rising wind. A sepulchral rumble was barely perceptible through the thick walls of the house.

Shannon said, 'When President Baumgartner was elected in 2000, there was a clear and pressing need for satellite defence. Everybody knew that South Africa had medium-range ballistic missiles with neutron warheads all emplaced to stave off any black invasion from the north. And everybody also knew that it was only the fear of more fallout that kept the Jihad forces from using regular nukes on Russia. The Jihad didn't have neutron bombs yet, but it seemed only a matter of time. And with delivery systems becoming cheaper and more easily available, virtually any little nation would be in a position to commit nuclear blackmail inside of a decade or so.'

They stood in front of the armour-plated door that lacked a knob or a latch. Shannon pressed her right hand against the inset golden plate and a chime sounded.

'For years now, Daddy's agents have abetted terrorism and acted as provocateurs, just so this satellite defence system would be built. His people helped the Armageddon fanatics get their bombs. They triggered the civil war in the Soviet Union and aided the Jihad movement in Africa. When Daddy's candidate, Baumgartner, won the White House, it was politically acceptable for him to resurrect the part of the old Reagan Strategic Defense Initiative that was most workable – the ground-laser satellite-mirror system called Zap-Star.'

Shannon addressed the door's voice-print identifier. 'Open up!' The metal panel slid aside and the two of them entered Kieran O'Connor's sanctum. An enormous banked control console took up one entire five-metre wall. 'When Zap-Star is complete in another year or so, it will consist of 150 battle-mirror satellites and twenty ground batteries of multiple excimer lasers. UN peace-keepers will control the system from a new command centre being built on Christmas Island in the Pacific. The Zap-Star system is being financed primarily by the United States, Europe, Japan and Korea. China has built its own part of the network independently, twenty mirrors and two ground bases . . . but all the other satellites utilize guidance systems manufactured by Daddy's multinational aerospace conglomerate. And each one has built-in override.' She indicated the console. 'Zap-Star can be accessed from here, cutting out the Christmas Island syscom.'

'Good God!'

Shannon sat down at the computer. 'None of the weaponry is on-line yet, of course. When it is, the access code will be Daddy's great secret – the one I presume he'll offer to sell you in exchange for your soul.' She laughed. 'Would you like to see how the thing works?'

She spoke into a command microphone and summoned graphics to a big liquid-crystal display. 'The white blips on the map represent the UN's worldwide emplacement of excimer laser batteries. The green blips are the Chinese bases. Notice the two red blips! . . . Those are Daddy's insurance policy – one in Saskatchewan and one in the Maldive Islands south of India. His own ground bases, in case the others should be destroyed – say, by the Chinese.'

'What do the ground lasers do – beam death-rays to the battle-mirrors?'

'It's not quite like that. In case of a nuclear-missile launching or other hostile action, the excimer fires bursts of coherent light at the high-orbit relay mirrors. They're the large blue blips. These transfer the beams to smaller, highly manoeuvrable battle-mirrors that have already locked on to targets. Depending upon the nature of the beam – and it can be varied from moment to moment – the target can be pierced or fried or simply have its electronic or electrical equipment rendered useless. The last option is the most versatile! A certain type of beam can mutilate the microcircuitry of chips and turn them into useless junk. It can deactivate missiles, aircraft, ships, Asats – anything at all with computer guidance. And it can do more! It can short out auto ignition, radio, video, even light bulbs and hearing aids and solar-cell watches and calculators. The Zap-Star system is virtually the perfect defence against any sort of modern warfare.'

Victor said, 'Or the perfect offence.'

'Oh, yes. Just imagine a modern city deprived of all electrical or electronic equipment. It would be the literal return of the Dark Ages – the end of modern civilization.'

Victor gestured at the mass of equipment. 'What's to prevent us from blowing the whistle on this setup?'

'You'd never be able to prove that it's anything except a horrendously expensive control system for some kind of satellite link. None of the incriminating details – the target cities, for instance – are accessible. There's no law against having descriptions of Zap-Star in your data bank – especially when your companies manufacture the guidance systems for the satellites. As for the uplinks . . . they could control *any* kind of satellites – weather-eyes, surveyors, comsats, relays. Daddy owns at least forty-six.'

'When will the Zap-Star system be completed?'

'Late 2013. A very unlucky year – or lucky, depending upon your point of view.'

Victor was frowning, thinking furiously behind his mental barrier. 'There are at least a dozen holes in your father's scheme for using this thing to conquer the world. The most blatant, of course, is the Chinese connection. They control their sats and they have their own excimer batteries. Suppose they were able to use that sigma-field thing as shielding — '

'Daddy doesn't want to conquer the world.'

'Then what — '

She whispered into the microphone. The screen went black. Victor felt his heart constrict. 'But that's lunacy!'

'It's his vision of the Absolute,' Shannon corrected. 'He'd

tell *you* that Zap-Star was a tool for world domination and offer it to you in exchange for your help in destroying the operant leadership. He knows that they must be on to him.' She paused, then got up and smoothed the skirts of her white dress, smiling slightly. 'He may even suspect who has betrayed him. But he's trapped by his love. He still hopes to convert me to the way he's chosen. And the child . . .'

'Love!' Victor made the word an obscenity.

She turned away from him. 'I don't come to this room very often. Just when I need to remember, to strengthen my resolve. He did it to me here . . . And always, when it's time to go, I'm afraid. What if the door won't obey my voice and open? Or what if it does open – and I find him standing outside, waiting, asking me to reaffirm the bonding?' Could I deny him? Have I already accepted?

No! he said; and she clung to him, letting the fear and fury drain into ice-glazed oblivion.

In time, she did open the door. And of course the corridor was empty. Through the window they could see that the grounds of the mansion were being wracked by a violent thunderstorm.

'My Ferrari!' she wailed, all the rest of it forgotten. 'I left the window open!'

They ran for the elevator together, laughing.

25

Lewisburg, Pennsylvania, Earth
6 August 2012

The superintendent of the federal prison opened the door to a small bare room with a metal table and two chairs. 'Will this do, Professor Remillard?'

'Is it bugged?' Denis asked in a level tone.

The superintendent chuckled. 'Oh, no. There's the usual window in the door – but Agent Tabata has already made it quite plain that no observers will be required during your consultation with the prisoner. Shall I have him brought in now?'

'Please,' said Denis. He put his briefcase on the table and opened it. When the superintendent left the room he quickly took out four objects that looked like featureless grey business cards and placed one in each corner of the room. If there *were* bugs, they were now deaf and blind.

Denis had had to explain to the President that there was no way that a redactive probe could be accomplished at long distance. In EE, it required arduous effort to overhear declamatory telepathy – the 'loudest' kind – passing among persons being observed. Probing their innermost thoughts, a virtuoso trick even with the examinee at arm's length, was totally impossible. The only way that Denis could check out the amazing accusation of Gerry Tremblay's wife would be to probe him in person. The probe might or might not succeed, depending upon the psychological tone of Tremblay. As to the ethics of the situation . . . Denis had given the matter careful thought. Since legislation that would permit mental cross-examination was in the process of being ratified, Denis would accept it as de facto – with the understanding that none of the information he obtained would be used as direct evidence in any case, nor would Denis himself be called to testify as to his findings.

The President had complimented him dryly on his prudence and perspicacity. Denis had responded that those qualities had taken on survival value, given the present mood of the country towards operants. The President had earnestly assured him that the mood was changing for the better, to which Denis had replied sadly that he, personally, had seen scant signs of improvement in operant–normal relations – and if Mrs Tremblay's accusations of a massive conspiracy by secret operants could be proved, the Sons of Earth and other bigots would have a field day, and the operant image would be tarnished almost beyond redemption. The President had laid a big hand on Denis's shoulder and urged him to have courage. After the November election it would be possible to take action in a number of important areas. But right now . . . Tremblay! Denis had promised to do his best, and report his findings only to the President.

The door opened, and Gerry Tremblay came in.

'Hello, Denis.' Here I am and yes I know I look like hell I've lost ten kilos and my colitis has turned my ass to a disaster zone and I'm even starting to go fucking *bald* and my wife is knocked up with some unknown operant's brat and my father-in-law says All's Forgiven What the Hell You Can Be an Arbitrager! and why the devil did you have to come NOW four days before I get out of this fucking hole? . . .

'Gerry I'm sorry to bother you. I know how you feel. We all do. But I must ask some important questions.'

SUREyoumust! WhatthefuckgotintomedidI*really*thinkI wassavingAllOperantsfromBAUMGARTNERTHEARCH FIEND? The arrogance! The lunacy! The friggingdipshit BOOBERYofit . . .

It was Denis's almost invariable custom to veil his eyes from those he engaged in conversation. His direct gaze tended to paralyse normals and throw operants into a state of near panicky screen-slamming. Even his family could be shocked into speechlessness when he inadvertently let the power flood out instead of reining it back behind the social mask that the real superminds were still learning to wear. As Gerry Tremblay's mental speech babbled on, all fouled with self-pity and mortification, Denis looked at the table top. He had placed a pen and a jotting pad there, useless props. The ranting continued and he picked up the pen and drew a square. Then he drew a star, and a circle, and a cross, and three parallel wavy lines.

Gerry said, 'Oh, hell. The Zener cards!' And then he was laughing and half crying, remembering the very beginning of their relationship, thirty-three years ago, when a weird twelve-year-old kid had come slogging down into a dusty granite quarry in Barre, Vermont, and asked him to put down his jackhammer for a few minutes and take a little test that could be really important . . .

Denis said: We used those cards. The old-fashioned ESP pack that Rhine had made famous. And you called them one hundred per cent Gerry and nearly wet your jeans because you had no idea. None at all.

Yeahyeahyeah! And the test wasn't for your benefit it was for me so I'd come away to Dartmouth with you and Glenn and Sally and Tucker and the rest of the Coterie . . . Oh God Denis how did it turn to this *shit*?

'Listen to me, Gerry. There's still something important you can do. If you like . . . do to make up.'

Gerry stiffened. 'What I did – I did because I thought it was right. That's what I'll say until I die, Denis. I won't disgrace us. It was a hell of a dumb move, maybe even crazy, but no disgrace to operancy.'

Denis lifted his eyes.

Gerry Tremblay's mouth opened in an unvoiced scream. He covered his face with his hands and his shoulders began to shake.

You know you know God you know —

I don't know all of it Gerry but I must. Shannon has confessed a lot of it. First to Nell Baumgartner and then to the President himself. Is it true that Kieran O'Connor is a powerful operant?

Of course not.

Is it true that he's been misusing his powers for years breaking every law in the book to build up a personal fortune manipulating politicians even coercing Baumgartner to run and then when he saw his puppet slipping away in desperation he —

NO NO NO!

Is it true that Kieran O'Connor has set up a clandestine control centre for Zap-Star?

. . . whattheHELL???

So you didn't know. Gerry sit up. Take your hands away from your face. *Do it.*

Yes.

I'm going to probe you. To get the truth of it as you see it. There will be no follow-up at all as far as you're concerned. When I've finished I'll wipe out every trace of this visit so O'Connor will never suspect what's been done. We'll nail him through conventional investigation. He can't have covered every trace of his manipulation if it's as massive as Shannon says. Will you consent to the probe? You know it has to be voluntary.

I – I –

I know O'Connor's done something to you Gerry. I can see it a kind of command-inhibition compelling absolute loyalty. But I think I can crack it. I'll be as careful as I can.

I – I – Denis I love him. I love him and he's a filthy swine a madman —

Be calm Gerry.

Can – can you wipe *that* out too?

I could try. There's a chance that he'd know and it would be risky for you because you wouldn't remember any of this. But I think I could retain a semblance of the bondage. I'll try.

Thank you Denis thank you all right DO IT God do it help me get him out of me —

'Gerry, I'd like you to sit back in your chair and relax. Take deep breaths.'

'Okay.'

'Close your eyes now. If you like, you can farsense these Zener figures I've drawn on the pad. But see nothing but them. Think of nothing else.'

'All right.'

Gerry Tremblay closed his eyes and summoned up the familiar old markings.

Only a moment or so later, when he opened his eyes again, a guard was at his side and he was walking back towards his cell. He wondered whether he was losing his marbles. For the life of him he couldn't remember why they'd fetched him out of his cell.

Oh, hell. What difference did it make? Come Friday he'd be out of here for good, and he could pull his shit back together and make a brand new start.

26

From the Memoirs of
Rogatien Remillard

I went to the Hanover post office to do my regular first-thing-in-the-morning pickup. It was just across the street from the bookshop and, in those days, provided more convenient service than electronic mail or parcel express – as well as being considerably cheaper.

It was 24 September 2012, two days after the calamitous Metapsychic Congress in Oslo. Because it was a Monday the box was full of letters and cards and junk mail, as well as several videograms and the inevitable 'Please call at the window for package' notices. I joined the long line of patrons and began to sort my stuff, at the same time carrying on half a conversation with Elijah Shelby who was standing just ahead of me. He ran a desktop publishing company out of his home on River Ridge Road and patronized my shop fairly often.

'Tough about the way things fell apart in Norway,' Shelby said.

'Serves the heads right for scheduling a symposium on operant political activism,' I said. 'They asked for a reeraw and they sure as hell got one. I warned Denis not to force the issue.'

'Reckon your nevvy'll be coming home with his tail between his legs. Media kinda made mincemeat of him, didn't they?'

'Denis is no coward,' I said shortly. 'Takes balls to stand on your principles . . . and you don't want to believe everything you read in the newsplaques, Lije.'

'Mf!' said Shelby. My mention of the great innovation in communication struck a sour note with the publisher. The programmable liquid-crystal reader-plaques had already spelled the doom of printed periodicals and paperback ephemera; and the newer large-format plaques with improved colour-imaging that had just come out of China were bound to take a nasty bite out of conventional book publication.

One of the videograms addressed to me was from a plaque outfit. They were haranguing booksellers, urging them to install the latest top-of-the-line state-of-the-art super-glamorous reader-plaque recorder-dispenser unit – priced at a mere $189,000.00 if you hurried to take advantage of this one-time-only special offer. I deep-sixed the expensive advertising piece in the post office's waste bin, along with the rest of the junk mail.

The second videogram, a jumbo floppy, was from Denis, origin Oslo, transmission time last Saturday. He always conscientiously sent me the proceedings of the Metapsychic Congresses even though most of the papers and panel discussions were far over my simple head. I rarely bothered to play them – but I'd play this one, all right, and bring plenty of popcorn.

The third and last videogram was from Ume Kimura, origin Sapporo, transmission time 1915 hours tomorrow . . .

No!

I clutched the little disk in its flimsy envelope with both hands, letting the rest of my mail tumble to the floor. *You didn't. You couldn't. Not because of what happened at the Congress . . .*

'Hey, Roj?' Elijah Shelby was picking up my stuff and eyeing me askance. 'You okay? You look like you seen a ghost. Bad news?'

But momentary hope burst over me and I thought: Ghost! *Ghost! Stop her stop her you can stop her —*

All around me the banalties of a small-town post office crowded with patrons, and the good old gaffer now radiating anxiety as he realized that something was really wrong, and I walked away still mind-shouting, pushed open the door, stood outside in the early morning sun yelling around the world into tomorrow's night.

Then I ran, through the parking lot and across South Street to my bookshop, and fumbled with the old-fashioned key, and tripped on the sill, nearly dropping the precious disk. To the back room. Power up the player. (No. I couldn't print it. I never could.) Slip the videogram into the slot and fall into my old swivel chair. No longer shouting to the Ghost but pleading to the kind-eyed naked-hearted Jesus whose picture had hung on Tante Lorraine's bedroom wall. Don't let her! Don't let her! But I knew she had.

Her image smiled at me. She wore a plain Japanese robe and sat on her heels in front of a painted paper screen set in some outdoor courtyard or atrium. A small maple tree with spidery maroon leaves was visible behind the screen and there was a tinkling of falling water. Ume spoke to me with formality after the initial smile and bow of her head.

'Roger, my dear friend . . . I have just returned from the Congress in Oslo. You know by now that there is a serious division among the operant leadership, brought about by our increasing despair over the unending violence that afflicts the world. The dream we once shared of leading humanity to permanent peace now stands revealed as mere arrogant presumption. How did we operants dare to think that we would succeed, when all throughout history well-meaning persons have tried again and again to foster peace, only to fail?

'We tried to show humanity a fellowship of the mind, a new society where suspicion and fatal misunderstanding could be banished from political relationships, fostering a climate where peace might flower. But instead of this, we opened a chasm wider than before – a gulf between operant and nonoperant. There is no fellowship, only envy and fear. There is no peace, only ever-spreading war.

'You know how previous Congresses of operants would reaffirm, at the start of the proceedings, the ethic of love and nonaggression exemplified by the illustrious martyr, Urgyen Bhotia. This philosophy, together with its correlate – that operant minds have an obligation to love and serve selflessly those minds who stand a step beneath on evolution's ladder – was never seriously challenged during the twenty years of Metapsychic Congresses preceding this one.

'O my friend! Now the challenge has been made.

'It seemed so innocent, didn't it, when the symposium on political activism ended in an implacable deadlock! On the one side were Denis and Jamie and Vigdis, championing nonaggression, and on the other side, insisting that operants must now defend themselves and their countries with mental as well as physical force, were Tamara and Zhenyu and – the shame! – Hiroshi. My own countryman! And Tamara, the mother of us all! My soul turned to ice as these three revered ones opened their minds to the assembly and showed the reasoning that had led them to abandon the precious heritage of Urgyen.

'Yes . . . one may see the logic. The Soviet operants have suffered more terribly than any. Now that the dictator is dead and the Politburo begs them to return and unify their collapsing nation, how can they say no? They are offered great political power. Once before they were betrayed, and they vow it will not happen again. One may see the logic!

'But from it flow the consequents.

'China fears the Soviet Union. It is rich in food and technology and its great northern neighbour starves for both as the civil war drags on in spite of the capitulation of Iran and the coup in Pakistan. And the rest of Asia contemplates with horror a conflict between the giants. What can save us? The Zap-Star net is unfinished. Now its defences may be turned into weaponry! The EE adepts of every nation will survey the great laser batteries with increasing trepidation, wondering which country will first dare attempt the conversion . . . Japan fears that China may already possess this capability – and that it will be used as a preemptive strike against the Soviets . . .

'Like an avalanche in my Hokkaido mountains, it has begun with a tiny slippage downhill. Soon it will be an unstoppable monster. We operants will lend it momentum. Yes. It was already happening in Oslo as we raised mental walls against one another, feeling the former mood of trust and goodwill begin sliding into an abyss. All of us, seeing the logic; forgetting the love and the dream.

'I am saddened and shamed. In my pride I had culti-vated tsuki-no-kokoro – the mind as calm as the moon. I tried to lead and teach. I never coerced. But I cannot create within myself that selfless power, that Centre of vision that my people call the hara, that would give me courage to continue. I am a proud and foolish woman who long ago turned away from her own family, and again and again my mind shows me a small girl bringing humiliation upon her father. I must escape this girl and her shame.

'O my friend! The pleasure we shared was good. The comfort we gave one another must be your remembrance of me, and not this image of pain. Burn the disk, Roger. Nakanai de kudasai. Sayonara.'

She knelt silently then. There was no mat beneath her, only polished flagstones. She closed her eyes and her body tensed and I knew she was summoning the psychocreativity from what she called her Centre.

There was only a split second of flame before the video recording went to black.

She had told me to destroy the disk: I could not. She had told me, in Japanese, not to cry: I did. But I did obey her request to remember our sharing; and I remember it now and possess, for a little while, my own tsuki-no-kokoro.

27

Pittsburg Township, New Hampshire, Earth
31 July 2013

'You wanta wait here on the deck, Mr O'Connor, Vic should be back from his swim in a jiff. Coolin' off nicely out here now that the sun's down. Varmints be comin' down to the water. You might like to catch a scan of 'em. Visitors often do.'

'Thank you, Mr Laplace,' Kieran said. 'That might be interesting. What kinds of wildlife do you have in these parts?'

'Moose, bear, panther – Vic even reintroduced woodland caribou couple years ago, when he first closed off Indian Stream Valley to the public. These north New Hampshire woods'll soon be back the way my ancestors knew 'em. Damn good thing, too.'

'You're descended from the voyageurs?' Kieran inquired politely.

'Them – and the Abnaki. Figure I got my long-sight from the Redskin side of the blanket and my coercion from the Canuck.' The grey-haired caretaker nodded towards an impressive instrument mounted on one of the deck railings. 'Now some heads – uh – some operants like to use the spotterscope for spyin' wildlife if their long-sight gets a mite bewildered by the woods and the lake and all. Feel free. That there's a light-amp with optional warm-body targeting adjustable to the 'proximate size of the varmint you wanta scan. Try around four to six hunnerd kilos for moose, seventy to one-twenty-five for whitetail deer or bear . . . or a man.'

Limping slightly, Kieran went to examine the scope. 'Does Victor Remillard find much use for this?'

Laplace let out a pitying guffaw. 'You gotta be kidding!' Then the mien of exaggerated civility was back in place and he said, 'Well, you just make yourself t'home while I take care of a few things. Like I said, Vic'll be along soon.'

He turned and started to shamble away, then turned to say, 'Not that I wanta give you a hard time, since Vic *did* say he was expecting you. But you had your orders from Mr Fortier. Those heads of yours in the limo – they were told to go all the way back to the main Pittsburg road and wait. They ain't done that. I think you better flash 'em your telepathic high-sign.'

Kieran said, 'I'll do that, Mr Laplace. A misunderstanding.'

This time the operant yokel's deadpan expression was clearly contradicted by the contempt of his mental undertone. 'And while you're at it, give a shout to them four fellers pussyfootin' this way through the woods along the south shore. Tell 'em to get their asses and their arsenal back the way they come from before they fall into a bog . . . or somethin'.'

Imbeciles! Adam Arnie damnyou didn't I tell you I'd handle this on my own get out and call off those piss-artist commandos!

Kier we only wanted to maximize our options in case —

GET OUT! 'Well, I'm sorry about that, Mr Laplace. An overzealous subordinate took it upon himself to countermand my explicit instructions.'

'A damn shame. But no harm done, I reckon. I try to see to that, Mr O'Connor. We're just a little two-bit lash-up compared to your organization – but we get along.'

'I appreciate that. You might say that's why I'm here this evening. I've transmitted to my people direct orders for withdrawal. I intend to fulfil Mr Remillard's conditions to the letter. You will let him know that?'

Laplace smirked and spat over the rail into the lake. From somewhere out on the water came an eerie warbling cry like demented laughter.

'An owl?' Kieran asked.

'Nope. Loon. Alias the great northern diver, *Gavia immer*. Kinda relic of the late Neogene avifauna. Been yakkin' it up in these parts purt' near five, six million years. Long time to hold on to a sense of humour, but I reckon it helps a critter survive. Be seein' you, Mr O'Connor. You be sure to tell Vic I was on the job.'

'I'll do that,' Kieran said dryly.

The gangling old fellow clumped off into the lodge's interior and Kieran let out a long sigh of pain. He closed his eyes, summoning the soothing black momentarily, and let it cradle him. Serene, he banished suspicion and anxiety and the gnawing in his groin; and when he opened his eyes he saw four bulky shapes wading out from a small heavily wooded cove a hundred metres or so down the shore to the right.

He flicked on the spotterscope and swung the barrel. A cow moose and her nearly full grown triplets were feeding on water plants. He watched them for nearly ten minutes. The sky had gone to deep purple and the loons were cackling excitely over towards the northern reaches of the lake, so Kieran aimed the light-amplifying device in that direction after programming the infrared mode to detect bodies in excess of ninety kilograms mass. The driving mechanism took over and Kieran kept his eye to the scope as it scanned the opposite shore, about twelve hundred metres away.

The target-grid flashed on. Gotcha! And Kieran zoomed in and found himself looking at another moose. But this was one of the most uncanny beasts he had ever seen, an enormous male standing half concealed among the dense second growth of balsam fir. His colour was not the usual dark brown but burnished grey, like pewter; and the great rack of antlers, still dangling shreds of velvet, was whiter than bleached bone at the pronged edges and translucent with startling blood-veins in the broad, palmate centres and towards the base. The moose rubbed his fantastic skull adornment vigorously against saplings to scratch what must have been a colossal itch. Then he glared at Kieran from eyes like smouldering coals.

'I've named him Glaçon. Rather frivolous for such a massive brute, but it fit when he was a calf. He's a special pet. Genetically engineered albino. I always wondered what one would look like.'

Kieran continued his calm surveillance through the eyepiece. His farsight superimposed the image of Victor Remillard's face in the black forest portion of the visual field. 'Glaçon . . . that means ice cube, doesn't it?'

'Or a cold-hearted devil of a person,' said Victor Remillard.

Kieran lifted his head from the scope. 'He's beautiful. In this forest preserve of yours, he might even live to a ripe old age.' He didn't ask Victor if he would like to use the instrument. In farsight, the younger man was clearly his master. But that was not the metafaculty that mattered . . .

They faced off, the burly forty-three-year-old at his physical and mental prime and the dying old man. Kieran O'Connor's once olive skin was now sallow and deeply furrowed beside the thin-lipped Celtic mouth. The eyes were sunken, having the same insatiable ardour as Shannon's eyes; the mind behind them, however, had none of her fire but instead a beckoning well of unending night.

Come to me, said Kieran.

To me! Victor commanded.

Neither man moved.

The whooping of the loons reflected the laughter that flooded the aether. They disengaged and stood back.

Kieran shrugged. 'We had to try. But it isn't really a stand-off, you know . . . You've won.'

Victor was wary. 'Explain.'

'I must sit down,' Kieran said.

They moved to a couple of bogus Barcelona chairs and Kieran lowered himself with exquisite caution. 'You know my physical condition. I will continue to survive on will power, however, until it suits me to end what I began. You are also probably aware that both the FBI and the Justice Department are rooting feverishly through my data banks, using methods both licit and illicit, determined to find or fabricate evidence that I am guilty of treason, conspiracy, racketeering, grand theft and multiple counts of murder.'

Victor nodded.

'Do you know that your older brother Denis is responsible for this embarrassment of legal activism?'

'No . . .'

Kieran smiled sourly. 'He and his partisans are also behind the recent spate of bills introduced into Congress that will empower operant investigators to meddle in the affairs of persons like you and me. The amendment permitting mental cross-examination was only the beginning, you know.'

'I know. All these years, they couldn't touch us. Denis knew what I was doing, but there was never any way he could prove it. He couldn't even prove I was operant – much less that I used the powers to take what I wanted.'

Kieran said, 'A mechanical aura-detection device – ostensibly for use in identifying and classifying the faculties of operant newborns – is undergoing tests at the University of Edinburgh. Professor Jamie MacGregor will be demonstrating it at this year's Metapsychic Congress.'

Victor said nothing. But his mind transmitted both a query and an image of an intricate control console emplaced in a blind tower in the countryside west of Chicago.

'You want an explanation of that.' Kieran smiled and nodded almost absently. The pain was far away for the moment. 'I should have thought it would be obvious. It's the key to ultimate victory. Once the victory would have been mine. Now I'm offering it to you.'

Kieran spoke on, slowly and simply, clothing the ludicrous notion of ruling the world through the Zap-Star's threat with a glowing plausibility, but at the same time making certain that Victor recognized the scheme as the fever-dream of an ageing megalomaniac. The crude brain of the self-centred entrepreneur would be immediately aware of the gaping flaws in logic. He would visualize other ways of using Zap-Star, feasible ways. He would humour the madman, intuitively accepting Kieran's genuine need of him, but never grasping the hidden motive. As to the goal of the Absolute . . . its apprehension was as far beyond Victor Remillard as were the stars that had begun to twinkle in the summer sky of New Hampshire.

'It can all be yours. I've completed the instruments of transfer – of merger, actually, granting you control of everything I own. Once I'm gone, the feds have nothing. My corporations exist as independent legal entities and they're as legitimate before the bar of justice as any American business. All you need do is help me finish off our mutual enemies.'

'Denis? His Coterie at Dartmouth?'

'*All* of them,' Kieran said. 'The metapsychic leadership of the world. The operant meddlers. They'll be right here in New Hampshire in mid-September having their annual confab. Even the breakaways from Russia and the Orient have agreed to send delegates for one last meeting. I can't touch them . . . but you could. I could show you how. Help you. My agents will see that the local chapters of the Sons of Earth are armed and equipped. You and your people – completely unknown to the government agents – provide the leadership and then disappear, leaving the mob to take the blame.'

Victor said, 'And then?'

'I die. And you take everything I have. I've worked out the details in a way that should satisfy you. Three of my closest associates – the men who were with me from the beginning – are prepared to brief you on the entire operation, beginning to end, mind-screens down. You have as many of your people sit in as you like.'

'When can these associates of yours be here?'

'They're in the limousine that brought me,' Kieran said, 'the one that your efficient long-sighted caretaker made certain I sent back to the Pittsburg Junction before you put in your appearance.'

Victor laughed. 'Pete Laplace is the best farsensor I've got. Loyal as a Labrador retriever. With him and his old twelve-gauge hanging around, I'm as safe out here as a baby in a cradle. It's just a damn shame that his IQ's only around eighty-six.'

'He seemed sharp enough to me . . . Well, Victor – what's your answer? Will you put those spoilers away for me and let me die happy?'

'Kieran, I'm only sorry I didn't think of the idea first! Let me get on the phone and get a few of my boys up from Berlin. It won't take more than an hour. Your bunch can follow them back in here. Meanwhile, you might like to join me in a little snack.'

Kieran closed his eyes. Sequestered behind impregnable walls, safe in the secret depths, he gave thanks to the Black Mother. *In the end is the beginning. In death the source of life. Let Thy belly the void take us in. Dam dham nam tam tham dam dham nam pam pham* . . .

'Pete?' Victor was shouting. 'Pete, you rapscallion – where are you hiding? We've got company coming and I need – oh, for God's sake! Kieran, you want to come in here and get a load of this? He's out like a light on the sun-porch couch, with the Browning tucked under his cheek and an empty bottle of Wild Turkey clutched to his chest! I guess I'll have to do my own cooking.'

28

*From the Memoirs of
Rogatien Remillard*

In August 2013 I encountered the Family Ghost again – at the White Mountain Resort.

The sprawling white-stucco wedding-cake hotel at the western foot of Mount Washington seemed hardly to have changed at all from the days when I had worked there as its convention manager. It was as ridiculously posh and Edwardian as ever and served the same sumptuous meals, and in spite of America's depressed economy it was still crowded with virtually the same type of clientèle – upscale young families, hiking fanatics with sybaritic base-camp tastes, and herds of nostalgic oldsters on expensive guided tours. The latter now arrived by X-wing airbus instead of the diesel motor coaches of my day; but they still wore lapel badges, and they were still escorted by pretty young women, and the old ladies still cheeped and tittered eagerly while the old gents looked glum and resigned.

I had come to the hotel on business, to consult with the youngster who occupied my erstwhile position, one Jasper Delacourt. Ten years earlier the Twelfth Congress on Metapsychology had been held at the resort and Denis had roped me into making the arrangements. 'Who,' he had asked me reasonably, 'could do a better job of it?' And so I did, and the hotel's Olde New England kitsch had charmed the socks off the foreign scholars, who found it a refreshing change from the modern university locales that had characterized most of the other Congresses. The cog railway had been a big hit, and the more able-bodied operants tramped around on Mount Washington during their spare time, marvelling over the relict ice-age flora and the oddly portentous ambiance around the summit.

This year's Congress (which many people at Dartmouth feared would be the last) was also scheduled to be held at the resort, and so it was only natural that I should do a reprise of my 2003 duties. I had made most of the arrangements by phone and data-link months earlier; but as September approached I drove over to wrap things up in person.

Jasper Delacourt bounced up from behind his desk as I entered his office and wrung my hand. The hotel was extremely happy to be hosting twenty-eight hundred delegates during the somnolent post-Labour Day season.

'Roger, you old sonuvagun! God, you look great. Ten years, you haven't aged a day, my man!'

'You look pretty fit yourself,' I lied. 'The Congress committee over at Dartmouth is really very pleased that you could accommodate us, given the more modest budget this go-around.'

Jasper sighed. 'Things are tough all over. I can level with you because you used to sit in this seat, right? I have to hustle my ass off scratching up tours and conferences and sales meetings to keep this hulk topped off. If we had to depend on straight vacationers, we'd belly-up.'

I chuckled. 'It wasn't all that different in '90, when I left.'

He studied me narrowly and I could see his mind doing calculations. 'Jeez – that long ago? But I thought – How the hell old are you, anyhow?'

'In a week I'll be sixty-eight.'

'Holy moley,' Jasper groaned. 'What – d'you get your seltzer from Pounce de Leeon's fountain, man? I'd of said forty-five ten years ago and say the same now. I mean, you got that lived-in look and Miss Clairol never made a dime off those silver curls – but *sixty-eight*? No shit?'

I shrugged. 'Kind of runs in the family. I reckon I'll fall to pieces all at once at seventy . . . But don't let me waste your time. I know you've got a lot to do. Mainly, I want to noodle with you on the matter of our big Saturday night banquet on the twenty-first. Our attendance will be a couple of hundred short of last time, but you remember how we had tables packed cheek-to-jowl in the Grand Ballroom, and out in the hall, and even filling up the Fern Salon. There were closed circuit TV monitors spotted around so the speeches could be heard by the nonfarsensitive. But, Jasper . . . metapsychic operants want to experience the full nuance spectrum when somebody sounds off! Conventional sensory input *and* ultrasensory. Is the speaker delivering with a straight tongue and mind – or is he or she peddling tosh? Listening to a TV just doesn't cut the mustard with an audience of heads. We've got to think of something else – and I *don't* mean a buffet.'

'Roger! Roger!' he chortled. 'I'm way ahead of you, my man.'

With a flourish, he produced a folder bound in fake leather and smacked it open on the desk, pressing the upper right-hand corner. Ta-dah! A twenty-by-thirty plaque, playing a full-colour loop showing a series of lap dissolves of a luxurious mountaintop restaurant: exteriors at sunset, in sun-drenched daylight, in a majestic snowy night; interiors showing the place tricked out as a cabaret, hosting a bar mitzvah, wining and dining some affair of the New England Medical Association; close-ups of Lucullan feasts and après-hike fireside cheer. The book-plaque even had background music, for God's sake: Edward MacDowell's *New Ergland Idylls*.

'The Summit Chalet!' Jasper declaimed. 'Dine in opulent grandeur far above New Hampshire's White Mountains. Visit the fabled haunt of the Great Spirit, where even today flying saucers have been seen wafting through the crystalline air!'

'I remember now,' I said. 'When they demolished the obsolete antenna farm and transmitter complex four or five years ago, they granted the hotel a concession to build the chalet. Is it paying its way?'

'Not yet,' Jasper confided. 'We went way over budget on the environmental adaptations. You know – to keep it from blowing off the mountain when the wind's three hundred kloms an hour. The engineers finally licked it, though. A tornado couldn't budge that thing now. And what a showplace! Those globetrotting heads of yours'll eat it up, Roj.'

I was dubious. 'We're talking about moving nearly three thousand people up there from the hotel, Jasper. In maybe an hour. And then getting them back down after the banquet.'

'No problem. We bring in ten X-wing shuttle buses, make three trips.'

'Who eats the transport costs?'

'Goes with the deluxe dinner package: prime rib or lobster, BP and veggie, sabayon dessert, nonvintage champers, gratuity included – ninety bucks a head.'

I whistled. 'Jasper – the budget! Do you realize that Dartmouth is so strapped that they're remerging the Department of Metapsychology with Psychiatry again? My nephew, the Nobel laureate, is getting shucked of two thirds of his staff! The research grants are gone, the endowments are gone, and this will probably be the last time the Congress meets for Christ knows how long.'

Jasper leaned towards me. 'Then make it a whangdoodle. Take 'em out in *style*.'

'I don't see how I can justify — '

'Do me one favour. Go up and look the place over.'

A van trundled me half a klom to the X-wing pad, which was tucked behind a sound-baffle wall hidden amidst greenery. In less than five minutes the versatile aircraft that combined the speed of a fixed-wing with the limited-space landing requirements of a helicopter whisked me to the top of Mount Washington. We landed in a bowl newly cut on the eastern shoulder of the summit. I recalled that environmentalists had bitterly protested both the landing facility and the new restaurant, demanding that the old Sherman Adams Summit Building, a graceless structure built in the 1980s, be retained as a historical monument and the rest of the summit be left 'in a state of nature'. However, since virtually the entire top of Mount Washington was covered with trucked-in rubble, and had been humanly modified in one way or another beginning in the 1820s, the natural-staters hadn't had much of a leg to stand on.

The Summit Chalet was designed to blend with the lichen-crusted granite and dazzling hoarfrost that characterized New England's highest point. The building was trifoliate, the three lobes having armour-glass windows all around, providing maximum windowside seating. Its rock-strewn roof was surmounted by a wide turret with an observation deck and open balcony, mobbed with tourists on that balmy summer afternoon. On the level below the restaurant were boutiques, souvenir shops, and a small museum, together with more open balconies. A covered tunnel led to a new sheltered terminus of the little old cog railway, which was exactly as I had remembered it. After a short inspection tour I was admitted to one of the lower balconies by the chalet's manager and left alone to think things over.

One of the primitive steam locomotives was toiling upslope from the vicinity of the White Mountain Hotel, pushing its coach. The trails crisscrossing the summit had the same yellow-paint blazes. The grasslike sedges were desiccated, but here and there tufts of alpine herbiage grew green and indomitable, speckled with tiny flowers.

. . . The shivering boy standing at my side, pointing, his mind detecting the first empowered mind not of our own family.

. . . Hikers ascending in a line from behind the cog track, and little Denis's farsight lending me a glimpse of the second miracle: Elaine.

It had all begun here. It would be an appropriate place for the farewell.

The wind was stiff that day, blasting in from the west, and my eyes misted over. I felt again the strange aetheric vibrations and an eerie sense of looming presence. The mountain that was sacred. The mountain that had killed so many. The mountain that had heard foolish dreamers crying out to the uncomprehending stars, and nurtured wild tales of frost-demons and Great Carbuncles and flying saucers . . .

Bonjour Rogi!

I started violently. 'Est-ce *toi*?!'

Arrange for the Metapsychic Congress to have its last supper on the mountain.

'Hah! And should I tell them who decreed the final squandering of their treasury?'

You will be able to convince Denis that the site is suitable. Your coercion is more effective than you think. After he has agreed and all the arrangements are in train . . . yes, you may tell him about me.

'Grand dieu – you can't mean it!'

Be subtle. Choose your time well. Perhaps you can tell him that you have long since accepted me as a minor delusion – a harmless unconscious projection of hope. Of *reasonable* hope, not one forlorn on the face of it.

'You haven't been around here for a long time, mon fantôme. We Earthlings have made a botch of it!'

Perhaps . . . Tell him anyhow. Tell him that he is right in clinging to the ethic of nonviolence and service. Tell him he is wrong about wanting to retreat to a low profile. The Mind of Earth must not fragment but coadunate – grow and flow together in a sublime metaconcert of goodwill, a renunciation of selfishness that coerces the Intervention of the Galactic Milieu at long last!

'Now?' I cried. 'When it's all fallen apart? You've got a weird sense of humour.'

The Ghost said: Your nephew Denis can scan your mind and apperceive the reality . . . if you yourself believe it to be true.

'Go away,' I whispered, looking out over the western valley. 'Leave me in peace. I'm only an old fool and no one listens to me, and there isn't a hope in hell that Denis or anyone else would take such a fairy tale seriously. Extra-terrestrial redeemers are an old-fashioned aberration to psychiatrists like Denis. Jung even wrote a book about it! It's the perennial human desire for a fairy godmother or a deus ex machina to save us from our mortal folly – and I *don't* believe in it. So there!'

The invisible thing seemed to sigh in exasperation. It said: I hoped it would not be this way. Obviously it *must* be. Le bon dieu, il aime à plaisanter! Always the humourist . . . So! Tell me Rogi: Do you still have the Great Carbuncle?

'The key ring?' I blurted. Digging in my hip pocket, I pulled out the silvery chain that held my shop and apart-ment keys. The little red-glass ball of the fob winked in the powerful sunlight. 'This thing?'

That thing . . . At the Congress, when the moment seems appropriate, you will once again urge Denis to unite his colleagues – and the Mind of Earth – in prayerful metacon-cert. As a token of your serious intent, invite him to scru-tinize the Carbuncle with his deep-sight.

'Just like that!' I laughed bitterly. 'And how will I know this magic moment?'

The Ghost said, rather ominously: It will be self-evident. Do it without fail. And now, au revoir, cher Rogi. We may meet again soon!

A deathly chill smote me. I gasped, and my breath exhaled in a white cloud, and I realized that the temperature of the air had fallen precipitously. Stumbling, I turned to the sliding glass door behind me and hauled it open, flinging myself inside as if the frost-demons themselves were on my tail.

The manager of the chalet was there, and he said, 'Oh, there you are, Mr Remillard. When you didn't stop in again at my office, I thought you might have left — '

'We'll have our banquet here,' I said. 'I've made up my mind. Let's go to your office and draw up the contract.'

'Wonderful!' he said. 'You'll be glad you made this decision!'

'Somebody will be,' I growled, and followed him back upstairs.

The following week I drove to Concord, where I had made an appointment with a consulting gemologist. He was understanding when I said that I'd like an appraisal of the Carbuncle while I waited – and watched. But as it happened, I was out of luck. He rather quickly ascertained that the chain wasn't silver, but a platinum-iridium alloy; it was also easy to determine that the flawless, transparent ball was not glass, but some other substance with a hardness of ten on Moh's scale.

'Now, ordinarily, that would suggest that we have a diamond,' the gemologist said. 'But a blood-red diamond would be fabulously valuable, and no person in his right mind would polish one into a spherical shape rather than facet it. So this may be some very unusual synthetic with a similar thermal conductivity.'

My mind had gone numb. 'Yes. That's probably just what it is. An old friend of mine gave me this. A chemist. Dared me to find out what it was. I think this is his idea of a practical joke.'

The gemologist said, 'To tell what this stone is, we'd have to do a crystallographic analysis with special equipment. That would run into money and take a while.'

'No, no,' I protested. 'Why don't you just put down on your appraisal the bare facts you've told me. No monetary value of the stone, of course.'

'Well, if that's what you want. You know, if this really

were a diamond, it'd weigh upwards of twenty-five carats.
Because of the rare colour, it'd likely be worth a couple
million.'

I forced a laugh. 'Well, the joke's on me, isn't it? . . .
Now how much do I owe you?'

The fee was fifty dollars. I paid it gladly, and tucked the
appraisal paper into my wallet and the Great Carbuncle
into my pants pocket. Then I went back to Hanover to wait
for the third week in September, when the last Metapsychic
Congress was scheduled to begin.

I didn't say anything to Denis about the Family Ghost,
not even when the Carbuncle seemed to burn a hole in my
pocket. The Ghost was welcome to make a fool of me if it
could; but I was damned if I would make a fool of myself.

29

Bretton Woods, New Hampshire, Earth
21 September 2013

Swiftly, before any early risers who shared Ilya and Katie's
apprehensions could spot him and detain him, old Pyotr
Sakhvadze slipped outside the grand hotel into dawn
silence. He hurried across the dry lawn, noting that the
absence of dew probably signified that rain was on the way.
The sky was bright with a high overcast. It would be too
bad if lowering clouds spoiled the view from the Summit
Chalet during the banquet that evening, but a bit of
thunder and lightning might actually liven things up.

Here and there among the beds of chrysanthemums and
the formal evergreen plantations lay incongruous masses of
litter – broken placards, torn banners, scattered leaflets,
some beer and pop cans and snack-food wrappers –
mementos of the crowd of antioperant pickets that had
invaded the resort grounds last night. All throughout the
week-long Metapsychic Congress there had been small
groups of Sons of Earth demonstrators parading outside
the main entrance of the complex; but several hundred had

shown up on Friday evening, and the hotel security force had finally had to call in the State Police to clear them out. Pyotr's grandson Ilya had been quite alarmed at the sluggish response of the local authorities. He had warned Pyotr not to go outside alone on the final day of the Congress, when even more serious confrontations might be expected. However, the old man had no intention of forgoing his morning constitutional. The antioperants, he reasoned, would hardly be up and about at six in the morning. They would be sleeping off the Friday-night fracas and doubtless renewing their energies for a more climactic face-off tonight . . .

Abandoned placards blocked the pathway and Pyotr flicked them aside with his walking stick *tsk*ing disapproval of the impudent sentiments. WE ARE HUMAN – ARE YOU? one sign inquired. Pyotr chuckled at another that proclaimed SUPERBRAINS INVADE YOUR INNER SPACE! By far the majority of the professionally printed placards echoed the Sons of Earth chant, 'Off With the Heads' – which was often abbreviated in a sinister fashion to 'Off the Heads!' The meaning of one slogan, WHERE IS KRYPTONITE NOW THAT WE REALLY NEED IT?, eluded Pyotr completely. He was relieved when he came to the turnoff at the X-wing pad and was able to head into the thick woods along the little Ammonoosuc River, which threaded the resort grounds.

Down by the brawling stream there were no traces of the demonstration. Sugar maple trees were just beginning to turn colour in that amazing North American fashion that was – typically – so much more spectacular than any Europe or Asia had to offer. But Pyotr was really hoping to rediscover another tree that he had taken note of ten years earlier, during his first visit to the White Mountain Hotel. On and on he walked, without catching sight of it, and he began to fear that it had perished, perhaps toppling into the river during a spring freshet. But no . . . there it was. A solitary mountain ash laden with marvellous great bunches of scarlet berries, the very image of the beloved ryabina trees of Pyotr's native Caucasus.

He paused and contemplated the scene with a full heart.

The rushing stream, the magic-tree, the mighty mountain looming darkly to the east – all so reminiscent of his old home that it made him want to weep with the loss.

No, he told himself, and forged on. What a fool you are, Pyotr Sergeyevich! You have lived ninety-nine years and you are still vigorous and in control of most of your mental faculties – meagre though they be – and you have a safe home with your loving grandson Ilya in Oxford, and a wealth of memories and experiences to share with your great-granddaughters. You are as fortunate as the patriarch Seliac Eshba – even though not so tranquil, or so wise.

The path turned south, away from the river, and passed along the boundary of the resort's beautiful golf course, through an open area where the long rampart of the Presidential Range still hid the sun. The air was utterly calm. No birds sang and no civilized noises intruded upon the immense quiet. It seemed almost as if the entire New Hampshire countryside were holding its breath in anticipation.

Pyotr paused with his eyes lifted. The disasters had been many, but they had come and gone as surely as the seasons turned. In the future lay fresh perils, especially for his dear Tamara and the other operants now engaged in the struggle for power in Moscow. What would the simple Seliac think of such matters? Would he offer another homely metaphor from the abiding Earth as a symbol of hope? And why must it always be hope, rather than fruition? Must the small-souled and the evil always appear to triumph while the peace-lovers were left with only their dreams?

He walked on, brooding, towards a small pavilion where he thought he would sit and rest for a time; but the peculiar air of psychic tension was growing, together with a small but persistent pang just behind his forehead. He stopped again, rubbing his eyes, and when he looked back towards the mountain he stiffened and uttered a gasp of shock.

The rocks on the vast slope shimmered in green and violet, and the crest of Mount Washington seemed crowned with a golden tellurian aura.

Pyotr thought: It can't be! These land-forms are ancient

and stable. Surely they don't have earthquakes in New England!

He waited, frozen in place, expecting the tremor; but no seismic movement occurred. Instead, it was his mind that seemed to tremble on the brink of some stupendous discovery. What was it? He strained towards the insight that the mountain seemed to hold out to him, his eyes fixed on the brightening skyline —

And then the first dazzling limb of the sun topped the range, and he was momentarily blinded. He cried aloud, and when he could see once again the hallucination of coloured light had vanished, along with the mysterious pregnant tension that had enthralled his brain.

'Usrat'sya mozhno!' he cried. His knees threatened to buckle and he barely caught himself from falling. Leaning heavily upon his walking stick, he hobbled towards the little summerhouse. In his frustration and vertigo, he did not notice that the place already had an occupant.

'Dr Sakhvadze – is something wrong?'

A tall man who had been sitting in the deep shadows started up and took him by the arm, guiding him to a bench. Pyotr peered at him and recognized Denis Remillard's uncle, an enigmatic personage who acted as the Congress liaison with the hotel, but otherwise had little to do with operant affairs.

Pyotr sat down heavily, pulled out his pocket handkerchief, and mopped his face. 'A little bad spell. Nothing physical. I am sensitive, you see . . . to certain psychodynamic currents in the geosphere.'

'Ah,' said Remillard, uncomprehending. 'You're sure you'll be all right?' He displayed a miniature telephone unit that he had taken from inside his jacket. 'I can call the hotel and have a golf cart brought out. No trouble at all.'

'No,' said Pyotr sharply. 'You needn't treat me like an invalid! It was only a passing metapsychic event, I tell you. It shook me up. I'll be all right again in a moment.'

'Just as you say,' Remillard murmured, tucking the portaphone away. 'You're abroad rather early, Doctor.'

'And so are you,' Pyotr retorted. Then, regretting his

615

brusqueness, he added, 'I felt particularly in need of a ramble today, to set my juices flowing and sharpen my wits. There are a number of important papers and talks being delivered that I am anxious to take in – most particularly Jamie MacGregor's demonstration of the prototype bioenergeticfield detector. Auras of all types are of great interest to me. And of course, there is tonight's banquet to look forward to — '

'Along with other unscheduled diversions.'

Pyotr eyed Remillard with trepidation. 'You think there will be serious trouble?'

'Some kind of trouble. We're doing our best to make certain that it's not serious.'

'One would think that in a great and powerful country like the United States, such threats to public order would not be tolerated.'

Remillard laughed shortly. 'We have a saying: "It's a free country". And it is, Dr Sakhvadze – for better and sometimes for worse. The Sons of Earth and the other antioperant crazies can demonstrate against us to their heart's content just as long as they don't trespass on the private property of the resort. They got a little overenthusiastic last night, and a few of them ended up in the slammer, but the mob was still unfocused. Disorganized. What we're afraid of is that another element may be moving in – a more professional type of troublemaker.'

'Why don't your EE operatives investigate and forestall these – these — '

'Goons,' Remillard supplied. 'I'm sure that New Hampshire is doing its best. And my nephew's people have an informal group of EE watchdogs keeping an eye out. But it's the old problem in EE surveillance, Doctor – given a limited number of pEEps, where do you look?'

The old psychiatrist rose to his feet. 'Quite so. Well, I think I shall go back to the hotel. It would be prudent of me to return before my grandchildren miss me. The demonstration last night was very worrying to them. They warned me not to go out alone.'

Remillard still sat on one of the benches, tossing a key ring with a colourful fob from one hand to the other and frowning thoughtfully. 'They're quite right to worry. It was a nasty moment when the pickets broke through the outer line of security guards and charged down the hotel driveway. The mental vibrations scared the hell out of me, I can tell you . . . It was really a primitive kind of metaconcert, that mob mind. A mass mentality with an identity and a will of its own – just for those few minutes, until the impetus faltered and the thing shattered into individuals again. Thank God there weren't more than a couple of hundred out there . . . I couldn't sleep a wink last night after it was over.'

'And so you came out here.'

Remillard nodded. 'A long time ago I worked for the hotel. This little shelter out on the golf links used to be one of my favourite thinking spots.' He flipped the key chain high, snatched it out of the air with one hand, and stuffed it into his pocket. 'But I guess I've thought enough for this morning! Time for breakfast, and then I'll have to make arrangements for a special power-source for Professor MacGregor's doohickey.'

'Shall we walk back together?' Pyotr suggested. 'Then I will have complied with my grandchildren's directive at least partially, and they will have no occasion to scold me.'

Remillard hauled himself up and stretched. 'Those young fussbudgets give you a hard time, you just send 'em on to me! Let's go.'

Pyotr laughed. 'Fussbudgets! Doohickey! What a colourful language English is.'

'I don't know that those words are English, Doctor – but they're sure Yankee. Just like me.'

Pyotr's eyes gleamed. 'Yes . . . I do recall now that you are a native of this region, Mr Remillard. Perhaps you will be able to tell me whether or not there are ever any earthquakes hereabouts?'

'Why, yes. We do get one, very rarely.'

'I knew it! I knew it!' Pyotr exulted; and then at the puzzled expression on the other man's face, he apologized. 'I will explain my strange question in just a moment. But, please – first I have one other urgent query: What is kryptonite, and why do the Sons of Earth covet it?'

Rogatien Remillard exploded in laughter.

'But it was on the placards of the demonstrators!'

Still chuckling, Remillard asked, 'Have you ever heard of Superman?'

'Nietzsche's famous Übermensch? Most certainly.'

Remillard regained his composure with some effort. 'Not that Superman. Another one, a kind of American legend.'

'I have never heard of him, no. But I would be most interested to learn about this folkloric hero. I presume there are mythic analogues to the operant condition in the American Superman's tale?'

'I never really thought about it that way – but I guess there are.'

Together, the two of them started back for the resort hotel, with Rogi telling the story slowly and carefully so that the old man would be sure to get the joke.

'The Gi! Of course it was the Gi,' Homologous Trend said. 'One is most vexed with the silly things! What *did* they think they were playing at?'

'No real harm has been done,' said Asymptotic Essence. 'Let one's tranquillity prevail. There was only a minimal matter-distortion effect. One doubts whether any seismograph in use among the Earthlings would have been able to record the anomaly at all.'

'How in the world did they do it?' Eupathic Impulse was more intrigued than appalled, now that it was plain that no calamity had taken place.

'The phenomenon was generated by an empathy spasm of the collective Gi conscious,' Noetic Concordance explained, 'that took place as they commiserated with the aged Earthling's poignant meditations. The harmonic passed from the mental lattices to the consonant geophysical ones, setting off the tremor. One notes that the *reverse* of the phenomenon is common enough. Trust the Gi to come up with a unique twist.'

'Trust them to come up with arrant nincompoopery,' said Trend. 'One is strongly inclined to excuse the Gi Fleet from further participation in this convocation. Given the delicacy of the approaching climax, the consequences of its lapse could have been extremely serious.'

'The Gi are contrite,' Essence said. 'They have taken our rebuke to heart. They pledge that they will henceforth control the racial tendency to emotional ebullience.'

'They'd jolly well better,' Trend declared, 'or they can watch the finale from the backside of Pluto! Don't they realize that Unifex is in the process of exerting Its ultimate influences? As It draws the skeins of probability taut, the slightest skew off the median may confute the solidifying nodes.'

'Surely not,' Eupathic Impulse protested. 'Not on the very threshold of Intervention!'

'The resolution rests now with the operant Earthlings,' Trend told the other three, 'and possibly with the great Interloper Itself, whose ways remain as mystifying as ever. The rest of us are permitted only to watch and pray. Join with me, fellow entities, to remind the fleet of this solemn fact.'

The four Lylmik minds projected the thought, using the imperative mode; and it was affirmed by each and every one of the invisible starships hovering expectantly about the planet Earth – ships of the Krondak Polity, the Poltroyan, the Simbiari, and even the penitent Gi – summoned from every part of the 14th Sector of the Galactic Milieu in hopes of hearing the Intervention signal that only Atoning Unifex might utter.

Together with the great living cruiser of the Lylmik Supervisors, the convocation of exotic vessels numbered twenty thousand seven hundred and thirty-six.

The main dining room of the hotel was crowded for breakfast; but because most of the guests were operants who exerted effortless subliminal compulsion upon the hardworking waitrons, things ran very smoothly. None of the service personnel realized that they were being gently coerced. Nevertheless, because their minds were in a receptive frame, they were able to visualize the needs of the patrons even though they themselves were normals. There were no miswritten orders, no tables that were neglected while others were overserviced, no perfectly cooled cups of coffee topped off on the sly by overzealous pot-wielders. There was not even much noise, since the delegates who had gathered for this final day of the Metapsychic Congress did most of their conversing on the intimate telepathic mode – cool and smiling on the outside while they voiced their apprehensions or complaints mentally.

Rogi came into the dining room after seeing Pyotr safely to the elevator and waved off the maîtress d'. 'Thanks, Linda. I'll just join my family.' *But send somebody pronto to take my order I'm starving to death there's a good kid . . .*

Lucille and Denis and their three oldest children were well into their meal as Rogi slipped into the empty chair at the big round table near the window, sitting between Philip and Severin. A waiter appeared at once and Rogi ordered oeufs dans le sirop d'érable and hot sourdough bread.

Yucko!

The telepathic critique slipped out of the mind of ten-year-old Severin as the rest of the family greeted Rogi verbally. Lucille looked at her son and the boy gave a start and sat up very straight. He said, 'I beg your pardon, Uncle Rogi. It was rude of me to make such a comment.'

'De rien.' Rogi smiled. 'Eggs in maple syrup are an old-fashioned Franco dish. Even though they aren't on the menu, the chef knows well enough how to prepare them. When I was a child my Aunt Lorraine used to make them for us on special occasions . . . when our spirits were in need of a lift.'

'It's that kind of a day,' Denis conceded.

'The vibes,' Philip observed, 'are mucho malific.'

'And two carloads of deadheads just showed up at the main gate to start picketing!' Severin added.

Lucille said: Sevvy. How many times must I tell you not to use that epithet particularly in vocal speech when there are normals about who may hear you . . .

The little boy sighed. 'I'm sorry that I used the insulting expression,' he mumbled; but his farspeech, imperfectly directed to his two older brothers, belied the apology:

Well they *are* dead from the neck up and they hate

our guts and right this minute do you know what they're hollering at the delegates coming in from the other hotels? they're hollering FREAKS&HEADS! FREAKS&HEADS! YOUR MA SHOULDA KNOWED YOU WERE BETTER OFF DEAD! so who's really the deadhead huh? maybe we are to let 'em get away with that shit we should do like the Russians and show 'em what Heads can do to defend themselves if Assholes mess with us —

Denis said: *Severin.*

Severin said: Oops.

Philip and Maurice, their eyes on their plates and their barriers in place, sat very still.

Denis said: Severin your Mama and I felt that you were mature enough to come to this Congress to participate in the life of the adult operant community at this crucial stage in our evolution. Some of the input you've experienced here is positive and some is negative but all of it should nurture mental growth.

'Yes, Papa,' Severin said. But I wish there was some way we could *make* the normals stop hating us *make* them like us for their own good and ours too — !

'Learning to like someone,' said Severin's oldest brother Philip sententiously, 'as opposed to the spontaneous good-will experienced between compatible personalities, may take considerable time and require a large expenditure of psychic energy. Tolerance is particularly difficult for normals — who lack the insight faculties that we operants tend to take for granted. Normals almost invariably form value judgements according to prejudicial or superficial criteria.'

'For example,' Maurice chimed in, 'a normal would look at Severin and see only a scowling young pipsqueak with egg on his tie . . . whereas we, using metapsychic perceptions, can scrutinize his very soul and realize that beneath his unprepossessing exterior lurks a truly depraved little pillock!'

I'll get you guys! Severin declared.

Boys! said Lucille.

Rogi laughed. 'Yes, they're boys, all right.'

Denis glanced at his watch. 'Professor Malatesta's

symposium on psychoeconomic vector theory starts in five minutes in the Gold Room. Philip and Maurice – you won't want to be late.'

'No, Papa.' Still chortling mentally, the pair bade courteous farewell and sauntered out of the dining room. At sixteen and fourteen, they were both already taller than their father. Philip was doing postgraduate work in bioenergetics at Harvard. Maurice, winding up his BA requirements at Dartmouth, was toying with the notion of taking a degree in philosophy before entering medical school.

Rogi said to Denis and Lucille: There was an ugly undertone in that little bit of by-play among the boys. I think all three of them are scared silly.

Denis said: You're right of course.

Lucille said: None of them has ever had to face such a concentration of enmity before. You know what an operant sanctuary Hanover is. Philip's had a few disagreeable experiences at Harvard but that place is really too hyper-civilized to permit any serious incidents. This encounter with the Sons of Earth in all their deep-dyed yahoo splendour has shaken my babies rather badly. One's first meeting with hatred en masse is apt to do that.

Rogi said: You might want to consider sending the kids home.

Denis said: The security people will keep the situation under control. The boys will have to face situations like this sooner or later. They may as well do it with the support of their mental peers.

Rogi said: Even Sevvy? Denis he's *ten*!

Denis asked his son, 'What do you think about going home from the Congress a little early? You've had five days' worth. Phil could drive you and Maury to Hanover — '

Severin's face crumpled. 'And miss the banquet on top of the mountain? When it might even *storm* up there?'

Denis tried not to smile. 'I was concerned that the unpleasant aetheric nuances from the demonstrators might be upsetting.'

Severin glumly stirred his cold scrambled eggs with a fork. 'I can cope, Papa.' . . . But those ol' Sons better not mess with me!

Lucille said, 'If you do stay we'll expect you to behave like an adult, Sevvy. An operant adult.'

'I promise to do my best, Mama.'

'Good. Finish your breakfast then.' She glanced appealingly at Rogi, posing a mental question: Would it be too much trouble for you to keep him with you for a while? Both Denis and I must sit on a rather boring panel.

Rogi said, 'If you two would like to abandon us, feel free. Sevvy and I will take our time eating and meet you later.'

The waiter arrived with Rogi's meal as Denis and Lucille left. The boy showed immoderate interest in the big dish of eggs poached in hot maple syrup. They were accompanied by a goblet of freshly squeezed pink grapefruit juice and a smoking-hot loaf that sat on its own miniature breadboard. Rogi smacked his lips and tucked his napkin boldly into his collar. He turned the loaf on its side and sawed off a couple of aromatic slices, passing one to Severin.

'Look here, young man. Your food's gone stone cold and I've got more than enough for the two of us. I know these oeufs look weird, but they smell good, don't they?'

'Yeah . . .'

Without another word, Rogi divided the eggs and showed the boy how to moosh them up and eat them with a spoon while sopping the bread in the delicious mess. Severin was delighted with this confounding of bourgeois table etiquette. He tied his own napkin around his neck and fell to.

'I've got an idea for when we're done,' Rogi said. 'I have to help the building engineer fix up the big downstairs meeting room for Professor Jamie's show-and-tell at one-thirty. We'll bring in high-voltage power cables from the transformer room and set up an auxiliary board for the demonstration. You want to help?'

'Wow, yo!' said Severin, through a mouthful of eggs.

Rogi said: Keeping busy is another good way to damp the bad vibes. At least I've found that it works.

You mean you got the fantods too?

Doggone right. Off-key goblin bassoons whooping in the pit of my stomach and thousand-leggers skating up the back of my neck.

. . . Some of those Sons out there really *would* like to kill us.

I know Sevvy.

Would you let 'em? Rather than hurt them in self-defence?

The Ethic you've been taught tells you the answer.

I know the Altruism Ethic I want to know what *you* would do.

I'm just a primitive sort of head not in the same league as you and your parents and the other giantbrains at this Congress —

Answer me straight don't futz me like a little kid!

Nonviolence is a wonderful ideal but dangerous it's amazing that so many people do opt for it. Me I don't think I'd have the strength.

If those militant doodoodomes aren't *fought* they get worse!

The dilemma will probably remain academic thank God.

No but the whole thing really bothers me a lot I've tried to understand Phil & Maury say they believe AltruismEthic just like Mama & Papa but *I can see into their minds* and they're not sure either.

Lord I believe help my unbelief . . .

Sort of. The Ethic does seem right from the point of view of alloperantstogether because it's noble you know it catches the attention of the normals FatherAndy calls it moral suasion but it's not something you have to do is it *I* don't see what's wrong with the Russian heads saying they'll defend their country mentally what good would it do them to be noble and a beautiful example of nonviolence if they all *died*?

Tough question. If you ever find a good answer Sevvy tell me.

As Lucille and Denis passed through the crowded lobby she said: Let me just stop at the newsstand for a moment before we go on to Vanderlaan's panel . . . Good heavens! The entire portico of the hotel is swarming with police!

Denis said: The hotel security chief is calling in virtually every off-duty officer in northern New Hampshire – and a few from Maine. It will cost us a bundle but I authorized the expenditure.

. . . Even though none of the pEEps detected any unusual activity?

Especially because they didn't.

Lucille said to the clerk in the hotel boutique, 'I'll take this little package of aspirin. And do you have a PD of today's *Pravda* in English?'

'American or Eurasian format?'

'American, please.'

'I'll call it up in a jiff,' the girl said, turning to her register console.

Denis said: I told you I'd excurse to Moscow and check with Tamara late tonight.

Lucille's tone was irritable: Quick reassurances don't tell me enough. I want the background. The differing viewpoints.

There's nothing we can do to influence events over there. If the operants win they win and it will probably be more of a disaster in the long run than if they are forced into exile.

'Cash or charge?' inquired the clerk brightly.

Lucille handed over her credit card. 'Charge.'

Denis said: If the Red Army and the Party survivors agree to a coalition with Tamara's operants it will only be one based on force . . . coercion to control a panicking population or to intimidate the enemies of the state.

'Eight sixty-three, please, no sales tax in New Hampshire but we have to add excise for the plaque-disk of that particular newspaper. May I have your thumb here? Thanks a bundle — and you have a lovely day.' The clerk handed over the purchases and Lucille tucked them into her purse.

A lovely day! she reiterated ironically. The loveliest sight I can imagine at this moment is the National Guard rolling in the gate ready to camp on the golf course . . . But instead there are more demonstrators showing up I don't even have to EE outside to know it I can feel their thoughts mindlessly massing: *Off the heads off the heads off the heads* . . .

Denis reached out and enveloped her in redactive

comfort. The chanting faded, along with the small head-ache that had plagued her since rising. Delegates arriving from the other hotels swarmed all around them, heading for the different function rooms, but they were soundless, and even their movements seemed diffident and ghostly.

Denis said: You are not to worry. By evening it should all be over. We'll dine among the thunderclouds with serene minds and the conflagration of ions will wipe out all remnants of the haters' farspeech leaving us in peace.

You really don't think the demonstrators will try to follow us up the mountain?

No. They'd have to use the Carriage Road and the State Police are prepared to barricade it at the first sign of trouble. We'll have to endure their taunts throughout the day and there may be a few skirmishes if the pickets try to sneak on to the grounds again but there's no danger. You want proof? Jamie's daughter Katie claims to have the Sight you know and when I spoke briefly to Ilya this morning he said his wife sees nothing but great things happening today . . . Now all we — 'Damn,' he said out loud. 'My pager.'

Full-sensory reality claimed Lucille with painful sudden-ness. Denis pressed the stud on his watchband that halted the persistent prickling, then studied the message crawling across the Omega's digital strip.

'I'm to call the President,' he said.

Lucille stared at him in blank dismay, then burst out: Don'tyouDAREgotoWashingtonyou'retheChairofthisaffair youhavetoSPEAK tonightI won'tdoit foryouthis timedamnit youcan'tgoyouhavenomorecleanshirts!

He kissed her cheek. 'Don't worry. Go to our panel. And try not to let anybody catch you reading your newsplaque during the dull bits.'

Then he was off for the hotel manager's office and the secure landline that had been set up for a certain contingency.

Kieran O'Connor turned up the gain on the painkilling device that had been spliced into his nervous system, hating himself for the cowardice at the same time that he welcomed the wondrous semiorgasmic numbness that suffused his lower body, releasing him. It was ten minutes until noon and time to pull himself into shape for the showdown with Victor. Fortunately, that wouldn't take long.

Forgive me Black Mother soon I will return. Dam dham nam tam tham dam dham nam pam pham.

His farsensory faculties returned and he was once again able to experience the crashing waters of Upper Ammonoosuc Falls as it ramped and plunged over shiny granite ledges and boiled whitely through the monstrous potholes it had drilled in the tough bedrock. A blustery wind had sprung up that ripped the cascade's mists into furious wraiths that would have soaked any tourist brave enough to venture on to the small observation platform. But nobody was there. The parking lot of the modest roadside park was empty except for the silver Mercedes in which Kieran O'Connor sat alone.

He had rented the car at Dorval Airport in Montréal and driven it to this specified meeting place, along Base Station Road not far from the Mount Washington cog railway's lower terminus. He was thankful that all but thirty-five of the 345 kilometres of the drive had been on pilot-stripped auto-routes or freeways, giving him a chance to sleep off some of the jet lag. In order to foil the Justice Department surveillance team he had travelled from Chicago to New Hampshire via Seattle, Krung Thep, Bombay, Johannesburg. Fiumicino, Gatwick and Montréal – shedding the last pEEp agent in the chaotic concourses of Aeroporto Leonardo da Vinci. He was certain now that none of the government investigators would be able to trace him to this Congress – much less uncover his connection to Victor Remillard or the local branch of the Sons of Earth. The only potentially weak link had been Shannon – and just as Kieran had anticipated, she had been painstakingly discreet since betraying her pathetic dupe of a husband. Even more than her father, she wanted no hint of Victor's involvement with the O'Connor empire to come to the attention of the Attorney General.

Kieran's eyes filled, surprising him, and he realized that

for the first time he was mourning her loss. It should have been the daughter to inherit the night, not the daughter's daughter. But Kali would have her jest . . . *O Mother of Power, forgive her as you forgive me.*

She would be coming, even though he had forbidden it, eager for the final treachery. So be it. *Devouring Mother I would give her to you myself if I could. But I dare not waste the least spark of my dwindling powers. Please understand. Dam dham nam tam —*

'Are you asleep?'

Kieran opened his eyes. Victor Remillard was standing beside the closed window of the Mercedes. His dark wool Melton storm coat and close-cut curly hair glittered with mist droplets. A large orange van belonging to the New Hampshire Highway Department blocked the entrance to the waterfall's parking lot.

Kieran pressed the window button. 'You're on time. I presume those are your wheels.'

'The way the cops have the resort area sewed up, I figured something official might come in handy. Especially later.'

'Everything's in order?'

'I told you it would be and it is. But you're not getting any details, Kieran.'

'I don't want them . . . It surprises me, though, to perceive that you plan to oversee the operation personally. Aren't you concerned about being recognized?'

Victor laughed. 'I can fuzz my identity. You mean you can't?'

'The late Fabulous Finster, a valued associate of mine, once attempted to impart the technique to me. But I just didn't have the knack. I've had to make do with other mental expedients.' The old man's shadowed eyes lifted and barely reined coercion flashed in their depths. 'I thought I told you to meet me here alone.'

'I need Pete Laplace. He knows every back road and abandoned track in these parts and I've got other things to do besides study road maps. I'm running most of this goddam hit word-of-mouth and message-to-Garcia. No

628

farspeech, no electronics. Not until the tail end, when it'll be too late to stop us.'

'You've made the arrangements for my participation?'

'Yes. But I think you're crazy as a fuckin' bedbug.'

'Never mind,' Kieran said amiably. 'Humouring me in this final matter will have no effect at all on your part of the operation. But it's an old Irish custom to join the dance if you've paid the piper.'

'Which brings us to fork-over time.'

Kieran picked up an attaché case made of black light-weight metal and passed it through the window. 'It's not locked. You'll wish to programme the locking device and the built-in security mechanisms after checking the bona fides of the instrument of transfer with your people at Chase Manhattan. But I assure you that everything has been arranged as we agreed. My assets will become the property of your dummy Canadian corporation upon the completion of certain legal formalities at – at four o'clock this afternoon. Sixteen hundred hours. You see – I trust you to fulfil your part of the bargain.'

'What about the Big Cherry?' Victor prompted. 'And the last condition?'

Kieran lifted one hand in a reassuring gesture. His smile was pained. 'I told you that my final request wouldn't be difficult for you to fulfil – and a fair exchange for the access code to the override system of Zap-Star.'

'Well?'

'My daughter Shannon is at the White Mountain Hotel. In spite of my strictest orders to the contrary. She expects you to kill me, as you agreed to do in return for her favours. What I want you to do is show her the documents and the gigadisk data that are in the case I gave you. Get into the hotel computer and let her see the corporate transfer confirmed. And then, use the computer to confirm your access to Zap-Star as well – but without revealing the access code to her. Then you may question Shannon tactfully on what role she plans to play in tonight's operation . . .'

Victor's gloved hands tightened on the metal case. His mind was an impregnable fortress. 'Why?'

Kieran began to laugh, but then his body convulsed and

he groaned through clenched teeth and fumbled desperately inside his coat. Victor could see that the old man's shirt was partially unbuttoned and a flattened plastic control mechanism with numerous electrode wires was taped to his upper chest. For a brief interval Kieran writhed helplessly, until his fingers reached the device's key-pad. He summoned maximum analgesia and fell back in abrupt relief.

Presently, Kieran said, 'Sorry. Your question — ?'

Victor's face was expressionless. 'I don't understand why you want me to confirm my – my takeover to your daughter. It's only what she expects.'

'Tell Shannon that she never really had any secrets from me. Tell her that I knew all along about her duplicate mind-screen and had access to her secret heart. Tell her she was free only in her fantasies. My pathetic little girl! I was sadly mistaken about her and it nearly cost me my – my life's goal. But I was shown another way . . .' *Thank you Mother thank you dam dham nam tam —*

Victor demanded: *What do you mean what the hell are you saying and WHO IS SHE who is that?*

'My Mother. I pray her mantra.' Kieran's eyes closed and he lay limp against the soft leather seat. The rain had finally started and plump silver pearls danced among the lesser misty splatters on the waxed hood of the Mercedes. Kieran said, 'Go away. Do the things I've told you. Shannon's reaction will show you what my last request of you is. The Mother has compassion on my weakness and pardons me from having to do the job myself. And she doesn't need me to bring the final Blackness, either. It will all happen as it must happen. Dam dham nam tam tham dam dham nam pam pham . . .'

'The access code! Is that it? The mantra?'

Kieran's eyes opened and blazed. *Will you do as I say with Shannon?*

'Yes.' Victor's mind opened to confirm the truth.

Kieran nodded slowly. 'Another thing . . . She also fantasizes that her child Laura is yours. Disabuse her of that at the end, will you? It will bring home the point. You may want to take Laura away from Gerry Tremblay and bring her up yourself . . . Or perhaps you won't. You don't want to share, the way I did.' The eyes closed again. Kieran's face was yellowish-grey and he breathed slowly through his open mouth. 'I loved her, though. I loved them all. But not you and that's why you are my heir to the night.'

Victor reached out with his coercion, exerting it with delicate care: *Kieran. Don't sleep yet. You must tell me the access code. The satellite access code. Tell me.*

Yes yes this is the phrase without any punctuation FOR BEHOLD HENCEFORTH ALL GENERATIONS SHALL CALL ME BLESSED the key to bring about the final death of energy the final dark . . . I must sleep now but I'll wake this evening I'll wake in time to see it through it's all right now Mother I've done it now rest . . .

The mental image. Victor saw it again in the instant before Kieran slipped into unconsciousness. It was a great wheel of black petals with fire at the heart, held within the belly of a barely perceptible female figure. But Victor Remillard had never heard of Kali, and so all he did was swear in French as the vision faded.

Then he opened the door of the Mercedes and brought the window up. He closed the door, locked it, and left Kieran O'Connor to sleep beside the thundering waterfall until the operation began at 1930 hours that evening.

Shannon Tremblay attended Jamie MacGregor's lecture as openly as she had the other Congress events that interested her, confident that a severely tailored suit, eyeglasses with tortoiseshell rims, and a short black wig hiding her auburn hair rendered her unrecognizable. The concept of a mental signature, a personal thought-pattern as distinctive as a fingerprint, was quite unknown to her; and so she was badly startled when someone called out as she left the meeting room:

'Oh, there you are, Shan. Would you let me have a word with you before you go on to the next round of papers?'

It was a tall, balding academic, a man she had never seen before, and she regarded him frostily and said, 'You've mistaken me for someone else,' and would have walked on. But coercion took hold of her and forced her to turn and accompany the man into an alcove, and she did not dare protest and call attention to herself.

'I've been looking all over the hotel for you,' the man said. For a split second his ascetic face flickered and another underlying set of features took its place.

Victor!

The coercive grip tightened to the point of pain and she whimpered.

'Use regular speech,' he ordered in low tones. 'Your telepathy has always been incompetent in focusing along the intimate mode.'

She winced at the pressure. 'Let me go, damn you! What do you *mean* by accosting me — '

'You're supposed to be in Cambridge.'

She reseated her glasses and turned away from him. 'I can go where I please.'

'So you couldn't resist being in on the kill, eh? Never mind if somebody spotted you and put two and two together! Don't you realize this place is swarming with FBI and Justice Department agents?'

'They're not looking for me,' she retorted. 'They're looking for Daddy – or his known associates. Daddy disappeared three days ago, you know. *I* was the one who put two and two together and deduced that he must be on his way here, to this final Metapsychic Congress. It was the perfect occasion for him . . . and for you. Of course I wanted to be on the scene for the finale.' She lifted her chin with a triumphant smile. 'Are these Sons of Earth militants your idea? What will they do – try to burn down the hotel? The old place is a real tinderbox. I'm staying at the Horse & Hound in Franconia, so feel — '

'Shut up,' he hissed. 'Do you think this is all some entertainment put on for your benefit?'

She laughed softly. 'For both our benefits.' Then her expression hardened. 'Daddy has made the deal with you, hasn't he! You arrange for some convenient Sons-of-Earth-sponsored disaster to befall this hotel full of operants, and he says he'll hand everything over.'

'That's right.'

'You're a fool if you trust him. He'll never give up his

power until he's dead, and he won't die until he's ready to. The doctors can't understand how he's been able to survive this long – but I understand! He wants to offer a holocaust of operant minds to appease some horrible fantasy, and if you help him he'll find some way to finish you off with all the rest. You'll never get the best of Daddy unless you kill him. I told you that at the beginning.'

'Your father will die tonight.' Victor held up the black metal attaché case. 'And he's already turned over everything to me – including the access code for Zap-Star.'

She gasped. 'I don't believe it! He's lied to you.'

'There is that possibility. Which is why you and I are going to check things out before my big production number goes any further.'

He took her arm again and guided her up a wide flight of carpeted stairs to the main lobby. They might have been colleagues chatting familiarly after a long separation.

'Did Gerry know you were coming here?'

'Of course not,' she said. 'He knows better than to question me about my affairs.'

'What's he doing these days – househusbanding? Baby-sitting, perhaps?'

'Pulling his head together before going to work for a Boston branch of Carns, Elsasser, Lehmann, if you must know. He took it hard when Griffith kicked him out of Roggenfeld Acquisitions.'

Victor chuckled. 'Too timid to swim with the sharks, I heard. How are you two getting along these days?'

'Gerry is civil, and he's afraid of me, and there are times when I'm certain he's hiding some ghastly secret – but my redaction is no good against a trained operant like him, and I've never been able to pry it out. You'll have to. Afterwards.'

'How does Gerry get along with your baby, Laura? The kid's about nine months old, isn't she? And big-brained?'

Shannon said coldly, 'Aside from his little character defects deriving from overweening ambition, Gerry is a decent sort of man. He knows Laura isn't his, but he doesn't hold it against her. He's kind. He's certainly more interested in her than you seem to be — '

They had passed out of the lobby into the executive offices of the hotel and now paused before an unmarked door. Indicating mentally that Shannon should keep silence, he opened it and stepped inside. It was a suite of rooms that obviously housed the computer functions. A young man in shirtsleeves working on a sheaf of print-outs looked up in surprise and opened his mouth – then froze as Victor's coercion took control of him. Without saying a word, the young man got up and led Victor into an inner room where the equipment was kept. Victor said:

Your work for the day is finished. Go home now without speaking to anyone. You will not remember having seen us.

The young man turned on his heel and marched out, closing the door behind him.

Shannon said, 'What are you going to do?'

Victor had seated himself at the manual console and began to rap expertly on the key-pads. The display said: CHASE MANHATTAN BANK DATACEN. GOOD AFTERNOON MR REMILLARD. PLEASE BEGIN UPLOAD.

Victor took the thick plastic gigadisk out of the attaché case and slotted it. Then he waited.

Shannon's eyes were glued to the display screen, which now said: WORKING. She whispered, 'He couldn't have. I don't believe it.' And then the screen said: TRANS-ACTION VLNX2234–9–21–2013 PRELOGGED AND READY FOR FINAL EXECUTION 1600 HRS. DO YOU HAVE INSTRUCTIONS?

Victor typed: PRECIS.

And the computer obliged.

Shannon gave a strangled little joyous shriek. 'It's true! He's done it! My God, it's totally unbelievable!' She would have thrown her arms around Victor, but his coercion flicked her back as casually as an insect. 'Wait. We have to confirm the other.'

Thanking and dismissing the bank, Victor retrieved his disk and replaced it in the case. Then he typed out a certain telephone number with a northern Illinois area code. The screen said: YOU HAVE REACHED A PRIVATE NUMBER. PLEASE INSERT ACCESS CODE.

Victor typed: FOR BEHOLD HENCEFORTH ALL GENERATIONS SHALL CALL ME BLESSED.

The computer said: ENTER.

Victor typed: DIR.

The computer said: ZAP-STAR OVERRIDE 1MARY.KOC. THIS COMMAND FILE IS VALID BUT NOT OPERATIONAL UNTIL 12–25–2013 AT WHICH TIME THE ZAP-STAR SYSTEM COMES ONLINE. DO YOU HAVE INSTRUCTIONS?

Victor typed: NO GOODBYE. And then he erased all record of both the calls, using an old hacker's trick, and turned in the seat to face Shannon.

She said, 'It's true. He's capitulated completely . . . unless he plans to cheat you some way at the last minute — '

'I don't believe that he does.'

'Then,' she said, 'all that's left to do is finish him off.'

'*And* the Metapsychic Congress.'

'Oh, there's no need for that! Only a paranoid like Daddy would believe that the mass murder of a couple of thousand leading operants would leave people like us with a clear field. What about all the rest of the heads in the world? If we kill this lot, others will eventually take their places. No . . . Daddy's famous "edge" is obsolete, and so is yours, Victor. You should have seen the apparatus that Professor MacGregor demonstrated at his lecture! It was the first aura detector. All it does is shine a beam of something-or-other at a person and analyse the reflection – and it can tell whether or not that person is hopelessly latent, or suboperant, or operant. And it even quantizes the degree of operancy! One of the subjects MacGregor used in his lecture was the ten-year-old son of Denis Remillard. Would you believe the boy sent the analyser right off the scale? . . . So you see, with a gadget like this available, it just won't be possible for people to keep their operancy secret. Even casinos will install these things — '

'There are other edges,' Victor said.

Shannon looked at him mutely, her mind incredulous. Finally she said, 'You can't mean it!'

'I'd call Zap-Star the ultimate edge. Of course, it wouldn't be used in the clumsy death-ray scenario your father dreamed up. Its use would be very selective.'

'But it's not *necessary*, Victor! Any more than killing these operants is necessary. Once Daddy is dead you'll have all the power and wealth that any man could want — '

He shook his head. Slowly, he rose from the chair and came to her. 'He said you disappointed him. You've disappointed me, too.'

She didn't try to flee. Proudly, she said, 'I see. You don't need people the way Daddy did. You're self-sufficient. You don't need – or love – anyone but yourself, do you, Victor? Not me. And certainly not our child.'

'Laura is not my child. We've never had physical intercourse. You were quite right to call me self-sufficient.'

'Good God. Not yours . . .' Her eyes were fixed on him as the truth of it slowly broke through. 'Yes, I see. You're impotent.'

Victor laughed at her. 'Not in any way that really matters. Not the way your father is now, powerless because he still loves you. He asked me to tell you that you were never really free of him. He was always able to penetrate your double screen. I suppose he let you keep the illusion in hopes that it would shore up your ego. Keep you from suiciding.'

'And it suited his plans when I came to you.' Her eyes had gone dull. 'Of course. He had to manipulate both of us. He must have known he could never bond you . . .' She straightened, proud again for a moment. 'Neither of you will use Zap-Star, you know. The government knows the system is penetrated.'

'All they know is what you – and my brother Denis – have told them. I'm willing to gamble that the President won't be able to stop the system's activation on schedule. Not on the word of two dead heads.'

His farsight roamed the area, then lit on a small storeroom that opened off the computer room. He compelled her to follow him to it, opened the door, and flicked on the light.

'This will do. No one will come in here so late on Saturday afternoon. It won't matter tomorrow.'

She said, 'You aren't going to do it quickly.'

'I have some time to kill,' he said, laughing, and took off her black wig so that the long flaming hair tumbled out. Her face and mind were calm. Eventually he would give her what she wanted.

He asked her to kneel, and she sank down without protest. Then he cupped her head in both hands and pressed her against him, and stopped her heart for the first time.

30

From the Memoirs of
Rogatien Remillard

For more than a year, since Denis's interrogation of Gerry Tremblay, government investigators had sought in vain for hard evidence that would connect Kieran O'Connor to the sort of grandiose conspiracy that his daughter had accused him of perpetrating. It was easy enough for EE adepts to search his offices and his residence – and the presence of the elaborate satellite uplink equipment was duly noted, but conceded to be quite legal. The heavily guarded data bank beneath the O'Connor mansion undoubtedly held the key to the mystery; but EE adepts could scrutinize its library of disks until doomsday without knowing what they contained. No search warrant could be served because no probable cause of felonious action could be demonstrated, and US law forbade 'fishing expeditions' as unwarranted invasions of privacy.

One of the Zap-Star battle-mirrors was plucked from orbit and taken to the ON–1 habitat for examination. A problematic chip was indeed found, one that was unauthorized in the original specifications. However, engineers of the O'Connor satellite consortium maintained that the component was entirely innocuous, designed to improve guidance system response to groundside commands. If the chip did contain an override, the thing had been hidden with surpassing cleverness and would probably display its true colours only when activated by a coded signal.

One could, of course, haul in each and every one of the 130 non-Chinese battle-mirrors and – using exquisite care – remove the dubious chip. The fix would take approximately four years and cost $7.2 billion, and in the meantime the independently operated Chinese units would remain fully operational.

The allegation of conspiracy was based thus far only upon the unsupported word of Shannon O'Connor Tremblay. Denis's mind-ream of her husband had yielded only tenuous confirmation – and that legally inadmissible. Subsequent investigations of the O'Connor empire had turned up no evidence whatsoever of any Zap-Star conspiracy – and precious little else that was even remotely actionable. The only taint was a distant one: back in the 1980s certain O'Connor subsidiaries had been strongly suspected of laundering Mafia funds. But this had never been proved and the Mob was dead and gone, while these days the O'Connor organization seemed guilty only of the immoderate gobbling of smaller corporate fry . . .

At least that had been the status of the government's investigation up until 20 September 2013.

On that day, an alert bureaucrat in the Securities and Exchange Commission took note of a routine notification of a transfer of assets from an American conglomerate to an obscure Canadian holding company. The SEC woman was struck by the enormous size of the transaction, and even more interested when she recognized the conglomerate to be a key-stone of the intricate O'Connor organization. A fast check with Montréal (Canada having less of a penchant for financial confidentiality than the US at that time) yielded up the name of the man behind the dummy corporation. The SEC woman informed the Attorney General and he informed the President of the United States – who in turn called up Denis to inquire why his younger brother Victor was being handed control of virtually everything that Kieran O'Connor owned.

*

'I told him I was just as flabbergasted as he was,' Denis told me. We had met at the conclusion of MacGregor's lecture, and now he and I and Lucille stood in the back of the nearly deserted hall talking the thing over. Naturally the President had asked his people to brief him on Victor; and he had been dismayed to discover that the Nobel laureate's family harboured a sheep who, if not exactly black, looked decidedly grubby around the edges.

And was a familiar of Kieran O'Connor's daughter.

'I'll give Baumgartner credit,' Denis said. 'He called me himself and he was straightforward about Victor. He told me that the government had a file on him dating way back to when Vic and Dad first started Remco. Tax fiddling, and later on some quashed indictments for interstate transportation of stolen property. The feds have never been able to get the goods on Vic, primarily because no one would testify against him. Lately, he's seemed to be clean – but the feds looked him up again after Shannon sprang her blockbuster. Naturally she was investigated with her father, and her relationship with Vic muddied the waters considerably. I was approached last spring and asked to mind-ream both Victor and Shannon. Of course I refused.'

Lucille and I said nothing and kept our thoughts to ourselves.

'Now the President has personally appealed to me to interrogate them mentally – especially Shannon – to find out whether the threat to Zap-Star is real. If I can get confirmation from Victor, it will preclude the possibility that Shannon is suffering some delusion.'

'But why do the feds think Vic would know anything about it?' I asked.

Denis said, 'Because Kieran O'Connor has terminal testicular cancer. If he's passing his empire to Vic, as the Canadian connection seems to prove, he's probably passing the clout along with the assets.'

'Christ!' I said. '*Vic* with a handle on Zap-Star?'

Denis said, 'O'Connor evaded both EE and normal government surveillance and has disappeared. As far as the feds can tell, Vic is innocently at home in Berlin. Shannon

Tremblay was traced to this Congress. The agents are certain she's here in the hotel.'

'And the President wants you to find her,' Lucille said, 'and turn her inside out?'

'That's about it,' said Denis.

'It's monstrous!' she exclaimed indignantly. 'The whole thing is incredible! That wretched woman corrupted Gerry for some squalid motive of her own, and then when he was caught in the Coercer Flap she invented this other thing — '

Denis silenced her. 'All I know is what was in Gerry's mind. *He* doesn't believe she's deluded. His impression — the impression of a trained psychiatrist — is that she is eminently sane in spite of a neurotic love-hate relationship with her father. Deep in his mental core, Gerry recognized that Kieran O'Connor was a paramount metapsychic manipulator, a man who had used his powers for self-aggrandisement all his life. The Zap-Star net wasn't Gerry's province. He knew O'Connor's consortium built the guidance systems for the net and he had a kind of instinct that it figured in some scheme that the old man was cooking up. That was the only verification I could give the President after my ream of Gerry. It was sufficient to launch the full-scale investigation, which yielded nothing . . . up until now.'

'So where do you go from here?' I asked.

'I did a quick farscan of the place,' Denis said. 'I have Shannon's mental signature — in a rough approximation, I'm afraid — from my mind-ream of Gerry. I swept the hotel from top to bottom and found no trace of her. For what it's worth, I found no trace of Vic either! But that doesn't mean they're not here. Vic's a devil of a screener and Shannon's probably no slouch either. I'm going to go very quietly to the top scanners attending the Congress and ask their help in watching out for both Shannon and Vic. They may let their guard down.'

'You're not thinking of confronting your brother — !' Lucille was aghast.

'I'd rather not,' Denis replied dryly, 'but there seems to be little choice. If he shows up, I'll play it by ear. But I don't think he will show.' He looked at his watch. 'By now, he's the new owner of O'Connor's billions, with more profitable ways to occupy his time.'

'And Shannon Tremblay,' I said archly, 'is probably helping him get in the mood to romp through the money-bin.'

Lucille said, 'If the government agents tracked Shannon today, they can track her another day and take her into custody for your interrogation, Denis, you will have fulfilled your promise to the President when you notify the other scanners to watch out for her.'

I could see that my conscientious nephew was mulling this over, trying to decide whether to remain in the hotel on farscan alert rather than join his colleagues at the banquet, where he was certain to be distracted by his own speech-making – to say nothing of the emotion-charged atmosphere.

Impetuously, I said, 'Look. My farscan hasn't much range, but I know every nook and cranny of this old place. Pass me Shannon Tremblay's mental signature and I'll spend the rest of the afternoon and the evening combing the hotel from cellar to rafters. Hell – I'll get a passkey from Jasper Delacourt and search the place physically when the delegates are out. I'd rather do that than go to the banquet anyhow. Farewell speeches depress me and thunderstorms rattling around mountain peaks make me nervous. Any old backpacker will tell you the same.'

Denis eyed me doubtfully. 'Uncle Rogi, if you should find Shannon – or, God forbid, Vic! – you are to do *nothing* except notify me telepathically.'

'I swear!' said I, rooting in my hip pocket. I dangled the talisman and clapped my right hand over my heart. 'I swear by the Great Carbuncle.'

All day long the Sons of Earth pickets, a couple of hundred strong, marched up and down Highway 302 in front of the resort entrance. They chanted and flourished their placards and banners, and now and then numbers of the more dedicated lay down on the driveway when shuttle buses brought in delegates who were lodged at other hotels in the area.

The police didn't bother to arrest the lie-ins; they just toted them out of the way and deposited them very gently in a handy culvert flowing with storm run-off. Along about dusk, when the big X-wing transports came in from their base at Berlin, a band of more determined activists tried to infiltrate the resort grounds by moving through the forest that lay between the hotel and the cog's Base Station Road. Police detection equipment sniffed the invaders out before they had penetrated two hundred metres. A SWAT team of State Police rounded up the antioperant commandos, who were armed with nothing more lethal than paint-pistols, and removed them to the hospitality of the county jail over at Lancaster.

By the time the delegates were ready to depart for the Summit Chalet, the heavy rain had discouraged all but a handful of diehard demonstrators out on the highway. I had completed my search of the hotel's lower reaches and was just coming up to the main floor when Denis trans-mitted a mental hail:

Uncle Rogi . . . We're almost ready to leave for the banquet I presume and pray you've found nothing.

In the boiler-room was a poker game that I was strongly tempted to sit in on and in one of the empty salons a delegate from Sri Lanka and one from Greece were inter-rupted in the midst of researches into comparative metanooky. There is no sign of Mrs Tremblay and no sign of Vic dieumercibeau'.

None of us has sensed their presence either. Lucille's probably right when she says they cleared out long ago if they were ever even here I've notified the President he gave me a goodwill message to read at the banquet one could almost believe he was sincere . . .

Buck up mon fils. Go have your feast my only regret is not getting to see the boys tricked out in black tie.

[Image: Interior X-wing skybus. Dim flashes of lightning through rain-streaked small windows. Multiethnic delegates in formal dress settling into seats. Whispers and apprehensive giggling. Lucille smiling white-faced TWO GAWKY PENGUINS STRAPPED IN ON EITHER SIDE OF A SMALL CHUNKY ONE.]
There. I'm sorry they don't look more cheery.

Mille merde Denis what a glum and qualmish crew all you need is a band playing 'Nearer My God to Thee'. Go! Go! It will be all right! Follow your damned gleam my son Follow the Great Carbuncle to the uttermost height!

Au revoir Uncle Rogi.

Standing there at the head of the stairs in the fast-emptying lobby, I heard the first of the X-wings take off for the mountain summit. It was full dark outside and the rain was only moderate, with faint growlings of thunder. On top of Mount Washington the weather was bound to be worse; but the transports were so reliable and sturdy that they could have made the trip safely in a hurricane. The storm would provide a piquant contrast to the luxurious surroundings and the good food. After the banquet they could all gather around the four fireplaces in the chalet's main lounge and promise to mend their battered ideals. With a little bit of luck even Tamara Sakhvadze far away in Moscow would soul-travel to the festivities and take heart . . .

Well, it was time for me to renew my futile quest. I checked my watch and noted that it was nearly seven. The business offices of the hotel would be nearly empty now, as would the delegates' rooms. The only dense collections of people would be in the hotel kitchens, where the cleaners were still at work, and in the two bars where a few media types and other nondelegate hangers-on had gravitated. The hotel's Security Chief, Art Gregoire, came in the main entrance shaking raindrops from his jacket and spotted me.

'Hey, Art. What d'ya say?'

'Is that you, Roj? Thought you'd be up at the big feed.'

'Got business to take care of. Things looking OK?'

Gregoire shrugged. 'Once we get the folks up the hill, we figure it's pret' near all over. Only a handful of half-drowned pickets left. Me and my gang'll keep an eye on the X-wing pad and cruise the hotel to make sure no loony-tune tries to torch 'er. The county mounties and the rent-a-cops went into town to grab a bite and dry their socks. We need 'em, we know how to get 'em.'

'Any action over on the other side of the mountain – by the Carriage Road?'

'State fuzz says there ain't diddly. Nope, the Sons've given you heads a free pass tonight. You lucked out with the rain.'

He went off to scrounge supper in the kitchen and I headed towards the executive offices to get on with my search. As if Shannon Tremblay would be hiding among the file cabinets . . .

I stood outside the manager's office with my eyes closed and let my scanning ultrasense rove into the nearest rooms. There was no trace of any mental emanation on the operant 'band' and no clearly farsensed vision of normal people lurking about, which I would have perceived had any operant been deliberately suppressing his aura.

But there was something.

I unlocked the computer centre with my passkey and turned the lights on in the windowless rooms, and at that moment I heard a noise – a faint scraping sound – and realized that it came from the storeroom on the far side of computer operations.

I tried to farscan through the storeroom door. I couldn't.

Rooted to the spot, I probed the mysterious obstacle. Behind the wood and plaster lay psychic energy of an appalling absorptive kind. It was not a barrier – the little room was filled with it, and it was opaque and magnetic and colder than death.

I think I knew at once that he was inside. I tried to give telepathic warning to Denis – to anybody. But as I uttered the mind-shout I knew it had gone no farther than the boundary of my skull. I walked without volition down the neat rows of desks with their VDTs and data cabinets and posture chairs and stood before the closet, waiting for the door to open. In there was insanity and a lust that had no relation to any natural human appetite. In there, something had hungered and fed and still hungered. Even though it wore the shape of a man it had metamorphosed into something altogether different – and done it by its own will.

A barely heard click. The knob turned and a long shadowed streak grew as the door swung inwards. Not a single beam of light from the computer room penetrated that palpable blackness – but nevertheless, I saw Victor holding her. Both of their bodies were lit with a flickering blue-violet halo. Only his lips were bright, drinking the final dying scarlet radiance from the four-petalled energy-flower that seemed to be imprinted at the base of her spine.

Then it was finished.

The devouring darkness vanished. Room light shone on Victor, who regarded me without surprise and beckoned me to come closer and admire what he'd done. It was as if he knew I would recognize the pattern as the evil opposite of Ume's fulfillment of me. He was fully clothed in a grey suit, but every stitch had been burned from the corpse of the woman who lay at his feet. The body was charred and crackling, and up the spine and on the head were seven stigmata of white ash, marking where he had fed from each psychic energy-font in turn – beginning with the most rarefied and continuing to the root. I had no doubt that in place of Ume's joy there had been excruciating pain.

'There'll be more,' he told me calmly. 'Only I won't have to exert myself in the burning. It's interesting that you understand. I want – I want to know more about what it *is*. I think you may be able to tell me. Am I right?'

'Yes.' *No no no no . . .*

Victor laughed. 'Come along with me and watch.'

In my nightmare, I followed him docilely out of the hotel. We went without being challenged to one of the hotel parking lots at the north end of the grounds, where a highway department van stood in the shadows. The rain had nearly stopped but there was still a good deal of lightning flashing in the east, in the direction of the mountain.

I was dimly aware of another man sitting behind the wheel of the van. It was old Pete Laplace, who had worked at the cog during my years at the hotel. I got into the back of the van and we drove off.

Vic said, 'The boys ready to take off on sked?'

'Ready as they'll ever be,' said a dour Yankee voice. 'Poor stupid bastards.' He cackled, then swore as the van hit a pothole and lurched. We turned to the right and I knew we were on the back road leading to the cog base station.

'We're going to take my Uncle Rogi along with O'Connor,' Vic said. 'You three old gaffers ought to enjoy the fireworks together. You get steam up okay?'

'I know what I'm doin',' the oldster snapped. 'Just hope t'hell you do, Vic. Still say you shoulda gone in the airyplane.'

'Not on your life, Pete. That mob of heads claim to be pacifists, but you don't catch me betting my ass on it . . . Slow down, dammit. We're almost to the Upper Falls turnoff.'

My personality seemed to have fragmented. One portion was howling in panic-stricken horror, while another quite calmly submitted to Victor's continuing coercive hold, acknowledging him as my master whom I would serve without question. And then there was a third psychic chunk. This was the smallest and shakiest of all, stomped to a frazzle and nearly buried in the mental cataclysm that had overwhelmed me. This part of my mind told me to hang in there and wait for my chance. It was the damn fool part of my personality, so of course it won out. I've often wondered whether other heroes were made that way, too.

The van made a sharp turn and screeched to a halt. Vic and the poisonous old party climbed out. When they returned they were supporting a tottering form. Far be it from the richest man in the world to ride in the back of a muddy van, so they strapped him securely into Vic's seat, and my nephew came back to sit silently with me while we travelled the last few kilometres to the cog railway base station.

The place was dark as the inside of your hat, without a sign of life. But one of the antique engines had its firebox aglow and the steam up, and its smokestack threw sparks on both sides of the track that sizzled as they hit the puddles. Old Pete clambered into the engine cab, and Vic and O'Connor and I got aboard the unlit coach that travelled ahead. No blast on the whistle marked the train's departure. It simply hissed like a fumarole, clanked, and set off chugging and rattling towards the cloud deck that hid the summit.

Victor and O'Connor ignored me completely as they conversed on the intimate telepathic mode. I discovered only one of the infamous secrets that the dying old villain passed on to the hungry young one. God only knows what other bizarre thoughts they shared. They were both madmen by any civilized standard, and yet sane enough to recognize and still embrace the evil that their minds created. They were not mistaken, not misguided or deluded; they were only terribly and mysteriously bent and I have long since given up trying to understand them. The little train climbed valiantly into the sky, taking one to death and the other to oblivion. I could only huddle in my seat, half frozen now that we approached the tree line, praying that one of the unsuspecting operants in the chalet above us would turn his mind downwards, penetrate the dense granite bulk that blocked line-of-sight view of this part of the track from the summit, and sound the alarm.

The coach tilted more and more steeply and the little engine undertook its most severe challenge – a trestled section called Jacob's Ladder with a grade of more than thirty-seven per cent. My night-sight, dimmed by Victor's coercion, saw that O'Connor was clinging like a limpet to the seat in front of him, a grimace of what I took to be excitement distorting his wasted features. We had been passing through dense cloud ever since beginning our ascent of the ladder; but now we broke free as we approached the Westside Trail crossing and there were sudden flashes of lightning from the towering cumulus massed to the east. In another moment it would be possible for us to see the Summit Chalet silhouetted against the skyline . . . and the people in the chalet would have a greatly enhanced chance of farsensing us.

But Victor's elderly henchman knew his stuff. The deafening clatter of the cogs gripping the steel rack between the tracks diminished to a portentous clickety-clack, then stopped as the engine ground to a halt. The smoke cloud, blasted by high winds, raced uphill ahead of us. Surely someone would see it —

'It doesn't matter now,' Vic said. The locomotive clunked

and wheezed and in a moment the rear door of the coach opened and Pete thrust himself in, grumbling about the chill.

'This is it, Vic. Get 'em up here damn quick before we're spotted.'

'Higher!' Kieran O'Connor croaked. 'I want to see the chalet go!'

'Shut up,' Victor said. 'Look there – to the north.'

O'Connor keened: 'Aaah!'

'Now you can get 'er rolling again, Pete!' Victor's voice was triumphant. 'Our own Xs are on their way in!'

The old man dived for the rear door, which was still open. And at that moment Victor's hold on me eased as he broadcast some powerful farspoken command to the approaching aircraft. I flung myself from my seat, rolled downhill towards the door, and was outside feet-first and tumbling down among the frost-encrusted granite boulders before Vic could stop me. Somewhere in my trajectory I had smashed into that aged rascal, Laplace. I heard his wail echo thinly among the crags, then cut off abruptly.

God – now what? Uphill! Keep as much rock as I could between me and that young devil, Vic, and yell my brains out:

DENIS!DENISTHEY'RECOMINGFORTHECHALET INAIRCRAFT! DENISDENIS FORGOD'S SAKEVIC& O'CONNOR HAVE ARMEDAIRCRAFT ATTACKING CHALET –

I hear you Uncle Rogi.

Coughing and gasping with the cold, I toiled upwards over the rockfield. Behind me, I heard the engine give a mighty chug, then start uphill once again. Vic had probably taken the controls himself. There were two X-wings and neither of them had navigation lights. Up above the cloud deck, there was enough fitful moonlight shining between the thunderheads to show the planes approaching fast around the shoulder of Mount Clay; but they weren't gunships, they were ordinary domestic transports, half the size of the ones used to ferry the Congress delegates up the mountain.

DENIS THEY'RE GOING TO LAND! STOP THEM!

ZAP THEM SOMEHOW USE CREATIVE META-CONCERT!

I heard for the first time other minds – hundreds of them – but the lightning-fast moral debate was incomprehensible. The pair of X-wings hovered nearly over my head, their roaring drowning out the howl of the wind. Only my continued scrambling kept me from freezing.

DO SOMETHING! I pleaded.

Another mind-voice, one of surpassing power with a signature that was completely unfamiliar, said:

Together! Hit them together! Let me show you how . . .

A white fireball soared against the sky, arching over the crest from the direction of the chalet. It struck the central boss of the X-wing rotor housing on the lead aircraft and seemed to be absorbed soundlessly. But the sudden drop in the noise level was the aircraft's engine cutting out.

That's the way! Join with me again. Together . . .

NO! another voice pleaded, and I knew it was Denis.

A second ball of psychocreative energy flew up like a meteor and zapped the other X-wing. Both ships were in uncontrolled descent, windmilling with the deactivation of their engines. They pranged in not more than five hundred metres away from me, down the northwestern flank of the mountain. There were no explosions and no flames, and although my ultrasenses were impeded by trauma and the intervening crags, I knew that the occupants of the aircraft had survived and were pulling themselves together to begin a ground assault.

I cried: DENIS THEY CRASHLANDED YOU DIDN'T KILL THEM —

He said: I never tried. Most of us didn't.

I was scrambling uphill as fast as I could. Fortunately, at that point there was a footpath along the right-hand side of the cog track. As I came out of a hollow I saw the train again, chugging slowly along the skyline and trailing its spark-shot plume of smoke.

VICTOR IS DIRECTING ATTACK FROM COG! HIT THE TRAIN!

I heard laughter in the aether: *Yes. Hit the train. Together with me now!*

Another bolide arose. This time I saw it materialize just above the chalet roof and move purposefully in a flat trajectory towards the little train. But it faltered in flight and began to wobble, and instead of hitting the engine it bounced along the roof of the coach and then dove down on to the track ahead. There was a sharp flash. The coach bucked and slewed and fell off to the side. The sound waves reached me moments later — a detonation followed by a prolonged grinding crash as the coach left the track and toppled on to the icy boulders. The engine had slammed on its brakes. It screamed to a stop before reaching the damaged section of track and stood silhouetted against moonlit thunderheads on the skyline above me. Its firebox glowed hellishly and the rising gale blasted smoke over its trailing tender. A figure jumped from the engine cab.

UncleRogiDUCK!!

I did — just in time. A bullet fweenged off a rock a few centimetres above my head. I had completely forgotten the crashed X-wings and their complement of armed thugs. The warning had come from little Severin, who now told me:

They're creeping upon you they have infrared GET OFF TRAIL!! I'llhelpcreatedecoybodyglowCOMEUPMOUN-TAINHURRY!!SLEETSTORMCOMING . . .

I said: Putain de bordel de merde!

Sevvy said: You can say that again.

Another bullet struck, far off the mark to my left. Bruised and shivering, I resumed my climb uphill.

31

Mount Washington, New Hampshire, Earth
21 September 2013

Victor Remillard grasped the old man by the coat lapels. The head lolled and there was a bleeding gash across the forehead. But Kieran O'Connor was alive.

'What the *hell* did you think you were doing?' Victor shouted. 'I should – I should —— '

Kieran's eyes opened and he smiled. 'You should kill me. But it's totally unnecessary. Let me warn you, however . . . one touch of probe or coercion, and I'll never answer your questions. And you do want the answers, don't you?'

They saw one another in the shadowless eeriness of mental vision and ignored the strengthening wind that whistled through the broken coach. Victor was aware for the first time of a deathly stench emanating from the body of the dying man. Through the open shirt, he could see that the telltales of the painkilling mechanism had gone dark. No agony he could inflict on Kieran O'Connor could surpass what Kieran had already freely embraced.

'You took charge of those operants when Denis wouldn't.' Victor was accusative. 'You knit them together in some kind of mental unit and squeezed out those globs of energy that downed the aircraft and derailed the train.'

'The procedure is called metaconcert,' Kieran told him. 'An idea quite foreign to *your* mentality. I wasn't at all sure that I could work it. With my own people, the results have generally been unsatisfactory. But these fully operant minds . . . marvellous!'

'You fucking old bastard! You shot down my men – tried to kill them!'

'Nonsense. The craft are engineered to soft-land in case of power failure. Only the incompetence of your pilots and the rough terrain caused the damage, and most of your people were uninjured.'

'Then *why?*'

Kieran indicated the Summit Chalet, blazing like a jewel box on the mountain above them. 'They needed teaching, these silly pacifists. A revelation of their own power. The Russian operants have already learned the lesson and so have a few other groups. But these idealist leaders resisted the inevitable. They were too much influenced by your brother and MacGregor. An aggressive metaconcert was unthinkable for such minds – until they were given suitable incentive.'

'We'll knock them out! Your scheme – whatever the hell it is – can't work. The main vanguard of the local Sons of Earth took out the State Police barricade at the same time that the X-wings took off from Berlin. They're coming up the Carriage Road in trucks and four-wheelers right now. Even if that bunch in the chalet has called for outside help, it can't get here in time . . . and you won't pull your metaconcert trick again.'

Kieran was chuckling soundlessly, his breath forming small puffs of vapour in the freezing air. He said: Of course not it's no longer necessary NOW THEY KNOW HOW they are consecrated to the Mother without realizing it O Her jests O Her infinite wisdom behold the final generation shall call Her blessed —

Victor let go of the old man's coat. Kieran slumped back against the cracked windowpane, eyes closed, breathing in raspy bursts. Victor said, 'I'm not going to waste any more time listening to your crazy shit. Whatever scheme you cooked up – whatever way you planned to use me and my people – it's not going to work. I'm calling off my men from the X-wings and we're getting the hell off this mountain. The Sons can watch their own asses and take the blame — '

The mind-tone was wheedling, tempting: Don't be a fool my boy do you want your brother Denis to get away? And the other American operants the ones who will perfect MacGregor's aura-detector and use it to bring down you and your associates oh no oh no here they are together never again such a golden opportunity . . . I've had my moment. Now I leave the rest to you.

'What is the rest?' Victor raged. 'You bug-fucking old devil – what have you *done*?'

The mortal stench was now almost unbearable. Victor shrank away in the frigid darkness, braced himself against the tilted seats, heard the first rustle of sleet strike the coach's metal skin. He couldn't stay here any longer. His inside man at the chalet was supposed to have sabotaged the delegate transports. Could one of them be repaired? They could still make the hit and get out before —

His racing thoughts were interrupted by the old man's

voice, suddenly strong again. 'I thought I would be the agent of destruction. And then it seemed that you would be Her deputy. Now at the end I see the truth – that humanity will destroy itself without our impetus. Even these superior minds! We are all children of the Black Mother dam dham nam tam tham — '

The voice dwindled away to an exhaled breath. And then Kieran O'Connor's eyes flew open in thunderstruck surprise, and he screamed and died.

Denis Remillard gripped the lectern. He had to coerce them into silence, then plead with the ones who had left the main dining room to return.

He said: *You must not leave the chalet! The temperature has dropped below freezing and another storm front will be here any minute. Please! Come back to the dining room and we'll decide what's to be done . . .*

Jamie MacGregor, wearing a borrowed parka, came striding through the dishevelled banquet tables. 'Every one of the fewkin' air-buses is out of commission. Someone got to 'em while the crews were eating in the lower lounge. Some of the handier delegates are outside trying to fix things, but it looks bloody hopeless. There are cars belonging to the chalet staff, but not nearly enough to evacuate all of us – even if we managed to get past those buggers who're on the way up . . . Is help on the way?'

'Not from the police,' Lucille said. She and most of the Coterie were gathered around the speakers' table. 'The officers who had staked out the road on the Pinkham Notch side of the mountain were ambushed by the Sons. There's no way the police on the western side of the mountain can reach us without aircraft.'

Denis said, 'The President said he'd send an FBI special team – but it has to come all the way from Boston. The Governor's called out the National Guard. It will take two hours to mobilize.'

'Bloody hell!' Jamie exploded. 'Why don't they roust out the Marines or the Army Antiterrorist Unit?'

Lucille said, 'Because this country doesn't handle riots that way.'

The Scotsman snorted. 'This is no riot, it's a soddin' siege — '

'Jamie, please.' Denis's knuckles were white as he continued to grip the sides of the lectern. *We don't have much time. We must decide what we are going to do.*

Young Severin Remillard, unnoticed in the press of anxious adults, piped up: 'The only thing is to keep on like before – like Uncle Rogi and that other guy said – and clobber the sonsabitches!'

Lucille took the boy firmly by the shoulder and turned him over to his older brothers.

The Coterie turned away, returning to their seats. Other delegates who had dashed up to the observation turret or to other parts of the mountaintop convention centre returned to the dining room as Denis had requested. Some sat at the tables. Others stood around the perimeter of the huge room, their farsight probing the exterior darkness. The clouds had thickened again and freezing rain ticked against the thick glass in the western lobe. The corps of servers and the white-clad kitchen personnel, normals all, huddled in a separate group.

Presently, Denis spoke into the microphone: 'Ladies and gentlemen, we have called for help, and it is on the way.' There were murmurs and scattered applause from the normals; but the operants were under no illusions. 'It now seems clear that there are at least two forces of domestic insurgents belonging to the antioperant Sons of Earth group advancing on this building. About sixty are coming from the two crashed X-wings on the western slope. More than a hundred more are on their way up the Carriage Road on the eastern side, travelling in light trucks and cars. The motorcade seems to be equipped with rifles, shotguns and small arms. Many of them are under the influence of one thing or another. They can be characterized as a run-of-the-mill lynch mob – and aside from blocking our escape down that road, they offer a very minor threat to our safety.'

A voice yelled: 'Du gehst mir auf die Eier, Remillard, mit diesem Scheissdreck! Was können wir *tun?*'

'He's right! What *are* we going to do?' another voice shouted.

'That other lot from the aircraft aren't minor! I pEEped automatic weapons and at least one grenade launcher — '

Again, unwillingly, Denis coerced them to silence.

'Please listen . . . The airborne group *is* heavily armed. They have explosives with them as well as heavy weapons, and the only reason they aren't outside the chalet already is the sudden change in the weather . . . and they've temporarily lost touch with their leader. For those of you who don't already know, that leader is my younger brother, Victor.'

The room vibrated with a blast of wind. Some of the chalet workers were whispering among themselves.

Denis said, 'The real instigator of the attack is a man named Kieran O'Connor. Many of you know him as a pillar of the multinational military–industrial complex. O'Connor – like my brother – is a powerful natural operant who has concealed his metafaculties and used them to his personal advantage. For years O'Connor has worked secretly to destroy the operant establishment – not only because we might expose him, but also because peace isn't profit-generating to his line of business. Our globalism threatens him, just as it has threatened fanatics and dictatorships all over the world . . . just as it seems to threaten good people frightened of fellow human beings with higher mind-powers. And the normals *do* have good reason to be frightened, as long as operants such as Kieran O'Connor or my brother Victor exist.'

A Chinese delegate, Zhao Kud-lin, exclaimed, 'This is precisely why operants must be politically active – to ferret out and deal with such vermin!'

There were some murmurs of agreement. An anonymous mind-voice shouted! *Let's stop this palavering and whomp up another concert Denis! Come on pull us together again and let's start picking the dead-heads off!*

Denis said, 'It was Kieran O'Connor – not I – who led some of you in the aggressive metaconcert that downed the attacking aircraft.'

Sensation!

A woman delegate cried: 'Then three cheers for Kieran Warbucks!'

'No! No!' others shouted in dismay. 'Shame!'

Denis said, 'Kieran O'Connor knows we're divided in our attitude towards psychic aggression. I don't believe that his primary intent is to trap and destroy us here. He really wants to discredit all operants everywhere in the eyes of the normals by forcing us to abandon our Ethic. Some of you who joined his metaconcert probably reacted instinctively against a perceived danger. Others . . . did not. But we must all understand that we face the most critical choice of our lives here and now. We represent the operant leadership of the world. We will have to choose whether to adhere to the Ethic that has inspired us ever since our first meeting in Alma-Ata – or to do as certain of our fellow operants have already done: use our minds as weapons . . . I say that if we do this, even in this situation of obvious self-defence, the normal people of the world will ultimately condemn us as inhuman, a race apart, a monstrous minority too dangerous to share the planet with.'

The audience was still. Momentarily, the lights flickered. A few people cried out, then fell silent again as the illumination steadied.

'Make no mistake,' Denis said quietly, 'we could very easily die in support of our principles. But I believe there are two honourable courses open to us. The first is simply to wait for rescue, utilizing what passive defences we can muster. The second is to unite in a very different form of grand metaconcert – not only embracing those of us here, but also every other operant that we can summon telepathically from all corners of the world, *and even the normals*. Yes! I believe that we must try to gather them under our aegis as well. The focus of our grand metaconcert must be our enemies, the enemies of peace and tolerance everywhere. But we won't try to destroy them or even to coerce them. We'll try to reach their hearts.'

Out of the stunned hush, Jamie MacGregor's voice was imploring. 'But could it work, lad? It's a brave notion – but could it possibly move them?'

Denis had lowered his head. 'I don't know. I don't even know if we can put together this type of metaconcert. In aggression, mind-melding is easy. Mob rule! But this other kind . . . demands that one surrender part of one's individual sovereignty to the whole, and to do so leaves the mind vulnerable. I myself find the idea of metaconcert frightening. Invasive. I've only conjoined with my wife, whom I love more than life, and with my uncle, who has acted as a father to me. I don't know whether I would be able to do it with all of you or not. There's a potential for damage – very serious damage – to the coordinator. But I've decided that I'm willing to try, if this group asks me to do so. If it choses to uphold the Ethic.'

Denis lifted his eyes slowly and swept the room. 'Of course, you're quite free to choose the other way. I know you'll want to think it over. But please don't take too long.'

Victor had managed to rally most of his scattered force in the lee of the Gulf Tank, a landmark next to the upper section of the railway where the cog locomotives once took on water. Sleet coated the old wooden structure with glistening rime and whitened the rocks; but little of it stuck to the huddling men, who were dressed in electrically heated suits and helmets.

The most telepathically talented of the attackers had eavesdropped upon Denis's speech, and when it was over the aether clanged with their contemptuous laughter.

Victor shouted into the roaring wind, not caring who heard: *A prayer! That's what they want to zap us with boys! Not mental lasers or great balls of fire but a goddam prayer!*

When all except a few stragglers had assembled, Victor got down to business. He projected a mental map pinpointing their location – some six hundred metres from the chalet as the crow flew, if one would have dared on such a vile night. The disabled transport aircraft that had carried the delegates up the mountain and the twenty or so vehicles belonging to the restaurant staff were in a sheltered bowl on the other side of the summit. One small squad of men would go around the north slope, secure the vehicles for the group's escape, and dispose of any persons in the vicinity. The five-man demolition crew, which Victor planned to lead himself, would advance on the western side of the chalet under cover-fire from the rest of the force.

'You guys get up two, three hundred metres from the building, and make like the Battle of Gettysburg. Never mind trying to hit anything. Just fire high and fire a lot so those heads don't have time to think about anything but their precious skins.' Victor projected a farsight view of the western half of the building, which jutted shelflike above a small precipice and was supported by stout piers anchored in bedrock. If these were undermined, the entire structure would topple downhill into the vast gulf of Ammonoosuc Ravine.

'Once I'm certain the charges are placed right I'll activate the timers,' Victor said. 'And then I'm going to yell *go-go-go* over the helmet intercom, and telepathically too. You hear that, you haul ass for those cars. You'll have ten minutes from the shout. Whatever you do, don't mind-yak to each other – especially about the explosives! Remember these are heavy heads inside the building and they can use your thoughts to target you if they change their minds about doing a pray-in. Everybody understand?'

They muttered into their helmets. A few of the men, wearing older models with low wattage, were already having to scrape ice from the visors.

One querulous voice asked, 'Vic – you *sure* we can get down the mountain with that other bunch coming up? Seems to me — '

Victor cut him off. 'We got us a shit-trip. Nobody knows it better than me. But if push comes to shove we can walk off this rock-pile six different ways. Anybody starts wetting his pants better think hard about the one million cash he won't be getting if he screws up. I'm gonna come through this thing and so will you if you do what I told you. Now get going!'

32

From the Memoirs of
Rogatien Remillard

As I robbed the body, I cursed my late adversary for being
built like an ape instead of a proper beanpole.

This meant that his electric suit would have to be slit
around the upper inseams and crotch in order to fit me –
a mutilation that fortunately did not damage the thermal
wiring – and the embarrassing fore and aft gaps filled in
with a ludicrous loincloth rigged from my cut-up jacket.
His high moon-boots closed the ankle gap nicely, however,
and once I had turned up the suit's heat full blast, pulled
on the warm gauntlets, and settled the helmet into place,
I was no longer at imminent risk of death through exposure,
an expedient that had seemed all too likely before I had
encountered this straggling mercenary and chopped him
across the back of the neck with a sharp wedge of granite.

I had managed to bash my head and bruise my left leg
severely in my escape from the train. The injuries, together
with the arduous scramble that had preceded my ambush
of the mercenary, had reduced my mental faculties almost
to zero. Not only was I dead beat and only slowly
recovering from hypothermia, but I was emotionally torpid
– certain that nothing I could do would be able to help the
twenty-eight hundred operants trapped in the chalet above.

I had no farsight and I had no farspeech. The helmet
was equipped with the usual intercom radio, but to use it
would only alert Victor and his minions. I could expect my
neurons to revive as I thawed out – but the storm was
intensifying, and with the increased wind velocity and
precipitation the atmosphere was becoming loaded with
wrongo ions. Trained operants could project their thoughts
through such muck, but hardly the likes of me.

I knelt to study my victim's weapon. It was thickly glazed
with ice and unfamiliar in aspect, resembling a cross
between a large electric drill and sections of the chromed
exhaust system of a small motorcycle. I hadn't the faintest
notion where the trigger might be, and the thing's weight

was formidable – no doubt the reason why the desperado had fallen behind his companions, only to be dispatched by me in very cold blood. I decided to give further armed combat a miss and concentrate on saving my life.

I began to work my way across the slope in a southerly direction, having a vague notion of outflanking Victor's force and approaching the chalet obliquely by way of the main portion of the Appalachian Trail. On my left, the chalet blazed with lights, and I thought: Boobies! Don't you realize you're sitting ducks? Blackout! Blackout!

But then I realized the foolishness of my futile shout. Victor and his operant henchmen were not handicapped as I was; with their farsenses, they could perceive the chalet as readily with illumination as without it. I was the booby, as usual.

I crept into the teeth of the wind, more often than not going on my hands and knees over the icy, boulder-strewn mountainside. My mind drifted back to the time so long ago when I had been marooned in the Mahoosucs in another storm, only to be rescued – if I really had been – by the Family Ghost. O ingenious figment of my imagination! Where are you now – off on some interstellar jaunt? Or given me up as a bad job? . . . How could I blame you, Ghost? I disobeyed your orders. There I was, at least three times feeling the irresistible compulsion to tell Denis the tale of the Great Carbuncle, and on each occasion cringing at the banality of it . . .

O Ghost, you picked a loser. You told me I would know the appropriate moment to urge Denis to unite his colleagues and the Mind of Earth in prayerful metaconcert. And if this isn't the moment, I don't know what it is! But here I am and there Denis is, and Lucille, and their three boys, and all the rest of the good-guy operants, and I've blown it, and so have you.

Ghost, mon ami, let me try to make small amends. I will pause in the shelter of this blasted crag (since I'm in need of a breather anyway) and at least attempt to fulfil your esteemed orders. I will squeak into the hurricane and perchance le bon dieu in his mercy (if not you in yours) will bring a happy ending to this comedy:

Denis! This is your Uncle Rogi. Listen my son. I have been told to give you an important message. Unite the minds of your colleagues in a metaconcert of goodwill. Renounce violence. If you do this beings from the stars will no longer shun our poor planet but will come and be our friends . . . This sounds incredible? Bien entendu! Nevertheless I have been told many times that it is true. Denis! Do you hear me? Answer if you do.

I waited.

The first thing that happened was that every light in the chalet went out.

The next thing was that all hell broke loose.

Victor's men began to fire at the building with their automatic weapons from a long line of attack strung across the slope just above me. Tracer bullets stitched the curtains of sleet with scarlet smudges. I heard the sound of smashing glass, then exploding grenades. The howl of the wind was almost drowned out by the racket of the weaponry and I crouched in numb horror for several minutes – and then unaccountably felt infused with fresh energy and impelled to get moving.

I came upon some kind of trail. My impaired night-sight showed me the cairns quite distinctly, together with the slightly less rough rock surface that passed for a designated pathway on the Spartan slopes of Mount Washington. The shooting was really nowhere near me, but to my left. I began to move rapidly uphill, and the trail slanted away at an angle that put the wind at my back. I judged that I was probably approaching the chalet by one of the steep short cuts that gave access to the summit from the southwest. The thump of grenades had stopped, although fusillades of bullets continued unabated. I was moving up a gully and could no longer see the tracers. I had no idea whether Vic's troops were advancing or standing pat.

Then the gunfire became muted by the lay of the land, and once again I was acutely aware of the hundred-voiced wailing of the mountain wind and the hiss of freezing rain. My personal aether was a tangle of ionic chittering and sibilance, as meaningless as static on an untenanted radio frequency. I heard nothing from Denis, no Ghostly reassurances, only my ragged breathing and the pounding of my pulse. Slipping and sliding on the ice. I climbed upwards. My semiexposed rump, with its inadequate covering long since soaked through, had lost all sensation. My legs worked automatically. I had some vague idea, I think, of coming up beneath the overhang of the building and working my way around to the service entrance.

The ground began to level out. I was in an area of enormous jagged rocks, heaped around the massive concrete pillars that supported the western side of the chalet. My farsight provided a faint greyish view for a radius of a few metres. Beyond that was blackness.

Until I saw the blood-red glow.

A frisson of dread passed through me. Had Victor set the chalet afire? But the patch of radiance was too small for that . . . and it moved. Heaven help me, I thought of the *real* Great Carbuncle, that will-o'-the-wisp of Mount Washington folklore that lured stormbound hikers to their doom. But what would it be doing flitting about the foundation of the chalet? The bulk of the building now loomed above me, every windward surface plastered with a heavy crust of rime. I could dimly farsense that most of the western windows were broken. There were no telepathic thoughts to be discerned.

The magnetic carmine gleam drew me towards it. The worst of the sleet was behind me now that I was beneath the overhang, but there was a kind of frozen fog swirling through the cavernous dark that disguised the source of the red glow until I was nearly on top of it.

Suddenly, my ultrasense went off like an alarm clock, telling me that the thing I had perceived wasn't a light at all. It was an operant's aura, and the mind generating it was powerful, pitiless, and all too familiar.

I saw Victor.

He was recognizable in spite of the cold-weather gear he wore, unscreened and heedless, ablaze with anticipated triumph as he strapped the last of three packages of explosive to one of the piers of the chalet. Before I fully realized what he was up to he had finished the job. From a nearly empty backpack laying on the ground he took a device like a pocket radio, flicked switches, and tapped out some code. Then his voice was loud in my helmet phones:

'Go-go-go!'

The gunfire stopped, and at the same moment there was an abrupt lull in the wind.

Victor turned and saw me standing there, not ten metres away. My mind was paralysed by his coercion even before I realized that he had spotted me.

'It took you long enough to get here,' he said. Carefully, he tucked the little electronic gadget into the pack. Then he came for me. He didn't say another word, didn't transmit a farspoken message; but I knew what he was going to do. During that trip up the mountain in the cog, Kieran O'Connor had passed on to Victor the terrible secret of mind-bonding. Kieran had used his body as a tool. Victor wouldn't have to. The ultimate result on me would be the same . . . and if I refused him I'd finish up as Shannon had, incinerated as my psychic energies revitalized this creature that had once been a human being.

Victor had taken his helmet off and cast it aside. His eyes were like bore-holes into lava. And I thought, Jesus, I can't let him take me and I *won't* be a martyr. I'm going to try one last out-spiral —

Victor stopped.

Deep within the mountain was a sound, a slow and swelling vibration. The rocks around us began to shine with a barely perceptible greenish fluorescence and there were clashing tinkling chiming noises everywhere as their ice coating fractured like glass. The terror and hopelessness I had felt was wiped from my mind and in its place came an uncanny sense of warm benevolence: a beckoning bright calmness. Victor seemed to be feeling it, too. His raging aura dimmed and he flinched as if he had been struck, then looked frantically about. The expression on his face was one of a furious, perplexed child. Poor Victor! Something seemed to urge me to reach out to him, to show him where help lay. But I was too old and too wary and I resisted —

The phenomenon cut off as abruptly as it had begun. The banshee wind, carrying thick snowflakes this time instead of freezing rain, smote us with renewed vigour. It had gone pitch black except for Victor's red halo. I cringed before him and before the storm and heard him laugh.

'So that's the best they can do, is it?'

Then he was coming at me again. One blow of his fist knocked my own helmet off, and then he clamped my skull between hands like the jaws of a vice. The deadly eyes! My vision was a flaming blur and my heart leapt behind my breastbone and I shouted *NO* and summoned my body's core-energy and made it spiral around and around and around and out . . .

Victor was lying there at my feet. He had no aura but he breathed. His face was dark, bruised profoundly. His gloved fingers made small scrabbling noises in the icy detritus.

A voice said, '*Quelle bonne rencontre.*'

I gave a violent start and looked behind me. Someone was coming through the blizzard, carrying a powerful halide lantern that threw vivid orange reflections on the wild scene. I recognized Victor's villainous old sidekick, Pete Laplace, and would have ducked away — but my psychocreative zap had so drained me that I was incapable of moving a muscle. Pete limped up, shone his lamp briefly on Victor, then unwound his Ragg wool muffler and stuffed it under my nephew's head.

The vibration in the mountain started up again.

Old Pete looked about, smiling thinly. As the rocks went phosphorescent he shambled over to Victor's backpack and began stomping all over it. I heard breaking noises along with a fresh chorus of glacial tinkling.

'That's enough of *that*,' old Pete declared. 'Now let's see if those folks upstairs and their brain-pals around the world and a few other souls on this perverse little planet have got what it takes.'

I felt once again the pervading flood of calmness; but its joy and serenity no longer invited me — they passed me by. I experienced it but I was not really part of it. I seemed to see faces — the delegates, Lucille and the children, Jamie, Pyotr, members of the Coterie; and I saw others whom I knew were elsewhere — Oriental and Slavic faces, blacks and Latins, natives of America and Australia, the hawk faces of desert tribes, urbane Europeans. There were Caucasian elders and suboperant school-children from the Indian plains, academics, operant peace officers, scientists, government officials. I saw Ayeesha, the kind Syrian nanny of the Remillard household. I saw Jamie MacGregor's grandmother. I saw Tamara Sakhvadze, weeping, with her grown children Valery and Anna. I saw Gerry Tremblay. I saw Elaine . . .

So many of them in free coadunation, operants and normals, and Denis extended to his uttermost mental limits holding and guiding the prayer. I could not hear what they said. It had nothing to do with the stars and everything to do with Earth. It was not my prayer, nor was it affirmed by every mind on our proud and stubborn and foolish world. But it sufficed.

Old Pete came up to me, reached out, and seemed to take something that I had. He said, 'Come on,' and headed out into the open. The thunderous vibration was gentling and the wind fell so rapidly that by the time we were out from under the chalet and heading along the down-slope trail towards the south the air was dead calm and the snow had dwindled to a few drifting flakes. Pete had left his lantern behind. The sky was oddly bright, and when I stopped and looked back at the chalet I saw that the entire structure was clothed in auroral brilliance.

'This is far enough,' Pete said. He held something up above his head with one hand. I saw it was the Great Carbuncle.

'You!' I said.

The thing flared like a nova, blinding me. I felt someone take my gloved hand, slap something into it, and press the fingers shut.

'You can have it back now. But take good care of it. This is only the beginning, you know. Au 'voir, cher Rogi.'

When my vision returned he was gone, and the New Hampshire sky was filled with the thousands of starships of the Galactic Milieu, and the Great Intervention had begun.

FINIS

VINCULI

EPILOGUE

Hanover, New Hampshire, Earth
26 April 2113

Rogatien Remillard looked at the last words on the display of the transcriber, hit both PRINT and FILE, and then treated himself to a luxurious yawn. The cat Marcel, sitting at his elbow on the battered deal desk, pricked up its ears and stared alertly at an empty corner of the bookshop's back room.

'Is that you?' Rogi inquired of thin air.

Naturellement!

'Checking up on me, eh? Well, I've finished this bit. Don't think it was easy, even with your help.'

My congratulations on a satisfactory job.

Rogi grunted. 'Let me ask you a question or two off the record. Were you responsible for Vic not killing me when I found him and Shannon at the hotel?'

No. He wanted you. In spite of all his power, he was an ignorant man. He hoped, pathetically, that you would somehow be a mentor to him, as he perceived you had been to the young Denis.

Rogi shook his head. 'Too damn psychological for me . . . Another question: Were you always Pete Laplace?'

I assumed the personas of living humans when it was convenient, setting them . . . aside until the guise was no longer needed.

'Did you do that kind of thing very often?'

I confess, it did tend to become habit-forming! You must try to understand that, at the beginning of my direct participation, I was unsure how much adjustment of the probability lattices would be required of me. Meddling by an incorporeal Lylmik seemed marginally riskier than manipulations done in human disguise. In time, I came to realize that my doubts were merely prideful resistance to the promptings of the Cosmic Afflatus. My actions, though quite freely willed, were demonstrably preordained in the larger Reality, which is mystery. Keeping this in mind, I just got on with it.

'And even enjoyed yourself!' Rogi's tone was accusing.

The Ghost laughed: We Lylmik take our Olympian pleasures where we may. I assure you they are few and far between.

'I'll just bet,' said Rogi sardonically. Then he asked, in a more serious vein. 'What really happened to Victor? In retrospect, I don't hardly see how I could have zapped him without your help. I was just too far gone.'

I helped.

'Why didn't you kill him outright instead of trapping him inside his skull? My God, he was blind, deaf, deprived of all tactile sensation and every metafaculty but self-awareness. And the poor bastard lived another twenty-seven years.'

The tenderhearted may regard cerebral solitary confinement as too harsh a purgatory for any entity. I assure you that, for a mind such as Victor's, it was not. He was vouchsafed a period of reflection ... just as I was. Unfortunately, *his* final choice was the wrong one. Priez pour nous pécheurs, maintenant et à l'heure de notre mort.

Rogi sighed. 'Well, I'm going to take a vacation before I start in on the next part. Yours. Get in a little skiing before spring strikes with a vengeance. Might go to Denali. That was one of your favourites, as I recall.'

The Ghost was chuckling. Marcel flattened his ears as the printed paper pages in the transcriber's receiving rack riffled, as though flicked by an invisible finger.

The Ghost said: So you are quite sure now, are you, that you know me?

Rogi nodded complacently. 'Haven't figured the why of it – much less the how. But I guess I'll worm it out of you eventually along with some other parts of the story that always mystified me a bit.' He cut the power to the transcriber, stood up, and stretched. 'I'm outa here and up to bed.'

The Ghost said: Good night, Uncle Rogi.

Rogi said, 'Good night, Marc.'

THE END OF INTERVENTION

Appendix
The Remillard
Family Tree

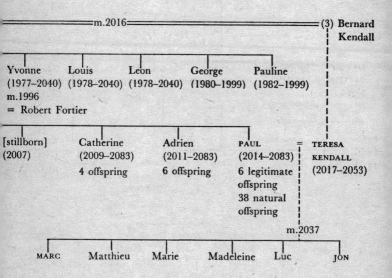

=========m.2016=========(3) Bernard
                                                                    Kendall

Yvonne   Louis   Leon   George   Pauline
(1977–2040)   (1978–2040)   (1978–2040)   (1980–1999)   (1982–1999)
m.1996
= Robert Fortier

[stillborn]   Catherine   Adrien   PAUL   =   TERESA
(2007)   (2009–2083)   (2011–2083)   (2014–2083)   KENDALL
               4 offspring   6 offspring   6 legitimate   (2017–2053)
                                             offspring
                                             38 natural
                                             offspring
                                                        m.2037

MARC   Matthieu   Marie   Madeleine   Luc   JON

(see continuation on next page)

O'CONNOR
GENEALOGY

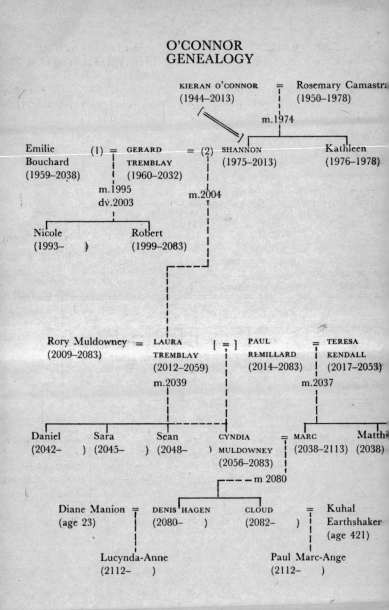

SAKHVADZE
GENEALOGY

MACGREGOR
GENEALOGY

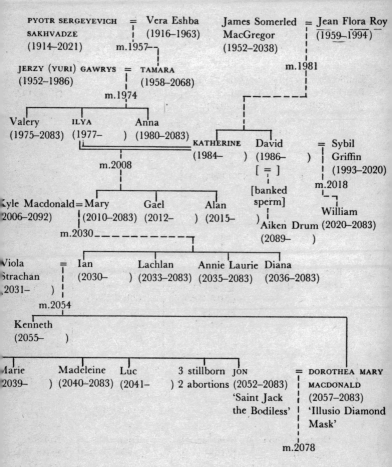

PYOTR SERGEYEVICH = Vera Eshba
SAKHVADZE   (1916–1963)
(1914–2021)   m.1957

James Somerled = Jean Flora Roy
MacGregor   (1959–1994)
(1952–2038)

m.1981

JERZY (YURI) GAWRYS = TAMARA
(1952–1986)   (1958–2068)

m.1974

Valery   ILYA   Anna
(1975–2083)   (1977–   )   (1980–2083)

KATHERINE   David   = Sybil
(1984–   )   (1986–   )   Griffin
            [=]   (1993–2020)
            [banked   m.2018
            sperm]
                         William
            Aiken Drum   (2020–2083)
            (2089–   )

m.2008

Kyle Macdonald = Mary   Gael   Alan
(2006–2092)   (2010–2083) (2012–   ) (2015–   )

m.2030

Viola   = Ian   Lachlan   Annie Laurie Diana
Strachan   (2030–   )   (2033–2083) (2035–2083)   (2036–2083)
(2031–   )

m.2054

Kenneth
(2055–   )

Marie   Madeleine   Luc   3 stillborn   JON   = DOROTHEA MARY
(2039–   )   (2040–2083) (2041–   )   2 abortions   (2052–2083)   MACDONALD
                                                     'Saint Jack   (2057–2083)
                                                     the Bodiless' 'Illusio Diamond
                                                                    Mask'

m.2078

Julian May
The Many-Coloured Land £2.99

Book One in the Saga of the Exiles

The year 2034 was when a French physicist discovered a one-way
fixed-focus timewarp into the Rhone valley of six million years ago. By
the start of the 22nd century, there are those who seek to escape a
world of technological perfection – the misfits and mavericks of the
future, who pass through the doors of time and enter a battleground
of two warring races from a distant planet.

'Grips the readers and doesn't let go' VONDA McINTYRE

The Golden Torc £2.99

Book Two in the Saga of the Exiles

Exiled beyond the time-portal, six million years in the past the misfits
of the 22nd century become enmeshed in the age-old war between
two alien races. In this strange world, each year brings the ritual
Grand Combat between the tribal Firvulag and the decadent city-
dwelling Tanu, possessors of the mind-armouringnecklet, the golden
torc.

Altogether enchanting and engrossing . . . I was captivated by its
glamorous, sinister movement through the misty forests of Earth's true
past' FRITZ LEIBER

Julian May
The Non-Born King £3.50

Book Three in the Saga of the Exiles

The dominion of the Tanu has been broken, and in the aftermath of cataclysm Aiken Drum seizes his hour to grasp control of the Pliocene world. Some, human and Tanu, rally to him – and others fear and hate him. The Grand Master, Elizabeth, the mad Felice, the goblin hordes of the Firvulag – all are thrust into a violent and stormy struggle for irresistible power.

The Adversary £3.99

Book Four in the Saga of the Exiles

Aiken Drum is king of the Many-Coloured Land. . . . The last chapter in the saga of the Exiles has begun. The Firvulag are rising, and the children of the metapsychic rebels are racing to reopen the time-gate back to the Galactic Milieu. Marc Remillard, defeated leader of the rebellion, takes up his destined role in the power play, determined to keep the gate sealed and to create the new race of Mental Man. Which side will he aid when Tanu meet Firvulag in the last great contest of the exile world?

A Pliocene Companion £2.50

The Saga of the Exiles, the critically acclaimed science fiction quartet, has become an international bestseller. *A Pliocene Companion* now follows, and it is essential reading for all followers of the Saga. It contains a descriptive listing of all the characters, a chronology, the author's original maps, two interviews with Julian May herself, and much more. The book offers the reader a chance to explore further the surroundings of a world six million years in the past.

The Galactic Mileu Trilogy

INTERVENTION is the prelude to Julian May's
brilliantly imagined new
GALACTIC MILIEU TRILOGY
which she is currently writing.

The Trilogy will consist of volumes entitled:

Jack the Bodiless

Diamond Mask

Magnificat

All Pan books are available at your local bookshop or newsagent, or can be ordered direct from the publisher. Indicate the number of copies required and fill in the form below.

Send to: **CS Department, Pan Books Ltd., P.O. Box 40, Basingstoke, Hants.   RG21 2YT.**

or phone: 0256 469551 (Ansaphone), quoting title, author and Credit Card number.

Please enclose a remittance* to the value of the cover price plus: 60p for the first book plus 30p per copy for each additional book ordered to a maximum charge of £2.40 to cover postage and packing.

*Payment may be made in sterling by UK personal cheque, postal order, sterling draft or international money order, made payable to Pan Books Ltd.

Alternatively by Barclaycard/Access:

Card No. ☐☐☐☐☐☐☐☐☐☐☐☐☐☐☐☐

Signature:

Applicable only in the UK and Republic of Ireland.

While every effort is made to keep prices low, it is sometimes necessary to increase prices at short notice. Pan Books reserve the right to show on covers and charge new retail prices which may differ from those advertised in the text or elsewhere.

NAME AND ADDRESS IN BLOCK LETTERS PLEASE:

....

Name ————————————————————————

Address ———————————————————————

————————————————————————————

————————————————————————————

————————————————————————————

3/87